T0381476

Brothers and Sisters

authorHOUSE®

AuthorHouse™
1663 Liberty Drive, Suite 200
Bloomington, IN 47403
www.authorhouse.com
Phone: 1-800-839-8640

First published by AuthorHouse 1/12/2009

ISBN: 978-1-4389-4141-7 (sc)

Printed in the United States of America
Bloomington, Indiana

This book is printed on acid-free paper.

Photo Credits

Front cover photo: The Gordon children, from the Graham family collection.

Back cover photo of author: by Sarah Reede

Contents

To my wife, Gwen.
A perfect blend of nurse Ratchett and a guardian angel.
With love, Russ.

Prologue

Near Washington D.C.
October 1864

The Virginia countryside seemed sullen and somber. He and the driver exchanged few words as Kavanaugh ran the rosary through his fingers. The enormity of his loss came to full realization as the men at graves registration off-loaded the four bodies and lined them neatly in a row.

"Can you identify these men, corporal? The man waited patiently and gently asked again. "You on the wagon, did you hear me? Can you identify these men?"

Slowly Kavanaugh dismounted, his legs barely holding him. He leaned back on the wagon wheel. "Yes, sir I know them." Slowly he recounted the names as the officer peeled the blankets from the faces. After the chore, he felt nauseated and weak, sat on the wagon step-up, and dropped his head to his hands. He was startled as a short Sergeant, with bristly whiskers and kind brown eyes approached.

"Looks like you could use this." He offered a cup of hot tea.
Kavanaugh took the mug in both his hands. "Thank you."
"Those were friends of yours?" He asked nodding toward the bodies.
"All of them," He quietly replied.
"Do you know where to send the bodies, maybe some one wants them embalmed? If you do, I'll make arrangements. It may take awhile, they are busy these days. They can be buried here or back at the big cemetery in Washington."

Kavanaugh thought for a moment, "Washington would be alright. But before you bury private Moran please contact Mary Cleary at this address." He handed the sergeant a business card Mary had given him.

"There is a big cemetery there on Robert E. Lee's old farm. It is going to be a national memorial they say. Do your other friends have any relatives someplace?"

"Back in Minsi, New York, but there is not anyone who would want them, except for Liam, the one in the middle there and Moran. I think Li would prefer to be buried with his friends."

"When you finish your tea, I will arrange for a ride back to your quarters."

When he reached his tent, despite his weariness, Kavanaugh changed from his bloodstained clothes into his dress uniform and asked permission for two days leave. He left camp and hitched a ride on a settler wagon into Washington. To his good fortune, the route passed near to Mary Cleary's bordello. He walked the few remaining blocks and paused at the circular carriageway.

"God give me strength for the task ahead, I ask in Jesus' name." He prayed silently. Evening shadows cast the colorful doorway into funereal tones. Slowly he circled to the back door and silently entered the kitchen . Evelyn was sitting peeling apples and filling the pie shells set before her. She smiled a welcome as he entered.

"Well mister Pat, you come early. Didn't 'spect anyone 'til tomorrow night. Where mister Donal? Why you look so sad? Her smile turned to concern and sensing the reality, she rose with a look of anticipation. "Oh no! Oh no!"

Pat's voice clotted with emotion. "I have some very bad news, they're gone, Evelyn." Despite his best effort, he began to tremble. "Gone, --all of them!"

Her eyes brimmed with tears and Kavanaugh could no longer contain his. She opened her arms to him and they stood locked together. She soothed him as her own grief poured down her cheeks. Evelyn took a halting breath. "Mister Donal?" She managed.

"All of them, -- Dolf, Liam, Sweeney and Donal".

"Oh lawd, Miz Mary gonna die with them. She loved that man. We must tell Miz Mary. She likes bad news right away and the news can't get any worse. I will go get her; ---she out front playin' cards."

Kavanaugh watched her disappear through the door and sat down heavily on the bench beside the table. He blew his nose and stared at the coat tree. One of Donal's caps still hung there. It seemed like forever before Mary appeared.

There was a bustling sound and Mary entered with Evelyn close behind her. She was smiling broadly.

"What a pleasure. You guys aren't supposed to be here until late tomorrow." She paused as though sensing danger. "Where is everybody?"

"I have some bad news, Mary." He rose to greet her.

"Has Donal been injured?"

He did not reply, but looked down instead.

"Oh no," her voice was a high- pitched wail that dropped to a dolorous choking tone. "Oh no, is Donal dead?"

"Yes, Mary they all are, Dolf, Billy and Liam too." He could barely articulate the words for the feeling rising in him.

"Oh my God!" She nearly fell as Evelyn steadied her and the two of them eased Mary on to the bench. Kavanaugh sat down beside her and Evelyn stood and braced Mary with her leg, her hand on Mary's shoulder. Tears flowed in long streaks down Mary's cheeks. Kavanaugh and Evelyn encircled her with their arms. Slowly her spasms decreased. Kavanaugh thought his heart was ripped from him. Evelyn patted both their backs as she wrestled with her own grief.

After a while, Mary stopped crying and looked at him through swollen eyes. "What happened, Pat?"

"Raiders, they set an ambush and we walked right into it. It was… it was…" He was lost for words. "It happened so quickly, like a lightening storm. Suddenly they were all around us. They were on horseback we hardly had a chance. They shot Donal from the wagon seat. His last thoughts were of you. He said to tell Mary -- tell Mary that I love her."

She looked at him this time a trace of anger in her voice. "I knew it! I knew it. I knew it was going to happen, I knew it and there was nothing I could do to stop it. I just knew it! We were too damned happy together. I knew something would happen."

Evelyn walked to the stove and returned with a bottle of brandy and filled two tumblers, then as an after thought, filled a small glass for her self.

Mary took a full swallow from her glass cleared her nose and wiped at her eyes. "I want to know all that happened."

"Well, there was some torn up track and we could see where the Rebs had made off with the rails. Liam tracked down the wagon they used, Donal drove up, and Dolf found something that Billy had stolen from a farm and told him to take it back. Billy set off on Lil and they hit us. Billy saw them coming and tried to warn us, but he went down and then they were all around us. It was a sharp fight – it all blurs together." Kavanaugh's voice choked and he became silent.

It became very quiet in the kitchen. The sounds of the dance floor drifted to them. He quaffed his brandy and sat silently his head down on his hands.

"I don't know how I escaped it all. I am so sorry, Mary --so sorry! If only I could have done something. I tried to get to Donal they were all over me. It all happened so fast."

Mary had regained her composure. "I know you would have if you could, Pat." Mary looked out the doorway. "He was a good kind man. This goddamned war goes on and on! He never seemed a part of it." She passed her hand over her brow. "Want to stay the night"?

"No. I should get on back. There may be some questions. I have a pass, but it is only good for tonight. There will be a lot to do, so I am going back and see if I can look after their stuff. I will have to make some kind of report. I told them to contact you about burying Donal." He rose from his seat.

Mary stood with him. "Thank you I will take care of it. I'll arrange for a ride. Evelyn, see who is available to take him back. Sit down a minute, Pat." They both sat back down on the bench. "What will you do now? Your enlistment must almost be up. It ends next week, doesn't it?"

"Yes, I don't know what I am going to do. There was a captain from the cavalry that relieved us – too late of course. He said to see him and that he would be proud to have me serve with him."

"Haven't you had enough, Pat?"

"Well, Mary, what else can I do? I have nowhere else to go."

"You can come to work for me. There is always something that needs to be done around here. I will pay you well --a hell of a lot better than Army pay!"

"Thank you, Mary, but no. It probably would not be good for either of us. Memories would wash over us again and again. I want to get away from here --not from you, Mary, you have always been so good to me, and Evelyn too. But, I am not a city man or someone to stay in one place for long. I don't want to go back to Minsi and the railroad. I have had enough of railroads. You have been kind and caring to us all. I just need to get away."

She looked down at his hands and covered them with her own, then looked to his eyes. "You will always be welcome here." Her eyes again began to fill with tears.

"I know that. I may well be back again one day right now I feel like I did when I left Ireland for America --sort of regretful and sad. I know now what I knew then. I have to be moving along. I'm not sure of the future, but real sure of the past."

"Well, Kavanaugh, there is something to be said for being in one place among people who love you. I just hope you are not going from the frying pan into the fire."

"Me too, I don't know what I am in for but it can't be much worse than what I have already been through."

Evelyn reappeared in the kitchen with a black man at her side. "Jacob knows the way," she said.

"Well, I'd best be going." Kavanaugh rose from the table and opened his arms to Evelyn, kissed her gently on the cheek. "You look after Miz Mary."

"Yes, I will. You look after you' self."

Mary was standing with her fingers over her lips watching carefully. The tears were once again streaming down her cheeks. Kavanaugh took her in his arms and held her close feeling the emotion pulsing through her. He kissed her on the cheek.
"I'll not forget you, Pat Kavanaugh."

"And I will always remember you Mary Cleary." When he released her, the tears were still trickling down her cheeks, gathering on her chin. "Be good to yourself, Mary." He picked up his cap, and with Jacob trailing behind him, stepped toward the door. He looked back. Mary was buried in Evelyn's arms sobbing quietly. Evelyn looked up. He nodded toward her and slipped out the doorway into the ominous darkness.

Part I

1867-1869
The Skin of Sorrows

Chapter 1

Fort Wallace, Kansas
June 1867

The dawn opened like a purulent wound, with a mauve-yellow haze behind the distant hills that bled red in long stringy strands across the eastern sky. He had been up all night attending to delirious patients and talking with other sick soldiers in his care. Finally, he had found an empty tent stool and was slowly slipping his rosary through his fingers, praying for the delivery of the two souls recently departed and for rain to raise the oppressive heat and the illness from his comrades.

It was going to be a warm day for June. The prairie was arid as the days turned toward July's heat. There had been very little rain, which added an unsettling anxiety to the ever present fear of Indian raids. Kavanaugh stared at the gently undulating canvas flap that shaded the sick. When the illness began, the men believed it was just a stronger strain of "the shits", but it was not long before the stool was straw colored water that just wouldn't stop running. Corporal Waltz came down with it in the morning and was dead by evening and from that point on it had steadily galloped about with a death every few days. Kavanaugh and some volunteers had put up a makeshift hospital of cots and tent-flies, at Pond Creek Station, about two miles west of Fort Wallace. On this June day, there were eighteen men beneath the waving shadows of the canvas. Not too many men by most counts, but a large piece of the 50 cavalrymen and hand full of infantry left in the fort area. The rest of the cavalry had ridden off with Captain Keogh to guide General Hancock to Denver.

Then it happened at the speed of a prairie fire; instead of a new patient every day or so, it became five or six, as fast as some recovered, others fell ill. Doctor Turner, the fort's medical officer, confirmed cholera. He saw the streaking vibrios passing like meteors across his microscope slide. To make things worse, Roman Nose, a Cheyenne war chief, and George Bent, a half breed, had been raiding all along the Butterfield Overland Stage Line and adjoining settlements. A driver killed here, a family there; they were chasing the stagecoaches, attacking wagon trains, and stealing horses. A greater part of the 82 miles of the Smoky Hill Trail was aflame from the raids.

All that would be needed to fix things finally at Pond Creek Station or at Fort Wallace; it would be a prime for the raiders to show up here. All that was left for active defense were twenty cavalry troopers and a few infantry, many of whom were very ill. A couple of scouts were left, to keep the Indians under surveillance, but even with all available men, there would not be much of a deterrent to an attack.

Kavanaugh had been waiting for Surgeon Turner for nearly an hour and had been moving among the patients giving encouraging words, strong tea, and hardtack. He was not sick himself but he was very tired - right to the bone. He looked up with a wane smile as the surgeon approached. "Sergeant, how are they doing?"

"Morning sir, Wyllyams is back on duty, went back to the fort this morning-early. The worst of them is McKee. I don't know whether he's gonna make it or not."

"I see you been boiling the sheets and bedding-that's good. Burn the pillows if you have to and we can disinfect the cots later."

"One thing sir, I been missing the rest of my duties; I have privates doing sergeant's work and corporals doing my work. Sergeant Brock has been complaining."

"Kavy, being a top sergeant at a time like this isn't easy, but I want you here with these sick soldiers you seem to reassure them. You have no signs yet do you? Are you feeling well?"
"Tolerable sir, I had a puffy belly, but I'm alright now-gas, I guess."

"Let's hope that's all." Turner looked toward the spreading plain and the rider who was approaching full throttle. "Who's that rider? Can you make him out? He's in a mighty big hurry."

Kavanaugh squinted in the direction of the boiling dust. "I believe that's Decker sir. He sure is flying, I don't like this."

"Who's in command here?" Turner asked with concern.

"Lieutenant Madigan, Decker's going right to him."

"I'd better get back to the fort. Lieutenant Bell is there with only a few soldiers. What's that way over there?" The surgeon pointed toward the East, this time with alarm in his voice.

"That, sir is a big cloud of dust made by a lot of horses and I think we're in for it." There was no panic in Kavanaugh's manner. "I think you had better head back to the fort. Right now, sir, and spur it."

The two men hurried toward the officer's tent; by the time they arrived, Madigan was already calling orders.
"What is it Deck?" Kavanaugh caught him by the arm.

"Indians, I mean a hell of a swarm of them-it's Roman Nose's band. There're a couple hundred of them they're headin' this way, and it ain't to trade blankets."

Madigan was yelling orders, "Get a barricade up, whatever you can hide behind, move those wagons! Set a line! We have big company coming." The small detachment around the hospital was spread very thin.

"Who's that over on the other side, Kavy?"

"Its Sergeant Brock and about fifteen men, sir."

"Bugler, sound assembly," Madigan ordered. The bugle blared into the gathering dust as the men scrambled toward the training area.

"Brock, roll some wagons out there, make a skirmish ring as best you can. Take it over to brace the hill; sharp shooters to forward positions and get us a line out there!" He turned to the side and pointed. "Set up some sharp shooters in the stable to cover the rear. Every man takes extra ammunition and tell ordinance get it here now! They're coming. Get into your defensive positions, now! Hurry men!"

A brisk mayhem followed as the ordinance wagon rolled from beneath its tent and rumbled to a stop. The men rushed for cartridges and ran to follow the Lieutenant's commands. Madigan continued to shout orders and remained alertly calm as he turned to Decker. "Well, Decker, what do you expect?"

"Sir, they're goin' to ride right at us, flare, then ride around and if they find a crack, ride in through it."

"What do you suggest?"

Decker reviewed the wagons drawing up front and back toward the hill. "You've done good sir, but you're gonna need every man you can spare right over there." He gestured toward a space behind the wagons. "And right over there, you're gonna need something," he pointed toward the stable, they will know there's horses in there."

Madigan looked toward the ordinance wagon. "You three men get the cartridges off that wagon and set up over there-between Brock and the stables."

The ordinance men quietly unloaded their cargo, helped themselves to ammunition, and took their assigned position in the rifle pits. Decker continued, "They will go for the horses, you can bet on that. Get as many of them inside as you can and check that corral they will try to run them off. You ought to have a couple of sharp shooters over there."

"Kavanaugh, take a couple of men."

"Sir, I'm not a sharp shooter. I can't hit a barn door."

"You join him Decker."

"Yes sir, we have a half hour at best, but they'll get here!"

Kavanaugh looked to the wavering tent-flaps as a brisk breeze suddenly lifted them. Four men looking more dead than alive reported for duty although they could barely carry their Spencers, they drew extra cartridges and took positions among the wagons.

Kavanaugh looked at the great cloud dust rising to the west. He couldn't see a rider yet, but a shiver worked its' way up his spine. They had barely reached their position when the first riders could be seen. They were streaking to the flank, bent forward over their mounts and raising a river of dust, positioning to form a wide circle of racing horses. They were met by a few shots, but the range was too great and there was no apparent effect on the circling movement. Then the next riders appeared, about thirty in number, and split their direction. They too, passed unscathed. As Kavanaugh watched the first riders appeared much closer and a general firing began. Decker rose quietly and fired his Henry. One rider was lifted high from his horse's back and flopped into the dust.

"Good shot, Deck." A rifle ball showered Kavanaugh with dust and a second grazed off a large rock beside him. Decker fired again and suddenly there was a storm of lead striking all around them.

Kavanaugh aimed at a rider and sent three shots then a general firing started. Soon there were clusters of braves everywhere and the shooting became intense. Some of the braves had reached Brock's wagon and there was a fierce hand-to-hand mêlée around it.

"I haven't hit anything but the dirt"

"Don't shoot at the riders. You can hit a horse, can't ya? Shoot for their knees."

Kavanaugh flinched as two more bullets struck nearby, showering them with splinters. He picked out a horse and fired at its legs sending it down and its rider sprawling ahead like a bobsled in the dust. The Cheyenne began to withdraw and in a great turn started toward the distant fort. All signs of their presence disappeared into dust, only a few dead and dying horses were left as evidence of the furious half-hour encounter. The men at the station were relieved and cautious they would return, but beneath the fear there was also a gritty resolve; if they were attacked again, the attacker would pay a dear price.

On June 24, company G of the Seventh Cavalry arrived at Fort Wallace, much to the joy and relief of the battered defenders.

The raids on the fort were suspended as the Indians turned their fury on the outlying settlements, the stage line, and the miner's camps. The U.S. Cavalry was drawn into numerous hot, but fruitless pursuits.

Kavanaugh reined up his horse to the side of the long column of horses filling the sky with dust. He was weary of riding and sweat streaked the dirt on his forehead and face in a wavy dark pattern. He had tied his bandanna around his face in an effort to keep from swallowing the large particles and, as he pulled it down to breathe easier, his face looked pearly white beneath the soiled veil. They had been chasing leads all along the Smokey Hill Trail, but by the time they arrived at the raid sites, the Indians were long gone and following their trails was an exercise in frustration and exhaustion. In five days, with the temperature hovering near 85 degrees, they chased the Indians over a hundred miles of crisscrossing dead ends. One day they spotted a lone rider who rode with ease over a rise in the plain, just out of rifle range. He seemed to be taunting them. Then, he too disappeared into a trace of dust. The men were tired, thirsty, and touchy, and the horses were near exhaustion. They still had 15 miles away from the fort, with no water in between except what they maintained in their canteens.

Kavanaugh took a pull at his canteen and watched a blue rider, covered in dust, approaching.

"A hot one, Deck," He smiled and replaced the canteen cork.

"Yes, I'll be glad to get to a creek." Decker took off his hat and beat off the dust on his thigh. "What do you think about Custer pullin' out?"

"Heard he headed to Fort Riley to be with his wife," Kavanaugh laughed. "He sure is something. Let's ask the captain, he's coming now."

An officer was approaching at a brisk pace, erect in his saddle, so covered in dust that it obscured his rank. He reined up beside the two men, his dark eyes flashing above the bandanna he pulled down from his face.

"Just what are you two up to? If you're tired of riding, I can arrange for you to walk." He teased.

"Captain Keogh." Kavanaugh nodded toward him and touched his cap.

"Capt'n, we was just talkin' about Colonel Custer. I heard he was headin' into trouble."

"And you would be heading into trouble too, if you left your men."

"What's going to happen to him?"

"Who knows? I know what already happened. The Army suspended him for a year without pay."

"Captain, had it been an enlisted man he would have been shot, at least flogged."

"Take care Pat, do you want my job?"

"No sir, not one hour of it." Kavanaugh laughed, "Wearing bars would change me."

"Suspended Custer, huh?" Decker spit a stream of tobacco juice.

"Yes, Decker, suspended." Keogh replied. "I never served with him, but I've been around the Seventh from time to time, for a long time. The colonel is a driven man. Took off to see his wife and that's what he told me. It wasn't very good judgment."

"From what I've heard, if an Indian don't kill him, one of his men will."

Keogh smiled then a stern look passed over his face. "I didn't hear that, Mr. Decker." Then he smiled again. "Has it been on your mind?"

Decker didn't reply. For a long moment they sat quietly watching the riders file past the hollow eyes and angular faces reflected their fatigue, some were barely able to stay in the saddle. "What kind of a man is Custer, Captain?

"Ah, Pat, I don't know the man well. He is driven; quite vain, barely a tad of conscience, but man enough for good company when I've been around him."

"Is it true he wants to annihilate the tribes?"

"He's a hard man to be sure - annihilate is a harsh word." There was an edge to his brogue.

"I don't believe in that."

"Nor do I, Decker. I know Tom Custer, his brother, he is a different man. Two Medals of Honor and doesn't carry the arrogant reputation his brother does, though he's proud. He knows what he's doing. I think pride may bring George down, perhaps it already has, thinking he's above it all."

"What's this I hear 'bout a winter campaign?" Kavanaugh asked.

"It's true, Sheridan is eager to get on with it." Decker added.

"It's been talked about, of course they don't consult me," Keogh laughed. "General Sheridan thinks that chasing the Indians around all summer isn't going to stop the warfare. He thinks if we can find their winter camps and trap them, they won't be so likely to get away."

"I sure don't fancy chasin' red skins through the snow." Decker spit at a fly perched on his horse's ear.

"Nor do I, I don't like the cold and thrashing around in the snow, freezing to death in the damn wind; that I dread."

Keogh laughed. "Aye Pat, not much like Ireland, if I could spare you I would, but your men wouldn't want anybody else leading them." He rose in his saddle and glanced toward the end of the column.

"Captain Keogh you'll be lucky to keep half the men if we start this winter business."

"There are no orders yet, but the men will do their job. They won't like it none, they will complain like hell, but they will follow."

Decker spit a stream of tobacco juice at some flies that had gathered themselves on his horse's neck. "Ain't likely to desert in winter, Pat - spring maybe, winter no."

"I don't believe we will do much this year, but it's on the docket for next winter." Keogh observed.

"You know captain, finding Indians in winter will be like finding hen's teeth. Once Bill Comstock and me was scoutin' out of Fort Riley. It was winter and snowin' hard. Bill smelt smoke so we stopped to look around. There it was, a whole camp of Sioux, the first wickiup wasn't thirty yards away. We didn't see the camp through the snow. We turned and lit out of there. It ain't easy finding Indians in the winter, and when you do, well, Bill and me was in the camp before we saw anything."

"Sure that close, you're lucky you still have your hair! Well, I won't be here for it, if it does start. You'll soon be getting a new commanding officer, Kavy. I'm off eastward for furlough, don't think I'll be back here, at least I hope not."

"Know who your replacement will be yet, sir?"

"Brevet Major Tyne, I think."

"I know Tyne. He was with Chivington - a real mean son-of-a-bitch."

"Now, now Mr. Decker, I didn't hear that either."

The line of horsemen slowed and began to press one another closely.

"Do you know for sure captain, I mean, you being re-assigned?"

"No. Who knows anything in the cavalry? I'm going to ride up ahead and see what the slow down's about. With my luck, I'll get re-assigned to Custer. I'd rather be in New York!"

Keogh touched his cap and raised his bandana over his nose. Kavanaugh saluted, and soon Keogh cantered into the swirling suspended dust.

They both watched him disappear. Decker turned to Pat. "Keogh's a good man Pat, right off the boat like you."

"True enough, he grew up not twenty miles away from me in Ireland. I'd rather he'd stay, he's a man you can talk to."

"Small world ain't it?" He spit another stream at the flies, and then cleared his mouth with his fingers.

"He likes the ladies and a drop or two."

Decker laughed and explored his pocket for his tobacco twist. "He's a soldier's soldier." He proffered the twist to Kavanaugh who declined it with a turn of his head.

"I'm going to give Duffy some relief. Want to ride back?" Pat stretched back in his saddle and turned his horse.

"No, I'd better get on up ahead and make sure we get to the fort so I can get about my business."

The two men began their ride in opposite directions along the thick column of choking dust.

In late 1867, General Phil Sheridan replaced General W.S. Hancock as the Commander of the Department of the Missouri. Sheridan was convinced the only way to ultimately defeat the Indians was to campaign in the winter when the roving bands would be isolated by weather conditions. He sought to destroy their winter stores before they could flee where they would be difficult to find. He believed the plains tribes could be starved into submission and confined on reservations. However, the plan did not materialize and in May, 1868, several more raids were made on the railroad, stage lines, construction camps, and wagon trains. Various sightings of marauding bands of warriors kept the cavalry busy, but no large aggregates of hostiles were spotted.

Life at Fort Wallace was active in the pursuing of the raiders, and peace emissaries were sent to lure the various Cheyenne villages to reservation life. For a while, life at the fort was restored to a harsh monotonous routine with Reveille sounded ten minutes before sunrise and Stable Call, Sick Call, and Water Call following in quick succession. Breakfast was at 6:30 AM, Guard Mounting at 8:00 AM, Duty Recall and Dinner Call at noon; all seemed to press together with duties ending at sunset, and Taps at 8:30 P.M. Days were filled with quarrying stone for new construction or reconstruction of the fort and out buildings, and bringing in supplies from distant places. Punishment details went out to bring in firewood or wood for shoring-up of defenses. The few women at the fort continued their laundry duties and serving officers. A few supplemented their income with 'personal services', discreetly delivered. Generally, the horses received more attention than the men who labored in squads at the infinite number of tasks to keep a fort functional. Garbage details, kitchen and latrine duties were sandwiched between training details and quick starts to hunt down an enemy rarely seen.

The Sutter Store, run by Val Todd, was the focus of much of the men's attention. There they could purchase personal items like soap, sweets, and articles of clothing, tobacco and whiskey, when not prohibited. Alcohol was banned from time to time, or limited in distribution, to help preserve order. Drunkenness, fighting and dereliction of duty were often side bars to alcohol consumption. The men had their ways of acquiring 'spirits' from a variety of sources, sometimes making it themselves.

A large vegetable garden was carefully cultivated by the fort's company, and provided a break from Army rations. Stringy beef with boiled beans and potatoes were usually served at mess. Deer, antelope, and buffalo meat was a welcome change.

Recreation was provided through reading from the library, card games, dominoes, and checkers. Small rivalries flurried between cavalry and infantry and among soldiers in their own ranks. A few enthusiasts, including Kavanaugh, enjoyed fishing in Pond Creek and adjacent streams. Generally speaking, it was boredom spiced with bone weary chases of an elusive enemy.

Sheridan continued to be convinced that a campaign could destroy the wild harvests the Indians made and break their resistance. Killing of buffalo and other game was encouraged. As a result, game near the fort was becoming scarce, requiring hunts farther and farther away

Chapter 2

Agate Creek, Kansas
August 1868

The August sun was in a high haze and the winding Pond Creek was shrinking in the heat. Rocks now showed that had been swirls of water in July. It was not especially hot on August first 1868, but despite the mild weather, there was a growing concern at Fort Wallace. Lieutenant Madigan, a very popular officer, had taken out five men to hunt some fresh meat for the mess. The group left a little after first light and was expected back by noon; it was now almost two o'clock. There had been two or three distant shots around ten o'clock, which were attributed to the hunters. Major Tyne assigned Decker to go look for them. Kavanaugh had just finished a close order drill with the company when he spotted the scout approaching. He wiped the sweat from his eyes and smiled at the lanky man as he rode out to meet him.

"Pat, I've been out a ways lookin' for Madigan. There are a lot of tracks out there and a lot of them ain't shod."
"Would hostiles be in this close?"

"I'm sure of it - three or four anyway. I'm goin' to need some help. Think you can get another rider to go out with me?"

"Alright, let's get out there, it's getting' late. I'll round up Corporal Harper and take a mule in case they shot a buffalo and are having trouble getting it in."

They had been searching two hours, spread out within eyesight of one another. Kavanaugh watched as Decker cantered toward him and drew up to his side.

"There's something wrong Pat. We ain't got six trails now, looks more like twenty, twenty-five. Horses ain't shod – Indians for sure. They could be cross-tracked, but I don't like the looks of it."

"Over here! Over here!" Harper shouted.

The shout startled them both; they wheeled their horses and rode to where Harper was trying to control his shying horse.

Lying naked, face up in a swarm of flies, was a disemboweled corpse. The face so badly mutilated as to be unrecognized. The body bristled with arrows, the genitals had been hacked off, intestines pulled out into a pile; where eyes once were, bloody black sockets pointed upward. A deep slash crossed both the throat and chest and the chin was a bloody stump. The man had been scalped and hacked, his right wrist to elbow had a large chunk removed, and his index finger was missing.

"There's two more over there." Harper pointed to a bristle of arrows.

"Jesus wept, Deck, there are two more just over the hill."

All six bodies were mutilated almost beyond recognition. There was not a scrap of clothing or a personal item present.

Decker drew up beside Kavanaugh. "What a mess! They all are here, Pat. There's some matted grass and blood clots over yonder, looks like they may have got one. He nodded to the body closest to him. "They are Cheyenne arrows."

"That's the lieutenant over there, or what's left of him." Kavanaugh pointed to another body. An arrow had gone clear through his throat, three protruded from his pubis, and a mass more protruded from his body like a macabre porcupine. His legs were spread clearly showing the gashes between them and both his thighs were cut.

"That's Dick Chance." Harper indicated. "Had a big scar on the back of his hand, otherwise I wouldn't know."

"That's Finney; I know Art Finney and he had real black hair. God look at him; his mother wouldn't recognize him."

"That's Brownell there with the arrow in his head and O'Brien beside him."

"Jesus wept, Decker. How did they get them all without a fight?" Pat shook his head in disbelief.

Decker spit a stream of tobacco juice. "Cheyenne war party was waitin' for them. Near as I can figure they was laid in here just beneath the brow in the high grass, their horses was probably over on the other side of that hill over there," he pointed past Harper. "Cheyenne must have seen them comin', hunkered down and raised up with a shower of arrows. Madigan would never have seen them; somebody got off a couple of shots, ---that was it. The injuns got to their horses, caught ours up, and headed south." He gestured toward a trail weaving through the grass at the bottom of the hill.

"Tom get on back to the fort, leave the mule. Get a wagon and some men, six blankets and tell Tyne we found them; best move it - it is almost dark!"

"What about you guys -suppose they come back?" Harper asked turning his horse in the direction of the fort.

"Hell, they're probably clean down to Arkansas by now. They got what they wanted-scalps and horses." Decker spit and dismounted. "This could be the work of that bastard Running Bull and his band of cut throats. The ones that did this were not a full size war party just a band of raiders."

After Harper left, the two men continued to look at the bodies, bristling with arrows, grotesquely mutilated with fingers missing. All were scalped.

"I saw a lot in the war Deck, rows of bloated bodies at Gettysburg and a lot after that, but I've never seen anything like this." He shook his head in despair.

"Cheyenne and Sioux cut them open and mess them up. They hate the whites, Kavy and they think by doin' this," he gestured toward the bodies; "they cripple their spirit, and make them cripples in the next world."

"What the hell should we do now?"

"We might as well pull out those arrows, no sense in everybody looking at this mess. If we find the parts just tuck them inside somewhere I doubt we will finish before Harper gets back."

The body of O'Brien had both the hands and feet removed and these were placed upon his chest. As the flies rose in buzzing masses, Kavanaugh and Decker began to assemble the other pieces scattered over the area.

Kavanaugh dumped the shovelful of manure into the wheelbarrow then started at the voice behind him.

"Muckin' out the stables again, Padric? What did you do this time?"

"Decker you have to stop sneaking up on me. You scared the hell out of me."

"Not likely, I came by to drop off the dollar I owed you."

Pat rested on the shovel and looked blankly at him, "What dollar?"

"You loaned it to me Friday."

"You been playing cards ever since?"

"Yeah, well you know. I play when ever I can. "

"Thanks then. I forgot about it."

"Thank you for the grubstake. What's that four maybe five times now?"

"Hell, Deck I don't keep track. You play till you win. I know I'll get it eventually."

"What's the stable detail for?"

"Nothing in particular, got a little drunk."

"That's not what's around. You wouldn't try to fool a friend would you?"

"Well, it started when I got a little drunk."

"I heard you bashed that bastard Brock around. And that Major Tyne would have busted one of you, but he couldn't decide which."

"Well I didn't loose a stripe and neither did Brock."

"I heard the major had the two of you for more than an hour."

"Sure, Decker, you're so nosy. Are you always spying on people?"

"That's my job." He leaned to the left and vigorously scratched under his arm. "I heard that Brock got the worst of it."

"I don't know, Decker, you know everything else, so you can find that out too. I haven't seen the man." He scraped the shovel into a manure pile.

"I don't think he wants to show." Decker chuckled. "It is a good one though. The two tops into a brawl with all the troops looking on."

Pat loaded another shovel into the wheelbarrow and wiped back the sweat from his eyes. He did not reply.

"And both are doing stable duty." Decker shook his head and smiled.

"What have you been up to?"

"Oughton and I located a band of hostiles Wednesday. I came back, he's still out there, and still the major can't figure out what to do – he wants reinforcements."

"I could have guessed that. He's careful anyway."

"You know Kavanaugh, these people, these hostiles; they've been here a long time. We're the ones that are puttin' them out. No wonder they fight."

"Yeah, we haven't had sense enough to leave them alone. We've thrown out the people who really have right to this land, destroyed their homes, left them to starve, and then wonder why they are so hostile." He knocked some manure from his spade and leaned on it. "So, you think we will be riding out in force?"

"Yeah, it was a large village, didn't spot many horses though. You can bet there's a war party somewhere. I hope we find them before they find us."

"I think we will be ridin' out. I saw Brock in there with the major. We will all be going, I suppose."

"True, enough I'll be showin' you the way." There was a twinkle in his eye.

"That's what troubles me, Decker. We will probably find them." It became quiet both men lost in their thoughts.

"There's a bad feeling here, Kavy, ever since we found Captain Madigan. Feels like a thunder storm comin, a sort of hair trigger and everybody's touchy."

"That's true; Captain Madigan was a good man and a good officer too."

"Not the usual combination." Decker chuckled.

"I feel the men's need for vengeance but it won't do anybody good."

"I know you liked Madigan and Brock badmouthed his memory. That's what the fight was about, wasn't it?"

"It was partly about that, and partly because I just don't like that shoneen son of a bitch. He reminds me of a game keeper I once knew."

Chapter 3

Indian Village
1868

They had been riding single file along a route that was parallel to the river. Some aspens, already showing yellow were scattered ahead like an abandoned bouquet. A breeze with an autumn touch laid down the grass in long shimmering waves. The sun was warm and the sound of creaking leather and the smell of horses assailed Pat's senses. The column halted before a long ridge stretching west, the trooper ahead turned in his saddle and called to him.

"Pat, we are dividing the command. The major wants you to take a column left and form up a line. Hostiles are just over that ridge along the river. Better look it over."

Kavanaugh turned to the men behind and spread the order down the column. The last rider raised his arm noting the message in a sense of fear blended with anticipation. Pat followed suit and signaled 'flank right into line and halt'. He turned his horse and walked it as the men in front of him split to the right. Soon they formed a long blue line just below the ridge.
He hissed at the man beside him "Let's take a look, Harper."

The two men dismounted and carefully approached the crest. The village that lay spread out before them was being taken down a flurry of activity. There were drying racks loaded with fish and meat and the odor of the smoking fires carried to them.
"What do you make of it Harper?"

"They are moving on, Pat – probably know we're near. This is a fish camp, kids and women most likely. Some tents are already folded. No lookouts, don't know why that is."

"See any warriors?"

"No. They have to be around and we had best be careful." He looked down the hill. "Christ, Pat s the Major is coming."

Kavanaugh turned to the noise behind him and beheld Major Tyne, florid from his climb up the ridge.

"Well, Sergeant?" he puffed.

"Women, old men and children, sir and they are breaking camp."

"I think it imperative that we attack at once. Get down the hill and form up your men. Fan your men in a longer line down the ridge. I want to turn in the corners and sweep the camp." His eye glittered like a wolf's. "Keep them all in."

"Sir, there are no warriors. We can surround them and gather them up. Make them take some supplies and march them off."

"They are very vulnerable! We will take advantage of that. Slip your men up and hold beneath the crest, attack on my signal. Now prepare, I want to kill them all, you understand? "

"Sir, they're women and children." Kavanaugh protested."

"All the better, sows make pigs and nits make lice."

"Sir, we can round them up, the only question is where to take them?"

"You let me worry about that, Kavanaugh. If nothing else, we will draw out the war party."

"That's a comforting thought." Harper injected.

"God damn it, Corporal Harper! Remember why we are here. Remember the miners, prospectors and their families. You were the one who found the women, and wasn't it you two who found Captain Madigan? Remember them?" He spoke in a hard determined whisper.

"Yes, sir," Harper turned to look the major in the eyes.

"I remember the Captain well, laid out on the grass with his private parts missing and thirty arrows in him. Thirty! Do you remember him? You remember Madigan don't you Kavanaugh?"

"Yes Major, I remember Captain Madigan. I said many a novena with him."

"Well then, let's hope his prayers counted. T he men's blood is up. And by God, these savages will learn their lesson! Now Sergeant, form up that line!" The Major shifted to his hands and knees. "I want this to be an example by God! Show those savages they can't get away with that." He began down the hill.

"Major," Pat enjoined, "I don't think vengeance is a good idea. The men…"

"Frankly, Sergeant, I don't care what you think. Now get on down the hill and form up. Brock is already moving into line!"

"Sir, I just don't think this is a good idea."

"God damn it! I don't give a fart about what you think; I am giving you a direct order!"

"Yes sir," Harper responded. He looked toward Pat and shook his head as if to warn Kavanaugh to end the discussion.

"I'll form them up," Kavanaugh resigned. The Major slid back from the crest and then trotted down the hill.

"Jesus, Pat. You've got an order. Let's get on with it."

"He means to kill them," Kavanaugh's jaw was set. "He means to kill them all. You heard him."

"Come on, Pat, he's nearly down to his horse."

Pat maneuvered the long line of horseman to his left and stared right to where the Major was slowly walking his horse up the rolling hill ahead. He raised his arm and signaled advance as they approached the crest the bugles sounded charge. He spurred his horse up and over. Pure panic was spreading among the villagers as he galloped down the hill, driven on by the men shouting. The shooting started almost at once. A young brave appeared before him and he rode him down. He saw a woman shot down before him as he galloped through the tents still standing. The shooting intensified as Brock's men were slaughtering the Cheyenne, the confusion of screams and shots filled his ears. He rode to the far side of the encampment as his men joined the carnage.

Three old men with bows had run to the center of the camp and were trying to make a stand against the wave of blue riders approached. He saw the Major shoot one of them and, in an instant; the other two were ripped by multiple shots. One trooper leaped from his horse and caught a running woman and they both tumbled inside a tent. All about him, children and women were being shot down. He reined his horse back and saw a saber flashing, one woman pierced through, a second dropped by a slash across her neck. His line of riders caught the van of the cluster of natives who had prepared to flee and there was a fierce firing from the left. He rode to the edge of the river and reined toward the sound of the shots.

There was a movement below the bank; two Indian women were crouched in the grass. One was carrying a baby, and the other was helping an old man who was limping heavily. Pat quickly dismounted and motioned with his pistol. The women froze on the spot, terror playing over their faces; he led his horse toward them and urged them back toward the village site. The crescendo was fading into more isolated and deliberate shots. Across the camp, he saw three children running from the village; they were shredded by bullets. He reined up and motioned for the woman and old man to stop. Slow deliberate shots punctuated the dying and the cries of the wounded. He looked up and saw the Major bearing down. Kavanaugh extended his arm and pushed the women behind him. The old man straightened to meet the Major and without hesitation, the Major raised his pistol with an angry look.

"Sir, I've taken these…" Kavanaugh began.

The pistol leveled. Pat flinched at the flash as the old man fell backward. The two women screamed and turned to their fallen comrade. The Major raised his pistol again.

"Sir," there was a loud click in response as the hammer fell on an empty chamber. "Sir, these women and child are my prisoners."

"I told you no prisoners today, Kavanaugh, step aside." He holstered his pistol and drew his saber, "that's a direct order."
"No sir, I won't step aside."

"You are refusing to obey a direct order? Get out of the way or I'll have your stripes you stupid Mick son of a bitch. You are on report!"

Kavanaugh moved more in line with the Major's movement to better cover the cowering women. The baby began to cough and cry.

The Major raised his saber to strike Kavanaugh with its edge, the horse shied and the flat of the blade fell across his shoulder, Kavanaugh caught the hand guard. The Major's horse reared back; with all his might he twisted the Major's saber and jerked him from the saddle. He bent the arm until it was across the Major's body and with sustained strength, forced the blade down. The Major grabbed the blade as it cut through his hand into his cheek, and fainted as the steel passed through his nose and then cut his eyebrow to the bone. Bright blood began to pulsate

20

from the slash.

"Come." he motioned to the women and they slid down the riverbank and began upstream under its cover. The sun burst through the clouds as they ran parallel to the steep bank. Behind them, the clamor had faded and the steep bank sides no longer protected them. They approached a long shallow ford and Kavanaugh led them across the river, and looked back. Nearly a mile behind them he could see the blue-black smoke rising in a great wavering plume. The women also looked toward the smoke. There were no tears on the fright-lined faces and, for the first time, Pat reviewed them carefully. They looked small and dark in the sunlight.

"I'm sorry," he said "sorry, you go now." He swept his arm toward the wood. "Go now, I am so sorry."

The women recoiled and cringed as he waved his arm. "I'll not hurt you but you must go, soldiers will come."

"No go. We go there." She pointed back toward the camp.
Kavanaugh was taken aback at the broken English.

"I, Sada."

Whatever the exact word she said Kavanaugh heard only 'Sada'.

"Sada, we cannot go back there now, we must wait; the soldiers killed everybody."

She did not reply her deep dark eyes fixed on the billowing smoke. She was tall for a native woman; petite with a straight proud nose, her black hair was knitted into a single long braid frayed from the flight. Her skin was smooth and dark, a shade darker than her doeskin smock. Her small breasts swelled beneath the garment she wore.

Pat followed Sada's gaze and solemnly, slowly shook his head. "They lost control." The other woman still clutched the whimpering child. She slipped a strap of her smock off and began to feed him. Kavanaugh wearily passed his hand over his brow "Jesus wept! What a trouble!"
"We go back."
"Let them leave, Sada, let the soldiers go away first; we'll go when they go away."

Sada turned toward the other woman now crouched still nursing the baby and said a few words. The woman stared fearfully at Kavanaugh and turned back to her task. Sada caught his eye.

"Maha fear. Fear you kill baby. Kill us."

"No!"

"I tell her. She think yes."

"We must move farther into the brush and trees, I will not harm you. Come, or they will see us."

He led them back from the river's edge into some screening alders and willows. They raked out a place under the thick brush and watched quietly. The women huddled together speaking in low tones. A lone blue rider appeared on the opposite side of the river slowly walking his horse. Kavanaugh recognized it was Oughton the other scout.

"Be very quiet, Sada. They are looking for us." She passed the message to Maha who visibly cringed and pressed herself and her baby into the leaves.

Oughton continued toward them and Kavanaugh drew his pistol. The light was beginning to fade and as the scout approached the crossings a distant bugle sounded recall. Oughton drew up, turned, and trotted back, disappeared over the horizon formed by the edge of the riverbank.

Pat gave a sigh of relief. "We can start back soon Sada, but we cannot spend much

21

time.   They will come looking for me tomorrow.   Look Sada," he loosened his pistol belt and cast it into the river, "do not be afraid of me."

It was approaching dark when they reached the ruined camp and the two women made their way through the carnage.   Bodies lay strewn where they had fallen in the pornography of death.   Pat walked slowly through it while Sada and Maha moved about the camp calling quietly, but in vain; the slaughter had been complete.   The ground was littered with small bodies and many women scattered across the camp site. The food and skin tents were still smoldering and, at times, the fire flared up casting a red-yellow pall over the destruction.   Kavanaugh tripped over a woman's body spread eagled in his path.   A sullen anger rose in him as he came upon a little girl who's back showed a splotchy bloodstain between her shoulders.

Skibbereen, Ireland, Gettysburg, Pennsylvania and the scene on a lonely Virginia road crossed and re-crossed his mind and blended into a macabre memory.   He sat down on a log and reviewed the flickering surrealism that surrounded him.   He dropped his head to his hands.

"Come.   We go." The voice startled him.   "All dead come we go."   She touched him lightly.   "Not you work.   Other soldier's work."

"Sada, you and Maha and baby go.   Soldiers will come for me.   I don't want them to find you."

"We go. You come."

"Where's Maha?"

"Father killed - he spirit man.   Come we go."

She tugged him from the log and they walked through the decimated village.   Soon Maha and the baby joined them.   Kavanaugh looked back at the bizarre light.   "This surely is a scene from hell," he thought.
"Come. They dead, we alive."

They crossed the ice-cold river at an island and walked through the night.   At first light they found themselves at a fork in the river, forded it and started north again.   The women had to swim the last few yards, but Kavanaugh waded across holding the baby over his head.   Finally, they rested in a deep thicket full of rustling sounds, but nearly impervious to the spreading light.

Sada produced some dried fish from a small skin bag she had picked up in the village, it was damp but sustaining.

"We go there."   She pointed up the river.   "Long away.   More my people there.   Get horse. Then you go."

They continued walking, until the river path gave out to heavy undergrowth.   In the morning, they found a second path that broke occasionally into grassy areas from the thicker trees.   It was on the edge of the trees when Sada stopped, looked back, and pointed.   A lone rider had appeared, and evidently had spotted them; they quickly retreated into the woods.

"Run, Sada. Go fast.   He looks for me.   Go now!   Go!   Don't look back."   Kavanaugh wrenched a stout sapling from the ground and snapped off its limbs.

"Go now Sada!"

The two women vanished into the woods as Kavanaugh positioned himself for ambush on the path. The horse had broken into a trot and was bearing directly down on him.   Kavanaugh braced himself sighting around the tree trunk. The rider looked familiar and as he entered the path into the woods and he recognized him, it was Decker.

Pat stepped onto the path.   The horse reared but when it came down Decker had his pistol drawn.

"Hello, Deck." He grasped the horse's bridle.

"Jesus, Kavanaugh! This time you scared the hell out of me!"

"Now, that would be hard to do." He smiled up at the rider. Decker dismounted and holstered his pistol.

"The whole damn brigade is looking for you." They shook hands and Decker chuckled. "Christ, Pat, you are in a world of trouble."

"It's the story of my life." He laughed and steadied Decker's horse." Did the Major die?"

"No, but his nose is near off, and three fingers, he lost an eye, you almost cut his face in half. You should have killed the son of a bitch, because now he sure wants to kill you."

Kavanaugh shook his head. The forest sounds swelled as the men stood quietly. "What the hell happened back there, Deck?"

"No control, the men went wild, I saw it once before at Sand Creek. They become madmen, just crazy madmen." He shook his head in despair. "They cut those kids down like hay, and bashed-in the heads of the babies." He passed his hand over his forehead. "Madmen, the two women with you are the only survivors so far as I know. Private Clarke thought he saw one down by the river, but we never found him." He turned to his saddle bags and felt around then produced some packets. "I brought you some jerky, a packet of coffee, a bit of bacon, some dry beans and some salt."

"Thank you Deck. One of the women has a baby, so there are three who survived. Obliged for the supplies, how did you know you would find me?"

"Unless you disappeared into the blue, I'd find you. The supplies are the least I could do. You're gonna have to hide out a long time." He paused scratched at his neck and continued. "There's also a pint of whisky, a pipe, a couple plugs of tobacco, a mess kit and a compass. And", he paused," a stuffer bag to carry it."

"Thank you, Deck." He gathered the packets and put them in the bag. "Won't you need the compass?"

"Hell, Kavanaugh, I've been riding this country so long, I just go in one direction till I find some place I know. That's a good briar pipe though, couple of plugs of tobacco my niece sent it from Boston --never used it. I'd rather chew." He paused and took a long look toward the east, brushed at some gnats and pushed his horse's nose away from the tobacco plugs Pat held. "You know, Pat. You might head east to Boston."

"Lots of Irishmen in Boston." Pat smiled.

"Yeah and Pittsburgh's, a good town too. You could get lost out here." He swept his arm west. "But it's no life for a man like you. Goin' east are some fair sized towns. You'll come to Independence first. Don't stay too long there. They will be looking for you there for sure. They will look for you clean back to Minsi. You must be careful crossing the big river, men are often posted there." It became quiet as the forest sounds echoed and flooded, faded and creaked.

"Ever think of home, Deck?"

"No, not really, might if I'd ever had one."

"It was some relative of yours that built Decker's Fort near Minsi, wasn't it?"

"Yeah my great grandpa, I grew up just outside Minsi near Prosper. You ever been to Prosper?"

"Yeah, just up the old plank road from where I lived."

"That's the place; I was born there, but didn't stay long. Ma died of the smallpox, both my brothers too. I had an older half sister she married and moved away. My old man and me headed out."

"Over to Milford, you said once."

"Yeah, then we went up to Fort Franklin, then down the Allegheny to Pittsburgh. We was doin' well in Pittsburgh, but the old man had itchy feet." Decker shook his head. "Headed for Ohio after that, I ended up in Independence Missouri 'cause my Uncle Mort was there."

"Did you live in Independence?"

"Well, I didn't live there much; he was guidin' trains out the Oregon and the Santa Fe Trails. I started to work with him."

"That's how you became a scout, I guess."

"Yeah, my father's horse dumped him one night, he was probably drunk and he dropped the reins over her. She stopped --he didn't, broke his neck."

"Long time ago?" Pat passed his hand over the stubble on his face.

"I was eleven, --I think. It happened when I was up the trail with Mort. By the time I got back they'd collected his stuff at the tavern where he spent a lot of time. I ended up with a watch, a pocket knife, a ten dollar gold piece and half a bottle of whisky." A slow and thoughtful smile passed over his face.

Kavanaugh also smiled. "What happened to your Uncle?"

"Comanche got him, they're fierce bastards. I fought them once or twice and Kiowa too." He shuffled his feet and leaned to his horse. "It's a long way to Boston and winter's coming on."

"What if I headed west? You have been to Oregon territory?"

"Yeah, a few times, also down the Santa Fe trail. Herdin' people who think they'll be gold rich or have the best farm in America. But west would not be so good, there's always the Army, go back get lost in the city someplace. Less likely to find you there I think."

"I think you're right."

Decker took a deep breath and extended his hand. "I got to get goin" Kavy. I'd hate to have them come lookin' for me and find you." They shook hands.

"Thanks, Deck."

"You're going to be in Sioux country 'til you hit Independence there's different Sioux, you know. And you know them was Cheyenne back at the village. There likely is a war party out and close. They will also be lookin for you. They ain't likely to forget what happened back there at Agate Creek."

"Yeah, I don't blame them what about the Sioux?"

"You got Arkansas, Omaha, Kansas, Miniconjous, and Ogallala; aren't much left of some of them now, government stole their land and turned their life upside down. They are all a little different but all can be dangerous. If you spot Indians just hide as fast as you can. Kavanaugh did not reply and Decker squinted east then west. "You be careful, Pat, the Sioux, maybe they kill you, maybe not. If they was Comanche, you'd be dead 'fore you knew they were there. And those Cheyenne, well, you be very careful of any of them."

"I will, Deck."

"Take care, Pat Kavanaugh. I'll see you in hell, maybe sooner than later."

He reached into the pack. "I forgot here's some long underwear."

They laughed and again the forest sounds overcame the silence. Decker had assumed a serious demeanor, looked down and kicked at a wandering ant.

"Pat, you are in very, very big trouble --life time trouble." He released a long breath. "The Major's already placed a reward on your head, --a hundred dollars, dead or alive."

"So . . ." Pat smiled nonchalantly.

"So, listen to me, God damn it! There're a lot of men would like that money and every bushwhacker and blue belly in the damn country will be after it. It's already on the telegraph."

"I've had a price on my head once before."

"Never mind that, Kavanaugh that was then! Damn it, I'm talkin' about now, don't be so damn cocky, if I could find you so can somebody else! You got the Army, the Indians and every law enforcement officer and every bounty hunter in the territory will be lookin' for you."

"How did you find me?"

"I volunteered; first we looked for your body, found your horse, thought you was dead. Oughton said he thought he saw you hidin', and the Major, said you was probably alive. But Oughton outsmarted himself, figured you would double back and go down river. He took half the company with him to look for you."

"Thank you, Deck."

"That's too many 'thank yous, you're making' me nervous."

Kavanaugh smiled. "Want a sip of my whisky?"

"No, you're gonna need it." Decker took a deep breath and turned to look along the bright shining river. "You got more trouble than you know, there's a big Cheyenne war party around here somewhere. Second company lost a scout. Horse came back without him, so he's dead somewhere. The hostiles ain't gonna take lightly that slaughter back there on the creek. There's gonna be a lot more killing, just make sure it ain't you."

"Nor you, Decker."

"I got to move on, Kavy, I don't want anyone followin' my tracks out this way." He picked up the reins of his mount. "Listen, Pat, head east, head to a city or town, somewhere you can blend in, like Boston, or New York or maybe even Washington; Pittsburgh's a good town."

"I thought that might be good idea. A city I mean."

"Stay away from people, stay off the skyline, know the shortest path ain't always the safest one, and get a rifle somewhere first chance you get. Where's your pistol?"

"I dropped it in the river."

"Jesus, Pat, winter's comin' on. That wasn't smart you ain't got any protection. You strike out east right away and you will probably make it before it gets too bad. Stay out of frontier towns 'cause there's always well informed bounty hunters there." Decker paused. "That is if the hostiles don't get you first." Decker swung up on his horse. "Be careful with your fires light only during the day and spread the smoke through. Travel at night if you can, don't talk to strangers, and get rid of that uniform."

"Wear the red underwear?"

They both laughed aloud. Decker caught Pat's eyes in his own.

"Damn it, Pat! I'm gonna miss you."

"No more grubstakes to poker, huh?"

"Well that, too. Take care of yourself Kavanaugh, maybe when all this is over we will meet again."

"Maybe, thank you Deck."

"East is that way," Decker pointed. "When all else fails look at the compass."

Decker turned his horse, trotted to the end of the forest path and urged it into the stream. He splashed to the other side, surged though the sand bar and disappeared over the bank. He never looked back.

Pat watched the spot where Decker had disappeared. Feelings of isolation and Dey je vous slowly worked their way into his thoughts. He rehearsed Decker's advice and remembered back to Ireland and his first time on the run, the advice had been much the same then. Pat hoisted the bag over his shoulder and walked down the path where the women had disappeared. The prospect of a journey did not trouble him so much but where he should go? He had gone about half a mile without a sign of use. He thought to himself, "The women must have headed off. I hope they find their way home." He took a deep breath. "I wish I could too, if I only knew where it was." He smiled on the recall of Decker's comment.

A voice started him as he approached the crest of a small hill buried in underbrush.

"Kav-van-naw."

He froze in his tracks as Sada stepped out behind him. She had positioned herself to observe Decker's movements; when he left she returned to the trail.

"Sada you startled me." He caught his breath. "Where are Maha and the baby?"

Sada pointed ahead. "There; come, we go!"

"Go where?"

"Village my people. Come, we go. Get you horse."

It was evening before they stopped and built a fire. Kavanaugh shared the jerky with the women, and in the morning, before light, fried a lump of bacon carefully cutting it into three equal pieces. For three days, they followed the same routine, huddling together at night to share their heat Kavanaugh laid between the two women with the baby tucked between him and Maha and Sada wrapped around his back. The position and a small fire each night kept the worst of the cold off. At first Kavanaugh was taken aback about the matter of fact way the women dealt with their basic functions and thought on one occasion Sada showed him a little more than she had to. She smiled at him, but he looked away. Still he recalled the event as she pushed up against his back at night.

Mid morning of the fourth day, Maha cautioned them to stop and cocked her head to listen. All three of them heard the far off sound. At first a murmur, soon the dull sound became louder, more distinct and all three clearly could hear the hoof beats of many horses. The riders appeared suddenly from a swell in the uneven plain, Kavanaugh gasped, the riders approaching were in full paint, shining with feathers and weapons.

"Sada, a war party, run!"

"No run."

"They may kill you just because you are with me."

"No, my brother chief."

Four riders had flashed out from the larger party and were bearing down on them. Sada stepped in front of Kavanaugh and raised her hand. Suddenly they were there, the first rider reined up but the second slanting in from the side struck Pat full stride. He was aware of the heat of the animal, its smell and as he was lifted and rolled backward dully aware of a hoof striking his head. Kavanaugh fell into a deep dark tunnel with a kaleidoscope of color bursting around him bright orange, fluorescent greens and blues then a dark stripe of red. Faces of long-dead companions flashed by; Sergeant Menzel was there, impassive as ever, and Moran smiling. He felt himself slipping away, and then Liam was there, a look of concern on his face, that faded to dim light.

He was next aware of being jostled around, fingers tearing at his shirt, trousers and boots then pinning his arms behind him. As he struggled to consciousness, he felt a noose drop over his head and tighten to his throat. His first image was a dark face wreathed in hatred staring into his and a line extending upward. He knew he was hurt and felt very dizzy with a racking pain in his chest when he breathed. He was aware of strong arms lifting him to his feet as he wobbled upright his head was yanked fiercely to the side. Pain engulfed him but he managed to stay on his feet and when he was able to focus his eyes he saw a warrior in full paint poised on his horse above him, a long length of rawhide drooped from his hand.

Slowly they started, with Kavanaugh, naked, staggering behind the horse, hands tied behind his back, and the long length of rawhide cutting into his neck. There were still flashes and bits of light passing through his senses and he tripped and fell head long into the grass. Again, he fainted and felt vaguely the arms dragging him to his feet, as his head flopped helplessly to the left; he saw Maha and the baby walking beside him. He vaguely wondered where Sada was and fell into step behind the horse. As he stumbled along, he became more aware of the noose around his neck and the pain in his side.

Chapter 4
Cheyenne Territory
1868

The large band made steady progress through the day. It was approaching dark when he heard some whoops from the vanguard, the pace quickened and Kavanaugh was forced into a shambling run. When the rider towing him stopped, he fell forward gasping for breath and in pain. Two warriors grasped his arms and forced him ahead, in the quickening darkness he saw a tall stake illuminated by the light from a large fire. The two warriors wrestled him down and bound him to the stake. He could not stand; a long length of rawhide tied his legs together and to the post. Kavanaugh passed in and out of consciousness and was dully aware of the commotion around him. Despite the discomfort, he closed his eyes and drifted into sleep.

He was next mindful of the early morning camp sounds ushering in the light. The women were tending fires and cooking pots, their voices punctuated by dog barks and the occasional shrill sound of a child. He could hear a greater blend of voices and the smell of boiling buffalo meat drifted to him causing pangs of hunger. His only perspective was a narrow view down the row of tepees and lodges. He seemed to be at the cross paths. Kavy smiled despite himself as one of the frowzy braves blundered by wearing his red underwear later he caught view of his blue coat worn by a young warrior.

The first few women came at full light they looked at him curiously and seethed with hate. They stood at a distance in a rough semi circle and they seemed particularly interested in his genitals leaning toward one another, giggling, and pointing. One older woman glared at him. She held a long pointed stick and he noticed some of the others had sticks too. Pat wanted to turn to his side but also wanted to be in a position to watch them. Three approached cautiously and Kavanaugh, aware of his nakedness, had little success trying to cover his genitals with his leg. Others, with pointed sticks, joined the three, and surrounded him. He ducked aside just as one of the points cut into his eyebrow and opened it to his nose. First one stick, then three others thrust into his chest and shoulder and they began to jab his chest, back, face, arms, and legs. He did not cry out but could taste the blood from his lacerated eye. The particularly malevolent woman came with a long smoking stick and thrust it at his front as he turned to dodge; and felt the stick penetrate deeply between his shoulder blades. Involuntarily, his legs uncrossed as he leaned back against the pain and pressure. When he straightened out, other women in front of him thrust forcefully; one staff cut up the inside of his leg and pierced his scrotum. He cried out in pain as a second gouge followed the first, lancing deeply into his thigh. The pressure in his back was excruciating, and then sudden relief as the stick was withdrawn. Two more women thrust pointed sticks deep into his chest and the wounds bled profusely.

Just as suddenly as they had come, the women disappeared among the tepees. He reviewed his wounds as best he could. He was bleeding quite heavily from his arms, thighs and chest; the blood was still oozing steadily into his eye and more blood ran a warm stream down his back. A brave came by and tied his ankles closer together.

A cloud shaded the sun and he was grateful for that, but late in the afternoon the women came back again. He could see that they were carrying faggots of sticks. "They are going to burn me alive," Pat thought in fear. However, most of the sticks were deposited near a large, apparently empty lodge a few yards from where he was tied. One woman bearing a burning branch did approach him and held it to his feet. The fire licked around his feet as he tried to avoid the thrusts. She managed to blister the soles of both his feet and toes and left a long angry burn up the side of his leg. When she left he quietly prayed, trying to ignore the persistent, agonizing pain that engulfed him. His feet throbbed and were red with large blisters and his toes were burned black. He continued in prayer but passed out, sliding down the stake, breaking the blisters on his feet and tearing flesh away from his toes.

Later, when he regained consciousness, Kavy could see braves entering the big lodge in front of him. He spotted Sada's brother in full feathers and from the different dress, paint, and hairstyles recognized that the men were from different tribes.

Near dark, a throbbing drum set the entire village dancing and milling around the area of the lodge. The activity lasted well into the night, he dreaded each minute thinking they would come to burn him. Kavanaugh was grateful he did not have another encounter with the women before dark and drew his legs up as best he could to conserve warmth. He was almost asleep when a quiet voice came from the deepest shadows.

"Kav-van-naw, I come help."

"Sada," he replied weakly. He felt her hand exploring his back pausing over the burning wound there. She kneeled behind him.

"Kav-van-naw big hurt?" She moved to his side exploring the cuts and scrapes to his chest down his abdomen and around his genitals, then down the inside of his legs. Kavanaugh flinched as she touched the wounds to his scrotum and thigh.

"Oh, Kav-van-naw big hurt," she whispered. "I go, come back."

He heard her moving off and was nodding in sleep when she returned a half hour later. She held a gourd to his lips.

"Drink," a look of concern laced her face.

He swallowed three big gulps she poured the remainder over his back. He felt her plaster a cool damp poultice on his back a similar one between his legs.

"Eat." She placed a piece of boiled meat in his mouth and he chewed while she carefully spread a strong smelling balm on his chest and arm wounds and the gash in his eyebrow.

"What will they do to me, Sada?"

"Tomorrow come many chiefs here. Many tribes. Big medicine."

"Will they kill me tomorrow then?"

"Don't know. Big medicine. Come Emo'ôhtavo Ma'hahko'e. You say Black Badger."

"Black Badger, --you mean like Sitting Bull of the Sioux? "

"Yes, big medicine man."

"Will the women come back with their sticks?"

"Don't know, yes," she looked at him. They call you Ema'o Nahkohe."

"Ema'o Nahkohe, what does that mean?"

"Red Bear. My brother bear too. He Etâhpe'o Nahkohe, Big Bear you say." She dabbed more balm on his feet.

"Sada go. Come at moon. Eat," she placed a bitter mixture in his mouth.

He settled back against the stake as he heard her footsteps retreating and the pain seemed to ease. A great loneliness filled him and he thought back to Ireland. Bittersweet memories flowed into him, then a bright green void passed behind his eyes and he drifted into sleep.

He was next conscious of full light, at the same time the sting of a switch across his cheek. The women were there again, but only one had approached. A warrior suddenly appeared from the lodge, growled something at the woman and she stopped. Again, the brave said a few words. Kavanaugh turned up his face just as the switch caught the cut eye. He felt it begin to bleed again. Another stern warning came from the warrior and the short, fat woman reluctantly left, looking hatefully over her shoulder.

A few hours passed and his wounds stung from the sun's heat. He saw four warriors approaching, his eyes focused on the tomahawks hanging at their sides. One brave moved behind Kavanaugh a sharp knife in his hand. The other three surrounded him. Pat closed his eyes and began and began to silently recite the Act of Contrition. The brave behind cut the thongs binding his wrists, moved to the front and cut the bonds on his feet. The others hauled him up and they started toward the lodges. He struggled to walk but mostly they dragged him past the large lodge to a tepee across from it. Kavanaugh was aware of the solemn looking warriors in full feathers watching him trundled into the tepee.

Inside there were some buffalo robes spread on the dirt floor. The warriors unceremoniously dropped him on to them. Two braves stayed, one at the tepee flaps the other across from him. He glanced over his body it was cut and bruised from hundreds of blows. He rolled over on his side, pulling the robe over his nakedness, and fell into a light and weary sleep.

He waked up as he felt the robe gingerly lifted off him. He rolled to his side and saw Sada was leaning over him. She began to dress the wounds on his side and shoulder and he rolled to his stomach and winced as she again worked over the deep wound in his back. He rolled over again and Sada continued to dress his cuts, she bent toward his lacerated eye. The two guards closely watched her.

"No kill you Kav- van- naw," she whispered.

"What are they going to do with me?"

"No kill you. You big medicine. No. Black Badger say no kill you."

"How do you know?"

"Brother say me. You now big medicine," she leaned over him and patched a cut below his other eye. "Black Badger tell Sada come. Bring water. Clean you blood."

She returned with water in skin container and with some soft deerskin began to bathe him.

Slowly she washed the blood caked between his thighs and washed the wounds on his arms and face. Sada gently cleaned the back wound, and as she worked she whispered. "Running Bull come, he talk English. He tell you what." She paused and looked at his feet. "You feet big burn."

It was just after dark when there was noise outside the tepee. The two guards became attentive as the flaps were pulled back and Big Bear slipped through. He pointed sharply at Kavanaugh and motioned him to follow. Pat slipped from under the robe and slowly stood up. Big Bear motioned toward the robe. Kavy pulled it around his shoulders and gingerly walked on blistered feet as he followed to the big lodge, the center of activity. There was a flaring fire outside, outlining many warriors gathered there. In the smoky light of the lodge he could see a number of them in feathers gathered separately from the others. The large lodge was crowded with men tightly packed together on three sides surrounding a small fire. Big Bear signaled him to stop. He could feel all the eyes turning toward him.

A slender brave with piercing eyes and a triangular forelock stood to greet him. The other men made way as Kavy followed Big Bear forward. The man with the forelock turned to the chiefs and pointed out a small dark somber man with a single feather who nodded assent and turned toward Pat.

"I am Running Bull. You are Kavanaugh, yes?"

"Yes."

"Be very polite, I will talk for you. This is the most important meeting of your life for it depends upon it. You understand that?"

"Yes, who are these men?"

"This is a council of chiefs from all 10 Cheyenne bands, plus a couple of Arapahoe and some Sioux."

"What am I here for?"

"They are looking for a messenger. If you fit, you live. If not, they will probably burn you alive. I will tell them you understand."

The somber man began a slow and sonorous speech stopped, and pointed to Kavanaugh. He listened carefully to the old medicine man. "Black Badger says you have been spared your life. It can be taken away just as easily." Running Bull interpreted.

"Yes, I know and thank him for his generosity."

"There is nothing generous about it; they have a task for you." He turned to the Chiefs and replied in a few quick sentences.

Black Badger looked at Pat and nodded. Then he began another rapid tirade and abruptly stopped.

"Black Badger says you are the 'bright' man. He has had a vision of a bright man to carry a message. Take off your robe."

"My god man, undress here?" Kavanaugh tightened the robe around him.

"Yes, he wants to see you. The women already have, so don't be bashful. Take it off, NOW, Kavanaugh, do you want to live?" Running Bull's voice was firm.

"Yes of course I want to live."

"Then take off the robe and step toward the fire. You wait much longer and your red hair is going to be on somebody's lodge pole."

Kavanaugh let the robe slip off and stepped into the brighter fire light. All eyes focused on him. The heavy red hair that covered his body glowed like a sunset.

Black Badger sat straight up and spoke excitedly to the men on both sides. He looked to Kavanaugh and nodded, a stir passed through the men present.

"Put the robe back on, white man; you are big medicine." Black Badger spoke this time looking directly into Kavy's face. There was a tone of assurance, but it was a short statement.

"Black Badger says you can put your robe back on, ---you are the bright man from his dream." Running Bull interpreted again.

The old medicine man broke into a long animated speech which Running Bull summed up in one sentence to Kavanaugh. "Black Badger and the Chiefs here want you to carry a message to the president and his soldiers."

"Running Bull, I can't go to the soldiers. I am a wanted man for what happened at the village. You might as well kill me now."

"That could be arranged! Quiet, let's hear what else he is saying."

Black Badger spoke again, this time stretching his arms to both sides, then bringing together his hands. "All the Chiefs here," Running Bull translated, "agree that you are to take a message about all of our troubles to your chief and appeal for peace, and ask for return of the rights to our land."

"I don't know. That is not the Army's business, it's the responsibility of the Office of Indian Affairs, I think, and I don't know anyone there, --- that's all the way back in Washington D.C."

"Kavanaugh you said you wanted to live. They want you to take this message on the "skin of sorrow," to someone who can help them. I will tell them you must take it to the Great White Father across the big river to the great waters."

"You want me to take this message to the President of the United States?"

"Yes or to a representative who has his ear."

"That would be the Director of the Bureau of Indian Affairs. I don't know how I am going to do that."

"It doesn't matter how you do it. Do you agree or not?"

"Yes, I agree to try."

"Good enough. They want you to go sit by them on the end there. They are going to smoke a pipe."

Running Bull addressed the assembled chiefs and guided Kavanaugh ahead. He gestured toward a place to sit.

"Kavanaugh, I think this is shit, I would sooner kill you. Keep yourself covered or they might change their mind." He smiled quickly, guiding Kavy to his appointed place and returned back into the assembly.

A stone tobacco pipe wrapped in deer skin began making the rounds. Kavanaugh observed the protocol and took his turn. He picked out Running Bull who was observing him without a sign of emotion on his face.

It was early the next morning when Sada entered the tepee. She had a bright red blanket, a breach cloth and a leather dish full of balm.

"Must put clothes on, Kav-van-naw. You go many chiefs Running Bull say. Running Bull comes soon." She quickly inspected his wounds dipping balm on them and gently rubbing it in." You very white where clothes were red, red hair".

Kavanaugh stoically took her ministrations, but became uncomfortable as she dressed the wound on the inside of his leg and scrotum. Sada continued industriously and Kavanaugh fought off an erection. Intuitively Sada leaned to his ear and giggled.

"You Etâhpe'o Nah Koe, too Em'oNahKoe," she laughed quietly as Pat blushed. The braves in the tent looked on curiously.
"Hurry, clothes. Running Bull come."

Kavanaugh knotted the breechcloth around his waist and slipped the blanket over his shoulders. His feet still hurt him and large seeping raw patch had replaced the blisters. Clumsily he sat down.
"My feet hurt Sada, I can't stand very well, can't walk much."

With a look of concern she left and quickly returned with some buffalo hide and leather strips she fitted over his feet and with her awl deftly made a few holes ran the rawhide through it and tied the ends over his ankles. Just as she finished the tie, the tent flaps pulled back. Big Bear and Running Bull stepped in.
Big Bear spoke a few words to his sister who solemnly listened.

Running Bull smiled, "you are going to have company Kavanaugh. Big Bear there just told his sister to look after you."

"She already is."

Running Bull smiled, "It may get better. She's a pretty one too."

"What is going to happen?"

"We are going to the chiefs again; Black Badger is going to tell us about the skin of sorrow."

"What is this skin and who is Black Badger?"

"Black Badger is big medicine. Hears Heammawihio, can foretell the future. The skin is a picture story. It's like a history lesson, and it shows what's happened the last five years. Black Badger has been keeping it. I haven't seen it, but that's what I hear." Big Bear motioned them to follow. Pat slowly pushed himself up. The hide sandals did protect him and slowly he limped through the flaps.

The chiefs again assembled with Black Badger seated in the center of a circle. Pat and Running Bull sat down across from him while Big Bear sat down among the others.

Across Black Badger's lap was a white deerskin pictograph with a large number of characters, some were repeated, some were not. He began in the middle in a staccato style following the characters in a circle pulling the robe and pointing.

Running Bull began to translate, "That figure he's pointing to is the man with the spots. That's small pox ---twenty-seven died. He's motioning to his face, see the scars? Pox marks. He says he died and lived again."

Kavanaugh shifted uncomfortably, "White men brought it, right?"

"Right the tepee with the arrow in it is a raid by Pawnees. Six children, six women taken and three old men were killed. Those figures with the arrows are prospectors killed. Now, the man with red spots, measles, I think. He's making a point. This war is white man's fault." Running Bull paused. "Another raid, they retaliated wiped out a whole village of Pawnee lost three warriors (one was my cousin). Next picture shows more died of disease, eleven children."

"These Pawnee, they don't get along with the Cheyenne?"

"True, most of the time, but you see that man there with the red and black face and all those ear rings". He pointed "He is a real Pawnee warrior and chief. He hates the whites, is called Blue Jacket and he is a big war chief. He is under protection of Black Badger but he doesn't like us much. The U.S. Calvary has used Pawnee scouts for a long time. The three over there with all the feathers" He nodded." are Sioux, all war chiefs. The three beside them are Arapahoe."

Kavanaugh looked toward Black Badger's pointing finger, "That's more disease that next figure?"

"Yes smallpox again, thirty-seven died. Another outbreak the following spring, twenty died. Are you picking this up Kavanaugh? It's too many to be accidental. "

"Yes, I can follow the pictures."

"You figured out the next one - ten blue men?"

"Soldiers who were killed, right?"

"Yes."

"That would have been the raid at the Terrell homestead."

"Yes, the Cheyenne lost some too - a dozen. But they burnt the place, a massacre right?"

Kavanaugh smiled, "I guess for them it wasn't."

"A simple victory; next picture, more disease, no spots, or pox showing, probably was bad whiskey, six died, all braves."

Patiently Running Bull translated each picture as the tale unfolded. The story went on for two hours. All the chiefs were attentive when Black Badger suddenly stopped. The chiefs shifted in their blankets adamantly speaking, with more curious and sullen glances in Kavanaugh's direction.

"Kavanaugh," Running Bull whispered, "Black Badger is speaking directly to you. Look him right in the eyes. He's asking if you will take the message of sadness and speak to the heart of the Great Father of the white men." Running Bull added in undertone "Be careful how you answer."

Kavanaugh looked at the old chief across from him, "Tell Black Badger that many dangers and trials will be waiting, but I solemnly swear I will do the best I can."

As Running Bull translated all the eyes of the chiefs were turned to him. "Good answer Kavanaugh." Black Badger nodded his assent and spoke to the chief.

"They're taking a vote, Kavanaugh and it's in your favor. Blue Jacket has asked if they trust you. The general consensus is no, but why not try?"

The powwow seemed at an end when Black Badger passed the white hide around the circle. It finally ended up in Kavanaugh's hand. Running Bull translated.

"You are so charged and you will leave soon. They will probably let you heal awhile. You will take the skin and they will make a peace sign for safe conduct. Say yes, Kavanaugh."

He looked at the aged medicine man. "Yes, I will do my best Black Badger. I promise you I'll try."

The chiefs regarded him as Running Bull translated. Again, there was some banter between the chiefs.

"You're out of here alive, Kavanaugh. Be happy for that. If you get to Saint Paul in your travels, that's where I was born. Now they're going to have a pipe. I think it's your tobacco," he smiled.

When Kavanaugh painfully made his way back toward the tepee it was almost dark. There was some smoke rising from the top flaps and when he pushed inside the two braves were gone and Sada was boiling some meat in a well-blackened pot. She looked at him blandly. "Big Bear tell me. Help you. Want eat?"

He settled down beside her and touched her shoulder. Kavanaugh noticed a frayed Army blanket, and on top of it were his rosary, his pipe and a plug of tobacco. The rosary was broken. He counted the beads, they were all there. He drew a thread from the blanket and carefully mended the beads.

Sada was watching him curiously, "White man's medicine beads?"

"Yes."

"Eat Kav- van- naw," she offered him a piece of buffalo meat.

"Thank you Sada."

She smiled at him, "Red Bear good man Sada like." She smiled, "Yes, Kav-van- naw?"

When they finished eating, they sat together as the fire burned down. Outside it was windy and away from the fire it was chilly in the shelter. Sada unrolled the sleeping robes, slipped out of her smock, and stood naked in the flickering fire light that blinked over the nipples of her firm small breasts.

Kavanaugh looked at her as she slipped between the buffalo robes. He sat for a while longer and felt her eyes on him while he said his rosary. He lifted back the robes, slipped in beside her and pulled the blanket then the robes over them. He rolled to his side, his back toward her, and felt her warmth.

"Sada like Kav-van-naw," she whispered.

After ten days, Kavanaugh's feet had nearly healed, and with Sada's ministrations he was somewhat restored to health.

"I go see Maha, ---she come soon," Sada broke the silence as she went about her work.

"So that's where you were this morning; how is she, is she alright?"

Sada did not reply busying herself with the fire.

"She come. She Running Bull's woman."

At midmorning, Sada started as the tent flap popped open. Kavanaugh too was startled.

"Hello, Maha." Kavy reacted. "What do you have there?"

She nodded respectfully toward him and at once became engrossed in a conversation with Sada. She gave her some carefully folded garments and left. Sada inspected them smiling.

"Maha sew good."

"Are those buckskins for me?"

"Maha say you try. She make better than me."

Kavanaugh slipped out of the breechcloth into the breeches. The waist fit perfectly but the leggings were up to his shins. With his teeth set against the pain in his back he pulled on the jerkin. It fell over his shoulders short in the sleeves. As he straightened the shirt he noticed the beautiful intricate beadwork.

"Big Red Bear," Sada laughed, "Give Sada." She held out her hand as he shed the buckskins. Sada quietly studied his wounds and then, leaving Kavanaugh standing naked inside the tent, stepped outside. He adjusted his breechcloth and followed her but she was no where in sight.

The sun was bright a very warm day for September. A few women were passing by, and spying him, began to talk among themselves. The bright sunlight shimmered off the beard and the red hair that was creeping down his neck toward his shoulders. He started to walk slowly through the village. He could see the tepees were in a rough circle and he was about in the middle of it. There were many lodges and he became uncomfortable thinking about the last, smaller village the cavalry had destroyed. Suddenly she was beside him smiling up into his eyes.

"Maha make better fit. Go river?"

"Go river," he smiled, "Now?"

"Yes." They set off slowly and stopped often. Ahead he could see the willows that lined the stream. They stepped into the cool water that eased the pain in his burned feet.

"You better Kav- van- naw?" Sada nodded toward his feet.

"Water feels good."

"Black Badger say to Big Bear you must go soon. Before snow come."

"Where is Running Bull? He was supposed to fill in details."

Sada looked blankly at him a smile playing across her face.

"Where is Running Bull?"

"War party gone. Brother gone. Running bull gone. When come back you go soon."

Pat looked up toward the sun as it passed behind a huge towering cloud. A chill ran down his back and he moved to leave the stream. He sat down on the bank his feet in the water Sada sat behind him bracing him with her legs.

"Sada like Kav- van- naw much."

He touched her hands and she wrapped around him. "Kavanaugh like Sada very much."

"Into me Kav-van-naw?" she slipped her hands to his groin. "Into me, now, Kav-van-naw."

"What if someone sees us?"

"See us?"

"Some women from the village," he gestured with his head.

"Big Bear give me you. Women like man." Kavanaugh turned toward her and they rolled from the waters' edge.

"Sada, I have never been with a woman before you."

"Into me, Kav-van-naw." She smiled and pulled him down and hunched under him. Slowly steadily, Kavanaugh pushed down and in. Sada first grimaced then sighed. She pushed her hips up. Kavanaugh made three thrusts and then convulsed.

"Ah, Kav-van-naw, it good no hurry."

"Oh Sada I think I love you. I've never loved a woman, you are the first." He stroked her face and hair and slowly withdrew.

"You like?"

"Oh yes, Sada. I like."

They lay together by the stream that murmured them both to sleep.

Over the next few weeks as Kavanaugh's wounds healed. They often returned to the stream to lie in the lush grass and talk together. One day they were there when Sada stopped their conversation and abruptly sat up. It was first a vague sound, and then became louder. Far beyond the river he spotted a cloud of dust rising. They stood up listening intently. Sada leaned into him, her arm around him.

"Big Bear come. We go now."

When they reached their tepee, advanced riders were already in camp and there was a great stir of excitement. Sada listened to the shouts and shrieks and gravely took in the puffs of dust growing closer. In the tepee was a neatly folded black and red striped blanket, his pipe and a plug of tobacco.

"Dance tonight," she tugged at her hair and crossed her forehead with her finger.

"Scalp dance?" Kavanaugh picked up the pipe, sliced the tobacco plug, and tamped it in.

"Yes three soldiers."

Kavanaugh drew a deep breath, "I hope they don't decide to make it four."

The short afternoon was warm, they rested together speaking quietly Sada was leaning against his side as he slowly drew on his pipe.

"Where did you learn to speak English, Sada?"

"Mission told me."

"What mission?"

"Mission at river."

"What river?"

She looked blankly at him.

"Never mind, how did you get to the mission?"

"When little," she held her palm parallel to the ground and signaled small. "Great dry, two," she made a circular gesture.

"Two years?"

"Yes, many die. Mother," she cupped her breasts, she signaled little again and touched her heart, "Give me mission."

"She left you at the mission?"

"Yes, take brother. Take my brother"

"You had a brother?"

"Born with me. He die."

"You had a twin brother?"

Sada's face lit up. "He be chief now, like Big Bear, but he die".

"He would be like the man with all the feathers." Kavanaugh placed his hands on his head, wriggled his fingers.

Sada smiled, "Yes, like Big Bear old brother. I at mission three," again she made a circular gesture.

"So that's how you learned to speak English."

"Not good."

"Sada, you speak better than a lot of soldiers I knew at Gettysburg."

"Getta, Getta, no can say word," she tried.

"Big fight, some there spoke only German."

"Ger, german," she shook her head. "Many words can no say"

"Never mind, Sada, it's of no matter. What happened? How did you get back to your people?"

"Big Bear come get me."

"Did you like the mission?"

"No."

"Why."

"Long knives there."

"You mean cavalry soldiers?"

"Yes, some hit Sada hurt me. They have scalps. No like me."

Kavanaugh gave a shudder as he recalled Brock's hatband and the other soldiers who had scalped the dead. "Ah, Sada some people are cruel - bad."

"Yes, not you, Kav-van-naw, you good." The sounds of the scalp dance seeped through the tepees, a drumming, shouting, and discordant music.

"It will be cold tonight," he wrapped the blanket over his shoulder, picked up a piece of wood and adjusted it on the fire.

"I am cold now."

"We will put down the robes."

"I sleep you Kav-van-naw. Make warm."

"That's a good idea." He smiled at her.

"It cold," She smiled back.

"Come in carefully," he arranged the robes within reach of the firewood. They curled up under the warm skins.

"You good Kav-van-naw, you man." Sada slowly moved her hand to Kavanaugh's thigh then to his penis. Slowly she stroked him.

"Sada maybe you should stop."

She continued and Kavanaugh ejaculated over her hand. She lifted the robe, "Look you make, four day I go to woman's place." She continued to rub his penis, "No hurry Kav-van-naw," she loosened the breechcloth and turned back the flap. She continued to rub him for an hour coaxing him; when he was again erect she sat astride him and pushed down.

"Sada, Sada, you feel so good"

She pushed down firmly, "You come in, no hurry."

"Oh Sada," he convulsed once, and again. "Sada, Sada."

She bent to him and touched his lips, "You good Kav-van-naw. I your woman now."

They lay down together listening to the drums.

It was dark when they rolled from the robes. The dance still throbbed on and the noise outside the tepee made him curious. He stepped through the flaps and noted a great pile of firewood burning in the empty area beyond the lodges. The men were dancing in circles holding long poles adorned with scalps they thrust up at the sky. A long spire of sparks reached into the dark. The thumping drum, gyrating dancers, and solid undertones of the women, were punctuated by loud cries that presented a weird scene, moving both joyously and ominously. He stepped back into the shelter.

"It is a big fire tonight, Sada?"

"Yes, big fire." She was busy boiling pieces of a prairie turnip with some dried buffalo jerky. They had just sat down, sharing a gourd of the hot stew, when the flap opened. Big Bear and Running Bull pushed inside.

Sada got up and went to her brother. In a show of affection that surprised Kavanaugh, he gave her a warm and lengthy hug.

"Well, Kavanaugh," Running Bull began, "you will be leaving here in five days or so. How are your feet?"

"Tolerable."

"You won't be dancing tonight. Fresh scalps," he squinted and with a crooked smile added, "probably friends of yours. They brought you a saddle. A scout and three troopers ran out of luck today."

"A scout was killed?" Kavanaugh thought of Decker.

"No, he got away. The other three blue bellies weren't so lucky. Don't know what they were doing so close. About two days out. They may have been looking for you."

"What did the scout look like?"

"A white man with a plain face and black hair, about your size – skinny though."

"What happened to him?" That's Decker, Kavanaugh thought.

"Found his horse and have his saddle and bags but he just seemed to have disappeared. They intend to give the saddle to you and a rifle. It's a breechloader a 45-90, Government Issue. If the Army catches you with this stuff, they are not only going to kill you, they will probably crucify you."

Big Bear and Sada had been speaking all the time that Running Bull and Kavy had. Now he called to Running Bull who listened nodded his head and turned to Kavanaugh.

"You leave day after tomorrow. Sada's going with you as far as she can toward Saint Joseph. Big Bear thinks two of you will blend in better than you by yourself, a trapper with an Indian woman, a squaw as you would put it. Maha, my wife has made you some buckskins and a hat to cover your nice red locks. Without the blue and boots, you will easily pass as a trapper, whiskey peddler, or a bum."

"How far is it to St. Joseph?" Kavy looked toward Sada then to Running Bull.

"Five maybe six days, it could be longer," he broke a knowing smile. "You could make it longer of course with those feet of yours," he laughed aloud. "Course you'll be on horseback."

"Very funny," Kavanaugh disclaimed.

"Anyway you will have that skin, wrapped in the red striped blanket, a saddle, rifle, a couple of horses and Sada. Hell, if I were you I'd keep going across the big river and hide someplace."

"I don't think Sada would do it."

"Best not try anything, Kavanaugh. Sada is Big Bear's sister. He would hunt you down and cut out your heart. There will be shadow riders and night visitors all the way to Saint Joseph. And keep that bright blanket rolled up behind you. That's your safety pass."

"I considered running; I don't think Sada would come."

"She won't, but you could come back. You'd be crazy, but you could. You are learning. If you had answered that council differently, they would not have believed you. If you fail, you could come back and tell them. You could settle in. I am not advising you to do that. Personally I think we just should have killed you."

"How will the other tribes know to leave me alone? Is that blanket going to be seen easily?"

"Yes, the word went out the same night you agreed to go. You will be well watched. That skin has to be rolled inside it and put up behind the saddle. Remember that."

"But there's cavalry we might have trouble getting around them."

"Ah, Kavanaugh you worry too much. This will probably be the safest part of the whole damn journey."

Big Bear gave a nod toward Kavanaugh, said a few words to Running Bull who replied so that Big Bear and Sada laughed. Then the two men turned and left.

After the men departed, Kavanaugh once again joined Sada in sharing the soup. Kavanaugh sipped lightly at the broth and watched the flickering fire.

"Kav-van-naw, sick?"

"No darlin', I am just thinking."

"You think friend?"

"Yes, I hope Decker got away."

"Decker big friend?"

"Yes, he was my best friend."

"He man at river?"

"Yes, we were good friends. His home was in New York and close to mine."

"He safe, eat."

"What did Running Bull say that made you laugh?"

Sada smiled and sipped at the soup.

"Well?"

"You," Sada nodded, "Piss pants when they come in."

"Not so," Kavanaugh laughed and kissed her cheek and she settled into him.

"Sada go with you."

"I know. I wish it were all the way to Washington."

"No want Kav-van-aw go."

"I may come back. I don't want to leave you behind."

She smiled but her eyes were very soft, "No, Kav-van-naw, you go. You dream Kav-van-naw, you dream much, wake me, and scare me. Talk dream, you in the big war, dream talk tell you never happy. Go, come, and go come all time. No will stay Sada."

Kavanaugh saw her concerned expression, "What did I say, Sada?"

"Who Mary?"

"Mary," Kavanaugh looked into the fire, touched his rosary. "Mary, Mother of God, Sada."

"No god mother, Kav-van-naw. Who Mary Carry?"

He broke into a smile. "That would be Mary Cleary, a dear friend."

"Your woman?" Sada smiled back.

"No, she was the girl friend of one of the soldiers I served with years ago. I have never had a girlfriend, except you."

"Why you talk, Mary? Soldier friend go 'way?"

He was killed, very near to me." Kavanaugh's eyes began to fill; he blinked away the tears then watched the flickering fire.

"Lose many friends, war. Why you fight war?"

He leaned back into the robes, "We fought for ideals, and then we fought for one another."

"Ideals, where ideals?"

"It's not a place, they are the ideas that we care about."

"Fight war for ideas? Don't know."

"It's hard to explain. Ideals are things we most believe in, that help guide our lives."

"No understand why fight war for ideas," she continued adamantly. "We fight for food keep us safe. Other tribes come to hunting grounds. We fight. Others come to take women, child, we fight. Keep people safe. No fight for ideas."

41

"I understand that kind of a fight too. Your reasons are better."

"Yes," she snuggled under his shoulder and placed her head on his chest.

"I'll try to come back."

"Yes," she smiled, "try come back."

A drizzly rain had wetted everything in the village when Maha returned with the buckskins. They were well tailored; the front was an open fold that the breechcloth covered. There was a beautiful beaded pattern over the chest. She had also fashioned a cap out of buffalo hide with flaps for his ears that fit loosely over his head.

Big Bear and Running Bull showed up at the tent leading two horses. The saddle and scabbard bore the name 'Decker'. The other horses carried the saddlebags and buffalo robes. Sada joined the group riding her own horse. Maha came to bid them off and six warriors rode with them a short way, then went on ahead in different directions.

The first day passed uneventfully and the Cheyenne riders were often in view. On the evening of the second night they made camp by a large spring the source of a rill that ran jaggedly down a fir rounded hill.

They had finished their evening meal of dried meat and a kind of tuber that Sada harvested from near the spring.

The sound of horses approaching at first did not alarm Kavanaugh who thought it was Big Bear and Running Bull, but Sada appeared frightened.

"Not Big Bear, white men; horse sound white men."

Two riders appeared where the rill from the spring broke into heavier cover. They had evidently seen the smoke from the small fire curling up through the willows and alders.

"Hello, the fire!" The big man called. "Mind if we share?" Without waiting for an answer they started toward them. Sada withdrew behind him.

"Long ride. I'm Jim Whit," he extended his hand. "That's Harry Koonz."

Kavanaugh shook his hand but noticed that both men were looking over toward Sada.

"I'm Pat."

"You are a long way from home." He paused, looking hard at Kavanaugh. "You're Irish ain't ya?"

"I'm an American now."

"Well, yeah we all are except maybe her. She's a looker. Where did you find her?"

"She's my wife."

Koonz began to chuckle, "Had two or three myself. Used to do a little trappin' up on the Colorado - Crows they were, meaner than hell them women!"

"From what I know of you Harry, they probably had a right to be."

"Traded one for a colt pistol and I still have it. I doubt like hell if my trading partner still has her."

They moved closer to the fire extending their hands for warmth.

Pat picked up the conversation, "On our way to Independence, going to work on the rail road."

"I did a little of that." Whit's eyes flickered about the gear spread by the fire, pausing for a moment on the saddle, then back to Sada.

"I got some coffee. Harry, why don't you go fetch it and the pot". He gestured to Kavanaugh. "You're welcome to share."

The pot was soon boiling filling the air with its acrid smell. Whit passed a cup to Kavanaugh. "Nuthin' like a cup of coffee, Pat?"

"It's been awhile."

"What's your woman hidin' for? She want some coffee?"

Kavy turned toward her, "Coffee, Sada?"

She shook her head negatively.

"She sure is pretty for a squaw. My, oh my, it must be nice," Koonz looked her over carefully.

Whit settled back sipping from his cup, "Well now, And Pat, we was fair to share our coffee. What about sharin' her?"

"Look. I appreciate the coffee but you can stay on your side of the fire. She's my wife, not a chance of that kind of sharing."

"And you was married by the pope," Koonz and Whit both laughed.

Kavanaugh felt the hair rising on his neck. The rifle was well back among the saddlebags and he was caught with just his eyes to guard them.

"Noticed that saddle there, I know who that saddle belongs to. Or should I say 'used' to belong to?"

"It belongs to me."

"That saddle belongs to a guy named Decker. Was scoutin' for the Seventh last I know."

"Then you also know he is from Prosper, New York and likes to play cards."

"That's true."

"I staked him many times. This time he lost it all, so I took his saddle."

"Is that right? I think you're lying, Pat. I know that Decker would never give up that saddle. And I think you stole that saddle. You're a deserter ain't you Pat? Stole the saddle and lit out, didn't ya?"

Kavanaugh did not reply.

"I did a couple of trips down the Santa Fe with Deck and his uncle. We had big Comanche trouble on one trip."

"Sure, Deck told me about that." He shifted uncomfortably at the man's questions.

"You're lying, Pat. I think you killed Decker and that Cheyenne bitch you're with knows it too. Get the woman, Harry." They both stood and moved quickly.

Whit jumped back from the fire and drew his revolver. Koonz moved toward Sada and Pat moved to block him, he felt something go past his face hissing, splitting the air and piercing Koonz from throat to spine. As he flinched away he caught sight of Whit grasping at his chest with one hand and staggering back, the revolver dropped and he grasped the arrow shaft with both hands and fell to his knees with a surprised look.

Koonz kicked a few times, twitched and lay still. Big Bear stepped from the shadows and with a swift, powerful blow struck Whit at the base of the skull with his tomahawk. Behind came a voice Pat knew well.

"I damn near killed you, Kavanaugh you were right in the way," Running Bull laughed. He lifted Koontz's head by the hair "Following you around is sure adding to my collection."

Sada rushed to her brother in a gush of talk. He put his arm around her, moved to the white corpse and turned it over with his foot.

"Jesus wept!" Kavanaugh blurted, "What the hell, I never suspected them!"

"We saw them a while back. We made it to the spring before you did. We've been waiting."

Kavanaugh stepped back as Running Bull drew his knife.

"I'm gonna collect some hair." He seized Koonz scalp, deftly cut a circular pattern around the top of the skull leaned forward and skinned a little back from the forehead and with a quick pull tore off the hair leaving the bone exposed. He examined the dripping prize, scraped off some flesh that still clung to it and proffered it toward Kavanaugh. "The horrors of Indian warfare, Kavanaugh."

"You made your point, I can't believe it. Jesus wept! Trouble just seems to be my shadow."

"It's all the same no matter what side you are on, the important thing is to live and suspect everybody. Do not trust anyone or you will not live long with a price on your head." Running Bull wiped his knife on some grass.

Kavanaugh looked at the body with the arrow still protruding from its throat. "Yes," he replied, "to live."

Running Bull was scraping more flesh from the scalp drawing the knife toward him, he saw Kavanaugh watching. Big bear also began to take his prize.

"I'm cleaning up this scalp."

"I see that, grisly business!"

"So was the village on the creek."

Kavanaugh shook his head, "I still can't believe that bloody mayhem. I thought I knew those men, they went crazy."

"I know kill crazy, they wanted to kill everybody. Sada told the whole story, It happens."

"Running Bull how the hell did you get here?"

"I'm a real American, Kavanaugh, born near Saint Paul, Minnesota." He turned the scalp in his hands. "My father took to the white man's way," he smiled, "Sort of anyway, he worked for a printer. My mother was a servant in the house. The wife was an abolitionist lady, very much an abolitionist lady. She also helped with a lending library and taught me and my mother to read. Hell, Kavanaugh, she spoke better English than you do. Better read than most politicians and she encouraged me to read and write."

"Is she still in Saint Paul?"

"No, both died with pneumonia, been 15 years or so ago. They were good to us, the printer and his wife."

"How did you get here?"

"My father was cousin to Hump Backed Wolf. Heard of him?"

"No."

"He was probably the greatest Cheyenne war chief ever, a warrior-chief not like those back at the council. I do not like the peacemakers – Civil Chiefs – shit! Big Bear there, "he nodded toward Sada's brother, "He's a war chief."

"But, it was big medicine that council, Black Badger and all?"

"Yes, big medicine. But don't trust those Pawnee. I don't. The ones at the council are riding just ahead of us. We will be riding with you for a while; you're safe almost to Saint Joseph. It's still a long ride, another day at the very least. We will not be with you all the way."

"I'll be more careful about who I talk to," Kavanaugh shuffled his feet.

"You'd better, or that red hair could be buzzard food or hanging on a Pawnee lodge pole. Travel only in full daylight. Get out early in the morning; avoid strangers." He waved the red edged scalp toward him, "You see what happens if you don't."

Kavanaugh backed away, "Yes I see."

Chapter 5

Near St. Joseph, Missouri
October 1868

Morning began when a crimson streak cracked the sky like a slow powder fuse and the high clouds burst to pink. Kavanaugh collected the revolvers belonging to Whit and Koonz and placed them carefully into his saddlebags, tied the blanket wrapped skin behind his saddle. They rode southeast, Sada following behind him. They made camp in a copse of poplars near a small brook. She was quite solemn, without her usual smile and chatter. The light of the fire flicked shadows over and between them.

"I no go with you tomorrow, Kav-van-naw."

"Not go. Why?"

"White man big fort tomorrow. Big Bear tell me."

The snapping of the fire became very clear and one small bough caught brightly then quickly faded to dark.

"Oh, Sada, I will miss you very much."

She smiled, "Sada like Kav-van-naw," she turned to him and he gathered her in his arms and clumsily kissed her.

"Sada like Kav-van-naw," she nestled under his arm as they watched the fire burn down. Soon there were only glowing coals and Kavanaugh felt the emptiness growing in him. He fingered the rosary around his neck, removed it and began, "Our father" Sada watched him her head against his chest and his huge arms around her. "Who art in heaven hallowed be..."

"Big medicine beads, Kav-van-naw?"

"Yes big medicine. I got them many years ago at another time when I was out of hope."

"Woman gives you?"

"Yes, then she died."

"I make you medicine bag. Give you tomorrow Cheyenne medicine."

"Thank you Sada."

He finished the rosary and they slipped between the skins. He reached for her and kissed her passionately.

"Kav-van-naw in Sada now." She raised her skirt.

"Yes," he rolled her to her back and penetrated her. They fell asleep locked together.

An angry jay was berating them in the morning light. Sada slipped from the robe and went off into the poplars. Kavanaugh stirred the old fire though only a few small coals remained. He sprinkled some birch bark and dry leaf mold over them and blew gently. The bits began to smoke. He was stoking in some twigs when he felt Sada behind him. Her head was crooked to the side.

"Kav- van –naw big back many marks," she smiled and passed her hands across her behind. "Look funny."

He smiled and pulled her to him, "Why don't you come with me Sada? I love you."

"No go, no like white men. They not good," she placed a pot of water over the now racing fire. "Better here. You come me when moons bring grass."

"I don't know if or when I will return."

"You come me," she smiled. "Think Kav-van-naw's baby here," she patted her stomach and smiled again. "You come. No come, Kav-van-naw here," she continued patting.

"You're going to have a baby? My baby?"

"Think yes."

"Then you must come with me, Sada."

"Where Sada go? No place Sada go."

"No, we will find a place."

She smiled into his eyes, "You come Sada when moons bring grass."

"I will try."

"Sada know not easy. Moons," she motioned folding her fingers, "moons never same people never same." She placed the medicine bag around his neck, "Keep Kav-van-naw safe."

They finished their meal and Kavanaugh dejectedly began to saddle up. Sada folded the Army blanket over her horse and deftly swung up on its back.

"What will happen when I leave? How will you get home?"

"Brother, Running Bull come, and look you see them. You go now Kav-van-naw," she pointed toward a small hill rising in the distance. "There go."

Kavanaugh followed her point, mounted, and caught up the reins of the pack horse. They touched palms. He fought the sadness and despair rising in him. Sada sat close-lipped; a tear began to run raggedly down her face.

"Go now Kav-van-naw. There," she again pointed.

Kavanaugh tried to speak, but he could not. His vision was clouded and his throat contracted. He finally managed to speak "Goodbye, Sada I will try to get back."

She turned her horse and rode slowly back over the trail they had recently traveled together. She stopped after a few hundred yards and waved. Two riders joined her. He waved back, directed his mount toward the distant hill, and started out of the poplars into an uncertain future. His heart was heavy, but he did feel a sense of mission.

His first business was to get a pair of boots, a blanket, some bacon, tea, and coffee, a small sack of flour and some salt. He hoped to trade the revolvers and buffalo robes for supplies. Then, he would be on his way to Washington, and if he ever got there, head to Mary Cleary's. He knew that she would help him. He remembered back to the last time he saw her, when he told her about Moran's death. She thought God had punished her for her fast life by taking away her only love. Yes, he mused: there is a law of limited good there are only small gains in life ---big ones are balanced by loss.

A light but steady rain began to fall shortly after Sada disappeared from sight. He silently thanked Maha for her skill and the extra overlay on his shoulders and the long fringe that deflected the water from his back. He saw the smoke of city long before its smell and sound, and entered the outskirts cautiously, avoiding what he perceived to be the main thoroughfares in the sea of mud. He was amazed at the signs of commerce around him and felt as if he had been lost in time.

The streets were thronged with people, so much mass confusion and noise to his ears after the solitary, silent, plains. At first, he felt everyone was looking at him, and then realized everyone was in their own world. He noticed a large plainly painted sign 'Fronmeyer Mercantile'. Down the short street piano music from two saloons clanked and clunked and interior voices carried to him. He fondly contemplated a drink then dismissed the thought. He felt he had changed somehow then realized the world had too.

There was no one else in the store as Kavanaugh pushed through the door, but as he closed it, a short middle age man with a thick curly hair and glasses stepped in from the back. "Can I help you?" The man waited for Kavy's response.

Kavanaugh did not reply struck at first by the polite man's voice and wire rimmed glasses that made his eyes look huge. He caught up to his surprise.

"Sorry, I've been away for awhile. Yes, I need. I need some things," he paused, "Mostly I need some boots or shoes."

The man peered at the clumsy buffalo slippers Kavanaugh was wearing. An inquisitive look quickly passed.

"We have a pretty good selection of shoes, but if you want good boots there's a cobbler down the street."

"No, I haven't got the time. I'm heading east."

"What size do you wear?"

"Fourteen or fifteen I think"

"Oh my, I'm not sure we…" He looked at Kavanaugh's feet thoughtfully. "I'm not sure but I think I have a pair almost that size, just a moment."

The serious little man disappeared and Kavanaugh began to walk around the display of merchandise. He looked up at the sound of the voice.

"I have one pair, a very good high top shoe. They are very heavy, but durable, yes,

48

durable, made in New York and very durable."

"I need some socks, a blanket and an oil skin too. I have something that can't afford to get wet". He glanced to the shopkeeper "I have a list, but I don't have any money."

The man looked surprised, "You are a stranger, and how do you expect to pay? I don't give credit to strangers."

"I have two buffalo robes and one of them is very large, plus two Colts to trade for the boots and the rest of the stuff, bacon, flour, salt, coffee and tea and socks."

"I don't often trade. I prefer cash money."

"I don't have any money and it is very important I get to Washington."

"Well", he thought for a moment. "Are the revolvers in working order?"

"Yes and the skins are prime-tanned."

"Bring it all in; guns are in demand these days."

"I have a couple of horses, but I may need them."

"Oh dear, no, I don't deal in horses."

Kavanaugh brought in the robes and revolvers and piled them on the counter. Fronmeyer carefully studied them, first the robes then the guns.

"Well, these guns are in excellent condition. I assume you are trading the holsters and the bullets in the belt?"
"Yes, of course. I could use some .45/90 cartridges as well, that could be an even trade".
Fronmeyer looked over his glasses, "The guns, of course, and those three buffalo robes are worth more than all you want to buy, but I don't pay cash."
"That's alright," Kavanaugh paused, "How much is it to cross the big river?"

"To cross the Mississippi costs a dollar for a man and horse, fifty cents for a pack animal. That's what it used to be. But it's a long way from here."

"Is my stuff worth a dollar more?"

"Yes. I'll allow a dollar and a half. I can make a small exception."

"Then, that's a deal, the stuff on my list and a dollar and a half, deal?"

Kavanaugh slipped on the boots and walked slowly toward his horses. His feet were still sore, but the boots did fit him well. He began to stow the packages and buffalo slippers in his saddlebags. The merchant had followed him to his horse.
"You forgot your bullets," he saw the name on the saddle, "Mr. Decker."

Kavanaugh did not reply but nodded and watched Fronmeyer disappear into his store. Kavy heard a commotion behind him. Two local ruffians were towing a thin, terrified Chinaman toward the hitching rail. One brandished a tomahawk and they both had a drunken glitter in their eyes. The Chinaman fell, the man holding his cue jerked him to his feet.

"Out of my way, Red, I'm gonna collect me a scalp," the one with the tomahawk croaked. He twisted the cue toward the rail; the other man was laughing holding the flailing arms.

The Chinaman wailed, "Please do not cut my hair. Please, No." he looked toward Kavanaugh terror in his eyes in a silent request.

They had him stretched, his cue over the rail. He began kicking ineffectively at his tormentors. The tomahawk was raised when Kavanaugh caught the wrist that held it.
"He said, no."

"Come on Red, this is none of your business we're just havin' a little fun, he's just a Chinaman."

"He's not havin' fun. Let him go." The man was as tall as Kavanaugh but slightly built, the other was considerably smaller. Both were obviously under the influence.

"This is none of your business."

"I'm makin' it my business," Pat quietly rejoined.

"Shit, just what I need to run into a Mick jack ass like you."

"I just had a scene like this with a couple of your brothers not long ago. They're both dead."

"Let go of my wrist, Mick or I swear you'll be the next one dead."

Kavanaugh tightened his grip, "Let the Chinaman go."

The man holding the Chinaman's arms released them.

"Forget about it, Kirby. It ain't worth it."

"Please do not cut my hair Mr. Kirby."

Kirby released his grip and the man pulled free. "Alright, I've got more important things to do," he looked into Kavanaugh's face, "I'm gonna do you." He made a quick move and twisted away at the same time arching the tomahawk toward Kavanaugh's head. Kavanaugh again caught his wrist, grasped his elbow and pitched the man forward. Kirby was up in a flash and again swinging the weapon. Kavanaugh again parried it but this time caught the arm and twisted Kirby against the rail and with a sharp punch sunk his fist deep into Kirby's kidney. He dropped the weapon and began to slide down. Kavanaugh delivered a second blow and Kirby's jaw shattered beneath it.

"Now Mr. Kirby I'm going to give you something to remember my by." Grasping first one thumb and then the other Kavanaugh broke them like match sticks. He turned to the second man, who stepped back slightly. The terror of the Chinaman now showed in his face and he jumped up on the boardwalk.

"Listen Mick, I want no trouble."

"Want it or not you've got some." Kavanaugh reached for him. Quickly the man drew a knife and stepped farther back.

"You better know how to use that blade or you will wind up with it in your ass."

"Come on, Mick. Come on," he waved the knife and began to switch it hand to hand.

Kavanaugh smiled slightly and moved toward him. In a flash, the knife nicked high on his arm. He made another slash and another nick almost in the same place. Kavy backed away.

"Like that Mick? I'm gonna open you up and wrap your guts around your neck."

Another slash and another nick this time on the other arm and the man called Kirby began to moan and tried to stand.

The knife wielder looked toward him then looked back too late. Kavanaugh had his arm and stepped behind still holding the knife and clamped his other arm around the neck. As the man struggled, the knife fell away. Kavanaugh continued to choke until the man went limp. He turned him on his stomach picked up the knife and drove it to the hilt, into his buttock. Kirby was now on his feet, wobbling slack jawed. Kavanaugh struck him a blow to the chest, caught his limp form, and tossed him into the water trough.

The Chinaman had retreated deeper down the boardwalk and stood before the store. Then he sat down wide eyed and peered at the scene back at the water trough. Kavanaugh checked his wounded arms and saw that there was some blood running over his hand. He shook his head and looked back just as the man who had cut him, struggled up. Kavy kicked him under the chin and as he fell to his side slopping his head into the mud around the trough.

A voice called from behind him, "Mr. Decker are you wounded?"

"A scratch or two," He replied as he looked over the wounds.

Fronmeyer was beside him looking at the scene, "Here Mr. Decker, take this handkerchief. The cut on your arm is bleeding."

"Thank you did you see what happened?" Kavanaugh pressed the handkerchief to his arm.

"Yes all of it. They deserved it, been bullying people around here a long time."

Kavanaugh re-checked his wounds and placed the handkerchief over the one bleeding the most.

"Mr. Decker you had best is movin' on. The skinny one there, Kirby, has three brothers. All of them are no account, but kind of local heroes. There gonna come lookin' for you and that Kirby is the baby brother."

"I'd better be movin' on. Which way to the Mississippi? What town?"

"You want to get to Hannibal?" Fronmeyer pointed to a dusty road angling east. "You head for Chillicothe."

Wearily Kavanaugh walked to his horse. The Chinaman stood on his approach.

"Take me with you, Mr. Decker."

"Take you where?"

"East, I am going to Washington."

"So am I," Kavanaugh prepared to mount, "You know how to cook?"

"No."

"Do laundry?"

"No."

"What do you do?"

"I can pay you well."

Kavanaugh shook his head, "Just what I need. Take a train it's easier."

"I need to leave. Please let me ride with you. These barbarians; I have had many bad experiences."

"Know how to ride? I don't have a saddle for that horse."

"Yes, I can ride."

"Alright you can ride the gray."

"Mr. Decker," Fronmeyer called up. "When you get to the Mississippi you can cross over into Illinois at St. Louis or you can cross right at Hannibal. You don't have to ride all the way; the train will take you to Washington."

"Thank you, Mr. Fronmeyer".

"Good luck to both of you"

Chapter 6

Mary Cleary
November 1868

Half a continent away near Washington D.C. the sounds of the band drifted through the door of a room thick with cigar smoke. Five union officers and a woman were looking at one another across a long pile of chips in the middle of the table.

"I fold," she said and pitched in her cards.

Two of the other players also turned in their cards.

"I'll match your fifty general and raise you fifty." A captain ventured nervously as he fingered some chips and tossed them in.

"You haven't got anything captain. I'll pay fifty and call." He scattered the chips forward.

The general laid down his hand, "Full House."

"Four jacks."

"God damn it!" The general exploded and jumped up cracking his thigh into the table rocking it nearly over. The drinks tipped then flopped, and the bottle of whiskey rolled across the table gurgling out its contents into the poker trays.

"God damn it!" He repeated his face florid. All the players in turn had jumped back to avoid getting their drinks in their laps except the woman who stared fiercely at the general. There was a momentary silence sliced by her icy question.

"What is your problem, General? If you can't lose then don't play! You owe everyone here an apology."

"Apologize for what, Cleary?"

"A second one now; you apologize to the company at once and to me in your next breath or I will throw your ass out of here." Her voice climbed steadily to a controlled rage.

The general started for the door. Stopped and with grim lips and said "I am sorry gentlemen. Mary is right, I apologize, Mary."

"That's better. Do you gentlemen wish to continue?"

"I'm done, Mary."

"Alright 'Captain Jacks,'" she smiled, cash in your chips. I think Sally is over there now. Are the rest of you in?"

They drew their chairs back to the table. "I think General Getting owes the table a bottle of whiskey, don't you general?"

Again his face flushed, the junior officers did not speak.

"You're hard on a man, Mary."

"You make things hard on yourself." She turned to the man across from her, "When you pick up your chips 'Captain Jacks'," she smiled. "Send in a bottle of Pennsylvania bourbon and have Sally come in with a cloth to wipe the table up," she paused, "General are you going to play or going out?"

"Charge it to my bill, captain."

"Yes sir." The captain nodded toward the table and quickly left.

The bottle having appeared and the table wiped, they sat to resume the game.

"Let's have a new deck, major and ante up."

It was already light when the game broke up, some officers back to their hotels and others to waiting women upstairs in the brothel.

"Time to call it a night, general," Mary settled quietly into a floral sofa, the general followed and settled beside her.

"Mary, why don't you take that blasted black garter off your arm, put it around your leg and go to bed with me? I really want to get in your pants."
"What for I have one asshole in there already?"

If Getting was offended he did not show it. "For money of course, that's what drives you isn't it? And why not who was this Moran anyway? What did he have that I don't?"

"It would take all night, General." She looked away toward the band. "

"I thought he was your business partner. Instead, he was just a teamster, taking advantage of you."

"General, the only thing that Donal Moran ever did me wrong was to get himself killed in a war he didn't understand. He enlisted for six months from upstate New York and had one week to go before his enlistment was up. Now, do you want me to see who's available?"

"I want you, Mary." He wrapped his arms about her and pulled her close trying to kiss her mouth. She turned away. He began kissing her neck and shoulder and grasped her breast.

She struggled trying to pull herself away, "Come on, General, just quit. This isn't going anywhere," she struggled free of him.
"When Mary? I've been coming here for months, nearly every night."
"I know that, and the answer is never. I'm not in the trade anymore."

"I'll pay fifty dollars, that's a fortune for fifteen minutes work. Come on, Mary." He put his hand on her leg and slid it toward her crotch. She let him feel her then slowly pushed his hand away.

"General, I haven't turned a trick in years. I just manage things these days. I have no need for a man because I knew one and loved him and he loved me. It's just a business, a profitable one and I'll be soon out of it. It is a complicated sale and I haven't figured it all out yet, but I will."

The general released her and settled back into the sofa. "You have managed pretty successfully. How many whore houses do you own?"
"Entertainment centers, General; I'm in the entertainment business."
"I know you have at least five."

"Yep, five plus two hotels a couple of saloons and lots of property and I intend to get more. It is a buyer's market." She smiled.
"Jesus, Mary you must be worth considerable money?"

"Yes, I have a lot of money and I appreciate your help in keeping out the police. Even though you don't seem to get all you want out of the deal."

"Well, it might not last that much longer. Of course you could guarantee it."
"Like how?"
"Like going to bed with me."

"General, I have more miles on my ass than a pie wagon pony, but as I have said, I don't do clients anymore. I can arrange company for you – that's it."

"No, I want you! Come on, Mary," he reached up for her pulled her close and again tried to kiss her on the mouth.

Again she turned away. "Why don't you let me get Sally for you?"

"I've tried Sally and the belle of the house. What's her name?"

"Hope."

"She was good. But…"

"I don't think she's available, Sally is."

"Sally was last time."

"How about, Florence, the clients sure like her."

"Don't like red heads, none but you that is."

"General, perhaps you would like me to get a copy of Vanity Fair from the library and you can read for awhile."

Getting laughed, "You're pretty damned sophisticated for a simple whore."

"I may be a whore, but not a simple one."

They both laughed and the tense emotions were relieved.

"Sally will be alright. If you ever decide to go back to work Mary, call me. I'll give you one of my stars for a blowjob, the other for fucking you."

"Hell, that's not very generous. What are they worth, a nickel each?" She stood up and motioned Sally over. "Take good care of him Sally. This one is on me; he has had a bad night."

Sally smiled at the general. "I remember last time big fellah." She hooked his arm with her own, and then glanced at Mary, "Hope's been wantin' to talk with you, Mary. She's waitin' in the lounge."

"Thanks, Sal; I'll go see what she wants." Mary watched the two up the stairway out of sight; wearily she walked toward the lounge.

Hope was seated at one of the tables near the wall that featured an upholstered booth of rich dark leather. There was a bottle with two glasses before her. She spotted Mary as she entered.

"Lo, Mary."

"Ah, Hope. How's my girl?"

"The truth is not too well."

"What do you mean? Those diplomat guys rough you up?"

"No, he was a gentleman. By the way," she pulled up her purse and placed it on the table. "He didn't squawk about the money and gave me a fifty dollar tip."

"Wow, that's a lot of money!" Mary picked up the two bills from the table. "Was it a nice affair then?"

"Yes, a big dance - beautiful. Everyone was all gussied-up diamonds and gold jewelry. It was at the Willard. We went around, met a lot of people. Most of them spoke Spanish or …"

"Portuguese, you looked gorgeous when you left here, that pale blue and pink really set off your figure."

She smiled, "Yeah, Portuguese. We didn't last too long at the dance. We spent most of the night in his room. It was nice there too. He had boiled quail eggs and spicy tomatoes and good tasting little sandwiches and nice wine."

"Hors d'oeuvres."

"Yes, that's it orderves."

"Sounds like a good night. I can't tell you how many men wanted to be with you tonight.

They say you are good company. You were so pretty, worthy of a diplomat."

"Hell, Mary, you know I just make them. I don't know. I listen a lot."

"Good, that's the way to many a man's heart, not food, nor sex, nor beauty just listening."

"They seem to like it. My God, the things they tell me."

"They figure you won't repeat it to anybody they know." She poured a small amount of gin into the glass and slowly began to sip it.

Hope filled her glass and took a big swallow. "You know how much I appreciate you taking me and baby Sarah in and all. I was out of luck, Billy gettin' killed and all."

"Yes, I was just talking about Moran tonight. I still miss him, you know."

"Yes, I know because I still miss Billy. I know how much now, I mean with all the men I meet now."

"That's the truth," Mary sipped at the gin. "What's troubling you Hope? You maybe want to go off on your own?"

"Oh no, Mary, I feel so much at home here with you and the girls and Mary, Sarah loves you as much as I do. You treat me like a sister."

Mary laughed quietly. "That is because you are like a sister to me. What is it that is bothering you?"

"I've got the scab, Mary."

"Oh no - how long have you had it?" She fixed her with a concerned look.

"I noticed it tonight when I was washin' up. It's in my hair beside the lips, you know. I pulled hairs from it. Thought they might be ingrown or something. It doesn't hurt."

"This isn't good, it's probably the pox. The scab will go away in awhile. Is it hard like?"

"Sort of, there may be another one comin'."

"We will call Dr. Sims over tomorrow. Ramona has a rash so he can look at the both of you."

"Anything I should do?"

Mary laughed, "I don't think so. I got some ointment you can put on it. I think puttin' some gin on it would do as well."

The two women laughed quietly.

"I'm not feelin' too good whether it's the pox or not."

"It affects people differently. Why don't you take a few days off and get some rest? Do some shopping; go to the park with Sara - something."

"That would be swell, Mary."

"I'll get Doc Sims in tomorrow morning." Again, Mary sipped at her glass, "Hope, I'll be going away next week for a couple of weeks. Suppose you could act as 'Madame' hostess while I'm gone? It would give you a little break."

"Me, Mary, "she asked timidly, "I don't think I know how to do that."

"You can do it. All you must do is keep track of who is available when and line up the clients. The girls like you. All the patrons I've talked with know you and they like you. You can do it. A couple of patrons asked if you were my daughter."

"That's because you treat me so nice. People notice."

"Hope, I was wondering. I'm going up to New York state, like I said, I may be gone a couple of weeks."

"New York?"

"Yes, going up to Donal's home town, Minsi."

"You like it there don't you?"

"Yes, it's beautiful, especially this time of year. I'm thinking of buying some land there in Sullivan County. It's beautiful; has a river through it, rolling mountains, flat rich fields along it. I'm going to build a place there."

"Are you going to set up another house?"

"No, this time I am going to build a home. I think I'll put up a good-sized mansion. I'm thinking of building a kind of refuge for old whores, unwed mothers, and runaways." She paused a moment and focused on Hope's face, "I've been all those things and no body ever helped me. I sure could have used it. I think I'll call it Moran's Cloister." She grinned "He would have thought that to be a great joke."

"Gee, Mary that is a great idea. Can I come there too?"

"Anytime you want to."

"That would be nice Ramona's gettin' old. Her list is very short these days. But you know, Mary, she has been very kind to me and Sarah since you took us in."

"Bringing you here has been the best investment I ever made." Mary sipped at her gin. "I thought I'd take Sarah with me, if you don't mind?"

"Oh yes, Mary take her if you want. She would really like it and it would be a good trip, that is, if you can keep her from runnin' wild. She is so active, never wants to wait for anything. She wants to know about everything and those books you got her? She's gone through every one."

Mary rose from the table reached into her sweater pocket and dropped a hundred dollar bill on the table.

"For shopping, Hope, don't spend it all in one place and consider it a prepayment on the extra work ahead."

"Thanks, Mary. You don't have to pay me until you see if I did things right."

"See you tomorrow. If Doc Sims didn't get drunk last night, I'll have him here around ten."

Dr. Sims stepped from the bedroom his bag in hand, as Mary was passing down the hallway.

"How is my girl?"

"Which one, Mary? They are both sick."

"Hope."

"She has less severe syphilis. The scab is definitely a chancre. I gave her some ointment for it. Ramona has something else; I gave her an ointment for it."

"I know, doc. Both from the same jar," she laughed and walked away Sims followed her.

"You know, Mary, this business is bound to bring disease. This is a dangerous business."

"So is soldiering. Come by the office and I'll pay you."

"I was thinking I'd see Heather. I don't need any money."

"Whatever you say, doc, I'll be in my office. Heather is here somewhere. Try the lounge."

56

She hurried up the stairs to her third floor office with a view of the burgeoning city. She liked this catbird seat during the day but especially at night, the gas lights of the street cast an eerie glow over the busy thoroughfares.

She was well into resolving bills and tallying assets when she heard a tapping at the door.

"Come in." The door swung slowly open and looking over her glasses, she saw Hope and her little girl crouched looking gleefully at her.

"Hi, Aunt Mary, did I scare you?"

"No you didn't, darling, come see me," she pushed back from the desk and opened her arms just in time to absorb the joyful bundle into them. They hugged and kissed. "How did you know I was here?"

"I didn't. Are you countin' your treasure?"

"Yeah, don't know what to do with it all. Have to go to the bank today and get some money for my trip, ---or maybe our trip?" she looked questioningly at Hope who nodded her assent.

"Are you going away, Aunt Mary?"

"Yes, and do you know what?"

"What?" she beamed.

"Your mother just said that you can come with me!"

"I can? Oh!" again she hugged her. "Where are we going?"

"Yeah, good question. You'd better know before you agree to come."

"Where Aunt Mary, tell me, ---downtown maybe?"

"No, darlin' we're going on a trip up to where my friend Donal came from."

"Up to New York?" she gasped her eyes brightening.

"Yes, you are going to be my business partner, and we are going to take some long rides; be sure Mommy packs some warm things for you to wear."

"Oh, this will be wonderful," she clapped her hands and bounced up and down. "I'm going to go pick out some warm things." In a flash she disappeared down the stairs.

"Think she wants to go?" Hope smiled.

"It will be good for her." Mary placed her glasses on the desk, "you saw the doc?"

"Yes, he said I have syphilis. He said it would go away in a week or so."

"Well, yes the scab will. But you know Hope, some people can become mighty sick from it."

"I know, he told me. Most people get better, so I'll not worry about it unless I need to."

"Take care of that scab and rest while we are gone."

"Yes, I'm doin' that, you know Mary, I really love you!"

"Me too, kid. Now, let me finish these bills."

Hope turned and closed the door behind her. Mary carefully completed her ledger, eased herself back into her chair, removed her glasses, rubbed and closed her eyes. She smiled to herself about Sara's calescence concerning the coming trip. She wondered what had happened to her own enthusiasm. She thought of Moran, and she knew. She dozed, drifting off into a troubled recurring dream.

A long curving lane arched from the wagon road to the farm tucked into the side of the hill. The house was small and neat with a steep roof that sprung two chimneys - one at either end. It was made of stone, carefully set, and a root cellar was between it and a barn which appeared to be in good repair. A number of mature pigs lumbered along the fence; in the barn, there was a sharp echo of squeals and squawks. The roof over the barn entrance was newly built. It was the last repair work that Bill Cleary had done before his fall. Now he was watching from his bed his useless legs stretched out before him. Inside the barn a middle aged man with high arched brows, dark eyes and thinning hair was trying to catch a piglet. It managed to escape his grasp and ducked under the fence heading for the door.

"Catch that god darned thing, Mary. He's comin' right at you."

"I got him, Uncle George. He surely is a lively one."

"Well bring him, over. I swear I'm havin' one hell of a day, you got to help me hold them. I got enough cuts to bleed to death. You got a good hold on him?" He looked disgustedly at the old razor in his hand.

"Yes. He's a lively one," Mary carried the piglet to him.

"You little black bastard, I'm gonna slow you down. Stand by with that kerosene." Deftly he spread the piglet's legs and made a short slash cross ways to and behind, pulled out the tiny testicles and jerked out the two sperm cords cut and flipped them aside. The pig writhed in pain. "Squirt him, ow, Mary, damn it! Not on me, on him."

They put the pig down and it retreated with some admonishing squalls.

"Why we doin' this Uncle George, it full hurts them little pigs."

"Why are we doin' it? Because your father can't since he fell off the ladder."

"I know that. But why do we cut these little pigs?"

George picked up the testicles and placed them in the palm of his hand. "These here are pig's nuts. If you don't cut them out, the pig's meat will taste strong and you'll stink out the house cookin' it."

"What are the nuts for?"

"Your maw hasn't told you anything 'bout roosters and hens, bulls and cows, mares and stallions?"

"Oh," she smiled, "you mean when they get on top one another?"

George flipped the testicles toward her. She stepped back and did not try to catch them. Slowly she bent toward the floor. George watched her carefully.

"You don't have pants on huh, girlie?"

"No, Maw's makin' me some out of a flour bag they will be done soon."

He walked toward her a bit, placing the razor back on the stall rail.

"Hey, girlie you got any hair between your legs?"

"Some."

"Let me see it."

"I don't know, Uncle George. Maw might wallop me. I showed it to Danny Reidel and he showed me his. His ma told my ma and she made me cut a switch."

"Well, your Maw ain't gonna find out. I won't tell her, she won't be comin' here. Let me see it."

Mary lifted her skirt and displayed the sparse red growth.

"Well, look at that," George marveled. "I never' did see a red one. Come on over here girlie."

He caught up her hand and they walked over toward a stable filled with bedding straw. "What did Danny Reidel do?"

"He showed me his. Looked like a birch sprout."

"That's all he did?" George laughed then leered, "You want to see a real one, look here." He unbuttoned his fly and displayed a large erection. "Did you touch Danny's?"

"Well, yeah but it wasn't big like that. It was gettin' hard but…"

"Want to touch mine?"

"Why, it's really big. Danny's wasn't like that."

"He's just a boy. Come here, girlie. That's it hold it. I like that. Want to kiss it? That's it. Suck it a little girlie. That's it. That's it. Now lets you and I lay down here on that straw."

He slipped her skirt to her waist. "Now just lay still," he pushed the glans of his penis into her.

"No, don't, Uncle George it hurts. It hurts! Don't. No. Oh, you're hurting me. Oh, oh stop! Stop, Uncle George!"

He pushed with all his force driving the shaft deep into her.

"It hurts, it hurts, Uncle George. You're hurting me!" He made a few quick pumps and ejaculated.

"Ah, that's it girlie. Just lay still."

"You're heavy and you hurt me. Get off me now!"

"In a minute," he kept her pinned beneath him as his body jerked several more times. Finally, he withdrew.

"You did me, didn't you?"

"Yes, girlie, I did you. You been fucked." Now he stood up, buttoned his fly, and straightened. "That was good, don't tell you're Maw and I won't."

"I'm bleeding Uncle George. You hurt me bad."

"Ah, girlie it will go away. Here take this," he cut a piece of cloth from a feed sack.

"Hold that on it. We got one more pig to do. Come on now, girlie. Come on help me catch it."

"He ran out of the barn. We ain't gonna catch him today."

"Probably not, let's go on up to the house. I can't come back tomorrow got business in town. Now, when we go up there promise not to say anything. When I come back day after tomorrow I'll bring you some candy."

"Will ya?"

"Yes."

"I like that anise candy, can you get that?"

"I will on Wednesday." They began to walk toward the house; Mary discarded the blood stained rag.

Wednesday came and once again, the two started to the barn.

"Like your candy girlie?"

"It's good. I like anise candy better"

"Did you tell your, maw our secret?"

"No, but she and I took a bath Monday night. Maw saw the blood."

Did she?" he replied in alarm. "Did you tell her anything?"

"Not our secret, I kept the secret."

They entered the barn. The pigs sensing some disaster again began to snort and run, a big brood sow's squalls pierced the din.

"I caught the one we missed the other day."

"What did your maw say?"

Something about having my time of the month time, she says it will come every month now."

"That's all?"

"No, we had a long talk. She was real nice. Told me about her first time it came on her, she didn't know I was so close and all."

"What else she tell you, girlie?"

"She told me about what you did to me and the roosters and chickens like you told."

"That's all?"

"That's almost all."

"Want to do it again?"

"No, you hurt me, Uncle George and I hurt a little still."

"If you do it again it will be better and it won't hurt this time."

60

"Really?" She passed her hand to her crotch and lifted her dress slightly.

"Come over to the straw girlie. It will be better this time."

"Ma told me men pay bad women for what you did to me."

"Well, you ain't bad, and you already did it once. Come on over to the straw."

"I want five cents if I do."

George shook his head. "I can't believe it. You want paid? That's what makes the women bad, getting paid for it."

"Well, Uncle George, molasses drops ain't exactly anise candy. If I get a nickel I can go get my own."

"I only got three cents."

"I want five."

"Damn it, girl, look I'm in a bad way!" He gestured to his bulging pants.

"I ain't in a bad way. I still hurt and I want five cents."

"The hell you say, get over on to the straw." He grasped her arm, "Come on."

"You want me to go? You pay."

"I got three cents, you ain't worth more, and you're just a girl. What's this?"

"Uncle George, you let go of me or I'll cut ya." She had picked up the razor from the railing.

"Why you little bitch, put that razor down." He pulled her toward the straw. The razor made a quick arch and caught his thumb.

"Yow! You, you little bitch." He raised his hand to strike her.

"You hit me and I'll cut you good."

He dropped her arm and started to suck his bleeding thumb. "You got me good already."

"I'll get you more. Now, we gonna' cut that little pig, or what?"

He took his thumb from his mouth gathered up some spider web and packed it into the small slit.

"I swear, Mary you're gonna be something. I don't know what, but somethin'. Come on over to the straw I'll give you three pennies and bring you a nickel tomorrow. And I'll for sure get anise drops next time I'm in town"

Mary jolted awake, and thought for a moment. "Dreams, that sleazy bastard, I am glad he's dead! The world is never safe for girls like Sara."

Chapter 7

Minsi, New York
November 1868

The stage ride from Washington to New York took three days. They had not hurried and took time to review some local sights along the way. Mary had business in New York so she checked into the progress of her women's clothing store that featured French designs. She directed the proprietor to begin looking for a suitable site for a second store, then she and Sarah took a ride through Central Park and dined at a deli. The rail ride to Minsi had taken the better part of the next day. Sara followed Mary through the cemetery gates and down the long rows of stones to a plot surrounded by set stones and dominated by a gray monument of an angel in prayer. The large stone bore the name Moran.

"Who was he Aunt Mary?"

"The only man I ever loved, Sara --the kindest, best natured man."

"Don't cry, Aunt Mary. If you loved him, he was better off than anybody."

"My word, child, why do you say that?"

"Because you love me, so I know."

Mary gave Sara a hug and held her close. The sun sank past high noon and the once bright foliage took on the burnish yellow color of the oaks as the other colors faded toward dark.

"Let's go to town, darlin'. I'm going to buy you a new dress. Then we will look around the stores and see what else we might buy."

"Could we buy some licorice maybe, I like licorice very much?"

"Yes, sure, I like licorice too. Tomorrow, we will go look at the property I bought." She turned slightly and shaded her eyes with her hand and with the other pointed toward a lumpy low slung ridge line cloaked in faded maples and dark hemlock. The ridge was split by a stream that ran into the river curling around it. "That's supposed to be it, I think. Do you see the water fall on that little ridge? We will name them Sara's Falls."

"I like that. Did you buy the whole mountain Aunt Mary?" They clambered into the buggy and covered their legs with a blanket."

"Yes darling I bought the whole mountain. Get up there, gray, chuck, chuck!" The horse lurched ahead. Only the creak of the wagon and the horse's breathing stuttered the silence.

"Aunt Mary?"

"Yes, darlin'?"

"Did you know my dad?"

"Yes, darlin', I did," she rapped the reins again.

"What was he like?"

"Well, he wasn't much more than a boy, I mean a young man. He had black hair, and the brightest blue eyes I ever did see. He wasn't very tall."

"I mean what was he like?"

"Oh, Billy was adventuresome and kind of feisty."

"Feisty?"

"He was strong willed and determined, always arguing about something."

"Ma said he was brave."

"Yes, I suppose he was."

"Did he love Ma?"

"My gracious girl, what's this about love all of a sudden?"

"Did he Mary?"

"Yes, I suppose he did."

"Ma loved him."

"Yes, I know."

"She said they were going to go out west to Oregon, was that just a dream?"

Mary did not reply, guided the horse around a long rolling turn in the road then looked toward Sara's innocent eyes. "Yes, darlin', I think he meant to, in that year a lot of dreams died in just one day." The creaking harness seemed louder as a cloud passed across the sun.
"Dreams don't last very long, Aunt Mary. But they can be nice while they do."

"That's true, but we sure do wish they would. And sometimes it's important to believe they will," Mary smiled at her. "My little philosopher you are wise beyond your years."

Sarah reached across, encircled Mary's waist with her arms, and leaned against her.

"I love you, Aunt Mary. Don't be sad."

"And I love you too, darlin'."

Chapter 8

Kansas/Missouri
November 1868

The weather began to change before dark on the first day of their ride increasingly cold and snow began to spit into the freezing rain. They had ridden side by side, but the Chinaman did not say a word; after a couple of tries Kavanaugh accepted the silence. He wished he had kept one of the buffalo robes, for the Chinaman was wet to the skin and despite his stoicism, he was convulsed to shivers. They reined up in a small grove of trees.

"I'll scrape up a fire. It's too late to go much further. Why don't you get over to the dry side of that tree?" Kavanaugh nodded toward a large sycamore.

The Chinaman dismounted and dragging the blanket headed for the tree. Kavanaugh looked carefully at him bone wet in his dark suit that was much too light in weight for the freezing night.

"You're not very well equipped to cross the prairie, are you?" The man did not reply. "So long as we are going to be together for awhile, what should I call you?"

"I am called Wu." He made a small bow.

"Woo?"

"Yes, Wu Shen K'ung."

"Well, Woo Shen," he could not help but to smile, "I'm Padric Kavanaugh and you are the first Chinaman I ever had the pleasure to meet." Kavanaugh made a small bow.

"You do not sound like an American."

"True enough, I was born in Ireland and if I could go back, I would."

Woo smiled, "Yes, these Americans are truly barbarians."

"Take the blanket and oil skin and get out of those wet clothes, friend, you don't even have socks."

"Socks?" He looked blankly at Kavy.

"Stockings, you know," he motioned toward his new shoes.

"Are we going to camp here, Padric Kavanaugh?"

"Just call me Pat a lot of people call me Kavy, take your choice. And yes, we will camp here."

"Is there not a town ahead?"

"Probably there is one not too far."

"Why do we not ride on?"

"I kind of avoid towns, Independence was an exception. Take this oil skin while I make a fire and wring out those clothes and we will dry them." Woo looked at his fingers. "Wring, wring you know," Kavanaugh made fists and turned them.
"Yes, Pat I understand."

Pat found a small windfall of fir and after a few false starts there was soon a blaze. He gathered enough fir and oak branches and the two of them leaned to warmth of the fire. The snow tapered off at dark but it stayed overcast.

"What are you doing in America, Woo? You are farther away from home than I am."

"I am on a mission."

Kavanaugh stretched toward the fire, "What kind of a mission, if I can ask?"

Woo smiled, "You already have asked."

Kavanaugh laughed, "I guess I did."

"I am going to Washington and New York City to speak with trade emissaries."

"Trade, eh?"

"Yes, and I want to know why my people are not welcomed in America."

"Everybody is supposed to be welcome," Kavanaugh smiled, "Except the Indians. You know, if it wasn't for the Irish and Chinese there wouldn't be any railroad to connect America together. We ought to be welcome."

Woo smiled, "Why the Indians not welcome? Do others want their land?"

"A lot of greedy people see the Indians in the way of the development of America and their personal fortunes. Many think because we have a strong government it gives rights to those that support it. Many Indians are being killed and dying of white man's diseases, soon there won't be many left."

The image of Sada riding off momentarily blurred his thoughts. He stared blankly into the fire. Woo turned his tunic that was drying on a rack Kavanaugh fashioned from an oak branch.

"Are they drying?" Pat asked poking at the fire.

"Yes, I do not want to burn them up, I will turn them."

"You would be in great shape if they burned. Are they your only clothes?"

"Yes, I was robbed of my things and my companion killed before I left San Francisco. I had two horses and many gifts and I have only my coins now."

"We must get you some clothes somewhere along the way. I have two blankets but one is wrapped around." He looked toward the bundled skin, "Now, I can put the buckskin in and other stuff that in my saddle bags. I will bring you another blanket."

"I have money. We could stay in town."

"Woo, I will not be staying in any towns, only passing through. You can leave any time if you want to stay in town but I must stay out."

"I think I will stay with you."

"Alright, next town we get to we will get you some things. I'm going to make some bacon and beans. You can clean up. I cook, you clean."

Woo smiled. He liked the big generous man. He again turned to his tunic on the drying rack. The snow had stopped altogether and the damp area around the fire started to steam. Kavanaugh brought the other blanked and they settled near the fire.

Morning brought a cloudier blue sky and in halos of frosty breath, they cooked a hasty breakfast and broke camp. The ice covered potholes crunched like cookies and spilled their muddy fillings into the softened road. After a few miles, the way fare filled with commerce and the sound of voices, snapping whips and the creak and rumble of wagons. Once they had to ride off the busy byway to allow a squad of cavalry to ride by. Kavanaugh avoided their eyes. After a short ride, the town of Hamilton spread across both sides of the road. The streets were busy with people bundled against the cold and intent on morning shopping.

"You should be able to find what you need up ahead there. That store there," Kavanaugh pointed.

"You are not coming into town with me?" A look of concern passed over his eyes.

"No, not a good idea, get yourself another warm blanket and clothes and what ever else you think you will need. We could use some more bacon," he paused, "Woo?"

"What?"

"I wonder if you'd get me a bottle of whiskey."

"Yes, if they will sell me some."

"You had better get going, and don't worry. I will ride up to the edge of town so I can keep an eye on you."

"I always seem to attract attention."

"I know that's why I'm not going with you. I do not want any attention. I think you had best get a heavy coat, a warm hat and some socks-stockings. A wool shirt wouldn't hurt you either; you should probably get a saddle too."

Kavanaugh tethered his horse and sat down on the boardwalk where he could see Woo ride into town and set about his business. He tilted his chair against the wall and let the sun warm him. Then he scratched around for his pipe and tobacco, lit up and waited. He could see Woo moving in and out of the pedestrians hurrying along. An hour passed before he again spied Woo burdened by his purchases making his way back toward him. Pat noticed Woo's horse was freshly saddled. In fact, he did not recognize Woo at first, for he was buried in a dark blue mackinaw and a wool watch cap.

The two carefully made their way through the town's back streets and regained the trail east. It was four o'clock in the afternoon when they stopped inside a little stand of trees. They found an old fire site and gathered wood. Kavanaugh pushed down a dead alder and snapped off the limbs. Woo brought some water from a nearby rill and watched Kavanaugh kindle the fire and soon their pot was bubbling.

"You want some coffee, Woo?"

"No, I have purchased some tea. You like tea?"

"Yes, at home I drank more tea than coffee."

"Good tea, very good quality tea. This tea came from Woo Nu Quei a merchant from Guangdong. I know him well; I am here because of him and Wa Fung of Suchow."

"Small world somebody said."

"This tea was cured near my home in Guangdong. I know the trees from where it came." He turned the can so Kavanaugh could see the label. "The trees are on the slopes of Luofo Mountain."

"Is that right, from nearby your home?" Kavanaugh smiled.

"Truly," again, he turned the can in his hands.

"You said you know the men who sold this tea to America."

Woo smiled, "Yes, they are two very prosperous merchants. Woo Nu Quei and Wa Fung. They want to do more business with America. This can of tea came here from England, but the tea was raised and cured a few miles from my home. We would rather sell more tea direct to America instead of to the English." He poured two tin mugs of the tea.

"I am all for that. Don't trust the English with anything. They think some how they are the masters of the world." Kavanaugh sipped at the steaming brew. It was already turning toward a cold evening. Woo squinted through the firelight at Kavanaugh who sat with a blanket draped over his shoulders and hunkered toward the fire.

"Mr. Pat."

"Just Pat, Woo. What?"

"Pat, then, you did not tell me you were a desperado."

"A desperado," Kavanaugh laughed, "A desperado! I'm not a desperado, what made you think that?"

"Your face is posted on the wall of the sheriff's office. You, Padric Kavanaugh are worth $500. There were many pictures there; yours said 'deserter from the Army, attempted murder, thought to be armed and dangerous,' "Armed? What does that mean?"

"Have a gun, which I do."

Woo smiled, "You are not a murderer, I would know. You are a man of jing chaou"

"Jing chow, what's that?"

"Jing chaa-ou," He gently corrected. "It means persistent strength".

Pat smiled "I never have been told that before". He chuckled and ran his hand over his shaggy beard. "But for these times, what else can you be"?

Woo hitched a little closer to the fire. "Well said, Pat. How did you get here? Why do they offer a reward 'dead or alive'? You are not a mean man. You care about others and offer help even to strangers".

They sat quietly watching the sparks from the fire raise into the blackness. Kavanaugh fumbled for his pipe and tobacco.

"It is a long story, Woo. But, before I tell you my story, I would like to know how a rich Chinaman, ends up in the middle of America with just rags on his back and a pouch full of gold."

Woo did not reply immediately but sat slowly sipping his tea. "As you say, it is a long story."

"Well, I asked you first and we are not going anywhere this late. I think we are going to get some more snow and I have nothing else to do. I'm all ears"

"Four of us were sent to America. My companion and I traveled to San Francisco, two others to New York."

"What happened to them?"

"My companion was killed in San Francisco and all our merchandise was stolen. I was away when they came and when I returned I found him dead. Everything was lost except for the gold because I had carried it with me. I joined with a group of travelers by coach and paid the drivers well, but they abandoned me at Independence two days before I met you and took another traveler in my place."

"So you still want to do business in the east?"

"Oh, yes. There are many of my countrymen who will help when I get there. The two emissaries sent to New York may still be alive. If not, I must get the others ready - buy ships get crews, and make whatever agreements I may need to make. There is so much work, but if my counter-parts are already there, it will be much easier. If not, it may take a while to raise all the necessary capital. The gold I have is to start our venture."

"Woo you are talking about thousands of dollars many, many thousands."

"We are prepared for that, first, I must get there."

"I will put you on a train and you will be alright, much more comfortable."

"Comfort is not the question, safety is, and will you come?"

"No, not on the train, not yet, I can't. There may be people hunting me for the 500 dollars, once I cross he big river I could risk a train ride."

"Will it will take a long time to get to the river?"

"I don't know, Woo, if you have to go, take the train, you will probably be alright."

"No, I will go with you for awhile. This is a very dangerous place."

"Maybe, after we cross the big river, the Mississippi, it's ahead a couple hundred miles. Maybe we can take a train then."

"I will give you the money if you need it, now if you want it."

"Thank you, Woo, but I may never need it."

Woo did not reply, but looked deeply into the flaming fire. It was almost dark when they heard the clatter of riders on the road and as they watched, four riders reined up.

"You at the fire!" a voice called out. Woo jumped. Kavanaugh stretched out his arm to restrain him. "Wait here, Woo hide your gold out of the fire light." Kavanaugh whispered as he rose to meet the riders and stepped toward them. Woo scurried into the dark.

The four riders arranged themselves around the campsite. Two were young looking men. One dismounted the others held back looking warily to the woods around them.

One of the younger ones drew his pistol and pointed it at Kavanaugh's chest. "You got any money?" As emphasis, he cocked the hammer of the revolver.

"No, I don't."

Another rider dismounted and patted down Pat's chest and sleeves then around his back and looked back toward the mounted man.

"No watch neither, Cole. Check them saddlebags, Arch. He nodded toward Kavanaugh's horse and watched as the man fumbled through the bags and withdrew the skin, folded it over and studied the picture, then passed it to the other beside him. Woo reappeared from the dark into the fire light.

"Injun stuff, kind of pretty, what do you think, Buck?"

A rider separated himself, "Pretty drawings it's Indian alright."

"You want it?"

"No, what use is a damned old deer skin with some pictures on it. You have cash, Red?"

"No, I don't. But that skin is very important to me".

"Put it back, Cole."

The mounted man looked down on Woo who had returned to Kavanaugh's side. "I suppose you don't have money, either?"

Woo reached into his pocket and fished out a Chinese coin with a square hole in the middle of it.

The man called Buck laughed. "Look at this, Jess - a coin with a hole in it, reminds me of the Liberty Bank," he laughed. "Chinese money, eh it isn't even made of gold."

"You got coffee cookin' there?" The man called Jesse queried.

"No just water for tea, but I can make some coffee." Kavanaugh glanced to the fire still sputtering sparks.

"You got any whiskey, the chills about taken me."

"You got anything?" The young rider asked holstering his pistol, "You're an Irishman ain't ya?"

Kavanaugh looked straight at him. "Yes and so what?"

"So, I think you're a God damned blue belly. You in the war?"

"Yes."

"You fight for the Yank's?"

"Most of the time I fought to stay alive."

"You weren't with that bastard Custer?" The other young rider asked.

"No, I wasn't, I was with the Seventh Cavalry, but not with him. I'm just a soldier trying to get home. I seen all the war and all the killing I want to see."

"You're just a God damn blue belly to me. I just as soon kill another one."

"That's enough, Archie, they got nuthin' we want." The man named Jesse dismounted, stretched, and began limping toward the fire. "Whiskey maybe."

"You got any whiskey?" The man called Cole asked.

"Woo, do we have whiskey?"

"Yes," he nodded and hurried toward the saddle bags piled outside the firelight.

"Why don't you come over by the fire and warm yourself."

The others dismounted and all settled around the fire as Woo produced the bottle and handed it to the man beside him. Arch took a long pull and passed it on.

"You want somethin' to eat. We have some bacon and beans."

"No, we got to be movin' on."

"You're in too much a hurry, Jess."

"Well, Arch. If you had a woman like Zee you'd be in a hurry too."

"She is a pearl whose price has launched a thousand ships," Buck quoted Homer with a flourish of his hands.

The bottle made another round and the man called Cole threw some more wood on the fire.

"Winter's late, been savin' up to bury us. You, Chinaman, what you doin' there?"

"I will make tea." Woo disappeared toward his saddlebags.

"I ain't ever shot a Chinaman."

"You ain't shootin' this one either, Arch. We ain't with Quantrell anymore and these folks don't mean harm."

"You are gettin' a little soft Buck?"

"No, I remember what it was like tryin' to get home after the war, and these folks ain't botherin' anybody."

"Have another drink. Keep you from freezin' to the saddle," Pat offered.

They sat for awhile huddled together against the growing cold and finished the bottle between them.

"Why ain't you wintering in, Irish?" Buck asked.

"Want to get to Washington before winter."

"You've got a piece to go. Winter's goin' to beat ya! Come on boys, let's mount up. Weather's goin to beat us too if we don't get along. Leave these folks to their fire. We got a piece to go ourselves." He limped to his horse and swung on to it easily.

As the others stood to mount the one named Buck turned to Woo and flipped him the coin he had taken. "Best keep this. It's too far for me to go to spend it."

They mounted and the one called Jess touched his hat. "Obliged for the whiskey, Red, be very careful it's a long way to Washington."

They whirled and rode off the sounds of their horses disappeared and the woods were strangely silent except for the hissing fire.

"They were desperados," Woo said suddenly.

"Is that so? How do you know? You are sure spotting lots of desperados" Kavanaugh looked to where they had disappeared into the darkness. "There's no doubt they were thieves."

"I know their names."

"You know those men?"

"Two yes, their name is James and their pictures were on the sheriff's office just above yours."

"Jesse James, well I'll be damned."

The morning was clear, but very cold and the tea-water pot was layered-over with ice. Kavanaugh ministered to his morning needs and returned to the fire site. Woo had not moved and still lay curled in his new blankets.

"Are you still alive, Woo?" Pat teased. There was some squirming beneath the blankets as an answer. "I have to get some water. Gather some more wood, and we'll get breakfast started. I'd like to cover twenty miles today."

They soon finished breakfast, packed their gear, and mounted on the trail. The morning was gray and frigid, but they made good progress. In the afternoon, an ominous gray appeared and the wind was sharp. Later in the afternoon, it began to snow in earnest. Woo had not responded to Kavanaugh's attempts at conversation and only spoke when they had stopped. They reined up near a cross trail with a rough wooden arrow indicating Macon fifteen miles.

"Let's camp over there. There's a little creek and those trees are thick enough to break the wind. I'm afraid it's going to get cold tonight, a lot more snow too." Woo looked toward where Kavanaugh pointed. "There's a lot of wood in that old oak. We have to get started on some kind of shelter. Did you hear me Woo?"

"Yes."

"You don't say much, do you?"

"In my country it is impolite to talk while traveling."

"Let's get into those woods."

"Yes, Pat. We must get out of the wind and I will help with the shelter."

Woo selected two adjacent trees, and with some deft strokes of his newly purchased hatchet, cleared the base, strung cross poles and industriously built three walls of boughs.

When Kavanaugh returned with firewood he marveled, "You're quite handy, Woo. That lean-to is better than what a lot of people I knew lived-in back in Ireland."

"Yes, I have made these shelters ever since I was a boy." He laid away the hatchet in his saddlebag.
"It's gonna keep the wind off and I'll build the fire in front."

Using the saddles for backrests and the blankets draped over them, they were warm despite the dropping temperature. Woo made tea and they sat close together the wind shearing around them.

"This isn't exactly a hotel room, but it beats bedding down in the snow."

"Yes. It is not a very big house."

Kavanaugh sipped his tea and put another piece of wood on the fire.

"What's it like in China, Woo? I mean what was your life like in China?"

"China is a very old country - thousands and thousands of years so it has developed much culture most of which the west has no knowledge of. It is much larger than Europe travel and communication is difficult. I think Ireland would easily fit into Canton where I was a boy."

"Are you married?"

"Yes, I have a wife and two daughters". He sipped at his tea." You are not married?"

"Yes, I mean, no, I am not legally married. I have lived with a Cheyenne woman for

70

a little while. With all the soldiering, I haven't had time and I thought I was too young. I am almost too old now. In Ireland, men wait until they are in their thirtieth year, sometimes not until forty." He smiled and thought of Sada. "Maybe someday I will get back to my wife."

"One is never too old to marry. For a woman can be a great comfort what ever one's age".

They watched the fire dancing and licking through the oak and willow boughs, it glared bright as a puff of wind caught it.

"How did you come to America? I mean the merchants sent you, but are you a member of their family, a cousin or something? In the business, I mean."

"My father and mother were both servants of Wu Nu Quen, but my father's family was influential in the past and I was trained for government service."
"Trained, you mean to be a soldier?"

"No, I was trained for civil government for a province or city or for the emperor herself. I studied seven years and took an examination to determine my fitness for a government post."
"An examination, was it difficult to study and take it?"

"Yes, I studied with a friend I met at the examining place. His name was Hung Hsu Chuan and he said to me, "If we ever get government employment it was not because they want us to, or did not try to keep us from it." Woo smiled at the recollection.

"Did you pass?"

"Yes, with very high honors."

"What about Hung what's-his-name did he pass?"

"Not as fortunate, but I did not fear for his future, he became a leader of men and led many in the civil war just ended."
"He became a regular general, huh, so after the examination, then what?"

"I became legal advisor and minor administration of Guangzhou the place you call Canton. I did my job for fourteen years; I dealt with westerners who sought to expand trade."

"That's where you learned English."

"I learned French and Italian also."

"I don't have much use for the French, less for the English."

"In Guangzhou the French built a church on land that was sacred and caused much ill will. They looted, killed, and raped their way through the war; thousands upon thousands of my countrymen were killed in Peking - all for the sale of Opium."

"I remember a little bit about it. Just before the War Between the States, here in America. The English, French, Germans and Americans were all involved."

"The result is that many, many Chinese hate the West and consider all whites to be barbarians who know nothing of value."

"Barbarians, indeed I have seen it at its worst." Kavanaugh reminisced.

"Not you Pat. You are a kind man."

"You haven't known me long enough to be sure of that."

"Yes, but I know." He sipped at his tea carefully gazing at the fire.

"War and hardship make barbarians of us all," Kavanaugh said thoughtfully.

"After the treaty was made in 1860 some merchants saw an opportunity to collect more wealth. Others saw opportunities for new government and for the first time, foreigners were allowed into China beyond the appointed cities. That treaty ended one agony and spawned another, the great civil war."

"So, when the business with the West opened up, you went to work for them."

"I left the government to work for Wu Nu Quei; it was a great opportunity to accumulate wealth."

"Another Woo, huh, but you are not so sure right now it was such a good deal."

"You may laugh, Pat, but I thought so then."

The fire brightened up as another gust of wind struck the flames that stretched away and the gray embers turned scarlet.

"Was it worth it, I mean accumulating wealth? We would say getting rich."

"I have a fine home - a beautiful house in the countryside, with high ceilings, a fireplace in every room, servants, a beautiful garden that climbs the hill behind the house, ornate rugs and drapes, clocks, dishes of fine porcelain many things such as those."

"If I had a place like that, I would not want to leave it."

"It was a difficult decision, but when one accepts employment one must do his duty."

"My father was a Ferrier. We didn't have much where I grew up. I had a sister and a brother and lived in a thick walled house of three rooms, a dirt floor, thatched roof, one fireplace where we cooked, a table, a couple of chairs and a potato patch."

Woo smiled but did not respond. The pot by the fire began to boil over and Woo moved it. "Would you like more tea, Pat?"

"Don't mind if I do," he extended his cup. "What's your family like, Woo, I mean, your wife and daughters?"

"She is tall for a woman; does not have bound feet."

"Bound feet?"

"Yes, small feet are considered to be a sign of high society, but my wife's family does not bind the feet of their women."

"I don't know what little feet have to do with anything."

"It is tradition of high born Chinese families, I am happy my wife's feet are not bound and she is not crippled for she walks with me often. You have no wife or loved one?"

"As I said I left a loved one behind on the great plain. She was pretty, a Cheyenne woman caring and kind, and very brave and she had a wonderful spirit."

"The women and their ways, they are the secret joys of life."

They did not speak for a few minutes the snow was gathering along the back of the lean to and drifting on to the side.

"We will surely clear Macon by tomorrow, if the trail is not too drifted. I tended the horses; they are back a little way in the heavier cover. We ought to feed them up a bit in Macon. I don't think going to a stable is too risky and we could stop in somewhere and get a good steak and potato dinner."

"Yes. Dried meat what you call jerky?"

"That's it."

"It is not good food for a steady diet, but I do not want to risk your life."

"It would be worth a good steak; my fare isn't the best. Do you miss home cooking? I mean food in America must be very different from China."

"I miss the rice mostly."

"Never ate much of that. Do you think after you get your trade agreement, or if you get it, there will be more rice here?"

"We hope to convince Americans to export more to us, for famine is lurking in many

72

parts of China. You know famine, Pat?"

"I lived through one," he looked over at Woo from the rim of his cup. "You never forget it." He fingered the rosary chain of cross hanging on his chest, "Never forget it. There were true barbarians there, particularly the English, although some of the Irish wealthy helped. What else is new, what else is there about the English?"

"They have high noses, deep set eyes, are crafty, treat everyone shabbily, despise learning, are not at all polite and are contemptuous of all others. They are barbarians."

Kavanaugh sipped at his tea and smiled. "That about covers it, Woo. That about covers it."

Next morning after breakfast and watering the horses, they again set out for Macon. They were a few miles out when the snow began to fall thickly. They reigned up at a farm house; Kavanaugh spied the farmer carrying a large bucket toward the house, and called out.
"Hello the house."

The man paused and disappeared inside. The two riders approached then drew up short at the end of a double-barreled shotgun.

"What do you want?" The farmer glared and rested his thumb on the curved hammer on the receiver.

"We don't want any trouble, just a place to get through the night."

"Know how to milk?" He did not remove the thumb.

"I haven't milked a cow in a long time." Kavanaugh replied.

"It ain't somethin' you're likely to forget."

"Sure, I guess not."

"You can stay in the barn. Feed your horses; oats from in the big bin and I'll throw in some hay. I got fourteen head in there needs pullin'. You can help me in the morning or hit the trail now."

Kavanaugh looked toward Woo sunk into his mackinaw and shook off an involuntary shudder.
"I'll help you milk, be glad to."

"My boys gone off and hired help ain't easy to find. There's room in the barn so go on in."
They pushed through the door and closed it behind.

"It's warmer in here, Woo." The heat of the animals plus the absence of the cutting wind made it quite comfortable.

As they hung their tack and fed the horses the cows gazed at them quite disinterested in the activity.
"No fire tonight, Woo. Do you want some jerky?"

The side door suddenly opened and the farmer bereft of shotgun appeared holding a pot and two spoons.
"The Missus sent this out, got lots of soup but not many bowls, here's some bread."

Kavanaugh thanked him accepted the bread and steaming pot and two spoons. The farmer disappeared as abruptly as he had come.
"Were in luck," Pat smiled, "smells mighty good." He tore the large golden loaf in half.

Woo raised his eyebrows as Kavanaugh ripped his bread to pieces, dipped one into the pot and poked it into his mouth. Woo looked at his spoon.

"Try it," Kavanaugh directed through his chews sensing Woo's reluctance, "Go ahead, dip the bread."

Delicately Woo tore his bread and dipped the soup, but made no sign as he chewed it, then quickly dipped a second piece. They dug into the soup kettle with vigor spooning and dipping in the bread and sucking the soup from their fingers. They made short work of the soup scraping the last of the vegetables from the bottom of the pot. Woo sat back as Pat attacked the last vestiges of the soup.

"Where will you go in Washington, Pat?"

"Well, I must get to the Office of Indian Affairs."

"Where will you stay?"

"I have a friend there, her name is Mary Cleary. She will take me in and as soon as I finish talking with the commissioner about the skin, I'm going to head back West and try to find my Cheyenne wife."

"Who is Mary Cleary?"

"She is a very famous Madame of a house and one of my best friends."

"Oh, I see," Woo nodded solemnly. "Where is her, her business?"

"Outside of Washington toward Baltimore, many people know of her and especially the wealthy people and military generals and officers and such. It's really a nice place. She was going to marry a friend of mine and we visited her on week ends when we were stationed nearby. Let's hit the hay," Kavanaugh gestured to the hay mow. "If we bury ourselves in there with the blankets, we will be as warm as that soup."

As the night progressed, the wind came up and howled through the cracks between the barn boards. It was driving a heavy skein of snow before it and left white streaks on the hay.

Kavanaugh was first aware of morning by scraping sounds from the door, as it grated open. The farmer stepped in from the swirling snow dragging the door closed behind him. Kavanaugh rose from the hay.

"Good thing you was here last night, we got two feet of snow and it's still comin', and that wind cuts like a razor." He hitched at his suspenders. "You do know how to milk?"

"It's been awhile," Kavanaugh pulled up a stool to the udder of a large Holstein; soon the milk was rattling the pail between his legs, in long ragged streams. The farmer also had a pail that he set ringing, and a strange melody emerged.

By the time he reached the fourth animal Pat was aware of his audience; Woo, squinting from the hay and two large cats prowling the stanchions. Much to Woo's mirth Kavanaugh aimed a squirt at the cat, which stood up on its hind legs and danced its whiskers through the stream. Soon both cats were prancing as Kavanaugh's unerring aim struck them.

"The cats are dancing." Woo laughed.

"Good thing you're out of range, I'd make you dance."

Kavanaugh made his way down the row of cows alternating with the farmer. "What's your name? You know how to work."

"Pat."

"Well Pat, that's the fastest I think I ever got done with these critters."

"You might as well stay put-up here for a day or two; think that storm is fixin' to stay awhile."

They strained the milk into large cans and lifted them into the spring fed cooler. They dumped a ration of silage in front of each cow. The farmer reviewed the cows and after a moment, the man passed through the door toward the house. Kavanaugh followed and peered at the gathering snow, then closed the door and turned to Woo.

"There are a couple feet of snow out there and it's still comin' down." He rubbed his hands together. We never had much snow in Ireland; I've seen enough blizzards for the rest of my life."

"We never had snow in Guangdong; it was warm and wet all the time."

"I can remember a snow fall or two when I was very young. It didn't snow much, but when it came it was wet. Some times it froze and that was usually a big mess. Here, though, I've seen some wicked weather, lots, and lots of it."

"How long will the snow fall?"

"Maybe an hour, maybe a day, maybe a week, but it doesn't feel like a long storm. It could stop by noon."

"We must continue on?"

"There is hard riding ahead and we might be even worse off. We can stay here a day or so, but no longer"

The two men sat in the haymow propped up against the wall.

"Sure could use a cup of coffee."

"Or tea."

"Yes, Woo, or tea, we can't make a fire in here."

There was a rattling at the door. "Open up in there. Open the door," a muffled voice demanded.

Kavanaugh slipped from the haymow and pulled in the door. The farmer was standing there with a large skillet of eggs and bacon buried under several thick slices of bread. In the other hand, he held a pot and a cup dangling from his fingers.

"The missus sent this out for you."

Kavanaugh took the still warm skillet and Woo soon joined, accepting the pot and cup.

"It's tea," the farmer announced. He pulled out a milking stool and watched the two men devour the food. "Say, Pat, you want a job?" He asked adjusting his suspenders.

"No, I've got to get on to Washington, but I'll say these vittles sure are a tempting reason to stay. We could stay maybe another day and see how the weather goes."

He speak English?" the farmer nodded toward Woo.

"Better than I do."

"Thank you for the food," Woo politely cut in.

"Well, storm ain't as bad as I thought. You could be movin' on afore long. Best feed up your horses. You can take some oats with ya."

"Thank you."

"Leave the pot on this stool here." He extended his hand first to Pat then to Woo. "Good luck," he left and carried off the pans, pot and spoons from the night before.

Woo looked toward the closed door, "These Americans, they are strange people. First he was going to shoot us and then fed us and wished us luck."

75

They reached Hannibal, Illinois through drifted snow and stinging cold. The river was steaming along its edges and a bone chilling cold sifted through the busy streets; they stood together straining to sort the other bank from the rising mist. Kavanaugh acquired directions to the ferry and they edged their way through the streets to the dock. They were greeted by a sour looking man in a dark jacket with his hat pulled over his ears. He glared at their approach; Kavanaugh stepped ahead.

"How much is it to cross?"

"A dollar for a man and a dollar for a horse."

"Very well," he walked back toward Woo. "It's going to cost two dollars each. I've got my two."

"Take this money," Woo dug around in his purse and dropped it, some gold pieces spilled on the deck. Both the men hurriedly gathered them up. Woo tied the purse strings. Kavanaugh turned and spotted the ferryman watching them intently.

He offered the twenty-dollar gold piece, "You can make change?"

"I forgot today was Friday, it is five dollars for a man and a horse."

"Five dollars; you can't do that! You said two before, you already told us!"

"I can do what I damn well please. And it's Friday and it's five each or we don't leave the dock."

Kavanaugh glanced about hoping to find a sympathetic face, but they were the only three near the ferry port. He swallowed down his rage, his face was flushed a deep red; he made a tight fist, and then relaxed it. "Alright, five it is, but we want to go now."

"I need more for a load."

"There is no one in sight, so let's go. You've got your money."

He did not offer to make change. "Get on board and cover them horses' eyes. You didn't pay me enough for those nags to kick up the boat or shit all over it."

"Where's our change?" Kavanaugh turned back to Woo.

"You don't get any change; we are leavin' early for the other side." The man turned and started toward the ferry.

"Pat, you are angry." Woo noted as they followed the ferry captain.

"You're damn right I am! He took the whole twenty."

"Too much, but we want no trouble." They approached the boat.

"Way too much, cover you horses' eyes, maybe use that old black shirt you had. Horse may get jumpy over the water."

He secured his slicker over his horse's eyes and carefully led it aboard, Woo followed. The ferryman stoked his boiler, slapped it closed and as the wheel took up motion; he pulled into the current and aimed at the other shore. Ten minutes into the crossing, Kavanaugh could see the dock and soon they were moving up the opposite current. A barge barred their way and Kavanaugh stepped up to the wheelhouse.

The ferryman called down, "We have to stop for a bit. Lend a hand, let down that anchor line. God damn it, we started out too early! Now we have to wait till that barge clears the passenger dock."

Kavanaugh did not know how to release the line and struggled with it.

"Look out! You have to drop the anchor, just loosen the ratchet, let out the line." He pushed Kavanaugh to the side. "Christ, you can't do much, can ya? You been fightin' Injuns or diggin' too much, now when I say so, drag in the anchor slack. The small ferry straightened against its bow and laid into the current. The ferry captain looked down on them with disdain. "What the hell are you lookin' at Chinaman?"

"It doesn't matter what he's lookin' at, and if it's you - it ain't much."

"Hah!" he started back toward the wheelhouse when Kavanaugh caught his arm. "Give the Chinaman his change, ten dollars."

"You paid full fare and we left early so you pay extra, now let go of me."

"We paid double fare, you shoneen son of a bitch. Give him his money."

"No trouble, Pat. No trouble."

"There won't be any trouble, Woo, as soon as he pays your money."

"No trouble, Pat."

The ferryman wrestled free from Kavanaugh and drew a derringer from his pocket. Kavanaugh slapped it clattering to the deck, caught the man under the chin, and backed him into the wheelhouse.

"I ought to kill you, drawing a gun on me."

"Put me down. Put me down," he choked.

"I'm gonna put you down right into the river. Give him his money, or as I live and breathe they will be lookin' for you down in Saint Louis with a grapnel hook. I'll get this boat across by myself."

he man had turned from red to purple, and ceased struggling. "Alright, alright," he hissed.

"Pat. Pat …no trouble." Woo picked up the derringer and thrust it in his pocket. "I have gun, no trouble."

The barge ahead had drawn up into the dock. Kavanaugh let the ferry captain down. The man staggered for a moment, then regained his breath.

"Time to dock, isn't it." He held out his hand, the ferry captain paid up two five-dollar gold pieces, and he passed them on to Woo.

The ferryman began his approach to the dock, and pressed closer to it, there were three rough looking men securing the lines. After they disembarked and started down the dock, Kavanaugh looked back; the ferry captain was in animated conversation with the three men and pointed toward the two of them.

They cleared the pier and glanced back. "Well, we are across the big muddy. That river will take you clear down to New Orleans, lots of French down there. That way is east," he pointed. "I think were about halfway there, to Washington, I mean."

"Are there many miles yet to go?"

"Many, many miles, I think you can catch a train now or maybe we'll ride on up to Springfield and catch a train there."

"You will come with me?"

"Woo, I haven't the cash money to buy a ticket. I'll see you on board then ride on."

"I will buy us both a ticket."

Kavanaugh thought for a moment of the prospect of riding ahead and decided to accept the offer. "I thank you in advance. As soon as I get to Washington, I will pay you back. I can get some money there."

"Your lady friend will give you some money?"

"Yes, Mary Cleary, she knows I'm good for it."

"It is arranged then?"

"Alright, Woo I'll pay you back." Kavanaugh glanced toward the sun heading down into the gray hills. "Right now let's get into town, find a livery, and get us a couple of good steaks."

Cairo, Illinois was a bigger city than either had expected and the streets were busy.

"I think we can get a meal over there." Kavanaugh pointed to a bar with chairs set along its boardwalk and a large window sporting the word Saloon. Inside, the tables were rough but clean, and seated round with battered chairs. There were a few customers at the bar but none at the tables.

"I'm going to get a steak, some eggs, and potatoes if they have it. What do you want, Woo?"

"I'd like some tea."

"Tea," He replied in surprise. "This may not be the place for tea. What else?"

"Some meat and bread, I do not ever wish to eat that dried meat again."

"Alright," Kavanaugh caught site of himself in the mirror behind the bar, he did not recognize the image with the long, red hair and beard curling toward his chest. He continued on to the bar where a large man with a blooming rum blossom surveyed him seriously.

"Whiskey," Kavanaugh gestured toward a bottle. "And can we get something to eat?"

"Like what?" Came the droll reply; he sat a bottle and glass in front of Pat.

"A steak, a couple eggs and a baked potato, bread…"

"Fried potatoes, out of eggs, pot roast, bread's stale and that is all we have."

"Alright, fried potatoes and pot roast, do you have tea?" He swallowed down the whiskey.

"We got tea."

"Alright, a pot of…"

"No pots. Get a mug."

"Alright, I'll take this bottle too."

Kavanaugh drew up a chair across from Woo, settled into it, and poured a glass full. "They have tea, but nothing else we want. I think around here the rats get the best of everything."

Kavanaugh had just finished his second whiskey when the saloon door folded inward; four men entered, glanced toward them, and went to the bar. Kavanaugh watched them carefully and finished his whiskey. Occasionally one would look toward him, but when they caught Kavanaugh's glance, returned their attention to the bar and slouched forward talking quietly.

"I don't like the looks of those four, Woo. They were on the dock; friends of the captain, I'd guess." He poured himself a third glass.

The bartender called out, "Hey Red, your dinner's here." On the bar before him were plates heaped with meat and potatoes.

"You want gravy?"

"Yes."

"You'll have to wait a minute." He disappeared into the kitchen as Kavanaugh carried one plate and a large mug full of tea back to the table.
"Look out, Woo, this is really hot. I don't know how good it is but there is a lot of it."
As he turned to the bar, he recognized two of the four men were watching him. He gathered his plate and was about to sit down when the bar tender called to him.

"Gravy's ready," Kavanaugh started back toward the bar.

"I will get it, Pat."

"No, stay here, those men at the bar are up to no good."

No sooner had he sat down again than the four men left the bar, pausing for one last look, and disappeared from the window view.

"Do you want to stay in the hotel tonight?"

"No." Kavanaugh sawed away at his meat. "You can stay there if you would like".

"What will you do?"

"I'm going to stay with the horses."

"Then I will stay there too". Woo turned the mug in his hands "The tea is very good."

"This is probably going to cost us two dollars."

Woo produced five silver dollars, "This will be enough?"

"Oh, yes." He took the money and returned toward the bar, "I'll be glad to get on to Springfield. This place is not the best, I feel trouble coming."

It was close to dark when they started toward the livery stable, the streets were already deep in shadow so they hurried along. As they entered the stable there was a lamp burning in the livery office, otherwise only the warmth and smell of horses, hay and straw greeted them. Suddenly there was a sound of movement. Instinctively Kavanaugh turned from the noise and ducked but a heavy object struck him on the back of his neck and knocked him to his knees. He covered his head with his arms and a second blow struck heavily across them. He struggled to his feet and absorbed a third blow to the side of his face. He struck out fiercely at the figures close to him and knocked one sprawling to the floor he knocked a second one down a sharp blow struck his head and he fell to his knees and was vaguely aware of another blow as bright sparks burst him to unconsciousness.

He was vaguely aware of voices but seemed powerless to move. In the darkened livery stable the sounds seemed to be closed around him and he was aware of a single bobbing light.

"That bastard has a hard head."

"Yeah," the dark figure passed his hand over his jaw. "And a hard hand too."

"I can't find the Chinaman," chimed a third voice.

"He couldn't have got out of here."

"I know he's hidin' somewhere and I can't find him in the dark."

"Chris said he's got the money."

"God damn it, Jim! Why ain't Chris here?"

"Anse, let's leave this guy and we'll all go look. He's hiding in a stall some where"

"When we get ready to go, I'm gonna even things up with this Irishman."

"Yeah, yeah, Coe, right now let's find that Chinaman."

Kavanaugh felt that he was alone and tried to force himself to consciousness. The stable still turned in the dark, but the sounds of the shifting horses reassured him. He did not want to close his eyes because when he did, it felt like the world turned slowly over.

He was next aware of the sound of Woo's voice, "No money. No money."

79

"We know you got money, now, which of these saddle bags is yours."

There was the sound of flesh striking flesh and a gasp for breath.

"No money, please I have no money."

"You're lying Chinaman! You find that money by jingo; I'd just as soon kill you."

Again, there was a thump and a sharp gasp. When Kavanaugh was finally able to focus in the dim lantern light, he could see two men held Woo, while the third one was beating him, slapping first one side of Woo's face, then the other.

"I show my bags, no money, there my bag, I get it. I will go get it."

Woo was bent over as he staggered toward where his saddlebags were. He lifted them, dropped them, and then collapsed on them.

"Give me the bags." The man delivered a solid kick and dislodged Woo the three men bent forward in the dim light to see the contents that had spilled onto the floor. The can of tea was dumped; a packet of flour and each garment shook out to determine if anything was folded in them.

"Is there a saddle pocket?"

"No, Anse he's got nuthin'."

"God damn, maybe the Irishman has it. Let's check him out."

"My pleasure, maybe I can help him talk."

"Is he conscious, Jim?"

Kavanaugh felt the light close to his face as it grew brighter behind his closed eyelids.

"I don't think so, Anse."

There was the sound of riders in the street; the noise rattling close to the stable, but then fading away.

"Ollie is still outside watching' the town?"

"So far as I know, I got an idea. Maybe the Chinaman will tell us something if I killed his pal. What about that Chinaman?"

"No money, he has no money. I have no money."

"You're lying, prop up that son of a bitch."

"What are you doin", Coe?"

"Showin' him I mean business." He stuck the blade of his pocketknife up Kavanaugh's nose and sliced out. The blood began to run furiously over his face. Kavanaugh winced in pain and tried to sit up. He felt the knife on his throat. The man had him firmly stretched back with his arm locked around his chin.

"He has no money."

"Well then, where is it?"

The derringer flash temporarily blinded Kavanaugh. The grip on his neck loosened at the same time blood spurted warmly over his face. The second shot struck the man called Anse in the stomach he fell backward trying to pinch the wound closed. Kavanaugh jumped to his feet, in a rage grasped a hayfork, caught Jim under the chin through his neck, and pinned him to the loft post. Grasping a harness bar he brought it down with all his strength on the head of Anse. Blood was still running from his nose, mixing with the blood that now stained his buckskin to the waist. He delivered three crushing blows then staggered back and sat down heavily on the floor, he inhaled some of his own blood and coughed sprays on his thighs and knees.

"Did he cut my nose off, Woo? It feels like he cut my nose off."

"No, but he made a cut. You bleed fast, we must see a doctor."

"I don't need a doctor. I need something to stop the bleeding."

"You no, maybe I need a doctor."

Woo collapsed beside Kavanaugh who noticed Woo's blood soaked shirt. Slowly Woo uncovered the three deep slashes on his side.

"They wanted me to tell where the money is. They cut me too." Kavanaugh stood up and saw the pistol in Woo's hand.

"That's the ferryman's derringer."

"Yes I kept it and it has been useful. It is a pistol of simple design. I have seen many but have used none."

Pat examined the slashes on Woo's ribs and shook his head. "They don't look deep but they will be sore. Did they do this when I was knocked out?" Woo nodded. "We may not find a doctor at this hour."

"But we can find sheriff and tell of these men - these barbarians"

"I'm not too eager to do that. We would have a lot of explaining to do. But we had better do it. If some one were to find us with these bodies, we would never get out of this town."

Kavanaugh stood up and lifted the lamp and it was a macabre scene. The pitchfork still pinned Jim to the upright and the two others, sprawled on the floor, were awash in blood. He spotted a flannel shirt hanging on a peg by the office door and tore it into strips. Woo fitted one around Kavanaugh's head over the split in his nose. Kavanaugh carefully bound Woo's wounds. As he finished, the weight of Jim's body pulled it free and it fell to the floor with a thud.

The sheriff returned with them to the stable and brightened the lantern light. "Exactly what happened here?" He asked hitching at his gun belt. "It sure is a hell of a mess."

"Well sheriff, as we were coming in they laid into me with that single tree. They tortured my friend Woo and was about to kill me when Woo shot this one, and that one and I did that." He gestured toward the figure lying on the floor the pitchfork still protruding from his neck. I also bashed Anse."

"They tried to rob us."

"That right, Chinaman? Rob you of what?" He braced himself on a post and scraped his foot through the hay trying to remove blood from the toe of his boot.

"They thought we had money, and Pat had told you the truth. That is how this happened."

"It don't surprise me none." He studied his boot. "They all was trouble makers. That one there is Anse Gorman - a petty thief, hooligan, and brawler. And that's Coe Clayton, another no account n'er-do-well. The one wearin' the pitchfork is Jim Lingle; he always did talk too much -another drunken brawler. All three of them together don't amount to a pinch of punk. I'm surprised Ollie Owens ain't with them. He's a sleaze bag that would shit in church."

"What do we do sheriff?"

"Can you write, Red?" He scratched his backside and pulled his belt again.

"I can write, but not very well, Woo can."

"Write up what happened and sign it. I'll get Charley Atkins down here to take these boys away." He regarded the dead men, "Maybe you can pull out the pitchfork; Charley might be a bit queasy about that. He ain't no funeral man just a carpenter. Don't leave town 'til you write that out. You might as well follow me back; I got a pen and paper at the office."

"You go on over Woo and I'll join you."

Kavanaugh pulled on the pitchfork but it was tightly stuck, so he put his foot on the jaw and drew it out as he lifted the other bodies he went through their pockets. There were four silver dollars and a coin he dimly recognized; it was a pine tree shilling. "Must have been his good luck piece," he mused. "Well Jim, you bastard, you were going to kill me, now you're gone and I have your lucky coin. I will see you in hell."

He laid out the bodies, turned down the lamp and walked to the sheriff's office. There were six posters tacked beside the door. He bent forward to see, none were of him. He was relieved, straightened up and slipped through the doorway. Woo was slowly but confidently writing a note.

"You are not a desperado here," Woo whispered barely glancing up.

"They don't know I'm a desperado here," he whispered. "I have something for you money, old money." Kavanaugh tossed the coin on the desk. "Where's the sheriff?"

"He went away and said he would be back. What kind of coin?"

"Must have been Lingle's good luck piece, it's very old, more than a hundred years. It's a pine tree shilling." He passed the shilling to Woo and tossed the silver dollars on to the desk beside Woo's tablet. "These will help pay the burial costs."

Woo looked up from his writing reached into his pocket and presented Kavanaugh with a coin.

"It's got a hole in it. Looks old; is this the one Buck took from you and gave back?"

"Yes and it is about five hundred years old."

Kavanaugh laughed. "We will make a trade."

"Yes," he returned to his writing carefully lining out a detailed statement of the events. Kavanaugh sat in a chair hoisted his feet to another. "We cross all those bad lands, through Indian country, bears, wolves and rattlesnakes. We get into a town and people try to steal from us or kill us- ain't civilization great?"

"Yes," he replied without a look up from the writing pad.

Springfield, Illinois was a bustling town still full of talk about the election that resulted in U.S. Grant becoming president. There were crowds of shoppers and the snow had been plowed into low dark drifts down the middle of the streets. The raw wind carried a feeling of prosperity through the teeming streets. Kavanaugh became uneasy.

They drew up before a shop window adorned with a black draped portrait of President Lincoln. "Lots of people are looking at us, Woo." Woo did not reply but continued to look curiously about him.

"I think the railroad station is just ahead, there on the right, where that steam is rising."

Woo squinted ahead. "Yes."

"Woo, I think these clothes I am wearing are calling attention to me."

"Yes, everyone is wearing dark clothes, tall hats and they appear quite civilized. I think they are looking at your nose and all the stains on your leather suit."

A pair of women crossing in front of them looked at Kavanaugh and fled like quail through a passage in the drift.

"Maybe so Woo, I'll see what I can get for the horses, hopefully enough to buy a ticket to Washington DC. I think we can go all the way by rail now."

"I will give you money. Do you need money? I will give you some."

"You pay for your self; I think the horses should pay my fare. I need to get cleaned up though, a barber to cut my hair and trim up the beard. And I need to get some new clothes."

"I think I too shall get a new suit of clothes and dress like those around us."

"I think it would help. If you could spare me a few dollars, I'll get a new outfit; I'd better not walk around looking like a fur trapper - cut nose, bloody buckskins and all. People will think I'm looking for trouble."

They had progressed a short way on Adams Street when they came upon a barbershop, the barber gave them a long look as they sat down. He completed the scissor work on a man with a tonsured head of gray. The man paid and left with a curious look at the two strangers

"Who's next?"

"Me, I need a hair cut and a beard trim. Keep the hair shoulder length."

"Looks like you have been out a while." He flourished the striped cape over Kavanaugh.

"A long while, we need to sell our horses and buy train tickets east. Some place nearby to do that?"

"Where are you going east, Chicago, New York City, Philadelphia?"

"Washington."

"You need to get over to Jefferson Street. The St. Louis and Alton it will take you to Chicago; you can connect there to Washington on the Baltimore, and Ohio."

"We also need to get a suit of clothes and get cleaned up."

"If you need a tailor, there's a good one over on Jefferson Street. His name is Walton, Walton Tailors." He continued to shear away the long red hair.

"What about dry goods? We are in a bit of a hurry."

"I don't know, you're too big and he's too small. They don't stock many suits. I don't think Walton is too busy, you might be better off shopping there and tell him you need the order right away."

"You know Walton?" Pat asked looking at the barber's face in the mirror.

"He is my cousin and an excellent tailor. If you need boots or shoes, I know a good shoe maker that would be Walton Boots not far from here."

"We also need to sell our horses. Where do you suggest?"

"Jefferson Street, the livery is down near the depot – Walton Livery. My uncle owns it. He will make you a good offer."

"How long will it take to get to Washington by train - a week?"

"A week maybe, if the tracks aren't closed to snow - it can get really bad out there this time of the year." He gestured toward the east as he worked, quietly tilting Kavanaugh's head from time to time. Kavanaugh watched as the long red and gray curls fell down his chest. He reviewed the array of bottles and an ominous jar of leeches that dominated the counter. The mirror showed the dark scab marking the slash through his nose. He flinched as the barber began to trim his moustache.

"Got a sore looking nose there," the barber turned his head slightly. "Looks like somebody cut you."

"They did, be careful will you? I don't want another one. I swear, every time I look into a mirror, I look worse than before."

"You fellows look like you could use a bath." You can get one just down the street; the lady takes boarders just past the corner called the Alton House. She is a damn good cook and there is lots of hot water. Her name is Molly." He cut away at the beard. "This is damn near solid with clotted blood."

"I guess we had better get a bath before we get measured for a suit, Molly your cousin too?"

"No," the barber smiled. "But she might be yours, and I think a bath would be in order." He removed the cape with flourish and slowly spun Kavanaugh in the chair. "I get it short enough? What about the Chinaman with you?"
"No, he doesn't need anything, except maybe a bath and some clothes."

The lady at Alton House was a stout woman dressed in a faded blue calico dress; she gave them both a long look as they waited at the door. Kavanaugh felt a turn down was about to occur, but when she began to speak Kavanaugh caught the accent.

"Are you from Kerry?" he inquired.

"How did you know?" she laughed.

"I just guessed." He smiled, managing his best brogue. "It's been a long time since I have heard a Kerry note I am from near Listowel."

She opened the door to allow their passage. "Come on in then, room and board is two dollars a day, sheets changed once a week. Supper is at six, breakfast at seven and dinner is at noon. You smell like you need a bath, no charge for that. My husband, bless his soul, was a boilermaker so there is plenty of hot water. Doors are locked at eleven, if you're not home by then you will have to find another place to stay. I don't tolerate drunks, but a drink or two, well that's different. Leave your ladies behind, this is a respectable place."

They were ushered into a large room with two large beds and towels draped over the foot rails. A picture of Christ holding a shepherd's staff was on one wall and on the other a lithograph of Chicago; the windows on the third wall looked out over the bleak, white streets of snow.

"What did she say, Pat? She spoke so fast I did not hear and I did not understand her well."

"For two dollars we get three meals and a bed, the door is locked at eleven o'clock and we do not get drunk, and there is lots of hot water. The bathroom is across the hall, and there, my friend is where I am heading right now."

It was after dark when the two returned from their tasks. Kavanaugh had received a fair price for his horses, saddle bags and rifle and near the livery he purchased a small black valise. They had been measured for suits and assured they would be available in three days. After their trip to the tailor, they stopped briefly at a place called the Occidental Inn for whiskey and tea. When they arrived back at Alton House, supper was in progress. True to the barber's prediction, there was plenty of tasty food served with rich coffee or tea, and the pie was delicious. The dining room had been full, most of the boarders crowded around one table, Kavanaugh and Woo shared a table in a corner near the windows. By the time they finished dinner, it began to snow again.

There was a full crowd on this blustery December day at the railway depot in Springfield. Kavanaugh was confident that he would not be recognized and he moved about openly.

"You look fine in that suit, Woo."

Before Woo could answer, a voice drifted above the gathered crowd, "Chicago, all aboard for Chicago."

"That's us, Woo, time to go." Kavanaugh picked up his valise and walked toward the conductor. The coach was full of people of all persuasions and he felt even more at ease. He had selected a dark brown tweed suit, a white shirt and green tie. Woo wore a dark gray suit with blue pin stripes, a white shirt and gray tie with a fleur dé le pattern. To those who observed them, they appeared to be business men, on closer examination, one might wonder at Kavanaugh's sliced nose above his neatly trimmed mustache and thick beard. The derby hat that he wore was perched on his head like a bird's nest. Woo also had selected a derby, which gave him a rather odd appearance of elegance crushed into a hat. The ride to Chicago was uneventful; the snowy scenery absorbed both Kavanaugh and Woo.

In Chicago, they had to change trains; as the last light of day faded, they boarded the Baltimore and Ohio bound for Indiana. In Indianapolis Kavanaugh had enough of the suit and changed back into his buckskins, which were now less soiled thanks to Molly. A persistent snowstorm slowed the train to a crawl, and on the evening of the second day, they left the car briefly to buy some blankets. They could see their breath in the cold of the coach. They ate dinner on board the train during the longer rides, and eight days after they boarded the train in Springfield, they arrived at the Baltimore and Ohio depot in Washington D.C.

Kavanaugh changed into his new clothes just before the reaching the station. The depot was jammed with people when they arrived, among them were many soldiers coming from or going to distant places. The two sat down on a long wooden bench and quietly observed the crowd passing by.

"Well, Woo, this is the end of the line. Do you know where you are going from here?"

"I have an address of one of my business associates, and I will ask a coach driver to take me there."

"Will you be alright?"

"Yes, I will be alright."

"Washington is not as safe as you might think."

"I will take a coach to the address. Do not worry more about me. I will be alright."

"Well," Kavanaugh sighed. "I am going to miss you."

"I will miss you also; I will remember you each time that I look at this coin." Woo produced the shilling from his pocket.

"And me with this one." Kavanaugh fingered his medicine bag that now contained the Chinese coin Woo had given him.

"Perhaps they will bring both of us good fortune; good fortune on your mission and good fortune in my business."

"Yes, perhaps, I don't even know where to start now that I am here. I must find the right politicians and get in to see him. I have not done that before"

"We both have much to learn. I know you will manage, Pat"

"Come on, I'll walk you out to the coaches." He stood to leave.

"Wait, Pat, I want you to have this." Woo produced a small purse. "It is for your generous help you may need it. Will you ride with me? I will take you where you want to go --to Mary

Cleary's place."

"Thank you, but no, Woo. I'm not even sure where her place is or whether she is still there. Once I reach the Capitol Building, I can find my way. Thank you for the money." He put the purse inside his coat jacket.

They walked slowly toward the street. Several carriages were gathered near the depot entrance and they were quickly filling with passengers. It was cold, and the frosty breaths of passersby rose to a haze above the sidewalk.

"Good luck to you Woo; ---for the short time that I've known you, I never liked anyone better."

"Yes, we have had a great adventure together!"

Kavanaugh pushed the cab door closed. "You take good care of yourself."

"And you as well; ---we will meet again."

The hansom moved off into the traffic, the horses paced beside the trolleys. Kavanaugh felt a sense of loss as Woo's cab disappeared. He became aware that he was an island in the midst of a moving crowd; he gripped his valise, looked about, chose a direction, and started off.

Chapter 9

The Cleary House, Washington D.C.
Winter 1868

There were clusters of people moving around the Capitol Building and a cold wind drifted up from the Potomac. Kavanaugh was confused to his bearings since much had changed or was in the process of it, he recognized an old landmark, and started off briskly. He walked for over an hour when the familiar house with crescent carriageway appeared as though it had awaited his arrival. He made his way around to the kitchen door. Not seeing anyone inside, he slowly opened the door and stepped into the rich aroma of beef soup simmering on the stove. Pat paused by the long table and for a brief second was overcome by his emotions recalling all the faces of those who had once sat around it. It seemed so long ago, Moran with his smirk, dark Dolf smiling in anticipation of dinner, Liam with his ruined face staring at the stove and Sweeney chattering about before taking his seat by Moran. They were wonderfully warm times, some of the best times of his life, all together in the kitchen with the slowly steaming pots. A pang of remorse struck him as he recalled his last visit to the place. He could hear the band playing in the ballroom, the sounds stifled by the intervening rooms and distance. Wearily he sat down, his back to the interior. He heard her coming, talking quietly to herself. The muttering stopped and then the voice came sharply,

"What you doin' in my kitchen? Get on out now! Go to the front door if you want in this house!"

"I heard Mary Cleary owns this place." He replied without turning.

"She may own the house, but mister you in my kitchen! Now, you can git on out that door or I show you through it; and take off dat hat!"

Kavanaugh had not yet faced her. "I don't want to go through the door," he removed the derby and put it on the table.

"Well, you best move or I'll get my ladle and rattle your head; I show you the way!"

"I came to see you," he replied and turned toward her.

"Me? Why me? What business you got with me?" She stepped back, a frown set between her brows.

"Don't you recognize me, Evelyn?"

"No, I don't"

Kavanaugh rose to full height from his seat and looked at her full in the face.

"No, I....." She sputtered and stepped back, still wondering about the man before her.

"Don't you recognize the people that love you?"

She looked again," Oh my lawd! It's you Mister Pat! My lawd! My lawd!" They made a rush for one another, wrapping their arms tight. Evelyn delivered three big kisses to his cheek and Kavanaugh squeezed her tightly. "My lawd! My lawd! Mr. Pat where have you been? How many times I've thought about that table full of faces. Mr. Donal, Mr. Liam, Mr. Dolf. My lawd, my lawd! It's four, five years since I laid eyes on you. Miss Mary's gonna go up to the ceilin'."

"I've thought of you often too, and this place and the time when all of us were together." He could not repress the rising emotion; when he looked at Evelyn, tears were streaming down her cheeks.

"Oh, Mister Pat. Oh, I so glad to see you, praise the lawd." She wiped at her eyes.

"How's Mary?" He asked releasing her from his arms.

"Mr. Pat, she never stopped grievin' him, even now she talks sometimes like he was still here. Otherwise she is Miz Mary."

"She loved him, I guess."

"She love Mr. Moran like only she can love I know dat."

"Lots of things have happened since I was last here."

"Oh, yes. Miss Hope is here and she had a baby girl, Sara."

"Miss Hope?"

"Billy's friend, she came here with child and Mary took her in. How she love dat child!"

"Sweeney's girlfriend is here?"

"Said this was the place Billy told her go if there was ever trouble."

"Sounds like she's had some; ---Mary has once again shown how kind she is."

"I believe, but dat little Sara, well Mr. Pat, she is what keep Miss Mary alive. Miss Hope is big here now. Lots of customers just want her."

"Funny business, this business I don't really want to know much more than I already do."

"I go fetch Miss Mary 'fore I tell you everything dere is." She paused then gave Kavanaugh another big hug and kiss.

"Don't tell her it's me, Evelyn. I want to surprise her."

"She'll be surprised alright; I'll tell her there's somebody here to collect a bill." She paused at the door her hands wrapped into her apron. "Oh Mr. Pat, I'm so glad you here!" She turned quickly through the doorway. Kavanaugh resumed his position with his back to the interior. Presently he heard the two approaching in animated conversation."

"Dere he is, Miss Mary."

"Excuse me, sir," it was a blistering tone. "These are private quarters; patrons use the front door. Bill collectors also are received there between nine and ten each morning. If you have business with me, you should know it is well past hours, so you should leave."

Kavanaugh did not reply nor did he move in response.

"Did you hear me? I can escort you to the front rooms, but you must come now."

Kavanaugh beaming into a smile rose from the table and turned. Mary caught his smiling eyes, and then staggered back into Evelyn's arms, her hands crossed over her breast. She bounced from Evelyn, her arms outstretched; Kavanaugh opened his to the impact.

"Pat! Pat! My god, it's you, Pat!"

"It's me, Mary." They remained locked together holding tightly to one another. Mary sobbing silently as Kavanaugh held her tight, Evelyn watched, the tears again running over her brown cheeks.

"Oh my God Pat, where have you been? Why didn't you let us know?" Mary separated from him. She pulled a handkerchief from her sleeve and dabbed her eyes and cheeks. "God damn it! I should be angry with you! Never wrote, not a word, and now look at me, you've ruined my make-up!"

Kavanaugh laughed and again embraced her. "I've been lots of places Mary, mostly out west in Indian Territory."

"Why didn't you write to me or something? You disappeared like a god damn ghost."

"I thought the last time we met was enough, I didn't want to be a reminder."

"Oh, Pat I don't need you to remind me." They shared a brief kiss. "Have you eaten?"

"Nothing was very good since I left this place."

"Need a drink?"

"That too, I am a little dry."

"Evelyn, find Miss Sally. Tell her to bring back a bottle of Bushmills."

"Yes, Miss Mary. There's a good piece of rib roast left, or we got fresh pork chops."

"What's your pleasure, Pat?"

"Bushmills," he laughed.

"Not that." She waved her hand in dismissal." What do you want to eat?" She smiled. "Been drinking lots of dinners, Kavanaugh? That would be nothing new."

"I like, pork chops and I have not eaten any in a long time." He laughed but did not reply to her question.

"Evelyn, tell Sally to find someone else to take my place at poker. Pat and I have a lot to talk about."

Evelyn disappeared toward the bar and Mary looked Kavanaugh over carefully.

"A sore looking nose, been brawling again? For a peaceful man, you sure find your share of trouble."

"It's a long story, Mary, but I'm on a mission and I am in a lot of trouble."

"What kind of trouble? What kind of a mission is it for the Army?"

"No Mary, that's where the trouble is, I'm considered a deserter."

A look of concern passed over Mary. She licked her lips. "You, that's hard to believe. I thought you and Menzel had invented duty."

"It's a part of the long story." He sat down heavily and she sat across from him.

"It's been a long time, and I have a lot of time." She passed her hand over the back of his, "so tell it to me."

Kavanaugh quickly sketched his story about the massacre at the river, his capture by the Indians, the mission they sent him on his confrontation with the major and the adventures of his flight to Washington with Woo.

When he finished they sat together quietly for a minute and Mary shook her head in disbelief. "Jesus, Kavanaugh! You ought to write a book. You have more stories than James F. Cooper; Indians, shoot-outs, and saving Chinamen."

"Will you help me Mary?"

"Help you with what? You can stay here as long as you like, I don't give a damn about the Army's problems. I deal with them every night."

"I mean, Mary. You know people, important people. I need to get into see someone important in the Office of Indian Affairs."

"Well, the Bureau is over on Eighth and F Street. Not too far from the Capitol. I owned a couple lots over that way, that's how I know. But, Pat, I do not know anyone in the Bureau."

"Maybe you could get an appointment. Find out who I have to talk with."

I can ask Brice Randolph, he is old money and well connected. He will probably know who to see."

"I need to see the top man if I can, Mary, not a clerk or anyone like that."

"You know that Grant has been elected president? This time of year there's big changes goin' on in the government, lots of good byes and hellos."

"Yes, I know, I heard about it and it was in the papers. I read about it in Chicago."

"Well, I hope he is a little more careful with the country's money than he was with its young men."

"And a little less heavy on the Indians, there is a plan in force to annihilate them."

"Don't expect that, everyone who can is heading west, all land hungry and ambitious. That California must be something, I've even thought of moving, but I had a better idea; retire to the country."

"Will you help me get the message through? To the bureau I mean." He looked intently into her eyes.

"Of course, but I'm not sure how. Maybe you should wait until the new President gets all of his cabinet in order. With Christmas so near, there may not be many people around."

"I'd like to do it now, at least get it started, because it will take some time."

"I don't know, Pat. Grant has a lot of big money behind him and it is all looking west. There are some hefty investments being made ---railroads, land, and all. I don't know how sympathetic the new administration is going to be. Grant is a young man and wants to get his share. There is a lot of pressure to get the Indians out of the way. All I hear is 'kill all the Indians' like they were wolves some critter no one wants. Many of the Army officers think the only good Indian is a dead one and the way to resolve the Indian problem is no Indians."

"I know and heard it often enough I saw it being done. I must get this message through. I need an answer and return back there as soon as I can."

"It seems like you should have had enough." She brushed back her hair and smiled. "Pat, I will find out for you what I can. Here comes your bottle, let's have a drink and tell me all about being captured by the Indians."

Evelyn appeared with Bushmills and two glasses and set a place at the table.

"See there is somethin' left of dat bottle when you finish." She admonished and went to the stove to stir her soup.

Mary cocked her head toward Evelyn, "my conscience."

"You've got one after all," Kavanaugh laughed.

"Damn, you Kavanaugh! Pour us a drink and tell me about the Indians." She watched him pour two glasses half full. "You actually were chosen by them to bring a message to Washington?"

"Yes Mary, but it didn't start out that way --- they had plans to burn me alive."

They both turned toward the stove as a ladle clattered to the floor.

"Burn you alive, Mr. Pat? My lawd!"

Mary laughed. "My second set of ears, too. You better talk loud enough so she can hear."

Kavanaugh looked closely at Mary; beneath the mascara streaked down her cheeks was a uniquely beautiful woman. The image of Moran and her together, their obvious love and the recollection of Sada all blended together. When Mary again faced him full, he felt lightness inside and a rising warmth and comfort exchanged between people who care for one another. "Where do you want me to begin?"

"Pat, I am so happy you are here," again she stretched out her hand and passed it over his large strong forearm. "You are like a sunbeam come back into my life."

Over by the stove Evelyn began to hum as she filled the skillet with chops, the music from the band drifted in over their heads and the warmth of friendship filled the kitchen along with the smell of frying pork chops. Kavanaugh began to relate his story.

Kavanaugh stayed at Mary's for a week working around the yard, shoeing the horses, cleaning up the stable and generally helping with outside chores. Mary put him up in the library. He read some, but mostly he slept. Each evening he would sit with Mary for a drink or two in the kitchen, library or her office, but he never crossed into the rooms where patrons were present, lest he be recognized. Mary offered Sally as a 'bed warmer', but he refused.

The Sunday of the second week Kavanaugh removed his medicine bag and placed the contents on the dresser top. The care- worn rosary was there, Woo's coin, a swatch of black hair pasted together with resin, a wolf's tooth, a small piece of deerskin with a triangular design, a very bright sparkling stone, and some dried stems of leek that still bore a faint odor. He looked at the hair slowly massaging it between his finger tips. He knew was from Sada's own straight black strands. He thought of her rolled to his side and stroked his erection on to a handkerchief. When he finished he drew a tub of warm water and soaked himself and the handkerchief. He was so engaged when there came a sharp tapping at the door.

"It's Mary, I have some news."

"I'm in the tub."

"Well cover yourself, I'm comin' in."

Kavanaugh sloshed out of the tub and stepped behind a dressing screen wiping away the water with a large soft towel. Politely Mary waited in the bedroom. Presently he appeared with only his trousers on. She looked him over carefully observing the scars on his chest, and those on his back reflected in the dresser mirror.

"Well, now I think what I brought is appropriate." She produced a large box and plopped it on the bed.

"What's this?"

"Something you need."

He opened the box. "Ah, Mary, some flannel shirts; thank you."

"You've been working hard and you ought to have more than one shirt. Call it a Christmas present." She looked over the dresser. "What's all this?" She spread her hand toward the litter. "That's what was in my medicine bag."

"Hmm- I suppose some Indian woman made it up no doubt - a soothsayer or medicine woman? And you didn't tell me about her."

"That's right, Mary, her name was Sada. Now what is this news you got me out of my bath for?"

"That being as it may, Brice came by, --actually just left. He told me that the man you need to see is Nathaniel Taylor, ---he's the Office Director. Tomorrow Brice will make an appointment for 'Brice Randolph and friend' -- you are the friend. Brice will probably drop you off or leave once you're on your way inside."

"Thank you, Mary."

"Well, don't thank me yet. There's a lot of Army over there, many of them just in from the west, so you be careful. You never know where the spider is that bites you."

"I'll take my chances, Mary. When would the appointment be?"

"Brice said it would have to be on Tuesday; that's when he is free to go with you. He will tell me what time as soon as he knows."

"Do you think he can work it out?"

"When you have as much money as he does, and come from a Maryland planter family who just happened to be pro-union, and a big politico? Yes, he could get into the White House if he wanted to, whoever is in it."

He rose from the bed where he had been sitting and bent to kiss her cheek. "Thank you, Mary."

She caught his arm briefly held it and let go. "You be careful of those Army boys, if they catch you, you will probably get the lash, maybe even shot. You already have enough scars to qualify for a city map."

"Story of my life, Mary," he laughed.

"Still, be careful ---you never know." She smiled up at him. "Evelyn's made some pot pies. We will have dinner together, so as soon as you get your shirt on, come down. We will have the kitchen to ourselves. I swear there must be a big convention in town; my girls are going everywhere tonight -- only a few of them are here. I had to call them over from K Street."

"Oh, how the money rolls in."

"Yes," she laughed, "How the money rolls in."

Kavanaugh's eyes stayed on Mary as she left. "One of a kind," he said quietly. He carefully replaced the items in his medicine bag, keeping out the rosary.

Chapter 10

Office of Indian Affairs, Washington D.C.
December 1868

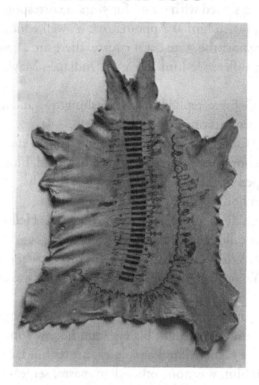

Brice Randolph was a tall man, shorter than Kavanaugh, but sparely built. He had black hair and a carefully trimmed mustache. His eyes were bright blue, and reflected a sharp intellect. He wore a dark blue suit, white shirt and black string tie. They boarded the horse drawn cab at Mary's and made their way across town.

"Well, Mr. Kavanaugh, Mary said you have important business with the Office of Indian Affairs."

"Pat, please and I do have business there."

He smiled. "Pat. Here is the plan. Our appointment is in a half hour and we will go in together, I will give the receptionist my card, wait for a bit and excuse myself. You will then be face to face with Nate Taylor, the commissioner."

"Do you know him?"

"I know him, but not very well. He is a petty bureaucrat who has become rich selling favors to land prospectors and railroads. He is much taken with himself and is a mild skeptic in these times. He is very personable and polite."

"Did Mary tell you why I wanted this appointment?"

"Not very much and I didn't ask more. Frankly, Mr.," he paused. "Frankly, Pat, I don't think you have much of a chance. The Office of Indian Affairs is primarily devoted to stealing the Indian land, making treaties to break and removing the red skins to reservations where they can starve them to death or kill them with disease. This Office does not have the Indians' interest at heart and its leaders are committed to becoming rich themselves."

"And the new administration, will they be any better?"

"There is word among people who are supposed to know, that Grant will choose Ely Parker as commissioner."

"Ely Parker? Who is he?"

"A Seneca Indian who served with Grant for years, a correspondent as I recall; supposedly he saved Grant's life and was with him at Appomattox. A well educated man from all accounts and at one time a warrior against the states. Of course, there are a few like him these days."

"That may make a difference-him being an Indian. Maybe he will get the message better."

"Don't count on it," Brice replied. "It's Washington, and money is what makes the difference. There will be enormous pressure on him."

The ante way of the Office was crowded with people and there was an air of last minute hurry; true to Mary's prediction, there were many gold trimmed, blue uniforms passing through the entrance. As they stepped inside the door Brice spoke quietly.

"Pat, you will have a half an hour to make your case, good luck."

They pushed through the door into the open ante way. "Hello Brice." A wealthy looking man seated in the far corner called. "What are you doing here?"

"Here with a friend, Patton. What are you after, a piece of Dakota?"

The man smiled, "Yes, a piece of the Black Hills." Brice walked toward his extended his hand.

The two men laughed together and began an earnest conversation. Kavanaugh reviewed the bustle, a man in a blue uniform caught his eye, and he saw something familiar about him. As Randolph approached the vaguely familiar soldier turned full face. Kavanaugh's heart froze, for the man looking back at him, was none other than master sergeant James Brock. Kavanaugh turned away quickly and they ascended the staircase. He glanced back, Brock changed position for better observation and Brock turned on his heel and disappeared into the corridor. Despite the quick exchange of glances, Kavanaugh felt strongly that Brock had recognized him. He felt he should turn around and get out of the building and the choice was tearing him apart, one side to fulfill the meeting, the other to run. They entered through a heavy oak door into a large pin- neat office with two desks behind a high counter. A man rose from behind his desk and approached the counter.

"Hello, Mr. Randolph. We haven't seen you here for awhile."

"That's true; it looks like you are getting ready to move."

The somber face burst into a grin. "You know how that goes in with the new out with the old."

"Cozdon, this is an acquaintance of mine, Padric Kavanaugh. He has a message for the Commissioner." He glanced past the clerk. "I'll say hello and be gone. I see that Commissioner Holyoke is busy or I would say hello to him as well."

"Come this way, the commissioner is expecting you. These last minute things and those last minute rushes add up." Cozdon nodded toward a large stack of boxes. "That's about half of it."

Randolph urged Kavanaugh through the portico and tapped lightly on the door before him.

"Come in," came a crisp reply.

The interoffice was a tangle of books, papers and boxes in all manners of disarray. The commissioner himself was buried behind a stack of papers on his desk. He stood smiling broadly.

"I must say Brice, it has been awhile."

"Hello Nate, way too long."

"Who is your friend? I was curious about your message."

"Padric Kavanaugh, meet Mr. Nathaniel Taylor, one of the last of the Lincoln line."

"Not the last by any means. Pay no attention, Mr. Kavanaugh, everyone chides me. I knew Mr. Lincoln before he became president. I sometimes passed him in the street. After I came to Washington I became acquainted Mrs. Lincoln's family, the Todds."

"I'm honored to meet a friend of Mr. Lincoln." Pat extended his hand.

"I was not exactly his friend, an acquaintance is all."

"I saw Mr. Lincoln once. He gave a medal to a friend of mine."

"That's interesting, when?"

"I will leave you two to talk. I must be on my way." Brice broke in.

"Oh, Brice, too soon, we need to talk some more."

"You know how that all goes." He replied in good nature. "Looks like you have a lot of work to do also."

"I am going to make a big pile and then I'm simply going to set fire to it." The commissioner laughed, "It would be by far the easiest way to clear out my office."
Brice took the commissioner's hand. "I assume you have employment prospects."
"Thank you for asking. Yes, I am going to work for the B&O railroad."

"Good choice, Nate. If you have time, there is going to be a little soirée at my place on Sunday afternoon. You're welcome to come. There will be a few folks from the departing administration there; some you may enjoy seeing. Come for dinner around four. It is a very informal affair."

"Thank you Brice. It will be a pleasure."

"Goodbye, Pat."

"Thank you, Mr. Randolph." Pat replied.

The door closed behind him as the commissioner moved from behind his desk to an empty straight back chair. Pat looked about. It appeared like the roof had caved and let in a flurry of books and papers.
"Please, sit down, move those books to the floor. Would you like some tea perhaps?"
"Nothing to drink, thank you," Kavanaugh briefly recalled Brock's look.

"Perhaps you prefer something stronger? No need to be nervous. To what do I owe this visit?"

"No thank you," Pat paused and began slowly, "I bring you a message form the Cheyenne nation."

"A message from the Cheyenne, I must say I did not expect this."

"Yes, sir, I was taken prisoner by them last September."

"Captured by Indians, you were lucky to escape, how interesting!"

"It wasn't very interesting, sir. Not at first, I was very frightened for my life."

"Oh, yes! I imagine so. How did you escape?"

"I didn't escape, sir, they released me to carry a message to you. It's here in my valise."

Kavanaugh drew out the skin and spread it on the floor before them. It immediately caught Taylor's attention.

"My word, this is a very interesting pictograph."

"This shows the sorrows that have happened to the Cheyenne in the past five years."

"Which Cheyenne, there seems to be an abundance of them." He scratched at his neck and leaned forward to better see the pictograph.

"This is from a council of all the tribes all, I think, sir."

"Tell me, what does it say?"

Kavanaugh went over the pictograph as best as he could recall the words of Black Badger. The commissioner was attentive throughout, and when Kavanaugh rested, Taylor sat back in his chair and fired up a cigar.

"This is very interesting; Mr. Kavanaugh, but we do have agent workers in the Missouri territory. This message should have come up through them."

"The Indians do not trust any of the agents and they believe that no one hears of their troubles. That is why they sent me to deliver this message to your very eyes."

"I thank you for the information but I must follow protocol. Besides, I am commissioner for only a few more days. What was their reason for selecting you as envoy, anyway?"

"That doesn't really matter sir, they did. They wish their hunting ground be undisturbed and for this they promise peace."

"Remarkable, Mr. Kavanaugh, remarkable. It is remarkable they spared you to this task and a remarkable journey you have made to bring this message to me."

"I promised them to try and I promised them an answer."

"Yes, yes. I am sure that you did. However, I can do little at this point. Who did you say sent you?"

"Black Badger, he is a medicine man respected by the Cheyenne nation."

"Oh, yes just a moment." The commissioner circled back to his desk, shuffled through some papers, and quickly appraised one. "Mr. Kavanaugh, I thought the name rang a bell, I received this message a month or so ago. Black Badger was killed in November."

"Oh." Kavanaugh ran his hand over his forehead and through his hair, shook his head. "That is unbelievable, I just saw him in October"

"Maybe you did, but it is true, he and the war chief Big Bear. Both were killed in the same engagement and quite a number of others also."

"Is there any word of survivors, or prisoners?" The concern plainly showed in Pat's voice.

"This report doesn't say. If it was a war party, I seriously doubt prisoners."

"Any word on a village, were any villages destroyed in November?"

"No village was mentioned. I assume it was a group of hostiles looking for trouble, and found it. A sizeable village was destroyed one day later. You look very pale, Mr. Kavanaugh, are you alright?" He straightened. "I am very sorry this news has upset you. Were these savages' friends of yours? What ever is the case," he straightened in his chair, "you didn't know. You have delivered your message and completed your mission, Mr. Kavanaugh."

"Big Bear and Black Badger were neither my friends nor my enemies, sir." It became quiet in the office; Kavanaugh looked out the window and wondered about Sada.

"What would you like to do with this pictograph? Would you like to leave it for Mr. Parker?"

The voice gave him a start. "I don't know. Maybe I should keep the skin a while longer and come back to see him."

"That would be wise; things are going to get lost around here." He paused and stared out the window for a moment longer then back to Kavanaugh. "I can make a tentative appointment for you. I would be happy to leave word and a note."

"Thank you sir, please do that. Slowly Pat folded the skin and put it back inside his valise.

"I would like to hear more about your exciting frontier exploits, but..." he made a sweeping gesture with his hand, "as you can see, I have much work to do. Cozdon will show you out. I will get a note to Brice about you're appointment with my successor. Perhaps I will see you at Brice's home?"

"No sir, I don't think so, thank you."

A sizeable crowd had gathered outside the office, Pat had to shoulder his way through it. As he reached the top of the staircase, he looked below. There was a throng of blue jackets, but Kavanaugh did not notice anything to alarm him. When he reached the bottom step a young lieutenant flanked by four other soldiers confronted him.

"Come this way." The lieutenant gripped his arm and with the help of two others, forced Pat under the stair well and there was Sergeant Brock with a crooked grin on his face.

"Is this the man, sergeant?"

"Yes sir, that is him. That's Pat Kavanaugh lately of troop A, Seventh Cavalry --- a deserter, a coward, and wanted for the attempted murder of his superior officer."

"You bastard, Brock, you no account murderin' bastard."

Pat twisted his arms free and grasped Brock by the throat. As Brock's face purpled, three of the soldiers twisted him off and pressed him against the wall. Brock retreated holding his hands to his throat.

"I'll get you Brock; someday, I swear we will settle up!"

"Seems you're the one's been got." Brock gasped, "You're the one caught."

"I'll see you in hell, you shoneen son of a bitch."

"I'll see you at the court martial, you Mick bastard. I hope they hang you by your balls." Brock pushed down his collar and straightened it, then leered at Pat, "Pig Irish bastard."

Kavanaugh pushed with all his strength, slipped partially away, and sent Brock skipping back. He could advance no further as the three strong men pulled him back, his hands behind him.

"Shackle him! Shackle him now, Hurling!" The fourth soldier produced wrist cuffs and snapped them closed. Before Kavanaugh knew what was happening he was locked in with a belt and a second set of clamps clicked over his ankles.

"Further altercations, Kavanaugh, and I will order you throttled."

Crowds of people had pushed to the sides of the entryway and were staring at the events unfolding. They hung back, leaving a wide space around the struggling men.

"Ain't you a sorry lookin' son-of-a-bitch? Kavanaugh, you had better start prayin'. They're gonna kill you for sure. I'm gonna piss on your grave and sow it with weeds."

The four soldiers forced Kavanaugh through the door. As they descended the stairs, Kavanaugh fell. He floundered helplessly, was jerked to his feet, and pitched head long into the jail wagon.

"Lieutenant, lieutenant, my bag, I want you to keep my bag for me."

"What bag? Sergeant Dewes, deliver this man to the provost. Confine him by himself, ten days on piss and punk. No visitors, no privileges, no nothing! Just another Paddy for your wagon, and this is a desperate man, so be cautious with him."

"Yeah, lieutenant, a real desperado, I'm a real desperado, but nothin' close to those butchers back at Agate Creek."

"Rather light aren't you, Kavanaugh? You will be up for court martial within the month. And if I know anything at all, dead by the end of the next one."

"That could be, but please, sir. That valise, my bag, it is very important to me. Please sir, would you get it for me?"
"Take him off, Dewes. Hurling's squad will ride with you."

"Yes, sir," The wagon poised as the four soldiers clamored aboard and lurched ahead into traffic. The lieutenant watched it drift into the crowded street.

"I shouldn't bother with that valise or turn it over to the Provost. Ah, what the hell, he did say please." He turned on his heel and walked back up the stairs and into the Office.

Chapter 11

Old Capitol Prison, Washington D.C.
December 1868

Kavanaugh lost track of the days in the near total darkness of the prison cell. The only light came when the guard opened the grate on the door. The guards brought him bread and water each morning and took out the pail that was his toilet. It was very cold; they took away his clothes and replaced them with a thin striped prison uniform -the number 1313 stenciled on front and back. The first few days he was chained to the cell wall and the shackles cut deeply into his ankles and wrists. The guards rarely spoke to him, except to give brief directions. One of them beat him with his fists on the first night, and another hit him with his keys, cutting his face. He soon acquired lice in his hair, under his arms and in his crotch. Once he started to scratch at them he could not contain himself. His underarms were already bloody and his scalp was full of scabs from his digging.

On the afternoon of the eighth day of his confinement, Kavanaugh thought he heard a woman's voice, but credited his imagination. However, a few moments later, the door burst inward blinding him with the light, and quickly closed as a slight figure slipped in.

"Ma'am, I can get in BIG trouble for this; I'm gonna have to lock the door. The guard changes in twenty minutes, so you got fifteen."

"Give me my basket, corporal. Don't worry I'll be out of here in time, you just come and get me."

Although Kavanaugh could not see her, he recognized the voice. The grate in the door remained open, allowing a small square of light to fall on his face.
"Mary, what the hell are you doing here?"

"Just what the hell do you think? She produced a small candle and a ghostly light illuminated the walls. "God, Kavanaugh, what a sight you are!"

"Careful of that bucket, Mary."

"I didn't know where the hell you were. When you didn't come back, I figured something was wrong so I finally got a hold of Brice. He didn't know anything either but he checked it out." She squinted into the dark toward him. "Jesus, Kavanaugh you are in a world of trouble."
"It's the story of my life, Mary."

"Well, maybe it's about time to change it! They are fixing to court martial you next week and they mean to kill you; either hang you for treason or shoot you as a deserter."
"I'm tired Mary, I'm very tired. I really don't give a damn!"

"Stop that shit, Kavanaugh! Quit this Mick fatale. There are many folks that don't want this to happen - me for starters." She dug into the basket. "I brought you some stuff. Here's some cold chicken, some biscuits Evelyn made, and she is beside herself worrying about you. Better eat this stuff fast."
"God bless her." He began to devour the food.

"Well, she is in tears most of the time worrying about you, so quit this shit about being tired. We are always worrying after you. I have a little whiskey here, had to put it in a crock bottle," she handed him what appeared to be a vinegar jar. "I told the guard it was salad oil." She sniffed loudly. "Jesus, it stinks in here." She moved the candle closer to him and winced as the light fell over his face. "They beat you up, huh?"

"A little," He passed his hand over the raw wounds on his cheek.

"And in chains," she clucked at him affectionately. "I wonder if there will ever be a day when I see you without a swollen nose or a black eye or a busted lip."

He sipped the whisky from the spout of the jar. "Want a drink, Mary?"

"No," she squinted toward him. "Pat, I don't know what I can do to get you out of here. You even made the papers, like some kind of…"

"Desperado," He sipped at the crock. "Ah, don't worry, Mary."

"You want to die is that it? Don't worry; what kind of advice is that?"

"Can't say I really want to, but I guess I'm ready."

"Well, I'm not! I had an interesting visitor the other day. Day before yesterday as a matter of fact - right after the news in the papers and Brice's account."

"Do I want to hear this?" he smiled.

She lifted her eyebrow. "Do you want to hear me or not?"

"Yes, I want to hear it, Mary. I'm happy just to hear your voice."

"A Chinaman dressed in gold and black robes, a hat with a big egret feather. The stuff he wore was pure silk - looked like a prince or a king or something."

"Woo."

"Yes, Woo. I told him you had talked about the trip and you were in jail and all and he gave me this," she reached into her bodice and produced the pine tree shilling. "Said not to lose hope you needed this coin for good luck." She handed the coin to him.

Pat held the coin to the light. "It's our good luck coin; keep it for me, Mary. If something happens to me take it back to him."

"I don't know where that would be." She extended her hand and Kavanaugh returned the coin. "Alright, I'll keep it for you. Ever since Woo left the house there has been a Chinaman outside the kitchen door just waitin' there. Evelyn feeds him and gives him a blanket everyday he is there."

"He is a messenger."

"Well, of course he is a messenger! You think I'm a dunce? Until today, I had nothing to send. And what the hell am I supposed to do? I can't write Chinese and this man doesn't speak but ten words of English - please, thank you, I am from Woo."

"You don't have to speak or write Chinese. Tell him I am alright and I thank him for his concern. Write it down in English, Woo is very smart."

"When he came to visit, we had tea in the kitchen. Evelyn was half-afraid of him, but he was polite and very serious. He spoke English pretty well; I didn't know he could read it. When I told him where you were, I mean are, he didn't say anything, just looked at me. Listen, Pat, I must go, I can't leave the basket so finish eating. I'll wrap the rest of the stuff in a napkin for you, and leave the candle. I'm going to inquire about who is the best defense lawyer in the Army and get another criminal lawyer to help from outside. I know a couple of real good ones."

"Thank you, Mary."

"Thank me if you get out of this." She leaned over and kissed his cheek. "God damn it, Kavanaugh! You could keep six angels busy getting you out of trouble. Are you done with the Bushmills?"

"Yes, and I think I know at least one angel."

100

She chuckled, gathered up the basket and bottle, and knocked on the cell door. "It's not me, not in your wildest dreams." The door of the cell opened, she disappeared through and it clanged solidly closed, behind her. The candle cast broad flickers of light on the wall of the darkened cell and he made out some initials and a deaths head etched in blood. He thought he heard rats squeaking and his mind rushed back to the famine scenes.

Quietly he began to say a rosary touching his thumb and index finger counting the beads that were not there. The time passed slowly and Mary had not returned, but one afternoon the guard slipped fresh biscuits, a cold pork chop, and a slab of cheese through the slot in the door. The guard muttered something about Mary then, "Three days, Kavanaugh, three days until your court-martial."

Chapter 12

Office of the Army Adjutant General
Washington D.C.
March 1, 1869

He'd lost track of the time but thought he had been in the cell for about six weeks and two days. One morning, rather than passing through the usual bread and water, the guards opened the door and lead him into the blinding light down a long hallway. He was doused with water, given a bar of yellow soap, and told to wash up. Then they dusted him with white powder and led him to a corner of the cellblock where a barber was waiting. "Sit down, Red, over here on this chair. They want to pretty you up before they shoot ya!"

Pat looked out the window and saw the capitol building shining in the distance. He derisively replied. "Yes it is very thoughtful of them."

The barber quickly sheared the long red locks to a close, military cut and trimmed his beard. He shook the hair from the towel around Kavanaugh's neck, dusted him again.
"I've been wondering where I am."

"You're in the Old Capitol Prison. When the British burned us out in 1814, the Capitol was right here."

The barber gestured him to come. "Follow me; you're goin' upstairs where they will give you a clean uniform."
"A clean uniform, what the hell do I need a uniform for? They are just going to hang me."

"This is a military proceeding. You must be in uniform, but no stripes, I understand you were stripped of them. You are still officially a soldier. From what I hear, you were a first sergeant."

"It seems like a long time ago." He fell into step with the barber leading the way. "You got a couple of lawyers waiting for you. Everyone's so busy with the new politicians you ain't hardly gonna be noticed."

There were two well-dressed men seated behind a table when Kavanaugh was ushered into the room. One was a captain in crisp union blues; the other, a civilian dressed in light gray pinstripe, a pale yellow shirt and a gray tie dotted with yellow crests.

"Sergeant Kavanaugh, I am Captain Will Sutter of the Adjutant General's office." He extended his hand and Kavanaugh felt a strong firm grip ripple up his arm. "I have been appointed judge advocate and assigned to defend you."

The second man extended his hand and smiled. "I am Don Sutter, hired by Miss Cleary to contribute to your defense." He cleared his throat, "If you are wondering, Will is my brother."

"My defense will be a family affair." Kavanaugh smiled and released his hand then sat down across from them.

"Will is going to take your defense before the court martial. I will help as best as I can from the, side line, so to speak."
"Mary hired you?"

"She hired him, and asked for me specifically," the Captain enjoined. "She must have had some influential friends. I was at the New York barracks and teaching at West Point and transferred here."

"I didn't even know where I was until today."

"It's the Old Capitol Prison, has quite a history. They hanged Henry Wirz, the Warden of Andersonville prison, right out there in the courtyard. You know about him I assume?"

Kavanaugh nodded. "I've seen some of his handiwork. I don't know how anyone could treat prisoners like that."

Will Sutter looked at his notes. "These are serious charges against you, assault on a superior officer that resulted in serious injury, desertion, and treason."

"The court will no doubt embellish the charge of assault and make it attempted murder. They'll surely ask for the death penalty for both desertion and treason." Don said.

"There is a good chance we can get that treason charge dismissed and perhaps the attempted murder as well," Will replied. "But there is the desertion of your post in the face of the enemy; that may be more difficult. They will trump that up to demonstrate cowardice to strengthen their case. In itself, desertion is a capital offense, but not necessarily."

"Treason has been added to assure the death penalty I presume, but there is a good chance that will not stick," Don added.

"I committed no treason." Kavanaugh said hopelessly. "I was trying to bring a peace message from the Cheyenne Nation to Washington, if that is what they call treason."

"You have been serving in the United States Armed Forces and you took a loyalty oath. The Cheyenne are our enemies, although no war has been declared against them." They will try to construe your agreeing to bring a message from the enemy, as treason - a capital offense."

"But I've never wavered in my loyalty to the United States, never!"

"I'll make a note of that, but you did take an oath of loyalty?"

"Yes, when I enlisted in the engineers five, six years ago."

"There may be a point here, but I doubt it."

"Did you serve in the late war?" Don inquired.

"Yes, I was at Gettysburg, then in Virginia. After my first enlistment I joined the cavalry."

"Gettysburg?" He turned the folder he had opened.

"Yes, sir, I was on Little Round Top before and during the Rebs assault."

"You have an otherwise undistinguished record."

"I didn't have a distinguished record on Round Top either. We fought for our life."

"Were you with the Irish Brigade?"

"No, sir, we were engineers from Harrisburg defenses. We straggled in through the enemy lines that on the north side of town." Kavanaugh took a deep breath and rubbed his forehead with his roughed hands. "I lost a couple of good friends there."

"Yes, of course. Well, what happened after that?"

"I lost the rest of my friends to Mosby's Raiders in Virginia."

"Don," he said turning to face his brother, "get what you can about it. Any details you can think of?"

"Any details, like what captain?"

"Were there any military contacts at the scene?"

"I remember riders from Kirkpatrick's Cavalry came after the raid. They scattered the Rebs, and got the ambulances to pick up the dead. They said we made a good fight, one of the officers came back to find me to get more details. His name was Gallagher and he told me where

103

to reenlist in the cavalry."

"Get what you can on it, Don. You can get most of this from military records, but it's the time factor again. Now, about the day in question and subsequent events, tell us what you remember."

"Major Tyne led the troops against a group of what he said were 'hostiles' - women, children and old men at a fish camp where they were drying fish and whatever the hunters brought in. They were quite peaceful."

"Peaceful?" The captain cocked his head, and then looked Kavanaugh in the eyes.

"I mean, there were no warriors. We attacked the camp and the troops lost control." He shook his head, "Lost control."

"Lost control?"

"Yes, Captain, they killed them all: the old men, the women, and the children. The dead were all over the village killed running away."

"Women and children, my God that was an atrocity!"

"Yes, sir, we even killed the babies."

"Where were you?"

"I rode through the camp and reined up; the killing went on and on! I saw some Indians trying to escape-they were two women (one with a baby), and an old man. I captured them."

"Captured, were they were unarmed?"

"Yes sir, then Major Tyne saw me; I told him they were my prisoners." Pat ran his hand through his hair and looked down at the table.

"And what happened then?"

"It is kind of confusing; the Major shot the old man and galloped toward us with his saber in hand. He hit me with it and I pulled him off his horse."

"His intent was to kill the women?"

"I believed so, yes, sir, and to kill me too!"

Don Sutter broke in. "Am I correct to understand that you struggled with the Major to protect yourself, the squaws, and the child?"

"Yes, we wrestled with the saber and I sliced him. I caught him across the face, put out his eye, and cut two fingers from his hand."

"What happened then?" Don queried.

"I and the women ran off. A Cheyenne war party caught up to us and took me captive."

"How long were you a captive?"

"About a month, maybe a little more; they had a big pow-wow and decided to use me to carry a message to Washington."

"So you became an envoy of the Cheyenne?"

"Yes, I guess that's true; they told me to do it, if I wanted to live. I brought the message they wished me to deliver, I talked with the commissioner himself but he didn't seem to care much - he was movin' out."

"You were arrested at the Office of Indian Affairs? You resisted arrest and ended up in prison, solitary confinement. For what, almost two months? Your nose and face are swollen, were you beaten?"

"I think, sir, that sergeant Brock keeps sending me messages."

"Sergeant Brock?"

"Yes, he was at the 'atrocity' as you put it. He was with the arresting officer."

"Don, see what you can find out about this man Brock, and see if there are some witnesses who will testify to corroborate this."

"Well, that settles that! You'll not likely find anyone willing to risk testifying for me, with Brock and Tyne around. It'll be my word against theirs. Hell, you might just as well hang me tomorrow!"

"Perhaps, but the Major has suffered a severe stroke. It is not likely he'll be able to give verbal testimony but you can wager he will draw great sympathy from the court, who will, of course, all be officers of experience."

"Will, remember what we discussed. If you push too hard, you are toying with that sympathy vote which will not be supportive of Mr. Kavanaugh's defense."

"Yes, it's your call. This Major has medals, service clusters and all. Every one of those officers will know about the Indian campaign."

The captain stood to leave. "By the way Kavanaugh, I have a certain valise of yours. A Lieutenant McCready turned it in and I have reviewed its contents; it contained a pictograph and twenty dollars gold. Was the pictograph the Cheyenne message?"

"Yes, sir that would be the skin of sorrow, the message I delivered. The one I tried to explain to the Commissioner."

"This was given to you by the Cheyenne council?"

"Yes sir, by Black Badger, a powerful medicine man and representatives of all forty tribes. He wanted to bargain, let things be, for peace. Unfortunately, like many peacemakers, he is dead"

"Sergeant Kavanaugh the bargain would not have happened. We will be in touch." He turned, "Guards, take him back and if there is one more scratch on him, even the width of a gnat's eyelash, I will court martial the whole lot of you, and when he is in his cell I want him out of the chains!"

Kavanaugh managed a salute. The two brothers disappeared down the corridor and he was quietly guided back to his cell.

Chapter 13

The Court-Martial

On the day of his trial Kavanaugh was transported to a building favoring Virginian style architecture. As he proceeded to the rear door he remained in manacles, but once inside they were removed. He entered the courtroom to the side and was ushered between the chairs. The front of the room was paneled in chestnut that reached to the ceiling and the floor was polished oak. The courtroom was nearly square, intersected by a railing that separated a small gallery from the bench and tables. He noticed that Don Sutter was up in the front row of the gallery along with a few men in blue. Brock was there grinning and leering at him, from an isle seat, and in the back corner; a Chinese man was somberly watching the proceedings. Two women dressed in black were also present, but he searched in vain for Mary.

Kavanaugh heard an exchange between Will and another lawyer, who said something about 'open and shut' but Will's response was lost in the crowd's undertones.

He walked with a guard on each side of him. As they passed Brock, he heard him hiss, "You Mick son-of-a-bitch, you're gonna get yours!"

Pat did not even glance in his direction as he was conducted to a table on the left side of the bench. Parallel to him was a podium and another table with two officers. Will Sutter was standing beside a lieutenant he did not recognize.

"Sit down Pat and bear up," Will motioned, "this should not take long." Forward to him a door opened and five senior officers filed into seats behind a balustrade perpendicular to the tables. A sergeant major with a well-worn face and a snappy uniform stepped to the podium. Behind the judge's chair, a door opened and a major general, his rank showing on collar tabs slipped through. The sergeant made a brief statement indicating that President of the Courts Martial, General Sean O'Neil presided.

A captain rose from behind the prosecution table and stepped toward the bench. The court rose in response.
"Captain Durcher, you may proceed to form this court," O'Neil directed in somber tones.

Durcher glanced at the papers in his hand, turned toward the court and began to read the names of the presiding officers.

"Brigadier General Thomas T. Holt, Commandant of Training Regiment, Washington Barracks."

The general rose and seated himself in the jury box, adjacent to O'Neil. The brigadier was a short sour looking man with a full, closely cropped beard. He glared at the court, nodded toward O'Neil, then straightened in his chair.

"Brigadier General Hector Paul Davidson, Fort Morgan Alabama, temporarily posted to the Baltimore Harbor Defenses."

The second man strode across the court and stepped into the box. He was tall, his face was deeply lined and tanned, and a slight smile emphasized the lines about his eyes and over his cheeks. He had snow-white hair with a neatly trimmed mustache and his well tailored uniform the gold buttons shined brightly against the blue.

"Colonel Francis C. Molloy, Strategic Planning Office for Kansas, stationed at Fort Wallace."

The officer rose and slowly made his way forward, showing a decided limp, with considerable difficulty he stepped into the jury box. He had a leathery appearance, with piercing blue eyes beneath a crop of thinning gray hair. As he seated himself, the light glinted from the Congressional Medal that he wore.

A murmur passed through the court as the gallery moved noisily to their seats.

"The court is now opened," O'Neil, informed.

Durcher raised his voice and read, "Headquarters, Adjutant General's Office, a Courts Martial is hereby appointed to try certain charges made against Padric Kavanaugh, former Master Sergeant, Troop A, Second Regiment, Seventh Cavalry, by order of General W.T. Sherman and signed Colonel Lloyd Green Assistant Adjutant General, for conduct in the vicinity of Agate Creek Kansas territory on August 20 and 21, 1868." He paused for a breath. "The court has been informed Lieutenant Harvey Veston, Adjutant General's Headquarters, is appointed Court Recorder and I, Captain Elmer Durcher, Trial Judge Advocate."

Durcher looked toward the defense table and again raised his voice. "Are there challenges or objections of this court?" He paused and looked around the courtroom.

"There are no challenges or objections. The court is formed."

"There being no challenge, read the charge Captain Durcher." O'Neil commanded.

"Charges are brought forward by Major General Solomon Kincaid, Commander, Fort Wallace, Kansas, on August 31, 1868 and served upon the defendant by Lieutenant Kevin McCready, Adjutant General's Office on December 30, 1868. Does the defense waive reading of the charges?"

Will rose, "No, we do not we prefer the charges be read." Slowly he sat back down and said to Kavanaugh, "We will hear what we have to contend with, and so will the press and the gallery."

Durcher collected the charge sheet from the table and began to read.

"Charge one, violation of the twenty-first Article of War, in that Padric Kavanaugh did commit an assault upon an officer in the person of Major James Tyne, in the area of Agate Creek on the twenty-first day of August 1868.

"Charge two, violation of the forty-seventh Article of War, in that Padric Kavanaugh did desert his post in the face of the enemy on the twenty-first day of August 1868 during the same engagement." He paused for a moment, found his place on the page and began again.

"Charge three, violation of the 21st Article of War, in that Padric Kavanaugh did disobey a direct order given to him by Major Tyne regarding the capture and confinement of Cheyenne prisoners."

"Charge four, violation of the first Article of War, treason, in that Padric Kavanaugh did enter into a pact with the Cheyenne Indians, a tribe hostile to the interests of the United States of America, to become a courier on their behalf."

"Mr. President, the charges, and specifications have now been read in the presence of the accused in open court."

"Let the record so indicate Lieutenant Veston. Captain Durcher, swear the court."

Durcher raised his right hand, the officers did likewise. "Do you swear that you will well and truly perform the duties of officers of the court in the case now in hearing according to the law or rules of warfare in like cases, so help you God?"

O'Neil, still standing, swore in Durcher who in turn indicated he would swear in legal counsel. "Captain Durcher is a member of the bar in Maryland, Virginia and the Federal system, and a member of the Judge Advocate Corp. For the defense, Captain Will N. Sutter a member of the bar in Maryland, Massachusetts, New York, Pennsylvania, and the Federal system, a member of the Judge Advocate Corps. Are these qualifications correct?" Durcher looked to Sutter who nodded affirmatively. "Very well, the court will accept the plea."

Sutter and Kavanaugh rose and O'Neil looked quickly, appraising them. "How do you plea?"

"Not guilty of all charges." Sutter looked steadily at O'Neil who responded.

"Be seated. Captain Durcher, proceed with the prosecution."

"Mr. President, Officers of the Court, on or about August 15, 1868, Seventh Cavalry scouts reported to Colonel Molloy, Commandant of Fort Wallace, that a village of hostiles had been discovered in the vicinity of the confluence of the Crooked and Agate creeks. After due deliberation a troop of Seventh Cavalry, under the command of Major James Tyne, was dispatched to destroy said village and take capture of the Cheyenne Indians living there."

Durcher paused and glanced about the court. "The command attacked the village and was engaged in a brisk fight. During this time, then Sergeant Kavanaugh, after refusing a direct order, did attack the person of Major James Tyne and, after severely injuring him, did desert his post in the company of hostiles. At some time later, he entered into a pact with said hostiles. He was apprehended on December twenty-ninth and has been confined until this court martial convened today." Durcher looked toward O'Neil, shuffled the papers in his hand, and walked obliquely toward his table.

"You will call your first witness, Captain Durcher."

"Mr. President, the prosecution calls Sergeant James Adderly Brock."

Kavanaugh heard the stir behind him as Brock rose from the railing and shuffled forward. Near the witness stand, he shot a look at Kavanaugh and stepped briskly to the chair. He sat very erect, the chevrons and diamond, bright red against his crisp blue uniform. His hair was slicked down with pomade and he affected the air of a neat, competent soldier.

"Sergeant Brock, you were present at the engagement of August 21, 1868, now referred to as the Battle of Agate Creek?"

"Yes, sir, I was there."

"What were your responsibilities?"

"I was Sergeant of A Troop, Seventh Cavalry."

"You shared these responsibilities with the defendant?"

"Yes, sir" Brock nodded forward and passed his hand over his hair.

"Recount as best you remember the events of that day."

"We raided an Indian Camp, there was a big fight, and we won." He looked toward the court. There was a ripple of laughter and he responded to it with a smile.

"Do you recall events surrounding the action in which the then Sergeant Kavanaugh, participated?"

"He was in charge of the left, sir, when we advanced over the ridge onto the camp."

The presentation was interrupted as the sound of the courtroom entrance door opened. A muffled exclamation passed through the court as all eyes turned toward the sound. Major James Tyne was wheeled forward; he appeared much too small for his uniform, and was slumped in the large wheelchair. His right eye was covered by a black patch and an ugly purple scar halved his face downward through his nose, to his chin. The orderly who accompanied him, dabbed at the drool that occasionally seeped from the corner of his mouth. There was a louder stir of voices in the courtroom as Tyne came into full view of the gallery. The panel of officers looked toward the broken figure that showed no sign of recognition toward them.

"Order in the court!" The gavel hit sharply, O'Neil glared about. "Any further murmuring, mumbling, or outright conversation and I will clear this court. Proceed with the witness, Captain."

"Sergeant Brock, continue."

"We cleared the ridge and tied into them. They didn't know we were there 'til we hit. In the middle of the battle Kavanaugh attacked the Major. Nearly kilt him, like to cut his face in half, put out his eye." He glanced furtively toward the wheel chair. "When we found him he was bleedin' badly. We thought he was gonna die."

"Would you identify the perpetrator of this act?"

"There, Captain." Brock pointed toward Kavanaugh, then settled back in his chair.

"When you found the Major so severely wounded, was the then Sergeant, Kavanaugh, present?"

"No, sir, he skedaddled and I never seen him afterward until last December when I seen him in the Indian Office."

Durcher turned from the witness and started toward the defense table, "Your witness, Captain Sutter."

Sutter stood, stretched his neck, and approached the witness chair.

"Sergeant Brock, did you see Sergeant Kavanaugh deliver the wounds to Major Tyne?"

"No, sir, I was busy in the fight. Major Tyne told us who done it."

"But you did not actually witness it Sergeant Brock?" Sutter looked toward the bench. "Is it not true that you had a personal dislike for Sergeant Kavanaugh?"

"We had our differences."

"Yes or no."

"Yes, I didn't much like him then, and I don't like him now neither."

"Sergeant Brock, isn't it true that the extent of your dislike incited you to contact the jailers responsible for the conditions of Sergeant Kavanaugh's incarceration and directed them to give him a lesson by chaining him to the wall of his cell and beat him?"

"Objection, objection! " Durcher was on his feet, red faced angry, "Prison conditions are not relevant here. This has nothing to do with the charge."

"I will allow the question; Sergeant Brock you will answer."

Sutter stood close to the witness chair turning slightly away, towards the court. "Yes or no Sergeant Brock, did you tell the guards to give Kavanaugh a lesson?"

"Yes, God damn it! Kavanaugh is a no good Mick son-of-a-bitch. Yes, I told my friends the kind of man he is. I told them no matter what he gets it ain't enough." Brock's face was red and angry; he glared first at Sutter then at Kavanaugh. "He is just pig shit Irish and there ain't any thing worse."

"The defense has no further questions of this witness," Will returned to the table.

O'Neil spoke up, "Sergeant Brock, before I dismiss you from the stand I want you to know that I did not appreciate your profanity nor your ethnic slurs. I hold you in contempt of this court and remand you to the provost guards to be placed under confinement until you can glean representation from the Adjutant General's Office. This court is in recess until eight o'clock tomorrow morning." He brought the gavel down firmly, stood up, and passed through the door behind him.

The men at the tables stood as the senior officers presiding left their seats, and the crowd spread as Major Tyne was wheeled out. Both Kavanaugh and Brock were surrounded by guards and whisked away to opposite sides of the courtroom and the area near the bench erupted.

Will Sutter shuffled his notes into a big case and looked to the prosecution table. "Open and shut case, Durcher? Now your key witness is in the pokey."

"It will be closed tomorrow."

"I'm looking forward to it. I expect you'll call on the Major since he was indisposed at the outset of these proceedings. Good luck."

"You seem to know. Your problem is you are too damned cocky, you Harvard snip."

"True enough, but I am curious about how you will get Brock out. Maybe you could declare…"

"I know the law as well as you".

"I'll see you in the morning".

Kavanaugh entered to a full gallery, the officers, counselors, and the president were already seated and conferring about the large gathering. O'Neil struck the gavel three times and the court quieted.

"Captain Durcher, let's get on with it."

Durcher rose and addressed him. "Sir, all parties to the trial present when the court recessed is now present."

"Proceed, Captain Durcher," O'Neil relaxed in his chair and glanced toward the activity before him.

"I call Major James Tyne."

O'Neil looked at him incredulously, and then tapped the gavel against the rising murmurs in the gallery. He leaned toward Durcher then glanced to Sutter. "Counsels will approach the bench." When they assembled, O'Neil continued in a low, stern voice. "Be careful here gentlemen. I do not want this witness harassed or extended beyond his current ability to bear. He is seriously disabled and he is retired with a fine service record. The extent of his disability is apparent. How do you intend to take this testimony captain?"

"Sir, the Major will provide verbal testimony."

"Verbal testimony, I have been told, Captain, that he is without the ability to speak, and can write only enough to sign his name. Was I incorrectly informed?"

"Mr. President, I wonder if this witness is competent to testify at all."

"Be careful with that word competent, Captain Sutter. You just show respect for this man. And you Captain Durcher explain please."

"The Major cannot speak sir, but he can sing his answers."

O'Neil straightened in his chair, and then leaned forward again. "What the hell do you mean sing? Sing but not speak?"

"Yes, sir," Durcher shifted his feet, looked toward Major Tyne, then up to O'Neil.

O'Neil leaned as far forward as the bench permitted and spoke vehemently. "Do you recall the last time you were before me in court? Outbursts from the gallery, three of your witnesses perjured themselves and there was a donnybrook in the hall. That does not bode well for you, and I don't like the sounds of this one."

"Believe me sir, Major Tyne can sing his answers sir, I protest should you bar his

110

testimony."

"I protest should his testimony be allowed." He saw at once the futility of the request.

"Be seated Captain Sutter. Proceed with your witness Durcher."

Durcher cautiously approached the witness chair and smiled at Major Tyne.

"Are you comfortable sir?" Tyne responded with a nod of his head. The near silence of the courtroom was broken only by a cough from the gallery.

"Major Tyne, on August the twenty-first of last year, you were present at the Battle of Agate Creek".

"I was there." A thin falsetto filled the silence with a squeaky, piping sound.

Kavanaugh swallowed back a grin and someone in the gallery sniggered and was joined by another.

"At this battle you were wounded and maimed by one of your own non-commissioned officers?"

"Yes," the answer was in two tones almost musical.

"Is that man present here?"

"Yes he is," the sentence sounded like 'doe, re, me.'

"Will you point that man out? " A wavering finger rose toward Kavanaugh.

"Then Sergeant Padric Kavanaugh?"

"Yes, he cut up my face and put out my eye and cut two fingers from my hand." The squeaky singsong tone was in gross contrast to the message.

In the gallery there was a stifled laugh that was accompanied by other choking sounds. General O'Neil looked hard toward the direction of the sound.

"Did this man then desert his post while the conflict broiled around you?"

"Yes, he was in-sub-or-din-nus and omin-us and tree-son-nus." The second bar came with a rhythm an octave lower; "He should be shot or hung."

Some men exited the court and their laughter could be heard in the hall. Major Tyne slumped in his chair. There were scraping and moving sounds as a general discomfort spread across courtroom.

"I have no further questions, your witness Captain Sutter."

"Adjutant will approach the bench." O'Neil glared at the gallery then narrowed his eyes on Durcher. His voice came in a malevolent undertone. "Durcher you should have spared this witness and Captain Sutter you will not badger him."

"You will allow this testimony, sir? I could hardly make it out."

"I will allow it, but Durcher, this court would have been better served with a written deposition. This man is feeble and he can't sing worth a damn. Be careful Captain Sutter. He waved them away. "Proceed with the witness."

"Major Tyne, with due respect sir, I have a few questions to ask you." Sutter positioned himself so the presiding officers could see the witness. "At the Battle of Agate Creek, how many warriors were taken?"

"There were many In-dee-ENS." The notes rose and fell in falsetto.

"How many warriors were there?"

"I do not remember, I do not remember and I do not remember," came in a musical cadence.

"How many warriors were there, Major Tyne?"

"I do not ..." He slipped into a stony silence, glared at Sutter, slumped in his chair, and released a long, wet sounding fart. The noise was obvious and two more men left the courtroom hurriedly.

Sutter looked at him patiently and stepped toward him. "Major Tyne, you are not going to answer my question are you, because the court would vilify it. Isn't that right, Major Tyne? Because the truth is mostly women and children were killed at Agate Creek. There were no warriors. Were you ordered not to take prisoners? Did you not order that no prisoners be taken? NONE. Did you strike at Sergeant Kavanaugh with your saber when he protected prisoners he had taken?"

The Major did not respond, the ugly scar twitching where it crossed the corner of his mouth. He gagged what sounded like "I don't remember". Tyne began to choke.
"Did you strike him, sir, yes or no"?

There was a bang of the gavel. "Captain Sutter, I thought we had an understanding." O'Neil interrupted. "This witness is dismissed."

"With all due respect, sir…"

"The witness is excused." The gavel came down with a shattering bang. "This court is in recess until Monday next at eight o'clock. I will see counsels in my chamber at once." He angrily bashed down the gavel.

Kavanaugh remained seated at the bench surrounded by the provost guards. In a few minutes the attorneys reappeared, Durcher was pale and Sutter appeared angry.

"I don't need another one of those sessions any time soon, Pat." He began to fold his papers away into his briefcase.

"How are we doing Captain?"

"Well enough Pat. Our defense will start Monday and Don has gone off to meet a train. We finally have another witness willing to testify for our side. A Corporal Adam Harper he said he knows you well and what really happened at Agate Creek."
"I know Harper sir, a very honest man, and a good soldier."

"Harper is no longer in the Army, thus willing to testify. We contacted others, but they would have been more of a problem than a resolution. Harper's service records indicate he was present and mentioned in dispatches."
"We will see what happens Monday. I'll be glad to see Harper again."

The provost guards shackled Kavanaugh and led him away. Sutter turned up the aisle with Durcher.

"Captain Durcher according to O'Neil, your last trial was a circus and this one a public spectacle. You had better stay away from O'Neil. Maybe you should go into another line of work, surgery maybe, or the carnival business."

"You Harvard snip. The verdict will bear me out. You might entertain a change yourself, Sutter, after they announce Kavanaugh's firing squad. I will press to execute him; I am convinced of the support."

Monday's trial began in somber tones. Major James Tyne had suffered a second and fatal stroke. The court was made aware through a vigorous admonishment for their behavior on Friday and was threatened that the first unruly behavior would result in it being cleared.
"Captain Durcher, you will proceed."

"Sir, all parties to the trial present when the court recessed is now present."

O'Neil nodded and settled back in his chair.

"I call Herbert Holyoke."

After preliminaries Captain Durcher said, "state your name."

"I am Herbert Holyoke, formerly first secretary to the Office of Indian Affairs, Nathaniel Taylor the Director."

"Were you present on December twenty-ninth of the past year when a man explaining his presence as an envoy for the Cheyenne nation appeared at your office?"

"Yes. I did not know he was an envoy at the time until Mr. Taylor told me later."

"So indicate the man."

Holyoke pointed toward Kavanaugh.

"You have identified former Sergeant Padric Kavanaugh."

"Can you tell us what this man, under his announced pretenses, was doing at the Office of Indian Affairs?"

"As I understand it he brought a treaty from the Cheyenne nation to end the war on the plains. Did he see the commissioner?"

"Yes he did. They talked for some time, and apparently Mr. Kavanaugh explained the conditions the Cheyenne sought for peace. I wondered what he was doing in the office. It is protocol for our agents bring forth such requests; of course, we would welcome the input from interested citizens and peaceful accords."

"Kavanaugh had no official reason for appearing and had circumvented the channels of authority so vested for the purpose of making treaties?"

"Yes sir, there was no official need."

"He was just representing the Cheyenne nation?"

"I assume so."

"Sergeant Kavanaugh's deeds do surprise me; he was still an official representative of the government. He had not been discharged from the Army and was carrying messages for the Cheyenne nations and that is treason! I have no further questions, your witness Captain Sutter."

"Mr. Holyoke, you served at the Office of Indian Affairs for how many years?"

"Eight years I am still employed there. I have served no fewer than five different commissioners."

"In your term of employment, have any private citizens brought forward petitions from the Indians?"

"Yes, many," he adjusted his seat in the chair. "Most come to us via our agents."

"So there is no law per se, prohibiting such action. Is the United States officially at war with the Cheyenne Nation?"

"Oh mercy, no, Indians themselves can bring petitions and grievances forward; we have not declared war on them."

"Were you present at the conversation between Sergeant Kavanaugh and Nathaniel Taylor, the Commissioner?"

"No, it was a very busy time. A new administration, President Grant, and there was a lot of chaos, last minute things that needed immediate attention and loads of paperwork. I was very busy."

"You did see Sergeant Kavanaugh and Mr. Taylor conversing. However, you did not hear what they said?"

"Yes, I saw them. Mr. Kavanaugh appeared rather discouraged when he left. Mr. Taylor commented to me that his, Mr. Kavanaugh's, cause was a lost cause."

"And that's all? You were not privy to the conference, so you don't know what was really said"?

"Objection the witness has answered the question."

"Yes, he has. No state of war exists between the United States and the Cheyenne nations. "Two men talking in an office and another person's perception of the outcome is hear say. I submit Mr. Holyoke's deposition is hearsay and should be stricken from the record and that the charge of treason is nullified."

O'Neil looked toward the other officers. "Gentlemen, an opinion please. " There was a brief exchange of words and General Hall leaned toward O'Neil.

"All officers of the Court, including me, have voted to strike the charge of treason. Lieutenant Veston you are so ordered. There being no further witnesses listed for the prosecution, this court is adjourned until one o'clock this afternoon when we will entertain witnesses for the defense." He firmly tapped the gavel, and the courtroom began to clear quickly. Kavanaugh faced Sutter.

"Thank you Captain Sutter. I never believed I was a traitor, I know what traitors are, and I have never set out to be that."

"That was an easy one, Pat, but we sure are in trouble with the other charges. "He changed the subject, "someone sent you lunch today. I have it in my briefcase. He produced a brown bag lined with buttermilk biscuits and cold ham. Sutter looked up as the provost showed interest in the bag. "It's all right boys; I'm just sharin' my lunch." He whispered to Kavanaugh, "I would have brought you a bottle of beer if I could have." They ate quickly, seated in the courtroom. Promptly at one o'clock, the court reconvened.

"The defense calls Adam Harper."

Harper rose from the gallery and walked toward the witness stand, a rustle of fabric and the creak of chairs greeted him as others in the court turned to watch his approach. He appeared tall and distinguished wearing dark blue suit over a white shirt and light blue tie. The crossed swords from his cavalry cap were pinned to the edge of his pocket. He glanced about, smiled toward Kavanaugh, and solemnly took the oath.

"Corporal Harper you don't mind my reference to your former rank?"

"Oh no, sir, I'm proud I served in the Seventh"; he smiled and straightened his pin.

"You were present at what is now referred to as the Battle of Agate Creek?"

"Yes sir, I was."

"Do you know the defendant?"

"Oh yes, me and Kavy served in the same troop. I know Sergeant Brock too."

"Would you explain the circumstances of the battle as you recall them?"

"It was a fish camp sir, the hostiles I mean. It was where they was dryin' fish and makin' stuff, jerky and such, getting ready for winter."

"They were not a war party?"

"Oh no, sir, they was dryin' stuff, they was mostly women and children, but we had reason to go in to destroy those supplies."

"Was Major Tyne aware of the activities at the camp and it was composed of mostly women and children?"

"I reckon so, sir. I think probably he knew before we was ordered out, and besides, Kavy and me crawled to the top of the ridge to get a look and Major Tyne, he crawled up too. He could see the whole lay out and what they was doin'. Him and Kavy got into an argument."
"What was it about?"

"Kavanaugh was worried that the men would lose control. They was fired up about Captain Madigan getting kilt. Kavy said the camp was peaceful and we shouldn't attack. Takin' away the people's food wasn't right - or somethin' like that. He wanted to surround them and march them off with their food to keep them."
"Kavanaugh protested the attack?"

"Yes, sir, we both thought there was gonna be trouble. We meant to try to capture them all. The major wanted to kill them. Kavy got it on with the Major 'because he ain't afraid of nuthin'. I told him to keep quiet, the Major was burning'. "Harper looked toward the officers, then to the President, and then to Kavanaugh.
"And what happened then?"
"We formed up and attacked, but there wasn't none to capture because we kilt them all."

Captain Sutter moved to the defense table. "I offer this account, the battle, as Defense Exhibit A. Permit me to read a portion; the report indicates that fifty-three hostiles were killed. There is no account of prisoners taken. How many warriors were killed, Corporal Harper?"
"If you mean men in paint, there were none, sir."

"This battle has recently been touted as a great victory; fifty-three hostiles killed, one trooper killed and three wounded."

"I don't know sir; Mullaly got an arrow in his leg - it was a boy that shot him. I kept his horse from runnin' off with him. Henderson got knocked off his horse, was trampled to death and Ellenby got shot in the foot. I don't know 'bout Ellenby, he shot his own horse out from under himself once."

There was laughter in the courtroom. O'Neil frowned in its direction. Sutter waited for the laughter to quiet and continued.
"Who were these fifty-three hostiles?"

"There was one or two old men sir and a few boys of ten or twelve years or so." He stopped.
"You say a couple of old men and boys, who were the rest of the fifty-three?"

"They was women and other children. The men went wild sir." There was a profound silence in the court as the gallery stretched to listen.

"How many women and children do you estimate?"

"Closer to forty than thirty, that's not countin' the papooses."

"Papooses, do you mean youngsters?" Sutter surprised by the statement.

"No, sir, I mean babies, they was found in the lodges. I think there was five or six. They laid 'em out for the weather to take."
"What happened to them?"

Harper took a deep breath and looked down. "Private Miller killed them, sir. They was lined up in a row and he just bashed in their heads with his rifle and threw them on the fire. I remember he said it was better than the frost getting them. They would have starved or froze. Nobody thought much of it; I don't think they was counted, I mean in the fifty-three."

"Your witness, Captain."

There was a stony silence; Durcher himself, impacted by the testimony, was slow to rise. In the courtroom, there were a few muffled sobs among the dark clad women and an air of shocked sadness drifted like distant smoke.

"Corporal Harper, how long did you serve with the defendant?"

"More than two years sir," he wiped at his nose and looked toward Kavanaugh.

"Was then Sergeant Kavanaugh a violent man?"

"Objection what is violent in a soldier depends upon a personal perception. You just heard the witness."

"Sustained, re-phrase Captain Durcher."

"Did you, Corporal, ever witness then Sergeant Kavanaugh performing a violent act?"

"Well sir, nobody under Kavy wanted to get on his bad side because he'd thrash them."

"Can you be more specific?"

"Well if one of his men didn't tow the line or shirked his duty, Kavy would straighten them out."

"So then, Kavanaugh was a violent man. Did he follow orders or was he more inclined to go his own way?"

"Oh he followed orders and made damn sure everybody else did too. Sometimes he didn't like it, but he did it."

"And when his men didn't, he thrashed them?"

"Sometimes, yes sir."

"He had a violent temper?"

"Objection, the Adjutant General for the Prosecution is calling for a conclusion."

"Sustained, where are you going with this Captain?"

"I want to establish that Kavanaugh was a violent man and scoffed orders as part of his general duties. Who would have thought little of assaulting an officer."

"Well you didn't; proceed with a different line of questioning."

Very well, Corporal Harper, did you observe behavior by the defendant that may have indicated his disregard for military policy?"

"Sir, Kavy was kind of a loner. He spent a lot of time prayin'. That was different and he never played cards, played dominoes once in awhile. Men used to joke about it called him Saint Patrick, not to his face of course that is if you valued your own. I knew he was a brave man, he wasn't afraid of nuthin'."

"Including the consequences of failure to obey a direct order?"

"Objection!" Sutter jumped to his feet. "Counsel is leading the witness."

"Sustained."

"Other than the fact he beat his men, was a religious fanatic and had a high disdain for orders, I guess he was a good soldier."

"Objection."

"Sustained, Lieutenant Veston strike that. I am warning you Captain Durcher to better direct your inquiry."

"I have no further questions of this witness."

"Any redirect from the defense, Captain Sutter?"

"Yes, sir I will ask additional information to enter in the record."

"Continue then, Lieutenant Veston take note."

"Corporal Harper, did you hear Major Tyne order the death of the hostiles?"

"Yes sir, I did. He said he meant to kill them all."

Sutter walked toward the witness chair. "Major Tyne disobeyed his own orders. Corporal Harper, you served in the United States Cavalry for twenty years. In your experience, was it usual for a Sergeant to discipline his men with physical punishment?"

"Oh yes, sir, I have done it myself; it was a common practice sir."

"Corporal Harper, did you serve with other religious men who were Catholics?"

"All the Irish I ever served with were Catholics or had no religion at all."

"Did any of them recite prayers, rosaries and attend church?"

"Oh, yes, sir - many. I remember Captain Madigan. We all liked him sir, he was one."

"In your experience has a commanding officer ever given you a direct order to kill hostiles without quarter?"

"No, sir, I had a Lieutenant order me to kill two wounded hostiles once. That is the only other time I recall."

"No further questions."

"Call your next witness Captain Sutter," O'Neil rejoined.

"The defense calls Padric Francis Kavanaugh."

Kavanaugh rose slowly to his full height and walked quietly toward the stand looking neither left nor right. A general buzz seeped through the court like a bees in bellflowers.

After preliminaries, Sutter asked directly, "Your initial military service was in the late war when you enlisted in "C" Company of the 144th New York engineers? Describe for the court your duties."

"We were assigned to dig the breastworks at Harrisburg in case Lee broke through, but we were reassigned on special duty to determine defensive positions on the route Lee was expected to come." He stopped and looked at Sutter.

"This special duty led you into the Battle of Gettysburg. The defense offers this document as Exhibit B. You were on Little Round Top, correct?"

"Yes sir, we ended up there after passing through the Reb lines. It was a hot fight sir."

"Your special detail was then reassigned to repairing rail lengths near Annandale Virginia."

"Yes, sir we kept what was left of us together. We buried the dead, stuff like that."

"Describe the events of October third, 1864 near Cow Crossing Virginia."

Kavanaugh slumped slightly forward in his chair and passed his hand over his forehead. "Mosby's men ambushed us there. We did the best we could but there were only six of us, and there must have been thirty of them".

"The defense offers the account of this action as Exhibit C. The document is signed by Colonel Fitzpatrick and notes Sergeant Kavanaugh for uncommon valor --he being sole survivor of that engagement. You transferred from Engineers to Cavalry in November of 1864 and were posted at Fort Wallace, Kansas in 1865."

"Yes sir. It was a busy place."

"And you were a busy man. Please describe the events of June 1867."

"There was cholera in the fort and the doctor needed help. Surgeon Smith asked me, so I did."

"Sergeant Kavanaugh, please describe the events of the great Cheyenne raid that June."

"Chief Roman Nose and about 300 warriors struck the fort. It was another very hot fight sir."

"Defense introduces as Exhibit D a report of those actions, again Sergeant Kavanaugh was mentioned in dispatches for dedication to duty in caring for severely sick soldiers at great risk to his own health. This dispatch was signed by Colonel Francis C. Molloy, who now is a presiding officer at this Court Martial."

"Yes sir, I know Colonel Molloy."

Sutter faced the panel of officers then stepped away, "what makes a good soldier change?" He turned to Kavanaugh. "What happened on 21 August last year?"

"Well sir, we attacked a village of women and children and a couple of old men. I had taken four prisoners: two women an old man and a baby. Major Tyne ordered that I surrender them; he shot the old man, drew his saber, and ordered me aside. I believed he intended to kill the women and the baby. I refused and we had a fight and I...., I wounded him."

"When Major Tyne tried to ride you down, were you in fear for your life?" Sutter stepped toward the bench.

Kavanaugh thought for a moment. "At the time I was more concerned about the two women and the baby, but I was a little afraid. He hit me pretty hard with the saber," he unconsciously moved his hand to his shoulder.

"What happened after the Major attacked you?"

"I jerked him off his horse and we wrestled for the saber that's when he was wounded". Kavanaugh leaned back in the chair with a visible sigh.

"After Major Tyne was wounded, you no longer participated in the atrocity?" The word hung in the air.

"No sir I took the women to safety across the river."

"You were subsequently captured by a Cheyenne war party that. They tortured you over a period of days and gave you a choice to carry a message to the Office of Indian Affairs or die. Is that correct?" Sutter turned toward the presiding officers who were intently focused on Kavanaugh.

"Yes sir, that's how it all turned out."

"Your witness, Captain Durcher." Will returned to the defense table, glanced at the presiding officers and sat down. Durcher approached Kavanaugh with his hands folded behind him. He began haughtily.

"Private Kavanaugh, you are a private, all rank removed because of your actions on August 21 of last year. The action on that date is now referred to as a battle. Captain Sutter called it an atrocity, perhaps counsel does not know what an atrocity is."

There was a loud sound of a chair going over followed by a sharp bang on a table. Durcher turned to see Sutter standing fists clenched, leaning on the table before him.

"An atrocity is an act of enormous savagery, Durcher, maybe YOU don't know that."

O'Neil brought down the gavel in three rapid bangs. "Order, gentlemen order, order in the court and sit down Captain Sutter! Enough of your vocabulary lesson, another outburst and you will be teaching Latin to the prison choir. Now, proceed with your witness Captain Durcher."

"On August twenty-first you attacked Major James Tyne, severely injuring him, yes or no?"

"Yes, I thought he was going to kill my prisoners and maybe me."

"Following the altercation with Major Tyne, you deserted your post and fled in the face of the enemy, yes or no?"

"Yes, I did, but there was no enemy present. They were all dead; the action was over."

"Did you refuse a direct order from Major Tyne to relinquish your prisoners?"

"I believed that he would kill them."

"Yes or no private, it has to be one or the other."

"Yes, I did refuse to let him have the prisoners."

"Did you then enter into a pact with the Cheyenne nation to become their messenger, thus committing a treasonous act?"

"Point of order, the evidence for the charge of treason has been dismissed; there is no point to this line of questioning." Sutter noted.

"Sustained," O'Neil crossed his arms and leaned back into his chair.

"So you refused to obey a direct order, assaulted your commanding officer, and deserted your men in the middle of a battle." Durcher allowed time for his words to be felt by the presiding officers and turning away from Kavanaugh announced, "I have no further questions."

O'Neil consulted his watch on the bench before him, glanced at the officers, then around the courtroom. "Court is recessed until one o'clock tomorrow at which time we will hear closing arguments." He struck the gavel once and the court began to empty.

Kavanaugh watched a fly preening itself in the square blotch of sunlight that poured through the window of the provost office. The March sun, warm and in its early intensity, cast lethargy through the office. He leaned back, closed his eyes, and was next aware of a guard shaking his shoulder.

"Come on Red, its show down time. I don't know what is gonna happen in there but good luck. They just now called us, so we had best move."

As Kavanaugh was led into the courtroom, he could see the gallery was packed; he cast around and did not see Mary, but the Chinese man was in his accustomed seat. He sensed the enormity of the moment and felt for the first time that the officers in blue might well condemn him to death. He was strangely resigned to it, for the truth of the matter was that he was tired, profoundly tired. If he lived it was all right, but the prospect of prison lay heavy on his consciousness. He thought, "if they find me guilty then let the sentence be death." The idea of prison and loss of his freedom was worse than death in his mind.

There was a tap of the gavel. "The court is open. Captain Durcher."

"Sir, all parties to the trial present when the court recessed, are now present. I do not wish to open and waive the privilege."

"Very well, Lieutenant Veston let the record so indicate. Proceed with your closing argument Captain Sutter."

"Officers of the court, the prosecution has made a strong proposal that you follow orders or not, you commit an assault or not and you desert or not. Let the facts speak. They are here, but it is the object of this court to go beyond facts to explanations of why." Sutter paused and again faced the officers.

"You have all had orders and I will wager that not all those you received did you follow in detail. You made decisions based on the circumstances; the answer was not always a simple yes or no."

"What motivates a man, a religious man, a valorous man, who otherwise followed orders, disciplined his men justly and was well respected by his comrades? What motivates him to assault a commanding officer, to disregard orders and to flee the scene of a battle that was really an enormous savagery? I suggest that Sergeant Kavanaugh was responding to a higher moral order. Is it the policy of the United States to exterminate the residents of our western plains, to kill their women and children, even their babies? Where is this written? Sergeant Kavanaugh protested the engagement at Agate Creek because he knew the camp was composed mostly of women and children who would be slaughtered like animals.

Of all the men contacted on behalf of Sergeant Kavanaugh's defense, only former Corporal Harper would come forward. I have a list here of those we contacted that were present at Agate Creek. One might ask 'why' to that also." He paused, "shame, perhaps? When the order is given to commit an act of savagery, it is the trooper's duty NOT to obey it. After being drawn into this conflict, and acting upon orders to capture the enemy and destroy supplies, in fact, Sergeant Kavanaugh was obeying the order that Major Tyne had been given."

Sutter walked to the defense table and sipped a glass of water. "Desertion, the Seventh Calvary has perhaps the highest desertion rate in the Army. Perhaps many of them also did not want to participate in enormous savageries. Sergeant Kavanaugh did absent himself. He did so to protect the lives of the prisoners he had taken, in fact, to protect them from his own commanding officer. What was he to do?" Sutter took sip of water. "In fact he was following the orders issued by Colonel Malloy."

"Major Tyne, it appears, was out of control and he did in fact attack Sergeant Kavanaugh who, while protecting himself, inflicted a grievous injury. One should ask why the Major shot to death, an unarmed prisoner and then set to attack the others. Why did he not follow his orders? But Major Tyne is not here to defend himself, and his judgment is beyond this earth."

"Sergeant Kavanaugh is guilty of disobeying orders to commit an atrocity! An atrocity! In attempting to protect his life and those of his captives from fulminating vengeance not condoned by this government, he left the scene of the atrocity to protect those prisoners. We have scrutinized acts of Sergeant Kavanaugh and no where have we found him guilty of actions not in the best tradition of the United States Army. Defense rests."

There was a general bustle in the courtroom as the gallery and officers adjusted to the break in activity. General O'Neil regarded the officers beside him and glanced toward the prosecution table.
"Captain Durcher carry on with the prosecution closing."

Durcher rose and positioned himself at an angle so he could regard both the bench and the officers lined beside him. "I begin my presentation with a heavy heart for, just a few days ago; this court was graced by the presence of a gallant officer no longer with us. Major James Tyne will be remembered as a gallant, honorable officer, quite different from the man on trial here. Indeed the opposite extreme, Private Kavanaugh, who, on 21 August of last year, assaulted Major Tyne and left him disfigured for life unable to use of one eye and one hand - marks he carried to his grave."

"Following this heinous assault, he deserted his men and fled the face of the enemy. To these facts Private Kavanaugh has admitted, in so many words. The defense asks why? Because Private Kavanaugh may be a man of valor, but he has no honor."

Durcher walked to the panel of officers. "You are all officers and you know about orders; Even if you don't like them, you follow them anyway. Orders are part of military life and we do not have the privilege to judge them either good or bad. We may not particularly like a commanding officer but we do not assault him. We depend on orders to make sense out of chaos. We do not desert our posts if it so happens we don't like the way things are going. It may be that then sergeant Kavanaugh was responding to a higher moral authority but it was not in the best interest of the Army of the United States."

"There is no need to belabor the obvious. It has been shown, indeed admitted, former Sergeant Kavanaugh refused a direct order, committed an assault on his commanding officer, and then deserted his post in the face of the enemy. These facts are the only ones that need to be considered here. Mr. President, the prosecution rests."

General O'Neil tapped the gavel lightly. "This court is recessed until nine o'clock tomorrow morning at which time the verdict will be rendered."

During the shuffle closing the session, Kavanaugh caught Captain Sutter's arm. "What do you think sir?"

"I don't know, Tyne was dying to testify and he did. There will be great deal of sympathy toward him I'm afraid. We are fighting for your life here, Pat."

Chapter 14

Cleary House, Washington D.C.
March 1869

Kavanaugh spent an uneasy night. He said a novena, settled on to the straw-filled mattress and tried to catch some sleep. At the same time, a very different scene was unfolding at Mary Cleary's Entertainment Center.

"You're losing heavily tonight, Mary. You sure aren't concentrating," General Getting observed.

"You sure you want to play on Miss Cleary? You have lost a big sum tonight. I think the General might be right," a Major said in a consoling voice.

"Ante up. Deal the cards gentlemen. Deal the cards." Mary gathered her cards noted the four fours peering from behind each other. It was a winning hand but winning was not on her mind.

"Bet two hundred," she ventured.

"Two hundred, I fold," the Major enjoined.

"Too rich for me," the fourth player ventured.

"I'll bet two hundred and raise two. I don't think you have anything, Mary."

"It will cost you to find out, General."

"Hell Mary, I just took you for four hundred. Four and now I'll raise you five hundred," he pushed the chips forward.

"That's pretty steep General. If you gentlemen would excuse us for a moment, I must speak with the General." She waited until the officers had retreated a respectful distance or disappeared into the bar.

"You remember when you asked if I ever decided to take a trick to let you know?"

The General leered at her and smiled, "All the way, Mary?"

"All the way, I'll bet a trick with you against what you have on the table."

"I don't know, Mary," he smiled. "There's more than a thousand dollars there."

"Oh what about those stars you were willing to bet?"

"You seem pretty confident. But I'll take the bet," he smiled, "it had better be a good one."

"You will enjoy it." Mary motioned the others back toward the table. "What do you have General?"

"A full house, Kings and Aces," Getting sat back with a satisfying smile confident he had won. Mary folded her cards and cast them face down on the table. "The game is over boys. The General and I have business. Drinks are on me." She waved to the bar tender and pointed out the men. General Getting hurriedly gathered his money, and pocketed it. Mary slowly gathered the remainder of the money and tucked it into her bra.

"Come with me General, this is going to be a surprise to the both of us."

Mary nodded toward a man as they ascended the stairs and into a room to the left at the end of the hallway. Inside was a bed with chains and cuffs folded neatly along the edge.

"What's this, Mary?"

"The way I like it. You will like it too."

"I never tried this - never in my wildest imaginations. Do I chain you or you chain me?"

"Trust me, you will like it." She undid the bodice of her dress and slipped it off and placed her money on the top of a dresser. "Are you going to take off your boots, General?"
"I am just fascinated by you." He shed his boots and began to undress.

"Loosen my corset will you." Getting fumbled with the hooks as Mary straightened to the task. "What a relief, you don't know what us women go through to be presentable."

"Mary, your skin is like peaches and cream."

"I guess the freckles must be raisins."

"Yes," slowly he worked his hand over her back and undid the last corset hooks and forced it down and forward. He grasped her breasts and slowly circled his thumbs around her areola. "Feel good? Oh, Mary you don't know how much I have longed for this night."

"It gets better." She stepped out of her panties and turned toward him, the red patch of her pubis was a tangled mass of curls.
He kissed her breasts, her navel, and buried his face in the hair.

"You better finish gettin' undressed before you poke a hole in the floor with that thing," she teased. He rose, slipped out of his underwear and settled back on the bed, his erection standing like a silo.
"Come on Mary."

"Not so fast General," She massaged his penis and kissed it lightly. "This is the way it is, I am going to chain you to this bed and get you and me ready then I'm going to sit on it. I'll give you another later, if this first one's not enough."
"It's a deal Mary. Get on with it."

"Spread your legs. There," she fastened the clamps, "now your arms." She clasped one and then the other.
"Come on, Mary, I need you."

"I need you too, General. She sat in the bed beside him spreading her legs and placing her hand on his penis then knocked on the wall. The door burst open and there was a blinding flash as the photographer set off his camera. "Smile, General," she teased.

"Jesus Christ, Mary! What the hell is this?" The bright light and smoke still blinded him and brought terror to his eyes.

"Welcome to my archive, General. You have been recorded for posterity; your wife can put the picture on her dressing table or you may wish to put a copy on your desk."

He began to thrash in the bed. "Let me out of here you God damn whore! Who do you think you are? You can't do this to me!"

"A whore, yes General, the god damn is waiting for me, and I'm not done yet." She rose, opened the door of the bedside stand, and withdrew a straight razor. "Ever tell you I grew up on a pig farm? I used to castrate pigs every spring." She flipped open the razor and sat it between the General's outspread legs. "Now you are going to do me a favor or I'm going to do you just like what I did to those little pigs."

"Mary for Christ's sakes, don't please, don't - oh, ow, ow! Oh my God, you have cut me. I'm bleeding."

"I just made a nick General not a stitch worth."

"What do you want? Jesus, Mary, please don't. Be careful with that razor. Please don't; please don't cut me any more. Ohh, what are you doing? Please Mary."

"All I have to do is stick my finger in here and give a pull and I'll have your nuts in my hand and then, I will turn you into a soprano."

"What is this? Jesus Christ, Mary. I will do what ever you ask. Don't cut me more. Take out your finger. I will do it. I'll do it. What the hell do you want?"

"For you to sign some papers," she stood up.

"Papers, what kind of papers? Please Mary be careful with that razor."

"Discharge papers."

"You cut me open to sign discharge papers? What the hell woman!"

"I have them prepared and I'm going to tell you whose name to write. I will let your one hand free. If you try anything or refuse, I'll take your cock off too."

"Alright, agreed! I agree. Please Mary take away the razor." She released his right hand.

"Be careful, I have only one copy. Write Padric P-A-D-R-I-C, Francis F-R-A-N-C-I-S, Kavanaugh K-A-V-A-N-A-U-G-H. That's good. The date, what's the date today?"

"Jesus Mary I'm bleeding. Please, please be careful."

"You be careful General, very careful. Let me think, the date," she flicked the razor, "March 9, 1868. No, make it March 20, 1868. Now sign it." She observed him carefully date and sign the document. "Thank you, General, I'll let you go. But first do you still want to get in me?" She leaned forward razor still in her hand.

"No, Mary."

"Maybe some other night?"

"You will never see me here again."

"I doubt that, General Getting, no one except a few of the officers who come in here even like you well enough to play cards with you."

She turned to the bedside table and removed a jar of ointment. "I'll dab a little of this on that nick. It will be healed by tomorrow or the next day, but you ought not to walk a lot." Gently she dabbed the ointment over the small wound. "I gave you a lot of money for this opportunity, General Getting, I had four fours and four of a kind beats a full house no matter how good it looks."

"That ointment stings, I will never forgive you for this."

"The sting is why it will get better. Now, I want to give you a little advice that you'd best hear. If you move to somehow cancel this paper or if you ever decide to raid my place, I will see that your wife gets a full size print of our indiscretion. You wouldn't want that to happen would you?"

"No."

"I have your word, General."

"Yes. You have my word."

"Good, I'm going to turn you loose. You're welcome to come back as you wish, tonight is our own little secret."

Slowly he dressed stepping gingerly into his clothing.

"Like I said General, I wouldn't walk around much."

"You are a whore from hell, Mary Cleary, and some day you will get your just comeuppance. Our friendship is over."

"Don't be too hasty General. I already got my comeuppance a long time ago. Hell, I'm just gettin' even. Don't let the door hit you in the ass on the way out."

The door closed behind the General. She carefully stored the paper and the razor, then opened the closet, shrugged on a robe, and headed down the stairs to the kitchen.

Adjutant General Headquarters

The gallery was once again filled with people. The court-martial had gained much interest as Harper's testimony was taken up by the press. Public sentiment was split with a majority concerned about the women and children killed, the other side proposing that the Indians got what they gave and it was time to eradicate them, no matter how the Army did it. The court house was jammed with a crowd that poured out of it and squeezed into the square around the entrances.

The court reconvened after preliminaries. O'Neil turned to the officer panel. "Have you reached verdict gentlemen?"

"Yes Mr. President, on all charges. " General Holt passed over a sheet of paper that O'Neil scanned quickly.

"Sergeant Kavanaugh, please stand." He paused as Kavanaugh reached his feet. "This court martial finds on the charge of disobeying a direct order, not guilty; on the charge of desertion, not guilty; and on the charge of assault to a senior officer, guilty as charged." The court burst into dozens of conversations, the talk drowning out the bench. O'Neil struck the gavel a dozen times before the clamor toned down.

"Order, order, order in the court, O'Neil shouted." The courtroom resolved to near silence. He folded the paper and set it down gently before him. "Sergeant Padric Francis Kavanaugh, you are hereby sentenced to twenty years confinement at the federal facility in Leavenworth, Kansas. You will be taken from this court and placed on the first available train to that destination. This court is adjourned." He banged the gavel down sharply.

Kavanaugh sat down heavily. "Twenty years, twenty years I'd rather be dead."

Sutter put his hand on Kavanaugh's shoulder. Sorry, Pat, at least you're alive. It's about the best we could expect, though I hoped that O'Neil would relent a bit. Don't go into great despair, the press is just beginning to chew on the atrocity. We can go for a petition of clemency. Remember where there is life there is hope, one is a long time dead and it is finality. If only Tyne had died before giving testimony or lived longer to have his own trial."

"I know you did the best you could, but twenty years is a very long time."

The provost guards led Kavanaugh away and Sutter walked beside Durcher. "How do you feel now, Mr. Harvard?" He was smiling like a Cheshire cat.

"Durcher, you got a conviction on one charge, public spectacle and all. You had better stay out of O'Neil's courtroom for a while."

"I am sure Private Kavanaugh will recall you fondly as he frets out his twenty years."

"I still think you might venture into the carnival business. Did anyone ever tell you that you were too cocky for your own good?"

"Harvard snip. You did your best and lost. They will be calling you Mr. Atrocity."

"Sticks and stones, I'll probably be seeing you again. What tops a spectacle, an extravaganza?"

They separated as they passed through the doors.

Chapter 15

Prison Train
April 1869

"Get on the train you Mick son-of-a-bitch or I'll stick my foot up your ass and finish the job. I lost a stripe because of you, you son of a bitch. I ought to kill you myself except it would be too easy."

The boarding stairs were steep and Kavy had to bring both feet to a halt before stepping up the next. He managed to get to the top step and was about to achieve the car landing.

"Get used to those shackles, Kavanaugh; you will see a lot of them at Leavenworth. I've got a couple of pals on guard duty there. I'll have them chain you to the wall for your whole damn life." Brock struck him on the back and Kavanaugh pitched head long into the car, striking his forehead on the door jam.

"Jesus, Sergeant Brock, don't you think you ought to hold back a bit? No sense shoving him around. We got to get him on this train."

"Hold back? He's on the train, ain't he? This Mick bastard cost me a stripe and I did hold back. I didn't kick in his head." He chuckled.

The two corporals lifted Kavanaugh to his feet, one moving ahead to force the coach door open. A trickle of blood seeped down Kavanaugh's cheek. They settled with a clump and clatter into the last seats on the coach.

"Wipe that blood off his face 'fore someone sees it. Hey Kavanaugh, you ain't said much. Are you thinkin' about a lifetime in the lock up?"

"I don't have much to say, Brock. You seem to be doing all the talking. I'll say a few words. You are a lying, no account, shoneen son-of-a-bitch and if I wasn't chained up I'd twist your head around backwards."

The resounding smack caused some passengers to look toward the prison squad. Brock prepared to strike him again but thought better of it because of the stares.

"You're a lucky son-of-a-bitch, Kavanaugh. They should have shot ya or hanged ya. I was hopin' for a hanging."

"Too bad, Brock, so long as I'm alive, you'll have something to worry about." Brock lashed out again, splattering the window with blood.

"Sergeant Brock, I think you better lay off somebody may report us."

"You don't have to think Corporal - either of you."

Kavanaugh noticed the first man passing by in the coach because of his size, six feet four if he was an inch; he also noticed with a start that he was Chinese. At about the time he spotted him, a second larger Chinaman sit down across from them and a third entered and positioned himself near the center of the coach. The whistle sounded a great hiss of steam swept the train cars and a faint "All aboard', drifted behind it. The squeaks, huffs, and squeals began and the train lurched ahead. After a small maze of switches, the scene from the window was a continuous run of wooden boxcars.

The Corporal closest to the window was already surrendering to a snooze encouraged by the regular rhythm of the cars slipping over the rail joints. On his other side the Corporal was staring down the isle and Brock was watching the stretch of yard as the train gained momentum north. Across the aisle, the large Chinaman, sitting by himself, appeared impassive to everything. As Pat looked down the aisle, he saw a bottle being passed among the ten soldiers. Vaguely he wished for a taste, then settled back to watch the boxcars flash by.

They made a few stops before passing over into Pennsylvania and the rolling hills were giving way to the snow-streaked farms. Kavanaugh relaxed into his seat as he watched Brock stoke up a cigar. The Corporal by the window was asleep and the other almost so. They both jerked semi-conscious as the conductor moved through the car, ushered in by a gust of cold air.

"York, next stop is York." There was a hiss of wind as he opened the car door and a metallic thunk as it closed. The train creaked and steamed to a halt and Brock rose, kicking the other two awake.

"I'm gettin' off; we'll be here for a bit. While I'm gone you watch this son-of-a-bitch!" He again kicked at the drowsy Corporal. "No nodding' off, that's orders." He rose, broke wind, and disappeared through the door.

"Well, Kavanaugh, Brock sure doesn't like you."

"The feeling's mutual, Corporal."

"What is it between you two?"

"Too long a story, it goes back a couple years. We both made Master Sergeant about the same time. I made it two days before he did. We ended up in the same troop, I was considered senior, he didn't like that and things got touchy. We had a couple of fights."

"Who won?"

"I don't think I lost." He stretched against his chains. "Mind if I stand up?"

"No, but you just mind us as well."

"They didn't feed me this morning."

"There may be somebody by, on a stop like this; usually somebody comes on board sellin' stuff."

"I'd like a piece of bread, maybe a piece of cheese but I don't have any money."

"I'll get you something." The Corporal sat back on the seat.

Many of the people had left the car; the three Chinese sat unmoving as though absorbed in themselves. A small boy with a large basket came into the car. The basket was piled with rolls and sandwich loaves, and appeared too heavy for such a small boy. The Corporal bought Kavanaugh a dark loaf. Pat tore it into small pieces, having difficulty with the cuffs, then bent forward and stuffed some into his mouth. The 'all aboard' sounded again, just as Brock bounded breathlessly into the car. He slipped into a nearby seat across from the three of them.

"Who gave him food?" he snarled. There was no answer forthcoming. "Did you hear me? Who gave him food?"

"I did Sergeant."

"I ought to put you on report, he doesn't have to eat!"

"Yeah, you do that, Brock," Pat muffled through the bread, "show everybody how powerful you are, what a bunghole you are."

The train was picking up steam leaving the York station yard and heading into the flat country beyond. As they passed over a crossing, muddied by melting snow, Kavanaugh thought he saw a man, his arm upraised, but he passed by so quickly Pat dismissed it. A moment later as the train was beginning to build speed; the huge Chinaman at the middle of the car stood and pulled the emergency stop lever. There was a great lurch and a couple of people spilled into the isle.

Suddenly the man across from them crashed his hand into Brock's face nearly lifting him above the window. Two more sharp blows and both Corporals were sprawling. Down the isle it appeared blue coats were flying everywhere. A woman was screaming hysterically and her companion rose from his seat with a pistol and was struck under the chin, his hat flew back three seats, as he flipped over it with the impact. One soldier drew a pistol in the melee; it arched into the air with him following shortly. Suddenly it was quiet except for the woman sobbing and a few groans.

The nearest Chinamen pitched the three guards into adjacent seats and drew a hatchet from beneath his coat, raised it, and brought it down with tremendous force on the chain that locked Kavanaugh's legs. Pat flinched and braced as the hatchet again descended, this time breaking the lock's hasp. The big man grabbed the chain twisted it until the link separated and Pat's legs were free. The Chinaman then grasped the chain to his wrists.

He raised the hatchet again and Kavanaugh flinched and gasped, "keys, keys," he gestured with his head, "Brock has the keys!"

The man rifled through Brock's coat and ripped the key ring from his belt. He quickly found the shackle keys, snapped them open, and dropped them to the floor. Kavanaugh rubbed his wrists and looked about; the car was in a shambles as though a great explosion had wracked it. There was a faint sound of voices approaching from the outside. Brock seemed to be coming out of his stupor. The big Chinaman hit his throat a shuddering blow. Brock's eyes glazed and he dropped in a gurgle of blood.

The towering Chinaman pointed to the carriage exit. "Get off the train."

Kavanaugh rushed down the aisle. The train had come to a stop just past the crossing of a rural road. He moved through the doorway and saw no one for the length of the train except one of the Chinamen, but there were many voices on the other side and the sound of a fight. There was a covered carriage parked not far down the lane and he began a dogged run toward it. As he approached, the door opened. Mary Cleary was smiling at him.

"Get in Kavanaugh. We have to get the hell out of here."

"What the hell is going on?"

"You're going home;" she quickly appraised him. I brought your buckskins. Get rid of those prison clothes, you don't look good in stripes." Kavanaugh slipped off the shirt and tossed it into the back of the carriage. He had difficulty getting the buckskin trousers on- both his ankles were swollen from the chains.

"They will follow. Do you have any idea of what happened on that train? I think that big Chinaman just killed Brock."

"I would say that it is a small loss, and so what if they do follow?"

"I don't want to get you into any trouble."

"What is it you say 'story of my life'? Look what I have here, an honorable discharge, signed by General Getting himself. You can hang it on your wall. You are not the Kavanaugh who escaped, and if anyone should ask, these papers will prove it."

"How, Mary, how did you get them? Never mind I really don't want to know." With a gesture, he dismissed any reply. "Where are we headed?"

"I bought the Sullivan land sections, and that's where we are going."

"Those sections north of Minsi? That is a long way away."

"Yes, I bought all three of them." She chucked the horses. "We have to make a stop; there is someone who wants to see you." The horse moved briskly. "I am building a mansion

129

right in the middle of it and set it up for ladies of the evening to recover, bring their babies, and help women who are pregnant and no place to go. I have a small house almost done and I plan to build another larger one. There will be lots of work. You're welcome to help, and I think you had better take my offer this time. I'll pay you well."

Kavy looked at the discharge papers. "You've already paid me." As they moved along they heard the tooting of the train's engine.

"That's true," she slapped the reins. "Lincoln, let's get going' - north!"

The Pennsylvania town of Reading was very quiet when they pulled into the livery stables.

"Why are we stopping here?"

"We need to get over to the Washington Arms. Someone there wants to see you."

"Who would that be?"

"It's a surprise. You like surprises don't you?"

"It depends upon the kind of surprise it is."

"You will like this one."

The lobby of the hotel was paneled in quarter-sawed oak giving it a rich and warm feeling. The fire place crackled with fir and maple and was flanked on three sides with dark leather sofas and chairs. Mary glanced quickly about, located the registration desk and walked smartly toward it.

"Sit down, Pat, I'll be right back. You want a drink?"

"Yes, of course, I've been deprived of late." He smiled. "Only sip I had was that jar a friend brought to me when I was behind bars."

"That jar of Bushmills was very expensive, Kavanaugh. The cost of the whiskey wasn't much, but bribing the guards cost me fifty silver ones!"

"Ah Mary, you know how much I appreciate that."

"Good, because I'm going to let you drive a while, as soon as I change horses. I want to be in New York and plan to stop only to eat or sleep. Ahead there are horses arranged for us."

"How far is the border?"

"It's about 70 miles to the border, two days and two nights if the roads are good. There's some snow to contend with. Once we get there and into Sullivan County nobody will bother us there. They know me well; I have half the county employed and three quarters of the rest owe me money."

"Know you well?" he laughed.

"Not by reputation, they think of me as a very rich widow; eccentric, but wealthy, and wealthy is what makes the difference."

"Seems like it wouldn't hurt, but I personally don't know."

"Most of Minsi works for me and half of Forest Port. I own the two banks and they call me Missus Cleary - with respect! You will be just another employee."

"Is that respect important?"

"Always has been, Pat. It wasn't always true, but I like it now. With money comes power and respect – in that order. You sit here and warm up; I'm going to order us a drink from the bar."

Pat watched her talk to the desk clerk then she disappeared into the bar. He rubbed his wrists and ankles, the blue indentations were still there. A waiter appeared and there was a flurry about the table before the sofa, he watched as it was laid out and a great flood of emotion struck him. There was a bottle of Bushmills, two glasses, and a teapot with one cup.

"I'll be damned, Woo is here." As he thought the words, Woo and Mary appeared from near the front desk both smiling and chattering together. Kavanaugh could not wait and rose to walk toward them, making a small bow that was returned, opened his arms, and crushed Woo to him.

"Woo! I figured you had something to do with the train when I saw those three huge Chinamen. Who were those guys? How did this all come about? How did you know where I was?"

"One question at a time my friend." He smiled and glided onto a sofa.

"We kept in touch during the trial; one of his friends is a reporter for the Chinese news and was able to get into the courtroom. Didn't you see him?"

"I saw a Chinaman who looked important, so I thought probably Woo was aware of what was going on."

"When we found out that you were going to Leavenworth instead of the gallows, Woo and I figured out a plan."

"There were many details it was necessary to know; the train schedule, where you would be confined, the time when you would leave Washington." Woo enjoined.

"So, I made some contacts and got word to Woo about the schedule."

"Once we knew when you were leaving, we selected a spot to interrupt your ride."

"I tell you Woo, it was not going to be as enjoyable a train ride as the one we shared."

Woo looked at him curiously, "What was so enjoyable about that ride?" He laughed, "Oh you mean the destination." He paused, "I would give you some money, but Mary said you will not need any."

"It is true, Woo, I will not need money, for with friends like you, I am rich indeed."

They all sat quietly watching the popping fire. An ember burst sending a bright red spark skittering over the hearthstones. The three sat silently sipping tea and whisky.

"Thank you. Thank you both, I thought I was a goner this time." Kavanaugh shook his head and smiled.

"We are not home yet, that man at the desk told me a fresh horse would be ready. This one is named Jefferson. He is motioning now."

Pat looked at Woo and smiled. "Speaking of money, I have something of yours. Mary gave it to me on the way here." He slipped the medicine bag from his neck and dug out the shilling.

Woo took it, looked at it and folded it away in his robe. "This is a very lucky coin for the both of us."

"We had best get moving, they will be looking for us soon." Mary stood up and shook Woo's hand. "It has been a pleasure, Woo. If you get up toward Minsi or Forestport, I'd be proud to have you stay with us."

"And for me, it has also been a pleasure. One never knows I may stop by. We are looking for places to site our silk mills."

Kavanaugh bowed to Woo. "Good bye my friend I know we will meet again."

"One never knows about these things, the world is not as big as once it was."

"Woo, you're welcome anytime. If I can ever be of help you, let me know."

"Goodbye, Miss Mary. Look after her; Pat and Mary you best look after him"

"If I can, Woo he is not a man inclined to listen." Mary and Kavanaugh walked out into the sun splashed snow and climbed into the carriage. Mary wrapped the robe around her; Pat picked up the reins and they started off north-east.

"Well Kavanaugh, it will be spring in a week or so, and that's when I think the New Year starts; a new spring, a new life, and a new hope."

"I hope so too." He chucked the horse and they lurched ahead.

Woo watched them from the hotel window and turned to the man who had joined them. He nodded and they hastened to bring up his carriage.

Chapter 16

Minsi, NY
Spring 1869

The road to the Sullivan County sections twisted through old growth oak and towering white pines and over a hemlock darkened brook. A few oaks had maintained fall leaves that rattled a greeting and willows along lowland rills extended fuzzy flowers.

Ahead of them a large flat wagon emerged from a curve reaching from the top of the hill. Two great Belgian horses were moving it easily it drew closer and stopped.

"Lo, Mary, I am glad to see you back."

"Sam". She nodded towards him with a smile "How you boys doin' on the little house?"

"The guy with the carpets came yesterday and they rolled them out. They trimmed out the kitchen and finished it yesterday, too. Your cook, Evelyn gave us lots of supervision with the kitchen. It's about done except a couple of inside doors; I'm going get them now."

"Has Karst finished the plumbing to the horse barn?"

"No, but they moved in a lot of furniture last week. The house plumbing is all done, but we ran out of pipe for the barn. I'm getting some of that too. All the lamps are up, it looks real nice."

"What's goin' on up the hill?"

"Oh, the clearing's done for the private residence and you're going to get a lot of lumber from clearing. Some of those white pines were big. I mean big, the saw mill is up and running."

"The big house is coming along then?"

"The hotel, you mean?" a crooked smile emphasized it.

Mary laughed. "It's coming along then?"

"It took a lot of stone we had three crews of masons, so it's all framed and roofed. Slater's left yesterday. It's a solid house Mary solid."

"Good." She passed her hand across her brow and stared ahead.

"You can't hear much from where we are now, but when you get 'round the bend there's so much hammerin' and sawin' it sounds like Pickett's charge."

Kavanaugh straightened in his seat as the memory of that charge flashed through his mind. Mary hurried to introduce him.

"Sam this is my friend Pat Kavanaugh, I've known him for a long time."

"Pleased to meet you any friend of Mary is a friend of mine."

"Same here," Kavanaugh acknowledged.

"Sam is my builder. He sees that things are planned and the work gets done. You'll be seeing a lot of him." She glanced at the man in the other wagon. "I want you to put Pat to work."

"There's a lot to do, finding work will not be a problem."

"Sam, you listen to him, alright? He will be telling you what I want when I'm not."

Sam laughed aloud. "Hell Mary, when will that be?"

Mary chuckled, "I'll be going back to Washington from time to time, so listen to him then."

The faint sounds of carpentry carried up the road.

"There is one thing, Mary. You know that Italian guy who came to quarry the stone and build the fireplaces?"

"You mean Guessipe?"

"He can't speak English, he just waves and hollers drove the masons crazy about layout. Gives everybody hell and I don't even know what he's shoutin' about. I don't speak Italian. Do you Kavanaugh?"

"No I don't."

"That ain't gonna be much help 'cause he only knows a little English and mostly curse words."

They all laughed.

"Where is he now?"

"Up quarrying more stone; he wanted more dynamite, but I didn't know whether I wanted him to have any more, you know - he's crazy, I think. Every time I turn around he's setting a blast somewhere."

"I can help there, Mary. I've set a lot of stone and sure as hell built a lot of walls. I don't know much about dealing with crazy people, though." They all laughed again.

"Sam, when you get back, take Pat up where ever he is quarrying."

"I guess he found some good limestone back in a way, still on your property. He looked for about a week and blew holes all over the place."

"What do you mean holes?"

"Some pretty good sized ones, Mary. I had to chase him away from too near the house. One bang was too close. I worried he would break windows."

Mary giggled, "well, I've got just the match for Guessipe."

"I hope so," he raised the reins and was about to start ahead. I almost forgot, that architect from the city was here just after you left; he said he had the final drawings of your residence and said he would have them in two weeks. He sure seems to know what he is doing. See ya, Mary." He urged the two great, gray horses ahead.

As Mary and Kavy rounded the curve the banging sound and the talk of the workers carried to them. Kavy looked up the hill toward the workmen and for the first time caught site of the huge scar cleared on the hill and the huge structure under construction.

"Jesus, Mary and Joseph!" He gasped. "That's no house it's a castle."

"Kind of big isn't it? I like it though, the bigger the better. I don't plan to live there."

Kavy cocked his eyebrow, "and how are you paying for all this?"

Mary popped his shoulder. "Pat don't you worry it is all paid for with cash. Know what a million dollars is?"

"No, can't say I do."

"Well, I didn't either I have one already or I haven't even sold all my D.C. property. I'm making more every day. I bought a lot of real estate when it was cheap. That 'Cloister' as I call it, will be my way of paying some of it back."

The banging and talk was apparent as a breeze blew down hill. A song sparrow burst into it's repertoire as they both watched the workers.

"Pat, I'd like for you to stay on until the house is complete - I'll pay you."

"I already owe you my life. I don't need any pay, just a place to stay."

"And you saved mine. I remember the day you told me of Moran's last words. I was hoping I could thank you someday." Her eyes filled with tears. She took a handkerchief from her sleeve and wiped at her nose. "The little house is already done. There's somebody there who will be glad to see you."

"Where's the little house?"

"There, over the hill," she pointed ahead. "I'll want you to stay there with me. Oh, don't be raisin' your eyebrows; there are three bedrooms and Evelyn's quarters."

"Maybe it would be best if I stayed with the men. Is that their tents, there"? He motioned in the direction of some canvas shelters.

"Maybe it would be best, but you're staying' with me anyway. You can go drink and carouse with them if you will, but I want a good man in the house."

"I don't know," he mused.

"Well, you can sleep on the porch then."

"Don't be angry with me."

"I'm not good enough yet Pat that you won't stay in my home? I save your dumb Irish ass and you still can't stay in the same house with me?"

"Ah, Mary cool down. I didn't mean anything by it."

"God damn it Kavanaugh, you stayed in my house before."

"Yes, well it was different. Everyone knew…"

"I belonged to Moran?"

"Well, yes."

"Well, bull shit, you thick headed Mick! Moran never thought I belonged to him, and neither did I," she slapped the reins and the horse jerked ahead. "So sleep on the porch!"

They continued on in silence. Mary reined the horse up beside the kitchen entrance. She stretched and looked eastward.

"God, I love the smell of these hills. It's a good omen Pat." She walked on to the porch and passed inside the door.

"That's true." Pat said behind her and entered the kitchen, empty of people, but with a long table piled with food and mouth-watering aromas from a large soup pot. Mary moved through the interior door.

Evelyn came into the kitchen as Mary passed. "Miz Mary," she smiled then she spotted Pat. "Well, look who's here!" She waddled up to Kavanaugh with a big hug. "My lawd, Mr. K you is a sight for sore eyes. We thought them goin' to shoot you." She smiled her eyes bright with tears. "I've made some biscuits Mr. K. I'se glad to see ya; it's gonna be like old times." She laughed and wiped at her eyes. "Yes, suh, it like the good old times. I missed ya. You was one that liked what I cooked."

Kavanaugh gave her hug. "That's true." He smiled and looked around the kitchen. "But what I liked most was you."

"Ah Mr. K you as sweet as ever." She gave him a big kiss. "It's so bad you ain't all here." She wiped her hands on her striped apron her kind face softened, "but," she said indulging in confidence, "best not to talk about Mr. Moran. Miz Mary has gone inside herself again. She done loved him and ain't over him yet. I ain't so sure about this place. I saw a bear!" She rolled her eyes. She moved to the large black stove and stirred the soup with a long wooden spoon. "She grieved some more when she first comes here but she better now." She laughed. "My, my and that little Sara, that little Sara is the dickens herself. She is Miz Mary's pride and joy. I know it could have been worst. She shore not afraid of lovin', Miz Mary ain't, just shines on out. That lil' girl gets it." Evelyn glanced from the corner of her eye. "My, my, Mr. K you are lookin' lean and hard. Miz Mary don't mind the men around and she knows 'em all and talks and talks. She wears pants out there! I had to sew 'em special. I'se glad you here. She paused and looked up the hill. "But them men they too familiar. Why you wouldn't believe the way she talks to them." "Yes, I would," smiled Kavanaugh," she always talked up her customers."

"Yeah, sure she did, but we up here in de woods. My, my, I am glad you here Mr. K. they gonna look at you and think twice. I'se glad you are here."
Kavanaugh looked thoughtfully up the hill to the flurry of activity there.

"They comin' to dinner soon, you want some early soup? Get some ham with your beans?"

He nodded and sat down. Evelyn dipped up a large bowl of soup opened the oven and withdrew a tray of biscuits. Pat's eyes brightened.

"I knowed you was comin' since yesterday. They brought a note clean from Forestport said you on the way. Bin cookin' and cleanin' to git ready."
"Mmm buttermilk biscuits and you make the best." He sighed and reached for the butter.

Guessipe was clucking about some stone Kavanaugh had cut. "Good cut, Kavanaugh. Look here. Look I show you something." He quickly chiseled a more precise edge, then stepped back and stared at the shaped piece, twisting at his black, curly beard. "We start big fire place today. What's matter for you? You say no word; Mary not home?"

"She came in late last night, after dark, she doesn't usually do that. Usually stays in Forestport." He continued to study the edge that Giuseppe had trimmed.

"Maybe you worry too much for her, she no come to you bed? What you mad for?" Guessipe beamed as bright white teeth gleamed against his dark face. "Smile, we build good here."

"You mean we pay attention to Mary's directions." Kavy replied laughing. He genuinely liked the stocky Italian, although a stickler for detail, he was an excellent craftsman, and a bit eccentric. He worked industriously, had eye for stone, and was not satisfied with just fit. He blended grain, texture, and color into the fireplaces. In the evenings Guessipe made intricate carvings of people's faces in walnut and cherry wood, and they bore a remarkable likeness to his subjects. "I suppose she will be up here before noon directing things." He aligned his chisel on the edge of a rock, struck it with the hammer.

"If no, you see her soon." Guessipe paused and looked into Kavanaugh's eyes. "Good you worry about Mary, keep you not lonely. Mary, she like you much, I know."

"I have to haul up some water." Guessipe nodded and Kavanaugh started toward the pump carrying two five-gallon pails.

Mary neither showed up on the job, nor for lunch or dinner. In the growing darkness of the porch Evelyn came bearing a candle. "Mr. K., Miz Mary wants to see you." She was quite somber, her face wreathed in concern.
"Is something wrong? What's wrong?" He looked for an acknowledgement.

She nodded. "It's Miz Hope. She is very, very sick. They go to bring her here. Miz Mary goin' back to Washington tomorrow."

"What's wrong with Hope?"

"The whorin' bizness, she awful sick."

"Does Mary want me to go with her to Washington?"

"I'se don't know but best you come now."

Mary was seated in the corner of the darkened parlor where several candles cast a soft light across her face. Even in the dim light he could see the dark circles beneath her eyes.

"Hello, Kavy."

"Did you get some bad news Mary?" He settled beside her.

"Bad news, yes the worst kind." The tears welled in her eyes. "Jesus, Kavanaugh, when's this going to end?"

"Ah, Mary, I don't know - when we die, I guess."

"All the people that I love are all going before me." She choked off a sob. "All of them."

Kavy sat quietly glancing first at Mary then out the window. "The house is coming along good; we will be finishing up in a couple of weeks. ."

"Kavy," Mary said quietly, "I don't want to hear about the house, I am too weary."

"Evelyn said you were going back to Washington?"

"Yes, tomorrow."

"Do you want me to go with you?"

She turned fully to face him. "I don't think so; it's not exactly a safe place for you." The tears began to run down her cheeks and she sniffed and wiped her nose with the back of her hand. "Oh, Kavy, I am so sorry about Hope." She buried her head his chest and began to sob.

"It's alright, Mary. It's all right."

"Nothin' right about it," she mumbled between her sobs, "nothin'!"

He held her until she stopped crying, and pulled a red handkerchief from his pocket.

"This probably won't smell too good, but it's all I have."

"Thank you Kavy." She blew her nose and returned the fabric.

"Sorry to be so damn childish. I haven't cried in a long time, but the last three days I can't stop."

"Will you bring Sara back?"

"Of course, she will be with her mother as long as we can keep her. I don't know how long that will be - she's already acting a little crazy. I'm about the only one she recognizes now. She shouted Sara out of her room the last time I visited; other times she asks for her. The poor child was confused and frightened." I'll bring them both back. I have some business to do in New York; afterward I'll finish in Washington."

"Are you sure you don't want me to go with you?"

"You stay here, see that things get done." She peered at him in mild frustration. "I don't want to take a chance on somebody recognizing you."

"I hadn't thought about that, I've felt so safe here."

Mary sighed and leaned back into her chair. "Evelyn is making up my room for Hope; it's the coolest with the best breeze. Help her if she needs to move stuff. Sara will go into what was supposed to be your room. That is, if sleeping on the porch still suits you."

"I'll drive you to the station."

"Alright, but don't spend the rest of the day in Owen Caulfield's gin mill," she smiled.

137

"I'll stop in to say hello is all."

"And half a bottle of Bushmills later, you will say goodbye." Mary brightened, "Kavy, I want you to find a horse for Sara."

"We have a few horses, Mary." He drolly replied.

"I want this to be her horse. She can learn to ride on that chestnut mare, the gentle one, but I want her to have her own horse. You ask around for a spring foal."

"How much do you want to pay?"

"I'll leave you five hundred dollars."

"Five hundred" He exclaimed. "What the hell do you want, a thoroughbred? Mary, I could buy three foals and a mare for that. I don't know if I can even find one."

"I want a colt from a gentle mare; keep what's left for your retirement. Don't argue with me about money. I want to leave tomorrow morning by six."

"Alright, Mary I'll be waiting." He caught her eyes for a moment and nodded in wonder. He turned and quickly strode away.

One week passed on to another and Pat talked to the local farmers until he located a foal he thought suitable and bought both it and the mare. He checked on building progress or helped with the stone work. He was glad to see the buggy bearing the women come up the hill. It arrived with mixed emotions. Mary was exhausted from the ordeal of travel and Hope was very ill, but little Sara was a ray of sunshine.

"Uncle Pat!" She yelled as she leaped from the buggy right into his waiting arms. "Aunt Mary said you would take me fishing!" She planted a kiss on his cheek. "When, when will you take me?"

"Hold on darlin'. You just got here. I'll take you fishing just as soon as we get everyone settled in." He swept her up onto his shoulders and walked beside the buggy toward the house. I'll take you Saturday.

They pushed through the tall grass between the trees to where the clear Navis River flowed brightly before them.

"Uncle Pat?"

"Yes, what is it darlin'?"

"Tell me again what we are going to do with this thing." She held up the square wire mesh rack by its handle.

"That's a clipper net, Sara, and we are going to catch some bait - hellgrammites."

"Hell-gram-mites what are they?"

"They look sort of like a big ant and live under the stones out there," he gestured toward the rippling water. "We're going to sneak up on them, I'll lift the rock and you put that screen under it."

"They look like big ants?"

138

"You will see, they are fearsome looking things." He smiled beneath his heavy red eyebrows. "They can pinch, so you let me catch them off the net."

"I think that I'd like to do that, so long as I am holding the net."

Kavanaugh laughed out loud. "Alright, but I'll show you how to pick them up."

They sat side by side, unlaced their shoes and rolled up their trousers and eased into the river. "I like trousers, Uncle Pat; I don't get all scratched up, wow this water is cold!"

"This water is definitely cold," Kavanaugh echoed. "Put the net in behind that flat rock." He lifted the stone and water rolled beneath it. "Lift it up quick, oh, look there - two big, fat ones. Don't dip the net, they'll get off."

Kavanaugh deftly plucked up hellgrammites from behind their collars. "Pick them up like this. You see those pinchers? Hold them this way so they can't pinch." He placed the larva into a can on his belt. "Let's go on to another rock."

"This is kind of fun but I got my bum wet."

Kavy laughed "I'll bet its cold. Wait till you feel a fish on your line, then the fun really starts."

They picked a dozen of the larva and moved to the long deep green pool formed by the confluence of the Minsi and Navis.

Kavanaugh cut and trimmed two crotched sticks to set the poles. "Remember, now, strip the line from the reel and run it through the eyes. I'll tie on a hook and a weight."

They prepared the poles and set them in the sticks. "Watch now, darlin'." Kavanaugh stripped the line from the reel, and then tossed the weight toward the middle of the river. It hit with a plunk and the line went tight, then limp. "Throw Sara," he stepped back. "That's it, good throw! You are a fast learner."

"When will I know there is a fish biting?"

"Just watch your line or the tip of your pole, it will dance a little. Then pick up your pole, take up the slack up to the reel like I showed you, and jerk the rod up but not too hard."

They settled beside one another, Sara intensely watching her line. "When will the fish bite?"

"There are lots out there, but it will take a little time. There are bass, walleye, catfish, rock bass all out there looking for something to eat."

"You tell me if I don't see the fish biting."

"Yes, I will." The sound of the current washing through the rocks became apparent. "How do you like your horse darlin'?"

"Oh, she's wonderful." She snuggled up to Pat as a chilly breeze set the eddy to ripples. "When will the fish bite Uncle Pat?"

He reached into his pocket. "Before you can finish eating this peppermint stick."

"Thank you Uncle Pat." She jabbed the stick into her mouth and again snuggled up to him. He placed his arm around her and they sat quietly watching the river coil its way toward the sea.

"I have some candy, Uncle Pat. Would you like some?" She pulled some butterscotch drops from her pocket and offered the bunch all stuck together.

"Thank you." Some far off crows were calling in unison. Sarah traced a pattern in the sand with her feet.

"Uncle Pat?"

"What, Sara?"

"Is my momma going to die? She hardly wants to see me. Aunt Mary says she's getting better and sometimes I hear her calling out. Aunt Mary doesn't always tell me."

Kavy did not reply watching the slowly turning water.

"Is she Uncle Pat?"

"Nobody knows what God has in mind. She may be better tomorrow, maybe not."

"Is she Uncle Pat?"

"Well darlin', I think maybe God's going to call her home."

"That's what I think too." The sound of the riff raised in the quiet "Uncle Pat?"

"Yes, darlin'."

"If momma dies, will I go back to school in Washington?"

"I don't know."

"I want to stay here with you and Aunt Mary."

"I don't know. I'll talk to Mary. I'd hate to lose a fishing partner."

She leaned her head against his arm. "Uncle Pat?"

"Yes, Sara, you sure have a lot of questions."

"I want to see Doreen grow up. Her mother lets me brush her and I brush her mother too."

"That's good for horses. They know when you care about them."

"Uncle Pat?"

"Yes, darlin'."

"I love you."

"I love you too, Sara".

"And I love Aunt Mary too and momma." The sun winked up from the ripple. "Uncle Pat?"

"What, darlin'."

"Do you love Aunt Mary too?"

Kavanaugh did not reply but smiled and focused on the trees across the river.

"Uncle Pat your line is moving." Sara pointed to the rod tip.

"You're right, darlin', that's a fish."

Kavanaugh pushed through the screen door into the kitchen filled with the scent of biscuits baking. It was Saturday and the men did not start until eight. He could hear their early morning preparations, but none had come in for breakfast.

Evelyn, busy at the stove, looked over her shoulder as Pat sat down at the long empty table. She set a mug of steaming coffee beside the creamer and slid the plate of biscuits beside him.

"Oh Evelyn that coffee is going to taste good this morning." He glanced into her face the usual grin was wreathed in worry. "Is there somethin' wrong?"

A big tear slipped down her cheek. "I'se so worried."

"Worried?"

"It's Miz Mary. She ain't come out of that room for two days. She won't eat nothin', been drinkin' tea, tea and that's all. I asked her, I told her, I scolded her. And Mr. K., she won't eat nuthin'."

"Where is she now? He scratched his head. "I've been wondering where she's been."

"In that room with Miz Hope, she bin in dere for two days, sittin' in a chair with nuthin' but tea. She's got big loops 'beneath her eyes and she weak as a kitten. And nuthin' but tea."

"She was in there all day yesterday?"

"Since Thursday Mr. K., and nuthin' but tea. I worried. Worried! It ain't like her I afraid we gonna looz them both."

"Ah now don't cry, come on now," he put his arm around her and gave a brief hug.

"I'se worried Mr. K. I'se worried. I don't want loose dem both. And Miz Sara, she's been wonderin'."

"Where's Sara?"

"Right now she in the barn with her horse. She help me here." Evelyn chased a way a tear. "That poor girl."

Kavanaugh sat in silence for a moment then reached out put his arm around her waist again. "Now quit cryin'. Fix up a plate of biscuits and jam and some coffee or tea. I'll take it up to Mary and see what's goin' on."

He tapped lightly on the door and, hearing no response, quietly pushed it open. His senses were assaulted with the strong smell of purulence and urine in the darkness, and it took a moment for his eyes to adjust.

"Hello Kavy," her voice was weak and distant.

"Mary, I brought you something to eat. Tea, biscuits, and the best blackberry jam in New York."

"I'm not hungry, Kavy."

He ignored the remark and set down the tray on the table by the bed.

"How is she?" He asked quietly.

"Not good Kavy. Not good."

"You've been in here since Thursday?"

"What day is it?"

"It's Saturday," he scolded, "and you are going to eat. You gettin sick won't make Hope any better, or Sara, or Evelyn, or me. We're worried about you."

"I think she is dying."

"She has been dying."

"No Kavy, I mean I thought so since Thursday. She hasn't eaten and won't let me feed her either. The damn doctor put those restraints on, and he was supposed to be here yesterday. I've been giving her the laudanum. She will take that, but I feel so bad, I got her into this."

Kavy regarded the young woman on the bed, her sunken cheeks and paleness stark against the faded light.

"She doesn't seem to know me anymore. She has sores all over her back and her privates are just a mass of jelly. On her behind there are two big ulcers.

I need to turn her. That goddamn doctor was supposed to be here yesterday. I have trouble doing it myself."

"Why didn't you call me, I would have helped

Hope stirred awake and focused her eyes. "Is that you Mary?"

"Yes I'm here." She said encouragingly.

She looked to Pat, "Are you a new doctor?"

141

"No, it's Kavanaugh. Do you remember him?"

"Yes, kind of, He was Billy's friend." She rose weakly against her restraints. "Mary, I don't want to be tied down."

"It's alright, Hope. We will let you up. Do you think you can you sit up? How do you feel today?"

Mary busily began to untie her. "Help me Kavanaugh. Undo her ankles." She leaned forward toward Hope. "Do you want something to eat? I have some biscuits and tea here."
"No Mary, I am cold, very cold. Where is my little girl? Is she alright?"

"She's fine Hope. She's down in the barn and has been helping Evelyn in the kitchen." Pat reassured.
"I'd like to see her."

"I'll bring her in as soon as she comes in. She's tired out today I think. I saw her riding yesterday, just around the barn." Mary smiled. "She's doing well."

"She's little to be ridin' ain't she?"

"Matthew is with her, watches her like a hawk."

"Do you want to sit up and eat?" Mary asked.

"No, but I'd like to look out the window."

She struggled to roll toward the sun peeping beneath the shade. Mary tried to help, but Kavanaugh rolled her easily into position and let up the shade. The smell of necrosis nearly gagged him. He held his breath and swallowed back hard.

"Kavy, do you remember Billy?"
Of course, I remember him well."

"I have been talking with him. He said he is waiting for me to come soon. He loves Sara."
"Of course he does." He adjusted the pillow.

"Kavy he says heaven is a wonderful place." She remained unmoving peering out the window.

"Yes, of course."

"Will you pray for me Kavanaugh? Pray that I will see him."

"Certainly," his voice softened.

"I think your prayers would count. Mary? Mary are you here?"

"Yes, I am here."

"You take good care of Sara, huh?"

"Hope, you can take good care of her yourself. We have this beautiful home and I want you to help with the girls."

"Take good care of her. I gotta go, they're waitin." Her voice faded and she lay very still. Her shallow breathing barely raised her shoulders.
"Is she gone, Kavanaugh?"

"No Mary, but it sure ain't good. Now, you get out of here for awhile and have a cup of tea and a biscuit. You can't do anything and she is asleep. Come on now." Mary turned from the bed, took a step, and collapsed. Kavanaugh quickly caught her and lifted her in his arms.

"Mary Cleary," he said quietly, "whatever else you've done, you have a kind heart." He bore her lightly across the hall into the room.
As soon as Mary touched the bed she opened her eyes and struggled to sit up.
"Kavy, I can't have her there alone."

142

"Don't fret; I'll sit with her awhile." Gently he pushed her down to the pillow. "You are looking as poorly as I have ever seen you. You need some rest. And don't be frowning and turning away. You know it. I want you to eat one of those biscuits. You hear me?"

"But Kavy, she…"

"But nothing, Mary Cleary what happens if you get sick? Who will build the house? And who will look after Sara? What would happen to Evelyn? You eat something now and get some rest. I'm going to bring that tray in here." He slipped quietly across the hall, held his breath, grabbed the tray and was back in a flash.

"I don't want her to be alone."

"I'll sit with her while you rest. Be resolved Mary, there is nothing you can do."

As he reentered Hope's room, the strong, smell overwhelmed him. He raised the shades and opened two windows; the flood of fresh air and sunlight put a different perspective on the frail figure in the bed. She seemed to be resting quietly. Kavy sat across from her, took his rosary from the small leather pouch in his pocket, and began to slowly turn the beads.

A light breeze stirred through the room; he could hear the men at work up the hill. After an hour he was starting to feel a bit drowsy, when Hope whispered faintly.

"Billy." Kavanaugh moved to the edge of her bed. She struggled to focus on him squinting into the light.

"Mary?"

"No Hope, it's Pat."

"Ah Kavanaugh, I've been talking with Billy."

"Yes I know; do you want to sit up?"

"No, I'm so tired; I've gotta go." She closed her eyes." They are waitin for me".

Kavanaugh stood by the bed for a few moments then returned to his chair. Hope began a shallow irregular breathing, a few short breaths, then silence, then a deep breath and silence again. He could hear the men working, occasionally punctuated by laughter. Kavy quietly prayed and observed Hope. He dozed and was roused by the dinner bell. He looked toward the bed to see if the noise had awakened Hope, but she was dead. Kavy chased a curious fly from her eyes, closed them, and covered her face with the sheet.

When he reached Mary's room, she was already perched on the edge of the bed wide-awake.

"How is she Padric?"

"She's gone Mary."

"Gone? Why didn't you call me?" She angrily slid from the bed.

"And what would you have done Mary?" He put his arm around her and stifled her sobs against him. He held her for what seemed a long time and recalled his own tears on the Virginian road when he lost his friends. After a time, she looked up at him, wiped her eyes and stepped back as though reality had seized her.

"Pat, where shall we bury her?"

Taken back a bit by the change, Kavy took a deep breath and thought for a moment. "There is that beautiful fork in the river where I have been taking Sara fishing. There's some high ground there above the flood line and we can get a cart in."

She thought for a long moment. "I was thinking I wanted her closer, but Sara has told me much about your fishing trips. It would be a nice place for her to visit."

"Don't worry yourself Mary, I'll see to it."

"Thank you Pat, and thank you for your kindness."

"Ah, Mary it's more than that."

"Yes?" She pushed away and straightened her dress catching a glimpse of herself in the mirror. "I look a fright."

He did not reply and prepared to leave the bedroom.

"You'll see to the grave, Pat?"

"I will dig it myself; you can make her ready. If you'd like, I'll tell Sara. We talked about this once."

"Yes, thank you Pat I appreciate that I am not very good at these things."

He turned to leave and quietly closed the door behind him.

Summer 1869

The rounded mountains were showing tones of blue and gray as the sun set. A whippoorwill was calling in the distance, in clear sporadic tones. Kavanaugh, in his short sleeves, had just lit his pipe, and with his feet on the porch railing, pushed back bracing his chair on the wall behind him. The whippoorwill was close when he turned toward the sound of the porch door opening.

"Hello, Mary, going to catch some of this cool evening air?" He noted her simple gray dress and puffed his pipe, "that's a pretty dress."

"Pretty my ass, it's a long way from feathers, pins and sequins."

"Plain suits you well, Mary." He smiled. "Not that your other dresses don't."

"Quick thinking, Kavanaugh." She chuckled and settled into a chair beside him listening to the plaintive whistle of the whippoorwill. The bird ceased for a moment and a silence complimented the darkening woods toward the West. She sighed but did not speak.

"The mansion is almost done, Mary and they are really moving along with the residence – much faster than I thought they could."

"Yeah, there will be another furniture delivery tomorrow. You and a couple of men should be standing by for that. The draper is coming tomorrow too." She passed her hand over her brow. "It's quiet and kind of melancholy tonight."

He did not reply, nodded, and puffed his pipe.

"Do you ever think of him?"

Pat folded his pipe into his hand, puzzled by the question. "Do I ever think of whom?"

"Donal."

"Yes, I do, I pray for them all every night." He could see her eyes became shiny in the growing dark.

"It's been five years, Mary." He puffed at his pipe, staring at the darkening woods.

"Do you suppose God hears your prayers?"

"Yes, every one. I'm sure he does."

"I always have trouble thinking about God, some man with a long beard. He is supposed to love us all, yet he's always ready to be angry and get revenge because people don't please him or thank him or whatever. Why the hell is God a man?"

"No one knows what God looks like. He could look like anything. He's also spirit and embodied in his son."

"Well, Kavanaugh I just visualize him as an old bearded guy with a big hard on, chasing me down the streets of paradise."

Kavanaugh looked at her quizzically. "Mary you shouldn't talk like that," he gently admonished.

"I suppose not; given my past life I'll never get to heaven anyway, so why should I worry about what I say?"

Kavanaugh laughed quietly. "Only God knows who will join him in heaven. I would wager you will make it."

Mary sighed, drew a deep breath, exhaled, and turned to face Kavanaugh.

"You know what I believe, Pat. I don't think there isn't any such place as heaven and hell is on this earth; I don't believe in God either."

He wagged his head. "Well, Mary what can I say to that? God is too complicated for me to imagine, but faith helps."

"It helps you. Once back in Harrisburg I met some Quaker ladies. They were talking to me real nice like. Asked me if I wanted to change, you know. We were talking and this one said to me 'God is 'love,' not a 'he.' It is something we all have inside us and it keeps us together. What do you think?"

"Mary, I truly do not know."

"Have you ever been in love, Kavanaugh? I mean with a woman."

"Yes. I think so."

"I never would have guessed it," she replied in surprise, who was she? Was it that Indian woman or someone in Ireland?"

"Oh, Mary," he shook his head in negation.

"It's alright. You don't have to tell me, some secret, huh?"

"No, it's not like that. I can talk about it, and it was not in Ireland."

"Then it was here?"

Kavanaugh smiled. "Aren't you the curious one?"

"Alright, don't tell me," she sulked and looked into the darkened hills.

"It was the Indian woman when I was out West. She was one of the two I saved from the massacre I was only with her for a couple of months."

"A squaw, I don't believe it!"

"Well good, now you won't ask me anymore. And squaw is not a polite word."

It became quiet again. Far down in the forest the whippoorwill called faintly and was answered by another.

"Pat, I am curious."

"I'm sure you are, I swear Mary, and sometimes you're worse than Sara."

"I guess I can be a little girl if I want," she said defensively, then laughed, "I just can't imagine you with an Indian squaw or woman what ever the word. You are so religious and then to fall in love with a heathen. I surely am puzzled."

"Mary, let's talk about something else."

"Alright, that Quaker lady who said God was love. I kind of believe her because love changes us, changes us to the better. We become more kind, even more helpful to people. Hell, Kavanaugh, people can pray all their lives and they are not one whit kinder. They go to church and feel as though they have met some obligation to the old man with the beard." She paused, "Let me have a puff on your pipe."

He passed over the pipe and she puffed it a couple of times.

Kavanaugh smiled at her vehemence. "You are a very wise lady, Mary Cleary."

She passed back his pipe. "Tastes like you packed your pipe with horse turds! I'll get you some good English tobacco next time I'm in Washington," she brushed her hand over her eyebrows. "I never told anyone about what I thought before."

"You have interesting ideas."

"Do you think that it could be? I mean could God be love?"

"I don't know, Mary. It could be and even if it's not, it is a beautiful thought."

She reached over and stroked the red blond curls on his forearm. "My love for Donal changed me. I know I believe it. And I miss him still."

The two listened to the night sounds.

"You know, Mary it's been five years. You have made yourself a martyr to a memory. If love is so important, you ought to try again. There are many men who admire you."

"Yeah, my money or my body; I'm considered shrewd in business, but no one really respects my ideas on anything else. I think most men are afraid of me, they know the power I have around here."

Kavanaugh smiled and patted her hand still on his forearm.

"There's nothing wrong with your ideas, Mary. Maybe God is love and if so, you have had a full share. You know as much about it as I do."

The sounding whippoorwills were nearer to the house.

Kavanaugh spotted Guessipe busily digging around a large oak stump the carriage road bent around. "What are you up to Guessipe?"

"Mary tell me blow out big stump here."

"It's a big stump alright." Kavanaugh cocked his head peering at the diggings at various angles around and under. "Looks like you packed a lot of powder though."

"Not much. No worry. Powder old, I think wet, not much good."

"Two casks that is a lot isn't it? No dynamite?"

"No worry Pat, old powder. The dynamite it's good one stick only have no more BIG stump."

"I get paid to worry. This isn't going to be another blast for the mother lode?"

"Do na' worry, we got good rock with big blast, no?"

"You said you don't think the powder is high quality?"

"Do na' worry it's been wet." He finished packing the roots with the casks.

"You're not going to put more in there?"

"Why not, we wake 'em up at the big house!"

He finished packing the powder and carefully measured, cut and twisted the fuses.

"I don't know." Kavanaugh said dubiously. "That is a lot of powder."

"Come Pat. We get back." He pointed to a small sunken spot as he played out the long fuse.

"I don't know, I think that it is too much."

"Ah, no worry!" He continued back peddling from the target. "Here I think. We stay here." He made a final snip of the fuse. "Get down now." Taking a match from his pocket he fired it with his thumbnail and touched it to the fuse. Both of them watched as the blue smoke fizzled toward the hulking stump.

Kavanaugh covered his ears. The sound of the blast was deafening and Kavanaugh watched the stump raise slowly into the air. The shock wave slapped across his face forcing him to his hind end. The stump disintegrated on its way down and a great gray cloud billowed out so it was impossible to asses the damage.

"Jesus wept, Guessipe! I told you it was too much!"

He stopped his tirade as a rain of rocks and wood pieces poured down nearly covering them. In the distant trees, they could hear the debris rattling through the leaves and a heavy echo from the hills. Pat flinched as a large piece of wood fell a few feet from him. The cloud of smoke gathered and seeped toward the forest. In the distance he could hear the men shouting epithets above the echoes. The smoke curled deeper into the woods, rose quickly and disappeared into the wind.

"Jesus wept!" He ducked again as debris dropped across the field.

"Not as wet as I thought! Big, big bang eh?" Guessipe's teeth flashed behind his beard and dusty face. "I think they awake at the house, no?"

Kavanaugh looked toward where the stump had been; the bend in the road was no longer. Instead there was a large yawning hole, rapidly filling with water.

Kavanaugh began to beat the dirt from his clothes and looked back toward the house where the men still hurled curse words in their direction. As he observed, the porch door burst open.

"Oh, oh, here comes Mary! We're in for it now. She's barely touching the ground!"

Guessipe followed his gaze. "Ah she comes, she still in her underwear!" They watched her rapid approach. "I think I leave."

"Oh no you won't you're not going anywhere!" Kavy caught him by the sleeve. They watched her determined stride, her bathrobe blowing behind. She arrived, red faced and furious.

"Just what the hell was that?" She cinched her robe closed. "What the hell was that?"

The two did not respond both looked toward the hole that was rushing water.

"Look at the size of that hole! Look at the road! You, you, -YOU crazy bastards! It's not there anymore!"

"Ah, Mary we misjudged."

"Misjudged? Misjudged? Is that all you have to say? I asked you to blow the stump out, not dig me a god damn swimming hole!"

"My fault Ms. Mary, I thought the powder was a no good. I didn't think…."

"You didn't think? You didn't think? What the hell! McGentry fell off the porch roof, you broke two kitchen windows, and god damn it, Evelyn was just serving me breakfast and dumped it all over me. Look!" She opened the robe and gestured toward her night gown. Guessipe leered at her cleavage and grinned.

"Not that look, you crazy Italian," she jerked his cap over his eye brows. "It is a wonder you didn't knock the house off its foundation! You scared the shit out of us!"

Kavanaugh glanced at Mary, her gown splashed with coffee and egg stains. She cinched the robe closed again. He shifted uneasily. "I'm sorry, Mary."

"Well, fix it! Get workin' on it now and fix it! There's furniture comin' tomorrow and there is no ferry boat!" She turned and left in a huff. "You're like a couple of damn kids playin' with firecrackers." Her words trailed after her.

With feelings of relief, they watched her leave. Guessipe lifted his hat from over his eyes, wiped his brow and smiled at Pat.

"She's a fine figure of a woman." He turned and assessed the spreading hole. "That was quite a blast," his eyes twinkled.

"It was a blast, alright. How are we going to fix the road? Look at the size of that hole. Any ideas about how we can fix it?"

Guessipe did not reply and continued reviewing the scene.

"Maybe we can re-route the road," Pat suggested. "I helped build a couple bridges during the war. Maybe we build a bridge or stone-up the hole. We will need some help and those carpenters aren't going to like it much." He shook his head in dismay.

They looked at one another and both began to chuckle. They could not contain their laughter. Guessipe sat down doubled over in spasms.

"That sure was a blast, Guessipe." Kavanaugh said holding his side and wiping his eyes.

Mary had reached the porch and looked back. They tried to contain their laughter and ducked out of sight.

"Let's look busy." Kavanaugh gasped.

The two walked toward the new spring bubbling its way toward the woods.

"I want you to take us tomorrow."

"It's a working day."

"Kavanaugh you work for me, and I want to take Sara fishing. She's been after me for a couple weeks. I have to go to Washington on Friday."

"Washington?"

"Yes, I had a letter that someone wants to buy a piece of property I own in Arlington."

"I thought that it was all gone."

"Not all, I bought this house a few years back. I was going to retire there and have a house for girls. It's a nice house with about two acres; but I'm here now, and this is where I'm going to stay."

"What about Guessipe, --I mean tomorrow?"

"What about him?"

"I was supposed to help him tomorrow. He's building that outdoor fireplace and it's a lot of work."

"I don't care what you were supposed to do – you are going to take us fishing. Besides, if he is building a fireplace by himself, maybe it will keep him from blowing the place up."

"Ah Mary, he is usually pretty careful."

"I know how careful he is -we have Stump Lake to prove it."

"Well? Do you think I should stay then?"

"No, I want you to take Sara and me fishing. I'll have Evelyn pack us a picnic basket."

"Fishing is best in the morning, Mary."

"What time in the morning?"

"Early."

"Well eight o'clock is early enough!"

Morning came with a bit of a chill in the air and they could see their breath when they set on the ride to the river. While he guided the wagon toward the river Pat listened to the chatter of Mary and Sara wrapped to their noses in a big blanket. They stayed huddled together while he baited the hooks. They tossed their lines and ran to the wagon to again in the blanket again.

"Why don't you make us a fire over there, Pat?" Mary gestured toward the nearby tree.

"Yes Uncle Pat, a fire would be very nice."

"Some fishermen the pair of you are," He laughed and began gathering wood.

They watched him breaking branches over his knee and snuggled closer under the blanket.

"Aunt Mary?" Sara asked wistfully.

"Yes, dear," Mary replied in the same wistful tone.

"How long will you be gone?"

"I think about a week."

"Oh," she sounded sad.

"I'll bring you a present, how about a new dress or maybe a red sweater?"

"A red sweater would be nice." Sara paused. "Uncle Pat needs a sweater. He needs some new clothes, Aunt Mary."

Mary curiously looked at the figure bent over the pile of wood.

"Well I could bring him a sweater too. He sure won't buy it for him self."

"You know Aunt Mary, Uncle Pat needs someone to take care of him too."

"I suppose so-he's a good and a kind man."

"I know he likes you very much Aunt Mary."

"I like him too little darlin'." She glanced toward Kavanaugh, he had made a small flame and wisps of blue smoke were curling up into the morning air. "Come on Sara, it looks like he has the fire going. We're supposed to be fishing. Let's take this blanket with us over to the fire."

"Will you bring him a sweater Aunt Mary?"

Mary laughed and stroked her head. "I think he has someone to look after him, already". She laughed. "Yes darling, I'll bring Uncle Pat a sweater."

The fishing was brisk with all hands busy and soon a string of rock bass and wall-eyed pike were turning on their stringer. The blanket was spread by the fire, though there wasn't a need for it Pat still fed it wood. He watched Sarah tending the lines.

"She sure likes to fish," he chuckled.

"That she does, I brought along a little whiskey; want some?"

"I'll just take a sip, thank you." He smiled at her scoffing look.

"A sip, huh? She looked toward Sara gathering some weedy flowers. Mary looked into his clear blue eyes. "She loves her Uncle Pat too. You sure have done wonders for her since and even before Hope died." She glanced to the grave site just beyond the wagon.

"I like young ones; they are the hope of the world. Hopefully, they will make it a better one."

"She wants me to bring you a sweater from Washington."

"Does she? I never said anything about a sweater."

"I told her I was bringing her one. She wanted you to have a sweater too. She said you needed someone to take care of you."

Kavanaugh smiled, "That little dickens."

The fire crackled and popped as it worked through some pine knots. They watched its progress content to be together.

"Sometimes I think "She stopped.

"Sometimes you think what?"

She passed her hand along his arm. "Sometimes I think I should let go of it all. We don't need any more money, hell I do not want all that was made. I'd like to get back to; I don't know what – but something basic. I would be happy with just my stores in the city. I am making more now than ever but the price in grief is too much."

"Mary, Donal's been gone more than five years and now Hope, --- people you dearly loved. That's enough grief for a life time. Maybe you should slow down and gather some strength."

Her eyes welled up and she brushed lightly at her cheek. She smiled, "You know he used to call you Saint Patrick."

"Well I suspect, Mary, that was one of the milder things he called me." Kavanaugh looked toward Sara. "Donal liked children, tried to father the younger guys around; first Steenie, and then Billy. Ah, Mary, all that seems like a century ago. You know Mary, Donal would have wanted you to be happy and to get on with your life."

"Maybe, Pat, maybe."

"Well, I know so, no maybe about it and I knew him longer than you did." A couple of delighted shrieks came from the riverbank.

"She has another fish."

"Do you need to help her?"

"Not unless she asks."

There was another shriek.

"He got away," Pat laughed.

"Oh Uncle Pat," came the cry, "He got away!"

"How's the bait?"

"It's alright he didn't get my bait. I'm going to catch him again. He won't get away next time."

"Alright you do that." He shook his head, crouched toward the fire and added some wood, poking at the fire as Mary held out the flask to him.

"Don't mind if I do." Pat smiled and took a swig from the bottle. Mary pressed close to him and they watched the fire work through the new fuel.

"Pat, what do you really think of me?"

"What kind of question is that Mary?"

"My question, I want to know."

"Well, Mary, I owe you my life."

"That may or may not be true, but that's gratitude. What do you really think of me?"

"I don't quite understand what you want me to say."

"Not what I WANT you to say, what do YOU say?"

"Well, you are very kind and I admire that. You are perhaps the kindest person I have ever known. You love Sara, I respect you and I like you."

"Like me?"

"Ah Mary, you're puttin' me on the spot."

"More than just mild affection or the way you like Evelyn?"

He paused, "Yes, Mary, more than just mild affection or the way I care for Evelyn. I also know you're still livin' in the past."

"I know Pat. I also know that you are perhaps the kindest man I know."

"Well Mary, there are a lot of people who wouldn't say that."

"I think it's true, I don't care what other people say." She passed her hand up his arm and kneaded the muscle of his shoulder.

"Aunt Mary, Aunt Mary, you have a fish on your line!"

Kavanaugh helped her to her feet and they hustled to the dipping pole.

"Lift up, Mary, and set the hook."

As she did the water down stream exploded upward and a large fish shook and disappeared under the water.

"My God, Mary, that's a big one! Hold on, don't let him go. Keep the rod tip up. Don't let the line go slack."

"Damn it Kavanaugh, you reel him in. He's pullin' like hell."

"Oh no, you bring him in yourself."

For five minutes Mary wrestled with the big fish, accompanied by gleeful squeals and solid advice. "Hold the tip up Mary, let him fight." As the fish weakened, she guided it to the bank and Kavanaugh caught up the line.

"It's a big trout, a big brook trout. Look at him." He lifted him from the water.

"Oh Aunt Mary, he's a big one!"

Mary leaned forward and gazed at the speckled fish with the dark, worm-like markings on its back. "Why, he's beautiful," she gasped. "I didn't know they had so many colors: red spots a beautiful gray-blue."

"He must be four pounds Mary."

"We've been fishing here a long time and haven't caught one as pretty as this," Sara chimed.

"He will make a fine meal, Mary." Kavanaugh lifted the large fish and disengaged the hook.

"Put him back Pat."

"Are you serious Mary?"

"Yes, put him back."

"But..."

"Let him go, Pat."

"Don't you want to show Evelyn, Aunt Mary?"

"No honey, I just want to know something that beautiful is still out here."

She leaned forward and touched the trout's sleek side. "Put him back Pat."

The three of them knelt on the bank as Kavanaugh placed the fish in the water. For a long moment the fish wavered in the current just beyond his finger tips, then quickly darted away. The swirl in the water danced along the bank edges and it, too, disappeared.

"That was a fine fish, Mary. Biggest speckled trout I ever saw. Near twenty inches, that one, and you let him go." He laughed. "I don't know about you Mary."

"That's what life is all about, isn't it Pat, holding on and letting go?" Doc Wayland has told me that a dozen times. There were tears in her eyes. "At least it's alive."

She turned to Pat and he opened his arms. They held each other; he could feel her repressing a sob.

"Oh don't be sad, Aunt Mary. You might catch him again." Sara piped and spread her arms reaching to embrace both of them.

Mary lifted her head up toward his, offering her face. He kissed her clumsily at first then pressed on her lips. The three of them stood locked together.

Down stream, the big fish surfaced again, and then dove to the bottom of the current and the sun burst warm on the threesome along the riverbank.

September 1869

Music filled the house and drifted into the surrounding hills. It was an Italian group recruited by Guessipe and tarantellas mingled with local folk music. The wedding march had been solemn, so it was a spirited session that followed as all the instruments played up a joyful air. Mary was beaming and Kavanaugh flashed between smiles and embarrassment as local folks, Guessipe, the workmen and their families all mixed together milled about the southern barbeque pit. An ox was roasting a great many of the town's people had made their way to the "big event at the mansion." Mary's businesses were prospering and the local banks were benefiting from her bloated accounts. Her money was the grubstake for many homes in the town and some marginal farmers knew prosperity for the first time. Tuxedos, store bought suits, calico dresses and home spun all blended in a rainbow of celebrants.

Kavanaugh was swallowing his third whiskey when a movement down the road caught his eye. Mary was holding his arm and talking to some of the guests. The musicians struck up a lively tarantella. Guessipe approached the newly weds.
"Mary, would you dance with me? I'm the best dancer here - I promise." "Go ahead Mary," Kavanaugh said absently. There's someone coming up the road, I can't make out who it is, but he looks familiar".
"It's just another late arrival. Some of these folks have come more than twenty miles."
"Go ahead and dance, Mary. I'll see to whoever it is."

Mary was swept into the medley as Guessipe whirled her about the wide and crowded porch.

Kavanaugh walked toward the hitching rail at the front of the house. There was something vaguely familiar about the approaching rider leaned slightly backward in the saddle with the reins held in one hand up to his chest. He was an accomplished long distance rider. He recognized him just as he came into hailing distance. It was Decker. He rode up to the rail grinning like he had found a new watch.
"Lo, Kavanaugh," he said before dismounting.
"Need a poker stake Deck?" Kavy smiled.
"Nope, I came out here to look into a weddin'."
As he stepped from the horse, Kavy opened his arms and they held a long, tight hug.

"Jesus Kavy, let go of me you're breakin' my back."

They both laughed and stood back, Kavy with his hand on Decker's shoulder.

"You're a sight for sore eyes, Deck. How the hell are you? How did you know I was getting hitched? How did you know I was here? How did you find me?"

"I'm alive and with my hair. I rode into Minsi and there was hardly anyone there. I asked the barber and he said everyone was at the Kavanaugh wedding. I knew you were from here, so I came out to take a look see."

"Welcome, I can see that you still have your hair. Where you been?"

"Well, since the last I saw you, more than a few places; up in Sioux country, clear down to Texas, and over to California, even made it up to the Oregon territory."

"Scouting' for the Army?"

"Yeah, I'm done now. I thought I'd come home - that is find one. I always liked it around here. They paid me off over eight hundred dollars. It's a good down payment for a place."

"You put in a few miles for that."

"Hell yes. If it wasn't for the calluses on my ass, I wouldn't have one at all."

Kavanaugh laughed, "Come on into the house, I want you to meet my wife."

"I never, ever thought you'd get hitched."

"I didn't set out too. It just happened."

"Don't trouble me with it Kavanaugh.

I will get to lookin' for a good woman myself. What's her name?"

"Mary, Mary Cleary."

"I just never figured you for being' a marryin' man, maybe a priest, but not a husband."

"Well I am just about two hours old at it."

"Well I'll be, and there's no way out now! A little earlier and I might have prevented it." He chuckled.

"Come on into the house. There is a lot to eat and some people I want you to meet."

"Alright, but before you go in, I got somethin' for you. Might be you won't think its important now. I probably should not give it to you at all except I promised I would." He turned to his saddle bags, extracted a bottle of whiskey, and a piece of buckskin. He lifted the bottle. "This here's a worldly present, best sour mash I ever tasted."

"Thanks Deck." He took a swig and noticed the buckskin roll.

"Well, maybe before I give this to you, we ought to talk about it."

The two men started toward the din rising from the house and paused on the steps.

"What is there to talk about?"

"Well, I got this piece of hide from an Indian woman down at Fort Supply in Oklahoma territory. I was there a couple days and finally finished up my discharge. She knew me from somewhere - asked if I knew you." Decker spit some tobacco juice over the corner of the step. "Kav- an- naw, she called you."

Kavy's joy began to fade into concern, but he did not speak.

"I said I knew ya."

"Where did you say this was?"

"Oklahoma territory, Fort Supply; they packed a bunch of trouble raisin Cheyenne there."

"She said her name was…."

"Sada," Kavanaugh finished.

"Yeah, so you do know her?"

"Yes, she saved my life."

"Well maybe. She was one of them you saved at Agate Creek wasn't she? Maybe I shouldn't say anymore things being the way they are now." He stepped toward his horse.

"No Deck. Don't think of leaving. Sada was one of the women I helped at Agate Creek. I want to know about her, and you're not going anywhere until we talk some more."

Decker pushed his hat off his head, uncovering a tangled mess of gray hair. "I was in the brig there waitin' the discharge and when I got out, one of the guards said an Indian woman was lookin' for me. He pointed her out. At first I ignored her, and then she saw me and came toward the fence. She said 'you Decker'? 'Yes', I said 'who are you? I know I don't know ya because you're too pretty to forget'. She did not reply at first. She looked at me curious like. 'You Kav -an- naw's friend she said. You could have knocked me over with a feather. I hadn't really thought much about you after we last met. I had not heard anything; I figured somebody had your hair on their lodge pole or the bounty hunters got you."

"No Deck, but it's a long story, a really long one! What's that buckskin?"

"It's some bead work." He unrolled the hide. Embossed carefully with beads were the figures of two boys, one in dark beads the other in blue. "She told me to give you this if I ever saw you again, or to send it to you if. I promised her I would. I kept it mainly as a souvenir."

Kavanaugh studied the two figures. "What does it mean Deck?"

"Well Kavanaugh, I think you was a father before you was a husband. Those two figures are two twin boys."

The noise of the music filled the stairway as both men quietly contemplated the beaded cloth.

Kavanaugh breathed out a long sigh. "Did you see them?"

"Yeah, Kavanaugh, I did. One's got dark red hair, tan skin; the other looks a lot like all the other Indian babies I have seen. They are both plump, healthy boys."

Kavanaugh wiped his forehead as though brushing away a wisp of hair, and sighed.

"It's true then Kavanaugh?"

"Must be, if Sada sent this, it's true. Jesus wept, if I had known…"

"Come on, you look a little peaked. Let's go sit down over there and say hello to this bottle for a bit."

They settled down on a bench; Kavanaugh took a deep swallow and passed the bottle. Decker took two great gulps and cleared his throat, "good stuff, eh Kavy?"

"Yeah, good," he looked at the bottle as though it were some distant place.

"You have grown particular in your old age? Better than that stuff the boys used to make out of taters."

"Yes better than that." They listened to the music for a while and passed the bottle. "What happened to you after you found me and headed back?"

"Just scouting, I tell you I had some close calls!

"You know what Decker? I had your saddle for awhile."

"My saddle, how did you come by it?" He took a swig and looked curiously toward Pat.

"Yeah, and I also had a fine Sharps 45-90 that belonged to one of your mates who didn't make it."

"Oh, must have been from Green Spring Rocks, we got hit by a band of Cheyenne. They kilt my horse and I had to run fur it. That was one of those close ones. I applied for discharge right after that. I figured I was beginin' to lose my luck."

"I knew some of those Cheyenne; one was named Black Badger, a big medicine man - the other Big Bear and a real character named Running Bull."

"We got both of them later at the Cedar Butte fight. Running Bull is still out there. We gathered up all that bunch after that. Big Bear near got me at Green Springs. That's how I lost that saddle. That day they shot my horse and killed Boyle and McCray and damn near got me!"

"What happened?"

"Well, I got off her before she died, grabbed my rifle and ran. There was no place to hide. I spied a bunch of buffalo carcasses."

He took the bottle and pulled at it, then wiped his mouth.

"Hell, I crawled right inside one, drew in my legs. "Bout then I heard this buzz; there was a big old rattler inside that carcass with me. He slid outside right over my ankle. I heard those Cheyenne comin'. That big snake slid back in right up along side me. If I'd breathed hard, I could have felt him. Him and me just stayed that way until dark and he slipped out again, no farewell needed. Cheyenne must have saw that snake and figured there wasn't anything else inside."

They both were startled by the voice. "There you are. I wondered what happened to you." Mary was flushed from the vigorous dancing.

"Mary, this is my old friend Bill Decker. I knew him in the Army out west. He saved my life."

"Yes, you told me about him." Mary stepped forward her hand outstretched. "Well join the club, I saved Kavanaugh too." They shook hands. "Are you hungry? There's lots of food. Come on in."

"Thank you Mary, don't mind if I do."

"You want to stay over? There is no room in the house, but there's a room in the stable no one has claimed yet. This man's gonna dance with me."

"Ah Mary, I can't dance!"

"Well you're gonna try! Welcome, Decker. What's that you got there?" She gestured toward the beadwork, while tugging Kavanaugh toward the crowded dance floor.

"Alright Mary," Kavy broke in, "I'll try to dance. I'll see you later Deck. Keep that buckskin for me would ya?"

Kavanaugh rolled to his side his shoulder lifting the sheets from the woman beside him. The movement bared her breasts, nipples still erect from the intimacy they had just shared.

"Sorry Mary, I tried."

"Sorry for what?"

"I mean I went too soon."

"Ah Pat, don't be bothered by that. Why does it trouble you so? It was longer than last time and I didn't marry you for sex, I love you Pat."

"And I love you; I just want to be the best."

"Let's not go down that road. You are a kind, caring, loving, gentle man and I feel loved. What could be better than that?"

"Well, Donal."

"Donal is dead, Pat, as much as we both wish he wasn't, so let's not go down that road either." He lapsed into silence watching the sun wrestling with the dark, a small streak of silver spread across the hills and pink was flooding in behind it.

"Pat, Decker seems like an interesting man." She adjusted up on her elbow so she could see his face.

Kavanaugh sat up against the headboard and Mary slipped under his arm. "He was one of our scouts, the best one. He could write a library full about his adventures. We always got along. I'd stake him for poker now and then he always paid me back. We had a few drinks together."

"What were you and him talking about? You sure were busy at that bottle."

"The old days, you know the fort, Indians, and such."

"What about that piece of buckskin he brought you?"

Pat lapsed into silence and focused on the sun. Pink gave way to gold and a flight of ducks, still silhouettes, waved toward the pond and splashed down among the reeds.

"You saw that?"

"Yes, what does it mean?"

"It was from Sada," he spoke quietly. "She had twin boys."

Mary sat up in the bed, the sheets fell away from her breasts and a dark red line of pubic hair burst over the edge of the covering. "Jesus, Mary, and Joseph, happy day after the wedding to you too, why didn't you say something?"

"Don't be grumpy, Mary. I'd have told you if I knew."

She followed his gaze out the window as the bright light flooded the hills. "You damn near didn't tell me this time." She set a steely stare and took a deep breath. "Are you sure they are yours?"

"Pretty sure, one of the last things she said was she had my love inside her. I would have gone back if I'd known, and I would have told you why."

"I know you would have told me, Pat." She watched the sunrise and turned to him. "Mary, I should have gone back to get her, but all the trouble and now being here with you, I would have, except I am in love with you. We have such a good life together, Sara and this place and friends."

"Oh Pat, only you would worry so. Most men would just say it's been nice knowing you - happens all the time."

"What should I do? I thought she died when they killed her brother and destroyed their village." He drew her tightly to him and she kissed him on the chest. "I love you Mary."

"If you're sure they are yours and if you still care about this woman, there's not much of a choice now is there?"

"What do you mean?" He looked into her hazel eyes staring up at him and smiling.

"We will go and get them!" The sun pressed up over the string of hills, fulgent and green; the room flooded with sunshine.

Part II

**Beginning Again
1869-1882**

Chapter 17

Fort Supply, Oklahoma
Autumn 1869

Kavanaugh and Mary Cleary boarded the train from Minsi to New York City and switched to connections west. The New York Central carried them to Chicago and the Santa Fe bore them toward Oklahoma. Crossing the plains into Dakota country a herd of buffalo raced the train. Some men pushed up the windows and emptied rifles at the herd, but the distance and movement limited any great effect; still, several buffalo were wounded and the claps of rifle fire had passengers flinching. One man set up a firing station on the seat behind them and was blazing away at the buffalo. The expended cartridge cases were raining on Mary's seat.

Mary called to Pat above the din of the bounding train and the bangs of the inept marksmen. "What the hell are they thinking of? What the hell is the matter with them? If one of those bullet cases drops down my neck, I'm gonna kick that son of a bitch in the ass."

"I don't know, Mary. They have to kill something, I guess. Don't pay it much mind." He flinched as rifle fired, close to his ear." They're a cluster of fools but no sense in getting excited. Those buffalo will soon be out of sight".

From the next seat, an excited shout punctuated Mary's pout.

"I got one, I got one, I got one!"

"I got one," she mimicked; I've got one, too! Every one has an asshole," she gritted, but you are all asshole!" Her voice rang out above the din of the train.

"Mary, for God's sake, don't start something," Pat whispered.

Another shot ripped out from the seat behind them, as the buffalo veered away from the train , a tall man with a carefully clipped salt and pepper mustache peered over the seat frowning.

"What is it you said, Madame?"

Before Mary could speak, Kavy broke in. "We don't want any trouble. My wife didn't approve of you shooting the buffalo. You know, just leaving the meat for the vultures."

"You look like Easterners; you don't know what the hell you're talking about. If you kill the buffalo, you kill the Indians."

"Well, why don't you save your shots for them, or are you worried they will shoot back?"

"Mary, let it go." Pat said under 'I risked my life for a shoneen the likes of this bastard.'

The stranger straightened his back at Mary's insult and fastened his eyes on her. "Lady, I've been killin' em since I was thirteen."

"Indians or buffalo, I guess it doesn't matter to you, you think neither has the right to live!"

"And the Indians do not have any right to steal my horses and cattle or to kill the white settlers and miners, scaring the country half to death! The only good Indian is a dead one!"

"Oh, bullshit, why do only white men have a right to this place? Is it because only white men have the right to say?" She turned away and faced out the window. "You're just a thief stealing what they have all rights to. Go back to shooting buffalo you're just a horse's ass and I haven't got time for you!"

"What you have is a filthy mouth, lady, and if I were your husband I'd..."

"This has gone far enough. Please just leave and go back to your seat. And Mary, please..."

The man looked down on Pat in disgust. "If I was married to that bitch, I'd say..."

In one motion Pat rose and pushed the surprised man aside. "Say what?"

"Well, I was saying your wife has a filthy mouth and I would…"

Before he could finish the sentence, Kavanaugh's left fist flattened his nose and he fell into the seat across from them, scattering two women and a man who had been listening in on the exchange. The man caught the tall stranger and pushed him to his feet. Kavanaugh's second punch shattered the man's jaw. He glared down as the man collapsed and curled across the aisle. The blood was quickly pooling at Kavanaugh's feet, the unconscious man began to convulse.

Kavanaugh called above the sound of the racing train. "Anyone down there know this man? Better come get him."

Two men had heard the ruckus and were coming down the aisle; they tried to raise him to his feet but could not, so they unceremoniously dragged him toward their empty seats.

"Jesus wept, Mary." He wagged his head in negation. "Will you ever learn not to be so damned irritating? Everything that crosses your mind doesn't have to come out your mouth!"

"Well, you didn't have to get so damned vicious with him," she observed, then smiled. "He is an asshole, Pat." She glanced down the car at the revival efforts.

Pat looked at his hands; two of his knuckles were skinned back and bleeding. He took a handkerchief from his pocket and wrapped them carefully.

"Are you hurt?" She asked with concern

"Not as bad as he is." Kavanaugh tightened the handkerchief.

"He shouldn't have talked like that." She adjusted her shoulders back and peered out the window. "He should not have talked like that!"

"Well, Mary," he replied in resignation. "It is not likely we will have to talk to him or anyone else in this car." Pat turned and sighted down the isle. There was a crowd gathered around injured man.

They took a stage the last few miles to Fort Supply. It was not much of a fort: Headquarters, barracks, some derelict storage buildings and a large fenced in area. Within the fence were some lodges, and a number of tepees, some showing smoking fires. Solemn, dark skinned men peered back from behind the wire. A cart parked to one side held two fifty gallon barrels of water, but there was no visible sign of sustenance. The place had a septic smell that permeated the surroundings like a ripe cow stall. A few children played in the mud around the water barrels. The area boded of illness, despair and defeat.

Kavanaugh had been anxious on the stage; concerned about seeing Sada especially in the presence of Mary. They dismounted the stage as a young soldier was passing by and Mary called to him.

"Young man, Private. Where is the headquarters building?"

He smiled, showing a missing front tooth, and pointed toward a nearby building. "Over there, ma'am, where you see the flag."

"Thanks." She rejoined and turned in the direction he had indicated. "Let's go see who's in charge. Come on, Pat, this place stinks."

"Maybe she's not here, Mary."

"And maybe she is. We will have to find out - if she's not here, we'll find out where they have taken her or where she might be." Mary gestured at the structures about her. "We have not come all this way to turn around and go back. This is not much of a fort, Kavanaugh."

"Yeah, Fort Wallace was better than this place." They began walking toward headquarters, raising scuffs of dirt. Pat pointed toward a signal pole. "At least they have a telegraph, if it's working, but not much else here".

There was a short corridor inside the headquarters building that split into a "T". A black corporal confronted them, looking sharp but hot in his uniform.

"What's your business here?" He asked politely.

"We're looking for someone." Mary replied.

"Well, ma'am, if you're looking for a member of the post you go left to the Sergeant Major's office."

"We're looking for an Indian woman."

"Among the captives," Kavanaugh inserted.

He hesitated a moment, it was a question rarely asked. "For an Indian woman among the captives you will need to see the Captain. Wait here; I'll see if he is busy".

The corporal disappeared off to the right. Pat paced nervously while Mary reviewed some of the skin shields decorating the walls. The corporal reappeared.

"The Captain will see you."

"Thank you, Corporal," Mary paused and looked him over. "That uniform fits you well."

The young corporal smiled shyly. "Thank you, ma'am, come this way. I'll take you to the office."

The short hallway to the office was lined with pictures of Union generals Meade, Sherman,

Sheridan, Thomas and McClellan. Mary and Kavanaugh reviewed each of them as they passed by. The corporal stepped to the side of the open door and gestured them in.

"Captain Payne, two civilians to see you, sir."

The captain looked up from his work and swept his arm toward two straight back chairs. "Be with you in a minute." An American flag flanked by Cheyenne skin shields were behind the light oak desk. A photo of U.S. Grant peered down them from one wall, and on the other, a photo of a military scene with Captain Payne amid a score of Union officers. Payne continued to write without looking up. Mary lifted from her chair and walked over to the photo. Payne looked up at the movement.

"Oh, that's Cumpy Sherman and that's you, Captain Payne?"

He looked up from his writing. "I beg your pardon, ma'am?"

"That's Cumpy Sherman, right?"

"Yes, that's General Sherman. The greatest officer I ever served under."

Mary cocked her head at the photo, studied it briefly and looked back at the captain. "Yes, well, he was a stubborn man. It was quite a while ago when I first met him."

"Mary," Kavanaugh enjoined, exasperation edging his voice.

She walked slowly to her chair and sat with her back straight, giving her a regal appearance.

Payne, more interested now, folded the ledger on his desk and looked steadily at her. "What business do you have here? I don't see many civilians in this god forsaken place."

"That's obvious." The slight did not go unnoticed and drew a frown. "I have no business in the strictest sense. I'd like to know, that is," she looked toward Pat, "We are interested to know if you have a native woman named Sada and her twin sons here at Fort Supply."

"She is a Cheyenne woman, about five and a half feet tall. She has two little boys."

The captain leaned back in his chair and lifted a cigar from a box on his desk and lighted it. "And what business would you have with her, if she was here?" He smiled at Mary and puffed a perfect ring toward the ceiling.

Mary stiffened at his voice, and smiled demurely. "Is she here or not?"

"I really don't know – she may be. What do you want with her? Did she steal something; kill one of your friends? Steal a horse, perhaps?"

"None of that, we want to take her home. Now, is she here or not?"

"You want to take her home!" Payne laughed out loud. "You can't just come in here and take an Indian home. These are hostiles, at least the ones behind the fence are."

"Are you saying that she is here?" Kavanaugh asked.

"She may be."

"Yes or no, sir, it is a simple question that requires a simple answer." Mary was becoming impatient.

"Yes, a native woman of that description is here."

"Goddamn it, Captain! Why didn't you just say so? "

If Payne was troubled by Mary's profanity he did not show it, except that his eyes narrowed. It became very quiet in the room. The sounds of cadence from drilling troops sifted through the open window.

"Can I see her," Pat broke the silence.

"What business do you have with her?"

"It's personal business, Captain, personal business; she is a friend who we want to take home with us. Just what do we have to do to make it so? Can you release her?"

"No, the woman you seek is incarcerated. She was captured with a dangerous band of raiders, and it's only because of my good nature that her boys are with her. Big Bear, her brother, led them I believe, along with a fulsome character named Running Bull. The two of them were responsible for raids that murdered miners, settlers and their families' men, women and children!"

Mary was becoming agitated at the lecture and replied in disdain. "I beg your pardon, Captain. I am sure she played a very bloody role. She was a particularly murderous kind - a woman with her babies under her arm and a tomahawk in her hand.

"There's only one kind of Indian that plays a good role and that's a dead one!"

"Whoa, whoa!" The argument stopped at the sound of Pat's voice. "Let's not get too far off now. Please, Captain. May I see her?"

Payne eased back in his chair." You can see her, but she's not going anywhere without a proper release from a proper authority, and I have neither the power nor inclination," he glared at Mary, "to do so."

"Who do we need to see?" Mary asked.

"Please, Captain, can I see her?" Pat implored.

"Yes, but only one visitor at a time." He leaned away from Mary and called out the door. "Corporal Madison, would you come in please?"

There was a rustle at the doorway and the Corporal slipped in and snapped to attention.

"Yes, suh," he said loudly.

"Take this man, what is your name?"

"Kavanaugh, sir, Pat Kavanaugh."

"Take Mr. Kavanaugh to see the Indian woman named Sada."

"To Sada, sir," he asked dubiously.

"Did you hear me?" He asked irritably.

"Yes, suh, follow me this way, Mr. Kavanaugh." Pat stood, cast a wary glance at Mary and followed the uniform into the bright sunlight.

The two made their way among the plank buildings, then through some tepees with unseen occupants. A small Indian boy suddenly appeared in the path before them and then quickly ducked behind the tent flaps. "They are not very friendly," the Corporal said over his shoulder. "And I don't blame 'em much."

"I know. They captured me once. It wasn't altogether pleasant; as a matter of fact, not pleasant at all." They continued to walk.

"Sada has been set aside."

"Set aside?"

Madison stopped and turned to face him. "She's pretty, you know?"

"And..."

"And the men, some were quite attracted to her. They visit her, you know? You know what I mean?"

"No, but I can guess." A sudden sinking sadness struck him.

"We - that is, they," he corrected himself. "They, ah, use her."

"Yes, they use her." Pat closed his mind to imagining the use and silently sighed. "She has those two little boys and she does what she has to."

163

"I imagine she would do that. I feel sorry for her sometimes. I always take her something, some rations. She's also helped me, made me a tonic when I was sick. They let her go out to collect plants and things, I let her out too, when I can get away with it," he smiled.

"That's mighty nice of you, Corporal." Kavanaugh shuffled his foot and studied it.

"I was sold from my mammy when I was six; she was a healer, too. Lucky I was just a little way away. I used to get to see her. I saw her workin', sometimes she would be along the edge of the field and I would be with her a little. I was lucky."

"I can understand how you might feel. Sada isn't so lucky and she's a long way from home." The Corporal laughed and again struck out across the camp. "She's lucky, lucky she don't have more babes to look after." They had progressed a few more yards when Madison stopped and pointed to a shack at the end of a tent row that once was a storage shed. "She's in there. Want me to check if there's somebody with her?"

"No, Corporal, thanks you have been helpful." Kavanaugh hurried toward the dilapidated building and pushed through the door. It was very dark inside; the only light was from the open door. He stood for a moment, his eyes adjusting to the dark. The place smelled of sweat and dirt and the musky scent of semen. He peered into the recesses and caught a movement. A wee boy completely naked crawled into the light of the doorway. Pat's heart jumped and a great surge of both joy and sorrow welled up in his eyes. A second baby crawled into the light and then retreated. Some waiting flies flitted in and lit on the first crawler's face. He swept the child into his arms and brushed them away and called quietly, "Sada." There was no voice in reply and, as his eyes adjusted to the dark, he saw movement. "Sada," he repeated, "It's Pat Kav-van-naugh." He slipped deeper into the heat and smell.

"Oh," a weak voice came from a dark corner. "Oh, you Kav- van- naw."

"Yes, it's me, Pat Kavanaugh - Kav-van-naw."

"Oh, oh!"

He saw her stand and set down the babe beside the other, who had crawled toward his steps.

Suddenly she was before him wrapped only in a robe. He took her in his arms.

"Oh, Sada, Sada, I have missed you so."

She did not respond but let him hold her.

"I've come to take you from here."

Quietly she spoke. "Kav-van-naw, I think you dead."

"I'm very much alive, and I'm going to take you out of here!"

"No, Sada stay, Kav-van-naugh; no want Sada now."

The tears were now streaming down his face. He blurted, "yes, I do." His eyes finally adjusted to the dark. A few streaks of light shined through the spaces between the planks and barely illuminated a mattress on the dirt floor. The only other object was a small stove that had an unlit candle on it.

"Jesus wept, Sada. What have they done to you?"

She did not reply but pulled away. He caught her shoulder. "Come, let's step outside."

"No Kav-van-naugh; no want Sada now." She tried to pull away from him.

"Stop it, darling, come outside with me." He knelt and picked up the baby boys. "Come, Sada; please come."

They slipped out into the light. Sada shaded her eyes and squinted. She drew the robe closer around her, and for the first time he could see her plainly. She was very thin, her cheek bones prominent over her deep set eyes.

"Decker told me you were here. I didn't know what had happened to you. I knew that Big Bear and Black Badger were dead. I thought you were too."

"They kill brother, Black Badger. Me, Maha, Running Bull run away. I afraid they come take boys from Sada, I afraid. But Sada live, I live for boys."

"I'm here now, and I'm taking you and the boys away from here. We have to make arrangements, but we are leaving here." He picked up both of the boys who squirmed against his strength, one grasped his ear.

"These boys are beautiful - beautiful!" Kavy beamed.

"They you boys," she smiled and staggered a step back, caught herself and slowly sat down.

Are you sick, Sada?" He knelt beside her. "Are you all right?"

"I tired, very tired."

"You need some water. What else do you need? Are you hungry?" He set the boys down carefully and they wobbled over to their mother. He sat down beside her, awaiting her reply.

Her robe fell open, displaying her breasts and both boys moved in, seeking her nipples. She whispered something in Cheyenne. They sat down and she pulled the robe around them. They both regarded Pat carefully. The one boy's eyes were black as shoe buttons peering from a dark, copper countenance. The other boy's eyes were a deep hazel with brown motes, his skin a pale tan.

Pat smiled and tickled them under their chins. The lighter boy recoiled at his touch, but the other one broke into a broad smile. The sun warmed the scene as Kavanaugh brushed back a new streak of tears.

"Sada, I have to go now. I must go back to see the Captain and start arrangements to get you out of here. We're going east, back to my home."

She reached out and caught his sleeve, holding tightly.

"Don't worry; I'm just going to see the Captain. I'll be back in a little bit."

"Kav-van-naw go?" She gripped his sleeve tighter.

"Just for a little bit I'll be back before the sun goes down, I promise."

Reluctantly she released him and studied his eyes.

"You wait right here."

"Kav-van-naw come back before sun goes?"

"Yes, yes, I promise." Sada's eyes searched his again. Pat stood quickly and slowly stepped back. "I promise, before the sun goes down." He backed up, turned and strode toward the headquarters building. He nodded toward Madison as he passed by, and then slowed his hurry as he approached the door. When he entered the room he sensed all was not well. The captain had returned to his ledgers and Mary was sitting stiffly peering out the window. They both turned to Kavanaugh's entrance.

"Well, Mr. Kavanaugh?" Payne ventured.

"It's her. It's Sada and the twins, although they don't look much like twins."

"Fraternal twins is the term, I believe, Mr. Kavanaugh."

Mary eyed Payne but did not reply and turned to Pat.

"It's her, then, Pat?"

"Yes, and not in such good condition, I think."

"Well, that doesn't surprise me, knowing as I do the good Captain."

165

Payne stiffened at the remark. "She has received the same treatment as any of the others, and as a matter of fact better."

"Come on, Captain. You've been using her as a whore, and we know it. Let's just get on with it. What do we have to do to get her released to our custody?"

"Usually it would be through the Indian Agent, but he's not here."

"Where is he?" Mary asked flatly.

"He's out in the field. Some negotiations somewhere and I don't expect him back this week."

"How else can it be done?" She asked truculently. "We can't be waiting here for a week".

"Well, she could be paroled by General Sheridan, but he's back in Washington. It will take a couple of weeks to get a message to him and back, sorry about that, the agent might be back in less time."

"Might be, but maybe not, and it's easy to see how sorry you are, about as sorry as a possum with a mouthful of shit.

"Mrs. Kavanaugh, I don't need to hear this and unless you refrain from your vehemence I'll have you escorted out of the fort!"

"Mary, please! Captain, we don't want any trouble, so please, can't you let her go? We mean to treat her well. She will have a home and those little boys will have a chance for a good life."

Payne sighed. "Mr. Kavanaugh, I can't do that. She's a hostile. Do you understand?"

"Yes Captain, I understand it well. I fought the Cheyenne at Fort Wallace and other engagements all across the Dakota Territory. I understand well, but she is not going to be near enough to make any trouble. We live in New York."

"You were in the cavalry?" Payne asked seeming to have ignored the rest of Pat's reply.

"Yes, I was. I also fought at Gettysburg and chased Mosby all over Virginia, or more correctly patched up his handiwork along the Orange and Alexandria."

"What is your interest, then, in this Cheyenne woman?"

"It's personal, Captain Payne, and you have said enough, Pat," Mary interrupted. "You say General Sheridan can release this family?"

"Yes, he could."

"Do you have a telegraph, sir?" Mary acidly inquired.

"Yes, we do."

"Can you contact Washington?

"Of course," he replied, adjusting some papers on his desk. "Of course I can contact Washington."

"Then please, I would like to send a message to the General, can you allow that?"

"I'm afraid these are military lines, for military business. And unless there is a better reason, I am reluctant to do so."

"My ass, you just don't want to cooperate."

"Please Captain", Pat broke in. "Could you make an exception in this case? Please."

"Well, it is not policy and I do not make the rules."

"Captain would you like to see those little boys have a better life?"

"Nits make lice, Mr. Kavanaugh, and you should know that." He busied himself at his desk opening a drawer and filing away a page of script.

"Do you have a family, sir?"

"Pat, don't beg the bastard. We can go into a town and get a railroad telegrapher to send a message,"

"Do you, Captain?" He asked, ignoring Mary's remark.

"Yes, I have a wife and child, "He smiled, "Eleanor and Ellie."

"This woman needs help. I can guarantee you the boys will not grow up as savages. We have a home for them, back in New York. Would you please reconsider?"

"Alright", he was obviously agitated as he got up from behind his desk. "The telegrapher is down the hall. He will send a message for you. Just for you, Mr. Kavanaugh. Your wife is out of control."

"No, it's for me and you too, I know what to say. I will spare you, Captain Payne. I know Phil Sheridan, and I will consider it a favor that will save me from seeing him face to face and making mention of how you treat private citizens."

"Spare me what? You are a most disagreeable woman!" He straightened from his desk with a murderous look. "Just who do you think you are? I doubt if you know General Sheridan except from a photograph."

She laughed. "Funny you should say that, I'm sure there are many who would agree with you. But Phil Sheridan is not one of them and he is a friend of mine."

They followed him to the telegrapher, who was carefully recording a message.

"Private Chenoway, this couple would like to send a message to General Sheridan's office. Please accommodate them."

The Captain turned and started out the door. "It will be at least a week before a parole, if there is one Mr. Kavanaugh." He paused and changed his voice to a more accommodating tone. "Perhaps the agent will be back. By the way, where were you at Gettysburg? I've studied the battle in great detail."

"On Little Round Top on the second day."

"You were with the Irish brigade?"

"No, Captain, I was there before they arrived and was with General Warren when he spotted the Rebs forming up for their charge."

"Oh? Well, send your message. There are no civilian accommodations at the fort." He paused and mused. "You were on Round Top on the second day? I know that was a hot fight. Sometime I'd like to talk with you about it."

"Yes, sir, I'll do that, but it's not a happy recollection."

"Well, Kavanaugh," he studied Pat for a moment, "there are a couple of empty tents, and we can provide some blankets. It's getting too late to travel now. I'll send Madison over to show you the way. I hope you don't mind Army rations again."

"Thank you, sir."

"I'll leave you to your message." He nodded toward Mary, who nodded in return, then left abruptly.

Chenoway offered Mary a piece of paper to write her message. She smiled at him and leaned across his desk to retrieve a pencil, her breasts pointing tantalizingly close. "Are you good at this telegraphing, Chenoway?"

"Yes, ma'am, I'm one of the best. Write down whatever you want to send," he grinned, "I'll get it off straight away."

Mary sat down and began to write. "I want you to send this to General Sheridan urgent and for his eyes only."

"Oh, wow, Miss, I don't know..."

"Yes, you do." She smiled at him and began to write.

"All right the Captain said to send your message." He smiled again and curiously watched her compose:

Dear Phil,

I am at Fort Supply, Oklahoma. I want to take custody of a Cheyenne woman and her twin babies. The Indian agent is not here. I was told that you can release them in his absence. Please do and could you do it very soon? I would like to get started back home. I hope you are well. I recall you fondly.

Mary Cleary

Chenoway quickly encoded the message and tapped frenetically at the key. He stopped and grinned up at her with a big smile. "It's done, Miz Cleary."

"Thank you, Chenoway." Mary reached into her purse and produced a five dollar gold piece. "I'll give you another five to get the reply to Captain Payne a minute after you decode it."

Chenoway looked at the gold piece. "Oh my, thank you, Mrs. Cleary. I'll take it to the Captain if it comes in the middle of the night."

They left the office guided by Corporal Madison and started toward the row of wall tents.

"Excuse me, Corporal. Do you suppose we can go back to see Sada on the way to accommodations?"

"Yes, ain't those boys' cute little buggers?" He smiled, "looks like Miz Cleary stirred the Captain some. He was in his office talking to his-self."

"You hear that, Mary? You satisfied now?" He did not expect a reply.

Kavanaugh glanced toward the sun disappearing in the west. The sky was full of red and gold, with a tall banner of purple fading to rose.

"Thank you, Madison. Mary, are you ready?"

"I'm as ready as I'll ever be. Let's go meet her."

Sada had worried and waited all afternoon. A dust storm blew hints of red and rose tones across the empty plain and for one shining moment the sun raised a scarlet rim before settling into purple and gray. Slowly she stood up from where she was lying between the tents. She did not return to the hut, because she might not see Pat approach. The boys were adventuring to the tent ropes, flaps and stakes. She called and they came running to her.

Kavanaugh had said that he would be back, but it was nearly dark and he was nowhere to be seen; a nameless anxiety and dread overcame her. She knew what her heart had settled long ago: she loved him, all of the hurt and loss had focused it. As she started toward the hovel that had been her home for the past year, Sada heard footsteps. There he was, looking foreign in his suit, so different from the tight fitting buckskins that Maha had stitched for him.

"Sada, Sada." He walked awkwardly toward her as the boys grasped her skirts more firmly. Through her tears, she clucked at them and they let go, positioning themselves behind her. "Why are you crying? I told you I'd be back." He opened his arms and she folded into him like a mouse to a nest.

"So happy Kav-van-naw come. Take Sada away. Want to go away."

"Yes, a long ways away, it will take a week on the iron horse to get there," he pointed east, "that way."

"Sada want go." She hung on to him. "Want go now."

There were some additional sounds in the grass just as the sun had pierced the darkening sky with bright red reaches.

"Sada, this is my wife, Mary."

Sada stepped back and observed the white woman carefully, then looked into Kavanaugh's eyes with a question as deep as the sea.

"Kav-van-naw now have wife?" She took a step backward.

"Yes. We were married a few months ago." He replied uncomfortably. He felt some how he had betrayed her - acid churned his stomach.

"Sada can no go, Kav-van-naugh. Woman not want other woman in tipi."

Mary stepped out to face Sada. "It's all right, Sada, I want you to come. Pat has told me about you."

"I didn't know what happened to you, Sada." She was uncertainly peering at him. "I didn't know about you or the boys. Do you remember Decker?"

She was hesitant to reply, looked furtively to her boys, and then back to Kavanaugh. There was no hostility in her voice.

"Decker you friend, I give Decker beads."

"Yes, that's right, and he told me. Mary and I were already married".

"Sada, Pat learned too late. He told me how much he cared for you and how you helped him, and I thank you for that."

Pat broke in. "When Mary found out that you were alive and about the boys, she said we should come right away to get you."

Sada did not reply but moved her bare feet in the dust, marking an S with her toe.

"I want you to come live with us. We have lots of room, many acres of land. There are beautiful creeks and rivers. It will be a good place for the boys to grow up, much better than here in the dust behind a wire fence. We will make a special place for you, if you want."

One of the babies was peering from behind Sada's skirt, half his face and one dark hazel eye showing from behind the hem. His hair was a dark auburn, slicked back over his large ears. Suddenly he smiled.

Mary got down on her knees and extended open arms.

"Come see me, little fellow. I'm your Aunt Mary. Look at that wavy hair. I really could be your Aunt Mary." She was beaming at him.

He demurely ducked back, then looked and smiled again.

"Come on, come see Aunt Mary. What's his name?"

Sada looked down but said nothing. Slowly the baby emerged from behind the buckskin in all his naked glory.

"Come on. We might as well be friends."

The child toddled over to Mary's outstretched arms.

"That's better." She hugged him, and not sure of all the attention, he patiently endured Mary picking him up.

Sada smiled and Kavanaugh remarked, "This place is no place to raise these boys."

"Who is this?" Mary asked again, wreathed in a bright grin.

"He Lame Wolf."

"Lame Wolf, there appears nothing lame about him."

"He a warrior," Sada watched as Mary hugged the child. "He fight – fight to stay in me."

The second twin emerged from the other side of the skirt. His eyes were black as coal, set within the deep copper skin. This twin had straight jet black hair, he also wobbled toward Mary who was still kneeling on the ground.

"What is this one's name"?

"He Gray Wolf".

Mary glanced from the boys to Pat, "My god, what beautiful boys, Kavanaugh! It's a wonder you had it in you".

Tears were tracing their way through the dust on his face. "Ah, Mary, God bless you!"

"Nice thought, Kavanaugh," she bantered. "It's far too late for that." She looked at Sada as Lame Wolf took a sudden interest in the breasts behind the buttons and industriously tried to get to them. "We are all going home together, right?" Mary asked, shifting the baby to her other arm.

"You will come with me, Sada with us? You can have a much better life for yourself and the boys."

Sada smiled at Lame Wolf's interest as she felt her own breasts begin to drip. "Yes, Sada go."

Mary lifted Lame Wolf from her bodice. "Sorry, little Lame Wolf, nothing in there for you. They're just big boy's marbles. What a cute pair of wolves."

"When go?" Sada enquired.

"Well, we don't know yet." He looked at Mary, then back to her. "We have sent a message. We will know tomorrow. It may take a week, maybe one moon."

She was quiet and looked back to Mary, who had released Lame Wolf to his brother's company.

"Hopefully it won't take that long."

"Don't worry, Sada, I'm not leaving if it takes a year." Mary said.

They spent the night in a tent nearby headquarters. Following dinner Mary retired and Pat and the Captain talked far into the night over a bottle of brandy. In the morning when they returned to headquarters, Captain Payne finished with a flourish, the document before him. "General Sheridan was quick to reply. This is a writ indicating you are assuming responsibility for three hostiles. You may remove them whenever you please. I enjoyed talking with you, Pat. He passed the document to Mary. I hope that there are no hard feelings Mrs. Kavanaugh."

Chapter 18

The Formative Years in New York
1869-1880

Once the boys arrived in Minsi they were given Christian names; Gray wolf became Liam and Lame Wolf became Billy. Over the years the boys grew strong and straight. At the outset it was readily seen that Billy was bound to be the taller and Liam had a talent for drawing. A sense of adventure and curiosity bloomed early in both the boys. The forest, streams and forgotten trails consumed their time. Fishing and hunting were their obsession. Sometimes Sara would accompany them, but more often she was busy with her tutor. Mary had her studying everything from etiquette to piano, --often to Sara's dismay.

School didn't start at Muskrat Hollow until the end of September. Grades one through six were housed in a small dilapidated-looking building in an area of small farms, and there were about twenty-five students in all. Each morning the three Kavanaughs set out on foot for the hollow, about two and a half miles from the big house. It was not long before the insightful new teacher, Miss Bales, singled out Sara and Liam to teach the younger children, and Billy was assigned to referee the rough and tumble lunch and mid-morning break. All three had outstanding academic ability, partly due to Mary's tutoring and partly because of Kavanaugh's command of numbers and English and parish schooling in Listowel.

When time came for them to attend the higher grades, an additional two miles was added to Minsi. They rode their horses to school. Often Billy would do riding tricks, standing on the saddle, sliding around the horse's neck, even doing hand stands. Sometimes he rode without a saddle, careening circles around the other two. He called it Cheyenne style; many of his tricks were from Sada's recollections and suggestions.

Sara out performed both boys in most academic studies and competition between she and Liam was apparent. She excelled in science, math and music and as most popular with the other girls. She also was interested in history and writing . Sara became the defender of the other girls, backed up by Billy who would tangle with anyone who threatened Sara or Liam.

Billy acquired two dozen steel traps and strung them out along the creek that wound its way to the swamp behind Muskrat Hollow School. He spent a lot of time with his mother and loved to hear her stories of the plains and Big Bear, Running Bull and the mysterious medicine man Black Badger who had saved his father's life. He often talked with her about going out west to hunt, trap, and pan for gold. "To see it before it was all gone." Signs were apparent to anyone who he talked with that he wanted no part of being a farmer, a lawyer, or a doctor.

Billy did tolerably well in arithmetic and geometry, but he excelled in history, general science and geography, and demonstrated a proclivity in foreign language. At Minsi Academy, they all studied French & Latin, and at home, Billy became fluent in Cheyenne. When he worked the land with Kavanaugh he became an astute student of the seasons and in the ecology of the fur bearers and big game–deer and bear. Most of the results of his hunts went to Sada, who taught him to skin, flesh and care for hides and how to make jerky and select edible plants. Billy and Liam and occasionally Sara hunted together. By the time Billy was thirteen he was already a legendary marksman, and won the rifle competition at the county fair. The prize was a boxed Colt Army revolver which he promptly gave to Pat.

Liam excelled at arithmetic, geometry, art, history, and handwriting. He eagerly assisted in Mary's business doing the books, spending time with Mary's lawyer, Haney, and making small purchases for the clinic. By the time that Liam entered eighth grade in Minsi, Mary turned over some of her books and ledgers to him relied on his help. He was "sharp with a dollar" and had an intense concern for accuracy. He still helped with spring planting, summer haying and the fall harvest, but Mary insisted that other farm chores were the hired help's responsibility.

All three children were growing beyond the land; it was simply a matter of time. As more chores were taken up by the three of them, Mary spent more time with Pat and complained it was difficult to "drag him away from the plow." Occasionally she could get him to go to New York City with her, after a couple of days he was ready to return home. Mary had more money than she could spend in three lifetimes; she made generous donations and poured money into the 'Cloister.'

At Home in Minsi, New York
Summer 1880

Billy and Liam quit the small eddy with the deep water. They had done well with three bass and a wall eyed pike to show for their efforts. They were sure they had quite enough for dinner. Evelyn would reward them on their return, with sugar cookies and tea. They had accepted the "white man" names that Kavanaugh gave them; but their mother still called them by their Cheyenne names.

As the two came up the river path they could see the stream bending in shiny light where the hemlocks pressed closest to the water. Billy held up his hand to stop as he spotted a figure in the water below.
"What is it, Billy?"

Billy turned, holding his finger across his lips. "Sssh, there's a woman in the water below us."

"Probably one of Mary's girls, there's lots of them these days. They sure are busy at the clinic."

"She's skinny dippin'." He crouched down and moved closer to the bank. "Maybe we can get a look," excitement creeping into his voice. "Get down - she may look up. She's washing her hair."
"Move over, let me see."

The woman in the water turned on her back, letting the water buoy her up. The long black hair spread and fanned out with the current."

"Billy, that's Ma!"

"She's got pretty big ones, Liam!"

"Billy, that's Ma! Let's get out of here. What if she sees us?"

"What if she does?"

"Come on, Billy, she might feel bad. She's starting to get out of the water."

"Ssssh, I want to watch."

"Come on, Billy. She might feel bad; I'm gonna close my eyes." Liam turned from the scene below and squeezed his eyes closed.

"Sssh, watch!" Billy's eyes remained fixed on the figure below. "Look at that!"

Liam remained quiet, but turned and opened his eyes just in time to watch as Sada slipped into her robe, sat down and began to pull a comb through her hair.

The boys carefully backed away from their perch, making a rustle in the leaves. Sada turned to look up as the two buried themselves in the grass. With a slight smile she returned to watching the river as she combed out her long black tresses. T he two boys beat a hasty retreat into the alder trees.

"Geeze, Billy! You think she saw us?"

"I don't think so. A woman's body is a beautiful thing, ain't it?" They continued side by side up the path, one carrying the poles, the other the forked limb holding the fish.

"Sure could see that black patch." He ducked under a reaching alder bough. "Did Sara ever show you?"

"Did she ever show you?"

"Once, she did - a long time ago. We were down in the barn when you had the mumps. Wasn't much to see, a puffy little slot between her legs."

"She showed me once too. We were fishing; you were with Pa and Mary. She had to pee, and while she had her pants down she showed me. I showed her mine too."

"I'll bet its different now. She's got hair under her arms and I'll bet she has some between her legs too."

"Probably, I don't think she'd show us now."

They passed through the trees and the meadow ahead was dotted with cows where pink cockle flowers were woven through the yellow mallow.

"Billy."

"Yeah, what?" He turned to face him.

"I love Sara." Liam stopped and shifted the stringer of fish.

"Love her?"

"I mean I want to be with her. I want to marry her. She's nice and warm and we talk about all kinds of things."

"We talk too - about the kids in school and stuff. She is our sister for God's sake."

"But it's different and besides, she is really not our sister not really. I like holding her hand and talking to her. She lets me kiss her too - sometimes."

"Rather be with her than fishin'?"

"Yes."

Billy took a deep breath and looked toward the unseen house marked by a blue plume of smoke rising from the chimney. "I guess I like to talk to Sara too, but I never kissed her. She tried once, I didn't want to kiss her and I'd rather go fishin.' She likes you better than me, I think, and I never kissed her." Billy squinted at his brother. "She kiss you back?"

"Yes." He shifted the fish again.

173

"Then you'll probably be seein' what she's got between her legs before I do." Come on, let's git going. She is just my sister and that's that!"

They resumed their journey across the field. Liam stopped again after a few steps. "I love you too, Billy."

"Yeah, Liam, I love you, too - and Ma and Pa, and Mary and Sara. I guess Evelyn has got to be in there too." He smiled and draped his arm over Liam's shoulder.

"I think Sara likes you better than me, Billy."

"Ah, I don't think so. Anyway, what difference does it make? Come on. We want to get home before these fish get too stiff. Want me to carry them for awhile?"

Liam smiled and they exchanged burdens. "Do you think Ma saw us?"

"I don't know, Li. What difference would it make?"

They continued on. The house appeared in view.

Sada rarely came to the house; she was more comfortable in the Wickiup Pat built for her down by the river. When she did come up to the house, she preferred to sit in Evelyn's kitchen. Evelyn knew Sada was partial to sweets; there always was something special prepared for her safe from the boys' searches. They'd talk while Sada sipped tea and ate the treats. When someone in the family was ill, Sada brought herbs or a poultice or some tea-like concoction. Evelyn believed the tonics to be better than anything one could buy at a chemist, which was probably true. Mary, however, was not so enthusiastic and did not trust them so much. Once passing by the kitchen, Mary peered in at the pair deeply engrossed in a conversation of Sada's broken English and Evelyn's heavy accent and wondered what was being understood, but she knew that they were both healers in their own special ways, and smiled at the exchange.

Sara enjoyed making rounds with Doc Wayland. At first she just observed, soon she began to help directly with the patients and became a trusted and beloved addition to their care.

She decided that she wanted to become a physician. She was out with him almost every evening and when school was finished for the summer, she spent many hours with him and his patients. She brought offerings of tonics and teas that Sada made which in some cases proved efficacious. Doctor Weyland reported that Sara not only had the mind for medicine, but also a healing touch. The terminally ill had a special regard for her, and he believed when she was present they were more at ease with their fate. Wayland once explained to Mary (while slightly anesthetized by a generous ration of gin), "she has a special healing spirit – better than prayers." Mary knew Sara well enough to believe there was something to his babbling, despite knowing the good doctor's poor regard for religion.

Sara liked to visit Sada every chance she got, and on this particular evening in early July, she spotted her busy outside her Wickiup. The sun was setting in the west, throwing a brilliant golden and pink-purplish glow across the horizon. The quarter moon was beginning to show bright in the sky above. Sada heard the sound of approaching footsteps, and looked up, smiling.

"Ah, Sara, come, we go river – now."

Sara circled her arms around Sada and squeezed her, a greeting Sada had begun to take pleasure in since everyone hugged her whenever they saw her.

"We go fish. Many long fish now."

Sara smiled and replied in Cheyenne. "We can catch many."

Sada laughed out loud at the sound of her language. "You good speak Cheyenne, but Sada want talk English."

Sara looked at what Sada was working on. It was a tangled macramé line that appeared to be one great snarl of loops and twists.

"Long fish make me work."

"Eels, they sure can make a mess!"

"But very good to eat."

"Oh, Sada, they give me the creeps. They're like snakes and I don't like snakes."

Sada smiled. "But not snakes -- better to eat."

"Let me help." They sat side by side untangling the line, both absorbed in the intricate task.

"Last night catch big one." Sada nodded toward a smoky fire that passed into a small grill-like smoke-house structure piled with pieces of eel.

After a short time, they finally mastered the tangle and began walking quickly toward the dark whirling eddy.

"Tomorrow can we go to gather medicines, Sada? I learn so much from you, better than school, and I'd like to learn more."

"Sada take Sara down river." She said, smiling as she bent to the task of baiting the hook and then deftly tossed the line to midstream. "We sit together." Sada spread her robe over them and the night reverberated from frogs in the water to frogs in the trees, punctuated from time to time by the sharp squawk of a night hawk. The soft darkness enfolded them, drawing them close. Sara could smell the herbs in Sada's hair.

"Tomorrow we find weed that bites," Sada ventured.

"Sting weed? I think we call them nettles, and they sting all right."

"Sting weed --yes, good -many things. Stop bleeding, stop baby bleeding," she gestured to her groin. "Root of sting weed good, old men, help pass water, make strong."

"I know where there are some nettles."

"Good, Sara, show Sada." She suddenly reached forward and picked up the line. "Oh, long fish, he come us." She quickly began to pull in the line hand over hand, the slack water swirling as the big eel fought against her. "Sara catch line, big, big long fish!" The line was strung down the water's edge. Sara caught it and dragged the eel onto the beach. Suddenly it was loose and writhing toward the water. Both women grabbed for it but missed. Sara got under it with both hands and tossed it up on to a sandy spot and Sada dispatched it with her knife.

"He almost got away! He is a big eel, I could barely toss him; oh, look at my hands – they're black, yuk eel slime!"

Sara sanded her hands rinsed them and wound up the line on a stick and they started back with their prize. For a long while they sat before the smoking fire as Sada skinned and cut the eel into to drying pieces and Sara scraped the remaining black slime off her hands.

"Sada," she asked, shrugging the blanket over her shoulders. "I bleed a lot during my time. Do you know what I mean?"
Sada looked back with no emotion. "Much bleed?"

"Yes, very much." She felt comfortable talking with Sada; the language barrier was difficult though they usually managed.

"Tomorrow we find tree --it help you. We find many plants tomorrow. We find bleeding tree, and plants stop bleed."

They undressed and curled together in the robe beneath the blankets. Sara liked to feel Sada's soft breasts on her back. It was a thrill not offered at the house, despite owning the best bed springs available; there was special warmth in being curled up naked next to Sada.

They'd been walking for hours, taking long stops as Sada selected plants and explained their usefulness. They found the nettles and the bleeding tree that turned out to be witch hazel, more a shrub than a tree. Sada explained that the bark made into a finely smashed poultice was also good for swelling of the eyes, while drinking of it as a thick tea stopped bleeding.
They also found ginseng; Sada smiled as she explained it was a general stimulant and served to "get man hard" and fight sickness of all kinds. Sara recognized bergamot; it was a flower known as Oswego tea. Sada explained it relieved tension when one drank it and cured rashes when used as a poultice. The lessons continued: pine needle tea is a cure for diarrhea; juniper branches had a diuretic effect when drunk and soothed arthritis pain when applied as a topical treatment. Rattle weed or Cohosh was used for post partum pain, expelling the placenta and encouraging breast milk. Mallow flowers made a good laxative and the whole hawthorn shrub, limbs, leaves, bark and roots, served as a heart tonic.

The sun was quite warm in the afternoon and the two stopped for a rest where a small creek flowed into the Minsi. Sada gathered some pieces of dill, the long green stalk topped by a feathery flower just showing spots of yellow.
"I know that plant, Sada. It's dill. Evelyn uses it to flavor pickles."

"More than sour for pickles." Sada smiled for she knew well the snappy taste of Evelyn's dills. "Sweet pickles better. Sada learn from white mother about pickles, but more than pickles."
"What does dill do, pucker your lips?" She scrunched her face into a sour look.

"Good many things. Chew seeds make, she blew and gestured her hand beneath her chin.

"It is good for your breath?"

"Yes, make breath sweet. Good for, holding her hands on her stomach she made a circular sign.

"It is good for pregnancy or calms your stomach?"

"No, no," she made a puffing sound and gestured toward her behind.

Sara laughed, "gas --farts."

Sada joined in her laughter. "Gas - farts," she carefully pronounced. "Dill good to make milk" she cupped her breasts. "Sada use dill, --much dill with boys. Two boys, one here, one here" she touched her breasts in turn.

They did not speak for awhile, both thinking of the boys but on different plains.

"It must have been difficult; Mary said it was very dry and dusty in Oklahoma. Were you thirsty a lot?"

"All time thirsty. Drink much water. When Kav-van-naw comes, give Sada beer. Good, baby good sleep."

Sara examined the dill stalk, tasted it and made a mental note. The warm sun made her drowsy as she watched Sada cut the weed to store in her leather bag.

"Sada, what was it like to have twins?"

"Hard time, we not live one place. All time go. Long knives hunt us."

"I've helped with some deliveries, even turned one baby. Doc Wayland asked me to help, my hands are smaller. It was all right for me, but a hard time for the mother." She studied her hands, and then looked at Sada's long lashed eyes. "Were you alone, Sada? Did anyone help you?"

"I know more one baby inside. Maha stay me." Sada settled beside Sara and looked toward the westward sky.

"Maha," Sara straightened to attention.

"Maha my friend; she wife of Running Bull. Maha do many things sew with beads, very good. She make good buckskins. She love Running Bull like Sada love Kav-an-naw, he no with Sada, Running Bull with Maha. We friends long time."

"Did you have a special place to bring out babies? Like when you monthly bleed?"

"Yes, Running Bull make place. Set tepee near camp. Maha come."

"All of the babies I've helped with came one at a time. The twins, did they both try to come out at the same time?"

"Think maybe. But Maha help. First baby Gray Wolf -- much water, blood."

"Liam?"

"Yes, but Lame Wolf, he fight, he fight." She leaned back against the warm and shaded bank and pushed a stray shock of gray hair back toward the shiny black braid. "Hard time." She smiled. "He want stay inside me."

"Were you lying down?"

"No, like this." She rose and squatted. "Like this. Maha help take Lame Wolf out. Soon, before Maha cut line, inside come out. Maha, very busy, Sada so tired. Maha give babies, then big fear." She waggled her head.   "Big fear comes."

"What happened?"

"Maha, Sada, alone. Big wolf come."

"Did he come right into the tepee?"

"Yes, he big gray wolf. He come, showed teeth -- grrrrr," Sada made the sound in her throat. "He take Sada insides and go."

"You mean the afterbirth?"

"Yes, take two. He is so close. Maha, she fight wolf. Sada fear he come for babies. Maha hit knife at him. He take insides, run, but he lame, slow. Sada heart goes fast, no breath!" She put her hand to her chest.

"That sounds so scary!"

"Maha fear too." She laughed. "We hear men come. Running Bull see wolf. Try shoot him but he go. He eat both pieces me."

"What a story.   He ate your afterbirth?"

"Eat, run away.   Not eat baby. Maha she scare wolf good." She paused in the telling and shaded her eyes. "Men think big sign. Much scare too. They think we all die. Maybe big wind come, or white man, guns. Many scare, many things. Wolf in camp bad sign."

"Did anything happen right after that?"

"Yes, bad things, big fight with white man who digs."

"Miners, you had a fight with miners."

"Yes. Maha killed. Running Bull very sad he go.   Big fight, soldiers find our place, kill many Cheyenne. Take us Fort Supply." She moved her head in negation. "Bad time, Kav-van-naw, Mary come, we go here."

"I remember when you came. At first I was afraid of you. You stayed in the stable and only came to the porch. Evelyn was always fussing over you. Uncle Pat tossed the babies so high, I thought he would scare them, but they crawled over him like ants."

"But you like babies. I know."

"I did! I was pretty small myself, but they were like dolls to me. Mary enjoyed them so much, I was jealous sometimes.   It's hard to believe that now we're all grown up."

"Yes, grow up. Sara still likes boys?"

"Yes, I love them both." She looked down at her mud covered shoes and smiled.

"Sada think you love Lame Wolf most." She made a quick rolling motion with her hand.

"Maybe a little more," she smiled.

"Lame Wolf warrior, not good love one, he love war."

"I don't know, Sada.   I love Liam too."

"You love Liam. He stay you, he kind, like Kav-van-naw. Billy go way to war. He like that."

"You don't think he might change?" She asked, shading her eyes from the setting sun.

Sada smiled a tint of sadness showing on her face. "No, he go way, he warrior."

The shadows where growing deeper, Sara shifted to her side and glanced upward.   In her heart she knew that Billy was bound away and Sada was correct. "Shall we go back now, Sada? I think it's getting late."

"You learn today?"

"Oh yes, you have taught me a lot today."

Sada rose and began to tug at some cattails.

"Are cattails good for anything, --a medicine?"

Sada smiled, "cattails good eat." She began to strip the outer skin from the stalk. "Taste good with long fish."

Chapter 19

September 1880
Changing Times

A new interest caught Mary's fancy; it was called women's suffrage. She said she didn't know what all women were suffering from, (she decided it was mostly from men). But no matter, they should have the right to vote. Upper and middle class women were holding rallies in Buffalo, in Baltimore and Chicago. Mary began a correspondence with Jean Brooks Greenleaf the president of the New York State Women's Suffrage Association. She learned that Greenleaf was going to attend a large rally in New York City and Mary decided that she would seek her out.

It was a stifling day in the city when Mary attended the large gathering of women at the City Library. The cause was not a popular one and the city's police force was gathered to maintain order. Many detractors and supporters, both men and women, had gathered to hear the speech. Mary had sent the New York suffragettes a hefty sum of money to help with the printing of the "Woman Voter." Her donation had not gone unnoticed. Greenleaf asked her to be on the welcoming committee for the event. Mary agreed; then judiciously placed twenty of NYC's constabulary about the crowd, tipped them well and indicated she would like their assistance. Clouds over the sun had reduced the heat when Greenleaf picked up the megaphone and began:

"Friends and fellow citizens: I stand here in the shadow of greatness. Shadows cast by Elizabeth Cady Stanton, Lucretia Mott and our beloved Susan B. Anthony."
The opening words were greeted with catcalls and jeers. She paused and began again.

"The preamble of our great constitution includes words blessing liberty to ourselves and our posterity. The authors of that great work were not only referring to the male gender; posterity was for the whole people – women as well as men. Indeed without women there would be no posterity. It is an equally cruel joke to speak of enjoyment of liberty while refusing women the use of the ballot, the only means of securing this liberty. To provide equal representation of all is the law of this land. ALL has no gender.

"To make gender a qualification for a ballot is a violation of the supreme law of this land. This republic is not for men only – like a private smoking club or a millionaire's drawing room. To the contrary, we continue to build a nation, not an oligarchy of men. Just as it is not an oligarchy of wealth, or race, or of learning. Yet women continue to be denied equal access to commerce, to education, to the laws of divorce, even to custody of the children they themselves have born. Even in the church women are excluded from the ministry and decisive affairs. Men have endeavored in every way they can to destroy the confidence, self respect of women and to force them to be subject to his whims."

Boos and catcalls resounded, and the first tomato arched out of the crowd; Mary, like a major league batter, smacked it with her megaphone, splattering the grand stand with shards of the juicy red fruit. There was movement in the crowd; she saw some night sticks swing and the crowd drew suddenly more attentive although a few jeers still emanated from the assembly.

Mary nodded toward the speaker. "I apologize for that, Jean." She brushed a few red stemmed seeds from her bodice.

"On the contrary," Greenleaf replied. "Better a bit than the whole tomato." Once again she raised her voice to the assembly.

"Not long ago as history dictates, we fought a bitter war to keep this nation from being divided north from south, freedom from slavery. It is now time to face an even greater concern a division in our very own homes where an oligarchy of sex exists. An oligarchy which gives fathers, brothers, husbands and sons power over mothers and sisters, wives, and daughters in every household. Men are sovereign - women are their subjects.

I call to all you present, men and women, boys and girls, aunts and uncles, husbands and wives to embrace the Declaration of Sentiments of Seneca Falls and to go forth and secure the right for women to vote in all elections in this land. Strike forth and reverse the idea of withholding from one half of our citizens the right to vote. Our women can not be denied - many of whom are cultured, revered and virtuous while unstintingly bestowing the vote upon men – many of whom are illiterate, debauched and vicious. Reverse the twisted precedent that the only people who can vote are men. Reverse the cruel concept that denies the right to vote to those who were not wise enough to be born male instead of female." She abruptly stopped speaking and sat down.

The large gathering was solemnly quiet; then a great round of applause struck the stand like breakers on the beach. Twice Greenleaf rose and bowed to the applause. The jeers and catcalls were far outnumbered by enthusiasm and encouragement. An all-woman band struck up the Battle Hymn of the Republic and the crowd surged forward as some of the bunting of the speakers stand was torn into souvenirs. Later at Delmonico's, a number of suffragette families gathered to share a meal provided, through Mary Cleary's generosity.

Mary seated herself by Greenleaf. She felt strangely empowered by the cause of women's rights and was stirred by the talk spreading among the tables. Greenleaf gave another brief speech.

"I want to thank you all for your support of this just cause. Today we sent a singular message to all those who oppose us. In particular I hope these words reach not only the recalcitrant men present at the speech, but also those in Congress. I wish you all to know that some suffrage debates will soon get underway on college campuses. I hope and pray that those women of the Anti Suffrage League will also hear us and change their hearts to our cause. Our sisters in England, the mother country of many of us, have long supported the women's right to vote. Those who imply that women's suffrage is a leap into the dark are most in error. Indeed it is a stride into the light!"

There was polite clapping and, as those in attendance began to pay more attention to their plates, Mary Cleary spoke to Greenleaf.

"You know, Jean, you have inspired, yes, inspired me today. You can count on my assistance in the future."

"Well Mary, your donations and your presence here are testimony to that. But our message must reach out to those in rural areas as well."

"I know what you say is true. The farmers I know are very unlikely to support the vote. They don't see any importance in bothering with woman voters. Many are more concerned about their cows than they are about their wives. They must get the message, but it will be a hard sell."

"Yes, Mary. Perhaps you could reach out to them. Perhaps you could organize a chapter." She smiled. "Give some speeches yourself."

"I don't know about speeches, but I know a lot about money, mortgages, and marriage. It might be an interesting mix to study."

The sun poured through the windows rimmed with lace and caught the dark tones in the young girl's hair. Sara was peering into the mirror above the rich oak dresser and giving herself a reassuring assessment. She leaned forward when she spotted the small red spot on her chin. She fingered it and was about to give it a squeeze when the door behind her opened.

"Well, darlin', Evelyn has finished ironing this dress. I like you in blue. There's a red paisley scarf here too, --a touch of color to brighten your cheeks." She paused. "My gracious girl, we will have to get you a new brassier soon."

"Mother!" She scolded. Sara called Mary 'mother' because it pleased them both.

"Well, it's true. Now pull on this dress and I'll touch up your hair."

Mary was still petite; a few lines creased her forehead and light lines crinkled at the corners of her bright blue eyes. She was spreading through the hips and her once red hair had faded to a suggestion in the waves of gray. It was Mary and Pat's thirteenth wedding anniversary and people were gathering from all over Navis County to help them celebrate the occasion. Their anniversary had become one of the social events of the year replete with food, drink, a band, and photographers. It also marked Sara's imminent departure for Hunter College in the fall.

Sara popped her head through the collar and wrestled her arms through the apertures, tugged and adjusted the dress.

"My hair is a mess; I got some burdocks in it yesterday."

"How did you do that? I see the snarls. My word girl, it is a mess!"

"Well, Billy and Liam and me got into a fight. You know we stuck the burrs together. We were only supposed to throw at the clothes but Billy hit me in the hair, the ball stuck there. I got most of it out."

"That Billy, he will be lucky if I don't hit him with something else like right on the ass with a two-by-four."

"He didn't mean it, mother. Besides, I hit him in the hair first." She smiled slightly at the memory of Billy's surprise.

"Well then," as she pulled the hair brush with a brisk stroke. "Maybe you deserved it. It's going to pull a little, it's quite a snarl."

"Ouch! Ouch!" Sara made a wry face against the pain. "Ouch, ouch, Mom, are you almost done?" She glanced into the mirror at Mary's resolute face, which burst into a smile.

"Almost," she began to extend in smooth strokes as Sara heaved back with them. "Would you happen to know where the boys are? Decker is coming and you know how he loves those boys. I hope they remember," she added with an edge of irritation. Some of my suffragette friends will also be here. I want you to look nice and presentable for them."

"They went hunting early this morning, said something about Sada wanting to make some jerky."

"Do they ever stay out of the woods? Billy and all that Wild West stuff, I tell you! Do you know how many times they have worried their father? Three times he sent people out to find them before they were ten. They ought to talk more with their father about the Wild West before they go exploring."

"That's when they were little. Now, they know their way around better than an Indian.

181

Do you remember when they found them both up in a tree --where they spent the night? They were ten then, weren't they?"

"Yes, I'm not likely to ever forget. Half the county was out looking for them. Even Sada and I were scouring the woods." She made a final pass of the comb, "do you suppose they're back?"

"I told them last night they should be back before noon." Mary lifted a necklace that dangled a small timepiece with diamonds at noon, three, six and nine. It was her favorite piece of jewelry, given her last Christmas by the mysterious Mr. Woo, a regular Christmas visitor ever since Sara could remember.

"It's ten o'clock." Mary noted in dismay and turned to the window. "People are arriving already. Matilda's here. You finish up now and hurry downstairs to help greet the guests. June is such a busy month, anniversaries, the boys' birthdays. You are my showpiece, you know."

"Ah, I should have gone hunting with the boys."

"No, you shouldn't have! I'll see you downstairs."

"Mother?"

"What, child?" She stopped nearly out the door with the comb still in her hand.

"Do you want me to go down to the Wickiup? See if they're back?"

Mary paused, pursed her lips and touched them with her fingertips. "No, Sara we will wait a little longer." She placed the tortoiseshell comb on the vanity. "Hurry on downstairs, they will finally show up. You look very pretty. I noted young Lassiter looked you over quite carefully last time he was here."

"Don't get your hopes up. He gives me the creeps. He looks at me like a prized cow or something."

"Maybe you're a stubborn tomboy donkey," Mary laughed.

"Maybe I am stubborn, but I'm not a tomboy."

"Whatever you say, young lady," she responded with a sage smile. "I think maybe you're sweet on Billy."

"I like them both."

"One of those two boys is going to have a broken heart one day. I think they are both wrapped up in you."

Sara glanced at the small snatch of hair that had been brushed out with the remains of the burr. With an edge of irritation she noted, "sometimes I wish Billy would show it more."

"I must get downstairs. Hurry now; do not spend all day in front of the mirror."

Mary vanished down the broad stairway flanked by the curving balustrade. Sara once more reviewed herself in the mirror, touched the tiny red spot on her cheek and decided against a squeeze. A booming voice and a throbbing good natured laugh echoed up the stairwell. Sara gave one final adjustment to her bodice and laughed with the laughter coming up the staircase. "They don't call her big Matilda for nothing."

She carefully aligned the brush, comb and hand mirror across the vanity and walked slowly down the stairway.

The old slate quarry road curved its way across the whole first section of Cloister land, passing in turn through a hemlock darkened forest, small meadows and large stands of sheep laurel. There were three bridges across clear quick running streams that were home to many small trout that would strike a bare hook with the right twitch. Just before the quarry itself was a small deep lake with water so cold it could turn a swimmer blue.

The big doe paused before stepping on the edge of the faded wagon ruts; a soft rustle in the leaves was all that announced her presence. Billy saw her first and slowly inclined his head toward where she stood. Liam followed with his eyes, spotted her, slowly raised his rifle and settled behind the sight.

At the sound of the shot, the deer flinched, turned and bolted for the woods behind her. Billy fired at the disappearing deer.

"Jesus Christ, Liam. What the hell's the matter with you?"

"I missed."

"You missed all right. You couldn't hit a bull in the ass with a bass fiddle. You flinched."

"No, I didn't."

"Yes, you did. I saw you."

The two began walking toward the place where the deer had vanished.

"What about you? You missed her."

"I think I hit her. I tried to get out front and she dropped her tail. Better check for blood."

They spread out searching the ground before them, looking for telltale spatters on the leaves.

"There's blood over here, Billy a lot of it!"

"Don't move 'til I get there."

They joined at the red stained leaves.

"I did hit her, bright pink, its lung blood. She won't be far," he looked ahead. "Whoa! There she is!"

The deer rose from cover about fifty yards ahead and was slowly moving away. Billy sighted, fired again, and the deer crashed into the cover.

"She's down," he observed calmly.

"I think I see her just to the left of that big oak! She's not movin'!"

When they reached the animal she was still. Billy prodded her with his rifle barrel; his second shot had shattered her neck just behind the head.

"Now the fun begins," Billy took a deep breath.

Liam fished a watch from his pocket and snapped open the case.

"We have to hurry. It's almost ten o'clock. I think it may have started already."

"It has, didn't you hear the horses greeting one another?" Billy took his knife from its sheath and bent to work. He carefully gutted her.
"I see you nicked her brisket." He fingered the wound on her chest.
"See, I didn't miss."

Billy continued cutting through the esophagus, trimmed out the diaphragm. "You didn't kill her either, she would have got away." He rolled the animal to its side, draining out the pooled blood. Help me turn her over."

They turned her over and Billy stripped out the viscera all of the organs spilled out. Carefully he trimmed around the anus and released the large intestine. They lifted the deer from the gore.

"Want to skin her here?"

"No, Li, we've got to get home. Ma can skin her. Besides it would be a mess by the time we got her out."

"I'll find a drag then. It's near half a mile to Ma's. We should have brought the mule," Liam grumbled.

"Well, we wouldn't have seen any deer. Old Jake makes more noise than an army wagon."

Liam cast about and spotted a maple limb that he trimmed with his knife. He inserted it through the slots Billy had cut in the hind leg tendons. "Ma will be glad to get this. But, Mary will be wondering where we are the party and all. Pa might cut a switch." He looked toward where the house was and shook his head in dismay.

"Yeah, it will make good jerky." Billy smiled. "I really like jerky!" The two deer slayers each took a side and began the tow home. "And don't worry about Pa. He won't want to spoil the party".

At the house Mary greeted Matilda with the enthusiasm saved for close friends, for she and the whole town respected the large good-natured woman who by herself had raised three girls on a hard scrabble farm.

"Ah, Mat, it is so good to see you. She took the big woman in her arms and gave her a big hug, getting a greater one in return.
"How are you, Mary"?

"Fine if you haven't cracked my ribs. Better get inside there, there are a lot of people you may want to talk to".
"I'll see you a little later."
The two women laughed and Matilda walked toward the assembly in the ball room.

Mary decided to look in on Pat, already involved in a pinochle game in the parlor. He sat smiling at the table, his sleeves rolled back, and she listened for a minute to the roll of brogues that accompanied the dealing of the cards. She loved him, sunburned skin, freckles and all, for underneath she knew it was kindness that drove him.

They had rescued one another. He had delivered her from despair and an empty life. She had delivered him from imprisonment and an equally empty life. Mary spoiled him a tad more than he could usually bear, but there was no picking and whining in him, and he never bore a grudge. She watched the game progress and the glasses filled a second time. He caught her glance from the doorway, and his red face broke into a smile that danced his blue eyes bright.

"Would you like to join us, Mary?" He gestured toward an empty seat.

"Hah, as if you'd have me."

"Come on, join in." There was a general agreement.

"I don't like pinochle and I can get a drink in the kitchen. Can you guys believe it, that Pat never played a hand of cards until he met me? You really do not want me to play. He often wins and I taught him."
There was a general nodding and chuckle that passed over the faces.
"Ah, Mary, it's the company," rejoined the man across from Kavanaugh.
"That being the case, O'Meara, I'm better off in the kitchen."

She turned away from the laughter as the players jibed O'Meara. There was still much to be done to prepare for company. She looked back as she was leaving.

"Pat, the boys are not back yet."

"Where are they?" He paused in picking up his cards.

"They went hunting this morning and promised Sara they would be back by eleven."

"Ah, don't worry, Mary. You know how their hunting trips go."

"Sara said she would go down to Sada, if we wanted her to."

"Oh give them another hour, if they are not back by then, I will go down to see Sada myself."

"If you are able," she added sarcastically.

"Well then, send Sara."

"She is already dressed for the party. I don't want her traipsing through the woods."

Mary heard a commotion on the porch and hurried to the window. She spotted the boys shadow boxing with Decker, soon he had the both of them wrapped up and they were squealing with delight.

She turned from the window." They're here, and they are a mess, blood all over their jeans and look like the wreck of the Spanish Armada. They are not going through the living room looking like that!"

"I told you not to worry." The players sorted their cards and arranged them as if they had not heard the exchange between Pat and Mary.

"I am going to catch them before they get too far." She huffed and started off.

"Mary, would you please send in another bottle of Bushmills?"

She threw a disgusted look at him fighting back a smile born of both relief in seeing the boys and amusement. "You are a wonder, Kavanaugh; I don't believe an earthquake can stir you from a game of cards."

O'Meara chirruped, "a wonder alright, he hasn't lost a hand."

Mary shook her head left the players and hurried toward the clatter on the porch and overheard Liam through the window.

"Ma really wanted that deer and she started skinning it right away. And we both got her, no matter what Billy says."

"Well your Ma will make that up into pemmican or jerky and you both will enjoy that."

"Say Deck," he paused rubbing his neck where Decker had held him. "Will you come over and go hunting with us some days?"

"Sure will, maybe next week."

"And will you tell us some more stories about scoutin' and chasing Running Bull and about the Comanche?"

"Well your father knows more about Running Bull than I do and so does your Ma. But I'll tell you some more stories if you like. Oh, oh, I see Mary looking out the window you had better skedaddle and get cleaned up."

A week after the anniversary party Billy, Liam and Sara decided to go exploring. The vast cloister-land was rich in opportunity and they were headed toward an abandoned Indian village rumored to be deep in the forest. The trail was steep and rocky as it wound through the heavy woods.

"Billy, will you slow down! We've never been here before. Where's Sara? "

"I don't know where Sara is, behind us somewhere. Come on; there's a big clearing up ahead, I can see it through the trees; we'll wait for her there."

"You went too fast ahead of me!" A voice echoed up the steep slope.

"Where have you been, Sara?"

"I stopped back there, and when I looked up you both were gone."

"Why did you stop for? Li just noticed you weren't with us, a few minutes ago."

"I had to pee. You could have waited; I didn't know where you had gone."

"How were we supposed to know you wanted us to wait? You should have told us you had to pee."

Sara climbed up the slope and breathlessly arrived beside them. A pileated woodpecker was filling the woods with sound.

Sara wiped her hands on her slacks. "Do you know where we are, Billy? We must've been hiking two hours." She swatted at a square tail fly perched on her arm."

"I'm not quite sure."

"We're lost. Are we lost?"

"No, Li. how can we be lost? We have been climbing up this mountain". He pointed behind him. "All we have to do is go back down again."

"But you don't know where we are, where would we come out down below?"

"Hell, Sara, what difference does it make? We wanted to explore, right? So how can we explore if we don't go somewhere different?"

"Are we still on our place?

"And what difference does that make?"

"I don't know, Billy. Maybe we should head back. It's already afternoon."

"You and Sara can go on back if you want, but I'm going to look at that meadow ahead. I think that's where that Indian village Pa told us about is."

Billy surged up the slope; his two companions hesitated, and then followed. After some steeper toiling they broke through the trees on to the meadow.

"Look at all the deer shit." Billy pointed to the ground. "Hell, this place is a regular deer meadow; lots and lots of tracks. Trouble is if you shot one here you'd have a hell of a time getting it out!"

"Don't swear so much, Billy."

"Sorry, sister Sara." There was a glint of sarcasm in his voice.

"Hey, look over there," Liam was pointing toward the distant end of the field. "It's a lodge or something. See it?"

"Yes, I see it! Come on, let's go over there." Sara and Liam fell in behind Billy's trot. "Last one there is a rotten egg!" They began to run toward the distant structure, all arriving at once.

Sara bent forward, leaning on her thighs. "I won," she gasped.

"If you say, so I think Liam beat us, Li beat us both."

"I say so!" she exclaimed.

"Then that's how it is – real or not." Billy laughed.

Liam was kicking over a large piece of flint with many fractures from where chips had been made to fashion tools. Cast about around the large stone were dozens of worked pieces in various stages of completion. Liam picked up a piece and studied it.

"Looks like the toolmaker sat right here and chipped out whatever they needed, arrowheads, spear points and oh my, look at this!" Liam lifted a beautifully worked stone knife from the grass.

"Wow!" Billy reached out to take it, but Liam pulled away.

"Let me look at it first, I found it."

Billy turned back and began to select pieces of flint from the heavy grass. "There are all kinds of stuff here!"

Liam was still turning the museum quality knife in his hands. He proffered it to Billy. "Here, take a look at this."

The three of them studied the intricate flaking and the feel of the stone knife.

"He had a soft touch, didn't he?"

"He could have been a woman," Sara rejoined.

"I don't think so, not very likely."

"But you don't know, Billy."

"No I don't, but neither do you."

"Come on, you two. What difference does it make?" Liam began more carefully to inspect the ground.

Sara now held the knife, studying it closely and turning it in her hands. "This is beautiful. Brown and gray and so carefully chipped."

"You can have it, Sara. Liam fingered a broken arrowhead in his hand. "There is lots more stuff here. You can have it. "

"No, Li, you found it."

"You can have it. Please. Keep it."

"Thank you." She put her arm around him and kissed him on the cheek. "It's a beautiful knife."

"Are we going to take a look inside this lodge or are we gonna stand out here all day?" Billy admonished.

Most of the roof of the lodge had fallen in but there was still enough to shelter them from the sun. One piece of the ceiling bark had collapsed into a dry spot under the standing roof. Sara took it by its crumbled edge to flop it over. She saw the movement too late as a large copperhead slithered to coil. As it raised its head to strike, Billy's boot flashed past her arm and crushed the snake's head under it.

"Jesus, Sara! Be careful!" Billy ground the head into the dirt, turning on his heel and then holding it down as it lashed around his leg. "Get away – it's a goddamn copperhead! He's got enough venom to kill us all!

Liam was frozen to the spot and Sara rushed to cling to him. Billy still had the writhing snake underneath the heel of his boot, continuing to crush it. Finally he stepped off. The large snake was dead.

"Jesus, Sara, he didn't get you, did he?"

Sara was still shaking, hugging close to Liam, as she studied the serpent.

Billy lifted the snake by its tail. "He's a four-footer. Biggest one I ever saw. He was so big he was slow."

In a tremulous voice Sara pleaded, "please, Billy, put him down."

"Put him down, Billy he's still twisting around."   Liam was supporting Sara, his arm around her waist.

"He's also dead!" He tossed the snake aside.

"I'm getting out of here." Sara rushed through the lodge opening into the meadow, and began to sob, catching deep breaths between the paroxysms that gripped her.

Liam came out and stood by her, and Billy watched from the lodge doorway.

"I wet my pants.   I have never been so scared!" She quavered. "Oh, Billy," she rushed to him and threw her arms around him. "Billy, I was so scared!"

Slowly he disentangled himself from her. "It's all right, Sara. It's all right. I was scared too."

The two boys joined together, locking Sara in their arms.

"It's all right, Sara," Liam whispered. "We all were scared."

"You saved my life, Billy." She burbled. "You saved my life."

"Come on, come on, it's all right. He didn't bite anybody."

Sara tried to kiss his lips, but he turned away.

"Come on, Sara, it's all right. Come on, let's go look around some more. There ought to be some good stuff here." Billy disappeared behind the lodge. A few moments later they started at his shout.

Sara was still frightened and Liam remained with her, his arm around her shoulder. "Hey come on over here. I found a whole bunch of pots; most of them are broke, but not all."

Slowly the pair moved toward Billy's voice. He had indeed found a collection of red clay pots, some with intricate designs.

"Oh boy, Ma might like to see some of these. Look at this one." Billy held a small squat jug that had an elaborate design pressed onto its outside. "This is really a fancy one. It's small but really fancy."

Sara studied the pot in fascination. Small aster-like flowers seemed to be pressed in careful symmetry. "Jeepers, this is a pretty pot." Liam watched, also enthralled by the design.

"It's a pretty one," he wiped some sweat from his eyes. "It must have been made for something very special."

"It is the most beautiful pot I've ever seen. We never found anything as nice as this pot before."

"Well, hand it back. You can't have it. This is mine and I'm gonna take it to Ma."

Sara handed back the artifact and cast her eyes about at the other broken shards and damaged jars.

"All the rest are broke," Liam noted.

"Maybe not, you look around some more. Hold this one for me, Li. I'm going to shinny up that big hemlock and see if I can tell where we are. We need to mark this place somehow."

"I thought you said all we have to do is go down the hill."

"Yeah, we do, but it would be better if we knew where we are going after that."   He handed Li the pot and swung up into the hemlock. The day warmed and they slowly made their way toward home.

Liam waited patiently at the open door to the office, hoping that the bespectacled woman would look up before he chose to disturb her. But Mary was engrossed in the ledger before her and refused to do so. Finally he knocked quietly on the molding of the door.

"Li, what are you up to?" She dropped the spectacles from her nose to her bosom.

"Hi, Aunt Mary, I brought you something."

"You did? Well, let's see it." She encircled his waist with her arm as he drew up beside the chair.

"It's a drawing I made this morning. It's not much, but..."

"Don't go there, young man! You know how much I like your drawings." She nodded to an image of a woodchuck carefully framed on the office wall. "What is it this time?"

"A pair of geese I saw this morning when I went down to see Ma." He handed her the sketch.

"Oh, Liam, these look so real. My god, boy, you have a talent! Maybe you ought to try to sell some of your sketches." She held the drawing at arm's length. "Liam, they look like they could take flight and sail off the page."

"You like it, huh?" He shifted his feet uneasily.

"Yes, thank you." She opened her arms and he leaned down to give and to get a peck on the cheek. "Thank you for the drawing." She put on her glasses again and reviewed it carefully, then set the drawing down. "I'll have Charlotte frame it. She was a painter, you know," Mary laughed, "among other things."

Liam smiled but said nothing.

"Is there something wrong, or something bothering you? You have a falling out with Sara? Fighting with your brother?"

"No, nothing like that, I've been waiting to ask you something. But..." he paused.

"But what, out with it, lad, I'm listening."

"Sara will be leaving for school soon, all the way to New York City."

Mary's demeanor changed slightly. She replied with a touch of reproach tinged with sadness. "You don't need to remind me of that. I will miss her so. We will all miss her so."

"Aunt Mary..." again he paused. "Mary..."

She frowned, and then smiled. "Cat got your tongue? What?"

"Aunt Mary, I want to go to college too."

"You mean you want to go with Sara to the city? I just sent a draft off to Hunter. You know it's a women's college."

"No, no, Mary. I want to study law like we talked about -a long time ago. Maybe I could become an apprentice first to see if I like it."

She glanced at the ledger books that filled one whole shelf of the large bookcase, "and I haven't forgotten, ---one day I'll turn all these books over to you." She paused. "You know I want you to study law. You are a very bright boy. You have already helped me a lot; you're a real wizard with numbers! Hell, if you had a law degree, there'd be no stopping you! The business would be booming. Your father wants you to stay here and run the Harden and Albright farms. I told him that would happen only 'if' you want it to. I'd like all three of you to see a little bit of the world beyond these farms before you get stuck in one place."

"I know, he told me that too. I could, but really don't want to be a farmer. I like doing the books, but what I'm really interested in is the law."

"Liam. I am delighted that you want to become a lawyer. Don't worry about your father.

I'll 'tend to that." She smiled and patted his hand.

"Mary, I hope they will admit me to a law school someplace. There is a one at Columbia University. I'd like to try there."

"Oh, it's in New York City." She smiled slyly. "Of course, that's where Sara is headed. Well, I know some people there. Also my attorney Haney ---he is a weasel, but he has made both of us a bundle of money." She paused a moment and rubbed at her eyebrows. "How would you like to work with Haney for a week or so to find out more about what it's like to practice of law? In the city I know Will Sutter's firm. I used the firm with Sol somebody, who helped me buy some property in Cuba. I forgot his name. Will himself defended your father in court. He was in the Army teaching at West Point when I recruited him. I have used the firm over the years."
"West Point, he must be a pretty important man."

"He's an expensive one. He was then, too." She laughed. "You know, your father got himself in a bit of a scrape. Not the usual kind – serious trouble."
"I know some of the story, Mary. That's when he met Ma and Uncle Woo."

"Well, they damned near hanged him. If it wasn't for Woo and me, I might add, he would have been killed. Will Sutter prevented the hang man, Woo and I prevented his murder."
"I'd like to meet him someday."

"I think you will. I will write Will a note and have Helen deliver it. She'll be going back to the city this week. A new shipment is in from France that I want her to check out, and I'll ask her to hand deliver the notes. I'll take you to the city myself and introduce you. If you like, perhaps we can work out an apprenticeship and you could attend Columbia as well."

"There's a lot of work coming up. Spring is on us and it's been wet. We have to start planting corn soon. We haven't been able to get the horses in to plow so we can't plant. We have to wait until the mud dries up, and we're supposed to go to Goshen, get us another bull and the corn planter has to be fixed this week and..."

"And that's why we hire help. Don't feel so responsible for everything. I admire that trait in you, but life is not all work. Take time to draw and bring me some more of your pictures. Your father and I are going to Goshen today."
Liam first smiled then laughed outright. "Aunt Mary, you need to follow your own advice."
A small frown passed quickly and she too chuckled.

"Well, Liam, if Haney and Will Sutter will take you on for a week or two, we will both take some time off. Ah, hell, we'll take Sara too. Make a holiday of it. I'd ask Billy, but I've been told he and his mother are making an eel rack, what ever the hell that is. I've been meaning to buy an apartment in the city in Manhattan so when we visit Sara we will have a place to stay. She might as well help pick it out. Sound good?"

"Oh yes, Mary – very good!" Some voices close outside the window drifted up to them. They could hear Pat shouting at someone in his best brogue. "What do you think about Pa?"

"He won't want to come with us either. He loves the farms, digging is his calling. God bless us, he's a simple and kind man, a blessing in this life! Don't you worry any though; he wants the best for you boys."

Liam could hear the sounds of his father's voice. "Sure you'll break your fool neck, Billy, doin' a handstand on a saddle–you ought to." The words were followed by a burst of laughter: "I told you so! Are you hurt?" Both Liam and Mary laughed at the inaudible invectives and mirth. Quiet again returned to the room.

"Riding practice, we should sell tickets," Mary laughed.

"Aunt Mary?"

"Yes."

"If I go to law school, it will cost a lot of money. I've saved a little bit."

"Oh, Liam," She dismissed his comments with a wave of her hand. "If you find out you like law, there will be money for your schooling. That is the least of your worries. You go ahead and apply to the school if you want - now. We don't have to wait on a reply from Will Sutter. I'll give you the note for Mr. Haney. You take it to him yourself, I'm sure that he will let you follow him around for a week or two, if he is not too scared you will find out he's stealing from me." She chuckled.

In the bright afternoon light, Sara was studying the man in the white coat walking beside her.

"Mary told me you want to be a doctor. That right?" He locked his eyes on hers. I can see why you might be. Do you remember your Ma being so sick, Sara? One of the reasons you want to be a doctor?"

"Yes, Doc, I do." She looked down from his gaze. "You know I do. I remember my Ma."

He glanced at her, and continued down the hallway. "Well, the medical schools aren't too keen on letting women in. It could change in time but not before you are ready."

"I know that, too. But Mary has…"

"So what do you want me to do?"

"I want to learn more about doctoring, not just helping deliver babies, more about disease and choosing drugs." They turned the corner that led to the small infirmary, the place with the most light in the Cloister.

"There are six patients in here, two of whom are very ill." He smiled, took a flask from his pocket and took a swig. "Both are likely to end up in boot hill."

Boot hill was the name given the small but growing cemetery on the knoll outside the clinic. Despite the jest about it each grave was marked and carefully kept by those patients able to do outside work.

Doc Wayland screwed the top of the flask back on and dropped it into his pocket. Inside the door three white coats were hanging; he unhooked one and proffered it to Sara.

She smiled and slipped it on and peered cautiously at the quiet beds spaced along the wall.

"These whores - women, I should say, get the best care they probably ever had. They also have the cemetery where with a name on their grave. The two most sick are dyin' of the pox.

"The pox," Sara peered toward the beds.

"Yeah, the pox – syphilis, some call it. It's the official name, I guess."

"Syphilis, I have never heard of that."

"Yes. They got it from their working lives. You know, sellin' themselves to anybody for a dollar or two."

"Mary's told me about that, prostitutes, right?"

"Yes, the world's oldest profession."

"Why the name Syphilis it sounds so peculiar?"

"The name comes from a poem something about a young swine herder. Fell in love with a lady that didn't want him. When he finally got her, he got the pox."
"The pox, that's another name?"

"Yes, the Great Pox, not to be confused with the smallpox that's been about of late. Then there's chicken pox, too. Remember when Mary called me in to see you?"
"I remember that. Liam had it; Billy had it, all the kids in school about."

"I don't know why they call it the chicken pox." He paused before approaching the beds. "Are you ready for to see your patient, doctor?"
"I guess so, yes."

"Okay, let's take a look at Maude Kindler. She's old now, but I'll bet she was a beauty. She's there in that first bed."

Sara looked toward the bed; the woman in it was lying on her side with the covers pulled up to her ears.

"Sara, she is in the last stages, not much I can do for her. I try to comfort her a little. She has lost her mind a bit --often thinks she's back in the trade. Talks with Jesus too, must have had some religion at some time." Gently he touched the woman's shoulder.
"Lo, Maude, we have a little angel of mercy with us today."

"Angel, Doc?" She smiled at him, her dull brown eyes staring up from beneath heavy black eyebrows. Her hair was gray, yet her face was still hauntingly beautiful.

"It's Mary's daughter, Sara. She's studying with me for awhile. She wants to be a doctor. I am showing her around."

"Mary's daughter," Maude struggled to right herself against the headboard. "Oh, yes. She must be an angel. Your name is Sara?"

"Yes, Sara."

"Will you see your mother when you leave here?"

"I'm afraid not. She won't be home until tomorrow. She and Pat just went to Goshen on business. But I'll see her tomorrow or the next day".
"Child, when you see her please thank her for me. Will you do that?"

"Yes." Sara shifted her feet and again looked into the beautiful faded face. "I will tell her."

"Maude, I want to take a look at you. We need to hike your nightgown up." He placed his hand on her forehead as she adjusted. No temp today, you feel cool to touch."

"I used to charge people to get a look." A wan smile creased her face. "That was a while ago. But my customers still come back; Saint Peter is one of them."

"Oh, I'd pay too, if I didn't have this job where I can get a free peek." The two laughed. Maude began to cough. "Oh you doctors" she began to cough again.
"Easy now, I didn't mean to get you all excited." He chuckled and she returned a smile.
"Where were you doctor before all this came on to me? I would like to have known ya."
"Don't know – probably doin' something I shouldn't. You know you're my favorite."
"Pshaw, Doc, you treat us all the same. We girls talk, you know."

"I can imagine. I might be too young for that conversation." He leaned forward to get a better view of her pubis as he folded back the cloth covering. "Come look here, Sara. This is tertiary syphilis. It's called a gumma."

Sara leaned forward and despite trying not to, involuntarily drew back. She thought at first she was going to faint, took a deep breath and looked again. In place of Maude's labia was a large sore with red edges and in the middle, a blister-like lesion full of cloudy fluid. The tissue was quite destroyed. Sara listened intently to Wayland's exchanges with the patients.

"Maude, when was it that you lost your ability to walk?"

"Oh, Doc, it's been two years. Sometimes I can still feel my legs. Sometimes I feel the..."

"You feel the evacuation when you urinate?"

"Yes, when I empty my bladder or bowels. But sometimes I can't. I so hate to make a mess, but there's nothing I can do. I call Angie and she helps."

"Angie's been good to you?"

"Most of the time, sometimes she's a little rough. I thank God I can still feed myself, poor Christine. She lapsed quiet and appeared confused. "Angie doesn't want any of my customers but Christine might."

He placed his hand on her wrist and took out his watch, studying the second hand. "We will see her next. I will ask her. What I am going to do is put a frame on the bed to hold the sheets up. And I want you to keep your nightie up around your waist. Let the air get to that sore. Can you do that?"

"Yes. You know I can do that. What about Saint Peter? What should I do?"

He began to withdraw from the bed. Maude caught his wrist.

"Tell him to be patient, Maude."

"I'm going to die soon, aren't I? You know, Doc, sometimes when I fall asleep I know. I don't think I'm going to wake. I have been trying to stay awake."

He gently unfastened her hand from his wrist. "No one knows when you will die. Keep your spirits up. I'll be by to see you tomorrow. We have to go now to see Christine and Angie."

"Jesus said he loved me."

"I'm sure he does, Maude. I'm sure he does. Sara, put your finger on her wrist right here. Now count the surges." A minute later he asked, "how many?"

"More than ninety, they were hard to count."

Slowly they started toward the second bed, when he stopped.

"You look a little peaked, girl. You sure you want to be a doctor?"

"I've never seen anything like that. Phew – I mean it was..."

"It was the trade off - grief or the poverty. That's why it's called a social disease. She has a very thready, weak pulse. Slower than yesterday and her heart is very irregular now. I don't think she has long. An irregular heart beat does not mean that much by itself, patients live for many years with arrhythmia but the combination with this illness usually means death is near."

"Oh." Sara passed her hand over her forehead and looked down at the floor, then back to the bed. Maude had closed her eyes. "She is going to die soon?"

"You will come to know the rhythm. That is, if you become a doctor. It's the eternal one – the one we learn first when we are in our mother's arms and it is also the last thing we learn."

"What do you mean rhythm?" Sara observed his face soften as he glanced toward Maude. "I call it holding on and letting go, the rhythm of life". They continued down the hallway.

Chapter 20

Minsi, New York
Summer 1882

Kavanaugh leaned back in the chair and watched the women working the two acre vegetable garden set out in orderly straight rows. The vegetables were used in the clinic and the household. Most of the women worked, naked to their waists, and their breasts bobbed along with the hoeing and cultivating in the mid-day sun. From the corner of his eye, he caught a glimpse of Evelyn approaching, drying her hands on her apron.

"What you doin' out here, Mr. Pat? She squinted toward the bare breasted women, then back to him.

"I am just enjoying the day," he smiled up at her, "enjoying the day!"

"You are enjoyin' the day alright! You out here watchin' them women hoe in the garden."

"Well, that too."

She fixed him with a scolding stare. "What Miz Mary think she know you out here?"

"I don't know. I suppose you could go ask here. She's the first one in the first row, down by the pole beans." He pointed towards the garden.

Evelyn looked toward the bean patch, and then shook her head in disapproval. "Look at dat. Lawd, she out there workin' like a field hand! What wrong with dat woman?"

"Well, you ought to know, you've been with her a long time, much longer than I have. She says she likes the sun."

"Sun don't like her none. She gonna get herself burned skin all wrinkled up, then you gonna listen her complain. She out there working, then they all go down to de pond and git in the water and no clothes on. She looked hard at Pat, "but I bet you know dat already."

"Ah, Evelyn, they probably like it, otherwise they wouldn't do it."

"Dat don't matter none. I first asked what you was doin' you watchin?"

"And I answered," he replied with conviction.

"You answered about the day, but I know you watchin' those tities swingin' around out dere. We had a master did dat, you should be ashamed!"

"Ah, I'm no master, Evelyn, besides it's you I love." He grinned and reached toward her.

She backed away. "Stop dat!" She feigned disgust. "I swear you ain't to be saved. Whatever happened to all dat prayin'? You done changed some!"

"It's all Mary's fault." He laughed at her disdain.

She feigned disgust again and rose from her lean on the railing. "Hmmm, I am goin' inside!" She walked toward the door with a smile Kavanaugh could not see. As she reached the threshold, she looked back at Pat, shook her ample rear, and disappeared inside.

Kavanaugh laughed quietly and reached for his pipe. He had just settled back to his review of the garden when there was a rustle behind him. Evelyn had returned with a mug of coffee and three large oatmeal cookies.

"You might-'s-well have all you wishes fixed. I baked this mornin' and de coffee's fresh too." Then she laughed out loud. "Mr. Pat you has changed alright."

"Ah Evelyn, you're the only one who hasn't."

They smiled at one another and once more she disappeared into the kitchen. He looked at the door, listened to her rattling around the stove, then looked away and slowly consumed the cookie. How fortunate they all were to have Evelyn's quiet love and loyalty. She was a confidant and supporter of Mary, and grand mothered the children with a kindness that never went dry. Thoughtfully he sipped at the cooling cup. He looked over the stable to the trees that lined the river, then caught Mary's eye and waved. He finished the coffee, knocked out his pipe, and stepped briskly down the porch steps. He'd not seen Sada in several days, and Sara told him this morning that Sada wasn't feeling well, so he decided to go check on her. Dropping one cookie into his pocket, he walked along munching on the other, as he made his way to the Wickiup in the woods.

Kavanaugh set aside the door skin and stepped into the smoky interior. Sada had been lying down and sat upright beneath her robes. A paroxysm of coughs rocked her. She smiled wanly at Pat.

"Kav-an-naw, why you come"? Again she began to cough.

"I came to take you to the house. Sara came to me and said that you were sick. And I can see that you are."

"Not sick;" she began to cough again.

"Not so, Sada, you're coughing. I don't want you to get pneumonia. I want you to come to the house. It's too cold in here."

Sada nodded to a small stash of wood near the door. Without a word, Kavanaugh carefully placed two sticks into the small stove and left the door open.

"No go house."

"Why not, for the love of God you're sick!"

"No go," she coughed, and then stretched her hand toward the fire flickering around the new fuel. "Big noise house two moons past."

Kavanaugh did not respond, but placed his hands in the warmth of the flames. He did not care to remind her or bring up the topic of the celebration activities at the house for fear of depressing her more.

She coughed quietly, engrossed in the fire.

"Sada, this is the coldest I can remember here at this time of year. We had frost last week and it's cold even now."

"House colder," she replied with a quiet cough.

"What can I do?" His voice trailing into frustration. "You must come. You are not well."

"Like you bring me tea," she replied and adjusted the robe.

"I'll bring you some tea, when you come to the house. Evelyn made oatmeal cookies with cinnamon and chocolate. I know you like those cookies. And it's warm in the kitchen." He waited for her to respond, but she did not. Gently he pressed his hands on to her outstretched ones. "I brought you a cookie."

"Sada, I love you. Do you know that? I always will."

"What such love you? You with Mary, I alone; need no man, want no man."

"But..."

"Only want you, Kav-an-naw only, for all time."

"If I had known where you were and about the boys I would have gone to you. I didn't know until after I had married Mary. I've told you time and again, I thought you had been killed with your brother."

She looked into his face and for an instant there was a bright flash in her eyes. Then she turned to the fire.

"Our time go when only you want be with me. I love boys. Lame Wolf is good hunter." She passed her hand in a waving motion over the fire. "Gray Wolf is good boy kind like you. I love Sara too,"

"Billy is a hunter all right." Kavanaugh moved closer to her and slipped under the robe. "It's cold here, Sada, you must come to the house." He encircled her thin body with his arm. "Did Billy tell you he wants to go west? He wants to go out to where you were born, see the country, hunt buffalo, pan gold, trap. What Liam wants to do now is to become a lawyer. He changes, but Billy has wanted to go west since I can remember."

"My heart there; it go with Lame Wolf." She began to cough, this time very hard. Kavanaugh drew her to him and absorbed the hacking deep throated sounds on his chest. After a few moments, she stopped and leaned away from him.

"Lame Wolf talks Cheyenne." She smiled. "He talks Cheyenne good." She touched between her breasts. "Sada teach." Her smile broadened. "Sada teach Lame Wolf good, Gray Wolf, ---Sara too."

Kavanaugh returned her smile. "Yes, Sada, you taught them all very well. They have learned so much from you."

She became very somber. "Long ride home. I no go with Lame Wolf." She watched the fire, settled closer to him. "You go house, Mary. Tell Sara bring tea."
"I am so very sorry, Sada," he gently hugged her.

"No sorry, Kav-an-naw." She straightened and slowly ran her hand through his thick hair." You good man. You come me when we no place go. Boys better here".

"The boys are your special gift. They are a great joy to me and to Mary." He straightened from her touch and brushed at a tear starting down his cheek. "And so are you Sada – a great gift and joy to me. Evelyn loves you all too."

"No sad, Kav-an-naw, we had time, long time pass. We had time." She placed a new splint on the fire, which popped with the heat and flared up orange. Evelyn good to me she kind to me."

"The fire feels good." He drew her closer and opened the robe to catch the new heat.

"Gray Wolf come me. Say he go away. Go to big city far away. Say he see Sara."

"Yes, he and Mary have planned a trip. Liam, Gray Wolf, wants to be a lawyer."

"What law-yur?" She regarded him curiously.

"Law...it's a white man thing. Treaties, land ownership..."

She looked at him blankly. "Gray Wolf wants make lies?"

Kavanaugh paused, realizing it was beyond an explanation. "Yes, that's about right."

Sada shrugged deeper into the robe and began to cough again. "No lawyur, better he stay here!"

Pat frowned at the sound of her cough and again drew her closer to him. "I think the real reason he wants to go to New York to study is because Sara will be there too. She wants to become a doctor."

"Sara comes me many times. She help get my," she gestured toward the dry flowers and

196

herbs, "my medicine."

He followed her gaze. "She has always wanted to be a doctor. The herbs are part of it."
Sada smiled and leaned on Kavanaugh's shoulder. "Sara is wife soon."
Kavanaugh gently slipped his hands beneath her breasts and cuddled her close.
"Time come, I go soon."

"No, Sada, you can't leave me. You can't leave the boys." He smiled at her and tightened his arm around. "What would they do without you?"
"Yes, Kav-an-naw, dream comes," she began to cough against his chest.
"I go land 'cross water. Soon owl calls Sada."

"Shush, don't say so, saying so may make it true." He leaned away and touched the end of her nose with his finger, smiling into her eyes. "So don't say so."
Sada smiled back and squeezed him with both her arms.

"What dream you, Kav-an-naw? You dream good? See old friends? You dream home?"

"Sometimes I dream of my home, Ireland, I mean. I wonder what has become of my old friends. Sometimes I dream of Kerry, but most of all, I think of my brother and sister, my nephews and nieces, grown now or nearly grown. I've never seen any of them. My father and mother are long gone".
"You dream of land, this land?"

"No, of Ireland, my home, where I came here from, it is across the ocean. I think of the green hills and small streams and trout fishing and a Guinness at the pub." A kind of fond recollection and reverie passed through him. "There is a beautiful vale in Kerry."
"What say?"
"A beautiful little valley, I remember the flowers there."

Sada rested quietly against him, and they both watched the fire sputtering yellow and orange flames.

"Yes, sometimes I dream of home. I think of horse races at Listowel, talking with my friends."

"Sada dream of land long time ago. I see brother, mother, Maha. You need go home, Kav-an-naw. Here house only. See sister. See brother."

"You're probably right." He kissed her lightly on the cheek and passed his hand over her slick black hair and down the braid. "For the last time, please come to the house."
Sada smiled and pulled away. "Sada no go house!"

It seemed to Liam they had been on the train all day. At Minsi the tracks were overrun by pickets bearing signs: "A dollar a day is not enough pay. Eight hours a day is enough."

Mary and Liam pushed through the crowd, entered the train, and adjusted the seat so they could sit face to face. Outside a great clamor of voices indicated that the strikers were being asked to leave the station platform. Three local policemen were trading voices with the organizers and when the shouting died down, the pickets sullenly left. The train lurched ahead; it was stifling hot inside the car.

"What a clatter out there! Open the window, please, Li. I'd rather face the grime than the heat." The train was gathering speed, rumbling through the busy rail yard. Liam adjusted the window and sat down. "Two dollars a day – that's a lot of money."

"Not really so much Li, although I can recall when a person was glad just to have a job, willing to work for nickels and dimes. There still are a lot of people who would just like to have a job." She folded the lace cuff back over the sleeve of her deep green dress, searched through her pocketbook and removed a folding mirror. After reviewing her face, she pushed back a lock of hair behind her ear and reset the pin.

"Do you think we should have brought Billy and Sarah, or Pa?" He crossed his legs and leaned back.

"No, Li. They all have work to do. They had their chance. Billy would not have come. Sarah's doing her work with Doc Wayland. And your father would rather dig, sow, cultivate, plow or whatever he's doing. Sara needs a break from the city."
"Do you know where Columbia University is?"

"Yes. It's quite a ways from Sarah's school," she laughed. "But there are streetcars. We will go out to Columbia; Will Sutter's office is out that way. The note Helen brought back was quite cordial and he wrote tomorrow would be an ideal day. He expects us at the Oyster House at one o'clock."

New York City

Li was fascinated by the city as they made their way across town. They had stayed at the Belmont in a large two bedroom suite with floor to ceiling windows heavily draped in a blue paisley print. It had a large ornate desk and two rich toned leather chairs. The room projected a solid, comfortable ambience. Mary ordered up an early morning breakfast, scrapple and eggs, coffee, fruit and toast. It was quarter past ten when they boarded the cross town trolley.

Liam bombarded Mary with questions about the people and places they passed. The sounds of foreign languages babbled about them and Liam tried to guess their origin.

"Gee Mary; this city is a big place, so many people, so many streets. Do you know where we are?"

"Of course, don't worry;" she laughed, "and I also know where we're going. We will change cars in about three stops or so. Then it's just a short ride."

"How did you get to know your way around so well?"

"I have business interests here. One of my dress shops is just down the street from where we will get off. I want to make a little surprise visit."

Li and Mary were caught up in the crowd that swept along the sidewalk and stopped before a shop window displaying blouses and scarves of bright hues and smartly tailored dresses of more conservative colors. The window had a small Gothic lettered sign in carmine red, Chez Marie. The shop was busy with patrons, and Mary began to review the swirl of scarves in a glass case before she became aware of Liam beside her.
"There you are, I thought you wandered off, maybe I should get a rope."
"I got caught up in the crowd. There are a lot of people shopping here."

"It looks like a good day." She returned her attention to the scarves and mused aloud, "I thought I would get something for Will's wife. A drab dresser, as I recall." She pointed to a burnt orange scarf made of silk. "What do you think of that one, Li.? Bright, don't you think?"

"Yes, but I don't know anything about..."

Their conversation was interrupted by a woman dressed in a royal blue blouse and ankle length navy skirt. Her shiny black hair was folded neatly back exposing high cheek bones and deep dark eyes.

"May I help you, madam?"

"Yes. What is your name?"

"Olga." She seemed pleased yet a bit embarrassed by the request.

"Olga, I like that orange scarf," she pointed to it. "French made?"

"Yes." She slid open the case and carefully lifted it out, allowing it to flow over her hands. "It's a French design, one hundred percent silk, and beautifully fashioned." She folded back the edge, exposing the stitching. "See how carefully it is done."

Mary slowly drew the scarf over her hand and carefully reviewed it. "I'll take it."

"Yes, madam, it is a bargain at two dollars."

"You'll box and wrap it, please?"

"Of course, would you like a card?"

"Yes, thank you. There is a slate gray dress in the window, with the white lace and piping."

"Yes, I know the dress."

"Do you have it in my size?"

"That would be an eight?"

Mary smiled. "I am much more comfortable in a ten."

"Hello, Mary" came a soft, good natured voice.

"Hi, Vivian," she replied jovially.

"You old fox! You sneaked in on me." She laughed quietly and opened her arms. They embraced and traded kisses on the cheeks.

"This is my stepson, Liam Kavanaugh."

"I am pleased to meet you, Liam."

Vivian turned to Olga, who was placing the scarf in the tissue paper of a monogrammed box. "Olga, I'd like you to meet Mary."

"Are you Mary Cleary, Mrs. Kavanaugh?" She asked in awe.

"Yes, I am all of those."

"This is Olga Fedderoff, Mary. She's just joined us three weeks ago."

"She is a Russian, from way up north in that country." She smiled at Olga.

"You are Russian?" Mary stepped aside to allow passage of some shoppers. "My, my I didn't realize they had such pretty girls over there."

"Yes, Mrs. Kavanaugh," she politely replied. "I am from Siberia."

"Siberia, my oh my, you are a very long way from home. Call me Mary, give her a raise Vi, she's good." She glanced toward Liam. "Olga, I want you to take Liam back to foundations. He needs a lesson in women's underwear. Most men do. Would you take him back there and explain some things? We will get back to the gray dress when I have finished speaking with Vivian."

Vi laughed and locked arms with Mary, and if Olga had been shocked by the request, she didn't show it. She led the red faced Li away without a word from either.

"That will keep him busy for awhile." She and Vi chuckled again." Let's go talk some business."

"I swear, Mary. You change but you're also the same."

The two old acquaintances moved into the back office where Vi put a teapot on her small gas burner. Mary peered out through the floor window and smiled as she spotted Olga holding a brassiere as Liam looked on curiously.

The lunch crowd at the Oyster House had thinned out by the time Mary and Liam pushed through the door into the plush interior. Mary glanced around quickly but did not see Will Sutter anywhere in the dining room. She checked her watch; it was five minutes to two. The maitre de' guided them to a small couch in the lounge. An oil painting of tall ships exchanging broadsides dominated the decor. The two talked about the detail the artist portrayed, then stirred to the sound of approaching feet.

A man with striking hawk-like features and thinning hair burst upon them.

"Hello, Mary!" He opened his arms and gave her a tight hug. "How are you?" He released her, stepped back and looked at her from head to foot.

"How do you do it, Mary? You haven't aged a day. How is Pat?"

"He is fine and shares the same blather! No wonder you win the juries. You're looking quite well yourself." She reached out to Liam. "This is Pat's boy, Liam."

"Hello, Liam." Sutter exchanged a firm handshake and smiled. "So, you want to be a lawyer, maybe?"

"Yes, sir, I'd like to know more about what lawyers do."

Sutter laughed. "You mean outside of settling estates collecting outrageous fees?"

"Yes, I want to know about juries and courts and judges and fees too."

Will looked at Mary with a grin that sparked his eyes. "I'm sure you had something to do with rearing this lad. Come on; let's go inside and get something to eat before we get started talking about this practice called law," he smiled at Liam." It might take a long time. I have a table reserved."

The cuisine was excellent, oysters on the half shell, red clam chowder, a salad of greens and tomatoes and each to their choice of fish sautéed to a fine touch. As the three mulled over their coffees, Liam reached into his pocket and withdrew a carefully folded page.

"I wrote down some of my questions, Mr. Sutter."

The two adults caught one another's eyes. Sutter winked and sat back in his chair. There were eight questions ranging from training to setting up a practice, and two hours passed in what seemed a flash before Liam finally folded the paper and slipped it back into his pocket.

"Thank you, Mr. Sutter. That's pretty much all the questions I could think of."

"Well, you did a good job, young man; your questioning skills will surely do you well in this line of work. Mary, what are your plans? When you wrote, you alluded to the possibility of Liam maybe staying for a while, and he is surely welcome to do so."

"I don't want to be too much of a bother, but I was hoping you have some accommodations where I won't have to worry about him."

"Nonsense, no bother, he can stay with us. We have a suite right adjacent to the office, and my wife said she would be glad for the company. We don't have any children, you know. We can show him a little bit of the city."

"That is very thoughtful Will, and I appreciate the offer. Would you like that, Li?

Liam smiled. "Yes, I think I'd like that a lot."

"It's done then. I have some business that could keep me busy a few days." She paused. "I also have a little trouble; I'd like to talk to you about, Will."

"That's not particularly new," he laughed. "How can I help you? You need some legal advice?"

"Not yet time to break out the checkbook." She smiled and became serious. "You know about the business. I'm much decentralized, as you would call it. My dress shops are doing well and I've sold out most of my other holdings, all but a few. I've been expanding a different direction."

"Oh?" He sipped at his coffee. "What might that be?"

"Well, I'm into gambling, a very profitable enterprise. It seems people are dying to throw their money away."

"Yes, and it also can be BIG trouble. You realize that I can't advise you to anything illegal."

"I have three parlors here in the city; a couple in the DC area, one in Atlantic City and you know I bought a large place in Havana, Cuba."

"Yes I remember Ryan and Sol handled that. So where's the trouble?"

"Here in the city --right here. What do you know about these Italians? Men with Italian names, Tony, Franco, Luigi – Italian sounding – stopped by my biggest place."

"So what's in a name?"

"They, three men with those names, came into the Fourth Avenue parlor, wrecked the place, and roughed up some customers. Told McDunn to pay up or they will blow the place up." She sipped her coffee. "And I've been reading some things about gangs – organized ones, Italians, explosions."

"Probably Mafia, Mary; they are not to fool around with. Their mode of operation is terror, and if I were the DA or someone in the Tammany Hall crowd, I'd get serious about it getting rid of them. Many call them 'the mob'."

"There was a man that used to work for me; do you remember Giuseppe, Liam?"

"I remember him. He was Pa's friend; I was really little, but I do remember he used to carve things from wood. I still have them."

"Well, anyway, I heard he is in this 'mob.' I would like to get word to him."

"What's his last name?"

"Innella, at least that's what he said it was, Giuseppe Innella."

"I don't know how you manage to find these friends, Mary, but Giuseppe Innella around here is known as 'Geep the Bomb'! And he is very high –at least in the local Mafia. His cousin is the big shot. I know this mob --they are without ANY scruples."

"Then you do know him?"

"Barely, I've dealt with some of his boys. I got three of them off two months ago. They had them but they processed them improperly. One paddy whacker, called a policeman, beat a confession out of one. We don't torture people in this country. At least the civilized half – we're not supposed to anyway."

"Could you get a message to him? Between the cops and the whops, I'm being bled dry maybe your brother."

Sutter smiled. "My brother works over in England now. But yes, Mary, I'll try to get in touch with him. Now, about this young man," he smiled toward Liam. "I'm in court day after tomorrow; two of my best people are working it. Liam can sit in on the prep and come to the trial if he'd like to do that. I'll probably attend myself, if I'm able. What do you say, Liam?"

Liam's smile lightened the somber discussion. "Oh yes, Mr. Sutter. I would really like to do that.""Good, call me Will and we'll call it a deal."

Minsi

The evening was closing about the forest and meadows in a light gray caress. Kavy was balanced in his favorite chair, leaned back against the wall. He was tired from cultivating corn all day, riding the metal cultivator seat that swayed and bounced and had left a diffuse but deep impression on his ass. He shifted to his side, balancing the glass of John Power's whiskey, trying not to spill it as he let the chair down from the wall. He had just settled in when the voice startled him and the whiskey went over the rim.
"Hi, Pa."
"Damn, Billy! You need to make more noise! You are worse than Decker at giving me a start. How long have you been there?"
"I just came in, Pa."

"Well, you spilt me whiskey," he broke into a big grin. "It was a tad full anyway. Sit down," he gestured toward a high backed chair he was prone to prop his feet on. "What brings you, boy? Did you and Joe finish those lower five acres today?"

"Hell, Pa, we finished that this morning."

"Where you been then?"

"I was down to see Ma. She was cookin' a muskrat, for Christ sake!"

"Billy, watch your mouth!" Kavy's retort was sharp, not only in response to the curse but also tinged with a little guilt. Sada lived on her own terms. He took a sip of whiskey, his reprimand passed. "I'm happy you go to see her. How is she?"

"Why aren't you telling me instead of asking me, Pa? She's still coughing - hard; she asked about you. We had a Cheyenne session, she said I'm doin' good. Did you know that she speaks Sioux as well?"

"If I recall correctly, she speaks Delaware too" Kavy sipped at his whiskey. "You want a taste?" He offered Billy the glass, and he took a sip and made a wry face.
"Jeepers, Pa! How the hell can you drink this stuff? It makes my eyes water."

"You're too young to appreciate it, and easy on the swearing." He took a swallow and brushed wiped his lips. "I've been too busy of late. I'm neglecting things I shouldn't. So what did your mother say?"

"Oh, she told me about living on the plains, her brother and Running Bull and Maha. Good stories, I've heard some of them before, but they are all so interesting. She said you knew them all. You were at the raid on Fort Wallace and at Agate Creek, you were tortured by the women of her village, you saved her and Maha and you know Running Bull well. How come you never talk about them? You have never said a word about it." He looked westward over the hills. "I want to go out there, Pa."

"Hold the whiskey, boy. I need to get mixings for my pipe." He handed the glass; Billy took another sip and waited for his father to pack and stoke his pipe.

"Your mother is a very special woman, Billy. I just think that most of my Army time is best forgotten. I don't like to recall it. Gettysburg and all that killing, I don't want to remember that time either. Your mother saved my life too. Did she tell you that?"

"And you saved hers, and Mary saved you both." Billy leaned back and tilted his chair to the porch rail. He watched his father puff a cloud of blue, still visible in the growing dark. "Pa."

"What?" Kavy picked a piece of tobacco from his tongue. "What?"

"I really want to go out west." He passed back the whiskey glass.

"West, do you mean to the plains, Indian country – that west?"

"Yes, Pa, I want to go."

"What on earth for, Billy? You have a great life here, all the advantages. You have land that you can work, farms are all set up. You have things to look forward to. Why west? I've been there and believe me, it is a hard place to live. Ask Decker if you don't believe me. Weather is fierce sucking heat in summer blinding blizzards and below zero in winter, all kinds of dangerous critters, hostiles, thieves, murderers, miles between water you can drink it's all out there. You find bones of people that no one knows who they are or where they came from and families still wondering about them."

"I appreciate all that you and Mary have done for me, Pa, really I do, but it's dull to me, Pa. I want to do something different: pan for gold maybe, or hunt buffalo and grizzly bears - you know. See some country; see it before too many people move out there. I want to see the Rocky Mountains. I want to see the Pacific Ocean. I'm not a farmer, hell it's dull! I want to find my roots; you know what I mean, Pa?"

Kavy sipped at his whiskey but did not reply.

"You know what I mean, Pa? You left Ireland for America."

"Why I left Ireland was for altogether different reasons. We rarely had enough to eat, the English were killing us, and thousands were starving. The roadside was littered with dead bodies," he gritted his teeth and fingered the rosary around his neck, "and I had to leave."
"I know."

"Well, what you may not know, Billy, is that all the work, the time, the money and the hope of Mary and me, this is all for you two boys and Sara. Like I said, I've been out west and it's still very dangerous! You think there is something great about Indian life, and the Cheyenne, but I can tell you it is not as wonderful as your mother remembers. We have very good land here, lots of opportunity."

"I appreciate that, Pa, but I want to see what's out there, what's beyond the hill I haven't seen yet. You know?"

"Could it be you're talking to Decker or your mother too much? Has she said something about going back?"

"Come on, Pa. She won't leave here. She's real sick." He paused, wiped at his eyes and looked toward the river, his voice trembled slightly, "she isn't going to last much longer. I know

203

it and it makes me sad."

"You're here and, Liam, she wants you to be here. That's why she's here to begin with. I haven't been down for a couple of days. Maybe I'll go there tomorrow, and have a talk with her."

"Well, me goin' west is not her idea – it's mine. If I don't go soon it will all be gone."

"It's not going anywhere, Billy and you have lots of time. It is still not safe out there. There are still killings and Indian raids a lot on miners these days. You can't take everything away from people and expect they'll not try to get it back. I can't blame the Indians altogether there is always lots of fear and hate to go around. Running Bull is probably still fighting – if he's alive." Kavanaugh sucked his pipe, exhaled and sipped at the whiskey.

A whippoorwill could be heard whistling in the night. They sat quietly listening to the sounds in the bonding evening.

"There's something else, Pa."

"Oh? What is that?"

"It's Sara."

"Sara? What on earth..." Pat sat the chair down with a thump.

"You know Li and her..." He stopped, afraid he had misspoken.

"Liam and her what, Billy is there something I should know that I don't know?"

Billy looked first at the floor, then into the distant woods.

"Billy, you raised something –now explain yourself about your sister."

"That's it, Pa. That's the way I see her –as my sister, even though she's not."

"She's close enough." He replied in agitation.

"Anyway, I feel trouble comin'."

"Trouble, what kind of trouble are you talking about?"

"Sara said the other day she loved me and wants me to marry her."

"Marry her? Why, she's just a sprite. She's what –how old?"

"Pa, she is seventeen. Hell, half the girls in the county her age are already married and some of them have a couple of kids. I told her, Pa. I don't want to get married and I don't want to marry her in particular."

"That was wise –honesty usually is best." He drew on his pipe and the smoke wreathed his head.

"That isn't all, Pa. You see, Liam loves her. He told me so. But she doesn't want to marry him."

The sounds of the night became more apparent and the sound of Evelyn rattling through her cooking pots drifted through the window.

"So you think if you go away it will all be resolved. You're going to ride off and then Sara and your brother are going to work things out."

"Not right away, but Pa, that's not all of it. I really do want to go out west. To hunt, see things, go to where you were. See Ma's people, what's left of them. Maybe live with them awhile, and then maybe I'll come back."

"That's all fine and good but they may not want you and just remember what will happen here if you don't come back. This home will never recover, and I told you all Cheyenne are not the same. Very, very few are like your mother. Most want to kill the white men like many white men want to kill them. I think it's a dumb idea, Billy."

"But, you wouldn't try to stop me from going?"

"I AM trying to stop you from going! I can't stop you from what you're set on doing, Billy. Tell me, when would you plan to go and how long do you plan to be gone?"

"I haven't decided when, --soon, I guess, but I don't know how long I'll be gone."

"Billy, you know that Sara wants to go to medical school when she finishes at Hunter College."

"And Liam wants to be a lawyer and he will be going to school."

"Things could easily straighten out when they're at school. You're good with growing things – workin' the land; you have the touch for it."

"Well, Pa, I don't want to go to go to college. I've had enough trouble in school already. Hell, Pa, I don't want to be anything, I just want to be myself." Billy rose from the chair and patted his father's shoulder. "You know what I mean? I'll see you in the morning."

Kavanaugh drained his glass, set it on the porch deck and leaned back in his chair. As he drew his pipe it made a faint gurgling sound. He released a sigh and looked to where Billy had disappeared. In the restless boy, he saw himself.

Billy approached the screened door quietly and carefully. He knew that Evelyn had started huckleberry pies earlier that morning and set them on the kitchen window sill to cool. The aroma had assailed him all morning for he had drawn the worst detail, he thought, the worst waste of his time and energies. Mary had directed him to plant flower bulbs in the large rock garden that stretched from the front of the house around the side and ended at the kitchen door. He slowly pushed the kitchen door open. His timing was perfect. Evelyn had gone into the house to supervise some of the women in preparing for the suffragette meeting that evening. He placed one hand on the side of the pie plate, the other underneath, when the voice behind him startled him.

"What are you doin', Billy Kavanaugh?"

He lost his grip and the pie slid dangerously toward going out the window. He deftly caught it and rearranged it beside the other two.

"What you doin' here," Evelyn repeated sternly regarding him with her hands on her hips.

"I just came by to see you." He smiled and walked toward her, putting his arms around her broad back and squeezing into her ample breasts. She hugged him back

"Now Billy, what are you doin' here?"

"Ah, Evelyn, the smell of those pies has been driving me crazy! Do you know what I've been doing all morning –planting flowers, for God's sake!"

She shook her head. "You be careful about whose sake you say you work for. And sass' Miz Mary is a good way for you to get lots of jobs you don't like."

"Can I have a piece of pie?"

"No."

"Ah, Evelyn, why not?"

"Them pies are too hot to cut and made for tonight, --Miz Mary's meeting."

"What's that all about? I hear you even go. Why do you want to vote anyway?"

"Yes, I go. I want to learn about voting'."

"Well, I don't vote."

"You is a boy now, but when you get older, you can. I cain't and Miz Mary cain't and we should." Evelyn twisted her hands through her apron.

"No pie, huh, would you reconsider if I went cat fishing tonight and brought you a mess - cleaned?"

"No, but I do have a couple of turnovers. There lots of berries, thanks to your mother and Sara, and a few of the girls. Nothin' to do wid you though, you was asked to help, I shouldn't give you anything."

Evelyn busied herself at the oven, opening and closing it, bringing out two very full turnovers. They were still warm.

"You want some milk?"

"No, I want some coffee."

"Coffee, you askin' like you thinks you a man and you just a sprite."

Evelyn brought a cup from the stove and sat down across from Billy. Billy took a generous bite of the juicy turnover. He asked, "my ma comes up here sometimes, to talk to you doesn't she?"

"Yes, she sit right where you at. She is a good woman."

He took another bite. "She helps you in the kitchen?"

"No, but sometime she brings me medicine, --mostly we talk."

Billy put down the pastry, licked his fingers and began to drain the coffee cup.

"That ought to be good, Ma and you talkin'. She barely speaks English and doesn't talk to nobody."

"Sometimes it don't take many words. Your mama and me, we git lots of feelin's out together."

"I wish I could take her back west. Does she talk about the west – going back?"

Evelyn became very solemn and looked out the kitchen door. "Your mama's not well, Billy. She can't make a trip out west."

"I know --I wish Pa would take her anyway."

"Your Pa has Miz Mary, and he ain't likely to go nowhere without her."

Billy sipped at his coffee. "I reckon you and Ma have something in common. You're both a long way from home." Billy smiled at the large lady across from him. She did not appear to be in a hurry to go back to work, nor was he anxious to return to the flower bed detail.

"Evelyn, what was it like where you lived?"

"Why, I lived in Washington wif Miz Mary. It's a big city."

"No, before that, before you met Mary.

"Oh, I live on a big tobacco farm, me and my family."

"You were slaves, right?"

"Yes. We had a master who owned us. I don't know where I been born. Nobody ever tell me. I worked for Master Stratton until I was sixteen, then I run away. Mr. Stratton a big man in tobacco politics. His father was good friend to Mr. Jefferson –Mr. President Jefferson."

"What was it like when you were a little girl, before you ran away?"

It was a big farm and de house was in a big bunch of trees. Dere was a big tree in the front yard and de master he made a swing on it. Tied up some rope and us chillun could go swing on it –we chillun all like dat swing. It had a seat but it was loose." She grinned. "I remember one day, Bobby Stratton was pushing me higher and higher, and that seat was loose; when he stop me, I fell right off, skirt up over me and Billy Stratton lookin' right down betwixt my legs. Lord, what a fall!"

Billy laughed with her.

"I never been so embarrassed before or since."

"Do you remember the war?"

"Of course I do. I remember your father in blue and Mr. Donal and all those folks."

"Was Mr. Stratton a confederate?"

"Oh yes, dat he was. I remember when the Yankees came. Young Mr.Chase Stratton come ridin' up yellin' about Yankees, there's goin to be a big fight. Master starts rapping with his cane and hollered git some food and blankets on de wagon right now. Just about then we see a lot of men comin' on the road; dey all dressed in butternut and brown. They was draggin' some big guns on wheels."

"Artillery —cannons."

"My, we all scared, we women just leave things right where it is, 'cept we put out da fire and grab up all de pots and pans. Some women run to get de mules and wagons," she paused, and then continued with great excitement in her voice. "I run right with 'em, start gettin' meat and corn out of de place we hid it to keep the scouts from finding. We all got ready to travel and young Chase all the time hollerin' ey-yah, e-yah. We was all scared. Lawdy, we was scared! We lit out..." Evelyn paused, her lips tightened and she shook her head, "down de road we go wit dem wagons, lickety split!"

"Well, what happened then?"

"We hear fightin' long about where the hedge was, right twixt the neighbor's place and Master Stratton's. Dem guns sound like horses runnin' over a plank bridge, smoke raisin' in de trees. Men on de road start runnin' ahead farther up de road. Horses was rearin', men shoutin' and all dem guns, --bang, bang, boom, boom." She lifted and spread her arms. "All dat noise, it starts to rain. Thunder comes more noise and more soldiers come. We cain't get out the road so we just strike out across de field to where de river make a big bend." She circled her arms. "Dat river got a place called River Cliff, we get in a big cave, and spend a whole day and night in it; we hear battle goin' on."

"The battle went on all night?"

"No, not all night long 'bout dark the Southern men folk pass to get away. Dey come up, ridin' by where we is and make no difference how much the head man yell at dem, he cain't make a slow up." She wiped at her forehead, the recollection still rousing her fear. "Lord mine, we was scared!"

"The Confederates were on the run?"

"Dat's right. Some of them jump in de river and swum across. After while here come de Yankee soldiers goin' back toward where the fight was. Pretty soon we see smoke back to de Stratton place."

"The Yankees burned your home?"

We thought sure they did, but when we git back dey ain't hurt nothin' much. Hogs was in pens and chickens come round. Dey burnt down de wagon shed wid three wagons in it. More Yankees come. De road was so crowded wid wagons and big guns and soldiers tramp up mud so bad, wagons stuck all de time. We find new graves not far from de house."

"They must have been Confederates who were killed."

"Yes dey was four soldiers." She paused and looked blankly over Billy's shoulder at the window. "Found out my brother Mark and his friend Simon lit out and went north. I waited two days, then my sister Arlene, Jane, my friend, and Martha, Simon's sister and Miz Cady, we all set out. My mother stayed behind."

"Stayed with Master Stratton? Why?"

"She don't know no other. We young, if my mother not dead, she still dere."

"You went to Washington, then…"

"All us girls got dere. Master Stratton, he had a slave catcher go after us. They took Miz Cady, Jane, and Martha back. Arlene, she find a job lookin' after chillun of Senator Fischer. I got kitchen work –I just a gir,l but was big even then," she smiled, "and knew my way around de kitchen."

"Slave catchers scare you? Were you afraid of being caught?"

"No, send no catcher for me. I guess Master giv up on me. He try me out with Simon's father five times, but I didn't take."

"Tried you out? What do you mean?"

"Try me out for babies, but I didn't take. I s'pose he figgered I wasn't worth much."

Billy sipped at the dregs of his coffee. "Well, Evelyn, the master sure would have taken you if he had known how well you cooked."

"No one want a big barren nigger woman." She mused for a moment. No catchers come for Arlene."

"Maybe your momma had something to do with it."

"Yes, maybe momma worked hard enough for de both of us."

It became quiet in the kitchen and Evelyn started to get up. Billy watched her rise but made no move to go. He caught her eye.

"Evelyn, I want to thank you for being so kind to my mother."

"Why, child, why wouldn't I be? Now you got a turnover and some coffee. Both is gone, you best hustle and git dose day lilies planted 'fore dinner. Or did you forget?"

"Naw, I didn't forget, and I won't forget your story either."

"Get on out of here now. I got work to do."

As she started to the stove, Billy caught her up in his arms, gave her a bear hug and kissed her on the cheek.

"Evelyn, you're the best friend this family ever had." He held her close, and released her with a big smile. He noticed her eyes were wet, but she neatly camouflaged it and turned away.

"Now, you git out of here Billy Kavanaugh, and git to work!"

"Yes, Miss Evelyn." He mocked.

He plunged out through the screen door, stopped and looked over his shoulder. Evelyn was dabbing at her eyes as she approached the glowing stove in the corner.

"If there is a God," he said quietly to himself, "he has blessed her and if there is a heaven, she will go there."

He walked down the steps, gathered up his shovel and the five gallon pail containing the day lilies. He sighted back over the planting, took a measured step and began an Irish tune. "Goodbye, Mershin Dwerkin, I am sick and tired of workin'; instead of digging praties I'll be digging lumps of gold."

Pat and Mary were alone together in the living room. Mary enthroned in a large leather chair while Pat paced before the fireplace.

"What are we going to do, Mary?"

"What do you mean 'we?' Do you have a mouse in your pocket?"

"He's pretty upset." Kavanaugh shook his head. "Just like a Dublin man."

"Dublin man or no, did you talk to Billy?"

"Not yet."

"Why not, when did you expect to do that?" She sat back in the black leather chair and began to file her fingernails.

"I ought to take him down in the stable and beat the bejeezus out of him."

"You do that and you'll lose a boy who loves you. So get that out of your mind, don't even think about it!"

"What do you think I should do?"

"Pat, he's a young man. Some his age are already married –the McCabe boy, for one."

"McCabes are shanty Irish, I'd expect that."

"And you I assume you think you're lace curtain Irish? A man who does little more than works the fields and who has a son who just got the neighbor girl pregnant?" The retort was sharp.

Kavanaugh did not respond but dug around in his pocket for his pipe and tobacco.

"I'll just beat the bloody hell out of him."

"Pat, Billy is a young man sowing wild oats. The Carey girl had a part in it."

"Sowing' wild oats all right –now he'll have a bitter harvest!"

"Where the hell do you get on being above it all? You didn't have a girl back in Ireland? Sit down and quit pacing. You're making me nervous."

"No, I didn't, Sada was the first woman and you are the second."

She waved off his remark. "You just yanked your wire and fantasized you were fucking the Virgin Mary."

A flash of anger passed to his eyes. He looked hard at her. "Mary Cleary THAT is no way to talk!"

"In thought or deed it is the same sin, whatever, but you had better talk to Billy. This is not the first time. Will you please sit down?"

"What do you mean?" He replied settling into a chair.

"I mean he was what the polite term is? He was 'consorting' with Doris, that cute Cajun girl who came here to have her baby. Do you remember her?"

"I do so."

"Wayland caught them at it in one of the patient examining rooms." She laughed, "and he was doing more than examining."

"Why didn't you tell me?"

"Precisely because of the way you are reacting now. I sent Doris on. She would like to have stayed."

He ran his hand over his hair. "What will I do? "

"Well, I'd talk to Billy, tell him that you know. Tell him you don't like it much. Then talk to Carey."

"I just didn't expect it."

"It's not the end of the world, Kavanaugh. We had what..." She contemplated briefly,

209

counting with her fingers. "We had fourteen young girls over the past year or so who got involved, got pregnant and no place to go. Most went back to their families after it was all over. Some went another way."

"It surprised me when Carey told me. " It made me mad as hell."

"Let's find out what pound of flesh Sean Carey wants for this. Does he want Billy to marry her?"

"He didn't say. I supposed that's what he expects."

"Tell him to expect something else. We can't have Billy's life put in limbo because one or the other can't count the days in a month."

"Billy wouldn't know. This might help to get those foolish thoughts about going west out of his head. Maybe it would be best if we did make him marry her."

"And it might just do the opposite. Billy made a mistake this time he hurt somebody else. A stiff cock has no conscience, but she should have. I would expect Celia Carey to teach her kids that much. She obviously knows, she has only two kids."

"Mary, Mary." He cajoled, shaking his head. "Such talk."

Mary did not reply but became engrossed with her nail file. After a few minutes she quietly noted, "I was worried a bit about Sara and Billy, Pat."

"What?" He flashed. "If he's been messing with her, I'll skin him alive."

"You will do nothing of the sort. It passed, anyway."

"What do you mean? What passed?"

"Sara loved him, loves him still, but not with the same intensity. Billy never responded – he'd rather hunt, fish and otherwise trespass."

Pat snorted, "Even on the neighbor's daughter!" They both began to chuckle.

"Billy wouldn't have anything to do with Sara, but I am quite certain Sara was ready to do something with him. I know she was thinking something. Of course I discouraged her."

"Sara? Our Sara Kavanaugh," he continued agitation showing in his voice. "And how do you know this?"

"Mothers and daughters talk, you know."

"I don't even want to know." He vigorously cleaned, then repacked his pipe. "Don't even want to know about those conversations."

Mary smiled. "She was mighty interested in his under parts. She was quite intense about it, but she got over it. She's a little more interested in Liam now."

"In Liam, she is interested in Liam?"

"It's a bit safer, I believe. Liam's been in love with her since just after he learned to talk."

Kavanaugh laughed. "I think I recognized that. But it was always Billy, Billy, and Billy with Sara."

"I know. Liam worries that she won't come back. Go off to medical school and forget all about what's here. Forget him, find someone else you know?"

Mary tightened her lips in a kind of wondering frown. "Isn't it always the way with love and romance? The woman is in love with some man, and the man in love with someone else - on and on, even among brothers and sisters. It has to be an ancient truth. Sara in love with Billy, Liam in love with Sara, all washed over in wet pants and erections."

"Mary, I don't want to hear it."

Mary smiled in satisfaction at his consternation. "About Carey, I'd offer to take the daughter over here. Tell him she will be well chaperoned. Summer is here, everyone knows we're hiring and we will just keep her on 'til after the baby. No one will be the wiser except, hopefully, Billy and Susan. It's Susan, right? The dark haired one built like a Guernsey?"

"Yes, the big girl."

"Tell Carey Susan can stay on and work here. We will pay her a wage and Wayland will take care of the delivery and setting up the adoption. Or Carey can forgive the girl and take his grandchild. Usually that's the course of events. Right now he's angry at Susan, Billy and the world. It will pass."

The sound of squabbling ducks could be heard from the spring lake. Mary continued working her nails. Kavanaugh knocked the glow from his pipe into an ashtray and for a moment watched the smoke rise in a long spiral toward the ceiling. He got up from his chair and moved to the hassock in front of Mary, his back to her, looking toward the sounds of the ducks coming through the window.

She laid down her file and rubbed his head gently, tossing his hair.

"You're getting gray as a bat, Kavanaugh. Maybe we should dye your hair. A red rinse maybe?"

"I don't think so, Mary."

"Does wonders for me."

"Ah Mary, you are the wonder. I think of you and the good life you have provided me." He turned to face her. "I love you, Mary."

"Well, that's a good thing!" She offered to lighten the conversation.

"All the things you have done for me."

"Come on, Pat, don't get morose on me."

"I'm not. I'm just thankful."

Silence gathered from the corners of the room. Far away the ducks began again.

"Pat, what have you done for me? You saved me from a barren world; no man would want me now. Those two boys and Sara are the light of my life. And you – you big Mick, are the sun! Boys will be boys – unfortunately girls will get the worst of it."

He stood up suddenly and swung her into his arms like a child would lift a bird.

"Put me down, for God's sake, Kavanaugh, before you break both our backs!"

"I will, on the guest room bed."

She laughed and kissed his face. "Getting spontaneous in your old age? All right, bring me to it."

He dropped her onto the bed, pushed up her skirt and pulled down her drawers as she fumbled at his fly. With one great thrust, he was in her.

Down at the pond the ducks were still squabbling.

Part III

**To Each His Own
1883-1914**

Chapter 21

New York City
February 1883

The cab drew to a halt before the Twelfth Avenue address. Mary braced against the February wind driving a fine dust of snow. She reviewed the note Sutter had given her, carefully refolded it, and placed it in her purse. The storefront was very plain block lettering across the window spelling out Ristorante Italiano, in the lower left corner: Peter Caioffa, Proprietor, Established 1879. She paid the cabbie and tipped him handsomely. He doffed his hat, smiled, and leaned to listen as she started talking.

"Driver, pull down the block a little way and wait for me, I'll not be very long."

He reviewed the bill in his hand, "Yes ma'am, I'll be glad to wait," he smiled broadly. "I could go back to Saratoga on this tip!"

"Just wait for me," she said with finality. "It should be no more than an hour."

She pushed through the door and was assaulted by rich aromas of Italian cooking: garlic, basil and tomatoes, mixed with the smell of wine. She paused for a moment and looked around the restaurant. There was a row of tables with red checkered tablecloths along the front window, and booths down the two side walls, plus some very busy tables in the center of the large room. At the far end there was a closed door. An older man was softly playing an accordion, the sound barely audible above the stir at the tables; he glanced up, spied Mary and squeezed into a zesty tarantella. Immediately a thin man appeared with a menu. He had a carefully trimmed, beard and dressed in a crisp white shirt, black vest, and sharply creased black trousers.

"Lunch for one, Madame?" He asked in a heavy accent.

"Maybe later," Mary smiled and shifted the purse in her hand. "I am looking for someone. I was told he is often here for lunch."

"Who might that be? Perhaps I can help;" he leaned forward to hear.

"I'm looking for Giuseppe Innella; I am a friend of his." She smiled at the waiter's surprise. "Is he here?"

"I am not certain." He glanced toward the closed door.

"Could you find out? Should he be here, please tell him that Mary Kavanaugh would like to speak to him."

"Mary Kavanaugh?"

"Yes. He used to work for me, but that was some time ago, at my home upstate in Minsi. I think he will remember me ".

"I will see if he is here, Mrs. Kavanaugh." He disappeared into the kitchen. The accordion player had taken a break and from the kitchen she could hear someone singing La Donna Mobile. It was a rich, full voice. The restaurant indeed had a festive air with animated conversations and laughter. She was studying the tables when the door at the end of the room burst open. A man appeared there still sporting a black checkered napkin. Though a little more rotund than she remembered, there was no doubt it was Giuseppe Innella. He strode toward her, cast his napkin, his face wreathed in a broad smile that showed his china white teeth. Another man, looking hard and oiled, shadowed him.

215

"Mary, Mary, Mary! What a surprise!" He opened his arms and she bore up bravely under a crushing hug. "Mary, Mary – how long a time?"

His loud endearments attracted the attention of the other diners who smiled at the greeting. She pulled back to arms length and appraised him like she was buying tomatoes, then focused on his eyes.

"A long time," Mary replied breathing easier from the release of the strong arms. "You look very well, Giuseppe."

"Come with me. I gotta' a table in back. Come, Mary, come!" He swept his arm toward the open door. The back room furniture consisted of three tables dressed in black and white checkers. Two men carefully observed her, separated, one taking a position behind her.

"Sit, sit." He gestured to a table with three plates of half eaten food. She chose a chair near a cleared area that had not been set for lunch.

"We just sat down to eat. When they say Mary Kavanaugh's here well, I surprised!" He beamed and gestured toward the large bowls of pasta, sauce and lengths of spicy sausage. "Come have-a something to eat. Tony, get her the plate, napkin from that other table there."
"No thank you, Giuseppe."

"No? The food here is very fine. A glass of wine?" He pointed toward two decanters in the middle of the table.
"I'll have a glass of the red."

"It's a good to see you. Howsa Pat? Howsa the boys? Billy, howsa the little tiger?" He looked at the wine, "Rosé is very nice, or would you prefer Chianti? Rosé? He pointed to the red decanter she had selected "I think good, you'll like it." He poured her a glass from the decanter.

"Pat is fine – busy on the farm. Billy is not so little anymore; he's as tall as Pat." She raised her glass to him and took a sip.
He smiled knowingly. "My God, been a long time, Mary! Howsa the little girl, Sara?"

"She's fine too, and also not so little any more. She's been studying in the city at Hunter College now she is studying to be a doctor."

"A doctor – a doctor want to be a woman doctor?" He topped off his own glass of wine and shook his head as though trying to clear it or to manage some unbelievable event.
"Those fellows there, I interrupted their lunch." Mary nodded toward the standing men.
"Donna worry, we make another order." He raised his glass. "Salute."

"Salute," she replied and sipped from her glass. Their eyes met for a moment, each searching the other for a sign of change. There was none save for the time and distance passed by old friends.

"Howsa the other boy?" He leaned back relaxing against his chair.
"Liam?"
"Yeah," he took a deep swallow from his glass.
"Liam is working with Bill Sutter."
"Lawyer Sutter," his curiosity showed through the remark. "He must be pretty smart to work for him."
"He wants to be a lawyer."
"That Sutter, he's a good man, a smart man. He should be the Mayor, or president, or something."
"He is something, a damn good lawyer! I was over there the other day. He's the one

who told me I might find you here."

Giuseppe affirmed with a nod and smile. "I'm-a glad you come to see me."

"He tells me they call you 'Geep the Bomb?'" Mary looked carefully at him to see the impact of the remark but there was none. "I didn't doubt it. I recall the pond you and Pat made."

"Giuseppe laughed. "Oh yes, I remember dat." He continued to chuckle. "That was one big bang!" He looked toward one of the others and made a slight motion with his hand. "Bene, bene."

"Found the best water in the county!" Mary chuckled, and then they both laughed out loud together. A waiter suddenly appeared and started gathering the dishes. The men that had surrounded the table followed him into the kitchen. The room was now empty except for the two of them. Mary sipped her wine and thoughtfully rolled the glass between her hands. She felt him studying her and she looked up from the wine and into his eyes.

The singing clearly carried to the table like a jubilant spirit suddenly set free. Mary listened for a moment and the voice stopped suddenly. Only the distant wash of customers talking and the sounds of clearing the tables remained.

"Giuseppe, I am really here on business."

He raised his glass, took a gulp and leaned back in his chair, his dark eyes dancing.

"Business, what sort of business?"

"Last week there was an explosion over on Ferry Street, a bar where people also played cards." She searched his face but it did not portray any emotion. "I just happen to own that bar and I still own what's left of it."

"So what, why do you talk to me?" He replied politely.

"You know why I am talking with you, Giuseppe."

He picked up his napkin and wiped the wine stain from his lips without even a hint of an acknowledgement.

"You understand that blowing up any place is bad for business, everybody's business."

"Sure, it would be." For the first time Giuseppe showed a slight uneasiness.

"I wouldn't want it to happen again."

"Of course not anyone would like that."

She picked up her purse and withdrew a sheet of paper she had folded away. "This is a list of the places I own in the city. There are 22 including O'Malley's – the place that will take about three thousand to repair. I don't want any money from you, but I do want your promise that there won't be any more trouble."

Giuseppe picked up the list and began to study it. He glanced over at her but said nothing.

"Giuseppe, I put you to work for me, I trusted you and you were an extraordinary stonemason. I think you told me you had thirty-five cents in your pocket and needed a place to stay." She paused, waiting for the words to sink in. "Isn't that right?"

"Yes."

"It wasn't that long ago."

He shifted uncomfortably. "Sometimes mistakes get made."

She continued crisply, "I know about mistakes, I don't want any more of them." She took a sip of wine. The singing from the kitchen once again carried in to them.

"I'm sorry, Mary. Sorry this happened to your place. How was I supposed to know your business?"

"Giuseppe, I don't want any problems, I didn't say anything to anyone, told the detectives I had no idea who would do such a thing. If I didn't care about you I would have told the cops, many of whom owe me loyalty. You don't owe me anything, Giuseppe only our friendship."

"It's-a bad thing for business." He picked up the decanter and refilled first Mary's glass, then his own.

"I've been in the city for a long time. There's big money to be made in gambling and girls but I'm slowing any expansion. I may sell off some of my interests so we may have to talk again, you might receive a great opportunity, without anyone being hurt. Think about it."
He nodded his head in affirmation. "I look at the list."

"In the meantime, I want you to know there are a lot of cops on my payroll, and I could put a lot more on if I have to. There are a lot of Micks on the force and as much as I would rather not think, a lot of resentment toward Italians. Funny how being in the same church doesn't help things."
Again, he nodded.

"And, Giuseppe, they could just make life miserable for my competitors. I know what's mine and I know at least a dozen places that aren't. So let's have a truce before any more bombs go off, or we could have some real trouble, good idea, huh?"
"Yes, Mary, a good idea."
"We understand one another then?"

"Yes, Mary. Yes." He brightened into a smile. "Let me buy you lunch. The ravioli here is fit for king or queen."

"Oh, Giuseppe, I do like you. I don't want any trouble." She reached across the table and patted his hand.

"Good, good, me either. I order you lunch."

"I don't like to eat alone and you have already had yours."

"Please, Mary".

"All right, I'll have lunch. Will you stay with me?"

Giuseppe fished a bright gold watch from his pocket and snapped open the case. "Ah, sure it's-a nice you here. This food, I can eat again." He turned and raised his arm toward the door. The waiter had been observing the scene through the glass and came immediately, and the order was placed in short, staccato Italian. Smiling broadly, he again filled the glasses.

"I'm-a so happy to see you. Mary, you are one of the most beautiful woman in the world, magnifica, here's to you." They touched glasses. "That Pat, he's a lucky man."

"I am a lucky woman as well, Giuseppe. Now that business is over, I'm even happier to be here."
Giuseppe laughed and leaned back in his chair. "Howsa the Indian?"

"Sada has been ill recently, but I think she is better now. We don't see much of her only once in awhile. The boys and Sara sure love her and they spend a lot of time with her, can't wait to get down there. I don't know what all they do; she tells them stories and has been teaching Sara about herbs and Indian teas and the like. She gives the boys reason to scour the woods hunting for her."

"She's a beautiful woman, too. Does she still live in a Wickiup?" He emptied his glass and began to refill it.

"Yes, she won't change that, I've tried but she refuses."

There resounded the beautiful tenor as the waiter appeared with a plate of bread in the one hand and a large antipasto in the other.

"My, that man can really sing. Who is it"?

"Ah, it's-a Peter Caioffa. He owns the place." The ravioli arrived and true to Giuseppe's word, was a savory salute. They finished the meal and Mary decided against desert and coffee, thanked him, and stood to leave.

Giuseppe accompanied her to the inner door. His last words to her, "Don't worry, Mary."

She smiled. "Oh, I won't worry, so don't you worry. Goodbye, Giuseppe, "It was a delight to see you again!"

As soon as the door closed the one from the kitchen opened, ushering in Giuseppe's companions.

"All right, Geep?" A surly dark eyed man inquired.

"It's-all right Franco." He reviewed the list Mary had provided and fingered a name. "Frank, we need go see Guido - now."

"What's up?"

"We don't do this one. He traced his finger beneath the name then tapped it.

"The Kirby Club, that's today."

"We need to tell Guido no." He stood straightening his jacket and tie, using the reflection in the decanter.

"Okay, let's go." His eyes questioned for a moment, they hurried outside the door, Frank leading and the others in tow. "Geep, who was that woman?" He asked as they stepped into the street.

"An old friend, and next to my mother, the smartest woman in the world."

Chapter 22

Medical School
March 1883

Sara's first year at medical school was less than pleasant even though she had delayed her entrance to school by one year so she could continue working with Doc Wayland in the Cloister's clinic, and learning about healing herbs from Sada. She had excellent preparation, but there were only three women in the first year class and none in the second and third years. Three women among all the men was uncomfortable, to say the least, so the three of them had become quite close. The upper class men scorned them and treated them like trespassers, most were distant, if not down-right hostile.

The women soon demonstrated to their classmates that intelligence was not just a masculine trait as they began to outperforming their male counter parts. This did not improve the situation and their performance was obviously being graded at a higher standard. During recitations, the minutest details of their responses were examined, while the men's were readily accepted without question, the discrimination did not dissuade them from continuing, it made them more determined. Sara, the most outspoken of the three, garnered more hostility or admiration to whichever proclivity the other students were inclined.

About two months into the school year, the three decided to room together and after some parental concerns that were ultimately resolved, they took up residence in a fashionable brownstone Mary owned, only a ten minute walk from the medical college.

Sara returned home for a weekend holiday as St. Patrick's Day approached and here presence was always a cause for celebration at the clinic. Pat and Mary's friends were coming for the day and small gifts would be exchanged all around. Mary also managed small gifts for all the patients and Sara busied herself delivering them.

A little later, Sara left the festivities, and checked with Evelyn to see if she could help, but was dismissed from the kitchen already teeming with Cloister girls. She made her way through knee deep snow, to Sada's Wickiup. She peered ahead and sensed something amiss; there was only a faint waft of smoke rising from the tent. Sara broke into a trot after calling Sada's name, and then pushed through the entrance. It took a moment for her eyes to adjust to the dark, but she recognized Sada's form huddled beneath her buffalo robes.

"Sada, Sada." She shook the blankets and turned the robe from over her head. "Sada, are you all right? It's cold in here." She shook her lightly and Sada opened her eyes slowly and gave Sara a fragile smile.

"Sara, you home. You come see me."

"Sada, you look ill." She placed her hand on Sada's forehead and felt the heat and sweat. "We have to get you up to the clinic, you have a fever."

"No go house."

"You must, you're soaking wet with sweat. We will go to the clinic." Sara looked about, found some sticks and wood and stoked the fire, then returned to Sada's side.

"I'll get Billy and Liam; they'll help you out of here."

"No go house," Sada weakly sighed. "Tell Kav-van-naw come."

"I'll get him too. We have to get you up to the clinic."

"Tell Kav-van-naw come."

"All right, now. You stay covered." She picked up the water jug and held Sada's head while she took a swallow. Once more she checked the fire and put in more wood and started it blazing.

"Fire feel good," her voice was nearly inaudible as she leaned heavily against Sara and held her arm.

"I'm worried about you. I'm going to go to the house and bring back a wagon."

"Tell Kav-van-naugh come. No go house. No wagon, she murmured."

"I will, I will take you to the clinic." She felt a panic building and stepped toward the door. "I'm going now. I'll get Pat and be right back in a few minutes. Don't worry, I'll be right back."

She strode forward, dropped the flap and began to run through the snow toward the house. Breathlessly she charged through the door into the gathering of friends sipping toddies and in good hearted conversation.

Mary greeted her. "Where have you been?"

"Pa, Billy, Liam, Sada is very sick. We have to get her up here. Is Doc Wayland here?"

The conversation stopped as Pat, Billy and Liam rose in unison.

"Get the wagon, boys, and follow. I'm going to hurry on down there." With three great strides Kavanaugh left the room, struggled into his jacket and hurried toward the Wickiup. After a few steps, he broke into a run.

When he reached the Wickiup, the warmth greeted him. Sada was sitting on the edge of her robes, her hands extended toward the fire.

"Sada, are you all right? Sara said you are very sick."

"Kav-van-naw come me." She smiled and weakly reached to him.

Pat sat down behind her, supporting her weight on his chest. She sighed and settled against him. They were in this position when the boys and Sara arrived with the wagon. Billy rushed through the door way and knew at once that his mother was dead. He touched her face lightly, then backed away from his father's tears, and as his sister and brother entered, Billy ducked out and put his hands over his ears to the cries from within. He set his collar against the wind and blinking through his tears, spread the robes they had brought on the wagon bed, and gently stroked the horse.

Soon Pat appeared tearfully carrying Sada's body, Liam followed, drawn and diminished, and Sara with tears streaming and snuffling. Billy retreated from their grief into the depths of his own. They covered the body, and with Liam and Sara beside it and his father perched on the wagon seat beside him, he slowly guided the horse towards the house.

"Take us home, Billy." Pat murmured, roughly wiping at his streaking cheeks. To himself, he said "I did my best, but it wasn't enough." From way off behind the ridge rising through the trees, a solitary fox barked, then cold silence.

Chapter 23

Nebraska
May 1883

Billy picked his way along the wagon ruts that spread to both sides of his passage. It was warm for May, but the evening's stillness had brought a chill. He had not seen a trace of game, but his saddlebags contained coffee, bacon and jerky so he was more concerned about water than food. There were groves of cottonwoods and alders scattered in front of him, and he could see a long, thin line of green ahead that wavered across the tracks and seemed to end abruptly in a stand of trees, a sure sign of surface water. He also could see some faint blue smoke against the gray sky, emanating from the green traces. He urged his horse ahead; the prospect of someone to talk with brought a sense of anticipation and the water would be welcome.

As he approached the grove, the silence struck him. No sound of a human voice or the whinny of a horse or bark of a dog, a single meadowlark was whistling, sending a rill into the silence. He stopped, leaned forward and patted Bucka's neck; she was nervous and took a quick skitter to the side, slipping slightly, her nostrils flared.

"Easy girl, easy, what's wrong? Come on now. Come on," he clucked. A dark movement caught his eye deeper into the stand. He froze as he noticed a large turkey buzzard rise into the lower limbs; immediately he spotted others hunkered in trees near where the first one had lighted.

"Come on, girl, easy, let's move up!" Billy squinted into the cover ahead. He could see a half burned wagon; a lick of smoke was rising slowly from it into the cooling air. He spotted the remnants of a second wagon, almost totally consumed save for the metal rims of the wheels. A small flicker of flame stitched its way across the ashes and the charred wood remains. He dismounted, drew his derringer, and walked slowly toward the smoldering fire. A breath of breeze passed over the side boards, bringing with it what smelled like burning pork. After a few steps the scene became clearer; he recoiled in horror. Lying a few feet ahead to the left of the clearing was what was left of a woman's body, her abdomen gone, her spine showing through, legs and breasts in shreds and most of her face gone. The body was swarming with flies, and her faded red skull emerged through shanks of black hair on either side. Two other bodies of young boys, also scalped, were akimbo behind her.

The wagon's contents had been ransacked, with clothing, tins and trunks' contents scattered across the clearing. Billy slowly made his way around to the second wagon. As he looked closer, he spotted the remains of two feet sticking up grotesquely from the edge of the ashes, the shoes mostly burned from them. He realized the mass of char in the center of the fire site was a man. All the flesh was burned from the skull lending it a grey grimace. The man's black and blistered hands had somehow escaped the worst of the heat and were outstretched toward the wagon. It appeared he had been tied to the wagon when it was set afire. The smell of cooking flesh again assailed him and, swallowing his choler, he stepped away from the putrid smoke. As he walked out of the clearing, he stumbled over another body half covered with leaves. It was a young woman spread eagled in a final obscenity, her dress pulled over her head. The buzzards had been at her legs. Gingerly Billy pulled her dress down to cover her nakedness. " J e s u s wept," he quietly said and staggered back to his horse. He found the small rill that spread into a larger spring, knelt and filled his canteen, he thrust his head deep into the water, straightened and shivered as water drained over his back.

Reluctantly, he made his way back toward the clearing. After a few minutes' search, he found a shovel and, with quiet determination, began to dig the graves. He worked steadily for three hours, and the sun was well down when he finally ended his labors. Taking a long handled ax from among the spoils, he set out to fell some saplings to fashion some crosses as grave markers. As he made his way toward a small tree, a brown leather purse caught his eye. It was pulled tight and nearly buried in the leaves. He picked it up and opened it; much to his surprise, it contained four twenty-dollar gold pieces. He assumed that the purse had been tossed into the woods at the approach of the hostiles or whoever. The robbers would think they had nothing to steal and left, the settlers could recover the purse after the thieves left. A good plan, but to no avail. He placed the purse in his pocket and finished his grave marking chore. Only then did it occur to him to find some identification of the unfortunate family. One of the trunks half consumed by fire bore a brass nameplate, Mosher. He pried off the plate, pocketed it, mounted up and removed his hat.

"I sure am sorry, Mosher family. If I'd been here I'd of helped. I'll report your graves first chance I get. I hope the spirits go easy with ya. I'm sure they will, because you had a real hard time dyin." Slowly he turned Bucka back toward the trail. "Come on, Bucka. Let's get out of here; too many ghosts in this grove."

The plains spread out before him; there was not a movement in sight except for the swaying grass and an odd peace descended over him. The demon of memory was resting, waiting for the dark and dreams.

Billy reigned up near the Livery sign in the bustling town of North Platte. After his encounter at the cottonwood spring, he had become more vigilant, and in a troubled sleep the scene vividly replayed across his mind. He was sleepless the first two nights following the event, drawn up to his saddle, his Henry rifle across his knees. Until his macabre discovery, Indian or any trouble had not seemed real to him, it simply had no face, no reality beyond the print of the prairie papers. His vivid recollections brought a serious question it could even have been Running Bull responsible for the murders at the spring?

A stop at Fort McPherson had not revealed much information about Running Bull. The enlisted men he talked to during his stay there had never heard of Running Bull, but they were full of stories of Cheyenne and Sioux deprivations. At the trading post where he gathered supplies, using some of the recovered money at the spring, he had agonized over the decision to report or not to report the event. He was concerned on the one hand that he might have to go back to the scene, and on the other that he right thing be done for the Mosher family. In the end, he decided that going on was the most important thing for him; he would report it later for it would not make any difference when to report the deaths.

Billy left his saddle and supplies at the livery and, carrying the Henry, started down the street to find something to eat. There were many clapboard buildings and tents in place. North Platte had been a major exchange in the building of the Union Pacific Railroad that had reached North Platte the year he was born. A few of the buildings were portables and could be struck like a tent to follow the railroad crews. When the owners found a profitable site, the temporaries became more permanent. It was one of those buildings that Billy entered. The Frontier Saloon filled the street with the smell of searing steaks. He entered and curiously assessed the people at the tables. Some were playing cards, others were eating and some were simply talking all under the gaze of a portrait of a naked woman with ample breasts inviting eyes, her hand cupped over her pubic hair. Billy smiled at the scene and settled into an empty chair; this was the west he had imagined.

There were some men seated at the next table talking, enthusiastically. The man nearest him was wearing a buckskin jacket and a wide brimmed brown hat. He had a flowing mustache and goatee; turned looked Billy over and returned to his conversation. In the brief moment their eyes met, Billy thought the man looked familiar.

"That's a mighty handsome Henry you've got there," the man noted a moment later. "I can't recall ever seeing a silver inlay like that before."

"It is a gift from my Uncle Woo." Billy turned the rifle so that the others could see the elaborately inlaid receiver.

The man broke into a smile and tugged at his goatee.

"A gift from your Uncle Who?" he laughed."

Billy laughed with him. "My Uncle Woo. He's a Chinaman."

The man responded with a chuckle echoed by the others at the table. He glanced around the table at assenting eyes then turned to Billy.

"You don't look like a Chinaman, and if you are, you must have come a long way." The men around the table cackled at the comment.

"All the way from Minsi, New York and it is a long way."

"New York? That is a far piece. I didn't know any train came in."

"I rode my horse." He shifted the rifle against an empty chair.

His interest piqued, the man turned fully to face him, his eyes cut to Billy's solar plexus. Recognition came with the force of a gale he tried but failed to contain his excitement.

"You look like Buffalo Bill."

"I hope so, I am Buffalo Bill. What's your name, lad?"

"Billy Kavanaugh, sir. I just finished reading your book, and have heard about your play." His reply was animated. "Your book is one of the reasons I decided to come out west."

"I hope I didn't drive you to that, leaving home." He laughed and turned to the others at the table who joined the mirth.

"No sir; I was bound to head out west anyway."

"I've got a place in Rochester, New York. Where's this Minsi?"

"Oh, it's a way south and east from there. It's about a hundred miles from New York City, on the Pennsylvania border. They call the area the Catskills."

"I've been through there, boy but not Minsi - I don't think. I've been to New York City."

"I've only been to New York City a couple times. My ma, that is my step-ma, has several businesses there."

"You didn't make this ride alone, did you, lad?"

"Yes, I did. I rode the train part way, but then went off on my own since St. Louis. I was with a few folks when I started out. Then I figured that I would be better off on my own."

"Well, I'll be. And you still have your Henry and still wearin' your hair. Didn't anybody tell you it was dangerous out here?"

"A lot of people told me that."

The other men at the table had been listening and Billy felt a surge of curiosity and respect.

"Mind if I take a gander at that Henry?"

"I'd be honored. Careful, it's loaded."

"I'll be careful." The entire table enjoyed a great guffaw.

Cody took the rifle and examined the silver inlay of a white tail deer. Inside the trigger guard formed by the lever mechanisms was inscribed Billy Kavanaugh.

"Know how to shoot this thing?"

"Well, Mr. Cody, I'd guess as well as any three men you can line up in a hurry."

The men at the table again were seized in mirth; Cody laughed out loud. "I'd believe you, Billy, but I know better. I like a fellow who has a lot of confidence though. Why don't you come join us," he motioned to an empty chair beside him.

As he moved to his new seat, Billy took full measure of this man, a legend of the plains. He had long, dark, gray-streaked hair that was beginning to recede from his forehead, and engaging, deep-set eyes.

"You passin' through or are you looking to settle around here?"

"I'm passin' through."

"Well Billy, I, that is we..." he gestured toward the men around the table. "We were just talkin' about settin' up a show - a riding exposition. We are tryin' to get folks more interested in the Wild West. We're lookin' for some riders, ones that can shoot too." He smiled and his good humor made its way around the table. "We have some good riders, but need a few more. Would you want to try out, maybe join in? You'd get paid a fair wage."

"What would I have to do?"

"Ride and shoot and holler like hell!"

"Well, sure, I'd be interested. I'd be honored to ride with you and you others too." He nodded to the men across the table.

"We're goin' to have a buffalo hunt with real buffalos, a pony express ride and an exchange station. There'll be Indians aplenty. We'll show Custer's last stand like we showed it on stage. It will be an extravaganza!"

"Mr. Cody, I never shot a buffalo."

"We can take care of that." He laughed. "I've killed a few."

"Over four thousand, that's what the book said."

"By my count" Bill stroked at his goatee and smiled.

"What kind of Indians?"

"Well, there are Sioux, Pawnee, whoever wants to join."

"Are there any Cheyenne in the show?"

"Not likely." He shook his head as he picked up a glass from the table and took a swallow. "You never shot a buffalo but you know about Indians, how's that?."
"My mother was full blood Cheyenne."

Cody looked him over carefully. "Well, I'll be. It sure don't show much; the eyes maybe." He paused. "Your mother's a full blood Cheyenne, you got an Uncle who's a Chinaman, and if I'm not mistaken, Kavanaugh is an Irish name. By God boys, we got a winner here." Cody laughed out loud, wiped at his nose and shook his head. "Billy Kavanaugh, I think you ought to be, no, I believe that you belong in this Wild West Show. You want to try out tomorrow?"

"Yes, I will."

"Well, good, do ye' have a place to stay?"

"I thought I'd bunk up at the livery."

"I'm goin' back to Fort McPherson tomorrow, but Jake here." He pointed to a clean shaven man across from him, "...will find you a better place to stay and show you the ropes. Welcome to the show." He extended his hand; Billy took it in a firm grip; a thrill passed through him.

"Jake will meet you at the livery. Somethin' I can do for you?"

"Well, I came in to get something to eat."

"Well, you came to the right place." He motioned to the bar keeper. "Charley, fry this man a steak. It's on me. You drink, lad?"
"I drink beer is all."

"Hey, Charley, bring this young man a beer as well. Jim over there", he gestured to the man seated at the end of the table – "speaks some Cheyenne but, he's half drunk – tell him somethin' in Cheyenne."
Billy rattled off a greeting that fit the man's stature and features.

Jim looked a bit surprised, "that's Cheyenne all right, but it's much too fast for me. You sure have got that lingo down good."

Cody shook his head. "Well, have another drink, Jim. We'll find out what he said tomorrow." They all laughed.

Billy looked at those around the table, their plain shirts, dust-covered hats and worn, lined faces. He smiled inwardly and sipped at his beer. This, he thought, really is the West.

Fort McPherson was busy. A train had arrived and there was much disarray among the pilgrims because the chief scout had decided to leave the train at North Platte so there was a scramble at the post as they tried to find a new one.

Jacob Just made his way among the rough hewed cedar beams that had been used to assemble the fort and its outbuildings. He found Bill Cody talking with the wagon master.

Cody was going down a list of scouts who he thought could assume the duties of the one who had chosen to leave to join his show. There was no written list, just the names that came to him and where they could be found in the area. Jake waited patiently for their conversation to end. "Bill, did you get them straightened out? There are only two scouts ready that I know of."

"I think so." He stroked his goatee, and watched the wagon master who disappear into his followers.

"What's the news?"

"It's about that kid we met yesterday."

"Uncle a Chinaman, mother a Cheyenne-Kavanaugh?"

"Yeah, that's him."

"Well?"

"He can ride all right. I never saw the likes of him except among the Cheyenne themselves."

Cody gave his friend a questioning look. "What do you mean?"

"He rides like the devil himself."

Cody chuckled. "Good! Sounds like he will, or should, fit in"

"I saw him this morning. We talked a bit and he saddled up and I say, 'show me what you can do.' He reared that horse, turned on the spot and went down O Street like he was on fire. He turned behind the Frontier and out comes the horse. Couldn't be sure he was on it. I tell you, Bill, his mother must've taught him to ride too. He comes flashin' past me like Spotted Tail himself; leanin' under, just his foot showin' on the saddle."

"A real Cheyenne trick, huh?"

"You bet, but that ain't all. He reined up in front of Sally's and damned if he don't come down the street doin' a handstand on the saddle, swings himself around lookin' out over the horse's ass, swings again and reins up right in front of me. There was a sod buster out there in front of the hardware. Kavanaugh kicks his horse and, as I live and breathe, jumped that wagon with enough clearance you could smoke a pipe under."

Cody listened, a frown knitting his eyebrows but with a pleasant smile. "It sounds like the Pilgrim from New York doesn't fit what one would expect." A trace of disbelief in his voice. "He must've learned somethin' somewhere, sure sounds like he has a good horse to boot."

"I swear, Bill. I never saw the likes; he reins up and says to me, 'tell Mr. Cody that I ride best without a saddle and I can shoot better than I can ride."

Cody laughed out loud and clapped Jake on the back. "It sounds like we've got ourselves a rider."

"Bill, he could be a feature."

"Hell, Jake. We got lots of trick riders, but we're goin' to be short on Injuns. We'll paint him up and let him have at it."

"I swear, Bill. He is one hell of a rider!"

"And coming from you, I believe it. Now, let's go have a drink. I know old Beauchamp has a bottle." They started off toward the enlisted barracks as Cody added, "Maybe, Jake, we ought to start lookin' for those three marksmen."

"I don't know, Bill. I wouldn't want to be holdin' a bet against this one."

"Well, sign him up. We got to get back to Omaha and get this show started, load it all up on the train in the morning."

Oregon Trail House
Omaha, NE, 1883

Billy, Jake and a number of the other riders were seated around a table in the bar. The Wild West Show had been a great success and after paying the group, Cody had invited them to get drunk and 'celebrate the female figure' at this small hotel with a polished opulent bar. For the moment, Billy had the great scout's full attention.

"Billy, you did right well, especially during the stage hold up. You sure were feelin' your oats!"

"Thank you, Mr. Cody." Billy blushed at the praise as powerful warmth pressed through him.

"You'll be stayin on, of course! You've got a part for as long as I have this show."

"Thank you, Mr. Cody."

"Will you call me Bill?"

"Yes, Bill," Billy smiled at the honor. "I thank you for letting me ride and all, but I think I'll be movin' on."

He ran his hand over his moustache while keeping Billy in his gaze. "What are you goin' to do?"

"I don't know quite, but I come too far to be a circus performer."

Cody chuckled. "Better than a circus, our animals ain't in a cage."

"Yes, sir, I mean yes, Bill." He sipped at his beer and smiled contentedly.

"What do you think about the show?"

"Well, I was surprised about the Indians, I mean they didn't seem so big and mean as I thought. Not fierce, just kind of quiet. Kind of kept to themselves, my ma was like that."

"Injuns can't be very well predicted. When their blood's up, they are fierce as anyone I've ever seen and believe me some Sioux are good sized men."

"I guess so. You know, Bill, I found a couple of wagons, or what was left of them, mostly burned up - a family. They were all dead, murdered, scalped and mutilated. I buried them, two little boys, their ma and pa and sister. It wasn't pretty I never saw anyone who was scalped before."

"I've seen it dozens of times – it's never pretty and it ain't always Indians that do the scalping. Some bushwhackers do it to cover their crime and get people to blame the Indians." Cody studied his glass.

"It looked like they tied the man to the wagon and set it on fire. I got an idea their name was Mosher – got this trunk tag." He displayed it. "I didn't know what to do with it. It was east after I'd crossed the Platte back toward Grand Island." Billy sipped at his beer. "It scared me some."

"It should. I hope it scared you into being careful. You never know when. Things can happen fast out there, when they happen. I'd take that trunk tag over to the fort. Somebody will be lookin' for word." Cody studied the name plate and passed it back. "I don't know any Mosher."

"Bill, you ever hear of an Indian called Running Bull?" Billy pocked the brass piece.

"Running Bull?" He leaned back in his chair. "Cheyenne or Sioux? I once knew a Santee Sioux named that."

"No, Cheyenne."

"Hmmm....yeah, I think there's a renegade Cheyenne by that name. There's a price on him - five hundred dollars, I think a Union Pacific bounty. He supposed to have kilt some train men -five or six, if I recall correctly. Nobody saw him do it, but they figure he probably did –he was seen near the place earlier, and the arrows they found were Cheyenne. Of course, he has done things like that before."

"Killed a crew?" A look of concern crossed his face.

"Yeah, I think he was at War Bonnet Creek too, but got away." Cody stroked his scalp thoughtfully. "That's where I got a new part in my hair. He's a lucky one, he is! He has fooled or got out of more traps than a three toed fox. He must be up in years by now, 'supposed to speak good English. He is related to Hump Backed Wolf - now there was a real warrior!"

"When was the last you heard of him?"

"Hmm, can't say as I remember. Let me think a minute." Cody leaned back in his chair and addressed his friend. "Hey, Jim, what have you heard 'bout that Cheyenne raider Running Bull?"

"Haven't heard much about him lately, Bill I think he's dead. He was in some bad business up in the Black Hills. Got his self shot, but guess he rode off. Last I heard he was somewhere near Deadwood, if my memory serves me right."

"Nobody collected the reward?" Cody squinted, raising his glass.

"Nope, not that I've hear of."

"Then he's probably still alive." He swallowed down the remaining beer.

"Could be, Bill, I haven't kept track of him. Real bad blood, that one! Danny Pleasant might know more – he came from out that way."

"You heard him, Billy. Running Bull could be five hundred miles from Deadwood by now. Or..." he laughed, "right over the next hill there." He gestured with his head toward the broken hill beyond the window.

Billy frowned as he sipped at his beer. "Could be any place out here."

"There's been some trouble lately over near Buffalo, Dakota Territory, raiders been attacking the rail repair crews and miners. It sounds like him. Why you so interested in Running Bull, Billy? You are fixin' to collect the bounty?"

"No, my mother knew him, is all."

"You'd be lucky to get close and if you do, he'll probably kill ya."

Billy took a swallow from his glass. "Yeah, that has occurred to me."

"Don't look so serious, get yourself another beer, it's on me, and think about stayin' on, Billy, you're welcome here." Cody smiled. "Why don't you take a try at one of them girls?" He laughed. "See Sally there, the one in the black dress with all the lace? She'll show you a better time than Running Bull, and a hell-of-a-lot more pleasant way to go. Get on over there, now and give her my greetings." He placed a gold quarter eagle on the table. "Have one on me."

Cody was taking a group of his performers and some local Omaha dignitaries to the Homestead Saloon on O Street. Billy excused himself promising to join them later. Although he would drink a beer or two to be polite, he avoided whiskey because he didn't like the taste or the feel of it. Cody's group had preceded him by an hour and as he dismounted in front of the

Homestead, he figured the group within would probably be pretty well oiled.

It was not hard to find them; there was a crowd around the table. He checked his Henry at the door and moved toward the group pontificated by Buffalo Bill, sharing his exploits as an Indian fighter.

"It was a fierce fight and Yellow Hair just popped into my sights and I dropped him in a flash, and raised his hair."

"I thought it was Yellow Hand Bill." A man who appeared to be the saloon-keeper, interjected.

"No, that's what the newspapers said - I knew of him before I killed him. He was a boisterous brave, and a braggart, but a great rider."

One of the men began to laugh. "Takes one to know one, eh, Bill?"

The men all laughed, including Cody.

"Well, anyway, his real name was Yellow Hair. He hadn't been at the Big Horn or Greasy Grass as the Sioux called the place. But he had a feather or two from settler raids." Cody looked up and saw Billy approaching.
"And speaking of great riders, here's Billy Kavanaugh, better late than never."

The men turned and Billy was greeted roundly and with good humor. He gestured to Billy to come back to the table.

"Gentlemen, and I use the word advisedly, yonder is a man with a Cheyenne mammy an Irish daddy and a Chinese uncle. Did you ever hear the likes of that?"
"And he looks most like an Irishman," a man enjoined."
"At least he knows who his father and mother are." chided another of the table mates.

Billy laughed. "That's a good thing probably more than a lot of you." He sat down amidst the laughter of his new friends.

"Give him a drink," Jake intoned from a nearby table and stretched his legs into the crowd.

A man handed up a bottle and another glass. "I don't want a drink, but I will have a beer, got some dust in my throat." The men acknowledged him and Jake raised his hand toward the bar keep who began to draw a glass of suds.

"No wonder, you should have some dust, what with ridin' upside down and circlin' like you do. You did well again today, Billy Kavanaugh!"

"Thank you, Bill. It was fun today, especially when that woman fainted and went bottom up right into the street. I damn near fell off my horse. She didn't have any underwear on."

Bill and the others laughed at the recollection. "And you thought you was the performer, those crowds are sometimes better than the show. Are you going to be with us tomorrow?"
"Well, sir...Bill. I stopped in to tell you that I'm movin' on."

There was a sound of dismay from some of the men around the table, the others quietly regarded him. The waitress brought Billy's beer and set the glass in front of him; there was a grave silence in the place.

"Sorry to hear that, Billy." Cody was studying him carefully. "Can't convince you to do otherwise?"

"No, sir, Bill, I've gotta be movin' on. I want to live a little more in the West, before I start make-believin' with it."

Cody threw back his head in a hearty laugh. "Well, Billy, that's good reasoning."

Once again, the table reverberated with good humor.

"When are you leaving?"

"Just as soon as I finish my beer," Billy's statement was met by a moment of disbelief and awe as those around the table sized him up.

Cody laughed again and shook his head. "You remind me of someone I knew once." "You," Jake broke in.

There was more laughter and the bottle made another pass among them.

"I must admit, Billy, you are one hell of a rider. Now, don't you lose track, I'm thinkin' of puttin' on another show or addin' another act – gonna call it 'Rough Riders of the World.' I'll get me a few more vaqueros, and more stunt riders. Hell, I might even get me some Cossacks from Russia or wherever they're from!"

"That sounds like a good idea." Billy replied setting down his half empty glass.

"We're going to take the 'Wild West Show and Exposition' on tour! That's right, gentlemen." He looked toward some well dressed men among the gathering, who nodded their assent.

Cody turned to Billy "I was quite a rider myself. Did you know that, Billy?"

"Pony Express, one of the longest rides."

"The longest ride," Cody said proudly. "I'm gonna miss you, Billy, but then I was just getting to know you." Cody reached into a leather bag he had over his shoulder and produced two double eagle gold pieces. "I want you to have these." He placed the coins in Billy's hand.

"What's this for, sir? The paymaster already..."

"This is from me, Billy Kavanaugh. Call it a retainer and when you get done Westernizing." He looked to the crowd, who joined him in laughter. "You find out where we are doin' the show, or stop by Scouts Rest near Fort McPherson and join up again. That's if the Westernizing' spares your hair." Again he turned to the crowd for their endorsement.

"Thank you, Bill. I'll no doubt be able to use these."

"Now a little advice from this old scout, if you're goin' after Running Bull, you be damn careful, lad! He's a slippery one and he is absolutely ruthless. He's the worst of the bad and he'll kill you soon as look at you. He has a bunch of cutthroats with him that would make a Comanche blanche."

"Yes, sir, I'll be careful."

"Call me Bill," Cody smiled.

Billy finished his beer and stood to leave. "I'm goin' now. Thanks again, Bill." He extended his hand and Cody took it in his own leathery grip.

"You remember, Billy Kavanaugh, you have a job as long as I have the show."

Billy turned, walked to the end of the bar, collected his rifle and passed through the door. He did not look back, instead, took a fix on the sun, mounted, and clucked the horse ahead. He had more money than ever, a new mule, provisions for at least two months, and a valuable new friend. He felt very well off.

Cody's eyes followed him out the door, and then he turned to the other men at the table. "I sure do like that kid. I sure hope he finds what he's lookin' for, I'm sorry it ain't here. I hope he finds it and lives through it," he paused, "but I'm not so sure he knows what it is, himself." The others sounded their agreement.

Billy trotted his horse out of town and set off toward North Platte; thoughts flashed rapidly through his mind. "Come spring, I'll look for Running Bull awhile, maybe get me some traps. Maybe a gold pan and digging gear. Hell, maybe I'll just go on to Oregon and see the Pacific Ocean." He smiled inwardly, "hell, I can do whatever I please."

Billy Kavanaugh rode west from Omaha following trails along the valley of the great Platte River. The Oregon Trail ran along the southern side of the river and the Mormon Trail on the north side. It wasn't long before he tired of the easy riding along the well marked trails and struck off to the treeless prairie and more rolling hills toward the north. He saw only an occasional spring, marked by cottonwood trees. Soon the sea of wither-high grass gave way to a more rolling landscape, a few canyons boasting small red cedar trees and some large stumps of trees that had been taken and hewed into beams.

When he reached the North Platte, he considered a plan for his future course of travel and bought bacon, beans, flour, dried peaches and a generous supply of buffalo jerky. He decided that if he found fur bearers he might trap awhile, so he bought a dozen steel traps. He also bought a bar of lead and a bullet mold to cast balls for the old Hawken rifle he'd brought along from home and a better mule saddle to carry the new belongings. His final purchase was a broad brimmed leather hat in the style of the frontier scouts. Confident he was prepared for any eventuality, he left North Platte, heading north into the Black Hills of Dakota. After visiting the bustling town of Deadwood, he continued west and north.

The ride took him through two small clusters of shacks, empty save for a few items no longer useful – a worn out prairie schooner from journeys past, a split shovel, several broken miners' picks, and rough made furniture in various stages of disrepair. There was an occasional rusty gold pan with holes that seemed to whisper of the miner's hopes that had passed through. Billy felt an uneasy sadness amid the abandoned shacks.

The surroundings seemed to hold the ghosts of the miners and their grand hopes, broken on the anvil of toil. He stopped at the empty shacks to gather wood to roast the rabbit or prairie chicken that he knew a brief hunt would bring. One slab was carved with a simple phrase 'Played Out 1852.' This sent a little shiver up his spine as he wandered along the creek near the shacks and spotted the placer claims fifty by four hundred feet. More junk was abandoned along the length of the creek, battered long toms, wheel-less barrows, and sluice boxes.

Billy realized he had only three months to find Running Bull or confirm his death before he would need to find winter quarters. He decided when the weather turned; he would head into a town, find what work he could during the winter, and decide what he was going to do. Although he occasionally missed home, the acuteness was gone and returning there was not in his plans. He rode on more alert than ever.

He had spied a crumbling stockade a couple miles before he came to it. It was a very clear day, uncomfortably warm, and he had been assailed by sand flies that made stopping uncomfortable. As he paused to review the old structures, he noticed there were some shacks buried into the trees along a small creek. He thought he would water the horse and explore the dwellings, and urged his horse in that direction. He saw the flash and smoke at the instant he felt his hat lift backward. He tumbled from his horse, at the same time drawing a Derringer from his belt band. He lay quietly setting the hammer on the little gun without disclosing his movement.

A voice came from the trees across the tiny creek. "Get up, you son of a bitch! You ain't dead. If I wanted you dead, I'd have kilt you."

Billy did not move but began to sweat profusely, trying to hold his position.

"Git up!" A second shot covered his hair with dirt. The horse shied away, leaving him completely revealed to the unseen man in the trees.

"Now you ain't gonna git me to fall for that old Cheyenne trick. I got me a nice shot at your future family and if you don't git up and talk, I'm gonna blow it away."

Billy quickly sat up.

"Drop the Derringer, right there." There was a pause. "How come you got no six-gun? Stand up, keep your hands high. You drop them an inch and you're dead."

Billy focused on the trees from which he thought the voice had issued. He saw no movement, then suddenly an old man appeared quite a distance from the shot. He was advancing slowly toward him, an old Spencer repeater ominously pointed ahead of him. When he got within twenty yards, he lowered the rifle.

"Hell, you ain't nothin' but a snotty nosed kid, what are you doin' here?"

"I'm just passing through." Billy involuntarily slapped at a biting fly and the old man responded by again leveling his rifle at Billy's chest.

"What you want here, boy?"

"I am just passin' through. Saw the old stockade and came, I thought I'd get some wood for a fire, water my horse and get out of the sand flies."

"Humph. You've got to be careful ridin' up on people, boy."

"Look." Billy laid his hands out palms up. "I didn't know you were here. I didn't even see the shacks in the trees 'til I was nearly on top 'em. I didn't know anybody was home."

"All right," The old man settled the rifle into the crook of his arm. "You got any whiskey?"

"No. I don't drink it much."

"You got any coffee?"

"I do." Billy gestured to the mule.

"You got anything sweet to eat?"

"I got some dried peaches."

"Good, let's have some coffee."

Billy resented the request and bent to pick up his Derringer. He heard the Spencer click.

"Be careful, boy. Break that open, drop out the load."

"Look, old man. I'm gonna pick up my Derringer and put it under my belt. And if you want my coffee, you'll just point that rifle in the air while I go get it."

"Feisty bastard, are you?" He watched Billy tuck away the Derringer and move to the mule saddle pack. "Bring some peaches, too."

Billy picked out the packets. "You got a pot, old man, or do I need to bring that too?" As he reached his hat he noticed the large hole in the crown. "Goddamnit, you ruined my new hat."

"Don't fret. I'll fix it." The old man began to gather wood.

"Why the hell did you shoot it in the first place?" Billy unloaded the coffee pot and two cups.

"Thought you was here to steal my pay packet."

"From the looks of this place you must not have much."

Billy struck a fire and soon his blackened pot was bubbling to the wave of the flames. The old man tentatively sipped at the hot brew. "There, we're even."

"Even with what, you shot a hole in my hat, I had to fall off my horse and you never asked a word from me until after you shot."

"I could have kilt you."

233

The two lapsed into silence, watching the flame die slowly downward to flecks of orange and yellow.

"What's the name of this place?"

"Don't have a name. When we was workin' it, we called it Glory Gulch."

"Was there gold here?"

"Some, but most all played out twenty years ago."

"What are you still doin' here?"

"I stayed for the silver. I still find a speck of color now an' again but silver had me stay."

"There's silver here, then?" Billy inquired over the rim of his cup.

"Some." The old man sipped at his cup and ventured nothing further. "It's gettin' late and time to think about cookin' somethin'. You want to stay?"

"Do I provide the victuals?"

"I got beans in the can and a haunch of antelope I smoked myself. You want more than that you will have to get it."

"I've no place better to go. I got dry beans, you rather", Billy smiled.

"Well, come on then; we'll go up to my shack and git started." Inside were two bunks, one with blankets, the other burdened with bulging bags that stretched around a tiny table to a wash stand. Atop a wood-burning stove was a large tea kettle, a smaller kettle and a long-handled skillet. A rough shelf had bean cans stacked along it, some empty bottles and a small sack of salt. There was a coffee grinder on the table; a second Spencer rifle and a double barreled shotgun were mounted above the doorway. There was a broom leaned in one corner and some rags hanging from wooden bar. Two spindly chairs completed the furnishings.

They had finished their supper the old man had made and were sitting at the table. The old man looked longingly at his pipe.

"I don't suppose you have – tobacco?"

"Yeah, I have a twist." Billy reached into his jacket. "Here, take a piece. I don't use it but to chew now and again"

"Bless yah, boy, I been out since two, maybe three months." He packed his pipe, lighted it with a splinter from the stove and regarded Billy through the haze of smoke. He puffed again and sat back in the chair.

"What are you doin' here, boy – besides just passin' through?"

"I wanted to see the west 'fore it was gone."

"You're too late – it's gone already." He chuckled. "You like the lonesome, eh?"

At first Billy did not respond, then thoughtfully added, "Do you ever get lonely?"

"You mean woman lonely?"

"No, just lonely, like do you miss your family?"

"I used to – was a long time ago. I had three sisters and a brother. Don't know..." He mused for a moment. "Don't know if any of 'em is alive. When I broke from home I broke for good. Better that way, then you ain't always wonderin' what's goin' on that's none of your business."

"You don't miss it, then?" he asked as he entertained the thought of never going back.

"Maybe once or twice, but I'm gonna take my poke in and cash out. Maybe I'll think about them then, maybe. But I'm goin' to town, I know woman's hard to find but I go back East. Maybe I'll find me one, look around some – saloons and such."

234

"If you go to town there's lots of places you might find a woman outside saloons – church be a good place to look, lots of women there."

"Them of the congregation that ain't bein' saved by the preachers, right?"

Billy laughed, "I don't know about that. I guess maybe. Still, church might be a place to start."

"Don't reckon church, never had much use for them or preachers. Most preachers get more ass than an outhouse seat and not too particular if the women already claimed and staked."

"I never was much for church either. I'd rather be outside on Sunday."

"I'm an old man now, just like an old dog, I'm gonna spend my time in the sun just lay there and soak it up. Hell, no matter what those churches say, in the shadow of a tombstone is only the cold. There's life and ain't nuthin' else."

Billy did not reply, listening to the wind rising through the old building. The man beside him tilted to his side and loosed a resounding fart.

"Now that," he guffawed, ain't cold. What are you really doin' here, boy?"

Billy looked to the russet and pink where the sun had settled. "My mother was a Cheyenne. She always wanted to come back. I guess I'm doin' it for her."

"Except for those hard eyes, you don't look like a Cheyenne."

"Ever see any of 'em? I mean wild ones – you know?"

"Once in a great while I see Indians. Don't know much about Cheyenne. My dealing is mostly with Sioux. They come by once in a great while to see if I have whisky. I always give 'em somethin.' Pickings are gettin' slim now. I'd give stuff I didn't need - a pot, a pan – something I saved from the other shacks or found someplace. They leave me alone."

"Ever hear of a renegade named Running Bull, a Cheyenne?"

"He's been around a while, raidin' and killin and runnin' off stock. As a matter of fact, Mort Montgomery, an old partner of mine, came in about a year ago with a Runnin' Bull story. He hit Gold Hole up on the Yellowstone, ran off some stock, and killed a couple of kids and Harry Knutson – feller I knew. Mort was there, decided to cash out. You wonder a little bit but more about time when it's runnin' out. Why risk it – ain't worth it no more."

"How long ago was that?"

"About a year, hell he could be anywhere now. You fancy collectin' the bounty'.

Billy did not reply but reviewed the littered cabin. "What's in all the bags?"

"That's my polk, boy. I got that other cabin there near full too."

"You have gold in all those bags?"

"No, it's silver ore. I got to take it on back to Lead, Dakota and get it assayed. Assayer will tell me what it's worth then I'll get it smelted or sell it."

"Can I see what it looks like?"

The old man opened a bag and poured some of the contents on to the table.

Billy snorted. "Hell, that doesn't look like silver. Looks like gray and flinty gravel. I didn't think it would be dark colored like that."

"That's pay dirt, boy, and look closer. You see those shiny little flecks? That's the silver and the more of those shiny streaks and flakes, the richer the assay."

"I'll be." Billy slowly turned the stone allowing the light to catch the silver streaks. "Gee, I never expected the color. It's sure heavy for a stone that size."

"You expect bars, maybe trinkets?" The old man laughed as he refilled his pipe.

Billy also laughed. The two talked long into the night and blackness was giving over to a gray dawn when the old man trundled into his bunk and Billy curled up on the floor.

He was first aware of the day as the sound of the coffee grinder.

"Slept in, boy, so did I. I did mend your hat. What the hell, I decided this morning I was gonna cash out."

"How you goin' to get the stuff - the gravel to Lead, Dakota for assay?"

"I got a couple mules out there somewhere. Ain't seen them lately, but they ain't far."

After a meal of bacon and beans, Billy saddled up to leave. "I'm movin' on now."

"Suppose you could keep an eye out for those mules, maybe send 'em this direction? They can be hell to find." He paused and pulled at his beard. "Boy, it's gettin late in the year. I wouldn't be chasin' after Runnin' Bull too much longer before winter. It can come hard and awful fast. "

"I'll keep an eye out for your mules." He leaned down from the saddle and extended his hand. "I never did get your name."

"I never tolt ya, you might want to stop in Belle Forche. It's a good town."

Billy shook his hand, straightened and smiled. "Take care of yourself and thanks for the advice." He started northwest, but he never saw the mules.

Chapter 24

Minsi, New York
July 1883

It was July the third and the town could barely contain itself for the big parade and fireworks. Fire crackers and rockets had been banging off at odd hours for two days. Mary was flustered and staring pitchforks at Pat who seemed not inclined to hear her. "Kavanaugh, you big mule! Why don't you get it? Women should have as many rights as any man who walks. We are suffragettes and we are serious."

"All right, Mary, go march the parade. You won't be happy until you do. I just don't understand - and what do you care for politics, Mary? Those politicians, most of the women you told be about are being' well cared for. Women don't know anything about politics."

"Tell me about it and I suppose most men do! Half these women are being cared for? The other half I know well, with their husbands humping them blue and poverty barking up their ass and him always on the watch for a woman in need he can take advantage of. It's not a matter of being cared for; it's their right to vote! These suffragettes are my sisters in equality, something I have wanted and worked for all my life. This is one thing I can do and by God I intend to do it!"

"It won't make any difference with the politicians, I know that. They won't pay any attention to you, your so called sisters and your parade."

"I remind them often it would be to their advantage to listen to me. Outside of the few teachers, the rest have been bankers or from families with money. They know me and they listen because many of them owe me a lot of money. I'm going to make the most of it, they have good reason to respect me, or perhaps fear me would be a better word."

"Sure, that should be enough. You walking down the street in your underwear with a placard, Women's Right to Vote, sure they don't care."

"Bloomers, Kavanaugh, God damn it, bloomers! And it's been men in charge! Always been in charge and what do we have? Businesses goin under, big business not paying their fair share to workers, strikes, riots and wars and people dyin' like flies with this disease or that one. Now, Kavanaugh, a woman might not do any better, but she sure as hell can't do any worse!"

"Ah, Mary, you have what you need, and what you want? Why not just let it go? The women can't know much about running the country or much else about politics."

"What about me?" Acid dripped from her voice, her eyes flashed and her face flushed. "What about me, Pat?"

"Well, you're no ordinary woman, Mary." Pat backed off quickly knowing he had crossed into territory he had never been in before. He settled for the storm.

"Ordinary or not, Goddamn it! The women have earned their right to vote. They have earned a share to govern this country. You're makin me mad, Kavanaugh."

"Ah sure, I can see that." He puffed on his pipe and looked away.

"Don't you turn away from me!"

"Ah, Mary, it's just that I think the women should stay at home. Keep their counsel for their husbands." He paused. "You know."

"No I don't know, Kavanaugh, maybe you should have gone down to the wickiup and moved in with Sada. She could do all those things. Hell, she could have even gone out and caught your supper, cooked it, then lit your pipe."
"Oh, Mary, I don't want to go down this path again."

"Pat, I have never been off it." She stood up and stamped her foot. She stared out the window for awhile and sat down. "You're right; we don't need to go there. The only woman I've ever been jealous of lived in a wickiup, didn't speak twenty words of English and was dark as a thrush."
"Peace, Mary, she is gone."

"Peace my ass." Her anger renewed. "Sada has nothing to do with our..." she paused, "discussion. It's the woman's place we're talking here." A menace crept into her voice. "And I'm saying ---whatever a man can do a woman can probably do better."

"Well, Mary, most women are happy with a home, a husband and lookin' after everybody." He tried to dismiss the tirade by angling away.
"You think they're happy, happy as compared to what?"

"Unhappy. And who are these suffergettes?" He asked drawing his pipe. "Are they all unhappy women?"

"Suff-ra-gettes – when are you going to say 'suffragettes' instead of 'suffergettes' and stop calling guns -goons? Christ, you have been in America long enough without falling over your brogue."
"Ah, Mary, you're testy, I was just curious."

She walked about the room and quickly sat down facing him. "Alright then I'll tell you who they are: there's Mary Haney, Helen Haney, and Sally Ha..."

"Oh, no wonder, --Mary is a mean widow and the two girls are old maids. That whole Haney clan is..."

"Stop it! Are you going to listen, or not? I don't care if I tell you." She sought his eyes and quickly looked away then began to get up.
"All right, Mary. I'll listen."

"Brenda and Mae Hanson," Kavanaugh started to reply and Mary pointed her finger. "Don't say a word about Mae." She raised her hand in warning.

He nodded, sucked his pipe and stared back at her awaiting further information.

"Matilda Reif."

"Big Matilda is one, really?" He appeared surprised. "I didn't think she was."

"Kavanaugh, do you want to hear the names or not?" She asked quietly. --he nodded. "Katherine Wright, Jenny Desmond."

"Jenny's sister, Katherine?"

"Yes, Kavanaugh, she is the wife of the newest banker."

"Go on, then. I won't say another word."

"Natty Williams, Patty Hoenig, Peggy Faye, Patty Cristwell, Eileen Mullaly."

"Eileen Mullaly, she's a Kerry woman!" He said in genuine wonder.

"To hell with you, Kavanaugh, if you're not goin' to join the parade, watch as we pass by; figure them out for yourself." She jumped out of her chair in a huff and scoffed, "I imagine you will march with your drunken friends; the Irish that saved the Union."

"Ah, Mary, I'm sort of duty bound to."

"Bull shit, I remember your duty and how the Army appreciated it. I'm agitated, I'm testy and those ladies represent a whole cross section of our society –housewives, mostly, but from all walks of life, even a teacher's wife."

"That would be Peggy Faye."

"Yes, Kavanaugh; now I've got work to do, is there anything else? I don't think we have changed anything in this discussion so best you prepare to be embarrassed. After the parade I'm coming home in the surrey, so if you expect to spend any time at Caulfield's, you better bring a horse."

On the following day, suffragettes were first assembled at the end of the parade behind the Navis fire company. The hawkers were out in mass, selling everything from firecrackers to hotdogs and cold drinks. Anticipation was stirring the townsfolk's excitement for the parade. The suffragettes were dressed in white bloomer outfits, but each wore a different colored hat. Mary approached the parade master, a prominent banker, who was bustling about arranging the final details with leaders of the various marching groups.

"Hello, Harv."

"Mary, I didn't know you were going to be here." A trace of surprise and concern expressed all at once. He studied her bloomer dress and bright red hat and was noticeably uncomfortable in her presence.

"That I am," she set the placard down, leaning on the handle.

"You're with the suffragettes?

"Yes, I am their leader and that is why I want to talk to you."

"I'm awfully busy right now." He looked desperately about to see if the nearby group of men had spotted him speaking with Mary.

"Harv!" Her voice was firm and rancorous with a questioning tone.

He dithered about, glanced at his list, and remained still, looking down at the parade order. "What is it, Mary?" He mumbled.

"Harvey, we are not marching last in this parade!"

"But Mary, the order of the parade has already been set out; see these pages?" He proffered.

"You set the order?"

"Well, the committee did. You know, Mark Hawkins, Pete Brownell, and Jake Turner."

"I know all those men, and all except Jake owe me money, as you do. We are not marching last, unless you want me to foreclose on those loans!"

"Well, Mary – Mary, I can't change the order this late."

"Yes, you can!"

"We've got the Veterans --Mexican War, Civil War; and the Fire Companies, the Young Republicans, --everyone wants to first! It's impossible!"

"Harv, you just work us in behind the veterans. There are about thirty of us and we won't take up that much space. I just had a discussion about this parade with my husband, and he lost. What will it be for you, win or loose, Harv?"

The parade was finally assembled with the suffragettes falling in step behind the Civil War veterans. Padric Kavanaugh was just behind the flag bearers. The Vets fell into a rough marching step, nodding and waving to the kids who gripped their balloons and noise makers. Some still had uniforms that fit; others bulged in different places. Some had no memorabilia of the war at all. Kavanaugh had the crossed swords that had adorned his cavalry cap, pinned to his lapel. Their expressions were sober, as the color guard advanced steadily down Perch Street to the corner of Main were the reviewing box was set. It was decorated with red, white and blue bunting and a large American flag was fluttering above it. The reviewers stood and loudly applauded the veterans as they briefly marked time in front of the stand before moving on.

As Kavanaugh passed in the rank before the stand, he overheard a conversation from the front row. Two men were looking at the suffragettes deploring the 'whores' and the slogans on their placards.

"Those goddamn meddling women!" One confided to his companion, he shouted, "Suffragettes are free lovers. Free lovers are whores."

"Meddling women nag over the stuff they don't even understand, dolts don't vote!" another shouted. The others began chanting, "suffragettes are free lovers. Suffragettes are free lovers." The police had anticipated that the suffragette parade order might cause problems and began moving through the crowd. Many men and some women were already jeering as the suffragettes made the corner. Someone threw out a string of fire crackers, but the women moved on resolutely as another string of firecrackers popped. The jeering grew louder. Pat stepped lightly out of the ranks as he and the Irish Brigade Veterans passed the reviewing stand.

Without saying a word, he climbed up and pushed his way to the dark haired man who had begun the chant, now almost hysterical, "Meddling women! Free lovers! Go home to your husbands! Take care of the children." His face was red, the veins standing out on his neck.

"Meddling women should stay in their kitchens."

Pat tapped him on the shoulder and as he turned, delivered a left cross that knocked him down two rows and dumped him on to the street just as the suffragettes were passing by. Big Matilda Reif sprightly skipped over him, and the review stand went silent.

Jim Hitcher, a candidate for the State Senate, looked apprehensively at Kavanaugh and raised a shout, "Hurrah for the suffragettes! Three cheers! Hip, hip, hooray! Hip, hip, hooray!" By the third cheer, nearly everyone in the stands had joined in.

The suffragettes continued down the street, standing tall, vigorously pumping their placards. Big Matilda could barely contain her laughter.

Chapter 25

Minsi
Christmas 1883

Christmas 1883 was a white one with below zero cold and a chilling wind. It had been snowing on and off for three days and the fields were covered deep and evenly and brightly flashed as the sun touched them.

Liam stepped in from the porch, leaving a trail of frosty breath. He looked toward town and broke into a smile.

"Someone's comin' I can hear them, and since we are not expecting anyone else, it must be Uncle Woo. I can hear the sleigh bells."

There was an excited response among the four watchers. Sara pressed toward the window that looked out over the road to town.

"I see them," she called shrilly. "Two sleds. I can't see Uncle Woo."

The others rushed to the window. Pat laughed, "You see that pile of robes in the first sled? That's Woo; he never did like the cold."

"I think I see Mr. Weng."

"You're right, Evelyn. That's him lookin' this way. Oh my, look at that second sled. It's full of stuff!"

"Closest thing you'll ever see to Saint Nick on this earth, Sara." Pat laughed.

"He a generous man!"

"You kind of like him, eh, Evelyn?"

"I do, I do. He be the nearest thing to a gentleman 'round here." She huffed.

Pat laughed in response and snapped his suspenders.

"With the exception of maybe, Mr. Liam."

"I appreciate the vote of confidence, Evelyn." Liam laughed.

"They're making the turn. Evelyn, why don't you put the pot on?"

"And Evelyn, you know how he likes your molasses cookies."

"Yes Miss Sara, we have two jars plumb full; I made dem yesterday!"

The two sleds drew parallel to the front door, the pile of buffalo robes stirred as Woo popped his head out, covered in a cap with the ear flaps pulled down.

Sara was first out the door, and as Woo's feet touched the ground she caught him in a big hug and planted a kiss on his cheek. He hugged her back.

"Well, Sara! Each time I come I find a more beautiful girl."

"Welcome, Uncle Woo."

"It is very cold!" The two started up the steps to the porch, where Liam was standing.

"Hello, Uncle Woo." He extended his hand. "I sure am glad to see you here."

"I would not miss the opportunity."

The door burst open and Pat stepped out. He made a pass at what might be considered a bow and Woo did the same, then with a great hug, Pat crushed and released him.

Woo was smiling after the assault. "I don't know, Pat. Each year you become stronger and each year I become older."

Kavanaugh laughed. "You're getting wiser for the both of us."

"Hello, Woo!" sounded from behind them. They cleared the way to the voice.

"Ah, Mary, keeper of souls, how are you, dear one?"

"I'm fine; we've all been waiting for your visit. Sara has been up since four thirty, trying to make it get daylight."

"Oh, mother," Sara was awkwardly demurred.

"But get inside." Kavanaugh hustled him toward the door. "Temperature's right around freezing."

"Way too cold!" Woo glanced back at the sled, "My man Weng, Mary."

"Evelyn's been waiting to see him. He can go right into the kitchen. Evelyn says she's going to enjoy another cooking lesson."

"I think she's sweet on him," Pat enjoined.

"Whatever Kavanaugh, you're getting to be a romantic in your old age," Mary replied.

Woo turned and said some brisk Chinese phrases, and Weng reached into the sled, withdrew his pack and started for the kitchen. The driver of the second sled took his place and headed toward town.

Woo made this Christmas visit every year; he'd been doing it since 1870, and the family always anticipated the event with excitement. Like clockwork, he arrived on December twenty-second and left on January fourth. The three youngsters looked forward to the visit like the end of school, and the Christmas holidays would not seem like holidays without him. Woo brought gifts for everyone: rich furnishings for the house, delicate China, silverware, decorative items, ivory pieces, ---even exotic spices for Evelyn, and always a personal gift for her. Mary had well prepared for Christmas: a twelve foot tree festooned with ornaments, strings of popcorn and strands of decorative tinsel. They always opened presents on Christmas Eve, for Pat still made his way into town for the early morning Christmas Mass, and then was gone until noon. Sometimes Mary and Sara accompanied him, but the boys, after their confirmation, refused to attend church. Pat, though disappointed, had accommodated their mother's wishes in the spiritual realm. He'd also visited Sada on Christmas evening, returning to the house well after dark. The family did not talk about it ---that's just the way it was.

The parlor looked like a department store show-room after they spread Woo's gifts, with their own, beneath the huge tree.

When Christmas Eve finally arrived, feelings were high, but this year, a shadow seemed to have spread over the carefully arranged gifts. Everyone felt it, but no one mentioned it and the opening ceremony was underway. Sara and Mary had ooohed and aaahed over the ceramics, and bolts of silk cloth; Evelyn, who had previously mentioned she liked ginger jars, now had three at her feet, plus a bolt of bright yellow silk. Pat had a cask of twelve-year old whisky and Liam an ivory chess set of intricately carved Chinese figures, plus a leather-bound set of Charles Dickens.

Woo sipped at his tea, basking in the appreciation and smiling inwardly about the large carved walnut box of antler pieces Liam and Sara had collected and sawed into angles for him. Weng smiled broadly as he opened the colorful knitted scarf that Evelyn had made for him.

Woo spoke as he was breaking a molasses cookie to bite size. "I brought an antique Chinese bow and arrows for Billy and a new knife of the latest design. I am sorry he is not here."

It became very quiet, an emotionally charged atmosphere, blended with sadness and regret.

z

242

Mary carefully placed her cup on the end table beside her chair. "We are all sorry about that, Woo. As I told you last time we talked, Billy left quite suddenly, after Sada died."

"I may have some knowledge."

There was a hushed silence.

"Is he alive, Woo?"

"Oh yes, Mary. Has he not written to you?"

"We have had no word," Sara enjoined, "Nothing!"

A puzzled look again passed over Woo's face. "I think he is, that is, I am told that he is working in a saloon in Belle Forche, in Dakota Territory ---The White Stag Saloon."

"Are you sure?"

"It is a mining town and some of my people are there. I had asked them to look for him since just after we talked about him leaving. I am sure he was there in November."

"Trust Billy to be colorful," Liam resigned. "It's an interesting sounding name."

"It is west of the Missouri River. A very busy place – miners, farmers; a brisk business place, no doubt," Woo added.

"Belle Forche ---I can't say I know where that is, but now we know he is alive, thank God. Let's have a drink; one winter out there may flush him home." Pat reached for a bottle from the silver service liquor holder.

"If the spring floods don't wash him away," Liam laughed.

"There's nothing funny about it, Liam." Mary was serious. "Pour me one, Pat. Would you like a drink, Woo?" He shook his head no.

"Maybe we should go out there and get him?"

"Are you crazy, Sara? It's so cold out there, and it's a long way to go. It would make him more determined to stay away."

Mary sipped at her whiskey. "Liam's right, Sara, I think so anyway. He has to want to come home. Pat, what do you think?"

"I think we should leave him be. Let him look around and get the Wild West out of his system. He will come home when he is tired of it."

"But you could write to him at the White Stag Saloon."

"If he is still there, ---Woo says it was in November." Mary took a deep breath. "What do you think? Should we all write in the letter? Tell him we miss him ---hold out a carrot. Maybe he would come back if we offered him the old Harmon place."

Sara answered, "I'll tell him I miss him. I do, you know, I really miss him." Tears began to well in her eyes.

Liam put his arm around her. "He won't be coming back for the Harmon place. He left for a reason, he will come back only for a better one."

"What a difference a year makes, eh, Woo?"

"Time has always fascinated me. Something we humans have created. We have clocks to remind us that it's all an illusion, yet we pace our lives by it."

"That's beautiful, Woo."

"It's also true, Mary."

"All I know about it is that I'm gettin' older." Pat stretched and swallowed his whiskey.

"And you become more cantankerous!" Mary confirmed.

They all joined the laughter at Pat's expense, and then sat for a moment in silence. The

243

tall clock by the staircase struck the half hour.

"Speakin' 'bout time, I best be gettin' on with dinner." Evelyn walked toward the kitchen, as the others acknowledged her departure.

Pat gazed out the window toward where Sada's wickiup had once been. "Oh, time," he said softly. "If only we could turn you back one year." Then he added aloud, "It's not the same this year with Billy and Sada both gone."

"Oh, Pat," Mary resigned. She then sipped her drink, following his gaze. She knew how much guilt and sadness he felt.
"Do you think he misses us?"

"Sara, if he doesn't miss us at Christmas, I'd be very surprised." Liam rose, patted his father's shoulder and disappeared up the stairs.

Belle Forche
Christmas 1883

Billy leaned back on the bed and watched Marigold slowly descend on him. "Oh, that's good, that's so good! Easy, Goldie, easy, stop, oh, stop."
In a deft move she lifted herself, settled deeper over him, and began to thrust.
"Oh oh the tension left him and he collapsed back on to the bed.
"Finish me, Billy. I can't finish." Billy reached up and began to manipulate her with his fingers.
"Oh, yes. Ahhhhhh." She came down full length across him. "For a kid you're sure good, very good. That was a shudder!"
"I've had good teachers."

She rolled from on top of him and kissed his lips. "Well, you sure been makin' the rounds; Merry Christmas!"
"You're my favorite, Goldie."
"That's what they all say. Helga sure likes ya," she said without a trace of jealousy.

"Merry Christmas," he stretched and looked out the frost-rimmed window. "A day off – that's great. I was surprised as hell Jerry shut the place down today. He said he's gonna pass out some presents later. You believe it?"

"Well, yeah --he did last year. The girls exchanged amongst us. See that beautiful lamp mat there?" She pointed to the table beside the bed. "Dot crocheted that for me last year."
"That's pretty. That's what they call a pineapple pattern." Billy offered.
"You're so full of information. You've have some presents, you know."
"No, I didn't know." He writhed uncomfortably. "I didn't buy for anybody."

"You don't have to -- it's just they appreciate you; everybody – all us girls since that big trouble last month. Somebody could have been hurt, even killed."

"He was drunk. He probably wouldn't hit anything but himself with that little two shot." Although he glossed over the event, there was more than an even chance someone would have been hurt or killed.
"After you rounded on him with that whiskey bottle, he wasn't gonna hit anything."

Billy smiled and rubbed at the stubble on his chin. "He went down, didn't he?"

"Out for three days, I wish the son-of-a-bitch had died after how he beat up Helga." Rancor still reviled her voice.

"I got there too late. I didn't see it until she went down."

"But you got there. The other bastards just stood round watchin' the fun."

"Buffalo Bill ought to put that scene in his Wild West show."

They both laughed. Goldie lifted a cigar from the lamp table. "Want a smoke?"

"You know I don't smoke."

"And drink damn little, but oh, the girls!" She chuckled. "You sure like them."

"I'm sorry I didn't buy anything' for anybody for Christmas." He looked out the window to the snow blown landscape, "I should have known."

"Well, there are four of us just buyin' for one, and you'd be buyin' for four. Don't be worried, just be there again should we need ya."

"I'll try but..." he rubbed at his ear. "I hope so."

"By the way, Billy, I already gave you my present and when you're rested up, I'll give ya another."

"Well now, it's gonna have to be later. I'm goin to run over to Milliken Grocery and fetch four bags of anise drops." He got out of bed and pulled on his trousers.

"Get molasses candy for me," she called as he disappeared out the door.

Once outside, Billy stretched, filled his lungs with the frosty air and slipped into the empty snow-choked street. He took bearing on the store and strode toward it. His travels set him up well, just over six feet in height; his months of riding had twisted him into a wire-strong physique. What had not changed were his slightly protruding ears and eyes that flashed like they would turn one to stone. He was regarded highly by most everyone who knew him for his riding, marksmanship, and fierce courage.

Belle Forche
March 14, 1884

It was a warm day for March; the promise of an early spring was in the air. Traffic in and through Belle Forche had resumed; farmers getting ready to put in spring crops, miners, and the usual bands of desperadoes, cowpokes and cavalry. The situation at the White Stag had changed, although Goldie remained. Helga had married a farmer in the next county. It took two new whores, gathered in from Yankton and St. Louis, to replace her. More traffic meant more fights and Billy had been prominent in many of them. The two new girls, Mary Beth and Micheline, a French Canadian woman, both had experienced his assistance. Micheline needed help when a drunken drover tore off the bodice of her dress and buried his face between her breasts, and Mary Beth, when Billy had demolished a local farmer who backhanded her face. Micheline was particularly grateful to Billy and often provided sexual favors to her erstwhile protector. Billy relished her attention. It was late in the morning when Billy made his way to her room bearing a small tray with pot, cups, and creamer and a bowl of sugar. She was lying naked on top of her

bedcovers when he entered. The otherwise austere room was draped with drying laundry.
"Ah, Billy, Mon Cher, how are you?"

"I'm fine. I brought you some coffee." He cleared a place on the bedside table and set down the tray.

"Oh, yes. Merci," she smiled coyly. "Did you come for a French lesson or a little French loving? Voulez vous couche?"
"Oui, Mamsel."

"Ah, Billy, your French is coming along well."   She adjusted to allow him some room on the bed.
"I'd like to have more practice." He smiled.
Micheline shifted her legs so Billy could review her mound of curly black hair.
"French or love? You can have both, but first the coffee."

Billy nodded agreement, smiled and slipped his suspenders aside, unbuttoned and dropped his trousers at the foot of the bed. The erection was sticking through his underwear like a beer bottle.

"Come," she said. "Lay down with me. I will have a sip of coffee and some of you, eh?" He removed his underwear, adjusted the pillow and slipped beneath the sheets, a bit self conscious, propping himself up against the large wooden headboard.

Micheline, while sipping the coffee, dribbled a large mouthful over her chin and down her front.

"Merde! Je donnait mes tetons un bain et ils n'avaient pas besoin d'un.....damn it!" She added in English.

"What did you say?"

"Nothing Billy, hand me that towel."

"You said something about your tits."

"Ah, you know that word, yes?" She vigorously mopped her breasts and belly and smiled into his eyes. "You know, Billy, I have known many men and I recognize a true believer - someone driven by a purpose."

"Driven by a purpose?" How do you say that in French?"

"Animé d'un ardent désir."

"Animé d'un ardent désir. ---Driven by a purpose." Billy repeated.

"Ah, trés bien. You have a skill for language."
"Oui, je peux parler le Cheyenne trés bien, un peu d'Italien, aussi."

"You are so young to know so much and to be driven as you are. Qu'est-ce que tu essaies trouver?"

"Trying to find?" Billy looked thoughtfully over his cup.

"Oui, quoi?"

"Je sais pas, Micheline, peut-être je le saurai quand je le trouver."

"Ton français s'améliorer." She laughed lightly.

"Mais, je veux á savior plus."

"Qu'est-ce que tu veux a savior?"

Billy lifted the sheet from her body and marveled at the smooth white skin against the sun shaded tones of his own. He caressed her breast with his hand and slid his fingers into the thick black curls that spread across her pubis and triangulated over her mons.

"I'd like to learn the body parts." He rolled closer to her and lightly passed his hand to her face touching her hair.

"Ceci? This?" He asked.

"Les cheveux."

Slowly he touched in order and Micheline replied:

"La épaule, la aisselle, le bras, le main, les doigts, le vender, la cuisse, la jambe, le pied, les orteils."

"Et ceci?" Billy touched her pubis.

"Le pubis, la vulve, le clitoris - ah Billy, doucement maintenant, le vagin."

Billy rolled astride and pointed at his erection. "Et ceci?"

"Un érection. Et oui, Billy." She smiled and spread her legs to better accomplish his entrance and closed them again to keep him tightly inside her.

"Et ceci?"

"Le sexe."

Slowly Billy undulated to her quiet responses, raised the tempo, and exploded into her, but continued to push until she tensed under him, seizing up, and collapsed with a sigh.

"Et ceci?" Billy breathlessly asked.

"Orgasme." She breathlessly replied, "Un vrai orgasme!"

"Quoi?"

"Un vrai orgasme, pas á convaincre quelqu'un mensonge. It's a real one, not to tell someone a lie to make them feel better."

"C'était bon?" She smiled.

"C'était merveilleux. Si, je était dans ma jeunesse, je t'aiderais á trouver ton désir, quelle que c'est."

It was later in the evening while Billy was tending bar that he heard Mary Beth yelp and saw the gray bearded man start to paw her. Glasses clattered to the floor and he had nearly pulled her blouse off. The few other customers gave way and Billy strode toward the couple now wrestling and shouting, clawing at one another.

"Hey there, old man, you turn her loose! You don't maul the merchandise in here. If you don't stop, I'll throw your ass out. You want a tickle, you have to pay."

The man released Mary Beth and she stepped back, then he regarded Billy's fierce demeanor and dropped his hands to his side.

"Didn't mean nuthin by it all I wanted was a little feel."

"Well, don't do it again. This isn't a fight arena; you want a fight? Go down the street and watch the dogs. You want a woman – pay for her."

The man recoiled from Billy's fierce eyes.

"Look, boy, I don't want trouble. I ain't talked to nobody in two months. I lost most my swag, damn near my life, and I was just funnin'." He gestured to a chair. "How about you talk to me?" He smiled, showing a mouthful of yellow teeth, half of them gone, that lent him a comic appearance. "I don't want any trouble – had enough trouble."

Billy looked back at the bar; the keeper had returned so with nothing better pressing to do, he sat down across from the old man. Mary Beth disappeared amongst the tables with a furtive glance over her shoulder.

"She's a pretty girl. Sorry 'bout the fuss. Are you sweet on her?"

Billy laughed – "No, not on her," he pointed to Micheline seated on the lap of a king-sized drover. "Her, and I hope I don't have any trouble with him."

The old miner laughed. "I'm Albert Kincaid; who be you?"

"Billy Kavanaugh."

"I'm pleased to meet ya, want a drink?" He retrieved a bottle and pushed the whiskey toward him.

"No thanks."

Kincaid took the bottle cork in his teeth and poured himself a tumbler full. "Like this whiskey," he mumbled around the cork, and replaced it, "ain't watered much."

"Not at all, it's how we get it from Nebraska. Where are you from?"

"I'm from a lot of places; had a claim up North most lately. I'm passin' through; sold my claim. I hit a pretty good streak about ten years back and was comin' to settle down. I always liked it around here. I went back for my last poke. There was quite a bit of silver I never touched."

"I ran into an old silver miner just last year." Billy broke in.

"There's a lot more interest in silver these days." Kincaid continued. "Used to be a bother, you know. I mean, it was gold I was lookin' for."

"Are you settling here, then?"

"No, decided I'm goin' back to St. Louis. I am tired of lonely." He took a deep breath and swallowed some whiskey. "That last poke would have helped."

"What happened?" Billy slicked his hair down and settled back for another story.

"Indian trouble."

"Indian trouble, what kind of trouble did you have?"

"Cheyenne they were. They're well known for it, but I never had any trouble before. A band of cutthroats if I ever saw one; I'm lucky I'm alive, --they wanted gold. I told 'em I didn't have none. I thought they was gonna kill me.

Then this leader, spoke perfect English – asked me if I thought I was lucky. 'Sometimes,' I say. He asked me for a coin. So I handed up a penny. He says, "heads or tails?" I said tails, and he flipped it. It was tails. "You win, old man," he says, "you're lucky, --- you're going to live." Then he took my mule and saddle bags. It was loaded with my silver ore and rich it was.

They just wandered off and dumped it all out - right there on the ground. Two, maybe three thousand dollars worth; wind blew and covered most of it. After they left I picked up what I could find but most was covered; I left a lot, I didn't have anything to carry it in." He raised his glass and emptied it. "I was just glad they didn't kill me."

"You say this Indian spoke perfect English?" Billy bent forward in renewed interest.

"Perfect - King's English, I know a little Cheyenne and one of 'em with him called him Running Bull. When I heard that I knew I was lucky to be alive."

"You said Running Bull?" Billy was on the edge of his seat.

"He's a bad one, that red nigger. Price on his head, but I'm glad I still got the hair on mine." He lifted off his hat, showing a tonsured dome with long hair growing from around a scabby bald spot.

Billy laughed. "Well maybe, Kincaid, he figured your scalp wasn't worth lifting.'"

They both laughed, and Kincaid ran his hand over his bald pate. He replaced his hat and thoughtfully added, "well, maybe. I'm alive anyway and I'm goin' to St. Louis or bust a cinch."

"Where did you have this run in with Running Bull? What did he look like?"

"Why, over near the Powder River, he's known to come there. He's weathered up, streak of gray hair, mean lookin!" He shook his head and poured himself another whiskey. "He had hard, hard shoe button eyes."

"You know, Billy, I bought myself a nice Winchester Rifle a short while back. A 44-40, and it shoots right on. You want to buy it? I'll sell it to you cheap, it's a center fire. I reckon a side arm would be better in St. Louis."

"In St. Louis you'd be better off with a pocket pistol. I got a Remington 41 over and under; I'll trade you even."

"I don't need that rifle anymore." He reached across the table. "It's a deal."

Four days later, true to their words, the exchange of firearms was made. Billy waited another week, and on the last day of March, with the sun warm on his back, he left Belle Forche, riding south and west, headed for Wyoming Territory. The territory was moving fast toward statehood, but within its vastness, many bands of native people still plied for furs, food and freedom. Billy was more confident now, he would find Running Bull and his band or they would find him, one way or the other.

Chapter 26

Cheyenne Territory
April 1884

Running Bull turned to look over the rump of his horse at the distant figure behind them.

"Is he still there Black Eagle?" He watched the far away figure closely until he felt sure the follower saw him looking back.

"He does not stop. I thought we were rid of him yesterday. He still comes. I'll take Blue Shirt with me and we will kill him."

"No, Black Eagle let's catch this following one. You see that hill beyond?" He pointed it out. "It is very steep and there are two little hills behind it. I will wait until he is closer and ride down the steep hill to between the two little hills. You, Sharp Axe and Blue Shirt, will wait behind the little hill on the right; Raven Feather and Spotted Horse behind the left one. I will whistle; you circle behind, I will be in front."
"Yes."

"If he wants to die we will see to it." He studied the distant rider steadily approaching. "They must have raised the price on me or that rider is simply stupid."
"All white men stupid."

"If that were the case, Black Eagle, there wouldn't be any in our hunting grounds and our streams would still be clear and not lined with them." He paused and again squinted toward the distant rider. "He may not be a white man; he rides well."
"We will kill him."

Running Bull shook his head in negation. "No, Blue Shirt, we will wait until he is a little closer. We will catch him and cook his feet." Once again he looked at the distant rider.

The horses snorted and milled a bit, then began to nibble on the tall grass. The midday sun had set the secret piles of snow to icy rills.

"I could kill him now." The warrior beside Running Bull shifted the rifle across his saddle and turned into the wind to test it.

"No, Black Eagle, he is out of range. I want him alive. He has troubled us enough to make him understand he is not welcome. Let's go on."

Billy reined-up on the hill where he had last seen the band of Indians. He sensed danger for, unlike the open prairie behind, ahead was a more vegetated, hilly area. There were a series of monoliths peeking through the forested terrain like battlements. Long alleys of conifers and aspens loomed like salient islands in a sea of grass. It was a steep hill descent before him to the swale below; the sod thinned out to a light beard of grass with purple patches of vetch that could trip a horse when its tendrils crossed its legs.

At first he saw no one, and then five riders appeared below, riding slowly. "Where's the other one?" He wondered. He started down the incline, lost sight of those ahead and was well into the swale before he saw the last rider disappear to the left. He spurred ahead, and as he made the turn he came up to three rifles leveled like a firing squad across the trail. Turning, he saw the other three riders coming towards him.

"Well, well, well. You caught up to us. What are you going to do now, kid?"

Billy did not respond immediately, and then in carefully intoned Cheyenne replied.

"I search for Running Bull. I want to speak with Running Bull. I know he will want to hear what I say."

Running Bull straightened in his saddle, and a murmur of surprise rounded among the other riders.

"You speak pretty good Cheyenne. I am Running Bull, what do you want with me?"

"You speak pretty good English."

A slight smile made a start, barely rippling his dark copper features.

"Black Eagle wants to kill you right now. What do you say to that?"

"That depends on you, I guess."

"What a cheeky little bastard."

"I am not a bastard, I am Sada's son."

This time his countenance was rocked by surprise. "Sada's son, Gray Wolf?"

"No, I am Lame Wolf."

Black Eagle raised his rifle and Running Bull gestured him to lower it. "He likes half breeds less than white men," Running Bull commented. "It's a pure blood question with him. It is a bit of a test. Sada's been gone many years." He lapsed into English. "Where is she? How is she and Kavanaugh, the great traitor? Where did you come from?"

"One question at a time, Running Bull, my mother Sada died about this time last year, I have come searching for you from New York State - a place called Minsi."

"Sada's dead?"

"She died about this time last year."

"And you came out here all the way from New York to tell me this?"

"Not only to tell you – if I found you. I wanted to come west before it's gone."

"You're too late. What is your Christian name?"

"Billy, that is, William, every one calls me Billy."

"A good name, there's at least one other 'Billy, --the Kid 'has the right idea about enemies in particular and white men in general." He added with distaste, "whatever happened to the shining man?"

"Shining man?" Billy looked puzzled.

"Kavanaugh, your father, Black Badger, a powerful medicine man, thought he would take a message for us to the great father across the river. Some message was supposed to go to that dimwit Grant, or was it Johnson? Anyway, what happened to him?"

"He's alive; a big time farmer now, controls hundreds of acres. I don't know all the details of the message from Black Badger, only what Ma - Sada and my Aunt Mary said. I know he got to Washington with it, before Grant took office. He was at the Bureau of Indian Affairs when they arrested him. They were going to hang him as a traitor for bringing a message from the enemy and for what he'd done to that Cavalry Major where he met ma."

"Arrested him?"

"Right there in Washington, that's when my Aunt Mary, his Christian wife, and a Chinaman named Woo planned to save him. He got loose on the way to Leavenworth Prison

– jumped the train. Got back to Minsi where he was from. Mary bought up a lot of property there – she has more money than God. The same year they married, they found out about Ma and went down to Oklahoma and brought her and I and my brother back to Minsi".

Running Bull smiled. The horses seemed restless, and across the expanse ahead thunderclouds were building a great mass of black bottomed anvils. The braves had gone back to Billy's mule and were searching through his possessions. Black Eagle pulled out the Winchester and was flourishing it about. Blue Shirt was brandishing the old Hawken, and Raven Feather was pulling out the traps and examining the gold pan.

"A Henry in the scabbard, a brand new Winchester and an old Hawken fifty, can you shoot those things?" His voice reflected skepticism.

"Probably better than you," he replied.

Running Bull leaned back on his horse and laughed. "My god," he chuckled. "I do like people of spirit. Let's set that gold pan out there and see. A half-breed from New York can shoot better than me? I don't think so!"

"I'd hate to ruin that pan I just bought it."

"We'll set it out far enough you won't be able to hit it and then we may kill you. Don't worry about the pan." Running Bull reviewed the burdened mule, "you've got rifles more than you need, a gold pan, and traps. Just what were you thinking about the west?"

"I wasn't sure, so I came prepared."

Running Bull switched back to Cheyenne. "Blue Shirt, take that pan to the rocks there." He pointed across the hillside then turned to Billy. "If you want to go ten more feet with me; you can leave that pan behind."

Blue Shirt placed the pan about 50 yards away and was starting back.

"Shoot, Billy, and shoot well -- your life depends upon it."

Billy yanked the Henry from the scabbard, set the hammer and fired, striking the pan dead center, then firing as fast as he could lever, sent shots skittering the pan up across and over the rock. The last shot struck the pan in mid-air.

All six of the Indians were transfixed as the pan popped over the rocks and out of sight.

Billy looked at Running Bull who, if he had been impressed, was showing none of it.

"Do you have any whiskey?" He asked as if the shooting exhibition had not occurred.

"No, I don't drink."

"Do you have any coffee?"

"Some."

Running Bull looked once more toward where the pan had disappeared, then stretched back placing his hand on the horse's rump and glanced at the mule.

"I do like coffee. Haven't had any for awhile. You can come along, Billy Kavanaugh – Lame Wolf."

"I prefer Lame Wolf."

"Very well, Lame Wolf. You might as well ride along with us. I'll show you my version of the Old West."

Billy smiled. "I'll bet it will be different than Buffalo Bill's."

"Cody is still alive?" He guided his horse closer to Billy. "He killed a friend of mine —years ago."

"Just saw him last year. I rode for him a couple days. He started a circus."

"I thought I killed that son of a bitch once over on War Bonnet Creek. I hit him in the head.

Too thick to matter, I guess. He ought to be in a circus in the freak show of liars." He motioned the braves to him.

"Lame Wolf will join us. He is Sada's son. Do you remember Sada, Spotted Horse?"

The man nodded his assent and studied Billy more carefully.

"Put back what you have taken and do not take from him until you ask of me. It's a long way to the lodges. I'd like to get there tomorrow." They urged the mounts to the northwest and set off. The party had only gone a few hundred yards when Running Bull joined Billy at the rear of the formation. They settled into a steady walk.

"Did your mother tell you I was there the day you were born?" He squinted toward Billy waiting for a reply.

"Yes. She said you drove off the wolf."

"Did she tell you of Maha?"

"Yes."

"She was my wife and I loved her." It was a matter of fact statement, almost bereft of emotion. "She and my son both died. Your father saved them to be killed by the miners. He glanced toward the west. "It is going to rain".

Billy did not register his surprise at the admission but looked ahead. They rode quietly for awhile, and then he said "I loved Ma, too. Pa and Mary brought us all to Minsi and we took good care of her. I know she loved Pa; sometimes I think it got real complicated for him because he loved Mary too."

"Who knows about love? Its like a great puma about the time you think you understand it, it tears you apart".

He glanced behind and back to Billy. "Kavanaugh is not as great a liar and traitor as I thought he was."

Ahead there were some craggy bluffs, sun bleached, in browns and tans with undertones of red. The long open vista was barred by stands of pine, and there were more far away crests that looked like hens' combs. Beneath his stirrups the soap weed stood like white lanterns patiently awaiting the right moths to fertilize their future.

Billy felt quietly content, even riding among strangers. Ahead Spotted Horse was leading and Billy felt a vague assurance that Running Bull beside him was prone to liking him. He was in the west, in the company of renegade red men and the notion appealed to him. He had no premonition that the choice he had made would change him utterly and that within days those great changes would fall heavily upon him.

It began to rain in earnest and lightning began to flash with great peals of thunder. They sprinted into a cluster of trees, dismounted, and sought shelter beneath the limbs.

New York City Vicinity
May 1884

Sara, Heddy, and Jane carefully studied the gate in the cemetery fence. The mausoleum was crouched like a cat just beyond the iron rails. Sara strained her eyes into the dark, leaning forward on the wagon seat. "I think that must be it. I think I see some fresh flowers. Do you see them, Heddy?"

"No." There was a pause. "Oh, now I do."

"Who has the bar?"

"I do," came the muffled reply, "it's too dark to see anything and this bar is heavy."

"I can see the gate is open, but there may be a lock on the door of the mausoleum. I think we can break it with the bar if we have to."

"How are we going to tell what is what? Isn't there usually more than one drawer in those buildings?"

"I don't know, Janie. We will try them all."

"Are you sure this is a good idea? I'm afraid, suppose we get caught?"

"You want to study anatomy – really study it, don't you?"

"Yes, Sara, but I didn't think I should have to collect my own cadaver."

"It's our cadaver. You know that the boys aren't going to share."

"They are really bastards, you know it." Heddy enjoined testily.

"They're interested in sharing bodies all right," Janie tittered, "our bodies, but they aren't likely to share the cadaver with us."

"Pete Mitchell isn't as bad as the rest, and he is very polite. He probably would have helped if we'd asked him." Sara pointed out.

"That's a big money family, the Mitchells. Maybe that is why he is so polite. My father knows Pete's father, Mason Mitchell."

"Pete is very smart, I mean not just about medicine – all kinds of things."

"That's true enough, Sara. He sure is head and shoulders above the rest of the pack."

Sara reined the wagon tightly and looked toward the high Iron Gate nearly invisible against the night sky.

"Are we ready?" Heddy ventured.

"I'm ready – you, Jane?"

"I'm scared. Suppose somebody catches us?"

"Supposed lightning strikes," Sara replied. "We need a cadaver, so let's get on with it."

"I'm having trouble with these trousers. If we get caught, they'll find out we're girls anyway."

"Better than bustles, I'm going to get me one of those bloomer outfits. That would cause a stir."

"Oh, Heddy..."

"Are you sure that the cemetery caretaker is at the pub, Jane?"

"Almost always is - he takes his supper now and I left a bottle of whiskey on his desk just as he left. I know he didn't see me. I put it down and got out of there. When he finds the whiskey he'll be gone." She looked toward the mausoleum.

"Well, now is the time. Shall we go ahead?" Sara asked. "We can still stop."

"Lead on, Sara that is a scary looking place."

"Who has the lamp? It's going to be dark in there."

"I have the bar, the lamp, and some matches, Heddy."

"Well?" Sara asked.

"I'm tired of those boys running us down, calling us names. They don't want us to be in medicine just like they don't want us to vote." Jane noted.

"Let's go." The three glanced apprehensively at the mausoleum in the dark distance.

"I hope it's a man. The body I mean. Let me take the lamp, Jane."

"It is a man. You read the obituary." Sara replied.

"Yes, a young man who drowned."

"Heddy..."

"Well, might just as well be young." The three laughed quietly and they rose, passed through the gate and ran quickly to the mausoleum door.

"What about the guard – the caretaker? I'm still worried about him."

"He's probably found that bottle of whiskey and well into it by now."

"To hell with him, I'm more worried about getting the body back through the fence."

Sara tugged at the door and it gave way with a creaking noise. Quickly they moved inside to the mausoleum, closed the door snug behind them, and stoked up the kerosene lamp. It lit up first blue, and then gave way to a steady sinister yellow glow.

"Bring it closer. Look here – this bottom drawer – it's a new tag. John Charles Brooks -1864-1884."

"That's it, that's it. I remember the name." Sara tugged at the drawer. It did not budge. "Give me a hand."

Heddy also grasped the handle, but it remained fast. Sara sat down on the floor, placed both feet on either side of it and pulled. It creaked slightly. Jane pried with the bar and it gave way a little more, Sara pulled again and Heddy put her back into it. "Come on, Jane, give us a pull. Everybody now, one, two, three pull. Again one, two, three pull." With a rasping sound, the drawer finally slid slowly out.

"Hold the lantern over here, Jane."

"I am."

Slowly they slid the drawer open, revealing the well-dressed corpse of a young man with sunken cheeks and funeral face make-up already peeling.

"Oh," Jane groaned, "oh, my – look at his face, yuck!"

"He has a ring on," behind Sara came a gagging sound, "and don't you get sick on us Jane. What about the ring?"

"Well, take it off, Heddy." Sara said tilting the light for a better look.

"I don't know about this..."

"Take it off," Sara whispered. "We will leave it in the drawer."

Heddy lifted the hand and managed to wrest the ring from it and said hoarsely, "it's off. God, his hand feels cold and awful."

"Of course, --he's dead. Come on, now. We have to get him out."

"I have to pee."

"For God's sake, Jane, not now." Sara replied in thinly disguised disgust.

"I have to go." She replied urgently.

"Well, go in the corner if you have to go. We can't stop once we get outside the door; we are going to have to hurry to the wagon."

Heddy spoke up. "Now we are going to desecrate this place."

"Isn't that what we are doing already? Go ahead and pee, Jane. Then we have to get out of here. Leave the lantern, we should carry everything away and leave the bar too. We have to move quickly."

Jane set the lantern down and struggled with her belt and disappeared from the lantern glow. Sara and Heddy could hear her splashing against the wall, and managed to lift the limp body from the drawer.

"He is heavy. Shouldn't we take his clothes off?"

"No, not now, what would we do if we got caught dragging a naked dead man down the street? What are you thinking of, Heddy? Let's get out of here, and undress him later."

"I hope the horse hasn't run off with the wagon," she mused as a worst-case-scenario.

"He's not going to do that –now, lift." Sara said. "Jane, are you done?" Jane appeared beside her. "Grab his legs. I'll take his shoulders. Get him in the middle Heddy."

Clumsily bearing the body, they pushed against the heavy door. "Turn off the lamp!"

They dropped the body unceremoniously on the floor with a dull thump. "Put the lantern and the bar in the drawer and push it closed. Hurry! We don't want anyone to see a light in here." She tried to focus on their burden in the dim doorway.

"He's heavy – heavier than I thought. I'll take the shoulders. Jane, you get the middle. Take the legs, Heddy."

With much effort they raised the body and staggered out of the tomb wrestling with the weight.

"Wait --wait, my pants are coming down. I didn't get my belt tight."

"Come on, Jane -- we're right in the middle, for God's sake."

Heddy tripped and dropped the legs. Sara fell over the body and Jane on top of her.

"Get up, get up, get up." Sara snorted horrified at being sandwiched between the bodies above and below her.

"Damn it, Heddy!" Jane chimed in, equally appalled at the pile-up.

Once again they righted the body and staggered toward the cemetery gate. "Don't drop his legs."

They reached the wagon and with a great heave dumped the body into the wagon box and covered it with a canvas. "We did it, we did it!" Heddy exalted.

"Yes, but we are not back to the lab yet. Stay focused." Sara replied as she clambered up to the wagon seat.

Heddy and Jane crept into the wagon box trying to avoid the crumpled form.

"Let's get out of here, Sara."

The three began to giggle part in success, part in relief. Sara picked up the reins and clucked the horse head. She smiled. "Anyone else hav'ta pee?"

Once more they began to laugh trying to stifle the sounds in their sleeves.

"No," Heddy replied, "but I already wet my pants."

As the horse surged ahead, the three began to laugh in earnest. Jane added between the peals, "what a night! Stay focused Sara."

They bumped along the cemetery road then on to a cobbled street leading to the medical school.

"I never thought I would have to do this just to become a doctor."

"Me either, but I'm more resolved now than ever."

"When we get back to the lab we will take his clothes off and cover him up with a sheet."

"You did get the donor form right, Sara?"

"Yes, I have the donor form. I told you I did."

"All signed and everything?"

256

"My mother signed it and wrote it was her nephew George."

"Will somebody check?"

"I don't think so; I told her that we needed a cadaver. She said when she signed the donor form that she didn't want to know any more about it."

"Gee." Jane said wiping at her nose. "I don't think my mother would have done it."

"Anyway, she doesn't have a nephew it was her uncle's name and I don't think the school will check. That is if they ever want another donation."

"Gee, your mom is really something."

Sara chuckled, "she's something alright, and she's something else." The wagon made a sharp turn and drew up behind the school – a light was on in the laboratory.

Chapter 27

New York City
April 1885

Peter Mitchell had turned into a great resource. He had accepted the women at medical school from the outset. From time to time he would come to their apartment, always bearing gifts, chocolates, flowers or some special snack purchased at the deli down the street.

It was obvious to Sara and the other girls that he was a lonely person, and they were not surprised to learn he was an only child raised in wealth by nannies and tutors. He had not gone to public school and though very polite, he was also naive and a little on the effeminate side. Peter's father came from a wealthy family and amassed a fortune manufacturing barbed wire and farm tools. He quietly supported a number of charities. Peter's mother had been strictly high society, born into a family of a shipping magnate. She was horrified and overprotective about the prospect of her son "giving out narcotics and sawing off legs." Medicine to her was filth and stink and she was aghast at Peter seeing "all those naked bodies!"

Sara was at first uncomfortable with Peter's attentions, but gradually she and the other girls came to accept him as "family." They enjoyed his tasty gifts and attention, but most of all they welcomed his intellect. He knew something about everything, and his close-to-genius mentality was well balanced by his quiet geniality. Peter tutored the girls on whatever they perceived needed to be learned. It was not altogether a surprise when he invited the three of them to dinner one evening, but it was a surprise when he invited Sara, alone, to dinner one week later.

After finishing their meal, where Sara felt her best manners had been tested, they retired to the parlor. It was impeccably decorated with a large tan and blue Oriental rug, and fresh flowers. A large portrait of Grandfather Mitchell was balanced by a dark Vermeer portrait on the opposite side wall. The furniture was dark leather and a slide rocker with green upholstery. Sara seated herself on the sofa and was joined by Peter, both patiently awaiting his father to fire a cigar.

"Would you like some sherry, dear? Do you drink sherry?"

"Not usually, Mrs. Mitchell. My mother does on occasion, but I rarely do."

"This is an occasion," his father piped nodding towards Peter through a cloud of smoke. "Pour Sara and your mother a sherry and," he held up his empty glass, "bring me another whiskey and get one for yourself."

"The lamb was excellent, Mrs. Mitchell. I enjoyed it very much. It was a real treat for me."

"I'm glad you enjoyed it, dear. You don't have lamb often?" A small, wooly white dog appeared and launched itself into her lap. "Ah, Pooky, precious," she lifted the dog to eye level. "You came to join us. We were just talking about lamb, you precious little darling." She began to stroke the dog that soon settled into her ample lap. "You don't eat lamb?" she continued, looking toward Sara.

"Not often," Sara was beginning to feel a little uncomfortable and wished she had not mentioned it. "We raise our own beef, fish from the river, and hunt venison, duck, and even an occasional bear."

Mrs. Mitchell placed her hand over her heart. "Bear meat, my gracious!" She said breathlessly. "It's a wonder it didn't make hair grow on your chin."

"Lots of people eat bear meat, Mildred. I've eaten some myself, fat and rich and bear fat makes the best pastry."

"Mother, Sara lives on a large farm upstate in Minsi, near the Delaware River."

"Venison and bear meat, I guess so. Those creatures are still about?"

"My two brothers were hunters. Only one is at home now, Billy went away more than a year ago, out west."

"Ran away?" The small dog suddenly appeared restive in her lap, licking her fingers and panting a frolicsome look.

"Oh no, Mrs. Mitchell, he's a wanderer, an adventurer, I guess. He always wanted to go, but I think he will back soon. He was upset after his mother died."

"His mother, I thought your mother was alive. The Director of the Medical School, Dr. Shaw, indicated that she had made a generous contribution to the school."

"Well, Mrs. Mitchell, they are really not my biological brothers. We were just raised together."

"Oh, I see..." Her curiosity more intent, she regarded Sara carefully.

"Their mother died about two years ago. She was a Cheyenne Indian."

"Oh?" The explicative hung in the silence like a shroud.

"My other brother is here in the city studying law."

"Here, mother – here's your sherry. Sara, would you care to try this? If you do not like the taste of it, don't drink it." Peter tried to deflect the conversation from family matters.

"What does your father do, Sara?" Mildred Mitchell pushed on.

"My father is dead. He was killed in the war - in Virginia."

"A lot of good men died there," Mr. Mitchell enjoined through a draft of blue smoke.

"Oh, what a shame," she continued. "Then you were raised by your mother."

"Not exactly." Sara's discomfort showed as she adjusted in her chair.

"Mother, why don't we talk about something else? Have you read about the developments in electricity?"

"I don't care about electricity, Peter. I am interested in your friend."

"Well, you should be interested in electricity. It's changing our lives."

"Pshaw!" She sipped at her sherry and bored into Sara with her eyes. "Are you an orphan?"

"For God's sake, Mildred, you're being impolite. She's our guest, this is not an inquisition. I apologize for her, Sara. Now let's talk about something else."

"It's all right, Mr. Mitchell, I was raised by my Aunt Mary."

"Your aunt? She is the Mary who made the..."

"Enough, Mildred, this young lady is our guest!"

"Yes, Mother. You don't wish to make her more uncomfortable." Peter acidly interjected.

"It's all right. I'm not." Sara smiled although uneasy in the exchange.

"Let's talk about school. How are you doing on the cadaver?" Peter asked enjoying the anticipated response from his mother.

"Oh, my God!" Once more Mildred placed her hand over her heart and exhaled audibly.

Peter Mitchell's father leaned further back in his chair and puffed some smoke toward the ceiling. "Yes, Sara, how are you doing with the cadaver?"

Dakota Territory
June 1885

"Speak English, Lame Wolf."

"You know, Running Bull, every time you call me in it's something different."

"I need the practice today." He gestured for Billy to sit down.

"What is it you want?" Billy sat down cross legged in front of the aging leader.

"I want you to head over to Buffalo and bring back some whiskey."

"Whiskey, you want me to ride all the way to Buffalo for whiskey?"

"Yes."

"That's a two day ride; you want me to ride all the way to Buffalo to get whiskey?" We have been riding hard for week. You have the money, I guess?"

"I have money here." He proffered a leather purse bulging with gold coins. "Take your mule and bring us back a couple of casks."

"Sounds like you are planning another drunk-up. Is anyone going with me?"

"No." He stroked his chin and thought for a moment. "Lame Wolf, also bring us some tobacco, two, no three twists, more coffee, fifty pounds of salt, dried beans and six boxes of 44-40's. See if you can pick up another 44-40 Winchester."

"Do you want flour also? Might just as well make it a big order," Billy added facetiously.

Running Bull flashed a long crooked smile. "If you think of anything else, I'll send a few Buffalo Robes so you can do some trading."

"No sense going empty – waste of a mule, right?"

Running Bull laughed at Billy's irony. "You'll share a pipe?"

"For a puff or two, when do you want me to go?"

"Today, I want you to leave as soon as you can."

"You're sure I can find my way back? I might take your money and go to St. Louis."

They both smiled at the ridiculous prospect. Billy had fitted in the first week he had arrived. Many evenings in the two years since he joined them he had shared stories of the white man's world, tales from beyond the great river. His knowledge and use of the Cheyenne language was now so complete that he had to think to convert to English.

He'd gone out with them on a number of hunts and raids to run off horses and throw a few shots at work crews or settler wagons, before riding off. Once when they were being pursued by cavalry, Billy had dropped three horses and shot a lieutenant from his horse almost three hundred yards away. He guessed he hadn't killed him because before he and Blue Shirt had taken to their heels, he saw the man run and remount. The sun and wind had turned Billy's complexion quite dark; only in winter could one determine him to be white.

"Running Bull, I have been meaning to ask you something."

"So ask," he puffed his pipe and passed it over.

"It's about Calling Jays."

"You mean, Woman Who Calls to Jays, and what?"

"I would like to marry her. Take her as my woman. Is that all right with you?" He returned the pipe.

"It's all right with me, but what about Black Eagle? She is his niece, you know, and he has raised her up. Her whole family was killed by a band of buffalo hunters. He is not likely to take kindly to the marriage. He thinks half breeds are worse than white men and he hates white men. You're doubly damned. He was just a ten year old boy fixing fish traps when your father and company came down on them at Agate Creek. He was the only surviving boy, and only because they did not find him. Arapahos picked him up; he lived with them awhile, and came back after the battle at Cedar Butte. He flat hates you – it's just that simple. He won't kill you because I told him not to. I would shoot him if he did, but he won't do you any favors either." Running Bull smirked at Billy's fallen countenance.

"There are a couple of eligible women here, Billy. Woman with Flowers; she is special. You could do worse. She is a little older, but wiser and she could make you glad she is there on cold winter nights."

"While I'm gone I was wondering if you might say a word or two, anyway."

"Not likely to do any good, Lame Wolf." I can speak, but I don't think it will change a thing. This is a family matter and I have no say unless asked. His feelings about half breeds like you are deeply ingrained." He scratched his head. "Woman Who Calls to Jays, I guessed you would have chosen differently. There is Red Apron Woman or Woman with Smiling Face."

"No." He paused, reflecting. Calling Jays came up to Billy's chest, she had beautiful dark copper skin, a round face, short, small hard breasts, and was a little rotund, with full but firm hips. She had a long straight nose flanked by large, dark eyes.

"You know that I have never done a single thing against him- nothing. I even caught a couple of his horses that had run off and I brought back to him."

"Lame Wolf, you are highly regarded here but not by Black Eagle. Why Calling Jays? There would be little problem with the other two. Red Apron reminds me of your mother."

"Yes, me too, but Red Apron and Smiling face are both pretty sour. Calling Jays is full of life, she has a very good nature, and she likes me very much. She also wants to learn English, I like that."

"Have you been tinkering with her, Lame Wolf?"

"Well, not really tinkering with her, I've touched her once or twice."

"Blue Shirt's boy had an interest in her, didn't he?"

"I know about Iron Hatchet. Calling Jays says she wants nothing to do with him or White Feather."

"You're tinkering could be a problem, if Black Eagle finds out about it, and it happens to be contrary to his family plans, there may be trouble."

"What should I do?"

"Talk to him, tell him you're concerned. Ask for his permission and don't forget to bring him gifts. How many horses do you have?"

"Six."

"Well, if that's not enough, I'll give you a couple of mine. It will take some doing, if he is inclined at all." He drew on the pipe and handed it over, watching Billy carefully. "Why don't you ask him today before you leave? Give him some time to think it over? Bring him one of your horses."

Billy offered the pipe back and expelled the smoke he had been holding in his cheeks.

"What do you think are the chances?"

"I don't know, Billy, he might be offended. He may talk to Calling Jays. Best you leave before he talks to her. If he becomes angry, your absence should give him time to cool off." He drew thoughtfully on the pipe. "He has killed four men I know of, you might be the fifth." He grinned.

"Thanks for your vote of confidence." Billy started to leave. "I'll go talk with him now."

"Offer him horses, if he takes it well, maybe he would relent a bit and maybe not.

Billy eased the horse down the steep hill, keeping a firm grip on the mule rope. At the bottom was a swale strung by tangled skeins of vetch, the bright purple flowers in contrast to the green and tan grasses about it. He had been thinking about Calling Jays since he so abruptly left for Buffalo. Black Eagle had refused his offer, but Billy was still determined to be with her. The return seemed shorter because of his familiarity with landmarks, and with a little luck he would make camp by morning.

He did not hurry, nor did he dawdle, but constantly scouted the route of his passing for signs of trouble. Danger could come from many sources, suddenly and seemingly from nowhere. For this was the no man's land of red and white and the cargo he carried would appeal to both. Wandering bands of Sioux traversed the area regularly, and renegade groups pursued by cavalry. Whites sometimes shot passing Indians merely suspected of being renegades, and thought little about it. He was packing two new Winchesters with ten boxes of ammunition, two two-gallon casks of whiskey and other supplies. If the Sioux caught him and he could not talk his way out of it, they would kill him for the whiskey and rifles; if soldiers stopped him, they would likely kill him for the Winchesters and ammunition and use the whiskey for a celebration.

The only riders he saw had been a way off; they had appeared to be Cheyenne in a hurry. Billy gathered some buffalo chips and a few twigs and built a small fire just before dark. Then, as the evening shadows reached into darkness, he carefully led the horses and mule into a small stand of trees half a mile from where the fire had been.

The wisdom of the move was apparent at first light for the spot he had left was being examined by a small hunting party of Sioux. He loaded the new Winchesters, cradled his own Henry under his arm and waited. One of the riders gestured towards where Billy was hiding, but after milling around for a while, they set off in the opposite direction, apparently with more important business elsewhere. Billy waited two hours before he resumed his course, evermore mindful of the danger.

At length he arrived among the circled tepees and rode directly to the one with thirteen black stripes, the residence of Running Bull. He kneeled and called into the shelter.

"I'm back, Running Bull."

"I can see that! Step through."

"Just a minute, I have a couple of things to bring in." He collected the two new Winchesters and took them inside.

"These forty-four forties were still in grease. I cleaned them up."

"Excellent, it took you long enough! Have any news or any trouble?"

"Not much of either. The town's full of talk, nesters and sheep men, are makin' trouble for the cattlemen and Cattlemen's Association is doing away with farmers; the miners are complaining about lodes and runs and whatever. None of them have regard for anything except greed."

Running Bull settled back and carefully examined the new rifles. "Miners, --there's real trouble brewing there." He enjoyed a moment of satisfaction as he ran his hand down the rifle stock.

"Good, maybe they'll kill one another off." Billy settled down on a folded buffalo robe. "I'm glad to be back. I ran into a Sioux hunting party. They didn't see me or else they didn't care to." He gestured toward his mule. "I've got the other stuff – whiskey, tobacco, beans and flour. They had sugar so I got some of that too."

The two men ducked outside and began to unburden the mule, completing the task silently and quickly.
"I thought I would find Calling Jays. Did you speak with Black Eagle?"

He nodded his assent. "He is not happy about this, Lame Wolf. As a matter of fact, I think he intends to kill you," he drolly intoned.

Billy blanched white and stepped back. "Why? I thought he was all right when I left, I offered him horses, thought he'd come around."
"He has made ready, he intends to kill you tomorrow."
"Tomorrow, can you stop him?"

"No, only you can stop it. He has named a place and watchers. Too bad he refused the horses, you could try again, but I doubt it will make any difference."

"I guess I should not have come back."

"I sent out some riders to find you, but no luck, so they came back."

"What do I do, Running Bull?"

"Well, you can hightail it the hell out of here. I can protect you if you stay away from her. Or..."

"Or what, I'm not just going to forget about her, so that's out."

"Stay and fight him then, but I don't recommend it."

Billy leaned heavily on the mule and shaded his eyes from the sun with his other hand. He sighed and looked toward Black Eagle's tepee.

"Running Bull, I've wanted to come here all of my life. I have wanted to be with you since my mother filled my head with stories about the West, the buffalo, and the plains. I am not going to run!"

"You could still stay out here – just stay away from here."

"I'm not going to run and I'm not going to give up on Calling Jays - I love her. So send word to that that son-of-a-bitch that I'll meet him."

Running Bull nodded. "I will. They have confined Calling Jays, but one thing I can do is to call her and her mother over here."

"I'll set the rest of the stuff inside. Are you going to pass out the whiskey?" He picked up the cask and started toward the tent.

"Tonight at the fire, Many Horns has made medicine; we will dance tonight. You can get killed tomorrow."

"I'll pass on the whiskey. Thank you for your confidence." Billy grinned despite the seriousness of the situation.

"Black Eagle won't pass on the whiskey. It could help if he gets lit up tonight". Running

Bull smiled and started for the tepee of Woman with Long Braids and her daughter, Woman Who Calls to Jays.

Billy watched him make his way and sat inside among the supplies. He drew his knife and slipped the small honing stone from its sheath, spit on it and began to slide the blade as if to pick a small slice from it.

"I'm not going back and I'm not leaving Calling Jays. Bring it on, Black Eagle, you sorry son-of-a-bitch."

The medicine dance lasted well into the night. All of the men shuffled to the sound of their feet and a dull repetitive chant with high emotion and occasional burst of eerie yells. The dancing stopped near midnight and, feeling exhausted and cleansed, they gathered at the striped tepee for libations.

Billy had spotted Black Eagle early on and purposely avoided him. After the first cask began its round, he promptly left to find Calling Jays. The night passed as if there would be no tomorrow, no recrimination or anticipated combat. Billy was hopeful that the matter might pass and some bargaining could proceed, so he had reassured Calling Jays.

Shortly before dawn, Running Bull ducked beneath the flap door. Billy was curled up with Calling Jays and did not hear him at first.

"Get up, Lame Wolf, get up. We must hurry; a messenger from Black Eagle has already called us. It seems he wants to get this over with."
"What?" Billy's sleepy stupor had not worn off. "You mean the fight is still on?"
"Yes, you must hurry! If Black Eagle knew she was here, he would be in a rage."
"We have to fight?"

"When you get there, challenge him. Bluff him if you can, he might not choose to kill you, but you're in for it. I think he is pretty well hung-over, so he might back off."
Calling Jays had been listening and tears welled in her eyes. "Oh, Lame Wolf, I fear."

"No matter what happens, you remember I love you and always will." He stroked her face lightly.

"You, woman, have caused lots of trouble. If Lame Wolf dies, I will kill Black Eagle and then I will kill you." Running Bull spoke with violence Billy had not heard before and Calling Jays cringed before the fierce eyes.

Billy tightened his buckskin britches and adjusted his knife scabbard. "Did you have to say that? Promise me you won't hurt her."

"She needs to be frightened." Running Bull replied angrily.
"Running Bull. I am scared enough for the both of us."

"Come! Black Eagle has chosen the place. We will make a large circle and you will fight inside it."

As they hurried beyond the round of tents, Billy noticed that only a few women and children could be seen. The warriors had formed a large circle beyond a small ridge where everyone appeared expressionless, and all were very quiet.

He approached the ring and could not discern Black Eagle from the rest of those gathered. Then some warriors separated and Black Eagle emerged from among them. There would be no parley. Their eyes met and Black Eagle, with a menacing move, came forward with his knife drawn. Billy was taller by a head, but Black Eagle was broad across the chest and shoulders. He was bare to the waist with a smear of yellow paint extending from shoulder to shoulder and wide white spots around his eyes. He made no sound in his sudden rush. Billy deflected the first slash, and the blades struck sparks. Black Eagle did not step back, and with a quick slice, nicked Billy's thigh. Billy flinched and stepped back. Black Eagle made a second rush, slashing at his face, but his momentum carried him past, and Billy kicked him aside. Black Eagle made a feint, and with a rounding motion, struck again. Billy parried the slash, and his own slash cut hair from Black Eagle's braid. Infuriated, the man struck back; again Billy blocked the blade with his own, but with a quick slash down and across, Black Eagle cut deeply into the back of Billy's hand and his knife fell away. Sensing the advantage, Black Eagle slashed at his side and the nick spilled blood. Another attack drew blood from Billy's arm. Sensing victory, Black Eagle took a chance, smirked and rushed for the kill. Billy caught up both his wrists, allowing the momentum to push them; then he dropped to his back kicked up and catapulted Black Eagle upward. There was a sailing shadow over Billy's face as Black Eagle made the apex of his flight, then fell behind. Billy, still holding the wrists, heard the sickening "whap" as Black Eagle struck the earth fully extended, the sound of his breath bursting outward. Quickly Billy released the wrists and, seizing Black Eagle's knife, put it to his throat while the man struggled for breath.

"I could kill you now, you son-of-a-bitch, but it would serve no purpose. But by God, you will remember this day." With a deep cutting slash, Billy ripped Black Eagle's chest from nipple to nipple. The blood spurted and began to run in a wide swath. Again Billy put the knife to Black Eagle's throat and in clear, concise Cheyenne, loud enough for all to hear: "Do you want to die?" He pressed the knife to the angle of the jaw until a drop of blood began to show. "Do you want to die?" This time he spoke louder.

Black Eagle muffled, "No."

"You now live because I choose to let you live." Billy stood up, threw Black Eagle's knife, sticking it in the ground close to his ear.

Blood was running down Billy's arms and his hand was dripping steadily as he looked toward his moccasins, and saw them filling with blood. Without saying another word, he limped toward the surrounding circle that opened as he approached. Running Bull fell in step with him. "Very good, Lame Wolf, but you should have killed him." He dispassionately noted.

"Well, I didn't."

"He will leave you alone, but he will always resent the embarrassment you have caused him. You didn't make a new friend today".

"That will be his problem. He can also remind himself that he lives with the scars, his old resentments have brought him to this place."

They plodded along in silence toward the stripped tipi. Billy, suddenly felt very weak, stumbled and Running Bull supported him.

"You're a cocky bastard, Kavanaugh, but damned if you didn't come through – nicked up and all. I thought he was going to kill you. I sure wouldn't have bet on you."

"Thanks for your confidence Running Bull, I am really inspired by it" he quipped. Again he staggered, almost going down a second time. Running Bull hauled him toward his tent. Inside the flap, Billy collapsed.

"Here, Lame Wolf, here; lie back. Take a sip of this whiskey."

Billy felt the clear fluid burn its way to his belly. He exhaled loudly and collapsed on the pile of buffalo robes. Running Bull's features started to fade to a grayish haze; he refocused.

"You're going to be all right. I'm going over to bring Woman with Long Braids; she's good with wounds - I'll be back."

"Calling Jays will come?"

"No, I'm going to set you a new lodge. I think the matter has been solved. Black Eagle will take three horses for her now. She's brought him bad luck. You can come for her later." He started out through the door flap, then looked back and smiled. "If he hadn't been hung over he probably would have killed you."

"Well, he didn't."

Running Bull chuckled and disappeared from the opening.

New York City
July 1885

Liam settled back in the large overstuffed chair and regarded Sol Rosenstein across from him. Often those in the firm, who were available, would gather in the library for afternoon coffee and a snack. The firm was overrun with business and both Sutter and Ryan were in court most of the junior partners were with them. Li busied himself slicing a piece of Brie cheese to apply to a cracker. Sol was engrossed in a magazine and had hardly looked up.

"What magazine is that, Sol? It must be interesting."

"It's an article on immigration policy."

"Labor troubles on your mind again?"

"No worse. This claptrap nonsense by John Fiske is, all about evolutionary theory."

"Do you mean Darwin stuff?"

"More political racism for monkeys and people, for instance, this expounds that cultural and social patterns are determined by heredity. Jews, Asians, Negroes, Indians and Middle Easterners have inferior blood and these inferiors are the reason for America's social problems ergo, they do not belong here."

"I don't believe that." Li derisively smiled and nibbled at the cracker

."There's more; Fiske thinks that human evolution culminated in the Anglo Saxon race. The rest of us are primitives since we did not originate in northwestern Europe.

"I don't think anyone knows where humans originated."

"These so-called scholars cite that the finer points of civilization are due to the Anglo Saxon race. They call this scientific evidence."

"Scientific evidence according to what they want to prove, what is best for them? What about the Egyptians, the fertile crescent and all that?"

"Precisely, there is always someone who has a scientific answer to support politics or profits. Did you know that you can tell a person's intelligence by looking at them?"

"No, but I'm interested, how do I do that?"

"Well, it's very scientific. You study the slope of their forehead."

"Really, and what do I study?"

Sol laughed. "Intelligent people are likely to have a high forehead according to Fiske."

"That would let me out. I can't keep the hair out of my eyes."

"Well, you see, that proves the point. As you no doubt have noticed, my hair line is receding rapidly. Soon I won't have a forehead – just a dome. Then I will really look intelligent."

Liam laughed as Sol swept his hand over his thinning hair. "I may never be intelligent, then? What a crushing blow, I thought I already was."

"Cow pies," Liam responded

"Of course since your mother was a Cheyenne, you have another strike against you."

"I'm seriously depressed about this prospect. What cow-pie logic that is." Liam laughed

Sol reached for his coffee, settled back, and crossed his legs. "You know, Liam, there is a serious sinister side to this. The evolutionists strike at the very heart of freedom. The very principles this country was founded on. Superiority of Anglo Saxons, the inferiority of all others, gives them the opportunity to fix blame. Why do you think this is so important?"

"Sol, you're much smarter than I am and I don't know, but I'd guess so long as you can blame evolution, you can throw up your hands and say we can't do anything about helping them, since they already are cursed."

"That's absolutely correct. There is a growing emigrant phobia here; not only are non-Anglos inferior in intellect - they also are the basis for American's social problems. These people can't reason."

"So, they are the root of all social evils - the tenement district, the pig market, railroad strikes and the Knights of Labor and Terrence Powderly, wow! What else?" Liam consumed his cracker and took a swallow of coffee.

"You will be interested to know that the population of the United States will rapidly become darker in pigmentation, smaller in stature, more mercurial, short-tempered, and more attached to music and art and given to crimes of larceny, assault, murder and sexual immorality."

"Wow! Is there anything else?" He sat back, crossing his legs and added derisively, "Sounds serious."

"One last thing: the ratio of insanity to the population will rapidly increase." Sol sat back in resolved satisfaction. "Our society will become sexually immoral, increasingly violent and prone to craziness."

"From the ideas of Fiske, the point is proven." Sol took another sip of coffee, set down the cup and settled deeper into his chair. He stroked his chin and became more serious. "I was down on Wall Street day before yesterday. There were a group of men carrying placards. The signs said things like 'I cannot read this sign, what right do I have to children?' and 'I must drink alcohol to sustain my life, shall I transfer this craving to others?' You know, they still don't have things in order down south, this long after the war. This eugenics stuff could also become an excuse for persecuting masses of people. It is already troublesome for the law."

"Signs on Wall Street why carry them on Wall Street?" Liam shook his head in disbelief.

"The social problems grow and the nation is changing so rapidly." Sol shook his head and stretched his arms.

"On Wall Street, one might expect something like that in the tenements or the Pig Market."

"That's not where the message will accomplish anything. They are on Wall Street because that's where the money and power are."

"The tenements are festering sores. Charity Lying In is near the market. Sara works and works, but there never seems an end to it."

"Well, bless her." Sol paused and hitched at his belt. "Have you been following the McCormick strike? It's been pretty hot last couple of days."

"No." He drank his remaining coffee.

"I wonder what the eugenics folks will say about this strike." Sol stood and brushed some crumbs from his trousers. "Their explanation should be a dandy."

Liam watched Sol leave the room, poured another coffee, picked up his magazine from the table and opened it. The contents listed an article on the scientific rationale for the restrictions of immigration. He turned to the page and began to read.

Across town Sara left the delivery room and went to the nurse's station to annotate a chart. It had been an uneventful delivery – forty minutes of labor to the mother's obvious joy at her second son. Sara reviewed the chart, made her notes, and paused to muse aloud.

"Well, young Ulrich. You will have a warm homecoming – five sisters and a brother."

She felt slightly faint so she sat down near an open window and reviewed the swarming street squalor below, then slowly passed her hand over her abdomen and pressed lightly on her umbilicus.

In a city half a continent away, events were developing that would cause a nation to stagger in her steps toward development, question the very basis of its founding and shake its system of justice to its roots.

Chapter 28

Sutter Law Offices
New York City, October 1886

Will was bent forward over his desk, flanked by piles of documents.

"You busy, Will?"

"Always busy." Sutter reviewed the man standing in the doorway to his office, a newspaper rolled tightly in his hand. "Come on in, Liam – you look upset."

"You're damn right I am! This can't happen in America, and Chicago is in America!" He shook the paper and tossed it on the desk blotter desk knocking papers awry.

"What can't happen in America?" Will blandly replied, after glimpsing at the paper with concerned curiosity.

"This, they found them guilty! They're going to hang them, for Christ sake!" He tapped the newspaper headlines.

"Yes, I read it," Will replied, "So? Why does that make you so upset"?

"Well?" Liam straightened, hands on hips. "I think the whole thing smells like a lynching".

"Liam, lord knows I have been in this business for a long time. The decision is a travesty of justice. Sit down; we can talk about it. This Haymarket business has troubled me for a long time. We've talked about it before and…"

"How could this happen? What happened?" Liam broke in. "I can't believe it!" They riot in Haymarket Square. Somebody throws a bomb and no one knows who did what, and they gather up some German emigrants, all but Parsons. The others were about straight of the boat and now they will hang them because they went to a labor rally? This is justice?"

"Well, Liam, you know what I have said many times. Cases are often lost before the trial starts. The press is often as much responsible for a conviction as a prosecutor; the press sets the stage for fear, panic, disorder, and misinformation, and a couple of months later are remorseful over their negligence."

"But this case - just being present they get arrested and hanged."

"The strike was against industrial powers - The Knights of Labor versus the McCormick Corporation. The press and would-be juries want to fix blame and support the establishment and the status quo. There is a majority of workers not involved with the Knights. They just want to keep their jobs and to hell with the eight hour day. This trial has been engulfed in a national wave of immigration fear. It gets further complicated because seven cops were killed and over sixty wounded. There was urgency for the police to make an arrest and take the pressure off them. Do you remember what happened when they arrested them?"

"Yes, it was like open season on German emigrants. They just rounded them up. Even here in the City there was a wave of anti German sentiment."

This is an extension of the emigrant panic. The people arrested probably didn't do a damn thing. There should not have been the arrests, there should not have been a trial and they should not have been convicted – and they sure as hell should not be condemned to death."

"That's right. I did not think the conspiracy charges would stand. I suspect that it had something to do with jury selection. The police rounded up some convenient suspects, the court tried them because they could find no one who actually threw the bomb. The people were afraid of the streets becoming less safe then they already are. The police brought these men forward, now they will be executed and Chicago will rest easier thinking justice has been served. It's a nice neat solution although an absolute reversal of justice. I am most afraid the results of this witch hunt will be less respect and confidence in the law".

"They are going to be hanged on the eleventh of November, all because they were present at a workers rally. They are being hanged for what they believed in, not for a crime they committed". Liam gritted his teeth. "We had a harvesting machine on the farm manufactured by that company. Damn! If I had known the kind of company it is, I would have told Pat not to buy from them".

"McCormick is not with out blame. They did lock the workers out and hired scabs. Their greatest mistake however was shooting into the crowd, those four that died in that violence set the stage for the bombing. You don't hear much about them in the press, they were innocents. The police who were the shooters became a target themselves."

"What the hell are workers supposed to do? Corporations make regular profits through their participation yet the workers barely break even. In some cases sweat shops and working conditions are appalling. Sara sees it every day working at Charity hospital. On the other side railroads fix rates, corporations conspire to monopolize to increase profits and banker's wheel and deal with peoples' money and sometimes fold with their depositor's life savings and none of them are held accountable".

"That's good for us, isn't it?" Will smiled. "These things happen. When I first started out in this business, I fancied myself a crusader I was going to champion the innocent. Then life became too comfortable. When I was younger I would have gone out to help them if only to protest it in the streets. In this case, perhaps I should have when I was asked."

"You were asked to help defend those men?"

"Yes, by Governor Ogelsby himself. He thinks the men are innocent, but he's also a politician and pardoning in this case is not a very prudent alternative. He cares enough that justice is served, he just doesn't want to be the waiter."

"Why didn't you go?"

"Liam, we are busy enough here, I would've had to be gone out there for weeks and leave the firm and my family. There are lots of competent lawyers in Chicago. The man name Altgeld is very good, better than me. It would have taken a lot more time than I had available - besides, the verdict was already pretty much decided. The jury was rigged, emotions were running high, and my presence would have served no good purpose. I would have been an out of town lawyer to whip up on".

"But Will, those men – Spies, Fischer, Engel and the others – they did not do anything."

"We really don't know that, but you're probably right. We do know that both Parsons and Spies were anarchists". He leaned back into his chair and looked thoughtful for a moment, then dismissed it.

"These men are going to die for what they believed in, not for anything they did. They were of German descent like many of the newest emigrants". Liam insisted

"Anything they were proven to have done". Sutter corrected. "The only one who knows who threw the bomb, is the one who did it".

"They all pleaded innocent to the bomb throwing and I feel sorry for the officers who died. But in this case they should not have fired into the crowd. Who were they protecting, the people or the McCormick Corporation?"

"They had badges, so they had license; they didn't have license to kill, of course, but people believe it to be so. Had I taken the case I would have made a point of that."

"Only one man threw the bomb and no one is sure who that was. You said yourself 'everyone is innocent until proven guilty in this country'." The trial of the Haymarket suspects had touched a deep chord in Liam.

"We certainly hope so." Sutter sighed and looked out of his office window to the building profiles across the street, bright with sunlight. "The defense was snookered by the prosecution that was riding the popular tide of anti-emigration, fear of socialists, anarchists, communists, and whatever. There's a general fear of foreigners with agendas that do not exist; agendas that if they did exist, would not succeed, anyway".

"What would you have done in court?"

"First I would have appealed the constituency of the jury. I would also ask for a change of venue, then I would have protested the press in the light of a fair trial and I would have tried to delay its beginning. That failing, I would have questioned every bit of evidence introduced, since it was all hearsay in respect to the bomb throwing. I probably would have assembled enough stuff to call a mistrial. Delay, delay, delay until that point when I'd push for a fair trial in a different location—after all of the speculation and accusations had settled down.

"It's not right, Will!" Liam tapped the newspaper on the desk before him. "This Haymarket affair makes a joke of justice. It stinks!"

"Remember, Li, fear drives people to desperate means and desperate actions. There is a fear in this country; I feel everyday, the fear of emigrants, that foreigners might be anarchists and will change our government for the worst; fear that a holocaust is in the making; fear of new ideas, new religious beliefs and atheists; fear of eugenic crazies; the press feeds this fear. I believe the fear to be baseless, but many others see it as real; too often jurisprudence supports the popular sentiment rather than the principles of fairness and reason that we know as justice."

"So fear turns justice upside down?"

"That's right – fear does. Sometimes there is no relationship between justice and what happens in a courtroom. If you want political support for an unpopular cause, or have people give up their basic rights under the US Constitution, scare the hell out of them!" He pushed his chair back from his desk and relaxed the frown that had appeared on his face. "Let's take a break, is Sol in?"

"Yeah, I saw him earlier."

"Well then, let's go prod the genius. He could probably do both sides of this debate, hell, he could probably do three sides. Let's go get some tea, and loosen him up."

Liam laughed as they walked through the doorway.

Will draped his arm over Li's shoulder. "I'm glad you're here, young man. This Haymarket affair has troubled me from the start. Now that you've made me think about it, it troubles me even more. You've got a good head on your shoulders."

They thrust themselves into Sol's office. He was not reviewing briefs as they expected, but was engrossed in the newspaper. He looked up. "Have you two been following this Haymarket thing?"

Will and Li looked at one another and laughed.

"Hell yes, Li and I have been talking about it all morning."

"It's a travesty of justice!"

Chapter 29

New York City
June 1887

Liam took the steps two at a time, then stopped before the door, straightened his cravat and pushed through. The secretary glanced up and nonchalantly addressed him.

"Hello, Liam."

"Hello, Joann. I'm late, I'm late." He smiled and started past her desk, but was pulled up short by her voice.

"Mr. Rosenstein wants to see you in his office; he is in with Mr. Sutter, and Mr. Ryan is in there too."

"Am I in trouble?"

The dark haired woman smiled. "You would know that better than me."

Liam walked past the reception room with its decorative palms, ferns and paintings. In the middle of the room was a delicate Italian fountain featuring two nudes the male seemed more absorbed by the running water than his female companion. The hallway that led to the interior was lined with pastoral tapestries. Each of the partners decorated their own offices. Liam had chosen some expensive prints for his walls. On one was a vivid Delacroix Liberty Leading the People. The lady looked like Sara and her bat eared companion bearing two guns was certainly Billy. On the other wall Bronzino's bold, neat Portrait of a Young Man. Some of the office clientele referred a visit to the Sutter office as 'A trip to the museum'.

The meeting to which he had been summoned was already underway when he passed into the room, all three smiled welcome.

"Ah, Liam, I'm glad you're here. We need some input from you." Sutter greeted.

"Sorry I'm late. I had lunch with my sister over by City Charity Hospital. She's working there now – didn't realize how long it would take to get back here."

"I think, Liam, its fortunate, very fortunate" Sol smiled, "That the young lady is not your biological sister."

"I agree, Sol. All this stuff about going to see his sister..." Sutter chuckled nodding his head in disbelief.

"Ah, come on, you guys. She sort of is my sister." Liam smiled in reply.

"It's your family, more precisely Mary's connections that might help us here." Sutter said in a serious tone. "We have been contacted to broker a truce and…"

"Mary's connections?" Li asked dubiously.

"You're aware of what's going on over in Chinatown?"

Before he could answer Ryan chimed in with a smirk. "The Italians tried moving into Chinatown, Guido, Geep and all..."

"I did hear about that and it sounds like trouble's brewing."

"Precisely" Sutter knocked the ash off his cigarillo. "There's so much trouble brewing over there that the courts won't be able to contend with it all, I can see it coming. There could be blood all over the streets."

"Yes", Liam agreed. " And equal and speedy justice won't be for all".

"Hatchets, knives, guns and bombs; we're talking a big scale thing. It won't be good for the city, it won't be good for business, and it won't be good for any of us." Ryan noted

"It won't be like the usual Chinese firework, that's for sure. Both the tongs and the Black Hand are better organized than a labor union and far more ruthless." Sol said scratching his head.

"Do you remember the Biondi case, Li?" Ryan asked.

"Of course, Will had me brief it. He killed Jim Heartso in front of twenty eye-witnesses and not one of them decided to testify. He's upstate for ten years, isn't he? "

"He's been paroled and was in here this morning, just after you left for your sister's."

"And what else, Will?" Liam was perplexed.

Will turned and tapped the table. "He told me it's going to get very bitter like a race war. He's reluctant to get involved although he is what's called a Capo, so he must be involved. The trouble is going to be 'bombed and bloody' - his phrase - and neither the Chinese nor the Italians want that kind of trouble. God knows the city doesn't need it".

"I inquired about it with a few of my contacts," Ryan began. "The Chinese want to remain sub-rosa and the Italians don't want to get any higher profile than they already have. Neither side really wants any big trouble."

"Since the two parties have so little in common, it is a surprise they want to talk at all."

Will nodded toward Sol. "Sol's right, we think we can head it off."

"They want a negotiator?" Liam sat in curious surprise and looked toward Sutter's desk. "Will, why don't you do it?"

"Chinese don't want me - they see me as Guido's man."

"What about you, Ryan, you have worked both sides?"

"They don't want me, either. Guido and company don't trust me; they think I'll side with the Chinese. The Chinese think I am Guido's man."

Sol laughed. "Ah, the public trust. What is law coming to? No one trusts anyone – it's going to be great for practice."

The three smiled toward the rotund genius perched in his chair.

"You want me to talk to Mary, see if they trust her, right?" Li laughed. "I don't know, she..."

"I've already talked to her, Li."

"What did she say, Will?" Surprise in his voice, Liam really did not believe that Mary would do it knowing her penchant for anonymity in business activities.

"She doesn't want to get directly involved. It appears no one does, she says she's too busy and negotiations are not exactly her forte. Also, there are some former agreements that might be, shall we say embarrassing for her should they come out."

"So?"

"So she said, 'ask Liam to do it'."

"Me?" He intoned; astonished that he would be asked to conduct such a task, but flattered at the vote of confidence. "What makes you think I can do it?" He realized how significant the request was and what the result of failure could be.

"Because all three of us know so," Ryan replied, "and Mary thinks so - said something about how you knew some of the people likely to be involved."

"Yeah, she meant I once knew them, Woo is a family friend," Liam smiled, "Geep, maybe."

"Of course we would like to broker a truce." Sol said "Were we successful, it would have great implications for future business and spare the city a lot of fear and grief."

"Sol's right Liam; if you pull this thing off, you'll be set in a lucrative practice for the rest of your life and it sure won't do us any harm either." Will affirmed.

"These guys don't forget, Li". Ryan added.

"What if it goes off the deep end?" Liam was still not sure.

"Ryan will sit in with you. Even if we don't get a perfect solution, we will be noted for having tried. We are in a no lose situation here."

"And, Sol ", Liam laughed, "None of you guys are going to be blamed."

"Yes. Will replied"

"That is right, even if nothing much comes of it, we succeed." Ryan smiled."

"That's true." Sol confirmed.

"You do know the protagonists here, don't you, Li?"

"I think so, Will. It would be Probably Guido, who I don't know, and Giuseppe – 'Geep', who I do know, and my Uncle Woo, right?"

"You are right." Sutter crushed out his cigar.

"We're working through Biondi for the Italian side, but no help from the Chinese side. We don't have a clue as to where Woo even lives and its mum down there; if they don't want to hear you, it's 'no speak, 'Engrish'."

"I know the way to my uncle's house. Funny, I just saw Giuseppe last night; he took Sara and me out for dinner to a great place, Caioffa's."

"We know." Sol smiled
"We even thought of joining you."

"Chaperones, Ryan?" he felt slightly annoyed.

"You wouldn't need one with your sister, now would you?"

"Nice remark, very nice, Sol." Liam feigned anger, and then laughed.

"We had good news for you." Will chuckled "We were going to share a glass wine with you, but decided not to."

"What news?"

"Well, you passed the bar, Li, with the second highest score in the state."

"What?" he said incredulously.

"It's true." Sol rejoined.

"We are all very proud of you." Ryan intoned. "You're one of the youngest ever to do it - first try and with that score. We're very proud of you!"

The three men descended on Liam to shake his hand.

"It's time for a celebration, and I just happen to have a little cognac here someplace." Sutter spied the bottle, opened it, then filled four glasses and passed them about. He raised his glass. "If you're old enough to pass the bar, you're old enough for this stuff. Here's to you, Li, many happy returns."

"Shalom"

"Salute," Ryan added." I do not know any Chinese toasts."

They lowered their glasses, Sutter slapped Li on the back, and each of them sat down around the small table.

"You passed the bar, Li – soundly! But you will have to wait a year before you'll get much respect in court - a lot of jealous and obstructing judges and lawyers out there. You're just nineteen, right"? Sol asked

"Yes, almost twenty"

"We are very proud of you. We would like for you to stay on with us. Of course you'll get a raise and a secretary as soon as you reach an age of maturity." He laughed, "when ever that might be."

"Wow – no more mountains of recording".

"It was good practice. You are the only one outside of the secretaries that still knows how".

"Well, Sol, I've had enough practice." He sipped his cognac. "I think we should get some of those new typewriters they could modernize the procedures around here and make recording much simpler"

The group lapsed into silence. The remote sounds of a bustling office could be heard.

"What do you say, Li? Join us as a junior partner in waiting? Will asked.

"Well, Ryan, Sol, Will - you have been so good to me. That bar-score, which is probably an error," he smiled, "Is as much a measure of all your mentoring as it is my performance."

"I think," Sol ventured," that if the score changes it will be adjusted upward."

"You did us proud," Ryan added.

"So, will you think it over?" Sutter asked sipping a small measure from his glass. "Both proposals, that is – one is not dependent on the other."

"I have thought it all over and yes, I'll stay, and if you would like, I'll get started with my uncle tomorrow."

"Not tomorrow, Liam. Tomorrow we are all going fishing."

"Fishing, what do you mean?" He asked in disbelief. "All of us tomorrow is a workday."

"You like to fish, don't you?"

"Well, yes – I'd rather do that than almost anything." He looked towards Sol and Ryan. "Both of you guys are going?"

"All the clans are going out on Long Island Sound." Ryan declared.

"Nobody gave me a hint, wait till I see Sara!" He grinned. "I've never been out ocean fishing."

"We will probably all get sick," Sol groaned, "I don't know how I was convinced to do this. What's worse, there's no way for me to back out. My wife, of all people, is looking forward to it."

"My wife's not so enthused, but she still insists on going." Will smiled. "She is afraid of missing the celebration for Liam."

"It's all settled then; we meet at six a.m. right here." Will drained his glass and set it down in finality. "I've got to get back to work. You know all that note writing".

There was laughter and a general consensus to the statement and the others suddenly left, leaving Li alone with Will Sutter.

"Thank you, Will, for all of your help. I'll do my best with Uncle Woo. Geep won't be a problem if Guido isn't. I knew Geep when I was a kid. He gave me some wonderful carvings I still have at home."

"Do your best, Li, I know that you will."

When Liam left the office, his spirits had never been so high, and a feeling of warmth spread within him. It was a great time to begin his career and Sara had to know about it. He trotted across the street and leapt aboard the cross-town trolley; a fifteen minute ride brought him to Charity Lying In hospital. Sara saw patients there most evenings. He walked through the door and hurried toward Ward Three.

At first Liam was at a loss to know how to proceed with the conference and then he decided to go straight to Woo. Woo had initially wanted the meeting to take place in Chinatown, but he reluctantly agreed to a neutral, mutually chosen, site. The following day Liam went to see Guido Innella; with the help of Dominic Biondi he was able to exact the same agreement. He returned to Woo's opulent home, the ante way of which had two twenty-foot tile walls decorated with a pair of bright red dragons on a royal blue background. Carved walnut balustrades led to the upstairs quarters, the landing of which was guarded by fierce looking ceramic warriors. He sensed the presence of servants, but saw only one who had a knee-length sword tucked in his waistband. Woo was seated on a small divan, dressed in simple black silk trousers and a bright blue jacket with gold brocade. He did not rise but gestured toward a mahogany chair.

"It is pleasant for me to see you, Liam. Will you have tea with me?" There was more formality in his voice than at other times and only a trace of a smile.

"It's good to see you, Uncle, and of course I would enjoy tea with you."

"I dearly care for you, Liam, but today is business." Woo said rather tersely.

"I figured it out by the chair, Uncle Woo."

Despite himself, Woo chuckled and leaned back reviewing the young man before him. "Oh? Well, I'll order tea." He pulled on a bell strap, still smiling.

"Uncle Woo, I am just here to arrange a place for negotiations, I do not represent anyone. I am here because other people with greater concerns are taking advantage of your long friendship with me and of course my family."

It was Weng himself who delivered the tea, acknowledging Liam with a slight nod of his head when their eyes met. He left without saying a word. Woo looked after him then back to Liam.

"The Italians, they are aggressive, ruthless, barbarians!" He sipped at his tea.

"Yes, and they fear you also, however, they are much more likely to act upon their fear."

"I do not wish to bring attention to myself now. I am almost finished here. I would like to depart this country with all in order, or as much order as I can confer. It is very troubling to me to have this dispute after nearly twenty years."

"Will you be leaving forever, Uncle Woo? I didn't know." A trace of concern based in sadness edged his voice." We that is my whole family will miss you".

"I have difficulties here, but there is enormous affliction, anguish and disorder at home. I must see to my family." Woo's face became set, his mouth hardened as if he had admitted more than he had wished. "My wife has already gone back. She could not tolerate this city."

"I'm sorry to hear of it." He sipped at his tea and solemnly viewed Woo over the brim of his cup.

Woo looked away briefly. "Again foreigners, the British, French, Americans, Russians, Italians- all, a very difficult time is approaching. There is much resistance to them. A great war is very near China will again lose much. Already we have lost Amman to the French and the prospect of loosing more is a near certainty ".

"Well, Uncle Woo, perhaps I can help ease a little of the trouble here." He spoke quietly and sipped at his tea, trying to discern the impact of his words; he saw none. Liam saw how deeply troubled the aging leader felt, and out of respect remained quiet.

Woo delicately set his cup. "My demands are quite simple. I wish our business interests not to be disturbed. We do not wish to pay fees beyond taxes and we want the bloodshed to stop."

"And what are you willing to do?"

"Nothing, but we will stop the retaliation. The other tongs agree, one of the few things we do agree upon."

"Last week there was a killing: Peter Marando and Anthony Sileti."

"That was Shen Tung Hsun – a difficult man, an agreement has since been made."

"The Inellas do not want fan-tan, faro and other gaming interests in certain parts of the city. The other businesses I don't think they care about. Mary had some trouble earlier, much like yours." Liam volunteered.

"I know. We have peacefully had carried out business in those neighborhoods dominated by the Italians. We must pay tribute for sweet shops, laundries, general merchandisers. Stop these tributes, and an agreement can be reached."

"And the gaming parlors, what will be done with them?"

"I will speak to the others of these." Woo appeared out of patience as though anxious to end the meeting. "Would you like more tea?"

"No, Uncle Woo, I'm going back to the office. Maybe later today I'll try to arrange a meeting with Guido Innella. I just would like to see it settled with everyone's interests considered. I'll no doubt have to meet with his cousin first." He paused then continued in curiosity, "Do you think the others would withdraw their gaming places?"

"It depends, perhaps, I will speak with them. Is it very important that they do so?"

"Maybe, Uncle Woo, you will be hearing from me very soon. Thank you for the tea." He rose to leave and Woo also stood. Liam gave a small bow, straightened and extended his hand.

Woo smiled. "Don't crush me, young fellow. I can barely withstand your father's embrace; I fear yours would do me in."

"Nah, he's stronger than I am, I hope to be back to see you soon."

As Liam moved toward the doorway, he again caught sight of the furtive male figure. He was watching impassively from behind a silken curtain. When he reached the street he was braced by a small breeze and a greater sense of relief.

After making two additional trips to each of the parties, Liam finally arranged for meeting at the Nolan Hotel located in a neutral area. Each party could bring a small staff and meet in a dining room that was out of the mainstream of business and commerce of the Bronx. Woo showed up with a small contingent, and Guido with a small bevy of stalwarts including Giuseppe.

Each had an interpreter: Dominic Biondi on one side, Si Weng on the other. Ryan and Liam were seated with the interpreters at a table between the other two. Neither Woo nor Guido was to directly exchange a word, and the negotiations were going well, each interpreter in turn speaking to Liam and Ryan. Each leader listened and replied accordingly. The talk was not animated, but factual and clouded with very little emotion.

"Liam, Guido would like for Woo to close a card shop over on Eighteenth Avenue. He says it is too close to his own interests there." Dominic said.

"There was nothing said before this about closing down a card shop. I believe Woo has given enough. I'm going to protest." Weng passed on both comments. Woo showed no emotion; the word that came back was no.

There was shuffling at the Italian table as if they were about to leave.

"Mr. Innella, Guido, let us talk more." Li sensed the eminent break-up. "This meeting is not about getting more. Rather, it is a meeting of what each of you is willing to give up in the interest of peace between you. The violence will only hurt business for everyone, people will be afraid to walk the streets. Law enforcement will tighten even more and it will be very expensive to everyone. So, what are you willing to give up? Woo has been reasonable – very reasonable. Are you prepared to allow other Chinese interests to be extended should the card shop be closed?"

The sounds of the kitchen and some loud orders descended through the heavy silence.

"And you know what else?" Giuseppe began and stopped as he saw Woo studying the molding along the ceiling and not looking at him.

The silence fell again but an unnerving feeling of hostility began to creep among the assembled. Giuseppe started to move back from the table but stopped sharply.

Li took the moment to continue. "You know what, you keep talking about the past and getting angry over it. Both of you Mr. Innella, Uncle Woo both of you, we should not be arguing over the past, rather what we want in the future."

All the eyes turned to him them in irritated attention. It became silent again.

"Isn't this the reason we are here together?" Liam queried.

No one replied, then Giuseppe leaned forward on the table turning toward Guido "The kid's right," he emphasized nodding toward Liam. Guido said something in Italian in response but did not alter his expression.

Woo's face showed no emotion, only a slight inclination of his head, throwing a glance in Liam's direction.

Giuseppe straightened in his chair." Maybe we could work things out." He fastened his hard eyes on Woo. "That is, if the Chinaman wants to,"

"If there is agreement to proceed we will work things out." Liam sharply retorted.

Weng translated. Woo then straightened in his chair, and nodded yes. A slight smile showed briefly as if Li's presence was a most valuable thing.

One of Giuseppe's companions, Tony, looked at Li and also smiled, "He's just a kid, but…"

"But, Tony, I don't have anything to win or lose here, the rest off you do. So, if you agree the future is what you are talking about – talk." There was the slightest twinge of an order in the young voice.

Giuseppe's smile fixed on Woo, "Well, Woo, about 57th Street…"

Guido listened to the interpretations, thoughtfully studied the faces around the table, settled back in his chair, giving an extensive reply to Biondi. Dominic related the message.

"Mr. Innella says he does not care if Woo sets up a dozen shops, laundries, restaurants or other business just no girls or money changers or gambling parlors. The one gambling shop he insists on closing is adjacent to his own shop."

Weng relayed the message. Woo nodded assent, then added commentary. Weng spoke to Liam.

"Woo asks that Guido guarantee the safety of his workers, do away with tributes, and the Italians entirely vacate all business interests in the area known as Chinatown."

Dominic in turn relayed the message. Guido looked toward Woo, raised his chin and simply said "Si." Woo nodded his assent and appeared impatient to leave.

"Very well, Li and I will draw up a general agreement. It will be in English. You will sign it but there are conditions. There is nothing legally binding, it is simply a witnessed agreement. You will be bound by honor only. It can not be a contract because the subjects are illegal." Ryan reached into his briefcase and withdrew a tablet.

Liam and Ryan waited until the room cleared. "I guess there won't be much in writing," Liam observed uneasy in the belief that things might be alright, for a short time only.

"Unless it would say an agreement was reached, we will just make up a kind of list, give them each a copy, file it for future reference and wait and see."
"Do you think either of them will sign it?"

Ryan laughed and clapped Li on his shoulder. "Sometimes you just have to assume one's word is their bond. But one thing is for sure; your reputation is secure among those who do not usually pay much attention to anyone outside their own. That was a nice little speech you gave. You have done a great job here."

"I don't feel like I did much of anything." It was not quite a true statement for he recognized deep inside himself that he had managed something important if both parties were true to their word.

"Property damage in the hundreds of thousands, deaths in the dozens, and grief that is immeasurable - that's what was prevented here today, however long it lasts. I'll buy you lunch."

"No thanks, Ryan, I told Sara I would meet her." He fished a watch from his vest, "... twenty minutes ago."

Ryan smiled and hailed an approaching trolley, then hopped on board. "Tell her when you see her to get used to you being late." He waved as the vehicle moved on. "You will be marrying her one of these days and she needs to know."

Liam waved off the comment, moved across the street and began walking briskly.

Charity Lying-In Hospital was just eight blocks away.

Dakota Territory
November 1887

The physical wounds that Billy and Black Eagle had inflicted, healed over time, but Black Eagle's hatred remained, growing steadily with each reminder of his defeat. He never exchanged more than a word or two with Billy and when he saw him, his eyes had a baleful look like a wolf awaiting a deer.

Billy's status as an outstanding and brave rider on buffalo hunts and the soldiers had grown in the eyes of his companions. Billy was thinking about that as he led his horse toward where the others grazed. Running Bull intercepted his approach.

"So, what will you call him, Lame Wolf?" He asked in his native tongue, as they walked.

"Are we speaking Cheyenne today, Running Bull?" Billy asked.
"Very traditional today, so what will be his name?"

"He is already called Red Shield. I think that is good. At first I was going to call him after my friend Bright Feather. If it is a girl, Calling Jays will select a name." Billy released his horse among the others.

"No, what will be his Christian name? He may well need one. The whites are everywhere; there will be schools along the Powder in a few years."

279

"I think Patrick Liam Kavanaugh."

"After your father?"

"And brother."

"It's a good, but I will call him Red Shield." Running Bull smiled. "Did you know that I helped name you? Did your mother tell you how the wolf came into the birthing place?"

"Yes. Your wife Maha was with her."

"Yes, Maha," he looked away from Billy toward the long low hills to the west. A sense of sadness passed between them. "So long ago - how old are you now, Kavanaugh?"

"I am nineteen, maybe 20." Billy wasn't exactly sure of his birth date.

"You were born in the late spring - but it was cold, very cold."

"So, I'll be 20 sometime next spring. I don't know the date." They turned and walked back among the lodges.

"Whatever. We were beginning to wonder if you would ever have a child. Iron Hatchet has a son and another on its way, and he took a woman right after you did."

"I didn't know you were keeping score," he quipped.

Running Bull laughed. "I keep careful watch on all of us, for we are getting fewer, the whites more numerous. These plains will soon be like the city of Milwaukee or worse. Towns everywhere and they keep getting closer."

"You worry too much. You usually don't seek me out unless you want me to do something. So what is it, another whiskey run? Are we going hunting – what?"

"Ah, you are unjust, Lame Wolf." He feigned offense, but smiled.

"No, just practical, it is usually one or the other."

"There are new miners down on Porter Creek."

Billy became alarmed. "That's less than thirty miles from here, how many?"

"Blue Shirt said at least ten. They are in tents now, but they have started to build a couple shacks, one shack is about done. There are two women, a couple half grown boys, and six men."

"What do you want to do?"

"I mean to go over there and kill them. Burn them out, whatever it takes."

"I wouldn't want to get involved with killing anybody. Maybe if we just run off the horses and mules, fire the tents, whatever. They will leave."

"You know better! They won't leave until they're ready, and it won't do any good just to run off stock. If we did that, it wouldn't be long they would be right here running off our horses, and you know it. They are worse than rats and they will bring havoc. They want to kill us all, I know this. Our women will not be safe." Running Bull rose and stalked about, the sound of his own words building his anger. "I know this I hate these miners most of all. It is best to kill them first – no miners, no problem that is what they say about us isn't it?""

"I know you're right," Billy resigned. "But I'm just not too anxious to kill anybody. They haven't done anything; I don't think we have to kill them."

"That's your weakness!" Running Bull turned to leave, anger still flashing across his face. "You don't have to go; you can stay here and guard the women."

Billy felt chagrined; he knew that guarding the women when a war party was out, always was assigned to old men and boys and would signal his own lack of manhood. He called after Running Bull.

"All right, I'll go. Maybe we could talk to them first?"

Running Bull stopped and looked disdainfully behind him, then proceeded toward his tepee.

The warriors had watched carefully while Blue Shirt sketched out the disposition of the miners and Running Bull planned the attack. They would ride into the wind until they reached the trees bordering the creek. Half would then proceed on foot until they could rush the length of the works along the banks and turn them into a trap. Running Bull and four others would ride in and sweep up any stragglers who avoided the assault, and block any flight down the creek. Billy rode with Running Bull and when the firing began they rode toward the widest part of the camp.

There were a number of tents spread before some half-finished shanties with canvas for roofs. The firing ceased abruptly and Billy reined up in view of the deadly scene spreading down the brook. Within minutes the miners had been shot down, some were still clinging to life in the current. He watched half in awe, half in disgust as his companions completed killing and began scalping the bodies.

A long curl of bright red was spreading in the water as the warriors brandished their trophies. The surprise was so complete the miners did not fire a shot, some had bolted into the stream, and their bodies were spread akimbo on its rocky shoals.

Running Bull was watching with a gleeful satisfaction as the bloody work progressed. He saw Billy shaking his head; Blue Shirt was dragging a body from the brook.

"The horrors of Indian warfare, Lame Wolf; I'm going down to check the damage myself." Billy watched him slowly walk his horse into the sickening scene. The braves were stripping off clothing and mutilating the bodies by removing fingers, slashing thighs and slicing into the viscera. He closed his eyes against the image and as he blinked he saw a movement beside and to the rear of the sluice boxes. Running Bull was intently watching the busy butchering party and let out a savage cry; as he lifted his rifle a shot rang out.

The bullet dumped his horse as his rifle careened away. The others looked up in surprise to see a woman, her fair hair flying behind her, rifle in hand racing toward Running Bull. Billy was surprised and his reaction delayed. As she closed-in and stepped toward the dead horse, her rifle leveled on Running Bull, terror set into the old Indian's features as he thrashed to get free of the horse. Billy shot her in the temple. She fell dead across the horse, her wound showering Running Bull with a torrent of blood and gore.

Quickly Billy dismounted while Blue Shirt and Black Eagle both sprinted toward the sounds, arms black with blood. Billy reached Running Bull first.

"Get her off me, Billy get her off me!" He was lying in a lake of blood, skull bits and brain pieces, get her OFF me!"
Billy took the woman's arms and dragged her over the horse. "Are you all right?"
"I'm stuck and I can't get out of here, my ankle might be broken. I never saw that bitch."

As Blue Shirt and Black Eagle reached them, Billy helped to roll the horse in order to pull him out, and after much straining and stretching, they did so. Running Bull rose and gingerly tried his ankle.

"I never saw the bitch." He looked toward the limp body now leaking crimson into the creek, mingling with the dull red of the others.

"I didn't see her either, at first. She was hiding under that canvas over there." Billy pointed out the shelter.

"She damn near accounted for me." His eyes met Billy's in a knowing way, but he offered no further comment. It need not be stated, all present knew that Billy had just saved the life of their leader. Running Bull stepped about a bit, trying out his ankle and rubbing his knee where the horse's weight had driven stones to bone. The other two men returned to their private, grisly tasks.

"You want her hair?"

"No, I don't want her hair. Goddamn it, this is madness! I don't even want to be here."

"Well, it's a good thing for me you were." He waved at the lifeless form. "Somebody else will take it." He limped over and leaned on Billy's horse. "Go down the creek and gather up the guns. That red bearded one has a Peacemaker; I can see it from here, it's yours."

"I don't want the pistol either," Billy affirmed. "Tell Blue Shirt to do it."

"Suit yourself," Running Bull acceded. "See if you can find a horse somewhere, I think they are in the trees across the brook."

"I'll see what I can find. They won't be far."

"Damn it, Lame Wolf. I didn't want to lose that horse."

Billy reined his horse around and looked down on Running Bull without a trace of emotion.

"Horrors of Indian warfare cuts both ways." He clucked his mount ahead. The other raiders were still busying themselves among the bodies. Billy looked at the first corpse. Black Eagle had cut the hands off and placed them on the chest. Billy could see the flashing of the blue flies as they began to gather. One landed on him; he frantically batted it away.

All the bodies had been stripped naked including the other woman who lay with both arms and legs spread. A brave named Gray Feather was industriously removing a second scalp of dark wiry pubic hair; Billy turned away and started for the trees across the creek.

On the other side of the creek, he looked back upon the gory scene. Two Drums' hands were deep inside the man he had killed. He suddenly jerked out the liver and began to eat it. Billy recoiled inside as he saw the blood running from Two Drums' mouth over his chin and down his chest. Along the length of the stony bar, the mutilation continued, blood running in rivers of red.

A feeling rose within him borne of revulsion, horror and a growing guilt. He had felt it before, long before when he sat in the back row of the schoolhouse and when he had been in the midst of festivities on the farm. It was a deep kind of loneliness, a separation of rootless longing. He felt the end of something, a realization that he didn't belong here either; certainly not here amidst the blood, and hideous abomination. Revulsion spread over him.

The image of shooting the woman returned vividly, her head exploding with his bullet, the sickening feeling as he pulled her back over the horse and the swath of blood it left. He shivered and again reviewed the men at the creek. Running Bull was leaning against a tree, also watching, but with an impassive demeanor, impervious to any sense of wrongdoing.

Billy mused aloud in disgust, "The horrors of Indian warfare just ain't me." The sound of the flowing water drowned out the voices of the men joking about Gray Feather's trophy. His revulsion deepened and guilt filled him to the core. In his mind's eye he again saw the woman with the burnished blond hair catapulting backward in a torrent of blood.

"This is it!" He said half aloud, "this is where I part company! I'm gonna get Calling Jays and the baby when it comes and we will get out of here." He looked over the stony bar at the warriors sawing and slashing with their knives. Two Drums was holding the liver in both hands attacking it like a hungry child would eat a slice of watermelon.

Billy fought the nausea rising in him and turned his eyes from Two Drums. The sluggish current was rimmed in red as he turned his horse away.

"No more of this shit," he said, "I'm done!"

For a moment the thought of going home flashed through his mind. He quickly dismissed it. Calling Jays and Red Shield will be his home and where ever he decides to raise a tent – that is all the reassurance he needed. He waved to Running Bull and spurred his horse toward the Cheyenne camp buried in the distance beyond.

Chapter 30

Minsi, New York
Summer 1888

Mary adjusted the green shade over her eyes and reviewed the man across the card table from her. He emptied the glass he held and poured from the bottle beside him. She continued to shuffle the cards and deftly began to flick them to his, then her side.

"Goin' pretty heavy on the Bushmills, aren't you, Pat?"

He swallowed from the glass, made a wry face and smiled. "I hadn't noticed." He studied his cards, separating two to the side.

"You haven't noticed? Well I have; what's left in that..." she nodded toward the glass "is the second bottle this week. And tomorrow is Wednesday, if you don't know."

"I know, Mary, and we're off to see Decker tomorrow."

"And that will be another bottle," she replied vehemently.

"Ah, so we'll break one down between us. No need to worry, Mary."

"I am worried. Ever since..." she poured a little into her own glass. "Ever since she died, you've been in the cups too much! Pat, Sada has been dead more than three years, and Billy has been gone that long too. I thought at first it was grief, but now I know better - you're just drinkin' too much."

Pat remained silent, picked up his glass and took a small swallow. She shifted about in her chair and laid down her cards to look into his eyes.

"It's just, Pat, I've seen so many go. You know? Go down the whiskey river, and it's a river of no return."

"Mary. I work everyday. I'm out there every day, I start in the morning and I finish after dark. I'm tryin' to do my share. Billy's gone, Li and Sara are in the city, and I don't have much help. So I like to have a drink."

"Well, you better be ready to go on Friday. We have to be at the Mitchell's on Saturday. Sara's expecting us."

"Ah, Mary, we have to go? He looked into her sharp stare. I guess so."

"Yes, we are going to meet Sara's potential husband. So, yes, you have to go" She paused. "And you need a new suit, so Thursday morning we are going shopping!"

"Mary, you wonder why I drink! Sara's going to marry Liam, want to make another bet?"

"No, don't you be lookin' at me so innocently. I'm not so sure about these 'uptown people' myself but I'm not drinkin' about it. Besides, I'm not so sure about Liam."

"I am!" He deftly changed the subject. "We'll be gone nearly a week. Work will lag and I won't get my share done."

"Kavanaugh, it's not about shares. It's about you and Sara and Liam and this family! If you need more help we will hire some. I don't want to loose you on that whiskey river. I see the signs, you drink every day. Not just a glass or two, it's half a bottle, and so far as shares go, I'm not cracking any whip." Her voice began to rise. "I don't care if you work a lick, I care about you!" He carefully studied his cards, but did not reply.

"You, don't you know I love you?" She reached out and covered his hand with hers, then sat back.

"Ah, Mary, I love you, too. It's just been hard. First Sada, then Billy, then Li, Sara, everybody's gone."

"Kavanaugh, I'm still here, I miss Billy too, but he's gone off to find himself, or whatever. Liam and Sara are nearby, only a couple of hours away on the train." She let out a deep sigh and reached across the table again. "I miss Billy too. Kavy, he wanted to go, but maybe he will come back soon, who knows?" She straightened. "Anyway, will you take it a little easy on the booze? Please? I don't want to loose you too."

Kavanaugh sipped from his glass, and then carefully set it down. "Alright, Mary, I promise I will,"

"And I don't want to hear anymore about your share."

He lifted the glass again, sipped and set it down. "It's just that I don't think I've done my share. The house, the mansion, when we were building I felt differently - like I was doing something toward it all."

"What are you doin' now? You're working three farms dawn to dark - said so yourself."

"But the money for this place, you know, I haven't contributed much."

She gave him a quick look, began to speak, and thought better of her words. "Well, give it up, I need you! I f it weren't for you..."

"What, Mary?" He rejoined in agitation. "What the hell do you need me for?"

"I need your companionship and your love."

"Ah, Mary, I know I'm the second choice. If Donal had lived, I wouldn't even be here."

"Come off it! If Donal had lived, we probably would have had a falling out by now. You sometimes do not remember that Donal liked money. He was about as straight as a crow's foot and, if you recall was not too backward about reminding his friends about his ambitions."

"But it was different."

"Different how?" She hotly enjoined. "Damn it, Kavanaugh, I don't want to get into this discussion again. Donal is gone and it is not likely anything would have lasted between us. He loved money more than me – I was a way he could get more and I don't want to go there again!"

Pat did not reply, sipped at his glass and smiled at her. "I'm sorry, Mary, you're right and I have been a little heavy with the glass lately."

She picked up her cards and let out a sigh. "All right, how many cards you want?"

"Two to win I have you beat this time."

"I don't want any, I've already won."

Pat stared at her beneath his bushy red eyebrows, his pale blue eyes twinkling as he set the cards.

"You think you always win." He slowly perused his cards.

"Or I wouldn't play."

They both laughed.

"What's your bet?"

"A quarter, no, Mary, I bet a dollar."

"I'll see you and raise you a dollar."

"Done," He stacked a silver dollar on the table, "And I call."

"Pair of red queens," Mary smiled. "One very rich lady in love is how I read that."

Kavanaugh grinned. "Wait 'til you see these!"

"I'm waiting."

"Pair of red aces, not a bad hand is it Mary?"

She waggled her head and adjusted the green shade. "Go ahead and rub it in I don't always win and I am happy to concede one game in ten to you."

"Well, Mary, you won me. What a prize!"

"Yes, you are just what I always wanted, a big raw boned Mick without a sign of sportsmanship, your deal." She tossed him the deck.

Kavanaugh scooped the cards, began to hum an Irish air, repacked the deck and began to slowly shuffle the cards.

Chapter 31

New York City
Fall 1889

The dinner was more like a banquet. The Mitchell's French chef had prepared duck flambeau, which when lit, had been an exciting moment for all involved. The courses included leek soup, green beans, candied carrots, and mashed potatoes formed into crusts and served with a dark sauce from the duck drippings. Despite their host's apparent friendliness, Kavanaugh felt out of place in the large pretentious dining room. The food was excellent, but he would rather be at the scuffed-up table in Evelyn's kitchen. Both Mary and Sara seemed to be faring better.

The two older couples withdrew to the drawing room for brandy, while Peter and Sara reviewed the well stocked library.

"Pat, were you in the war?" Mason Mitchell inquired over his snifter of brandy.

"Yes, Mason, I was."

"Call me Mace, Pat, all my friends do."

"Yes, Mace, I was at Gettysburg then followed Mosby around Virginia."

"The great battle that turned the tide of the war."

"It was a hot fight, that's for sure." Kavanaugh adjusted uncomfortably as he briefly recalled the events that had cost him so dearly.

"You were with Fifth Corps – General Sikes?"

"No, we were 144 New York Engineers – blundered on to Round Top the first night on a reconnaissance mission from Harrisburg."

"I served at Cold Harbor and Petersburg - a Shave tail in Second Corps, I was, and I managed to get wounded on June 22, 1864. That was the end of my service."

"Well, I stayed in a while; went out west against the Cheyenne – Fort Wallace."

"You had extended service?" Mitchell leaned forward and withdrew a cigar box from the humidor. "Have a cigar, Pat. I'd like to know more about the war with the Indians." He proffered the box and his cigar cutter.

"Men and the war, it sure dominates their conversations," Mary observed as she watched Pat fire up his cigar. "I was most interested when it would be over."

"Mason served with distinction. The way he talks sometimes, one would think he would prefer to still be in the Army."

Mary did not reply but watched the men continue to ignite their cigars. She turned to Martha. "Pat lost most of his friends in the battles; I lost in the war and gained from it too, after all is said and done."

"Gained from the war, Mary?" Mason intoned as he touched up his cigar.

"Good for business, wasn't it?"

"Yes, in a sad kind of way." Mason dropped the cigar cutter he had been holding and both men bent toward the floor to retrieve it, butting their heads in the effort. They both bolted back up, rubbing themselves and smiling.

Mary chuckled, "Let's see that again."

Mason joined the laugh while Kavanaugh looked at her with a benign malevolence as if to admonish her from further conversation. Unbeknown to anyone, the fiery tip of Pat's cigar tip settled into the crease of his vest.

"What kind of business are you in, Mary?" Mason asked.

"Yes, I am curious also. It must be a good one. I am aware of your contribution to the college. A considerable sum as I recall."

"Martha, she like us, was probably bribed into a contribution. I imagine yours was a little more rich, to enter a daughter."

"I am glad you have been spared a strong minded daughter," Mary replied. "She wanted to be a doctor and that was that. I thought when she went to Hunter she might change her mind. It was a costly choice, but it was her choice."

"Yes, I agree. It surely is bad enough to have a strong minded son. Don't you agree, Mason?"

"Yes, Martha." He paused and looked sharply about. "Is something burning? I smell smoke."

"It's you, Pat!" A small flame had appeared at Kavanaugh's waist. Without thinking, Mary threw her brandy on it, which resulted in a great burst of blue flame. Her glass shattered on the floor.

"My god," Martha screamed. "He's on fire!"

Pat stood up and began to beat at the blaze; Mary snatched the glass of water from Martha's hand and soused him with it. Everyone was standing by now. Kavanaugh, aghast, reviewed the large black hole through to his underwear. He made the sign of the cross, then stepped on the sodden cigar and slipped. He grasped at the chair to narrowly avoid a sit down. "Are you all right, Pat?"

"A bit singed, Mace, but I'm all right." He glanced angrily toward Mary. "What the hell were you trying to do, Mary? Set me on fire?"

"I was trying to put the fire out!" she replied defensively.

"Well, don't ever join the fire brigade." Pat brushed at the burned vest.

"Oh, my," Martha crossed her heart with her hand. "I feel faint."

"Sit down, Martha," Mary ordered, and still obviously shaken, she raised a fan from an adjacent table and began to vigorously flourish it in Martha's face.

Mason signaled for the maid, who quickly appeared at the door and ushered in Martha's lap dog Pooky that cavorted across the room. Martha was just opening her eyes when the dog appeared at Mary's feet lolling its tongue and wagging its tail. Pooky approached her and looked up like an admiring fan, barked, then dragged his bottom across the floor in response to Mary's warming look. He finished his whirls and advanced toward her leg.

"Sniff me, you little pisser, and I'll kick you into next week!"

Martha made a sigh and again lapsed into semi-consciousness.

Mason tried to subdue his laughter. The maid picked up the broken snifter pieces and began to sop up the brandy-soaked rug and puddle of water. Pat's trousers were soaked from the crotch down. The maid glanced at him suspiciously. Mary was fanning Martha at an increased pace, and Pat stood with his hand over the burn spot.

"Get that dog out of here and be careful with the broken glass. You'd better bring in a mop." Mason ordered.

The maid beat a hasty retreat with Pooky tucked under her arm. Calm returned and the two men who sat down while Mary fanned Martha, who blurred into full consciousness.

"Have another cigar, Pat," Mason offered the box. He regarded Martha with a benign detachment while Mary still fanned her face.

"I think one's enough." Pat protested.

"Hell, you didn't even smoke that one, have another." Still grinning from the conflagration, he handed Pat the box.

Pat lit-up the second cigar, removed the doily from the chair arm and placed it over the burn hole. Mason looked toward Martha still being fanned by Mary.

"Don't worry about her, Mary; she will be alright, these spells happen frequently."

A few moments later, Peter and Sara appeared in the drawing room.

"What's going on, Father? We heard a commotion and thought we smelled smoke." She looked curiously at Pat's wet trousers.

"A little accident occurred it was nothing very serious." Mason replied as Pat adjusted the doily.

"I'm glad you're back, Sara. I think it is time for us to go." Mary enjoined setting down the fan as Martha came to.

They rose to leave and Mason followed them to the hall closet to collect their wraps. Sara, for the first time, noticed the large burn spot on Pat's vest and trousers but said nothing. They waited for a moment, but Mrs. Mitchell did not appear.

Mason extended his hand to Pat. "I hope you'll come back, it's been one of the more exciting evenings I've spent lately."

"Thank you, Mace." Pat shrugged on his coat.

"And thank you, Mary," he extended his hand to her and she took it firmly in her own, "for a most entertaining evening."

Mitchell had provided a Hansom, and as they rode Mary related the details of the evening encounter, fire, dog and all.

"Well, you had more excitement than I did, for sure!" Sara laughed.

"I don't even want to hear about it." Pat replied.

"It's all right, Sara. You and I can talk about it later." Mary said stiffly.

"Are we going to see Woo tomorrow?" Pat asked.

"Yes, for lunch."

"Well, I'm going to stay well away from you when he serves tea," he said with a shine in his eye.

"That's unfair, Pat."

"Don't be miffed, Mother. From the sound of it, he has cause."

"She actually tried to set me on fire," Pat added, trying to keep down his chuckle.

"Tried, hell – I did."

The three laughed in unison and settled back into the ride.

Dakota Territory
Fall 1889

Calling Jays made her way to the edge of the brushy stream that coursed quietly into a large pool. She slipped the cradleboard from her shoulders and unlaced the leather bundle. Red Shield tumbled out and, though he could toddle about quite well, the walk to water was too difficult for him to try. She had just begun to menstruate again and greeted it with mixed emotions, pleased she could become pregnant again and concerned how the event would impact Lame Wolf. She withdrew a toy bow from her pack board and placed it in the boy's hand. Red Shield became engrossed with it, and then happily banged it against the frame of the cradleboard.

Calling Jays moved toward the stream's edge and bent to fill the water bag. She dipped in the bag and while doing so thought she saw a large shadow move in the alders, there was no sound. She let the bag settle into the water and turned to keep an eye on the baby; as she did so, she saw the alders shudder. A big grizzly raised, spotted her and dropped to charge. She began to run toward the baby and screamed once for Lame Wolf before the bear bowled her over and beneath him.

The first big slash of its paw struck her head, carrying away a large piece of scalp, and as she struggled the bear sank its teeth into her pubis, lifted her like a rag doll and shook her senseless. The animal continued to chew its way through her pelvis as she struggled in agony, then she felt the bear lift her again - her agony was replaced by a great red and black void. The bear finished feeding, and dragged her savaged remains back into the alder grove. There it hollowed out a place in the deep leaves and roughly covered her. The sound of the baby crying interested, but did not attract him; he turned and shambled off into the thicket.

Red Shield managed to toddle to the edge of the creek where a sunbeam had penetrated the valerian above. He reached out to catch it and fell silently into the water. The current was more brisk past the pool; it turned him over and over and carried him around the reedy green bend. Back in the grove where Calling Jays' blood dried in the grass, a sparrow began to sing.

Billy emerged from the trees and led the meat-burdened mule toward the tepee in the clearing. He wondered why Calling Jays had not come out to meet him as she customarily did and shaded his eyes studying the terrain. He called loudly. "Calling Jays, come. Where are you?" Again he reviewed the landscape that betrayed no movement.

No answer came, and the sense that something was wrong washed through him in a wave of alarm. He dismounted and ducked inside the lodge and saw the water bag gone. A sense of relief replaced the fear.

"She's gone for water. I'll unload this and go look for her." He thought aloud and untied the buffalo meat he had boned and wrapped in the hide. Knowing he would need wood for drying the meat, he led the mule toward the distant creek.

"Calling Jays!" he shouted. "Where are you?" There was still no answer. "We have work to do. Where are you?"

As he reached the creek, he noted the cradle board. There was clotted blood on the leaves

290

and a wide drag mark the bear had left reached into the woods. He found her half-devoured: her head, one arm, and a leg hung together with a string of meat. For days he desperately searched for the baby, until the weather turned so cold, he knew it was useless.

He created a bier in the fashion of the Iroquois and interred Calling Jays in a cottonwood near the teepee. He busied himself preparing for winter, fashioning a small tight stable for his horse and mule, and gathered extra wood, drying the meat from his hunt. In his heart he believed that a kind of divine justice had intervened because of his killing the miner woman. A heavy, lonely sadness engulfed him and, despite the busy work, each evening his eyes welled up with tears. The third week after her death, he tried to deal with his anger and searched for the bear, but he never found it. Billy's grief turned into a quiet resolution.

He saw the riders at a great distance; he could tell they were Indians and had ceased to worry about them. Visitors were rare and most passed by at a distance, but these riders were coming toward him. He recognized the rider in front, who at length drew up before him.

"Running Bull," Billy greeted in Cheyenne.

"Lame Wolf," he replied in English.

The riders dismounted and gathered in a semi-circle around him, exchanging friendly greetings except for Black Eagle, who gave a resentful nod.

"Where is Calling Jays?" Running Bull queried. There was a long hesitation and he recognized the tragedy before it was announced.

"She is dead." Billy pushed back his hat and pointed to the burial platform he had built in a large tree. "Grizzly caught her down by the creek." With an effort Billy controlled the contortion of emotion twisting toward his heart.

"Did he get the baby too?" Running Bull asked looking toward the forlorn platform in the distance.

"I think so, I never found him."

"I am sad to hear this." Softness spread over Running Bull's face. He looked to the trees and shook his head in disbelief. "She was a good wife to you." The others remained silent, looking at Billy carefully. Running Bull did not wish to dwell on Billy's grief. He turned from the trees. Black Eagle had witnessed the conversation, glared at Billy, jerked his horse about and rode off a short way.

"If looks could kill, you'd be a dead man Billy." Running Bull remarked as he watched Black Eagle ride off. "What are you cooking it smells good."

"Buffalo and beans, you're welcome to join me."

"No, it doesn't look like you were expecting company," he laughed. "As if anyone ever does." He fidgeted with his horse's reins. "Why don't you come back with me? Winter's almost here."

"No, but thank you, I'm well fixed." Billy shifted his feet uncomfortably.

"Well, you have a good spot for a camp. We have had to move twice; goddamned cavalry destroyed one of our drying sites - took all we had or burned it, but we weathered it out."

Quickly Running Bull turned and slipped deftly on to his horse. "I'm sorry about Calling Jays," he said in English. The other men also mounted up.

"So am I."

"Better break out of it. You sound very sad." Running Bull looked toward the platform.

"It took me quite a long time when..."

"I'm resigned to it now, I think. I'll be all right. I have extra jerky, take a bag with you."

"I will, if you change your mind, we are at the Willow Place. They haven't found us there yet." Running lifted a bag of the dry meat and draped it over his horse.

Billy pulled his hat forward again and drew himself to his full height. "Thank you for coming by," he smiled. "Keep your eye on the horizon. Shoot 'em where they're biggest."

Running Bull smiled back. "That's better. We will stop back come spring – if we don't see you before."

"Yeah, spring time, maybe then."

Running Bull turned his horse and with the other riders, paused for a moment, then galloped away. Billy watched them until they dropped from view.

"Today I am going to go fishing." He said aloud and rummaged about the saddle bags and picked out a long hank of line. He had fashioned a fly of buffalo hair tied around a hook and weighted it with lead. He studied the device, taking pleasure with the design.

He left the tepee and stared solemnly at the burial platform stripped of its leafy veil, stark against the tree in the fading November light.

"Loved One, I am not ready to leave you yet," he said aloud. He looked toward the creek, marked the place he was to go and fell in step. The autumn wind was cold; snow would soon fill the air.

Dakota Territory
Spring 1890 (May)

Billy had passed the winter of eighty nine setting short trap lines in areas nearby the camp he had made with Calling Jays. Although he had no regrets leaving Running Bull's band shortly after the massacre of the miners, he continued to think that the death of Calling Jays was retribution for his killing of the miner woman. In his fitful sleep were disturbing dreams, his wife and mother appeared together blurred, and balancing a baby between them.

Winter trapping was a challenge, but he cut through the thinner ice of the beaver ponds and suspended a roughly fashioned raft for his traps. He baited the willow or alder boughs then put them back in the hole that quickly refroze, holding his rafts in place. He also caught a number of mink near open water on the creeks, and foxes in snares he placed along the trails. He had collected sixty beaver pelts, all dried round on stretchers fashioned from willow wands. Scraping and fleshing hides filled his evening hours beside his fire. He also killed two buffalo, the hides of which were curing on the tepee floor and the meat in his smoke house. It was late May when he packed his hides started for the town of Buffalo to trade them for supplies. He left there with four months worth of supplies plus a cask of whiskey. At his camp he loaded his extra meat and set out for Running Bull's camp.

When he arrived, friends rushed out to greet him, raising hands to him and touching his horse. The clamor brought Running Bull from his tepee and he smiled widely, but waited to greet him, watching Billy work his way through the throng to his tepee.

"Running Bull," Billy phrased in careful Cheyenne and with a serious demeanor.

"Lame Wolf," He solemnly greeted and suddenly broke into a grin. He exclaimed in English, "I am glad to see you!"

"Just came from Buffalo and brought you a present." He dug through the largest of the pack bags and produced the two gallon cask.

"Ah, a gift indeed, we will celebrate. Care to share a pipe?" He gestured to the tepee.

Billy looked over the old warrior and laughed. "Why do you wear that white shirt? It would make a fine target." Billy noted adjusting the cask. "You tired of living?" He sat back on the robes.

"This is my new armor."

"What is the armor against, mosquito's bugs and such?"

"No, against the white man, have you not heard of Kicking Bear? He has had a revelation."

"He's a Bible reader?" Billy jested. "Who is Kicking Bear?"

"No! He is a follower of Wovoka." Running Bull began to pack the pipe.

"Who's he?"

"A Piaute medicine man has been to the other side. He has seen the future and Kicking Bear himself has talked with him."

"A Piaute, what do they know about anything?" Billy settled farther back into the buffalo robes and extended his legs toward the faint fire glowing in the center of the lodge.

"Yes, a Piaute, and he has foretold the dead will rise; we alive will not die. The buffalo will be back in their numbers, the white men will disappear. Our dead warriors will arise, we will be reunited with them and drive the white man away!"

"And you believe this?" Billy adjusted, following Running Bull with his eyes. "That surprises me; you have gone soft in the head."

"I believe the message but not what Wovoka has prescribed for bringing it on. Kicking Bear is big medicine and says differently. He is Sioux."

"Wait a minute here. You said this Piaute had a vision?"

"Yes. He saw it all from the other side. He has called for innocent behavior among us – no lying, stealing, cruelty or killing."

"I can't believe you are telling me this; and Kicking Bear does not agree with it? And what of Sitting Bull, does he not control the spiritual fate of the Sioux?"

"He is an old man; he does not dance but he has not stopped it either. Kicking Bear says we must rise up and strike with the thousands of warriors ready to fight the white man." After his outburst Running Bull sat cross legged and ignited the pipe, puffing it to a glow and passed it to Billy.

"Well, my friend, believe in what you will, but resurrection and reunion? I don't know about that. Sounds to me like cruelty and killing is about to get started."

"I have done the dance, Lame Wolf. I have seen the paradise to come. I met with Big Bear, with Man Hunting, with Humped Back Wolf and Black Badger spoke to me - it was so clear. I saw many others who have gone before." He wiped at his eyes as if to clear a phantom. "And Maha was there, and Lame Wolf," emotion betrayed his voice, "Your mother was there, too."

Billy did not reply, but studied the old warrior before him; obviously he had been touched deeply by whatever had happened. He became uncomfortable for a moment; he had never before observed Running Bull so deep in emotion. Billy offered no comment; spiritual matters were between the believer and the spirits. He had been touched by remorse, regret and sadness but those things never brought thought of an afterlife. The Latin masses of his boyhood had made no sense, and as they had droned on, he had read the missal trying to translate the sounds into words – the Latin to English. The two sat together in the quiet, the afternoon sounds of children playing, horses neighing, and the quiet talk of women working filled the space like sawdust. They smoked the pipe and sipped whiskey, saying little.

"Running Bull, I respect your beliefs - I wish I could believe in something but I'm afraid I can't believe in sacred shirts and help from the dead. When you're dead, you're dead! There's only one person I've ever heard of raised from death, and I don't believe that either."

"You must come and dance. At the last dance there were hundreds of warriors I had never before seen, so many gathered. We will drive the whites out. Black Badger himself so promised. He spoke to me in my eyes."

Billy realized the futility of further discussion. "Well, maybe I'll go with you one day. You want some more whiskey?"

"Yes, we will celebrate your return. Do you have any cartridges for the Winchester?"

"Yeah, I don't have many, but I can spare you a couple boxes."

Running Bull chuckled. "You don't need as many, Lame Wolf."

During the night, Woman with a Flower came to him in his tepee. She came through the door flap silently and sat across from him, then stared into his eyes.

"You are without a woman." She said in a matter of fact manner.
"I am happy without one." He said gently.

"I am without a man and not happy without one. Running Bull said I should come here, ask you to become your woman. He said you need one."

In the dim fire light he watched as she raised her dress over her buttocks, squatted, and turned her back to him. He could see the outlines of her labia spreading to the tension of her thighs. Slowly but firmly his erection built up. He undid the buckskin laces. There was a pungent smell from between her legs; this drove his erection stronger. He maneuvered behind her and thrust upward. She did not make a sound. Billy eased her forward and slipped his hand to the sparse hair of her pubis and began rhythmically thrusting. He felt his ejaculation spurt from him, and he fell forward on her back. Woman with a Flower cooed a near-breathless sound. Toward morning he was aroused again and turning her to her back, entered her again. Throughout the intercourse she bore a faint smile, her eyes closed. They fell back asleep and when Billy awoke, she was gone.

He made his way to Running Bull's tepee. The door flap was open, so he looked in.

"I'm leaving, Running Bull, got to get back. I have to pull traps, boil and wax them and store them away."

He raised his eyebrow in surprise. "I would ask why, but I know better. Lame Wolf; do not be in a hurry, this life is short so enjoy the moons. There are not that many you can waste in sadness. How was Woman with a Flower?"

Billy smiled in reply, "You are not one to talk about living with sadness. I have some coffee here and some sugar. Take it for your hangover. Some people believe it will take it away, I don't, but some people do, and," he added, "Woman with a Flower was fine."

Running Bull took the packets and placed them among the robes. "Why don't you think about coming to a dance? There will be big powwows this year. We are gaining strength. You must come."

"Maybe, I may come this winter."

"And Woman with a Flower, should I tell her something?"

"I'll think about it." Billy said and led out horse and loaded the mule, carefully balancing the burden. Running Bull stood by until he mounted up.

"Goodbye, my friend. Remember, you many not replace love with comfort, but it helps."

Billy slowly turned his horse and grasped the mule line. "As you say 'keep an eye on the horizon, shoot them where they are biggest."

Billy nodded and rode through the camp. He searched the faces that offered greetings, but Woman with a Flower was not among them.

Chapter 32

New York City
Spring 1890

Sara and Peter Mitchell selected a table by the window in Cohen's Delicatessen and settled back with their coffee and huge cinnamon rolls. Peter delicately pulled a strip off, ate it and licked his fingers; Sara was industriously plying hers with a knife and fork.

"This is really good stuff." He said licking at a bit of frosting still stuck to his finger. "You won't find a place like this in Minsi."

"You are right," she dabbed at her mouth with the napkin, "I will truly miss this place."

"Your decision is final?"

"Yes, it's always been my aim to go back to the Cloister Clinic to practice."

"You could stay on at Charity Lying In. I know they really appreciate you there and God knows you're needed. My father's on the Board, did you know that?"

"No, Peter, but they have already asked me back and I said no. I really do want to go home; I miss the trees and the river, my mother and Pat, and I really miss Evelyn's cooking." She popped a piece of pastry into her mouth. "I'm just not a city person. There is so much to do there, doctors are attracted elsewhere and my mother really needs me to keep the clinic going. You could come join us."

Peter blinked. "No, Sara. It's just that the years since graduation you seemed content at Charity."

"I've been waiting for Li. He has a good job and I'm looking forward to marrying him. We will both be going home because Mary needs him as much, maybe more than she needs me."

The noise of dishes jangling and the sound of muffled voices filled the space between them.

"Sara, I'm sorry it didn't work out for us, I really do care for you."

"I know that, Peter. I care for you too." She reached across the table and took his hand. "It just wasn't to be. You will always be a special friend. It's not like I am going so far away. Mary comes to the city often and no doubt I will accompany her from time to time and we can get together for lunch or for breakfast featuring cinnamon rolls."

"You know my family's concern; they really don't matter - to hell with them!"

"Oh, stop it, Peter, I understand." She laughed. "Remember the night Mary almost burned down your house." She laughed out loud.

"Turned your father into a torch," Peter smiled.

Customers at nearby tables turned their eyes toward the mirth erupting from the storefront table and smiled even though they did not hear the conversation.

"Are you sure you will be safe at the Cloister with Mary around?"

"No one's safe with Mary around." She chuckled, and then sipped at her coffee. "You are coming to the wedding, aren't you, Peter?"

"Of course I am. I would rather be in it, but I am going try not to miss it. It may be my last chance to see the three Femme Fatales; Heddy, Jane and you. One day I may even venture up state to work with you a few days. I'd like to see your home and the Cloister since I've heard so much about them."

"You will always be welcome there." She met his eyes with a knowing smile and he looked away. She knew he would never travel to the Cloister for the wedding and after it, she would probably never see him again.

The ceremony was brief and the reception resembled the city park on the fourth of July, replete with bands and a huge throng of guests. The only thing lacking was a parade. Both Woo and Giuseppe were present, and both wanted a private opportunity to speak with Li on business matters. Much of the talk had focused on the labor troubles plaguing the country, the Farmers' Alliance and government ownership of communication and transportation. Dire predictions were made about the influence of the Knights of Labor's, eight hour days, and increasing taxes. A couple of Kavanaugh's frontier friends showed up, including Decker his wife. Festivities lasted well into the evening after Li and Sara left for their honeymoon on a Long Island beach.

There was a somber sound to the waves across Oyster Bay that enhanced the damp within the cottage. Liam studied the woman standing naked before him; high, solid round breasts tipped with dark erect nipples, his gaze fell along the curves of her hips to the tangled black triangle that spread between her legs.
"Sara, you're beautiful."

"Like what you see, huh?" She stepped toward him and put her arms around his neck. "You're quite handsome yourself. And look at you." She smiled at his profile. "You must be ready for something."

"Let's get into bed." They slipped between the sheets and rolled close to one another. Slowly he explored her, rounding his hands over her breasts, slowly circling the areola until the nipples were stiff and erect.
"Oh, Li, that feels good."

"Do you know how long I've been waiting for this?"
"As long as I have, no doubt and oh, don't stop – it feels so good."

He slid his hand over her umbilicus and down to the scratchy edge of her mons; at first rubbing with broad strokes, then seeking the crevice of her labia. She raised her hips in response and searched out his penis, stroking it very slowly.

"You're big, Li." She began to caress the glans, slowly retracting the foreskin, then set a rhythm. "You're getting sticky," she observed.

"I want in you, Sara." He began to push as she guided him along, and then with a great thrust buried himself into her.
"Oh, yes!"

They lay quietly interlocked; he began to slowly pump and then with a desperate drive, released into her.
"Oh, Liam, I could feel that."
"Did I hurt you?"
"A little, but in a good way, it felt better than it hurt."
"Sorry, Sara, I couldn't..."
"Shhh, I still feel you so big, so good."

He withdrew from her and she rolled against him. "Oh, Liam, I felt you trickling down inside me."
"I always wondered why it was such a big deal. Now I know..."
"It was your first time, Liam?"

"Yes."

"Mine too, I wanted to before. Do you remember that day the three of us went swimming..."

"Down Alder Creek, I remember that well."

"We almost..."

"Oh, Sara - that image has stayed with me for so long."

"My breasts were beginning to show, I was embarrassed. I wish they had kept on growing – not much here." She rubbed her breasts against his back.
"Sara, you were beautiful then and you are beautiful now."

"I miss that. Wasn't that the last time the three of us went swimming together without anything on? Billy was always looking me over when we were swimming."

"I think so." He rolled to face her and encircled her in his arms. "And I miss that, too. Sara, I wonder where Billy is. Wherever he is, he's all right – I feel it."

"Oh, I just wish he would have been here for the wedding." It became quiet in the bed – only the sound of their breathing and the far off roll of the surf.

"Sara?"

"Yes?"

"If Billy had asked, would you have married him?"

"Well, he was my hero for awhile. He didn't ask and never would have." She kissed him lightly on the nose. "I got the best of the Kavanaugh boys, I love you, Li."
"And I love you, too."

When Liam and Sara returned, they took up residence in Mary's New York apartment. Mary provided a maid and a new cook, chosen with Evelyn's input and given two week tutelage at the Cloister. Liam settled back into a regular routine, enjoying his new status at Sutter, Ryan, and Rosenstein. Sara remained dedicated to the patients at Charity they knew it would not be long before they left for Minsi so together they zealously explored the city, where they had little time to so before. They took long walks in Central Park, investigated the water front, Ellis Island and the Statue of Liberty. Liam had much to do in preparing for the move to Minsi. Six weeks after the wedding, Mary arranged to visit. Preparations for her arrival were just underway when she walked through the door and whisked Sara away to lunch at Delmonico's. Mary was relaxed sipping whiskey and observing the rate at which Sara was wolfing down a piece of cheesecake.

"My, my, doesn't Liam feed you?" she paused and smiled, "It's not the new cook, I hope."

"I've been famished lately; I just eat and eat. This cheesecake is delicious!"

"Would you like another piece? I'm sure there's one available." Mary smiled slyly and sipped her whiskey as Sara was mopping the corner of her mouth with her napkin. "Are you enjoying married life?"

"Married life? Well, Liam is Liam. We are both busy." She then broke into a grin. "You mean the intimate part?"

Mary smiled and sipped her whiskey. "Whatever…"

"I don't know, mother, sometimes I think he wants me too much."

"Oh?"

"I mean the honeymoon was one thing two, three, sometimes four times a day. I thought he would get…"

"Get tired of it?"

"Well, yes. It's still twice a night and no sign of slowing down."

"Well, girl, enjoy it while you can." With a twinkle in her eye, "I'm lucky if Pat wants it two times a month. I don't really mind, you understand. Twice a night is a bit too much at my age."

"Oh, mother, you're so -so open!" she laughed. "I don't really mind, you understand?"

The two chuckled. Sara's eyes searched around the room for the waiter.

"Mother, do you think it would be a sin to have another piece of cheesecake?"

For a moment it was quiet at the table. "I would not call it a sin just a source of curiosity."

"Where did that waiter go? I don't know why I'm so hungry." Sara observed.

"You're a doctor and you don't know. What time of the month is it? Have you been sick in the morning"?

"I am not really sick, I am late, but only a couple of days, sometimes it happens. You don't think I'm pregnant?"

"You're the doctor."

"Hmmm, I'll not make any judgment yet." She raised her eyebrow in thought and smiled at Mary. "I suppose I could be."

"As soon as you decide you are, will you come home?"

"Actually I have been thinking about that, mother. Helping Doc Wayland with the girls is something I enjoy." She paused as the cheesecake was delivered. "But, do you think, I mean would you care if we sort of expanded our services? That is, my services?"

"Open a practice and have a real hospital-like clinic, you mean?"

"I would deal mainly with women, not many men would want to see a female physician anyway. I see that reluctance every day. I would not exclude men, but I would like to focus on obstetrics and pediatrics."

"What would have to be done? I mean – are changes needed?" Mary sat back and slowly turned her glass on the table.

"Doc Wayland and I talked some about it a while back when I was visiting. Not too much change; maybe do-away-with a couple of first floor rooms; convert them to examining rooms with a little privacy. Reserve, maybe six, rooms for people who are sick and might have to stay over. We could add a small wing, or we maybe just take out a couple of walls on the second floor and make a small ward. It would not be exactly a cottage hospital; a little bigger, you know." She smiled and Mary matched it. "We could take care of a dozen or so patients recovering from birthing. We would keep the one smaller room on the first floor just to deliver babies. It could be easily modified for a surgery and delivery room. I expect most deliveries would still be at home."

"Have you thought about equipment and such?" Mary smiled then continued, "You know during the war I used to help with the wounded in the hospitals down in D.C."

"You never told me." A look of surprise knitted her eyebrows.

"I never thought it was that important, I even met Mr. Lincoln one day at a Sanitary Fair."

"You did?" She registered her surprise just as the cheesecake arrived.

"It was a long time ago." Mary sipped her whiskey and watched Sara position the cheesecake. "I have no objection to the clinic or hospital idea so long as we treat the girls the Cloister was originally designed for. Lord knows I sure have resented the male physicians studying my female problems."

She rolled her eyes. "I always thought they were more interested in looking than treating."

"Men just don't know how to take care of women patients, so damned condescending and arrogant. Doc Wayland is the exception. They think delivering babies is no great feat in particular. You know, Mother, I have seen three patients since I've been at Charity who died in protracted labor, strained themselves to death. The babies just wouldn't come and we could not turn them."

Mary sat up then and leaned forward on the table. "That frightens me, Sara. I do not want you here if you are pregnant."

"Li and I already plan to come home in a year or so, he just wants to get a little more experience under his belt. I'll talk more with him; I could probably leave most anytime and come home for a while to plan with Doc Wayland about getting started. Liam might not be too happy leaving the city just now, lots of work right now."

"It's just a few hours away by train. Li could commute if he had to. Don't worry about Liam, he'll be okay, and I'm sure Doc would be pleased; Lord knows I have work enough for him. It will keep him busy as long as he wants to".

"I'll talk to Li, mother." She reached across the table and reassuringly pressed her hand. "I think he'll let me do it."

"It would be so nice to have you both come home." She smiled at the thought as she observed Sara searching for the last crumb of cheesecake. "I sure could use Li; he has a head for business as well as the law."

"I know he likes what he is doing very much, Mother. He'll probably not want to move until next year."

"Well I don't want to interfere. Would you like another piece of that cheesecake?"

Chapter 33

December 1890
Dakota Territory

Billy adjusted the two poles of the smoke flap, shutting it, and cinched the poles in place with lengths of rawhide. He checked the stones that weighted the skirt of his lodge and carefully pegged the oval door closed. He stretched then looked toward the burial platform in the cottonwoods.

"I'll be back, Calling Jays, I'm going over to visit Running Bull, and if all goes well, I'll be back around the first of the year. I am lonely, love of my life, and I miss you so. Woman with a Flower may come back with me. Don't worry; she may take your place among the robes, but not inside my heart." A sense of loss pervaded his thoughts and once more he reviewed the solemn platform in the trees. He swallowed down his sense of sorrow but not before his eyes rimmed over. "There will never be another like you," he whispered.

He turned his horse and mule southeast. He was well provided for, with food enough to carry him through the remaining months of winter and an abundance of meat to share. It was flurrying snow when he saw Running Bull's camp in the distance. He discerned activity near the striped tepee. He thought he had escaped notice when riders loomed from a swale to his left. Blue Shirt and a group of younger braves appeared. When they recognized him, Blue Shirt shouted aloud and they quickly closed about him in a torrent of Cheyenne and happy recognitions.

"You are here! It is as Running Bull said! Our great warriors would come." In an excited clatter they closed a circle around him. Blue Shirt sent a happy whoop toward the other riders at the camp. They immediately broke or mounted up and galloped toward them as if there was a great race.

"He didn't know I was coming, Blue Shirt." Billy intoned into the happy confusion.

"He saw you in his dreams."

"In his bad dream, most likely." The two men laughed. "What is all the excitement about?"

"Sitting Bull is dead. Now there will be many dances. Kicking Bear will…"

"What? The mention of the great medicine man chief was a magic word. "What happened?"

"The metal breasts killed him."

"The Indian police killed Sitting Bull?"

"Yes, Red Tomahawk, he went to arrest him and they killed him. Many of the Sioux are fleeing into the country of emptiness - some have come to us. The warriors will unite and it is the time for the ghosts to arise. Sitting Bull is now among them, he will lead in their coming."

The crowd of warriors clustered about Running Bull's tent. As Billy arrived, Running Bull emerged; his face was streaked in red and black.

"I knew you would come, Lame Wolf." A satisfied smile creased his countenance.

Billy dismounted and walked to his friend. "I heard that Sitting Bull is dead".

"Yes, killed - three days ago. He can now lead all those gone before." He paused and motioned eastward. "The white men are so afraid of our Ghost Dance, they strike out. It is also our time to strike out. We will go in with Big Foot and his band. There will be a big dance. The warriors will gather and meet Big Foot he is just north with the Miniconjous. We intend to go there and you must come."

"I don't know, Running Bull, I came to settle in for the winter. I was thinking of Woman with a Flower."

"You and the women, you can have her when we get back and your tepee will be here." He gestured to a place near his own.

"Don't expect me to dance, but I'll watch." He sensed excitement in the warriors around him. "Do you know exactly where Big Foot is?"

"Yes, and there's lots of cavalry around looking for him. The whites want to stop the Ghost Dances, and they will because it is something that unites us."

"Very well I will go with you." He reluctantly replied. He glanced toward the tepee of Woman with a Flower and remembered the last time he went against his better judgment and rode off with Running Bull. "When will we go? Are we headed into a fight?"

"We are ready but there will be a fight only if the Long Knives start it". Running Bull turned to Iron Tomahawk. "Go to Woman with a Flower; tell her to make ready the lodge of Lame Wolf for his return," The young brave rode off, leading Billy's mule then quickly returned. "Are you satisfied, Lame Wolf?" Running Bull mounted up. Billy nodded in reply.

Running Bull signaled, Blue Shirt and Black Eagle rode forward. Other braves spread out to the sides of the main group that cantered ahead. They found Big Foot's camp the following day. There were several hundred of his followers - they appeared starving and sick and greatly dispirited, and as they gathered to make camp, hundreds of other warriors arrived in small and large groups. Big Foot was very ill with pneumonia and greeted only a few of the new comers. Joyful talk was shared among those who had not seen one another in months or years.

Conversation focused on the great dance and many light shirts were in evidence, brightly decorated and patterned.

Rations were very short. Billy managed to supply two deer he had surprised at a spring and, other hunters supplied meat but not enough to meet the needs of all. After three days of celebrating; a large area was set up for the dancing. A muted excitement was strung through the gathering in an intensity Billy had never before experienced.

Billy withdrew from participation but watched as the men anointed themselves with sacred red paint and adorned themselves in pale colored shirts. Black Eagle's shirt was made of muslin with feathers sewn onto the sleeves. Across his chest was a large black circle crossed with red arrows. Blue Shirt wore gray bleached buckskin with red feathers surrounding the neck and two red circles each side of the chest. When Running Bull reappeared from his visit to Big Foot, he was wearing a white muslin shirt that flared over his hips, its only decoration thirteen broad black stripes. Hundreds of dancers had gathered. They, in turn, were surrounded by a mass of women. A shrill sound came from the medicine man named Yellow Bird.

Running Bull brushed past Billy, then turned and confronted him. "The dance begins; see, Lame Wolf? See all gathered, Sioux, Arapaho and us," he touched his chest. "Heammawihio above and Aktunowihio below will hear us. The sound of our voices will reach Heammawihio and the sound of our feet will be heard by Aktunowihio. Come dance."
"I'll watch this time, Running Bull, but may the spirits hear you."

"Each of us will die a little today. I will see the paradise to come. You will get only another stain of time if you don't dance."

Billy shook his head. "No, not this time." He watched the dancers form a large circle and began a slow counterclockwise movement that contracted and expanded the circle. Their chanting filled the air. He picked out the Sioux words: "We shall live again, we shall live again, and we shall live again! Warriors over the whole earth, they are coming. The buffalo are coming." The pace of the dance began to quicken; soon it was half shuffle, half trot. Around and around they chanted and whirled, the women and bystanders adding to the mantra. The dance gained another notch of pace and soon it appeared to be a great milling mass. Warriors began to spew out from the greater mass of movement like sparks displaced by a whirlwind. The dance continued to whirl at a frantic pace. Some fell to their knees; others staggered about in trance; others fell completely unconscious. The movement gained in speed and more dancers fell to the side; soon there were more on the ground and staggering than were in the central movement. Suddenly it stopped. Some men, breathing heavily but apparently not as touched by the ceremony, picked their way back into the crowd. Near Billy two warriors, one sitting, one kneeling, were offering prayers for the return of the buffalo. The fervency of their effort touched Billy in some primordial place.

He scanned the dance site that appeared like the aftermath of some great battle, some were on their backs others appeared wounded and stunned by the experience. He spotted Running Bull prostrated near the center, where the movement had begun. He started toward him, hesitated; started toward him again, stopped and turned away. Thinking aloud he murmured, "I don't understand this stuff. I better stay the hell out of it." He thought back to the beautiful Woman with a Flower'. She would be waiting for him at his new tepee. He saw that many of the women were still standing with their arms stretching toward the sky; they too were praying.

"Well, Woman with a Flower, if I'm gonna find paradise on this earth, it's you that's going to deliver me there, sex, power and money; people's paradises and I prefer one over the make believe ones."

Billy had hoped to meet the great Sioux Chief, Big Foot, but Running Bull told him that the old man was ailing, barely able to walk. In the predawn darkness the two had set out hunting.

"What did you think of the dance, Lame Wolf? You should have joined."

"Maybe next time," They rode a short way and stopped to listen. "Running Bull, did you have visions? I saw you down out there and I was going to get you up, but it didn't seem right."

"Yes, I had a vision. I had a vision about you."

"Me?" Billy said, surprised. "Me? Can you tell me?"

"I saw you dead, you returned to the white man's world. Soldiers took you and carried you off. You lived again, but among them."

Only their breathing and that of the horses could be heard, and the steam of the breaths flowed like veils between them.

"Not likely, Running Bull. I have no reason to go back there. I'm looking forward to getting back to Woman with a Flower."

Running Bull smiled and snorted. "We don't always get what we desire."

"True enough, but that's what I plan to do; it's all right with you if I leave and go back to my lodge near the little river?"

"Of course, I hoped you would stay with us but you know what they say about the best made plans of mice and men". He adjusted on his horse and more seriously continued, "Where was that spring you hunted the other day?"

"It's a couple of miles yet. There were a few antelope tracks there. I was by myself and I already had two deer so I passed them up."

"There are many hungry. Big Foot is heading back to the Pine Ridge today. We can stay awhile, but we should head back. The long knives press us even in winter."

"I'll feel a lot better bringing in some more food; everyone looked so poorly. Some of those Sioux had nothing to eat for three days. Those deer disappeared like magic. They were boiling the bones."

"Let's move along." Acknowledging the need, they picked their way ahead riding into the gathering light. Upon reaching the area near the spring, they dismounted and crept toward it. Three antelope bolted from the brush. Billy dropped the largest one, and the other two were in full flight. Running Bull hit the second, but it continued to run. Billy's next shot caught the one farthest away while Running Bull continued to shoot through the trees at the second. Billy hesitated until it passed into a small clear space and killed it with his third shot.

Running Bull looked over the three kills and in a voice born from admiration and astonishment remarked. "You haven't lost anything; you must be hungrier than me."

The two men laughed and Billy selected the event to tease the leader as they examined the last of the antelope.

"Well, you hit her two times, it looks like. What were you trying to do? Turn her into jerky before you skinned her?"

"I hit her, anyway." He replied defensively.

"Two out of eight I guess isn't that bad." Billy smiled. "You must get a rifle that holds a few more cartridges if you stay outside the reservation."

"You were lucky, Lame Wolf."

"No, I am just more accurate."

Running Bull laughed despite himself, and they began to gut the animals for t

"Listen, Lame Wolf, don't move. Listen."

The sound of metal clinking on metal carried to them.

"Calvary," Running Bull listened intently. "I think it's just a couple. Ease back into the trees."

"They heard us shooting."

"Or they're looking for Big Foot."

The sounds of another horse drifted to them. Running Bull adjusted to where he could see the riders.

"That first son of a bitch is Sioux. The rest of them are Pawnees, another Sioux traitor." He spat watching the first rider disappear up a distant slope.

"Do you think he saw us?"

"No, Lame Wolf, he didn't see us but he heard us. He's not by himself, so one of them may have seen us. He would have known it was two different rifles. They don't want to come too close. My guess is they have spotted Big Foot and are in a hurry to get back and report."

"Let's get these antelope back, tell what we saw and get out. There's going to be trouble - soon. They have killed Sitting Bull and I think they will be after all of the Great War Chiefs."

"Big Foot is going to head for Fort Bennett on the Missouri. They're moving toward there today, so we will shadow them a way; I don't want to be in the middle."

After returning to Big Foot's camp, Running Bull gathered his followers together. They ate some boiled meat then rode westward, bracing against the wind. As they cleared a ridge, Iron Tomahawk pointed back toward the camp. A squadron of blue cavalry was descending upon the encampment.

"Should we go back?"

"No, Lame Wolf, we were lucky to get out of there when we did. Let us listen."

They moved into a copse of trees and sat quietly, listening against the hissing wind. No shots were heard, so they set out from the cover of the trees. They watched the progress of Big Foot's band from a distance but never ventured close enough to attract the attention of the cavalry and their scouts. Billy reined up beside Running Bull.

"It's starting to spit snow, in case you haven't noticed. Think we should set an early camp? We need to hunt; our rations are low. At least mine are." He reached into his saddle bag and pulled out two lengths of jerky. He offered one to Running Bull, who accepted it without comment.

"You may be right. Take Blue Shirt with you and see what you can find. We will stay here."

The two men had ridden for more than two hours when they spied a second cavalry squadron that was making camp.

"Blue Shirt, go back. I'll keep an eye on these bastards."

Blue Shirt rode off and with darkness descending, Billy crept close to the cavalry camp and close enough to hear the men talking of home, women, complaining about the Christmas just passed and eliminating the Sioux. As he made his way around the men, he spotted three canvas covered caissons. Utilizing the darkness and opportunity for movement, he reached the first caisson and examined it. It was a Hotchkiss gun; Billy felt frozen within him. He had heard the stories about the gun's power, sixty rounds of exploding bullets per minute. These bastards mean to kill them all. Carefully he examined the gun's caissons, and then rode back to Running Bull.

"Running Bull. You must get word to Big Foot. That squadron is Seventh Calvary."

"That is Custer's old regiment."

"Yes, and I think they mean to kill everybody they were talking about it. They are loaded for bear because Hotchkiss guns are not for duck hunting. Get the word to Big Foot's camp and have him get the hell out of here. Tell him to Head for the Badlands, anyplace but get out of here. We have to get the hell out of here too. We ought to break up and go now."

Running Bull reviewed his men clustered in small groups through the trees. "Some have jerky, some do not."

"I've got some more. I'll pass it out. Go ahead and go to Big Foot. I'll look after things here."

Running Bull mounted, said a few words to Blue Shirt and Black Eagle, and vanished into the darkness. At length Blue Shirt appeared and they passed out the rest of Billy's jerky and returned to a small fire.
"This land is near Big Foot's old village. Big Foot has said he will go no farther."

"They'll kill them, Blue Shirt. I know it. I feel it; they want to kill Big Foot and all his people."
"Oh, Lame Wolf, you know the white men want to kill all Cheyenne, want to kill all Sioux."

"I hope Running Bull convinces them to move out." Billy said aloud in English. "They may attack them in the morning."

"What say, Lame Wolf?"

"That Running Bull's talk is heard and the Sioux go this night."

"Yes."

The snow began to whiten the blanket over Billy's shoulders and while he braced himself against the cold, Big Foot and his three hundred followers broke from the squadron of cavalry. In the middle of the night, they fearfully fled into the barren Badlands, but the snow was good for tracking and the band moved slowly. On December 28, 1890, Major S. M. Whiteside caught up to them and directed the bedraggled band, with their ailing chief, southwest to camp along a narrow creek called Wounded Knee.

Wounded Knee Creek
December 1890

Running Bull's group of warriors had lucked out. Iron Tomahawk, while hunting, had come upon fresh wolf tracks. He followed them to a sheltered gulch along a small rill. There he found three wolves attacking a lame buffalo sow. He quickly shot two wolves, then the buffalo. The men quickly, skinned the wolves, dismembered the buffalo, and returned to feast.

"We need to get some of this meat over to Big Foot. They must be in pretty desperate straits by now."

"It's going to be difficult, Lame Wolf. There are cavalry everywhere. Black Eagle saw four squadrons approaching from two different directions. We will wait. I think they will take Big Foot to Camp Cheyenne, then on to Pine Ridge. We will bring them food there."

Their attention was refocused on an approaching rider.
Black Eagle reined up and began speaking at once. "Soldiers are all around Big Foot's camp, guns with many barrels on hill north."

"Those are those Hotchkiss guns."

"How many, Black Eagle?"

"I think four guns - soldiers everywhere".

"Get down and get some meat. Iron Tomahawk is a great hunter now, he brought meat when we needed it"

The rider did not acknowledge Billy's comment and simply slipped off his horse, turned his back abruptly on Billy and sat by the cooking fire.

"Black Eagle doesn't say much, Running Bull".

"Not to you, Lame Wolf. He wears your scar on his chest and in his mind. He will kill you if he gets a chance. I don't intend to provide him with one."

"Maybe I should kill him." Billy reviewed the figure at the fire.

"You should have killed him when you had the chance. Now, Lame Wolf, there are more important matters."

Billy lapsed into silence, conscious of the smell of cooking meat and to the weak but warming sun.

"If trouble comes tomorrow, we must take those Hotchkiss guns on the hill. We need to ride out there and take a look."

"We will never get into the camp again, Running Bull. The cavalry will be as thick as fleas."

"You and I will go there we will look and then we will know."

The morning of December 29, 1890, was splashed with sunlight. Iron Tomahawk had climbed far up into a tree to get a clear view of Big Foot's camp. Upon the insistence of Running Bull, Billy also climbed the tree, but not as high and his view was obstructed by other trees and a low hill. Although he could see only the Hotchkiss emplacement he could see the tarps were removed and the crews stood by their guns.

Running Bull called up the tree, "What is happening, Lame Wolf?"

In turn Billy called to Iron Tomahawk.

"The warriors are surrounded by soldiers, who are in the lodges. All the warriors except Yellow Bird are sitting. The Hotchkiss gunners are at the ready"

Billy awaited further word and relayed: "The soldiers are searching tepees. They are all around the camp. Yellow Bird is making words." The shrill sound of an eagle bone whistle carried to them.

"The soldiers are pushing the warriors, throwing off their blankets. There..."

The sound of a single shot resounded and before its echo was heard, there was a fusillade.

"Long Knives shoot warriors. Shoot every body!" Iron Tomahawk shouted so they both could hear.

Snow began falling through the branches on to Billy. He looked up quickly to see Iron Tomahawk dropping from branch to branch like a squirrel. As he looked toward the hill, the Hotchkiss guns suddenly opened up. He could see the extent of the mayhem as the guns raked away. The screaming of the women and cries of the warriors could be heard, and the steady rat-tat-tat of the four batteries. Smoke was rising from the hill. Billy, too, began to swing down.

"They're killing everybody. I knew it– those sons of bitches!"

Running Bull and his followers leaped to their horses and began to gallop toward the hill. The withering fire of rifles was mixed with shouts and cries of combat. As they swept toward the firing, a woman ran by with her baby in her arms, a young boy running as fast as he could behind them.

Six Pawnee scouts popped up in front, rifles in hand. Recognizing them, Billy drew his rifle and swung to aim at the same moment the first scout fired at him; the ball struck him in the head and rolled him back over his horse. His final recollection was a sense of falling and crashing into the cold.

Wounded Knee Creek
Post Massacre December 1890

The young lieutenant straightened against the high collar of his buffalo coat and stared down the long, snow clinched draw where he watched a lone Indian riding toward him. He and his Sixth Calvary Ogallala Scouts had just a few hours before rode through the killing ground of Wounded Knee Creek. There were bodies curled in death, frozen in their last throes, arms reaching toward the sky, legs tucked under or widespread; he had not liked what he saw. Women spread-eagled, the skirts of their smocks lifted to expose them; children with gaping wounds, their frozen blood crystallized in the snow; and babies bundled in their blood. The corpses were all going dark blue from the freezing weather that had stiffened their limbs. The bodies were spread for more than a mile from the main center of the massacre and throughout the shredded tepees.

He had not said much to the Sioux scouts who had clustered about him in a loose but protective way as they toured the dismal scene. To those who knew him as the 'Man Who Crawls to Win', he was a fair man who treated them with respect. As they rode slowly through the gruesome horror, the lieutenant knew that this event was probably the darkest saga in the long black history of dealing with the Indians. Government neglect and treachery had added a bloody page, and he was not proud of it and even less proud of the Seventh Calvary's handling of this incident. It appeared that Custer's ghost had assumed command of his old regiment, with predictable results.

The lone rider drew up to him and guided his steaming horse beside him.

"What is it, First Sergeant Thunder Bull?" The horse shied a bit, and then relaxed.

"Lieutenant Pershing, Sir. We find a wounded white man. You come. Over there," the Indian pointed toward a string of trees set into a gulch. You see, Crow on Head? There."

The lieutenant followed the pointing finger and spotted the warrior a few hundred yards away.

"Very well, Sergeant Thunder Bull go ahead, I will follow." The two riders cantered toward the distant figure, the horses breaking through long, chest-high, drifts that alternated with barren and windswept ground.

Pershing dismounted when he saw the blanket covered body and the Indians kneeling beside it.

"Is he alive, Bear Nose?"

"Yes, he's alive, Lieutenant. Look here."

Bear Nose turned the blanket from the face and gestured to the long bloody black gash that had torn the hairline just below the crown of the head and ripped its way over the ear. There was so much blood that it had run over his face and neck and onto his chest. The man's upper body was brown as a nut, but his lower body was cream colored except for his feet that showed a legging line.

"Shot from front," Thunder Bull observed.

"I wonder who he is. What's under him?" Pershing straitened and shrugged deeper into his coat. "Is there anything to identify him, anything at all?"

"This," another of the scouts spoke out and reached toward him, with a small leather bag strung on a piece of rawhide. Pershing took it carefully and looked at the man who had proffered it. "You know this, Iron Cloud?"

"Cheyenne. Cheyenne medicine bag."

"Hmmm, I wonder where he got this?" He looked about.

"Get my blanket under him, cut a couple of those saplings and rig a travois." He searched the somber faces of his men. "Running Shield and Big Charger, take him back to base camp to the surgeon's tent. You know the place, take him to the major."

Thunder Bull made a brief translation, and the two riders rode toward the saplings and began to study them. They chose two of the straightest and began to cut them down.

"Well, Sergeant Thunder Bull, do they understand?"

"Yes, Lieutenant, they take him to camp."

Once again Pershing studied the medicine bag, and then slipped it over the neck of the unconscious man. "When he comes around, if he does, he will have some explaining to do." Pershing swung easily into his saddle despite the bulky coat.

"Was this man alone, Thunder Bull?"

"Tracks over there, ten, maybe twelve horses go north, Yellow Bear say, very fresh tracks."

"Well then, let's get about our task." He urged his horse toward the fresh turned snow.

"Yes, Lieutenant." The Indian turned his horse and spoke quietly to his companions. They had followed the tracks about three miles where they split into three divisions, each going in a different direction. Pershing and three of his men pushed after a set of them until late into the day, and as the light was failing he turned back toward main camp. Although very tired of fighting the cold and snow, he was equally curious about the young white man he had found. After seeing to his horse and storing his gear inside his tent, he made his way to the surgeon's post. The medical officer was puffing on his pipe, his feet propped against his stove.

"How are you, Jack?" He acknowledged.

"Major, I'm fine. A bit wind blown - cold out there today."

"Some handiwork, this like Custer himself was leading a vengeance."

"Ah major, it's a hell of a mess. They had no discipline, those Seventh boys – a bit of a disgrace, I'd say."

"God, Jack, I found six babies out there. A disgrace, I guess! I don't know how many women. I stopped looking after a while – I've been an Army surgeon for more than twenty years and I'll be damned if I ever could conceive of anything like this it makes me sick. It's a Goddamn travesty."

Pershing did not reply, but extended his hands to the stove. "So how's the patient my men brought in?"

"He's lucky to be alive. If that slug had been one inch to the right or a few inches lower, he'd have been a goner."

"He's going to live?"

"I think so. He was conscious a while back, speaking Cheyenne and English all mixed

309

up. Something about Sada, and mother, it is all gibberish I think he's probably been raised by the Cheyenne; maybe he was a captive. He might must be some kind of a trapper - trader."

"Perhaps, we will find out when he can talk."

"The only thing for sure, he's been shot in the head has a bad concussion maybe a depressed fracture." The major paused and stoked a piece of wood into his stove. "Want to sit for a spell? I've got a drink here – warm your insides, but you'd better put some water with it."

"The brandy's gone?" the young lieutenant asked.

"Yesterday, but this will suffice. It's not the taste that counts, it's the effect." He grinned and poured some clear liquid into a glass, then added water. "Good for what ails you, Jack."

"Whatever that might be – snow, cold, disasters and massacres of Indians." He resigned in despair, and then took a deep pull from the glass.

Billy was aware of the closeness of the tent and his aching, bandaged head when he awoke. He did not know where he was and could not focus well, but he was warm and could hear remote voices. It was like being lost in a fog. Slowly he rolled to his side in a wave of dizziness and saw a man across from him. The man was wearing a bloody sling, cradling a swollen discolored arm. The man caught his eye and called aloud.

"Major, Sir, the man across from me is awake."

Billy stared at the anxious voice, and realized he must be in a hospital and rolled to his side. His head ached with a pulsing pain and he was nauseous and disoriented. He rolled to his back when he heard other voices approaching from the inner recesses of the tent. Then he became aware of the slight medicinal-canvas smell and a faint odor of rot and for a moment he thought he would vomit. He closed his eyes, and heard two distinct voices over him - slowly he reopened his eyes to see a kind face regarding him. There was an oak cluster on the collar below the intense eyes.

"Well, young fellow, how do you feel?" The major leaned forward in a friendly manner.

"Where am I?" He became aware there were two officers peering at him. From long remembrance a respect modified his tone.

"Hospital tent, Sixth Calvary, near Wounded Knee Creek, you had a close call, lad."

"How long have I been here?" Billy rose up on his elbow trying to see through the fuzzy halo his eyes beheld.

"Well, Lieutenant Pershing here had his men dragged you in two days ago. Frankly, lad, I didn't think you were going to live. You have a very nasty head wound." The major leaned back, and the young lieutenant put down the camp stool, he carried, beside the bed.

"I have a few questions for you, young man. First," he began crisply...

"Take it easy with him, Jack. He could be very fuddled."

"Do you feel up to this, lad?" The lieutenant asked with forbearance.

"Yes, Lieutenant, I'm all right; just have a hell of a headache. Are you the one who brought me in?"

"Well, not personally. My scouts found you..."

"Thank you, Lieutenant," he said sincerely.

The grey eyes softened for just a trace. "I have some questions I want to ask you."

"Yes, Sir I'll do the best I can."

"First, what were you doing here?"

"I came down to watch the Ghost Dance," Billy paused.

"And...?" Pershing's question hung in the air for a long moment.

310

"I was following Big Foot in and some Indian shot me. I don't remember anything after that."

"When we found you, you were naked, lying in the snow. You hadn't been there too long, though. There were other tracks that were very fresh and one of my scouts caught sight of some Cheyenne fast disappearing over a ridge."

"Sorry, Sir, I don't remember a thing after I was shot. I remember that I think I saw the bullet that hit me, a kind of gray flash." He paused. "At least I think I did."

"What are you doing here so far away from a town? I mean, where are you from?"
"My home is in Belle Forche, Nebraska, but I'm from Minsi, New York."

"Your name?"

"Billy Kavanaugh."

"What are you doing out here?"

"Well, I did some trapping, trading with the Cheyenne."

"Trading with the Cheyenne? Does that explain the medicine bag?"

"No, my mother made that for me, Sir. She was Cheyenne."

"You sure don't look like any Indian I've ever seen."

"No, I know. Everyone says so."

"So you were out here trapping and trading?"

"Yes, Sir, I sold my pelts at Buffalo. Someone could vouch for me there."

"Why go to a Ghost Dance?" Pershing leaned back on the stool and crossed his arms.

"I lost my wife, Sir. I was hoping..." he stumbled in his speech then continued, "I don't know what I was hoping."

"She was an Indian?" His voice softened.

"Yes, Sir, a Cheyenne."

"Well, that's interesting. One of the most hostile tribes and you took a wife among them."

"Yes, Sir, I speak the language very well."

A slight smile showed at the corner of the lieutenant's mouth. "That's important, isn't it?"

"Yes, Sir." Billy closed his eyes as a great fatigue descended upon him.

"I don't have any more questions right now, better rest up and get some food in you. We know you haven't eaten anything in at least two days. I'll stop back later."

"Thank you, Sir," he whispered; his eyes squinted against the pain. He heard the lieutenant leave. A warm, rosy haze clouded his mind and he slipped into a deeper sleep.
"What do you think, Jack?" The major greeted as he fired up his pipe.

"He is a polite young man - shows some breeding. He says he is from upstate New York – Billy Kavanaugh."

"New York, huh it's an odd place to be from in this part of the woods. No Cheyenne up there I ever heard of." He sent a billow of smoke toward the ceiling.

"He has evidently had some schooling; even in his condition, he was very articulate – polite, respectful."

"Better recruit him, Jack. You need someone who can think to handle the general rabble out there. One in maybe twenty can read; most can't write more than their name, and speaking Cheyenne – a find I'd say."
"Come now, major. They're here..."

"And that's about all you can say for them. It's a little different from the parade ground at West Point. I must admit, though, those scouts of yours look sharp and they surely are loyal to you. Why, they wouldn't talk to the orderly, insisted they see me about our mysterious young man. 'Lieutenant Pershing said to see the major.'"

Pershing smiled. "It's amazing what a little respect will do." He stood and clapped his gloves across his thighs. "I have to get on with my duties. I'll stop back to see Mr. Kavanaugh this afternoon, or early tomorrow and I'll have another talk with him."

Billy woke in the late afternoon to the smell of soup. He propped himself on his elbow and watched the man with the bandaged arm struggle with the bowl before him. Suddenly Billy felt very hungry and tried to sit up. Although a little dizzy, he slipped his feet over the edge of the cot. An orderly with a soup pail had his back to him, filling another bowl. He straightened and turned.

"Can I have some of that?" Billy asked.

The man smiled. "I'll get you a bowl." He returned bearing a tin bowl with a spoon in it and poured it full, then dropped two pieces of hard tack on the cot. Billy ate eagerly and when he finished, he felt strong enough to try to stand. He did so with some difficulty and slowly worked his way to the end of his cot, where he could see the length of the tent. In a few moments the surgeon entered.

"Feeling stronger, eh, Kavanaugh?"

"Yes, Sir, a lot better."

"The lieutenant was in this morning and said he may be back to see you this afternoon." At that very moment the tent flaps opened with a blast of frosty air and Pershing entered his face purple from the wind and cold. He stopped by a cot nearer the opening, said a few words, picked up a camp stool and approached Billy.

"Well, major, it looks like our patient is up."

"He is, indeed. He's bull strong, I'd say."

Billy smiled at the reference. "I don't know about that, Major. Another hot meal and a woman would probably kill me."

Pershing and the major both broke into a guffaw.

"My gawd, Kavanaugh that tickled me." Pershing chortled.

"I worked in a saloon for awhile. One of the girls would often say that."

"You surprise me, Kavanaugh. You worked in a saloon also?"

"Yes, Sir, that was in Belle Forche. I also rode in Buffalo Bill's Wild West Show. Did a lot of trick riding, but I wasn't there long."

"You know Cody?"

"Yes, Sir, I do."

"Well, I'll be. You are a saloon worker, a trick rider, trader and trapper and Cheyenne speaker. What else can you do?"

"I am a damn good shot, had a nice Henry but that's gone now. Likely I'll not ever see it again."

"You familiar with the trap door Springfield 45/70?"

"I've shot them. They're all right for a pumpkin slinger – big bullet but slow to load. Half the Indians out here are better armed. Repeaters, you know."

"Yes." Pershing looked hard at him. "You can read and write?"

"Yes, Sir, I went to school until I was fourteen. Stepmother and father made me, but I didn't like it much. I would rather be hunting or fishing."

Pershing laughed. "I had a lot of pupils like you. I taught for a while before I went to

West Point." He leaned back and adjusted his feet.

"West Point's not far from where I lived, I thought about being a soldier once."

"You speak Sioux?" Pershing did not appear to notice the reference to soldiery.

As well as you speak Cheyenne?

"Some, I'm much better with Cheyenne."

Pershing smiled and rose from beside the cot. "You're going to need something more than a nightshirt now that you're up." He brushed at a twig that had twisted in his coat and carefully removed it, frowned slightly, then flicked it away. "Maybe you should reconsider becoming a soldier. With your background I can recruit you as corporal of scouts, consider the offer, Mr. Kavanaugh." He buttoned the great coat, looked it over carefully and walked toward the stove where the major was writing a letter.

Billy passed his hand to the bulging bandage on his head and pressed lightly along the swath of his wound. He began to bite gingerly at the hard tack. It hurt to bite down, but he was hungry. He glanced toward the two officers and smiled to himself.

"Why not, what the hell, she's gone now." He said to himself as his eyes began to fill. "Ah, Calling Jays, I miss you; there's no reason to stay with the tribe anymore." He thought for a first time about Running Bull. "He couldn't take me with him, probably waited until saw the scouts and dropped me off." He smiled despite the desperate thought. "We are even, old friend." He flinched at the vision of the miner's woman pitching over and Running Bull in the splash of brains and blood. "It's just as well that the chapter be closed. All this murder and despair, it's the end of something, I feel it." He folded himself back beneath the blanket on his cot and settled into his pillow. He closed his eyes and a deep sadness pervaded him. He adjusted his blanket, "And it's the beginning of something else." He entered into a deep and dreamless sleep.

The wound to Billy's head, though deep, had scabbed over, but the new cavalry cap he wore was tight enough to cause some discomfort. As soon as he could stand he was sworn into the United States Calvary as Corporal William Patrick Kavanaugh, service number 15074. The surgeon had given him a fit for duty report and now he found himself among the "Sioux Scouts." He communicated with a few Sioux words, a couple scouts spoke some Cheyenne, others spoke some English, and the rest was sign language. The lieutenant kept an eye on him, pointing out precise points of behavior and dress. He treated all the men with respect and consideration, and Billy's admiration grew for the tight lipped and stern commander.

The weather was especially cold, and fording the icy rivers, sleeping in the snow, in sleet and gale, in sub-zero temperatures was trying, even for Billy. On the trail his diet was bacon and beans, washed down with a quart of coffee, for breakfast and the other meals were whatever was in his saddlebag. In camp the fare was much better; supper was heaps of beef, potatoes and hard bread. Billy had not eaten so well for years and even gained weight despite burning the extra calories to compensate for the cold.

On the very first patrol out, Red Feather, one of the Sioux scouts, had crashed through a high snow drift and tumbled into a deep ravine. Billy was off his mount in a flash and edged down deep into the cleft; he locking the scout's hand in his own, and pulled him out. Getting the horse out was quite a project, but the two managed before the rest of the troop drew up. He had made a friend for life and a boost to his reputation.

They had been riding in every direction for about a week in the broken Dakota countryside. The area was quite suitable for ambush, and they were being particularly careful in their movements. They threaded through the steep sided hills and came upon the tracks of many riders and, before they could disperse the flankers, they rode right into the middle of a group of Cheyenne.

As they reined up, Billy recognized Running Bull and his raiders. In the hostile standoff, both parties were looking down their barrels into the barrels of the other. Billy rode to Pershing's side as the lieutenant was faced with a potential costly encounter. Running Bull balefully regarded them itching to kill them all.

"Lieutenant, Sir, we're in a bad spot. I know that chief, and what we are lookin' at are about half his men. There are about twenty ahead of us and probably three times that many closing in behind us. We're in a pretty bad spot. If we open fire, they will probably kill us all."
"I'm aware of the circumstances." Pershing was grim but did not appear afraid.

"I don't think so, Sir. Those men have revenge on their minds. They've caught us and have the drop on us. Maybe I can parley our way out of here."

Pershing did not reply but turned slowly in his saddle, his hand still upraised. It took only a moment to see there were braves near the crest of the hill, rifles waiting. He turned back toward Billy and saw more braves assembling. The only way out was to retrace the route they had come and, already, warriors were moving rapidly to close that option.

"You're right, corporal, we are outgunned." Slowly he lowered his hand. "See what you can do. I'll order the men to lower their rifles."

"Yes, Sir, I'll do my best." Billy slowly walked his horse toward Running Bull as Pershing's order held back the men. The Chief greeted him with a grim smile.

"Lame Wolf, so you are with them now." He said in Cheyenne. "Fancy blue coat and a nice horse you have there and new boots."

They continued to speak in Cheyenne. "Let's have a truce, Running Bull. We just ride north, you east or west or wherever."

"Why should I? You don't remember Wounded Knee? I mean to kill them all, but I might spare you. There are a hundred braves, many with rifles trained right now; one volley and lots of scalps."
"Some of your men will be killed, maybe you."

"Those Sioux scouts should be killed because of they betrayed of their own people. You're going to have to do better than fear for a reason for me to hold back."

"Then let it be our friendship and that of my mother, spare us. Remember the mining camp? I saved your life - that woman would have killed you for sure."

"Don't speak to me of the mining camp; I was the one who carried you from the field at Wounded Knee. I knew you would not be able to ride. We waited until we could see them searching for you. Waited for them to find you and take you to the white man's medicine. We barely escaped ourselves. I owe you nothing."
"I want to believe you but you could have left me to die in the snow."

"I could kill you now." He raised his hand as anger flushed his face and there was movement on the hill over the cavalry.
"Running Bull, please don't do this."

The great chief regarded Billy, his dark eyes fierce, unblinking, his mouth set tightly, his hand upraised for a signal to fire.

"For Maha's spirit and that of my mother, don't do this. We know you have us." Running Bull's horse was pacing, attempting to turn.

Black Eagle had been listening; out of respect for Running Bull he had said nothing but his loathing for Billy suddenly burst out.

"And the spirit of Calling Jays," He said in disgust. "She needs to be avenged also. You speak like you are one of us and you never were."

"She was my wife, Black Eagle. I paid for her with blood, both mine and yours."

"I will kill you one day, Lame Wolf, as I will kill other white eyes. We will kill you all."

Billy seized on the sentence. "Well, Running Bull, this man speaks for you now? A man whose wisdom is like a mouse and whose anger is like a bear's? He speaks for the Cheyenne now? What a poor choice!"

Billy observed Black Eagle tense in his saddle. All three men knew he had violated the basic protocol of brave to chief. He also could see Running Bull chaffed a bit at the event.

"The spirits of women drive us now? I will kill you one day, Lame Wolf." Black Eagle hissed.

"Well, Black Eagle, no time like the present. I spared your life once, too. You are no chief; you are not even a good follower."

The sun suddenly burst from behind its cloudy shroud, casting the scene in contrasts of stark black shadow on the blinding white snow.
Black Eagle once more began to speak. "I will..."

"Silence, Black Eagle! You have talked enough! We have talked enough. Your mind is hollow because of hate."

Black Eagle did not respond but continued to glare at Billy. Suddenly he turned from Running Bull and rode back toward the band of waiting warriors.
"You will go with them, Lame Wolf? I will no longer see you across a fire?"

"I reckon so, Running Bull. I have had enough. I think I will go back to New York as soon as I am able."

"You will go home, home to New York and the red one."

"I don't know about that –probably. I've had enough."

"Enough is when there is no more left to do and we are all dead." He looked toward the troopers, their carbines still drawn but across their saddles. "We want to pass west and we want no pursuit this day."

Billy scratched at his nose and spit into the snow. He looked toward the troopers, regarded Running Bull again. "I'll go talk to the lieutenant. The terms seem fair to me."

"Otherwise we will kill you all, this day." There was little emotion, just a straight forward observation.

Billy turned his horse about and rode the short distance that separated them, feeling all eyes upon him, including Black Eagle's hate. He reined up before Pershing.
"Sir, this is the message. We let them pass north and not take off after them today."

"Or?" Pershing looked past Billy's shoulder to the chief.

"Or they will kill us all; we could try to ride through them back there maybe. There are about sixty, I think, all around us. You saw those on the hill behind? We are sure to lose some men; they are eager to kill us all. I don't know about the back door, maybe twelve or fifteen braves there. I counted a dozen, but there are more I think. They will block us and it will close quickly,"

"I saw some of them, Cheyenne all?"

"No, I think there's some Sioux too. There was at least one Arapaho, Feather Stick, I know him. There's sure to be more with him." Billy also looked back to Running Bull.

"Very well, you carry my word we agree. It doesn't make me too happy, but we will probably fight them again under better conditions."

"I'll try to find out where they are headed. I better get back, they are not known for being patient."

Slowly Billy rode back to where Running Bull waited, and spoke in English.

"Lieutenant Pershing indicates he will do as you asked."

"Doesn't have much choice, does he?"

Billy did not respond but looked back toward the troopers.

"So we part ways, Lame Wolf."

"Yes, I'm probably missing an opportunity with 'Woman with Flowers.'"

"Too bad, you are a real killer. You could be the next warrior chief behind me and you will get lots of practice had you stayed with me." He smiled slightly. "I have your Henry." He tapped the butt of the rifle.

"I've had enough, Running Bull. I saw the rifle. I will always consider you my friend. Keep my rifle may it help keep you safe. There is a winter's worth of jerky back at my camp you are welcome to that too." He began to turn his horse when Running Bull stopped him.

"Billy, don't be so reckless with your life. These Army bastards don't care a wit for your life. They will be careless enough with it and they will kill you someday. It could have been today." He raised his arm and signaled.

Running Bull reined his horse about and rode back to where Black Eagle waited with a formation of warriors. Soon the others appeared from behind and beside the soldiers, riding toward Running Bull. Some of the warriors rode close enough to touch the troopers and glared at them as if their hate alone could kill.

Billy had stopped halfway as the riders rode past him without offering any recognition; their horses showered him with dirt and snow. He could see no more riders coming forward and quartered toward the bluecoats when a war cry from among the braves split the air. He turned back to see Black Eagle galloping toward him, rifle leveled. He looked down to draw his carbine as Black Eagle's first shot hissed past his cheek close enough for Billy to feel its passage; a second shot followed that thumped into his great coat but did not strike flesh. Taking a quick aim, Billy fired. Black Eagle's arms raised and his rifle sailed as the force of the bullet drove him from the saddle. Billy reloaded but there was no movement in the bundle of furs on the snow. Black Eagle's horse continued forward and stopped beside Billy's. He caught the animal up by its rein and slowly rode toward the large band of braves, directly up to Running Bull. Without a word he handed the reins to the old chief, nodded and rode slowly toward the troops on high alert. He heard Pershing shout, "Hold your fire."

Lieutenant Pershing looked steadily at him. Although grim, there was not the slightest inkling of fear. "Are you wounded?" He watched the war party intently.

"No, Sir, just a hole in my new coat." Billy turned his horse to look back.

"Mind telling me what that was about? It could have been a disaster."

"It was personal thing, Sir. He never did like me much; I had trouble with him before."

"Personal, well, young man, this man's army has no place for personal feuds. You have saved the day, but you have some explaining to do." He sternly regarded Billy. "I would like to know just who those Indians are and why you know them so well? And where did you develop your ability to speak Cheyenne so well? You'd better explain yourself." Pershing's lips were set, as he observed the braves removing Black Eagle's body.

"Do you want the long or short version, Sir?"

"I want the truth."

"Well, Sir, my mother was a Cheyenne and she taught me. The old chief over there was married to my mother's best friend. Also she was related to him somehow, so he is kind of my friend. That's the short version, Sir."

The Cheyenne across from them had rearranged their line of approach and were beginning to slowly close the gap.

A trace of a smile crossed Pershing's countenance. "Someday, Kavanaugh, I'll have to hear the longer version. But it is not appropriate at the moment." He turned toward the troopers and shouted, "Column of files, from the right, column right." Pershing raised his arm, turned his horse away from the approaching Cheyenne and motioned. "Forward!" The band of soldiers and scouts formed after him. Red Feather drew abreast of Billy and they rode out to point up the right flank. It would be a long ride before they were back at headquarters, it would probably be a good idea to avoid the lieutenant for awhile.

Dakota Territory
January 1891

"You wanted to see me, Sir?" He waited outside the open tent.

"Yes, come in, Billy." Pershing selected a cigar from his case and sat down on the camp chair, motioning Billy to the other. "How do you like this soldier's life?"

"I like it all right. Do they ever pay us?"

Pershing laughed. "Yes, of course. I heard yesterday we will get paid next week."

"I don't need the money, I was just wondering, I mean, what do I need money for?"

Pershing smiled and bent forward slightly as if to add an air of confidence. "Billy, I've been reassigned."

"Is that good news for you, Sir?"

"Yes. I am going to lead the Corps of Cadets of the University of Nebraska."

"That's at Lincoln isn't it? There's been some talk, sir that you might be leaving us."

"Yes." He lighted his cigar,

"I've been to Lincoln, not much doing' there." Then he smiled broadly. "Then, Sir, there's not much doing' here either."

"How would you like to go back there?"

"I'm to serve with you, sir?"

"Yes." Before Billy could respond, Pershing continued. "I will need some people like you to assist in dealing with a lot of young men who probably do not take their cadet experience very seriously."

"I'd be glad to help, Sir, but what would you want me to do?"

"Assist me in teaching marksmanship and riding."

For a moment Billy did not respond, then smiled. "I guess I could do that, sir, but I never fancied myself to be much of a teacher."

"I've been watching you. The Scouts regard you highly; you treat them with respect and they respond well. You're as good a rider as any one of them, although, sometimes, I think your antics will get you killed."

"I've been around Indians a lot, sir, my mother, my wife and the trading; they appreciate a little fancy riding, and you treat them right, they will treat you right. I think teaching cadets may be a little different."

"Yes, quite." Pershing smiled. "I'll not forget our little shooting contest we had last week I covered my group with my hat and yours with Captain Cronin's watch."

"Some people have a talent for that kind of thing. Yours were all in the black." Billy smiled. "Captain Cronin could use some help."

Pershing smiled. "And Billy, the whole troop witnessed the incident on the road with Black Eagle."

"I'm sorry about that sir. I realize that it endangered the men, but I didn't have much choice. Black Eagle didn't like me very much. He blamed me for my wife's death, he was her father. Not her real father in the sense of white mans father, but he raised her up and that's father according to the Cheyenne".

Pershing paused. "I'd forgotten you had been married." He glanced outside the tent then re-focused on Billy. "You're interested, then, in going to Nebraska?" He stood and walked toward his small writing desk. "The rest is none of my business."

"Yes, Sir, it would be a great privilege to serve with you."

"Fine, by the way, your promotion to sergeant is on my desk." He held out the paper towards Billy.

Billy was astonished, but stood and accepted the paper to review, then passed it back.

"A sergeant, I didn't expect that."

Pershing smiled. "You would have received it even it you hadn't agreed to go with me. You kept us out of a very serious scrape."

"A sergeant, my father was a sergeant."

"Oh." Pershing looked at him curiously. "You never mentioned that your father was in the Army."

"He didn't mention much about it either."

Pershing sat down behind the desk and looked up. "I am sure he would be proud of you." He paused. "I am sure that you could stay on here in the Sixth, but I think they will soon disband the Sioux Scouts."

"That would be a shame, Sir." Billy shifted awkwardly.

Pershing looked back at his desk, then to Billy. "Quite so, you're dismissed to duty, sergeant."

"Yes, sir," he turned on his heel and walked out among the snowy tents. "I didn't know it would be this easy. I should feel something different," he thought. "A sergeant – that's really something."

It began to snow.

Chapter 34

Minsi – Pittsburg
May 1892

Spring was doddering green and vibrant; the odor of flowers filtered through the windows. The honeysuckle filled the air with sweetness and bees were industriously working the flowers. Inside Mary's office Liam was uneasy in her gaze.

"Mary, are you sure you want, me, to go?" Liam was seated with his chair braced to the wall. "I don't know anything about boats."

"Nor do I, who else would you like me to send?"

"Mr. Haney knows your investments better, and he's a lawyer to. You are sure you want me to do this?"

"Gambling on the river is a good investment and Haney is a crooked lawyer. The boat that is advertised is a paddle wheeler, three hundred feet long, four decks, and a calliope with thirty two whistles. Handsome thing, look here at the picture."

Liam took the leaflet and reviewed it carefully. "Yes, it looks pretty, Mary. I don't know anything about river boats."

"Look, I have to send you. Bill Sutter believes you can do it, so do I. I can't go – I really need to attend some meetings. I don't feel up to travel. I have some other business problems I have to attend to much closer to home. There's nobody else I can trust with all that money. Haney would buy the boat for $30,000 and charge me forty. So just go and make an offer. You worry too much."

"I know that, it's just that I'm unsure - Mary, that's a lot of money."

She did not answer him directly but took back the photo and reviewed it carefully. "I want it. It sleeps one hundred seventy people, most of whom will be willing to gamble a basket full of dollars. There's no regulation on the water, and gambling other places is getting illegal. You can save me at least three thousand, Haney's commission. That's a lot of money, too."

"I don't know what kind of deal it is, but I guess I can do it."

"Yes." She took back the photo. "All you really have to do is deliver my letter of credit to Scaithe and Company. Stan Andrews, an old acquaintance, will meet with you in Pittsburg and show you the boat. He is honest I think and he does know something about Riverboats. He's brokering the deal and you will learn. I've dealt with him in the past, it was profitable. Don't you worry – I'm not. Enjoy the trip, meet with Stan, listen to him and find out what you can. I am thinking about hiring Stan and I will go over those details before you leave. If everything seems in order and you think it's alright, settle the deal. Otherwise say no and come home after you direct the bank to return the credit."

"They're selling the boat for a reason, Mary. Maybe they lost baskets of money."

"And maybe they were just poor business people. Here's a chance for you to get some experience."

"Boats sink Mary; have you heard of the Island Queen?"

"Yes, and lightning some times strikes a shithouse with someone in it, Liam. Do you have any other questions?"

The tone of her voice was turning sharp with impatience. "I have always fancied owning a Riverboat for gambling. It has always appealed to my – my adventuresome spirit, I guess. Now there is one for sale, I have the money and I am going to buy it or one like it".

Liam knew better than to advance any further argument.

"All right, Mary, I'll go to Pittsburgh, when do you want me to go?"

She walked over to Liam and put her arm around his shoulder. "We'll have to get ready and all. I should think in about two weeks, that will give us time to set things in order, how about the first of June?"

"All right," he set the chair down to the floor.

"You will need some new clothes. And my, my – there are some great new fashions for men this year. We will go to the city next week and outfit you. I want Pat to go also but that is like wrestling with sin. He may go, regardless, we can't have you go off to Pittsburg looking like some Minsi hick. Come on, now, Liam, I need you to do this.

He nodded his head and smiled. Alright, I'll go".

That's better - you're my boy with the magic smile; we'll enjoy a couple of days in the city. I'll get in touch with Bill Sutter and we'll have a night or two out on the town."

Liam rose and gave Mary a hug and a wet kiss on the cheek that obviously pleased her.

"Liam," she said in distraction.

"What, Mary?"

"You know what," she brushed at her eye, "you're all grown up."

"Smile, Mary."

Suddenly she laughed and surrendered to the attention. "Oh, Liam, you are so much like your father. I still miss him, and I am so glad you are here".

They encircled each other's waists with their arms and started toward the kitchen. Evelyn was making corned beef and cabbage and the odor was spreading through the house.

Liam arrived in Pittsburgh on June third and thoroughly enjoyed touring the site of old Fort Pitt, where the two rivers become the Ohio. He rested, ate well and prepared for his meeting with Stanley Andrews.

Stanley was a pompous man and his appearance lent credence to it. He wore a white shirt with a high collar with a winged "gates ajar" effect, a red polka dot cravat, a double vested waistcoat with velvet lapels, and pegged dark trousers with a buckled waistband, over less fashionable square toed shoes. His affected manner was enhanced by an ivory cigar holder that he waved and used as a pointer while he spoke.

"So, Mr. Kavanaugh, you work for Mary Cleary," he smiled and twiddled the cigar holder. "Err, how did you manage to come into her favor? Are you a gambler who ended up owing her?" He smiled at the preposterous proposal. "You appear very young."

"Mr. Andrews, I…"

"Stan, if you please," he broke in.

"No, I don't like gambling; I know that it has done great harm to those who gamble and to their families and I have a family myself."

"That's odd," Stan made a small flourish with his cigar. "Someone who hates gambling is thinking about buying a Riverboat designed for it."

"I work for Mary; I'm kind-of a partner that is, I hope to be one day. She has no compunction about gambling. "

"A kind-of a partner, what do you mean?"

"Yes, it's a family business." He spoke and tried to head off additional inquiry, but Andrews was not ready to give up.

"Really, I know that Mary's a mighty successful woman and very few like her in this country." He made another flourish. "Nor in any other, I would think. You're her nephew or something?"

"Or something, she is my step-mother."

"Mary's married"? He appeared surprised and puffed on his cheroot. "I didn't know."

"She has been married to my father for more than fifteen years."

"Stepson; the name..." He caught himself, and then blundered on. "You don't look like, err – I mean, Kavanaugh, that's an Irish name, and you don't look like an Irishman."

"That's because my birth mother was Cheyenne."

"Oh, gracious, I'm sorry, I'm a bit confused. I didn't know; I'm sorry to be so curious".

"Stan, I expect there are a lot of things you don't know about Mary Cleary Kavanaugh. Now if you don't mind, where do we find this Riverboat? I'm here to represent Mary's interests, so let's get on with it."

"Yes, Mr. Kavanaugh, of course." He was still a bit rattled, but obviously impressed by Liam's business-like manner.

The horse drawn cab wove its way through the trolley traffic and past the crowds of shoppers. The bridges that crossed the rivers were stirring with people going about their business. Liam opened the window to avoid Andrews' cigar smoke and to catch a better view of the spreading city.

"Are you familiar with Pittsburgh – our busy city?"

"Not really, I see lots of smoke, lots of people, and I know they make steel here."

"Yes, quite. Liam, sure you don't want a cigar?"

"Neither smokes nor gambles – interesting! Well, you're young, how about..." He paused. "I would like a nip, would you? I have a flask of some extraordinary cognac." He reached inside his waistcoat and produced a small silver flask.

"I don't drink before evening either, and before you ask, I'm married. I leave all the rest to my twin brother Billy, wherever he is."

Andrews chuckled. "A twin, oh my I'll wager he is all business too". He drew on his cheroot and exhaled a cloud of smoke. "As I was saying, Pittsburgh is a busy place. A great river forms here. The Allegheny from the north flows into the Monongahela and form the great Ohio. The Ohio flows into the Mississippi and that goes all the way down to New Orleans and the ocean. It's quite a trip; I've taken it many times."

"That's how you know so much about boats, Mr. Andrews?"

"Yes, I was also a pilot for a while - Port of Cincinnati, and in my younger days I was first officer on the American Line, the ship New Independence. We traded into Liverpool, England, mostly. I saved my treasure and even owned my own paddle-wheeler for awhile. I sold it for a tidy profit and started acting as a broker for other people interested in buying or selling boats of all kinds. I've brokered other international businesses as well. That's actually how I met your stepmother who was interested in buying some Cuban property – a coffee plantation, as I recall. The deal was in New York and she was represented by a Mr. Haney, if I recall that correctly."

"Yes, he still works for her, but he has slowed down quite a lot, he's an old man now."

"That Cuban property was a steal, I would have bought it myself if I'd had the cash. Your stepmother was a most charming, very fashionable lady and oh, so sharp. I am surprised she is not here herself."

"She is very busy, Mr. Andrews. She could be traveling all of the time if she wanted."

The carriage jounced along and Liam became absorbed in the passing landscape.

"Whatever happened to the Cuban property?"

"She still has it. She sold most of the coffee holdings to the worker's league, and then turned the hacienda into a casino."

"Yes, yes I remember that coffee plantation –it was an interesting deal. When I was first officer on the Independence, I often joined the Captain and guests at his table. One evening there was a Spanish couple, very nice people, quite fashionable; the woman was a dark beauty and the husband, Ricardo his name was." He puffed thoughtfully on his cheroot, his face brightening. "Her name was Rosandra, Rosandra and Ricardo Gardenda, were their names. She wore a beautiful yellow dress and…" He looked over at Liam. "Am I boring you? I would hate to be a bore."

"No, Mr. Andrews, I was just looking out at the city. I've been listening. Rosandra and Richard, you were saying?"

"Ricardo."

"Oh yes, Ricardo Gardenda."

"Well," he raised his eyebrows in emphasis. "They were leaving Cuba. They were having labor troubles of a sort - sugar and coffee workers." He puffed delicately on the cheroot.

"They didn't want more money per month, they wanted independence from Spain. A disorderly and brutal bunch of thieves and, I assume, idealists."

"Like Adams, Jefferson, and Washington?"

"Ho, ho, that's very good, Mr. Kavanaugh, and Jefferson Davis too – ho, ho, ho! That's rich, insightful, too, I think." He knocked the shrunken cigar from its holder and ground it out with his heel. "You are mature beyond your years, yes indeed."

"Getting back to Rosandra and Ricardo, what happened?"

"Oh, yes, well," he added, leaning forward to emphasize a confidence, "Their lives had been threatened. They were loyalists, you see, and the rebel leader, Cespedes, I think his name was, he knew it."

"Did he threaten them face to face?"

"Oh, no, Mr. Kavanaugh via a very secret society, I understand, quite secret. The Spanish authorities were seeking this man. "I know," he said with emphasis. "The Spaniards were particularly brutal. They tortured prisoners terribly so, beating, cutting them, burning them, trying to strangle the truth from them. And jail there – my gracious, absolutely atrocious!"

"I've read about some of that."

"Well, one night Rosandra heard a commotion outside. She roused Ricardo, but they did not venture out and sat on their bed with a loaded pistol, thinking someone was coming." He paused.

"Well?" Liam asked impatiently.

"The next morning they found the head of their foreman on the front porch of their house. It was just sitting on the railing and the whole floor was covered in blood. Evidently he had been an informer for Spanish authorities."

"I'll bet that scared them, all right."

"Indeed, Mr. Kavanaugh, indeed! They booked passage with us that same day. We happened to be in port, freighted to Madrid."

"You mean they just left?"

"With little more than the clothes on their backs and, of course, whatever money they had, which, by their standards, was not much so naturally they were anxious to sell the estate."

"They just up and left, that is interesting. Did they have any children?"

"A childless couple," He fitted another cheroot to his holder. "Anyway, we were at the Captain's table." He smiled reliving the event. "I had a nicely tailored uniform, fit me like a glove. They were resplendent: she wore that lovely yellow dress with a full skirt. She was nicely proportioned, and he darkly handsome." He drew a deep breath.

"What happened at the table, Mr. Andrews?" Liam drolly inquired.

"Oh, yes. Well, they were discussing their fate - quite convoluted, as I recall. They mentioned they wanted to sell their property and inquired if the Captain might be interested? Of course he wasn't, the sea was his life. He had a home in Pawtucket." Andrews paused and fired up his cheroot.

"And you..."

"I told them I was not personally interested but I would inquire around when I got back to New York. They said they would make it worth my while. I was thinking perhaps the owner of the shipping line, Mr. Ross, would be interested. He rather liked me and talked to me on occasion. He had a home in Cuba - some of our cargos both originated and were delivered there." He waggled the cheroot, puffed at it, then continued. "Mr. Ross wasn't interested, but he told me it was a great deal and referred me to his lawyer's office, said there may be someone there. They were over on Twelfth Avenue."

"That would be Sutter, Ryan and Rosenstein?"

"Yes, you know them?" He looked curiously at Liam. "Harvey Sutter an older gentleman was an outstanding lawyer."

"Well, I know Bill Sutter, his son best. He's a criminal lawyer. Rosenstein handles the corporate stuff; Ryan is kind of an all around guy, mostly real estate. I used to work in their office.

"That's where you met Mary?"

"Yes, less than a week later I had a caller who delivered a note for me to meet at their office. This was my first big deal, I wasn't officially anything. I knew how to contact Ricardo – that's all." He smiled, "I was quite bluffing it." He waved his hand.

"I guess it must have worked out all right. I'm not familiar with the details. That was before Mary hired me, I should say started to pay me."

Andrews laughed. "I must say your mother was splendid at the office. She wore a beautiful pale green dress, not bustled, quite svelte, and a gorgeous green hat with a white egret feather as I recall. Black ankle high shoes, she was charming, didn't say a great deal. A quick conference, Haney did the talking and carried on about foreign investment, you know?"

"How the hell do you remember all this stuff - hats, shoes, dresses? That was a long time ago."

"I pay attention to detail, young man. Anyway, Haney, that is Mary bought the whole place, house, coffee fields, outbuildings and stock for 65,000 dollars. I contacted the Gardendas; they accepted. It was done in a matter of three months and they awarded me four thousand dollars - more than I made in a year of sea duty. Needless to say, I gained in mind a new career." He puffed at his small cigar. "I didn't see Mary much after the Cuba activities."

"Like I said, Mary still owns most of it. Shortly after she bought it, she sold the coffee holdings to a group of workers who gathered up money from somewhere. Haney told me Mary gave them a very good deal. She calls the casino, Hacienda Patrones. She wants to send me down there sometime, but not this year I hope!"

"And no headless foreman," Andrews laughed.

Liam joined him. "There are no headless foremen, just a lot of misguided people who think that they can make a fortune at the turn of a card."

The cab approached an intersection jammed with picketers holding placards and chanting, "Three dollars a day for labor power!"

"What's going on out there? More labor trouble?" Li craned his neck to keep sight of the pickets.

"Oh, you wouldn't believe it!" He waved his cigar toward the window. "Lots of pickets, lots of labor trouble here, most of it now focused at the Homestead Works."

"Homestead Works what are they?"

"One of the Carnegie steel mills. The trouble has been building. He fired all his workers, put up a fence around the whole yard. Fisticuffs, shootings, and riots it's quite terrible. I would have thought you'd have heard."

"There are lots of labor troubles. I haven't been keeping track lately."

"Oh, but not like this. The workers are brawling with the strike breakers. Scabs, they call them."

"Where are these works?"

"Right over there," Andrews pointed out the area where great columns of smoke were rising from huge stacks.

"Maybe I'll go over there and take a look."

"What on earth for? It could be quite dangerous, you know."

"It's about money, I suppose?"

"Yes, of course, the workers want a dollar more than Andrew Carnegie is willing to give. It's like a fort out there. It's also a dangerous place to work, I can't say that they are without cause, long days; some are working seven days a week."

"It's their choice."

"Well, everything's more expensive to be sure, one must afford a living. There's also the north end of town where those who have money, the Melons, the Scaifes, Carnegie himself have substantial homes far away from the workers'. Most of the workers live in shacks and row houses - squalor. The city built a special street to the north for those fashionable homes and called Millionaire Avenue. Very large, beautiful homes and some," he flourished his cigar, "quite pretentious. The workers note the difference; not difficult to see why a strike."

"If they are pretentious to you, they must be quite extraordinary."

If Andrews felt the dig, he did not acknowledge it. They began to cross a long steel bridge. "Now, Mr. Kavanaugh, if you look out the window you can see the Steel City Queen. She is tied up along the waterfront just south of the bridge."

Liam leaned toward the window.

"Do you see her?"

"Holy mackerel – that's a big boat!"

"Yes, it is one of the larger ones. Shall we go look it over?"

324

The cab deposited the two of them near the dock where the stern wheeler was anchored.

"As you can see, Mr. Kavanaugh, she can use some paint and the iron work and railings repaired. When we go inside you will also note it needs refurbishing. All the gaming tables and other equipment have been stripped, but it is a very sound vessel. It cost over seventy thousand to build and fit."

They boarded the boat across the stage that stretched from dock to deck.

"You may note that the Queen has two stages - that gives her an interesting profile when in port."

The two men moved onto the deck, walking beside the wood and metal restraining rails. Liam looked at the towering decks above him.

"She has four boilers, thus four stacks, "he gestured upward. "Let's make our way up to the top deck; the pilot house is located there." They dodged the yawl boat and climbed to the pilot house, Andrews leading the way. "I have carefully inspected her – the guy wires are tight and in fine shape." He pointed to the lines running among the stacks. "Let's have a seat for a moment. I'm a bit winded." They sat down and Li reviewed the river while Andrews recovered his breath. "This is the place from where the boat is steered and what we are sitting on is called the lazy bench because all who choose to visit the captain sit down here while he busies himself in guiding the boat.

"Even river boat captains have spectators, huh?" Liam smiled and looked out the pilot windows.

"Precisely, many tales are told here, you can count on that. Let's go down to the fire box – top to bottom you might say and look over the boiler room. But before we go, note the powerful capstan; it is a very large one."

"That winch there?"

"Yes, lines are pulled with that – it is powered by steam and very efficiently. Just before docking the engine was overhauled."

Slowly they descended the stairs and Liam looked at the four boilers. "Are these in order, Mr. Andrews? That is, do they work well?"

"Yes. The hinge on boiler three's door needs to be replaced; a machinist will be required to do it. But the boilers themselves are very efficient, very sound. She was out fitted in Cincinnati; very best Ohio craftsmen are there. The Pitman arms are connecting rods to bring power from the boiler to the wheel and they are solid, well maintained. The power trains are excellent on this craft. Let's go to the paddle wheel, shall we?"

They strode the deck to the fan tail where the giant wheel towered over them.

"The wheel, as you can see, is about thirty feet high, and the bracket planks are made of alder and oak – the best, a very formidable boat. Shall we review the state rooms? I think you will be pleasantly surprised."

Some of the rooms had bunks, others one or two beds, an armoire and an easy chair. They were richly furnished, with side tables, desks, and some even had clocks. The walls were either paneled with wood or had floral patterned paper. There were oval framed scenes of Currier and Ives; others had Audubon birds in their stiff postures; and one room had an array of sunflower paintings. Liam critically examined each of the rooms. Following the tour the two men paused on the promenade deck.

"Well, Mr. Kavanaugh?"

"I'm impressed, Mr. Andrews; I was especially taken with the sleeping rooms the colorful carpeting and woodwork I can almost picture bright quilts and spreads I believe it was done by someone who knew what they were doing. The ballroom is beautiful and knowing Mary, there will probably be tables in there. I will need some photographs, can you get me some?"

"Yes. The Cincinnati firm Barres and Kroeler decorated the Queen. The calliope there, he gestured toward the bristling whistles, "Was also done in Cincinnati. I've checked below as well, the hog chains are intact; it's solid trussing to keep the ends of the boat up and the middle down. It is very sound and river worthy. Is there anything else I can show you"?

"Mr. Andrews, Mary considers you a very honest man. So tell me, is there anything in need of repairs other than boiler hinges, the gambling floor rail work and routine maintenance?" Does it leak or anything like that, serious stuff?"

Andrews laughed aloud. "I appreciate your confidence in me. Most boats leak a little, but this boat is in fine shape and any water taken in could easily be removed by the pumps. The boat is very sound. Trim and paint will do wonders for appearance. It is a beauty that, with a little care and attention, would have no rival on the Ohio and be among the best on the old Mississippi." He laughed quietly. "No need to worry about leaks, but that is an insightful and sound question."

"My best and only offer is $30,000 - cash."

"I think they are expecting more, but if that is your wish I will bring it forward."

"There is an additional three thousand for you, Mr. Andrews, should the sale be negotiated, and should you choose to oversee the refitting. Mary will have suggestions, but that's the deal. Some thing else for you personally may also be in the offing to which I can not say."

Andrews' eyes narrowed, and then he smiled. "Thank you for your offer; I'll present it to the owners. There are other interested parties."

"The offer is thirty thousand -cash, Mr. Andrews that is guaranteed."

He nodded his assent. "I will contact the owners this very day."

Liam was awakened before light by the mournful shriek of a steam whistle. It did not falter and filled the still dark morning. He clapped his hands over his ears. It was clearly not a shift change, rather a call to assemble. He looked out his hotel window and a small crowd of men, still tucking shirts in and tying shoe laces, had bundled into the street. Whatever the emergency was, two of the men were armed with rifles, a third man had a pistol. Liam quickly dressed in jeans and a flannel shirt and walked briskly in the direction where the men had disappeared. When he reached the cross street, there were people hurrying in the direction of the great steel mills. A tall man whisked by him in a determined stride.

"What's going on? What's the whistle about?" Liam asked, hurrying to keep abreast.

"It's the mill. Strike breakers are comin'. There's going to be trouble."

"I heard there already was." He fell in step with the tall man.

"They ain't seen nothing yet. If they want trouble, Goddamnit, they're gonna get it.

They're bringing in Pinkertons for Christ's sake!"

When they reached the works, a large crowd had gathered. Liam pressed closely, but carefully, forward. As far as he could see, a high board fence stretched around the enormous steel works. The twelve foot fence was festooned with electrified wire and ominous rifle ports cut through the boards. The boisterous crowd pressed forward and suddenly a large portion of the fence went down. Liam could see a steamer approaching with barges in tow, the decks crowded with men bristling rifles. As he watched, the advance guard of the mob was shouting and gesticulating, shaking rifles. Three men burst from the mob, turned and waved them to halt. Hatless and coatless, they seemed so vulnerable with their backs to the river. Liam could hear them shouting "Go back, go back!" There was a single shot from the bow of the boat, followed by a sheet of flames; a number of men in the mob went down. Then there was a second volley; Liam felt a bullet pass by his face. He worked his way into the crowd that fell back, and resurged. He was bounced around like a cork amongst the angry mob. More bullets whistled overhead.

"Holy shit, that was too close!" He dove to the sidelines at the same time the mob began to return fire. The Pinkertons were dropping back on the deck, two fell over the rail. They continued firing, but the numbers were smaller and dwindling to the shots pouring from the mob. The boat pulled out into the stream, the mob continued to blaze away, and the men on the boats sought shelter lying on the deck or behind the steering shack. Four men appeared from the river's edge bearing the blood-soaked body of a fifth. Liam could hear the rhetoric:

"Hang on, Tom. We showed those bastards. I'm goin' home and get my gun."
"Me too, Tom, they have done it this time."

"Don't you worry any, Doc Henderson will get those bullets out and we'll be right back on the dock. Those bastards! Goddamn it! This is America and we have a right to assemble!"
"They're all holed up now, Tom – couple of 'em in the river."
"It's gonna be hot; you're gonna be out of the sun but those bastards ain't."

"I'll tell Charley to put the oil on the river and we'll burn out those bastards. We'll cook 'em."

"And blow the heads off those that are swimming."

The wounded man did not respond to any of the comments.

The five men passed by and Liam could see the barges had reached midstream. The crowd continued to jeer and fire shots into the solid protection of the barge hold. More men arrived who carried rifles and other arms, some had their families following. The morning progressed, someone ran oil on to the river and ignited it, but the barges did not catch fire, although black smoke choked both those aboard and on the bank. As the hot May sun glared down, Liam could imagine the conditions inside the barge were stifling. Any perceived movement was fired at from shore. Again and again Liam saw a man cautioning the ranks and retraining the shooting.

Li stopped one determined looking man and asked "Who is that guy down there in the light shirt?"

"Hugh O'Donnell, he's union, but he's holdin' us back. If it was up to me, I'd get some row boats, and go out there and kill every one of those bastards! Send a message to Mr. Carnegie and his money. We're the ones that made it for him, and this is the way he treats us. It ain't right." He turned his hard eyes on Liam. "Who the hell are you?"

Liam opened and raised both his hands to his chest. "I'm just passing through."

"You're not one of them?"

"No, no, no. I'm here on business – nothing to do with steel."

"Look out there. Ain't that a white flag fluttering over that barge?"

A small boat made its way out to the barge, and a Pinkerton man appeared, stepped in, and was rowed to shore. There appeared to be some negotiation with some men on the dock and the detective returned to the barge. Shortly after, a signal was given and the steamer surged ahead and aligned with the barges along the dock.

The first of the Pinkertons came off carrying their wounded and a channel passage was carved through the crowd by men carrying rifles; slowly the Pinkertons walked through the mob toward where Liam was standing. Epithets from the crowd greeted them, some were bloody, most were trembling - they passed through stripped of their guns. They came closer to him. Li could see the fear in their eyes as they hurried toward a shelter that had been set up at the jail. The women were reviling the strike breakers and their voices added a shrill, hateful sound.

It began somewhere in the back of the line. A woman snatched a bag from one of the fearful men and pulled a shirt from it and began to wave it. The protective shield formed against the mob gave way. Stones and missiles began to fly as the crowd cheered the women on. Most of the men carrying bags were stripped of them, and shirts, underwear and socks were being tossed through the crowd like confetti. The guards who were herding the Pinkertons hurried faster, for they too were being hit by debris. The 250 Pinkertons still able to walk soon were out of sight. Although unhurt, Liam was shaken; the fearful, sweat soaked faces were etched into his memory.

Mary showed concern for all those who worked for her, but labor troubles were not unusual. Other riots had occurred and Liam wondered how her concern would be greeted in the future. Would it make any difference to those who perceived they deserved more? He felt that things were somehow going to change as a result of this day – for the better or for the worse, he was not sure. Somehow 'aristocrats and peasants' was not going to be the social structure of American society as it approached the turn of the century. Irresponsible people from both management and labor would be the new outlaw class. The mayhem caused was underway as a middle class of blue collar workers weaved its way into the fabric of America.

Liam, still shaken, was resting in his hotel room when he was startled by a knock on his door. Carefully he opened the door to the smiling face of Stanley Andrews.

"How are you, Mr. Kavanaugh? May I come in?"

Liam waved him to a chair. "Please do."

"Have you heard? " His usual smile passed to a serious set. "There was a bloody day out at the Homestead Works."

"I know; I was there."

A look of surprise spread to Andrews' eyes. "Really, then you likely know more about it than I. I heard there were eleven dead workers and seven dead Pinkertons and many others wounded."

"I don't know anything about the numbers, but I came close to getting shot myself."

"My, oh my, were you hurt"?

Liam tiredly sat down on a chair across from him. "No, I'm fine."

"I have news, but if you'd rather I'll come back later."

"No, Mr. Andrews, business is business as Mary would say".

"Well, quite." He paused. "Moy Reynolds, whom I represent, accepts the offer." He smiled and extended his hand. "And I also accept your refitting offer."

"Mr. Reynolds will have his money tomorrow. You will have half yours also and the rest when the job is done. We will meet at Scaife and Company and complete the transaction."

Andrews leaned back in his chair with a satisfied smile. He reached for his cigar, caught Liam's eye, and thought better of it. "I do enjoy doing business with a gentleman. I think, Mr. Kavanaugh, Liam, you have made an excellent deal."

Minsi, New York
June 1892

"Pat."

"Yes?"

"I've been thinking about taking a trip."

"So?"

"I want you to go with me."

"Where, you mean to the city? One trip there will be enough for awhile."

"No, Pat. I want to take you home."

He paused in the shuffling; an inquisitive frown set the lines of his forehead "Home, you mean Ireland?"

"Yeah, Ireland," She smiled "There's a lot of Irish in me, too, though I can pronounce an R.and a U when it's needed. Besides, its 1892, that's a lucky number for me."

Kavanaugh smiled and quietly laughed. "Suppose they've forgotten me by now?"

"Kavanaugh, you're the only man I've ever known who is wanted on two continents. But they can't bother you now, probably would not want to try. You're an American now."

"Ah, Mary, the English don't forget, they think they still own most of America."

"Let's not go down the road of 'up the Republic'. I'm not up to the couple of hours of what's wrong with England. As you often had said, one of these days the Irish will rise up - maybe. Still, it's rewarding to have some kind of cause. It keeps one from getting bored."

Kavanaugh began to deal. "I don't know, Mary."

"Well, I do. And I have a surprise for you."

"A surprise," He replied, kitting his eyebrows.

"It's your birthday tomorrow."

He teased, "I forgot."

It's time we did something for ourselves."

He laughed, "What's my surprise?"

Mary reached into the pocket of her sweater. "I have two steamship tickets."

He straightened in his chair, "To where and for when?"

"The tickets are to Ireland of course on September the first."

"Mary, have you gone daft? You mean next year? I have too much to do." He tried to dismiss it with a wave of his hand. "That's too close, maybe next year. I have too much to do."

"No, you don't, you work for me, remember? And I say we are going three months from today, get used to the idea."

He sat back in his chair. "Ah, Mary, how long have you known this? You know fall is one of the busiest times of year on the farm."

"I've been planning it for some time. Come on, Pat, think about it. We're getting older and we should go while we can, so I already wrote to your brother and sister-in-law about coming."

"What?" the exasperation showing in his voice. "You've written Margaret and Thomas?"

"Several months ago and I've written to your sister Meg too. I was not sure of her address so Thomas delivered my notes to her."

"Well, you could have told me, I'd have tried to add something." He ran his hand through his thick hair.

"It was a letter full of woman's things." She looked at him over her glasses. "They are running the Raven's Prey pub now."

"You don't say?"

"I do say, I sent them the money to buy it out of my private account. Not even Liam knew, and he still doesn't know."

"You did"? In a moment his face went to disbelief then wonder. "Sure, you are full of surprises." He sipped his whiskey and his eyes became tearful. He spoke in a quiet gentle voice "Ah, Mary that was nice of you to keep in touch and keeping the whole family together, but I can't go."

"Yes, you are going! If I hadn't known and loved you, I'd never had heard of the Raven's Prey Pub or Thomas and Margaret Kavanaugh, or Meg Kavanaugh, your sister. They hadn't heard from you for years."

Kavanaugh looked down, slowly shuffling the cards. Quietly Mary watched him.

"I always meant to write. I just...I just." He shook his head and became silent.

"Another hand, Pat, I'm not going to ask why you didn't write, but you should have, you know. And you wonder about Billy, two peas from the same pod, I say."

"Ah, Mary, I love you; thank you. No more cards tonight."

She reached across the table and patted his hand. He picked up his glass and took a slow swallow.

"I don't know about this, Mary," he replied dubiously.

"Well, I do and we are going.

Chapter 35

Ireland
Fall 1892

Pat and Mary disembarked the steamer at Liverpool, caught a smaller, packet, boat to Bantry Bay and then into the great docks at Bearhaven. The sky was traced with high strips of stringy white, like horsetails painted on the blue. The boat rail was crowded with people coming home to meet sweethearts, wives, or families left behind – all with stories of "America."

When the island first came to view, Pat had showed little emotion and restrained himself from the tumult of exhilaration or the tears that come with joy delayed. But when they started up the bay, the tears quietly slipped down his cheeks.

Mary gripped his arm but said nothing, as the boat slowly worked its' way through the myriad of fishing boats coming and going and some British men of war.

"Pat," she smiled, then reached up and brushed at his tears. "Are you alright?"

"Sorry, Mary I'm burbling like the bally fool."

"There's no shame, you big Mick – you've come home. I'm the only dry eyes on this whole boat."

"Ah, those Kerry hills, they pulled at my heart. I never ever thought I'd see this place again, but I always wanted to."

"Well, I did think so! I have wanted to see this place, ever since I met you and Moran. I don't really know why, except maybe that my grandpa was from Wicklow, and my grandma from Dublin. I don't remember either of them, but have been curious about those roots. Moran used to talk about Wicklow some, but not with any particular longing to see it again."

"Kerry is the heart of Ireland. You see those hills, there in the distance? Not the first set – they are the Caha Mountains, those further off?"

"Yes, they're beautiful, they remind me of Minsi."

"Those are the Magillacudy Reeks, that's the spine of Ireland."

"How far is it to Listowel?"

"Fifty miles or so as the crow flies, but nearly twice that far on the roads we will have to take."

"You know your homeland, I'll say that much. Ireland is simply beautiful!"

"I know it sure, from Bantry to Ballybunion. I've even been out to Dingle and Cahersiveen and that was a place I never wanted to be."

Mary smiled. "Why is that?"

"There was a big police barracks, not good to be transported out there."

"Not a good place seems you've ended up with more than your share of jail time."

"It's not all bad, there's also a fine lake out there, Loch Caragh. I fished it once when I was bolder - ah, it's a beautiful place. You've heard of the Ring of Kerry?"

"A hundred times at least mostly from you."

"Beautiful views of the mountains and there near Cahersiveen, Daniel O'Connell was born."

"The Catholic champion, and if I recall correctly, he was one of your heroes."

"Yes, 1829 began the emancipation, an examination of our 'civic disability.' Before that the English controlled our country by barring the Catholics, trying to convert us to the Protestant faith from the 'errors of Popery.' Kept us poor even tried to deny us heaven. Hell, they beat people for taking a pheasant; hanged people for poaching a deer, and treated us all like vermin."
"It sounds familiar like our own South and the slaves."

'Tis a shame, but the slaves probably fared better, at least they could count on a meal. They tried to starve us; would've hanged me, you know. I was not so innocent but many were hanged before my time just by being accused – never did anything. They would hang six or seven in the same day, often just because of friendship or association with another!" Pat's choler began to rise. "There would be arrests upon accusation, the solicitor would make his case, and then off to the gallows!"

"Well, Pat, we're here. I trust you won't be doing tirades in the streets or punching up judges or such."

Pat laughed. "No, Mary, I'm happy to be home, but the view is much better from outside a jail than in one."
She reviewed the cargo being deposited on the dock. "We'd best see to our luggage."

"Aye, we'll take a cart to Glengarriff. If we have the time, there's a beautiful waterfall near Castletown. We can take a coach to Kenmare." He looked about and indicated a nearby cart. "I'll rent that cart the driver is wearing a green arm band." He pointed to a nearby cart.

Mary cocked her eye at the donkey cart. "You think that donkey is going to pull the three of us in the cart with this entire luggage?"

Pat laughed, "If you think he's getting tired, I'll walk awhile. Don't you worry about that donkey, Mary; he is much stronger than he looks."

"I'll walk some, too, I guess." Mary replied, still unconvinced of the donkey's resilience.

"As you please," He lifted Mary from the boat to the dock. "Welcome to Ireland Mary Cleary."

For the first hour, the two walked hand in hand behind the cart, admiring the bay; then Pat lifted Mary on to the back of the cart. The donkey didn't seem any worse for the load, and trudged steadily along.

Passage to Kenmare was a rough ride by coach. When the coach finally stopped for lunch at Kenmare, Mary was anxious to stretch her legs. There was a pub across the square, so they walked over and settled down for a meal of mashed potatoes with a rasher of sausage and two large glasses of Guinness stout. The day had warmed since the cool of early morning, and now the tits and sparrows, in animated argument, worked the ivy and the shrubs outside the pub.

"You know, Pat, I have heard so many stories of the 'auld sod', so many tales I doubted the truth of them, but I am beginning to understand the sentimental hold it has on folks. Ireland is a beautiful place!"

"Mary, the best is yet to come. Wait until you see Kilarney, we should be there before dinner, and Tralee by dark. In the morning we will be in Listowel."
"You're looking forward to seeing Thomas and Margaret aren't you?"

"He was but a wee lad when I left, and she was a baby. He worked hard to take care of Peg and mother."

"You never speak of your father, Pat, what happened to him? I've heard often of your mother."

Pat took a sip from his glass and studied the rings of froth that marked his swallows on the glass, thoughtfully he turned it in his hand as though it was a portal to the past.

"The English hanged my father, Mary."

"Oh." Mary looked down. "I'm sorry – I didn't know."

"It's all right I have told very few. They hanged him; he was a stubborn man, my mother used to say. I don't remember much except that I used to watch him shoe horses and he walloped me a few times. They say that he was the best Ferrier in Ireland and a Republican nationalist like me. He wanted Ireland to be free and an end to the madness – equality and Ireland for the Irish. It was not a popular view with the English."

"Why did they hang him?" She lifted her glass and peered over its rim.

"They accused him of stealing and butchering some sheep, so they came and took him away. I remember that day. He didn't steal any sheep. Then they accused him of killing a man while he was in jail. It was not proven, but they hanged him anyway, not for the sheep or the man, but for being a Republican." He paused, his lips tightening to a string. "They wouldn't let us take him down." He shuddered. "My mother and I slept at the square until they let us take him down, two days we waited."

"Jesus, Pat – no wonder you got involved in a rebellion." She put down her glass concerned and sorry for a question better left unasked.

"Killing C. Terrence McGinty was a serious thing. God knows he needed it. I have seen so much killing since – Gettysburg, Fort Wallace, and Agate Creek - so it doesn't seem like such a big thing now." Pat took another drink from his glass and looked off toward the hills. "At Gettysburg I killed people I didn't even know and all the killing that bloody day at Sada's village – God rest her soul."

Mary exhaled. "Ah, Pat, you have seen enough trouble for a dozen men." She shifted her glance to the roadway. "It looks like they are getting the coach ready to go." She smiled into his eyes, "Let's look forward instead of back, Pat; it will be so good to see you brother and Margaret."

He quaffed the remaining dark liquid. "You're right, Mary. Let's go."

The road to Tralee passed by the shining lakes of Kilarney and then on into the town itself.

"That's Loch Leane out there, Mary; you can see the Reeks plain now."

"It's beautiful, Pat."

"There were red deer on those slopes, bigger deer than the ones the boys used to bag around Minsi; wild goats, foxes, hares and very good fishing. There also are several big caves nearby. The gap of Dunloe is truly beautiful, and there are some interesting scratched stones, sacred some say, supposed to be the most ancient writing in Ireland. They're called ogham stones; I don't know why they are called that."

"You're a regular traveler's guide, Kavanaugh. We should get you a job." Mary laughed.

"Do I bore you, Mary?"

"Not at all, I enjoy seeing you so excited to be home."

They spent the night in Tralee, a large industrial town stark in the midst of a beautiful landscape. Pat enjoyed the pub talk of the Land League and the Charles Parnell's incentive, and most especially, speaking 'Irish' with the locals. There was a fervent undertone of land reform, with two distinct sides - nationalism versus home rule. Both sides of the debate were well represented. After an evening of animated talk, Pat was as determined as ever of the need for an Irish republic - one that did not depend upon the vagaries of the British Parliament. Ireland would always be a hopeless hostage to political intrigues so long as control of the country, in any degree, existed outside of it. He had always known this, but now there was more open talk about it; to him it was Senn Fein – ourselves.

Mary enjoyed visiting with the ladies in attendance at the pub. They were screened off by a partition where their own lively conversation echoed that of the men, but also touched upon more domestic concerns. Regaling the women with talk of fashion, American politics, and the trials and travails of being a woman in business, Mary quickly became the center of information. By the time that they set off again for Listowel, Pat's interest in politics had been rekindled and Mary felt rather like a celebrity.

The deeply rutted road jarred their teeth and, on several occasions, threatened to tip-over the coach.

"Does this road pass by the place where you grew up, Pat?" Mary managed between bumps.

"Well, yes and no, you can see the road that leads off to it - my home was between Listowel and Ballylongford. I imagine that the house is gone by now. We could visit there, if you'd like; we could take a cart from Listowel."

"Another cart ride!" she laughed. "I still don't know how that donkey did it with me, all the chests and that large driver from Bantry."

"Ah, sure, don't worry - they can pull almost anything you can put in a cart." He pointed to a barely legible road sign. "That's Irish for Listowel - LiosTuathail." The coach continued to bounce along as Pat leaned toward the driver.

"That's a mouthful; this Irish sure is a different language." Pat did not hear her but she marveled at his conversation with the driver; not a single word of which she understood. Finally he turned back to her.

"There's a lot to see in Cork and Kerry." The coach took a particularly hard bump, sliding Pat toward the window and as he looked out he saw a tattered-looking figure on the side of the road, leaning on his cane.

"Jesus wept! Stop the coach! Stop the coach!" He was scrambling to get out before the coach even slowed.
"What the hell is wrong, Pat? You just stepped on my foot, damn it!"

The coach at first did not falter in its forward movement. Pat opened the door and shouted a third time slowly the coach jolted to a halt.
"What the hell, Pat?" Mary readjusted her hat and glared at him.

"I think I know that man back there." He slipped quickly from the coach and began to stride back down the road. Mary craned her neck to watch.

The man had resumed walking, then stopped and curiously regarded the approaching figure.

"Hello, Ci."
"You have the advantage. How do you know me?"
"It's me, Pat Kavanaugh. You don't recognize me?"
"As I live and breathe, the figure staggered from the impact of Pat's words. Pat steadied

334

him with his arm around Ci's thin shoulders.

"Pat, Pat, Pat. Jesus, Mary and Joseph – it's you! It has been such a long while. I never stopped thinking about you. Let me look at ya. By God, Pat, it is you! And in fine fettle, sure there will be some happy faces at The Raven's Prey today. How long has it been?" Ci studied him more carefully and shook his head in disbelief.

"About forty years. It may be hard to believe, but it's true".

"My God, Pat, forty years, that is a good long time!"

"When I left, you were on your way to jail."

"Yes, I got there; kept me five years to the day. They were going to transport me, but the wounds got me off."

"I well remember that day, Ci, it's burned into my memory. Come on up to the coach and meet my wife, Mary."

"So you got married, did you?"

"Yes."

"And how many children do you have?"

"Two boys, but that's another story."

Slowly they made their way toward the coach.

"I never did get married," Ci smiled, "Although I have tried a few times." They were both still laughing when they arrived at the couch.

"Surely this is a great day, Mary! This is my friend Ci Burke. He's the best friend I ever had."

Mary's face first registered surprise, then with a good-natured smile she said, "Pat has told me about you. Aren't you the one who got caught in a steel trap?"
"The same, the cause of me limp and Pat's trip to America."

"Well, I wouldn't have wished you any ill, but I'm glad he came. Otherwise I'd have never met him."

"We will all have some talking to do. How is my brother?" They boarded the coach and it surged ahead.

"Oh, Thomas is a fine pub master – don't play him at darts."

"And his wife Margaret how is she?"

"Ah, she's busy, and a real saint, all the time at the pub helpin', and she even taught me to read."
"Is that right?"

"Yes, your sister-in-law, she taught me. We have newspapers now, Pat. All about the going's on. There's not much business in Kerry we don't know about now."
"You say Margaret taught you to read? I'd think she was pretty busy to teach."

"Ah, she is, but Casey Quill, Mike Moore, Mick McEgan and me was talking one day. She said she could teach us and she did. I still can't write, except me name, but reading's good."
"Do you have any news of my sister, Margaret?"
"Your sister Meg is fine so far as I know but I don't see her often since she moved."

The coach arrived at the town square dominated by two imposing churches, St. Mary's – Catholic and St. John's – Protestant. As the coach stopped, a small crowd of people gathered around it. One tall red-headed lad carefully studied the embarking passengers. Ci tapped Pat with his cane and nodded toward the boy, then waved his cane to get his attention.

"That's you nephew there, he bears a good name, Pat. Sure he's your namesake." He called to the young man "Hi, over here, Pat – it's your uncle arrived from America."

The young man smiled and shouldered his way through the small gathering at the stage stop. He was nearly as tall as Pat, with a hand-grip like a vise.

"Uncle Pat, I am sure glad to see you." He said, a broad smile bursting.

"Well, Patrick. This is my wife, Mary." He gestured toward Mary.

"Hello, Young Pat." Mary smiled taking his hand.

"Ah, Mary, my mother lets me read your letters and my aunt Margaret too. When she visits, she always brings them with her I am very happy to meet you".

"Well, lad, how did you know we would be on this stage?"

"I've been meeting all the Kenmare stages for the last three weeks; we didn't know quite when you would arrive."

The driver and his assistant were unloading the trunks from the stage.

"I have a cart over there for your luggage." He nodded toward the sidewalk. "My father is sure going to be glad to see you. Aunt Meg will be here tomorrow or the day after"

They lifted the trunks on to the cart and young Pat began to lead the way.

"The pub is just around the corner; Mrs. Mullaly is going to put you up. She..."

"Sure, lad, I know where the pub is and I do believe I know Annie Mullaly. Come on, Ci, I'll stand you a drink. Hell, Ci, I'll stand you twenty drinks, it will take that many to hear the news."

Ci laughed. "Twenty, Padric that will get us only halfway, if we have one for each year you have been gone." They started ahead and joined young Pat leading the donkey, who was taking great strides down the narrow street.

Pat turned to Mary and saw her tears. "Ah, Mary, what are you sniveling' for? Come on, this is a great day. I feel like we both have come home!" He stopped and waited until she caught. Ci hurried ahead proclaiming Pat's arrival from America.

Mary took a handkerchief from her sleeve and loudly blew her nose into it. They walked slowly past the gawkers and good wishers toward the cart, now well ahead.

"Oh, Pat. I know it's a great day for you and I don't want to dim it."

Pat stopped and looked into her eyes, the tear stains not yet dry on her cheeks.

"Mary, what's wrong?" He grasped her by the shoulders looking into her eyes.

"It's young Pat, he looks so much like Billy just red hair instead of auburn black." Mary's voice was choked with emotion and despite her best efforts tears started weaving over her cheek.

For a moment the street's sounds surged as the crowd made their way past the churches to the streets behind the square. Mary snuffled, and then cocked her head toward Pat. "You know, Pat, I love you dearly."

"And I love you too." He gently squeezed her hand.

Young Pat was holding the donkey, patiently awaiting their arrival.

"Is everything all right?" The young man asked. "I thought I'd lost ya."

"Yes, we're all right," Mary replied smiling up at him. Her look of concern vanished.

His face softened into a spreading grin as he guided them on to the side walk. "My lord you're a handsome lad. Tell me something Patrick, how do you keep all the Maries, Megs and Margarets and Peggys straight? If the remark embarrassed him, he did not show it. He laughed as he guided the cart through the throng.

"I've got three little sisters bursting to you see you."

"Three?" Kavanaugh said in surprise.

"Yes and my little brother Kiernan Francis."

"That's a strong name." Kavanaugh gave a nod of approval.

"What are the girls' names?"

"The oldest is Siobhan, then Marguerite; everyone calls her Midge, and Olive. They all work at the pub."

Mary smiled. "Well, they won't be working for awhile tomorrow, I mean to take them shopping."

Patrick laughed. "They will like that. The pub is just around the corner..."

Kavy added, "I remember where it is and I have developed a hell of a thirst."

They gathered and turned to the side street just before Raven's Prey Cutaway. The door burst open; Thomas Kavanaugh and the entire family spilled out onto the sidewalk to greet them.

Ci smiled at Mary's look of wonder at why so many were gathered outside of the pub. "Good news travels fast in Listowel."

After Pat and Thomas held one another and the family lined up to hug him and Mary. A curious crowd was growing larger by the minute. Once inside Pat and Ci sat down and were soon joined by some friends of Ci. Pat put down a bottle of Bushmills on the table. Ci broke the seal on the large bottle and popped out the Cork. He contemplated it for a moment and flipped it to the bar. With a twinkle in his eye he looked at Pat.

"Ah, there will be no further need for that." He poured the glasses full. "Up the Republic" he toasted "And welcome home, Pat Kavanaugh."

Kerry, Ireland
Summer 1893

The Raven's Prey pub had an ante way that contained a short oaken bar and wainscot that carried into a large commons room. In the commons, paralleling a formidable bar was a second one that doubled for serving lunch. At the end of the bars there was a white stucco wall with a large fireplace. In a wing from the commons, stretching the length of the building was a dining area and a carvery.

The ante way bar had two casks, one of beer and one of stout, plus an array of two gallon stoneware jugs and brown labeled bottles. The larger commons bar also had two casks each. Behind each bar was a large mirror huckstering John Powers and Son whiskey and smaller mirrors advertising Bushmills and other whiskey brands and Clark's Perfect Plug tobacco. The commons was a dark but warm place, illuminated by oil lamps and candles on the tables. The large fireplace had a mantel that extended from above the firebox along adjoining walls. Mary placed photographs on the walls depicting various scenes from America. Whole families reviewed the photos, eager to see what America was like. Mary Kavanaugh was viewed with awe as a well traveled and wise woman.

Mary had also convinced Thomas to place tables on the walk outside the dining room entrance. Not many sat there to eat, but it was a pleasant place to have a glass when the weather was good and the flies were down – early October was often a perfect time.

Three men, Ci Burke, Jacob Crowley and Gavin McBride, were seated around the table slowly drinking pints of Guinness.

"Pat's late today," Gavin offered.

"He and Mary went fishing'," Burke enjoined.

"Did they take the Lartigue to Ballybunion?"

"I saw them leave this mornin'."

"It's good to have Pat back," Gavin took a sip and carefully replaced his mug on the wet ring on the table.

"That Mary is really somethin', isn't she?"

"Kind as the day is long."

"I heard she's been visitin' old Missus O'Neal who's been ailing' quite a while."

"Visits her, Eileen O'Hagan, Jennie Murphy, Margaret Gillhooly, – she's got half the sick in town under her care."

"They all get a meal each day, I know – I've seen the boys taking' the baskets".

"Well, she seems to have the money."

"It's not the money, Jake. There are those with plenty who have done damn little, and what's givin' to the church seldom finds its way to those in need, so far as I've seen."

"You sure can't count on much else. Nobody's helpin' the tenants."

"True, a good landlord is as rare as a white blackbird."

"Maybe Parnell's Home Rulers will change things. At least we'd have representation in Parliament. "

"Home rule, Gavin I think Parnell would be a dictator and little would change, we need to have the Republicans back – no ties to England - absolutely none!"

"We could use a dose of Fenian salts all right."

The three looked up as a donkey trap rattled down the narrow street and watched it disappear down the Mail Road. The sounds faded and the conversation resumed.

"Ci, did you know Kek Kavanaugh?"

"I knew him as Padric's father and remember the day they hanged him."

"Sure, I do too, most of Kerry was there, and half of Cork. They should never have let them do it. I was just a boy and it still made me angry."

"He was the best door stoop Republican in both the counties - someone should have done something and got him out of jail."

"I remember all the British Regulars surrounded the gallows, their bayonets fixed. There wasn't a sound, and when that trap door dropped, it was like cannon shot. I can see that face yet." He paused, shuttering and took a sip from his glass.

"That drop sounded like a cannon, alright. It should have waked us up to fight."

"Double guard for two days on that gallows. I remember Pat trying to chase the birds; they were sittin' on Kek's shoulders and head, pecking at his eyes, and Padric tryin' to climb up to chase them away. And him being just a sprout like me

"Was the second night that Shamus O'Reily and Jim Gill and the others cut him down."

"That's true; they took the widow home and wee Meg and Thomas in her arms. I know that Pat helped bury his own father, buried him behind my grandmother's house."

"I know the bastards came to look for a new grave down in the Abbey yard and were about to dig up old Tim Healy."

"Ah, that was a sight, I remember that." Ci smiled. "Widow Healy went to attack the diggers with her umbrella. I would not have guessed she even knew the words she was yellin' at 'em. Father O'Casey finally put a stop to it and they gave up lookin for Kek's grave then."

"Had Kek lived there would have been a different tune played around here. He was a natural leader, knew everybody – and everybody liked him."

"Wasn't long after O'Reily went to France and a bunch of others left Listowel – some of the best Republicans. I don't think they did much good there."

"Well, the likes of Kiernan Eamond Kavanaugh won't be seen around here again –I'd bet you."

"It's true. The land commissions have taken the sting from the Republicans."

"Home rule's better than nothin'."

"But not much better," Jacob Crowley replied. He lifted his mug and as he glanced over its brim, two figures appeared around the corner of the building. "Well, now, here comes Padric and Mary."

"It looks like they had a good morning."

Pat and Mary approached the table, each breaking into a good natured smile.

Pat nodded to the men. "Glad to see I've got some company – hate to drink alone."

"That's Blarney – how are you boys?" Mary smiled.

"We're fine, and that's a grand couple of cod there."

"Just like a woman," Pat smiled. "She caught them and I got to carry them, liked to have worn me out!"

Tom Kavanaugh materialized from the kitchen door with four glasses of stout, a bottle and several glasses.

"Tom, take charge of these fish, will ya?"

"Sure – we'll have 'em for supper, eh, Mary?"

"Why not, I'll see you later, boys." She gave Pat a peck on the cheek and followed Tom into the kitchen.

"Had a good day, Pat?"

"Indeed we did, Gavin, we caught quite a few more pollock, gave 'em to Francis." He poured a glass from the bottle. "Let's have one all around." He filled the other glasses and smiled, lifting his glass in toast – "Up the Republic!"

The men swallowed it down and Pat began to refill the glasses.

"May saints preserve us, Pat, we were just talkin' about the exact same thing."

At first Pat had a little difficulty speaking the Irish he had spoken but slowly regained it. He had dream in which Irish was spoken by its shadowy protagonists. He woke with a start, popping Mary awake, who responded with a muffled exclamation.

"Not now and leave me alone! It's two a.m. for God's sake."

"Ah, Mary, I had a dream. It gave me a start."

"I supposed you're going to tell me about it." She turned over to face him. "So get on with it."

"Everybody I knew was there, Moran even Dolf and Billy Sweeney, Crowley too, and they all were speaking Irish."

"And that's it?" She asked impatiently. "They are all dead, and I'm dead tired, so go back to sleep. You and your mates! You're up all night drinkin' Guinness and talkin politics."

Pat rolled away from her and hiked the quilt up to his ears. He was rewarded with a fierce jerk from Mary.

"Don't uncover me." She struggled a bit in adjusting the cover. "We are going fishing tomorrow."

"Yes."
"And then?"
"Well, I told Ci, Jake and Gavin I'd stand them a round or two at Lowry's."
"All right, up the Republic – now go to sleep."

Kavanaugh pushed open the door into the warmth of Lowry's. A peat fire was burning, its characteristic odor mixing with the smell of whiskey, beer, and fish frying in the kitchen. Lowry's was a warm dark place with a large, Guinness mirror centered over the shining bar. He rubbed the chill from his hands and made his way to a table, sitting down among the three men already there. He gestured to his friend Michael, who was keeping the bar.

"Sure and certain 'tis the fisherman," Ci greeted "you aren't carrying today."
"You picked a fine day for it – rain and all."
"Ah. Shamus it wasn't bad, a gentle rain, little sea."
'Tis a fact, it was quiet despite the drops." A man named Brendan added.
"Did you do any good out there?"
"Of course I did, but Mary caught a whopper ling cod, must've weighed thirty pounds. And as far as I know, it's makin' its way to Tom's kitchen right now."
"That's a big one."
"The fun was watchin' her catch it. I laid back and let her have at it. She finally got it aboard." He shook his head, "Neither she or the fish knew enough to let go."
The men erupted into laughter. "She must be quite a fisherman - 'tis a lot of fish!"
"She sat down after it – said she was done for the day. I couldn't get through the damn pollock to catch a cod. She said she had enough, so we came back."
Michael appeared with a bottle of Red Breast and he passed the glasses all around. He smiled at Pat.
"Mary showed you how to fish, did she?"
"Pay no mind to the cod – Pat's better at poaching' trout." Ci tipped up his glass.
The men all laughed. The story of how Pat and Ci had poached trout on the Jeeter's estate was well known. It was local lore that Ci had been man trapped and confined for five years because of poaching. The aftermath had propelled Kavanaugh's flight from Ireland – that too was well known among the locals.
Pat drained a glass of whiskey and poured another as the other men in turn took the bottle and filled their own glasses.
"Tis a nice whiskey," He cleared his throat "Those were the days, eh Ci?"
"Yes, good days to forget Pat Kavanaugh."
"Sure as we're sitting here we have changed, and we are also the same, but everything around us changes and it will never be the same again."
"True, Shamus." Pat took another gulp from his glass.

"Did you hear there's more talk – Republic talk."

"There's been that forever."

"All those Fenians from Cork and Kerry and Dublin are still biding' their time in France."

"There are a couple of young hotheads about, mostly talk, not much action."

"What about Parnell? To this day I can't quite make him out. At first I thought he was the hope. He wanted to break the ties yet wanted to keep 'em. It should have been one way or the other."

"He was about home rule and was popular and he got things organized – but was no republican."

"How many Irishmen are in Parliament now?"

"There's over a hundred – most of 'em landlords."

"How many Catholics are there?"

"More than seventy," I think.

"Parnell didn't give a damn about an electoral system – all he wanted was results that favored him."

"Probably was a Bonaparte at heart."

"Well, he did make the system better, but we don't need any Kings or dictators either."

"Do you believe he was behind the Phoenix Park murders?"

"No."

"I don't believe it, Pat, and the Piggott forgeries proved it."

"It was the bishops brought him down."

"And the damn liberals looking for a cause."

"Well, you know what they say," Brendan began. "There would be little trouble in the world if men minded better what's between their lips and their legs."

The men laughed and Pat again passed the bottle around

"To the Republic," Sean toasted, "Slante."

The men all quaffed their glasses and Pat again passed around the bottle.

"It's true," Ci enjoined. "If he hadn't been diddlin' Mrs. O'Shea that is what made things worse."

"Well, Parnell was never that popular here despite the rest of the country. The republicans – Sinn Fein will have trouble rooting out the home rule batch."

"The National League," Pat posed. "That may help the Republican cause."

"More land reformers," Brendan broke in. "They will stay in for awhile. The notion of a republic is borne on a peasant's cot, but men will forget it if their bellies are full. A republic is a great idea, but you can't eat it."

It became quiet around the table; the men slowly sipped their drinks. Brendan offered his glass to be refilled. The others became engrossed in the peat fire flickering blue and orange, edging the truth of the statement. The tables had gradually filled up around them and Pat looked in the faces and smiled.

"One day, and I am as sure of it as I am sure God exists, Ireland will be free; but before that time there will be troubles aplenty. I only regret I may not be here to see it, but maybe my boys will."

"Here, here," Ci quietly said and lifted his glass. The others followed suit.

"What do you say we go over to Thomas' place? I'll buy dinner - so long as it's cod."

They stood up together. Pat paid the bill and they exited into the brisk overcast day.

On The Beach in Ireland
Summer 1893

They had stripped off their shoes and stockings and had walked the sand, shoes in hand, until they came to the large promontory dividing the beach.

"That old castle there, Pat, who did it belong to?"

"That's Ballybunion Castle and was the home of a man named Fitzmaurice."

"They built them to last in those days. The walls must be six feet thick."

"Ah, but it didn't last; nothing really endures."

"Memories endure Pat."

He did not respond to her muse, instead pointed southward. "This was sometimes called the smuggler's coast because down that way, there are caves where smugglers traded."

"It's so beautiful here, Pat. I really like this place."

"It has a dark and violent past. Vikings came ashore here at Cashen Bay to plunder the towns nearby, and the Anglos – 'English'– also came ashore here. There were shipwrecks aplenty, and the clan wars of old were fought through here. There's a tall round tower not far from here – Rattoo. It was raised to search the sea to watch for wrecks and resist invaders lurking about. Then there's my time. The famine came hard here – the entire west and most of Connaught."

"Pat, how do you remember all this stuff?" She smiled. "The more I hear the better I understand your hate of the English."

"If you have history here, you have a calling; you remember places, people all have histories. Ireland had a history thousands of years before Christ, when there were still pharaohs in Egypt. Even you and I have a history, Mary.

She swatted him with her shoes. "I'd just as soon forget mine." She chuckled "I don't like looking back."

"You afraid something might be creepin' up on you"?

They both laughed and stopped to look at the surf. She suddenly threw her arms around him and gave a fierce hug. "Yes! Ah, Pat, you have made such wonderful changes in my life." Eventually they climbed up from the beach area and walked back to their cart, where a picnic lunch of boiled potatoes, thick sliced ham, bakery bread and four bottles of beer awaited. They spread the lunch on the cart and enjoyed the meal and the glorious sea view stretching westward from the mouth of the river Shannon.

Mary repacked the basket and began to amble along the cliff-top walk. The sea spread out below them, the white surf line marking the edge of the water, reflecting the blue sky above. A brisk breeze had risen and the sheep's heads were pocking the water as far as they could see.

"They call this the Nun's beach."

"Why do they call it the Nun's beach?"

"I don't rightly know, probably because it is so secluded – but I do know the story about that hole over there."

Mary looked toward where he was pointing as they both moved in that direction.

"That's Nine Daughters Hole and its a hundred feet down to the rocks and water."

"Nine daughters' holes – that sounds like quite a story."

Kavanaugh stopped before the aperture, hands on hips. "No, no, Mary. Saints preserve us, NOT Nine Daughters' Holes – Nine Daughters' Hole." He sounded peeved, but with a smile.

"I guess that makes a difference," Mary chuckled. "Either way, what's the story?"

"As legend has it," he began sonorously, "There was an O'Connor chief – the O'Connor was a very powerful clan; who had nine daughters and he found out that all nine secretly planned to marry Norsemen. He hated the Norsemen, so he tossed all nine of them down this hole here."

"All nine?"

"Yes."

"Well, that's a typical man for you; he should have been more interested in their happiness than his pride. That's not a happy story, Kavanaugh." She scowled.

"Ah, Ireland is full of unhappy stories."

"Yes, so happy in the morning, so sad in the evening, I've noticed that."

Carefully they picked their way down the steep slopes to the beach and finding a large dry log, sat down to contemplate the tides. Mary snuggled against him, bracing away from the brisk breeze off the waves.

"Do you like Ireland, Mary?"

"Oh, Pat, how much I love this land! It's so beautiful and peaceful. What do they say, just grand! "There is beauty everywhere: lakes and streams and vales and mountains all so unspoiled and warm, wonderful people."

"It's a beautiful place alright, but there is a dark side as well. Revolution lies in wait here and has been for many years. I know that too well.

Mary picked up a twig from the cluster of drift wood at her feet, and examined it for a moment before flipping down to the beach. "Pat, what happened back then? What did you do that was so bad?"

"I killed a gamekeeper named McGinty."

"Killed him, as in murdered?"

"Well, I didn't mean to, but there was murder in my heart, so I must've meant to.

"It just didn't happen; there must have been a reason."

"That's true. You know how Ci limps? That's because his leg was broken in a man-trap that McGinty set. And the day before that, the gamekeeper had shot a boy for taking two pheasant eggs from a nest on the Jeeters estate".

"It sounds like he needed to be killed."

"Ah Mary, I've seen so much trouble since then, it doesn't seem like such a big thing now. It was famine times and he was just doin' his job."

"But, shooting a boy for stealing two pheasant eggs? That sounds a bit extreme."

"Everything was...was... so unfair. The landlords could have helped, but obviously they didn't think us worth as much as their sheep. Many, many Irish died, but not so many around here; fishing, you know, but then they even tried to keep us from doing that. Some of the landlords, at least one that I know of, provided chowder made from American corn. He put people to work makin' walls. He pointed to the crisscross hills. It's one reason why there are so many of them". Kavanaugh smiled in recall.

"I think, Pat, that you were very different then. It sure has not been easy for you."

"Ah Mary, it was not easy for you either. Some things change, some things remain the same. It's the same with people."

"That's true; the whore's life sure changed me, some for the better and more for the worse". She lapsed into silence and stared at the far off gulls and slowly walked off.

Pat also watched the circling birds and after a few minutes, caught up her hand. "Don't be so hard on yourself Mary."

"Pat, as you look back what were the things that changed you?"

"Come on Mary, I don't even know."

"Yes you do. Tell me and...."

Pat smiled into her eyes and the laughed, "And what?"

"I'll tell you."

"Well, let's see, you, Sada, the boys and Sara, the war, and probably leaving Ireland in the first place." He turned expectantly toward Mary, "And?"

"I'm glad you said me first."

"And," He said asked with a smile.

"I've decided not to tell you." She rose quickly as if to run away, but he caught her wrist and she turned into him, throwing her arm around his neck, giving him a big kiss; then she squirmed to get away. He caught her and held her tight.

"And," He cajoled with a chuckle.

"God Pat, you are crushing me! And you, you have changed me the most."

He released her, "For better or worse?"

"Ah Pat, I love you. Your love has changed me most of all, and for the better. You are the love of my life Padric Kavanaugh."

"And you are the love of mine, Mary."

They sat on the log, bundled together, watching the gulls diving into the surf.

"Mary," Pat began again, quietly and stopped.

"What? What is it?"

"Mary, do you think, that is, have you ever thought we could come here to live?"

She sat straighter on the log and took his hand. "No, I never did until this moment."

"What do you think?"

"Well, Pat, you know the business still needs looking after. I mean that it takes my attention. Liam is getting very good at it – competent he would say, and he always was, but I still need to oversee things."

"What if you sold it all? The farms themselves would bring handsome prices and we could find a place here, start a different life. Let Liam run the rest."

"Oh, Pat. I do get tired of it sometimes Liam is a gift and saves me so much grief but he is young although not prone to mistakes. The ram and jam, disputes with the help, pay-offs to the cops and keeping the books; the Cloister and Sara's ideas, it is exciting. It is a challenge and I am blessed with being able to make money. I'm so involved with the suffrage".

"How much do we need, money I mean?"

"We have more than enough, but it's more than the money. I'm not so sure I'm cut out to be just a housewife. I need to keep busy doing things. And, there are the kids to think of–Sara, Liam and Billy and now Mary C".

"How much do they need?"

"It takes a long time to develop a fortune and but a short time to spend it."

"Maybe we could just live here 'most' of the time?"

"Pat, carrying on a business just a hundred miles away is difficult. A couple of thousand miles would be impossible. No, if I changed it would be finality. I don't think that I'm ready for that yet."

"What if you bought a business here, a small one, and a mercantile maybe? Maybe you could start a line of clothing using local cloth and lace, knitted things or something like that."

She leaned back from him. "Sometimes you surprise the hell out of me. What gave you that idea?"

"Just thinking," he looked to the sea and ran his hand over his chin to his neck, "You could keep a store in New York and sell the stuff there."

"It really is a pretty good idea, Pat. Really it is."

"So?"

She made an exasperated snort and laughed. "You know, Liam has really taken to the business and Sara is up to her neck in the clinic. But the baby needs someone to provide care while her mother works. Evelyn would help more but she is getting older, already has her hands full and she would stay behind. Sara talks about patients and plans and what-not all the time. Doc Wayland told me she is a better physician than he ever worked with. Says all the time she spent with Sada, she learned more about herbs and native medicine than he or any five doctors put together. She was a great teacher."

Kavanaugh did not reply, his sight fixed on the white caps stretching far away.

"You want to stay here, don't you, Pat?"

"Yes," he replied remotely, "but I don't want to be without you."

The two sat quietly studying the break of waves and the sound and smell of the ocean permeating the place between them. Suddenly Mary reached up and grasped his ear; he resisted at first, then she let go in exchange for a kiss.

"It could be done. Not this year, but why not get started? Liam could watch out better than old light finger Haney, and I could sell off some of my other assets, but it will take awhile. The Cuban investment is the only challenging piece; the money is coming in, but the politics are getting hotter. The Richmond house is the only property left down South plus a couple acres in Maryland. I could negotiate with Giuseppe for most of the New York gambling. My New York stores – there's always somebody looking to buy those. Gambling is getting tight except on the water and I am really not ready to give that up. The Steel City Queen has paid for herself three times over. But all in all, I think I could wrap it up in a year, maybe two. Can you wait that long?"

Kavanaugh laughed. "No."

"All right, one year then. We will see how Liam has fared with Haney while we've been gone. Haney is about done anyway; he is a greedy, but 'old' man."

"I swear, Mary. Why do you put up with Haney?"

"He has a nose for investment and he is not that expensive, even if he steals. I've calculated all of that in. But, he is getting old and he's not as sharp as he used to be."

"I'd like to beat him into his hat some days."

"Well, you just remember, if I would want to sell out, he would be the man to help me do it. And since a moment ago, I am seriously thinking about it, why not?"

"Ah, Mary, I love you." He encircled her in his arms and kissed her again.

"And I love you, Pat. So you don't have to throw me down nine daughters' holes."

"It's not nine daughters' holes! Hole is singular!"

They both laughed and lifted themselves off the log.

"It's about time I moved. My ass is getting flat on one side."

"Mary, Mary. On second thought I might give you a toss."
Arm in arm, they began to climb up from the beach.

Lincoln, Nebraska
May 1893

The day was bright with a few puffy clouds working shadows over the broad green fields. Billy had easily fallen into his training duties. Most of the cadets were already accomplished horsemen and many fine marksmen as well. Cavalry instruction was thus mostly tactics, but getting used to firing the trap door 45/70 carbine was more of a challenge. He had spent hours coaching the cadets to become sharpshooters and on this day they would officially register their scores.

After some individual coaching and practice rounds, Billy had just lined out the cadets along the firing line of the rifle range, when he spotted Lieutenant Pershing approaching. Quickly he called the men to attention.

"Sergeant Kavanaugh, are you ready for this day?"

"Sir, yes, we are."

"I'll take over the firing line."

"Yes, Sir," Kavanaugh took a step back, still facing the lieutenant.

"Any distinguished marksmen among them?"

"Yes, Sir, there are a couple of fine shots."

"Are any as distinguished as you?" Pershing smiled.

"Not yet, Sir," Billy cast a sly smile. "But they're working at it."

"Best you can hope for is to train someone who will exceed you."

"Yes, Sir, but it might cost me my job."

"Yes, don't that beat hell?" Pershing smiled.

Billy laughed, "Yes, lieutenant."

Pershing looked him over closely this time.

"You have a dusty uniform, dust up to your knees."

"I was helping one of the cadets into a better prone position."

"Next time brush yourself off. You can't stand before the men looking like some soddy-kneed kid, look like you are in command. Are they ready, Kavanaugh?"

"Noted yes, Sir, they are ready."

"I saw some prelim scores. They are shooting very well - not a single one failed to register below marksman yesterday?"

"They're doin' all right, lieutenant, but I swear they could do a lot better if they would listen."

"What is the difficulty?"

"Well, Sir, I tell them to adjust their sights. Some do and some don't. Most would rather adjust their point of aim. I tell them to take the same sight picture every time and adjust their position and/or the sights."

"What's the point, sergeant? It seems either would do."

"Taking a potshot at a running antelope or deer, that's one thing; but shooting at a stationary target is another." He gestured toward the row of bull's-eyes.

A trace of a smile on Pershing's face illuminated Billy's animated reply, but he did not speak.

"Targets, Sir, are more like buffalo. Believe me, I've shot both. But with buffalo you adjust your sights for range, hunker down and lock yourself into the rifle and squeeze them off."

Pershing looked down the line of waiting men and tapped his thigh with his riding crop. "Sounds like good advice, sergeant."

"Yes, Sir, I talked with Bill Cody about buffalo shooting and he agreed – said the same thing."

"Bill Cody?"

"Yes, Sir you know I rode for him in his cowboy Wild West show."

Pershing nodded his assent." Yes, I remember".

"But the boys are doin' better, Lieutenant. Yesterday, all qualified with two distinguished marksmen, six sharp shooters."

Pershing nodded his head. "You have done well here, Billy."

"Thank you, Sir. Would you like to get started with registration?"

"Yes, they may even do better today, I'll take over."

Pershing walked to the center of the firing line, assumed a commanding view. "Ready yourselves to the prone position." He watched the men adjust.

"Watch your targets. All ready on the right. All ready on the left. Load, ready; aim." He touched the cadet nearest him with his foot and whispered so only he could hear. "Fire your piece."

The cadet sighted his target and squeezed the trigger. The 45-70 banged, immediately followed by a crescendo of the other rifles.

Pershing stormed up to the next cadet in line. "Did you hear the command to fire?"

"No, Sir?" he replied in chagrin.

"Then why did you fire?"

"I heard someone else fire, Sir."

"Do you ALWAYS do what you HEAR other people do?" Pershing turned to Kavanaugh and approached him.

"Get some fire discipline around here, sergeant. You take over now. I must be in Chancellor Canfield's office. I do want to see the score cards. I also want to post the two best targets for the Varsity Rifles. And don't send me yours."

"Yes, Sir, I'll take care of it."

"You are dismissed to your duties, sergeant."

"Sir," Billy snapped a crisp salute.

Pershing returned his salute. "You know, sergeant, you keep having the success you have demonstrated with cadet marksmanship and you will be a sergeant major some day."

"Thank you, Sir. I hope they will shoot as well as you have taught them to drill."

Pershing turned and walked slowly away. Billy watched him sort out his horse and ride off.

"I sure would like to be admired like him someday," he thought. Then he turned back to his cadet marksmen.

"All right, men. That first round was practice. Go up and paste out that shot. From now on, listen for your commands and let's do this right. Let's see if you qualify to hit a bull in the ass with these Springfields. And if you think you're in trouble when you make a false step in drill, just miss one of those targets completely and I'll walk a mud hole in your ass."

Chapter 36

Listowel Ireland
January 1895

Everyone in Listowel was surprised by the crackling cold borne on the blustery wind. Then it began to snow; first big white wet flakes then a more sleety variety, hard and grey. Pat took quite a jibing, blamed for bringing in a blizzard from America. By mid-morning, a mantle of four inches covered everything; it thawed, but by afternoon the temperature dropped sharply and the snow crusted over with ice.

The streets were nearly empty, and the commons of the pub was filled with folks. Thomas had purchased oaken beams from a ship salvage yard, and had cut them into lengths which provided a nice, hot fire. Many people stayed at the pub because their own frigid hovels held no heat.

Pat announced that only he knew how to properly shovel snow, and since these were Irish shovels they would have to be taught, so he took up a shovel and attacked the white stuff industriously, clearing the L-shaped sidewalk from the front and side of the pub. Two hours later he came inside to enjoy a glass of whiskey, the warmth of the fire and the closeness of family and friends. After the shoveling, he was having a little trouble catching his breath; he attributed this and the tightness in his chest to muscle strain. He sat for a while, relaxed and sipped whiskey.

Mary had gone home to bed. She was very tired after accompanying young Patrick delivering food baskets. She then made a few rounds of her own. She visited Celia O'Neil, the frailest of her charges, ill in bed with out water. She'd hurried back to the pub, filled some gallon jugs, went back and made Celia some tea and headed home; she'd gone to bed early, in her heaviest night shirt, and hauled the goose down duvet up to her ears. Bundled down for the night, she fell into an exhausted sleep. She was awakened by candlelight.

"Is that you, Pat?"

"No, it's the devil himself."

"Oh, if that's who you are, you may just as well get in bed with me, it's too cold out there for someone who's used to such a warm climate."

"No doubt you could teach me a thing or two that would warm me up."

She felt his weight crush down on the bed, heard the tumble of his shoes and the rustle of his clothing plopping on the floor.

"Jesus, Kavanaugh, your hands are like ice."

"Ah, you have a warm behind – what else is under this shirt?"

"Damn you, Kavanaugh – if you've come to play I'm too tired! What is this, some kind of torture by icy touch?"

"Ah no, it is you who torture me. What are these bumps?"

"You're asking for it," she laughed. "If you really need it, I'll roll over, but I don't know – you're so cold you won't be able to find it unless you have a string attached. Damn, stop it now, your hands are cold!"

"What is it you say? Cold hands, warm heart?"

Mary chuckled. "Pat, you'll never understand – that's about women. I'm sure there's something about ice that would be more appropriate for men." She felt him on her chest. "Even your nose

349

is cold. Your romancing is over for the evening."

Pat laughed softly and kissed her cheek. "You know I love you, Mary Cleary."

"I love you too, Pat."

"I don't want to jump you, I just want to hold you, but you sure feel good."

"Smells like you've been into the Powers again."

"True, a little draught will do no harm." He gently squeezed her breast and rolled her nipple between his thumb and forefinger, wrinkling the areola and erecting her nipple.

"Now pull down my nightdress – you've managed to pull it clear up over my ass ---brrrr!"

He adjusted the shirt and passed his hand over her mons as he withdrew it from beneath her.

"I'm tired, Pat. I don't know how long Ceil O'Neil is going to last. Damn, I've grown fond of her."

"Her brother Desmond was quite a Republican, younger than my father. He went to Dublin; they arrested him, transported him to Australia - don't know what happened after that." He exhaled and drew a deep breath. "I'm tired, too, Mary. I wonder how the boys are and Sara, Mary C and little Billy"?

"I don't know, Pat, I think about them too. Do you suppose we ought to go home?"

"I don't know, Mary - winter crossings are dangerous; stormy times."

"I suppose they are alright, besides they have their own lives. They're not just looking over little ones. Sara's busy being a doctor; Liam is up to making me money. And big Billy..."

"Yeah and big Billy..."

"Somehow I know he is all right too, Pat."

"Sure, God is looking after him and unless he's changed a lot, he is still kind at the bottom. I sure would like to know".

They could hear the wind sighing outside the window in a kind of mournful resignation. She settled closer to him, curling into his belly.

"Are you going to blow out that candle?" she said.

She heard his puff and the satin darkness descended, only the faintest of light from the last of the peat flickered over the hearth. She closed her eyes, content to be in his arms and dozed off.

She became aware of a warm wetness and jarred awake. Pale light was edging in the frost white window. She then woke up with a start, struggling from beneath the leaden arm over her.

"Goddamn it, Pat. You've pissed the bed. What the hell? Wake up," she struck his shoulder fiercely, and then pushed hard. "Damn it, Pat – wake up!"

There was no response. Her anger dissolved into fear and she shoved his shoulder again. "Wake up, Pat," she said gently. "Come on, wake up."

But he was beyond the morning light, beyond the faded memories and beyond her desires and wishes. The realization struck like a bullet. She turned to him and cuddled his face in her arms, holding it against her as sobs rose from her depths. A brief but fierce anger rose then settled into the grief.

She smoothed his hair and gently chided "Damn you Pat, why did you have to leave me now?"

No answer was forthcoming, and a wave of remorse flooded her again. Quietly she stroked the pewter gray hair and slicked some behind his ear. Then she rose and shed the damp nightdress and shrugged on her robe. Outside the window it was snowing again.

The Cloister, Minsi N.Y.
March 1895

Sara knocked quietly on the door, and then carefully pushed it inward. Mary barely noticed.

"How are you, mother? You didn't come down for breakfast this morning."

"I'm not hungry." There was a sharp edge to her voice as she turned to the window. "And don't treat me like one of your patients, because I'm not."

"I can see you're not feeling as bad as I thought," she smiled despite herself and pulled up a chair beside the woman in black.

Mary exhaled in a sigh of resignation. "I'm sorry, darlin', I was just sitting here thinking, and I don't like the snow so much anymore. When I was a girl, we didn't get that much snow and we always enjoyed it – snowmen!" Her voice trailed off. "Do you remember how Pat would hook up the sleigh and we'd head off to Decker's or town?"

Sara noted the tear starting down Mary's nose. Quickly her mother wiped it away and continued to stare out the window.

"Yes mother, we all miss him." She stretched her arm over the black woolen shawl. "It is time to let up this grief that wracks you so. It is not healthy; you are skinny as a rail and we all are worried about you. Matilda and Decker have both been here twice and your other friends are asking for you. You have to give up some of this mourning."

Mary stirred angrily. "Give up my love?" She slowly passed her hand across her forehead. "You know we thought of moving to Ireland before…"

"Mother, you can still love his memory, but you must live better today. We all loved him and he loved us and nothing is better than that. You were so very fortunate, few women find it. Pat would not want you to spend your life in this room dressed in black and fluctuating between anger and remorse. He would want you to enjoy life. Enjoy the children, I wish I could help you understand that."

Tears were washing down both of Mary's cheeks, and she wiped them across her face with both hands, then withdrew a handkerchief from her sleeve and noisily cleared her nose.

"How's little Billy?" she snuffed.

"Into everything."

"And Mary C?"

"Oh, she's fine; do you want me to bring her in later?"

"I'd like to see her, she's such a darling. Reminds me of you when you were her age." She smiled slightly, turning from the window. "And where's that dickens Billy now?"

"He's playing somewhere; I can't keep track of him. Yesterday I thought he was in his room and one of the nurses opened the linen closet on the second floor ward, and there he was."

Mary laughed. "Do you remember when your brother Billy was so curious …"

"Yes, you mean the time he climbed up the chimney."

Mary smiled. "And Pat spotted him on the roof with his head out the chimney."

"And he spotted Pat."

"And before Pat could catch him, he was back down."

"And he ran across that beautiful white rug with his sooty tracks."

"And Evelyn chased him around the kitchen and finally he connected with that wooden spoon."

They both started laughing and Sara added, "The rug was ruined and Evelyn broke her spoon."

They became quiet as both savored the memory. "White is a poor color for a rug," Mary acknowledged quietly.

Outside the window, the darkened landscape suddenly burst bright, as the sun cleared the close-packed clouds.

"And I want to see that young man - today! He became quite creative the day before yesterday, got into my pen and ink and proceeded to engrave one of my favorite books 'The Scarlet Letter'. I didn't see him do it. So send him in when you find him, I want to talk with him about that."

Sara laughed. "I know he will get his just reward – like maybe one of those chocolates you keep in your desk?"

"Well, maybe - not until I give him a piece of my mind about drawing in other people's books." Although the message had a serious tone, Sara knew better. She took a breath and aired a really troubled thought.

"Speaking of books, business books, Li said you were thinking of sending him to Cuba". I was thinking about the trouble in Cuba. It's not just a little trouble; it's Revolutionaries versus Spaniards, and a stalemate not likely to be broken. It might be dangerous!"

"Spain is going to have to let go of her. She has too much trouble holding on."

"That's the point, mother. There's a regular revolution in progress there and..."

"And revenues at the Hacienda Patrones have not fallen off, so it can't be as bad as it's been painted. Americans are still going there in great numbers and it still is a favorite vacation spot for people with money."

"I'm just a bit worried." She frowned slightly.

"Then why don't you go with him? Go with him to Cuba. You have time to plan." Mary looked toward the window. "My big concern right now is if I can get the right price, I'll let it go. So go to Cuba with him, it would be a nice trip."

"You know I can't do that, mother".

She arched her eyebrow. "Why?"

"Because I can't go, not now anyway."

"Because of what? Tell me why you can't"

"Because of my patients, for one thing," She avoided Mary's eyes.

"Listen, to me," Mary broke in, "You can't let your work or diversions rule your life. Don't let them become your life instead of just a part of it."

"Medicine is not my hobby, mother! I am a physician, and these are people who need me."

"Then don't let your work rule your life."

"You should know, mother". It was a flippant reply she regretted and quickly looked away.

Mary lowered her voice "Yes, I should know, I spent most of my life nose to the grindstone. Yes, I should know. I know something else; don't ever, ever compromise those you love, for work

352

– cherish a good man. They will be gone all too soon; there will always be strangers in need."

"Mother, don't be so gruff. You have been helping people in need since before I was born, and you still are. The clinic is more yours than mine, I just work there."

"Well, don't let your work rule your life - that's all I'm saying."

They both turned their gaze to the window and the sun splashed snow. Somewhere in the recesses of the house they heard some playful shrieks and Evelyn's deep contralto voice.

"I really don't want to go to Cuba, mother. I'd rather be here."

"Then stay; but I could look after the children, Evelyn's here and..."

"No, I'll not go this time. I have so many things to do right now." She stood to leave, and then bent to kiss her mother.

"Are you going to your friend's wedding in Philadelphia?"

"I've been thinking about it; I certainly can't go to Cuba I can't do both and I'd worry about the children, the clinic and you too."

"None of that should stop you, especially not me. I can take care of myself."

"I know. I also happen to love you." She started towards the door, "I've rounds to make, mother – must get going."

Mary returned her gaze to the window. "My, oh my, this year is half gone. How the time flies." She sighed, "I'll see you later, dear."

"I'll send Billy up as soon as I find him and bring in Mary C after noon; and it's only February, mother." She closed the door behind her and hurried down the stairs.

Chapter 37

The Cloister, Minsi, New York
March 1896

Liam and Sara were seated at the kitchen table sipping coffee, waiting for the bacon and eggs, the preparation of which filled the air with a rich aroma.

"What are you doing today? I thought maybe we could ride into town; see the latest trappings of civilization."

"Can't do it this morning, the Kessler girl is going to deliver, I'm almost sure. She came in last night after you had gone to bed."

"But I wasn't asleep. I heard the clatter."

"It's her first you never know what to expect."

"Oh."

Liam looked out the window toward the Cloister that was now more a hospital. Sara's skill in obstetrics and the excellent reputation of the clinic had spread throughout the region and the patient census frequently reached sixty. She and Doc Wayland were handling the pressure of both obstetric and general medical patients with the assistance of four nurses, a housekeeper and a few volunteers. Although Mary had sold the brothels she still had property near Washington D.C. and in New York City had rentals, property exchanges, and retailing businesses. Managing these interests kept Liam bustling and often away from home.

He glanced toward Sara. "We are so busy these days, hell Sara, we hardly see one another. You're either out in the clinic with Doc Wayland tending patients or galloping off somewhere to visit sick folk at home."

"I know I am very busy, but so are you. There's no one else to help either of us. Doc Wayland is slowing down but the patient numbers keep growing. I haven't been able to find more help and you still haven't hired anyone to help you. That's the long and the short of it!"

"There's Jim Winters – that doctor over by Decker Fort." Liam ignored the reference to his own activity.

"Well, he's busy too, when he's sober. And, it's just not me; you are always off to here and there and everywhere. You haven't hired anyone either except for that Stanley guy and farm managers."

"I've made a lot of money for Mary." Liam did not reply further, but picked up his napkin as the maid came bearing the food. They ate in silence, each absorbed in personal thoughts.

"I've been meaning to tell you." He broke the silence.

Sara looked at him in anticipation. "What?" There was no response. "What?"

"Mary's been talking about sending me to Cuba".

"What on earth for? Have you lost your mind? Has she lost her mind? Haven't you been reading the papers? Why in hell does she want you to go there now?"

"The Hacienda, she's thinking of selling it."

"Well, isn't that just great! There is a revolution going on down there, and from what I read, it's damn dangerous! She should have sold when you suggested it."

"She wants to get out while she can. You know Mary she wants to get out with a profit."

354

"I can't believe it! She wants you to go down there. People have been relocated they're starving to death; they're dying like flies. Hell, it sounds worse than the stories your father told about Ireland. You will end up in the middle of trouble! What's wrong with her?"

"I raised the same questions but she insists that I go."

"I really don't want you to go there right now."

"I'm not excited about it. I really don't have any choice."

"How long will you be away this time?" There was a tired resignation in her voice. "Can't she be talked out of it?" He shook his head as she paused. "How long will you be gone?" "Not very long, I hope."

"And you talk about me being busy. Liam, I may be busy but I'm home every night. Isn't there someone else who can go?" She looked steadily at him. "Doesn't she realize that there's a war going on down there? Talk to her again, won't you please?"

"Sometimes I wish old Haney were still around. She wants me to go. You know Mary, once her mind is made up. I think she is getting over Pa's death a lot like her old self." "I have noticed that too she is very busy writing these days. Sometimes I wish she would just sell it all off."

"Well, Sara, it's her money that keeps your hospital going. It's not exactly a profitable enterprise." "Nor is it meant to be!" Defensiveness veined her voice. They both looked out the window toward the large stone building.

"The patients pay what they can and we don't exactly need the money." Sara quaffed her coffee and touched her napkin to her lips. "So when do you plan to leave?"

"In a few weeks, around - April first, I have to wrap up some business here, kind of straighten things out. It's not so easy to get there these days, so I have some details to work out, as well."

Sara appeared distressed and impatient for the conversation to end. "I have to get off to my rounds. You will tell me when you've decided where you're going?" She pushed her chair back and began to rise from the table. "I think I'll talk to mother about this."

"Wait, Sara, don't see her yet. You're not angry, are you?" She sat down, hands folded on the table.

"No, but a bit piqued and amazed that you're willing to be sent off to Cuba, the way things are down there. If you can believe the papers, it's mayhem and despair. The Spanish ought to just get the hell out of there and end all this cruelty and grief. They should have done it years ago and spared all this trouble".

"It's the old empire thing, if they give up a piece; they think it's like giving up everything." He relaxed back in his chair as Sara poured a splash of coffee into her cup. "To change the subject, how's your experiment coming? I heard you and Doc talking about it the other day." She smiled and the former querulous air dissipated like magic.

"You know, Liam, people have been using snake root or black Cohosh – rattle weed for years but my that is, Doc Wayland's and my investigation is going to prove that it works. We have used it for easing delivery and postpartum pain in twenty cases, and we're finding that it not only helps with pain, but has other benefits as well." "Rattle weed? Well, if people have used it, why isn't it used more?"

"Most of the information is anecdotal and has been passed down by word of mouth, not much has been written about it, and no one has demonstrated that it really works. We are doing a controlled experiment. You know Semmelweiz had controlled experiments on cleanliness and puerperal sepsis. He did a hand washing experiment."

"Puerperal sepsis what is puerperal sepsis?" He looked confused.

Sara smiled. "Childbed fever, anyway, it was his approach that gave me the idea to really study snakeroot. I, that is, Doc and I are going to write up our findings. We are being very careful in the study. I'm really excited about it. Doc Wayland suggested three groups to measure both treatment outcomes. If we can show that snakeroot..."

"Rattle weed, right?" He broke in.

"Yes, that's another name for it, that's what Sada called it. Anyway..."

"A rose by any other name, Ma knew lots of them; the Cheyenne words were real tongue twisters."

"Liam! Do you want to know about what we are doing or not?" She said in exasperation, and then returned his smile. I remember, the Indians have used it for years to help manage menstrual problems, so I have used it a lot in my practice."

"For what?"

"A lot of the same things the Indians used it for. It relieves menstrual cramps and childbirth pain, decreases postpartum pain; it also helps menstrual irregularity, prevents miscarriage. It also appears to increase the flow of breast milk. Even Sada took it herself and she gave it to me when I first started menstruating."

"Talk about a snake oil salesman, sounds like you think it's a female cure-all."

"It is NOT snake oil," her voice tinged with irritation; then she smiled.

"What is the experiment all about? Tell me about it."

"Well," she once more began in earnest. "There is a preparation made from ergot a fungus that grows on rye it's called Ergotamine. It is being used by many doctors to shorten labor and expel afterbirth by getting the uterus to contract." She squeezed her hands into fists to exemplify her point. "Problem is that there are lots of side effects."

"Side effects what kind of side effects?"

"Yes, some women hallucinate, others have vertigo, nervousness, fearfulness and muscle trembling. It can even cause gangrene due to the intense muscle contractions cutting of the blood supply; and severe pain."

"It can make them crazy?"

"Yes, so to speak. It's a dangerous tonic but an important one, and widely used to expel the placenta, and prevent postpartum hemorrhage.

"And the snake oil," She frowned at him. "Er.., the rattle weed stuff?"

"Liam, you're testing my patience again. The snakeroot, rattle weed root causes more natural contractions with none of the excessive pain and other side effects. So, Doc and I decided we would compare the two elixirs, with two groups: Ergotamine to my preparation and another group that gets neither. Patients seem to be doing better on my preparation."

"Which is?"

"Dried Cohosh Root dissolved in alcohol, about a gram to a milliliter, about four ounces to a pint of alcohol."

"And that's what Herb Sloan is doing with Dad's old still, making alcohol for your elixir?"

"Well, yes," she added, "might as well put the still to use."

Liam laughed. "Might as well, but getting Herb to do it? I hope you're not worried about controlling the quality of your concoction. Herb drinks most of the time."

"We have an arrangement and he is very good at what he does and the quality is consistent, we test the proof."

"An arrangement," He laughed derisively. "An arrangement it's like putting a fox in charge of the hen house."

"He runs me a gallon or two and gets to keep what's left over." Liam smiled but could see that she was approaching anger. He quickly replied "That's neither here nor there and it sounds like a good idea from what I understand you said. What's the future with Sara's Snakeroot Elixir? Are you going to market it?"

"It doesn't have a name, Liam." she said ignoring the question. "But now that you ask, the experiment is going very well. We're doing careful comparisons. The elixir works well; it eases the concerns of delivery and patients relax. Also our elixir appears to promote lactation, without concerns about side effects."
Liam became more serious. "It sounds good, Sara."

"We are keeping very careful notes on the comparison and other observations on all three groups - very careful notes. I am hopeful we will have enough data soon. We're trying for one hundred fifty patients: fifty on Ergotamine, fifty on the Cohosh Elixir and a control group of fifty on neither. We give the patients a hundred drops per day in water or tea. Of course, we still rub their bellies, but the difference is very noticeable. Patients say they have little pain and the milk output is up in almost everyone on the Elixir. Ergotamine has not shown even a trace increase in lactation plus we had some problems in a few cases. I mean these results are remarkable!"

"I don't understand it all, Sara, but it sounds like you are going to be very busy while I'm gone."

"We have very carefully collected a lot of data. It's very convincing. We could have a very positive impact on the whole practice of obstetrics."
Liam smiled. "Speaking of practice, would you like to go back to bed?"

"Come on, Liam – not now, maybe later." She smiled, walked around the table and kissed him. "You know I have to do rounds now."

He ran his hand over her buttocks. This is nice and round too, you sure"?

"Later."

"Very well, later" He laughed and patted her backside. "Why don't you get dressed? Come out to the clinic and I'll show you the data. I could use your mind on the numbers."
"All right, I'll be out in a while. Do you think Mary is up?"
"Yes, she is likely in her sitting room."
"She sure spends a lot of time there."

"Yes, since Pat is gone she is not the same – something seems to have left with him. The children are her main solace. She will see them almost anytime she is about. I know that Mary C and Billy sneak up there to see her, so she is not always alone. She sure doesn't see us much except to give you more work to do."

Once more they looked out the window at the Cloister building and the fields beyond, toward the river.

"She'll never get over him, will she? Much like Pat who never was the same after Sada died." She took in a deep breath. "I miss him too sometimes."

"One day I'm going over to Ireland. She said she never was as close as their time over there. She really loved him."

"And I love you, Liam Kavanaugh." She tousled his hair, kissed it, and walked from the kitchen.

357

Mary's New York Office
June 1896

Mary quickly examined the packet she had just received, sat down at her desk and extracted her letter opener. She sliced through the wax seal and turned the packet on edge. Four letters dropped to her desk, each with her red wax seal attached.
She sorted through them and selected the fattest of the group that was addressed to her. Each of the others was addressed to Sara, each one with a designated month, April to June.

She smiled and sorted them into a small pile and opened hers. She chuckled softly to herself. "Liam is a careful man and wanted to be sure I didn't open one by accident."

She had been feeling better since Easter. Woo had shown up to say goodbye and that he was leaving for China and would not likely see her again. It had been a bittersweet meeting. There had been no announcement. After a few choked up times and salutes to the empty chairs, Woo said that one of his minions had seen who they thought was Billy Kavanaugh at a trading post in Buffalo, Dakota Territory. He had traded some buffalo robes and came to his shop to buy some candy. He appeared to be well but said little. Mary took the news as the truth and celebrated, despite it being only a rumor and an old one at that. A few drinks and talk of the old days proved good for what ailed Mary. When Woo was leaving Mary, he had embraced her.

"Mary. I know that Pat is gone, but so long as I am alive you will never want for anything. Your whole family has jing chaou, the persistent strength that many have but few demonstrate. Pat and Billy, Liam too, but the greatest source is you, dear one."

"Well thank you, Woo." She commenced to give him a warm hug and replied, "And so long as I am alive, neither will you want for anything, Woo. Neither will you."

Sara observed that outside of Woo's smiles and omnipresent good nature, she had never seen him so touched.

A few weeks after Woo left, Liam was in Cuba. Only a note indicating his departure from Tampa was received there had been no further word. Mary and Sara were both concerned, and now this cluster of letters relieved Mary and she smiled at the prospect of carrying them home. Mary had been neglecting her New York City enterprises, and not spent much time in the New York office. She was feeling better to be back at work. Mary broke the seal on the letter, adjusted her glasses and began to read:

Cuba
June 1896

June 14, 1896

Dear Mary,

I have been here nearly three months now and I have had a good look around. The Hacienda Padrones is well kept and staffed and still has many customers, BUT I think you are right to sell, even if it is still making money. I've spoken with Maximo Hidalgo also — he is an excellent manager and he agrees.

Here's why:

First, there is a new general in town, Valeriano Weylon Nicolan. He has issued a decree of concentration—all the people of Sancti Spiritus, Puerto Principe and Santiago must leave their homes and go to military cantonments and he is enforcing it. Many are showing up here in Havana. Enormous disruption is pending.

Two: the mambeses — revolutionists, sort of like our minute men. They emerge from the woods at night, burn and pillage and before the army gets them, they're gone again. Orente province is really under siege. The rebels declared a Republic last July and they mean to keep it. They have not bothered the Hacienda.

Three: The Treaty of Zanjon with its promises is neglected, and more and more insurgents are joining up. Money's going down because of the sugar tariff of '94 that's now really taken hold. The money is going to go down more; the cane fields are being burned — no sugar, no cash, less local gambling.

Four: They killed Jose Marti last month, but not before he got things organized. We have an Invading Army and a Liberation Army, and though they killed Marti, both armies appear to be intact. No pitched battles, but they're working at it. Maceo the revolutionist is still here — he won't bargain with anybody and he has one army called the Invading under a man named Gomez. Although they are not really Armies, in the real sense, they are sympathizers and revolutionaries armed with little more than rifles and machetes, but raising hell.

Five: Although the revolutionary Cuban government is now called the 'government in the woods' by the Spaniards here, the locals believe it is highly organized and just waiting to take over. The Spanish regulars are singing a little ditty about making a broom from Maceo's beard to sweep the barracks with (good luck on that) and think the mambeses haven't anything to back them up. I'm not sure, for there are more and more reports of Gomez and Maceo making progress. There has been success reported since they got underway in earnest last October and it didn't slow down much until last month.

Six: I think the Spaniards are going to lose. They have made a big sort of road a couple hundred yards wide hoping to cross the island. It's called the Trocha. They think they can hem the rebels in on both sides of it. It has small forts pretty near together and it's already around Orente and there's talk it's going to be expanded. Anyway, you can't cross it without risking your life — as a matter of fact, travel anywhere is a problem. I've been stopped a couple times. Of course they assume I'm a local gambler when they pick me up, but the Spanish they throw at me is so fast I have to keep asking them over and over what they said, and that's making me suspicious to them. I can only travel after I get permission, and it's a bother.

In short, it's a mess down here, Mary, and in my opinion it's going to get worse. We can't count on Spain holding on despite what Canovas [monstruo here] said about holding on to the last drop of blood of the last Spaniard and the last peseta. The pesetas will go first. The morale of the troops is not very high and many are just boys. They die quickly here – malaria, yellow fever and the shits. I'll tell you true, Mary, I will be glad to get out of here.

Who's going to feed all those people who have been relocated? Most of them were feeding themselves where they came from. There is no organized support for them and some are starving; the more who gather, the more will get sick. It is rich ground for the recruitment of insurectos. Also the government forces are executing prisoners right and left Results have backfired and many more rebels are recruited because of the executions.

It's true the casino is jammed packed nearly every night of the week. Mostly Americans, it's like some kind of an emergency. I am treated very well; the locals bring me fresh fish every morning and fresh fruit every evening. Giving them the coffee trees was very effective, even though it was charitable; they have not forgotten you for it.

If we sell now there are still some people here with money; even more wealthy folks have been relocated and are looking for a place to buy, if nothing else temporary quarters. I think we can still get a fair price, but I think we must ask for U.S. dollars and not pesetas. And that is not going to be so easy. No one wants to pay our price. America is not going to get into this mess and getting hold of U.S. currency could be a problem here. Thank God for Cleveland's proclamation of last year. McKinley or Bryan or whoever wins is going to be up to the necks in problems at home, no time for Cuba, although I think we ought to reconsider our position. Innocents are dying here. The results of the bank panic of '93 will sure be top priority – that is reestablishing domestic business. Cuba will be second thought, even though there is a lot of US money here, including yours.

By the way, Mary - sometimes I wonder. Did you know that you have 180,000 dollars in the local account? Haven't you ever taken any money out of here? They wanted to give me pesetas if I withdrew it. So I asked for gold – they are working on it. I've left fifty thousand on deposit, the rest will be converted.

So, Mary, we need first of all to get the money out – gold being the best alternative. Next we need to sell the Hacienda while we can – it may take awhile to find a buyer. I am out of here the end of the month, no matter what.

Please get word to me as fast as you can – the sooner I get it, the sooner I can get out of here. Perhaps telegraph some one in Florida and have them forward the message by a courier or something. What price are you willing to take? How do you want the currency? If I don't hear from you, I'll just come home and we can work it out later. This is the longest time I have been away from home and I am tired of it. But don't worry about me, I am all right. I am at the casino each evening – there is a gifted piano player there. She even plays classics – Liszt, Brahms and Mozart – as well as the zesty Cuban stuff.

I consigned this packet of letters to Marv Rosenburg, I met him one evening. He appeared to be an honorable man, a lawyer, and was leaving for New York the following day. He promised me he would hand deliver the packet to you. Your office, he said, was not far from his and he said he knew Sol Rosenstein. I trusted this to him. It's a long letter.

Love, Liam

P.S. Give Sara and the kids a big hugs and lots of kisses for me.

Montana
October 1896

Billy dreaded the circumstances he was about to enter, for word had it that Pershing was leaving the Tenth. He braced himself mentally, and then ducked into the commanding officer's tent. Pershing acknowledged his salute and wasted no time in commenting:

"Well, Billy, it's parting time. I'm going on leave. I expect to be reassigned so I don't think I'll be back."

Billy had become very fond of Pershing through his service with the Nebraska Cadet Corps and reassignment to the Tenth Cavalry – a colored regiment. For Billy, it had been a great experience and he had learned to accept responsibility and leadership and was well regarded by officers and enlisted alike. The men perceived he was tough and fair, with common sense and good humor, much like their commander. Billy was not arrogant by nature and the Black Eagle incident had followed him and lent an air of mystique.

"Is there any word, Sir, where you'll be going?"

"No orders yet, but I think General Miles has something in mind."

"I liked the general, Sir."

"Yes, that little hunting trip at Fort Assiniboine was quite eventful."

"He's a fair-to-middling' shot, Sir," Billy acknowledged. "I won't mind going back to Assiniboine. Word is you're probably going to D.C."

"Well, I don't know anything for sure yet," Pershing continued. "I may be sent to Washington or I may be sent back here."

"Not very likely, I think. I'm going to miss you, lieutenant."

Pershing did not reply at first, and offered Billy a cigar from the small cache on his desk. "The new commander is liable to need some help. Can I count on you to provide it?"

Billy selected a cigar." Yes, Sir. Thank you for the cigar. I'll be glad to help however I can."

"I have recommended you be promoted to first sergeant again. I expect my request to be honored this time."

"Thank you, Sir."

Pershing leaned back in his chair and thoughtfully puffed a ragged from his cigar. "I think D troop is as good an outfit as any in the army. Discipline is excellent, but you must be alert to it. See to your deportment and dress." He took another thoughtful puff, blowing the smoke that gathered in a small cloud and dispersed toward the ceiling. "You must also be willing to enforce it."

"Yes, Sir, after you knocked that trooper into the Marias River, things have…"

"That's not generally the way to handle troops, Kavanaugh." A frown creased the lieutenant's brow as he fixed Billy with a stern look. It quickly passed.

"I know that, Sir. You show respect to any man willing to do his duty. You're highly respected in turn."

"Well, remember that when you're promoted."

"Yes, Sir, I will."

"You have a good way with the colored, even though you were not raised among them as I was."

"Well, Sir, I had an Aunt Evelyn. She was as much an aunt to me as anyone could be and she was born a slave."

"That reminds me, you never did tell me the long version."

Billy knew the reference being made, but feigned he did not. "Long version, Sir?"

Pershing broke into a smile. "Perhaps I really don't want to know that version."

Billy smiled in return, "Perhaps not, Sir."

Pershing looked out the tent flap, then in a soft voice replied, "Remember, Billy, the Army is one big family and the future in these times is difficult to predict; I believe our paths will cross again. Should an opportunity present itself, I would be honored to have you serve with me again."

A heavy stillness descended as their eyes met. Then Pershing turned away. "You are dismissed to duties, sergeant."

Billy snapped to attention and saluted. Pershing held his salute, snapped it away. Billy turned on his heel and left, the heaviness in his heart quickly replaced with the exhilaration of Pershing's comments. A lieutenant he did not recognize was approaching; Billy promptly saluted and hurried past, briskly dodging among the tents.

The big Montana sky was toned by clouds seemingly close enough to touch. The fall aspens were bright yellow against the darker conifers. To the north and west, a storm appeared to be brewing. Billy took of his hat and let his thoughts slip back to Running Bull and the burial platform in the trees. He sighed ran his hand through his hair, replaced his hat and walked briskly toward his tent.

In November of 1897, President McKinley had pressured Spain into granting Cuba some self government within its empire. The rebels wanted nothing short of total self government, and riots, deprivations, and atrocities resulted. Congress responded by sending the battleship Maine to protect U.S. interests and under suspicious circumstances, the ship blew up in February 15, 1898; war fever, fueled by the press, rocked America.

Chapter 38

Minsi, NY
January 1898

Sara looked up as Liam was descending the stairs. She could tell by the look on his face that he had just had another frustrating meeting with Mary. He dropped down in the chair across from her.

"You have a run in with Mary?"

He leaned back in to the chair, "you might say that."

"What is it this time?"

He shook his head. "Can you believe it? Mary wants me to go to back to Cuba."

"Cuba? Again! She looked toward him in alarm. "My God, you were just down there!"

"Cuba."

"My God, Liam, doesn't she know what's going on down there? Has she lost her wits?"

"Apparently, more likely she just doesn't give a damn."

"She ought to. There's a war going on down there. The newspapers are full of it. They want us to go to war, and it could happen anytime. What is the matter with her?"

"She wants to sell the Hacienda again. Not that it matters, but I told her two years ago to do it, so much for MY advice."

"Well I don't want you to go. Why the hell didn't she sell when you told her to? Now she wants you to go back? That is absolutely absurd! "

"I'm not thrilled about it. I don't think it will take me long to do it. There were a number of buyers who wanted it in '96, and I had another inquiry just last month."

"But you still have to go there?"

"Yeah, but it shouldn't take very long to close it. If you can believe it, they want the property more than the casino."

"How long will it take?"

"Getting there may be the problem, but once I'm there it will be a matter of a couple of weeks and I'll be out of there."

"I don't want you to go; remember the river boat? You ended up in a riot! Now she wants to send you into a war zone?"

"The Pittsburg thing was pretty much my own fault. It's not a war zone yet. It will probably be alright. I think I can get in there and out, so long as there is not a long delay in getting the commitment and the money. It could be just a week or so."

"A week or so, that's reassuring," She added peevishly. "You may get there, but will you be able to get back?"

"Of course, I'll get back! I didn't mean to worry you about it."

"I am worried and I think I'll go talk to mother."

"Don't get in the middle of it. The turn around time shouldn't be more than a month. I'll be home by Easter."

"Oh Liam, I don't think it's a good idea. I think I should talk to her."

"No, I have already talked to her and she is quite determined. Where are the kids? It's awfully quiet."

"They're down in the barn with Herb Sloan. He tells them stories."

"I'd like to hear them myself. He probably has some beauties."

Sara laughed. "Oh Liam, are you sure you don't want me to talk to Mary?"

"No Sara. I'm resolved to go. Maybe when I get back we'll go to New York for the Easter parade."

"The kids would like that and…"

"And we could see Will and Sol and what was your friend's name?"

"Peter. Peter Mitchell. I can't believe it, but he is chief of staff at Charity now. I read it in the Herald. I still get a note from him once and awhile. He is interested in my experiment."

"Maybe we will all get together for dinner - if you can find the time."

"I'll make the time. But maybe Peter will want to do a larger trial. He would have lots of patients."

Outside the wind whipped across the porch in a mournful whine. Its sure dark all of a sudden and the wind's up. I'll go down to the barn and get the kids."

"Dress warmly. I have to run over to the clinic in about fifteen minutes."

"That being the case, I'll just settle down and listen to Herb Sloan stories." They smiled at one another and Liam shrugged on his jacket and pulled a stocking cap over his ears. "How do I look?"

"Perfect for an Herb Sloan story."

Cuba
June 1898
Spanish American War begins

On April 19, two months to the day after Liam had arrived in Havana, Congress recognized Cuban independence. Six days later, the U.S. Congress declared a state of war existed between the United States and Spain. In June the invasion of Cuba began.

The convoy arrived at the debarkation point off the town of Daiquiri on June 20 and began the offloading of troops and supplies. On June 22, the first infantry went ashore. The same mass confusion reigned as it had in Tampa where the men and supplies were first loaded aboard.

Pershing had been appointed quartermaster for the Tenth, whose mission it was to fight as dismounted cavalry. There were many pack animals to be offloaded and immediate trouble developed.

The Daiquiri landing site had no real harbor, only a steel pier and a small mining dock. The beach was not defended; the landing was opposed only by waves and tide. Unfortunately, no one had foreseen the needs of getting troops and equipment ashore under such circumstances and General Shaftner, who had wished to preserve the Army's dominance in determining the campaign, did not want the Navy's help.

The men rode the boats until they wedged on the beach, then climbed over the sides, and waded to the shore. However, getting ashore was not an easy task; the men were burdened by their rifles, one hundred rounds of ammunition, blanket rolls, ponchos, canteens, shelter halves, and packs that contained food and personal items. The shorter men often found themselves in neck-deep water being pulled backward by tide and their packs. When the Tenth began their debarkation, two of the colored troops drowned - the first casualties of the war.

Billy was aboard ship and was beside himself when he finally found Lieutenant Pershing, busy searching a manifest.

"Sir, I need to talk with you."

"I'm busy, sergeant." Pershing glanced up and back to his papers.

"This is not a complaint about rot gut whiskey." There was an edge to his voice.

Pershing glanced up from the manifest and frowned. "Where's your blouse, sergeant? You can't be running around here like a goddamn Indian. You're out of uniform."

Pershing's comments set Billy's teeth on edge, but he controlled his urge to reply in anger.

"You're supposed to be setting an example for the men, not running around here naked to the waist"

"Sir, I have been setting an example! I've been in the hold of this goddamn bucket of bolts, trying to offload horses, Sir."

Pershing straightened against Billy's remarks, but a trace of a smile forged across his tight lipped stare.

"What is it, Kavanaugh? Make it quick."

"The horses are drowning, Sir."

"What?" A look of concern replaced his trace of amusement. "What are you talking about?"

"It's these Navy men, Sir; they don't know shit about horses. They decided they'd just lower them over the side and let them swim in. First, it's a fair piece for a horse to swim. Second, the horses are getting confused and many, too many, Sir, have swum out to sea. There's got to be a better way!"

"Horses are drowning? How many have we lost?"

"Quite a few, Sir, a number of dead ones have washed up on the beach already."

Pershing's concern turned to consternation. "My God – this landing is a debacle! This whole goddamn operation - hip, hip hooray; let's go to Cuba, like we were going to a goddamn turkey shoot. Do you know we are short on medical supplies, wagons, and artillery and signal units? Insofar as reconnaissance goes, we will have to do our own. The right foot doesn't know what the left one is doing, and now you say the horses are drowning."

"I've got an idea about that. If we roped five or six together, then threw the line to a boat, they could be led to shore. All I need is some kind of a boat. We could row them 'til they touch, then lead them off. Sorry about your frustration, Sir. You would not believe the confusion on that beach."

"Yes, I would. See to a boat then, I'll write you a note. See what you can do." Pershing searched his pocket for a moment. "Damn, Kavanaugh! I'll have to write it on the back of this checked manifest. We're even short of paper, I'm going ashore soon, and I want you with me!"

Billy took Pershing's scrawled note, searched about and finally located a chief petty officer to help him. Chief Taverton, a farm boy from Michigan, was also frustrated by the drowned horses. He commandeered a life boat then obligingly lowered it with a couple of sturdy sailors to row. Billy thanked him and walked back to find the lieutenant, but Pershing had left the spot where the two had talked. He looked toward the shore and smiled as he saw the boat towing a string of horses toward the beach. "Looks like an ant pile burying a snake; damn good thing nobody's shootin' at us. Guess I'd better put my undershirt on."

Billy filled his lungs with fresh air, and plunged into the stifling hold and the overpowering smell of horses.

The beach at Daiquiri was almost due east of Santiago de Cuba, the destination of the assault. Between the town and city was a wagon rut called the Camino Real which led through the San Juan heights. The heights were fortified protecting the eastward approach with a commanding field of fire over a long stretch of high grass land bisected by the San Juan River. Paralleling the river were tangled rows of barbed wire. In order to reach the foot of the heights, the troops had to pass through heavy jungle growth which was salted with snipers whose deadly aim, with their scoped seven mm Mausers, was extracting a heavy toll. The area was dense with foliage, and bunkers that loosed withering rifle fire mowed it down with the men who attempted its passage. The smokeless powder used by the Spaniards made locating sniper positions very difficult and seriously slowed the advance.

Billy was crouched behind a tree that had fallen across a dim game trail he had been following. He was intently studying the heavy cover before him and was startled at a voice; turning he saw Lt. Pershing leaning toward him.

"Billy, we have to slow this sniper fire. It's murderous – men are going down like tenpins. General Young has asked that I go find a unit that's strayed off somewhere in this mess. I am off to look for them." He squinted into the dense cover. "I have no idea where those snipers are, do you?"

"No sir, but I been shot at a couple times and you'd better get down, they damn near got me a little way back there. They shoot, and run. I haven't seen a damn one yet."

"I want you to take some men, find them, and clear our route ahead. Every tree or log can hide them. File off to the right through that heavy cover there," he slanted his hand down the path, "then come back toward the trail and clear them out. Re-file, go ahead and cut back again. Got the idea?"

"Yes, sir, I'll take Zeke, Joshua, Jubal and Isaac."

"Those four are your best?"

"Yes sir, they are all advanced marksmen. Zeke is especially good, and Jubal is an old buffalo hunter."

"All right, go and report your progress back to me. That path is supposed to lead to a big clearing along the river ahead – report to me there. If resistance stiffens like here, there will be hell to pay. Supply is already badly mixed up here, like Tampa only worse. Get to it!"

Billy organized his detail and filed into the trees. They had barely drawn parallel in their skirmish line and about to cut back to the trail when shots struck around them and they dove to the ground. The shots tore up the earth all around them and suddenly ceased.

"Zeke, did you see the flashes? I thought I saw it to your front. Look close."

"Didn't see him," was the exasperated reply.

"It's that goddamn powder. Josh, you see 'em?"

"I got the idea he's up in that swale up to de right by that big broke tree."

"Jube, you see 'em?"

"No sah, I didn't see nothin."

"All right, you watch that swale, I'm gonna give him a target. Cover me."

Billy jumped up, ran a few steps to the right, ducked behind some thick cover, and dove forward. A shot rang out, showering him with debris, then three replies from behind him. "We got him, sah." Isaac called.

Another shot was followed by a shout from Joshua. "Got another, they there, be careful, Sergeant Billy."

"Good, we have to get on and turn toward the trail - let's move out - now!" Billy jumped up. Two shots flashed from ahead and again Billy dove into cover. "Did you see them, Issac?"

"Yes, sah they in them logs."

"I saw two flashes," Billy called.

"You have a shot? Anybody have a shot?" From the distant heights came some intense volley firing, Billy listened to the fusillade, then called, "Josh." Billy became aware of the sweat in his eyes. "Josh, answer me."

But Joshua did not issue a sound; the two shots had struck him in the chest, his only sound, beyond Billy's hearing, was the blood rushing from his wounds.

"Zeke, Jubal, Isaac."

"I'm here, Billy," Jubal's voice faltered. "I think they got Josh."

"Jesus wept!" He wiped at the sweat and swallowed down the dryness in his throat. He was dimly aware he had given away their position with his calling. "Can you see anything?" "No, sah, it's too thick."

"I'm gonna make another try, gonna rush 'em off to my right. Watch close now."

Billy bounded up and started on an oblique angle to his right. A shot rang out to his left; another struck the ground in front of him. Three shots from behind followed by another to his front. He kept running to flank the Spaniards' position, then hauled up behind a large palm. He could see into their log structure, took a quick aim and emptied his Krag into the structure.

"It's clear," he called and reloaded "Move ahead." He heard the men running forward. He hesitated, and then ducked from behind the tree to the log structure. The glazed eyes of dead men greeted him and, for a moment, they froze his stride, then he jumped in among them. The other three men drew parallel again and Billy motioned them forward. Through the cover he spotted some uniformed men running ahead. All three fired, but the cover displaced the bullets and they escaped unscathed.

"Let's go, let's go, let's go!" Billy shouted, and the three pursued the fleeing forms.

Ahead all hell broke loose. Four flashes snapped followed by the sigh and smack of bullets slicing through the foliage. The four dropped in unison.

"Zeke, are you all right?"

"Yes sah, but Isaac's dead."

"God damn it!"

"There's works up there, Sergeant Billy."

"Jube, you get up here with me." In a few moments he arrived, wide eyed but willing.

"Are you sure about Isaac? Sure he is dead?"

"Yes sah, Sergeant Billy. He shot in the head. Zeke be alright, he is out on the left."

"Up ahead by that big leafed tree there's logs piled in there." He pointed ahead into the thick growth. "There's, a little higher ground, if we can get there we'll be above them. You see that rise?"

"I see it, but what about Josh and Isaac?"

"They're dead, Jube, let's keep from gettin' ourselves kilt. We will come back for them. We must be nearly back to the trail; can't be more than a hundred yards. We got to get those snipers out of there. If we can get some fire on 'em, I think they will run."

"I see where they am. They sure got to be as scairt as we is."

"Let's go, you stay close behind me. We're gonna make a run for it."

They burst from cover and four flashes from among the logs sent bullets scatting into the trees and thudding into the ground. Billy reached the place above, but Jube was not with him. The Spaniards had located him and it was getting hot - bullet furrows showered him with dirt and cut leaves were falling like snowflakes.

Suddenly from behind him Zeke poured a lively fire into the logs that protected the Spanish snipers.

Catching movement among the logs, Billy began shooting into them. Jubal drew up to him.

"I'se hit in the leg, Billy. It ain't bad though."

"I'll get a little higher and start blasting that log pile, you stay put." He hurriedly bandaged Jubal. "You'll be alright." Billy leaped up and charged the logs as Jubal began popping bullets into it. A Spaniard rose to fire from behind the barricade; Billy paused, fired a reply, that struck the soldier and he reached the pile without further resistance. One of the defenders was still alive, attempting to sit up. He could hear Billy's approach by the sound of thrashing foliage.

"Like to kill Americans, you son of a bitch?" He prodded the man with his rifle. "Do you like it? The man was in a trembling terror. "Well, you're gonna die for it." Billy shot him in the throat at almost the precise second he was showered with tree bark from two shots. He dived into the logs and Zeke piled in behind him.

"Jube's been hit, Zeke. I told him to stay." Billy turned to his back into Zeke's hard set eyes. "Did you see the bastards?"

"They right in front of us. One's by that log yonder. What about Jube?" He wiped at his forehead, still staring ahead.

"He'll be all right. I got a bandage on it – hit the side of his leg. We've only got a little way to go, and then we should be out of this thick shit."

"They thick as ticks in the woods." Zeke focused his eyes forward.

"I'm goin to the left this time." As Billy moved to spring out of the redoubt, a shot kicked up dirt beside him. He ducked, rolled to his side, and sprang over the logs. A shot greeted him. This time Billy saw the flash. Zeke's rifle replied; Billy searching ahead made another rush forward. Two more flashes and the whine of a round going past his ear caused him to dive into a shallow declivity.

Suddenly Zeke dropped in beside him. "There's two more ahead, one behind dat log. The other some past, didn't get a good look but I know 'bout where he is."

"I'm not sure of the other one either. Can you draw bead without gettin' your ass shot off?"

"I got a good lean on these roots."

"Well, watch, this son of a bitch is pretty good. Watch now."

Zeke began to sing a little ditty. "Here I am hidin' hind the log watchin' for the big white hawg..."

"Watch now, I'm goin' left again."

Billy sat bolt upright, quickly ducked in a fall away roll. The crack of the rifle was

368

inextricable from the buzz of a bullet and a jab of pain.

Zeke concentrated ahead. "Out came de hawg." Zeke squeezed the trigger, and there was solid whock sound. "And pop go de hawg," he whispered to himself. Zeke rose up and trotted toward Billy, smiling until he drew up to him and spotted his bloody ear.

We got him, Billy, but lawd, oh lawd – he got you!"

"Damn it, Zeke, I'm bleeding' I can feel it running down my face. Can you see?"

"I can see, a big round hole, 'bout half you ear gone." Zeke began to laugh quietly. "What's so goddamn funny? I'm bleedin' here. And get down before they put one in you!" "Dose ears, dey always did stick out too far."

"At least…" Billy saw the bullet strike Zeke as it passed through his chest bursting blood and sweat in a showery mist from his back. The force drove Zeke into the grass. A surprised look came on Zeke's face as he tried to stem the blood flow that pulsed from his mouth and through his hands. In the distance the volley firing from other Spanish positions again drifted through the woods. Billy knew it was a fatal wound. Sadness mixed with anger struggled to be expressed. He leaned over Zeke, trying with his own hands to staunch the blood that mixed freely with that dripping from his own shattered ear. In bubbling desperation, Zeke died with Billy's face fixed in his eyes. A great rage built within Billy. He wrapped his bandana around his wounded ear, plastering it to his head. A noise behind him caused him to roll aside; Jubal was crawling toward him.

"I told you to stay put, Jubal!"

"I's lonely back there and I hear the shootin' so I come here." He looked at Zeke and slowly shook his head. "They are killin' us, sergeant. They gonna kill us all."

"Jube, you get on back and tell whoever will listen what's happened here. You keep down on to your belly and get out of here. You head right down that rise there, stay off the trail. But first, let me tighten that bandage."

"What you do?" He winced as Billy tightened the bandage. "You are bleedin more than me."

Billy's jaw muscles worked in anger, then solemnly he said, "I'm gonna kill the bastard that killed Zeke and then I'm goin' on ahead and I'm gonna kill all of those sons of bitches I can." He looked into the quiet trees and tangles; only the distant volley firing could be heard.

"Stay down and get on your way. If you find Lieutenant Pershing, tell him I'm up here dead or alive. If I'm alive I'll meet him in the clearing."

Jube did not wish to argue against the resolved vengeance reflected in Billy's face him. He dropped down and disappeared into the lush growth. After Jube left, Billy waited and studied the terrain. A half hour later he rose up and moved cautiously forward, trotted, and suddenly stopped. Dirt exploded in front of him. He slipped behind a tree and once again looked over the terrain. There was a slight movement in the foliage of a large tree and Billy spotted a man braced there. He fired and with a grim satisfaction saw the man drop. He sprinted ahead to the dead Spaniard and kicked the body over. Lying a few feet away was a telescoped Mauser rifle.

"No wonder they're killin' us; I wonder how many of these are around?" He drew the bolt from the rifle and threw it as far as he could into the bracken behind him. There were sounds of a brisk fight behind and to his left; he eased toward the rifle fire. Ahead on his angle of approach he spotted several Spanish regulars withdrawing from the fight and coming toward him. He leaned forward against a tree and sighted the nearest man, exploded his head, then selected another. The unsuspecting soldiers made excellent targets and he began to drop them one after another. The effect was devastating and the men broke into a panic.

Billy ran after them paralleling their withdrawal. One man was kneeling, looking from where he had come and Billy killed him with a shot between the shoulder blades. He looked back and could see Americans moving toward him in the heavy cover. He waited and an officer appeared, walking briskly ahead of his men. Not fifty yards distant he caught another tree movement and fired at it. The Spaniard pitched from the tree. When Billy reached him he was struggling to stop the bleeding from his groin. Billy waved at the American officer who hurried forward; he drew up short when he saw the wounded sniper.

"Sergeant, how did you get here? That man" he motioned at the cowering sniper," He could have accounted for me"

"Yes, sir, Lieutenant Pershing sent me ahead to clear snipers. I've been paralleling the trail and got behind some of them. I picked this guy out of the tree right there, just about the time he was going to pick you off."

"Much obliged, Sergeant. You're Kavanaugh, aren't you? A trooper named Jubal said you were up here somewhere."

"Yes, sir, He is one of mine. Is he alright?"

"Yes, he is on his way to the medical tents you had best get to the wounded tent and take this man back too." He gestured toward the Spaniard reddening the leaves with his blood.

"I'm not taking him anywhere, Lieutenant, he's gut shot and gonna die anyway. The cover ahead is full of 'em near as I can tell. You can arrange to take him back sir, but not me. I'm goin ahead and kill every one of these bastards I can."

"Well, Sergeant, I..."

Billy suddenly leveled his rifle at the wounded Spaniard's head and killed him.

The lieutenant stepped back in shock and surprise.

"This ain't a basketball game, sir, and I've my orders to go ahead. Well, Lieutenant?"

"I guess you'd better get to it. He appeared to still be in shock at the killing of the Spaniard. "Go then, I must bring my men up."

"Yes, sir, I am on my way."

Billy turned and began to move, alert to every movement and driven by a powerful resolve.

Regiment Hospital, Cuba
July, 1898

Billy regarded the kind, bespectacled face that was examining the wounds on his arm.

"Looks like you have been busy, Sergeant Kavanaugh."

"I'm a slow learner, Doc. It could have been the same shooter that clipped me twice in the arm, never saw him. The one through the ear should have taught me somethin'."

"They're not serious wounds, but we must be careful that they do not become purulent. This climate, the damp and the dirt and the heat is ideal to encourage infection." He adjusted his glasses and continued with his assessment. "These wounds are quite clean, but need to be rebandaged. That's quite a hole in your ear. It doesn't get much closer than that. I guess you're one of Lieutenant Pershing's men?"

"Yes, sir.' He flinched as the doctor spread the edge of the wound on the crest of his deltoid, and relaxed as the doctor lightly touched the deep crusted stripe across his bicep.

Well, Sergeant Kavanaugh, you will be all right, but you're going to be bandaged like a mummy by the time I get through with you." He smiled. "Thank heavens we received more bandages today. We were a might short there for awhile."

"I saw quite a few wounded coming in, road's full of them. It took me two days to get here with all the damn downpours and confusion."

"Yes, unfortunately, quite a few sick and injured came today, but it's the yellow fever and malaria that's doing the most damage." The doctor paused for a moment, and busily wrapped from a bandage roll. "As a matter of fact, you are the second Kavanaugh I treated today. He is a civilian; at least we think he is a civilian, over in the fever tents, some locals brought him here yesterday. At first we thought he was one of our black troopers. Then one of the locals said he had been in jail someplace and they carried him here. They said his name was Kavanaugh."

"Lots of Kavanaughs in the Army and it's a common enough name."

"He is a pretty sick man." He tied off the second bandage with a small flurry and smiled; "Done!"

"What does the man look like? Don't happen to know his given name, do you?"

"The civilian has a dark complexion, that's why at first we thought he might be from the tenth. Name is Liam, I believe, Liam Kavanaugh.

"Liam, huh, where is he?" An uneasy feeling began to rise in Billy.

"He is in the quarantine tents, tent six, I think. I just saw him this morning with Captain Edwards."

"Any chance I can see him?" Billy asked.

"If you have a reason, do you think you know him?"

"Not very likely, Doc but maybe, I have a brother named Liam."

"You can go on over. Ask for Doctor Edwards, but go at your own risk. There are a lot of very sick soldiers over there."

Billy slowly made his way down the row of tents and stopped before a yellow quarantine placard staked in the middle of the muddy street. Two medical orderlies were crossing ahead of him carrying a blanket covered body. "Tent six?" he asked.

"Over there, Sergeant." The orderly nodded toward a tent to his right.

"Dr. Edwards?"

"He's over in eight – at least he was a few minutes ago. He's a busy man, hard to tell where his is now; they're dyin' like flies in here. This is our fourth trip to graves registration today. Just the two of us did twenty-six yesterday." The pair hurried past, steering the stretcher onto the muddy street.

Billy stopped outside tent eight. He could hear moans and cries from those inside. He lifted the flap and pushed through; he was not prepared for the scene or smell inside. Cots were crowded closely together, the fetid smell of feces and vomit was overpowering, and he quickly covered his mouth and nose with his hand. A man on the cot to his left rolled weakly to his side, and in a great gush, vomited a torrent of black on to the dirt floor, splashing Billy's shoes. Billy began to gag himself, struggling against the fecal smell and the groans of pain and anguish. In the half light he saw two men working among the sick. They had their backs to him, then turned and approached.

"What is it, soldier?"

"I'm looking for Doctor Edwards."

"You found him. What do you want?"

The man on the cot beside Billy turned to his side; this time the orderly with Edwards thrust a pan beneath the man's chin as he retched. On the cot to the left a man suddenly stiffened and shrieked in pain; his cry was joined by others down the cot line.

"Sir, I'd like to talk with you about a patient, but I've got to get out of here. I'm gonna get sick to my stomach."

"Come then, I'm heading outside."

Once outside, Billy breathed the fresh air in great gulps. "I didn't have any idea, sir. No idea it was this bad."

"It's not pretty. What can I do for you, sergeant?"

"When I was gettin fixed up – I got wounded couple days ago, anyway, the doc said you had a civilian in tent six named Kavanaugh, and I wanted to check him out."

"Yes, Liam Kavanaugh. Is he a friend or relative?"

"Well, I don't know, sir, but I thought I'd check. I'm Billy Kavanaugh."

"We can go on over." They began walking slowly toward tent six. "What's your unit? How are they holding up to the heat?"

"I'm with the Tenth Cavalry, Lieutenant Pershing sir. It's awful hot and the water, what there is of it, is putrid. We have a lot of men with cramps and dysentery's bad. Not too many wounded, but many with fever."

"Yes. You're with the colored troops – Tenth Cavalry. Your men did right well, so I heard."

"Yes, sir, the men fought well, sir."

"Brave men, but let me tell you, whoever thought that the colored troops would be resistant to yellow fever was wrong. There may be a token few who can resist malaria, but not yellow fever – febre amarilla, as they call it here. They are just as susceptible to it as the whites are, and we are losing lots of both."

They ducked into tent six; it was also full but quieter than the other. Billy followed the surgeon toward the back of the tent. He stared at the figure beneath the blankets; a dark, dirty yellow had replaced the once coppery tan. There were traces of blood around his mouth and black stains on his blanket, but he was breathing easily. Billy's legs began to wobble as he looked at the swollen face. He grasped the surgeon's sleeve.

"Oh, my." Edwards reached out and supported Billy with one arm; he drew a stool to the side of the cot. "You had best sit down, lad. You know this man?"

"Yes, sir – he's my brother, I haven't seen him for 15 -16 years, but it's him. He's my twin brother."

"Twin brother," He looked at Billy then to Liam. "There's not much resemblance."

"Fraternal twins, sir."

Well, I'll be, sixteen years, you say?"

"Fifteen, or sixteen – maybe more, I kind of lost track."

"They brought him in yesterday, very sick, in a lot of pain. He had been sick for three or four days before, probably caught it a week before that. Complained of pain in his legs and loin, bad headache, pulse was 115, temperature 103. I'm glad to see he's sleeping."

"How bad is he, Doc?"

"Yesterday I would not have given him much of a chance, but when I checked him earlier today and his heart rate was down to eighty. He's passing urine and that's a good sign. Temp is down today, a shade above 100. He vomited some time in the night, but as you can see he is sleeping easy now."

"Will he get better, Doc?" Billy cast a concerned glance toward the cot.

"I haven't had any experience with this fever before I came here; there's not much to do except nurse him along. But I think his crisis is past."

"Can it come back?"

"From what I've read, not often; but if it does, the news usually isn't good. If we can keep the fluids in him, barring something unexpected, I think he will recover."

"Good." Billy passed his hand across his forehead, then rubbed his eyes and swept away the tears forming. "I'm so glad to hear that."

"This is an odd place to find your twin brother. He was a bit delirious and called out for Sara and Billy. Is that Billy you?"

"I don't know, sir - could be, I guess." Suddenly Billy felt a vague sorrow descending as he gently moved his left hand up the wounded arm. "Sir, I don't want to wake him, but I do want to come back. Is that all right?"

"Of course, but it is to best stay away from here at night. We're pretty sure the mosquitoes spread this fever and they are more active in the cool of the evening. So why don't you come back in the morning?"

"All right, sir. I have to report in anyway. My lieutenant expects me back on duty, but I'm quite sure I can get some time in the morning."

"Very well then, I will see you in the morning. You don't have to look me up, but if you want to talk with me, I'll be somewhere nearby."

When they left Liam's bedside the sky was darkening, and it appeared as if another tropical downpour was on its way. Excitement mixed with worry thrashed through Billy's mind. 'Damn, Liam right here in Cuba. I can't believe it! What in the world is he doing here?' A passing soldier bumped heavily into his stricken shoulder. The sharp twinge of pain reminded him it was real.

Siboney, Cuba
July 1898

In the early morning of July 4, 1898, a tropical squall soaked the company compound but did little to dissipate the heat. When Billy asked Pershing if he could go back to the hospital area, he had assented with the proviso that the company muster be made before he left and that the morning details would be seen to. Pershing was aloof, stern, and a stickler for details, but he also had a kind, compassionate side, albeit well camouflaged behind his intense gray eyes. Billy commandeered a horse and rode back to the field hospital.

When he entered tent six, most of the patients were resting; breakfast kits were being collected to be boiled. Billy could see to the back of the tent where Liam was lying on his side facing to the rear; he did not hear Billy's approach. Billy sat down on the camp stool by the bed and touched the blanketed shoulder.

"Hello, Liam."

Liam turned to his back for a moment, but he said nothing, looking up at the smiling face.

"It's me, Billy. Don't you know me?"

Liam squinted up and slowly the recognition spread, a brightness coming to his eyes as though he was infused by a new spirit.

"Billy, it's you," he whispered in delight.

"Yes, it's me." He removed his cap and placed it on his knee.

Liam struggled to sit up; Billy supported him with one arm and lifted him into a hug.

"I can't believe it," Liam whispered in his ear. "I can't believe it."

Gently Billy set him down, tears streaking his face and choking his voice.

"It's been a long time," he managed.

"Oh yes." Liam collapsed back on his pillow. "I've been sick." He refocused his eyes. "Your arm's in a sling." He squinted, "and your ear is all bandaged."

"Yeah, I got chipped up a little bit." He smiled.

"You're in the Army, Billy?" He weakly noted.

"Yeah, I've been in the Army for eight years already, mostly out west."

"Why? Why didn't you write?" His voice was halting and thready.

"I should have, I guess, but I was a long way from paper and pen. I didn't have much to say. How's Pa?"

"He's dead, Billy, died a couple years ago."

"Oh." Billy straightened and wiped back the sweat from his face, streaking his hand over his wounded ear. "What happened?"

"He died in Ireland. He and Mary went for a visit - heart attack, died in bed."

Billy, fighting tears, turned his head toward the tent flaps that had suddenly given way to an orderly's visit.

"What about Mary?"

"She's about the same, kind of frail now. I came down here to sell the damn Hacienda Padrones Casino she owned."

"Sara?"

"Sara and I are married, Billy, she's a doctor now, runs the Cloister like a hospital. We have two children, Billy and Mary C."

"That's the Billy you must have been talking to." He smiled in recall. "I thought it was me."

"Who, what are you talking about?"

"Dr. Edwards said you were calling out to Billy and Mary and Sara, too."

"Oh, I was pretty sick, and I still don' feel very good. We named little Billy after you. "He paused and refocused." Why didn't you write? Last we heard you were in the Dakota Territory someplace"

"I was there for awhile. I joined up with Running Bull, moved around a lot."

"Running Bull, Ma's friend is he still alive?"

"Yeah, I was with him for awhile, but it turned bad." Billy again wiped at the sweat stinging his eyes. "I married a Cheyenne woman, but she died. I also had a little boy, Red Shield – he died too."

"Oh. I'm sorry to hear that, Billy." Liam struggled to sit up, and then rested on his side. "How did you get in the Army? That would be the last place I'd think you would be."

"I joined up right after Wounded Knee."

"You were there?" He cocked his head to see Billy better.

"Yeah, I was there. Lieutenant Pershing found me after I had a new part in my hair. I joined up after that, been in ever since. I like it."

"Oh, Billy, I could never see you being a soldier – orders and all that."

"It's not so bad. Sometimes I wonder myself- like these damn uniforms, I'm dressed more for the Klondike than Cuba. I'd like to take it off and hunt these sons-of-bitches in my underwear. Billy smiled, but Lieutenant Pershing doesn't see it that way."

"That's a cavalry pin on your hat." He noticed.

"Yeah, but we're being used as infantry here. We can't use horses here anyway except to haul the gear. Not many places we could maneuver –it is mud, mud, mud and so goddamn hot!"

"Pa was in the cavalry. Fort Wallace, wasn't it?"

"I think so, never been there, mostly I been in, New Mexico and Arizona; spent a little time in Montana and Nebraska."

"What happened to your arm? What happened to your ear?"

"We were trying to move up in the ridges. Some damn fool went up in a reconnaissance balloon and the whole damn Spanish army was shootin' at it. He fingered his arm. "Then the lieutenant sent me and a couple others ahead to clear snipers while he went off lookin for a lost unit. I got the ear then. After the jungle came the river and we got across that and into the high grass. The Spaniards were mowing it down and they mowed me with it. I was burned by a crease then hit the second time in the shoulder. Never did get to the top of the damn hill! I went to the field station; they put patches on me, but they were out of bandages."

"Kind of matter of fact about it, aren't you? You could have been killed." He said softly.

"It was a hot fight in that grass, not too bad for us but those Rough Riders on the right caught hell. We used to joke about them called them Teddy's Terrors but no one is joking much about them now. They really got chewed up. We couldn't get started - couldn't stand up. It was like a hail storm. I remember one officer tried, and he dropped just in front of me. Finally, I made it up to him, but the ants were already crawling over his eyes. Before that, I lost three men trying to clean out the goddamn snipers – two I was real partial to. I feel real bad about that. The shoulder wound didn't look good so they sent me here and that is how I found you."

Liam looked at him as Billy lapsed into silence. Half in amazement and half in incredulity, he spoke, "Jesus, Billy!"

"You want a drink, Liam. I got some boiled water here in my canteen." He offered the vessel to Liam, who took two long swigs.

"That's how I got here. Why the hell are you here in Siboney in the middle of a war?"

"I told you, Mary sent me down to sell the casino she had in Havana. I wanted to sell it before, but she didn't listen and waited." He paused. "Don't know why she didn't do it," he added in disbelief."

"You work for Mary, huh?"

"Yes, I'm a lawyer now. Mary asks me to do almost everything. God, she will be glad to know you are alive. So will Sara and old Evelyn; who rarely fails to wonder about you on every holiday for what, sixteen years?"

"I've been with colored troops nearly my whole career in the Army. I remember Evelyn often enough." He drank from his canteen and again offered it to Liam. "And Sara how is she?"

"Up to her neck in medicine she is even doing some research on herbs and stuff. She is really devoted to it - too much, sometimes."

"Research huh? How did you get to here? Havana is a long way from here. It's on the other side of Cuba."

"Things got very difficult in Havana, I got in all right, but travel was restricted. I got there alright and closed the sale but I couldn't get out of town, so I sent the money on, kept a few thousand pesetas and about three hundred American. I tried to buy my way east where the insurrectos had a good hold on things. That was April."

"April? That wasn't a very good time."

"Yeah, I know now; the blockade had started and the men I hired said they could get me out at Nuevitas, where they had contact with some men who had a boat." He paused with a troubled look. "We got started, but a Spanish patrol boat forced us ashore at Gibara. They found out I was an American so they put me in chains, sent me to Santiago, put me in prison." He caught his breath and frowned at the memory. "They didn't give us much to eat - a little water, rice or corn about every other day. I got sick. They were killing the men in the cells. They cut the throats of the men in the cells across from mine. I will never forget them screaming. I thought I was next. Then they abandoned the jail – sent the guards elsewhere, I guess." He lapsed into exhaustion.

"It's a wonder you're alive, Liam." Billy leaned back on the stool and took a deep breath. With effort Liam added, "they finally let us out. I barely remember it. They forgot I was American. The two men I hired helped me out and I remember it gettin' dark and we met some insurrectos. Don't remember much after that."

"They brought you in on a blanket. I know that, and you were very, very sick."

"I never had such pain, Billy. My legs and back had like cramps and I was throwing' up black stuff over and over. I thought I was going to die, and things just went dark. I want to get out of here and go home!"

"Don't be in too much of a hurry to get out of the hospital. Siboney, the town here, stinks; there are buzzards everywhere, filthy water runnin' in the streets, rotten garbage, rats, and bodies - nothin' but corruption and decay. Rest up for awhile, I don't think they will run you out because you're a civilian. Just don't say anything much."

"That Doctor Edwards been good to me and he seems to know what he's doin.' One man across from me died this morning, but..."

"He's gettin' lots of practice." Billy paused, thought for a moment and continued. "I'm going' to look around a little bit and find out a few things. I know some guys in transport. The lieutenant's been quartermaster and I got to know some people. I'm gonna get you the hell out of here, if I have to kill somebody to do it!"

It was five o'clock in the morning when Billy returned to tent six carrying a blanket under his arm and a small stuffer bag in his hand. Gently he shook Liam awake and bent closely to his ear.

"We're in luck, Liam. Do you think you can walk?"

"I don't know," he replied, the sleep still thick in his voice.

"That transport, the Leona, I came in on is sailing' in about two hours; we got to get over to where they're loading up. It's about a mile, maybe a little more." He helped Li sit up on the edge of his cot.

"Put this blanket around ya. I got a pair of shoes here in the bag. There's a pair of Army issue underwear, civilian trousers, a shirt and a pair of socks. Just put on the shoes and underwear now. You think you can walk?"

"I think maybe." He tried to push himself up, but failed.

"Let me help you get these shoes and socks on. If we can make it to the debarkation point, I'll get you on board; you'll be home in a couple of days."

"I'll walk, Billy, just help me get started." They struggled with the shoes and socks and underwear. Billy tightened up the shoe laces, and wrapped Li in the blanket. Liam stood with Billy steadying him but he nearly fell with his first step, straightened, and tried a second time.

"That's it, Liam. It's not far." Billy tucked the bag into his sling and with his other arm about Liam; they started down the muddy street.

"I told the orderly I was taking you out to a doctor's hospital and I got an evacuation tag in my pocket; picked it up down where they're loading up wounded. Some Navy guys I know are running the launch to the ship. They know we're comin'. So far as anyone else knows, you're just a soldier goin' home. We get to debarkation, and we will get you out of Cuba. This life sucking mud isn't goin' to help our walking, but at least it's not raining' – yet."

Liam did not reply but tightened his grip around Billy. He could make ten steps at a time, and then they rested. Slowly but surely they made their way to the evacuation area and fell in line among the wounded.

"I changed the name on this tag, Li; I put my service number on it, 150742. Just remember that 15-07-42. When we get to the launch, they will take care of you."

A medical officer was checking the tags before the men moved to the transport ship. The two came abreast of him and he cursorily checked the tag.

"Are you going aboard also, Sergeant?"

"No, sir it's not that I don't want to."

The officer grinned, "Then what are you doing here?"

"He's my brother, sir."

Liam's legs suddenly buckled and Billy caught his fall, wincing at the pain in the twist to his arm. He grimaced and steadied Liam who threatened to fall again.

"Soldier, you need to be put on a litter. From the looks of it we should get you both out of here." The officer called out to two stretcher bearers and helped ease Liam down.

"You're going aboard now." The officer checked his list name and looked to Billy.

"Billy Kavanaugh, that is Liam William Kavanaugh – everybody calls him Billy."

"Hmm, he doesn't seem to be on the list. No matter, the way things are around here, we're lucky to have a list; I'll add the name. Service number?"

Weakly Liam spoke, "One, five, zero, seven, four, two."

"Take him to the launch."

"Can I go down with him, sir?"

"Yes, of course." The officer again looked at the list, then to a large black man after him. "What's your name soldier?"

Billy strode alongside the bearers as they approached the launch and a wave of relief passed through him when he recognized the sailor at the helm. He placed the stuffer bag on the litter and smiled at the tired looking sailors.

"This is my brother, Liam, and his things. Tell Chief Taverton he's on board, will you?"

The nearest sailor nodded his assent. Why don't you join us, too, Kavanaugh, you look like a bandage bag? I'd like a chance to get back my three dollars." He laughed and said to the sailor next to him, "don't ever play poker with this guy."

They began to lift the litter, and Liam raised his hand to grip Billy's.

"Yeah, give Sara a kiss for me and the kids and Mary and Evelyn a big hug. Give them my all my love."

"Maybe you will come home after this?"

"Maybe," he gave Liam's hand a hard squeeze. "There's ten bucks in the pocket of the trousers. It's all I have or I'd give you more, but don't worry, I think I can get a poker stake." He smiled down on Liam and once again forced back his tears. Liam could not.

"Please come home, Billy," he pleaded and openly began to sob.

Billy bent down and kissed Li cheek and looked toward the launch and the waiting sailors. "Maybe after this is over I will come home." He looked away toward the waiting ships. "Look, these guys will get you to Tampa, but after that you'll be on your own."

"Don't worry, Billy. If I can get to Tampa, I can get home."

"See that you do." Billy squeezed his hand one last time as the bearers shifted the litter to the launch and the sailors adjusted their boat.

"Take care of your self, Kavanaugh," the nearest sailor jeered. "We'll get him on board all right and good luck on gettin' out of this tropical paradise."

Billy turned and walked back along the line of misery beside him. After he reached the officer checking the examination tags, he looked back again. The launch bearing Liam was headed out to sea. He fought his tears, and let them run. As he stared toward the distant ship, the clouds split into a torrential rain.

"Maybe," he mused aloud, "maybe I will go home." He swallowed down the memories, turned and made his way back through the tents and set out for his post, the ankle deep mud sucking at his feet. "Then again I have less reason to go there now than I ever had."

Kavanaugh Home
Minsi, New York
November 1898

Sara entered from the great room into the back parlor and sat down quietly behind Liam. The back parlor was his favorite room in the house. A small table and an easel were set near a large window. A massive grandfather clock, a sofa and three large leather chairs completed the

378

furnishings. Rifles and fowling pieces hung on the wall presided over by sets of deer antlers. Earlier, before first light, he had gone to the kitchen and fried cinnamon sugar toast and boiled some coffee. The coffee was long gone; only his empty cup and a single piece of toast remained. Sara had joined him and left at the sound of Billy and Mary C arguing. She returned shortly.

"What was that all about?" Liam did not look at her and remained engrossed in the birds sparring over the bacon rind dangling from the porch rafter.

"Oh, the usual, Billy teases Mary; Mary gets upset. Name calling this time Billy called Mary pimple puss, God he sure knows how to get down and dirty. She is in tears I sent him off to the barn to curry the horses, a job he does not particularly like."

He looked from the window to her face. "They both receive your wrath?" He smiled inwardly because it was rare for her to ever get upset by the children's quarrels.

"Billy started it. Sometimes I am so impatient with him. He is a good boy. He just refuses to listen."

"Sounds like his namesake in times past. Although I can't remember you ever crying because of anything either one of us ever said."

Sara did not reply, matching his focus on the warring birds. After a moment she quietly asked, "Liam, is something wrong? I know it has been a difficult recovery, but I thought you finally were over the fever. You don't seem yourself lately and you have been so short and so disinterested, like you are miles away. I know something is bothering you. Did I do something or the kids?"

Liam did not reply, nor did he face her question, he had hoped to see or at least hear from Billy but there was no word from him. Things were unsettling with Mary upon his return from Cuba and he projected on to her a loss of confidence in decision making. She appeared less interested in his ideas and there was an increase in arguments over details that previously meant little. Mary was relieved to hear about Billy, but was disappointed he did not write or come home. She also struggled with her guilt because she had sent Liam to Cuba. Mary said little about it but offered no apology. Liam in turn projected his own discomfort on to Sara and the children.

"The other night at dinner you were so short with me, and I don't believe you said ten words to me this week. I feel we are growing apart."

"Come on, Sara," he responded testily. "That's not true. I still don't feel that great, and I wish we heard from Billy."
"Well, it seems like we should hear something from him. You seem down, impatient, angry even hostile. You say very little about anything."

Why shouldn't I be angry? And you are the one that never talks and when you do it's all about rattle weed or Cohosh or whatever the hell they call it, and experiment this and experiment that. I just wish the hell you would be done with it."

"Li, I am doing a controlled experiment. I am going to make a second report at the State Medical Convention, and it's important to me. Three more large hospitals have tried the tonic and their success should be reported. They believe it is very important and have asked me to cooperate"

"I wish it were more important to me. You are the one who is distant – you're so damn busy all the time."

"I wish it were more important to you, too! You do not seem at all interested in it, and I don't talk about it as much as you say." She paused, her anger fading. "What is important to you, Li – anything at all?"

Liam lapsed into silence and slowly turned to face her. "Maybe you're right, Sara – nothing seems important to me. I don't have much to do that is important. You are finding work interesting, a great reward in it. Billy is off being a soldier. All I find in my work is money - there's got to be more than that. And, Mary is more and more difficult to deal with. I want to quit this job and do something more rewarding."

For a moment they both were quiet, Sara adjusted a long strand of hair from her forehead. Softly she replied to him. "I don't know how to answer that. Mary relies almost totally on your judgment now. It's her money that makes it all go here, the clinic, the house, our salaries, everything."

"Well, you know what she said," his voice rising. "Money isn't everything, but it's the best of everything. I don't give a damn about ALL the money I have made for her or us or anybody. If I had my way, I would sell out everything. Sell it all! Her holdings are immense. We have more money than we could spend in five, hell maybe ten lifetimes."

"Isn't that a great accomplishment in itself?"

"It's an accomplishment, but..." he returned his gaze outside the window.

"But what, Li, you have succeeded."

"I wish sometimes I had never gone to work for her. I really wanted to go into labor law. I really wanted to do that. I never wanted to be Mary's messenger boy whose advice was not followed very much. It's different now even Billy is doing something he enjoys; as much as I disagree with it, he is doing what he wants to do."

"I'm sorry, Li. I never thought..." she consoled. "I didn't realize the depth of your discontent. Yes, Mary has changed so much since Pat's death. Her work is everything now."

"You have your work and it has transformed you, I handle Mary's fortune and I'm tired of it. I'm just tired, I guess."

Once again from inside the house, there came the sound of angry cries, followed by a fiercer set. Then came a stentorian voice, then quiet.

"Thank God Evelyn's up. Billy must have given up on the horses."

The angry voices faded and were replaced by sounds from the kitchen. The clock in the parlor struck fifteen minutes to the hour.

"Oh, dear," Sara stood quickly, setting her cup on the table. "I must go, Li. I told Doc Wayland I would be there early and I am already late." She leaned forward and kissed his cheek, snatching up the remaining piece of toast. "We can talk more about the future later." She turned and hastened through the doorway.

Liam adjusted in his seat and watched the birds still dueling over the suet.

"That's it, isn't it, Sara?" He said aloud. "It's always later. Good old reliable Li can wait." He flinched as the great clock sounded out the hour.

Once more he watched the flighty birds around the suet. The battle had settled between the chickadees and the starlings, and the starlings were winning. He was still seated by the window when Sara returned. Once more she sat across from him and from her manner, Liam knew she was disturbed.

"Li, when I left earlier there was a lot unsaid. The more I thought about it the more it bothered me. You dismissed my concerns about you drawing away from us and I have a few things to say about that."

"Sara I don't want to get started. I do not have a woman somewhere. I am here most of the time. I am sick. I am disappointed about Billy and I do not like what I am doing at work-period. I do not want to talk about it any more."

"We have been over this a few times. We both have resolved to do better, but Li, you are spending less time with me and the children than before. You know how much I appreciate and have encouraged you to draw and paint, but we seldom spend time together anymore."
"It is a diversion that I enjoy. I don't have much of that, you know. It would be good for you to find a way to relax. The drawing is...' He stopped and looked out the window.

"It's what?"
Liam frowned, breaking the exchange. "It is a great satisfaction, just for me. I am able to get inside my own head and create something."
"The children are afraid of bothering you when you are drawing."
"They don't bother me. I have told them that often. I even told them they could watch."
"But they do not feel welcome to. It is not what you say, it is what you do. You are so absorbed; they do not want to disturb you."
"Well, how different is that from your research? Not much is it?"
Sara paused a moment to think of her next words.
Liam continued. "I took Billy fishing just last week
"No Liam, that was two weeks ago. Ever since you have been like a ground hog holed up in your office"
"Mary C came to see me yesterday."
"Reluctantly and at my insistence and she also came right back because you were so grumpy."
"I didn't mean to be. I didn't say a dozen words and she went off."
"Do you know we have not had a single meal together this week?"
"That is not all my fault."
"We do not even have Sunday dinner together, not for a long time. It used to be on Sundays we all went to church together. Now it is just me Mary and the children. You have changed from that too."
"Sara, I never believed in all that crap. You have known that since we were kids. Billy didn't believe it either. And it is only lately that it has really mattered to anyone but Mary. I am not interested in church or having my soul saved, or the gossip or supporting the pope. I am not interested in church —and I don't miss it either."
"Well, it's important to other people who know you."
"Why? I don't care about other people's beliefs any more than they should care about mine."
"But, Mary...."
"Mary is Mary; she has gotten a lot more religious since Pat died."
"The hell; I was home, the dutiful son, the compliant one. Billy went off, --he is happier for it. I stayed home and your father would want you to set some example for the children.
"I know my father would not approve of me now. I am not sure he ever did. He never said. He grieved over Billy, but cared little I successfully managed a bundle of money and am I happier for that? Not one wit! So much for hope and prayers and a father's love, he didn't care."
"He was a religious man. What ever you want to say about him, and he loved all of us."
"I know that. The only reason I went to mass was to please him. I never believed in hell or damnation or that the key to heaven was to believe in Jesus neatly mixed with the Holy

Spirit and his 'father'- God. What a nice blend and sleight of hand from the only one spirit Ma believed in".

"Liam that is blasphemous!"

"Blasphemous, what a word, since I haven't made my Easter Duty for at least five years, I am also excommunicated."

"All you have to do is see the priest for penance, perhaps there is a way to be absolved."

"The power of the church does not make a lie the truth. So forget about Sundays. I am done with all that. I have seen the bodies packed like garbage in the cells where they died. I have been tortured by good Christians, told them the truth and was beaten for it. I have heard people begging for their lives and heard the gargle sounds after their throats were cut or their gagging when the noose drew tight and wondered if those good Christian soldiers were going to hang me next. I saw people starved to death and mothers lugging infants that were just bags of **bones** whose next breath could be their last."

Sara did not say a word as Li vented his fuming grief, finally she replied. "Li that is not the church's fault."

"Is that right the king is supposed God's representative on this earth. Then the church wants prayers and money for the victims that their souls are saved to heaven. Like there is some great bank account above where souls are sorted and stored and donate a little to get them into heaven. I am done with all that and good riddance."

"But the church fundamentals are not the question rather what people do. The church is the answer not the question, its teachings are true."

"Not likely, when you start with a lie, you must layer it over and over, soon the truth just slides beneath it. I think that if Jesus ever returned he would be so busy throwing the hypocrites, the money changers and the power brokers out of the church, he would have little time for anything else."

"I can see there is little reason to continue with this conversation. You have changed Liam Kavanaugh. I am not sure I know you anymore."

"So have you changed, Sara. You talk about time with the kids. What about us and the time we should be spending with one another? When was the last time we had good sex? Frankly I can't remember."

She did not reply, slowly passing the accusation through her mind. Together they looked out the window, but their eyes were looking to the past, searching for the future. Both knew there was some truth to what the other had said.

She started toward the door stopped for a moment, looked back, turned and walked away.

Chapter 39

Beijing China
May 1900

At the close of the 19th century, China was emerging from a feudal society after centuries of imperial rule. The European powers were pressing for greater trade relationships outside the enclaves already granted. The Opium wars of 1800s. Woo had returned and was recruited to the service of the Dowager Empress Tsu Hse. Her court sought his expertise and experience after his long stay in the United States, the only member of the council who had ever been to the west. Woo was careful and reserved with his counsel for it represented an unpopular point of view.

"Woo, why do you persist in excusing these Western Devils, All these countries ravish our resources Russia, Germany, France, Italy, Japan and America waiting for an opportunity ? We have little control over our own resources!"

"Yes I also believe, Woo Shen that the trade treaties not only humble us, but also yield so many concessions that our economic wellbeing is threatened."

"They have torn our country into strips of influence where our citizens can trade only with the foreigners."

"I hear your concerns. But Kuang Yu, we have many problems of our own to solve before we can deal with the foreigners. The I HO CHUAN brotherhood is also plundering the country."

The Empress has withdrawn support from these murders and looters."

"Yes, but it goes on and on. The actions of the Boxers, as the West calls them, have outraged the Europeans. This group of looters kills Christians – our own people. They have been raising havoc for two years and the depredations are increasing"

"I agree that this is not desirable and provides the west with a reason to intervene with military action, which would be a disaster."

"Pan Pang despite the Dowager's condemnation, the Boxers have support some right in the Council "

That is true. I support them. I HO CHUAN is a secret society that has supported China's values for hundreds of years. We do nothing with our army to control them. At least they make the Christians and their sponsors feel unwelcome. They are simply the second devils of foreign control."

"The barbarians outrage me! They plunder our coal, pull in with their ships stoke them and carry it away at a rate we are challenged to produce. They pay next to nothing less than our own people pay, by the time the mine owners take their share, there is barely enough to feed the miners, an outrage!"

"Woo I also know a silk merchant whose warehouse was emptied. He was paid a price that did cover his cost of production."

"There are hundreds of stories, Woo – even the crops of our people depend on are taken off with little recompense."

"Our very life "We had reached a level of perfection these Europeans have yet to reach when they still were wearing animal skins. We had iron in quantity.

We made a mistake by not perfecting it into the manufacture of guns."

"All we want is to be left alone, if the Society of Harmonious Fists can help, let them."

"Gentleman, let me clarify. You seem to endorse the society? The society has spiraled out of control. They are killing people in the streets, riots, turmoil rule – our people cringe. They condemn the society."

"True but they also admired."

"Admired? When railways can not be operated and our communications are disrupted if not stopped. What about our future development? We require what the West can bring. We do not yet manufacture necessary materials,"

"Perhaps it is needed but not necessary and certainly not under these humiliating conditions. The barbarians restrict where we buy these essentials buy here but not there, all worked out among them."

"Wei Shu , we agreed to these conditions"

"No these current conditions are forced on top of the agreement."

"Woo some may think you are a Western sympathizer."

"Sympathizer no, I am a business man. I have lived in America. I was there to arrange rice sales and to help our businesses that were already established."

"And KuanYu, he was successful in helping others and imports from America did increase at fair value."

There was a brief and uncomfortable silence as the members adjusted to the truth of Woo and Pan Pangs point. Wei Shu asked.

"Woo Shen, you have an advantage, for you lived in the West particularly America. What are the Americans really like?"

"They are mostly barbarians. In America they treat us much like they treated their slaves."

"Why do you defend them then?"

"So that is why you assist the barbarians, the basis of your support?"

"They are not all barbarians, they can be reasoned with. I became close to one family and they treated me very well. The family took the place of my own before my own joined with me."

"So, Woo?"

"They are mostly barbarians. They are yet to join in the plunder, and that is why we must review our actions carefully."

"But the current trade must be abolished."

"And if the society, Boxers as they are called, then so be it."

"Ah, Kuang Yu, if we become engaged in open conflict with the West, we will be crushed and suffer even greater burdens."

"Well, Woo Shen, it makes little difference now. The empress has declared all China resist."

Woo left the meeting with a sense of anxiety. In his heart he knew the counselor's cogent comments were correct, and had to a large extent agreed. He also knew that open hostility with the Europeans would mean disaster would ensue, and a greater calamity would follow. Uneasiness crept through him that one of the counselors might denounce him as a traitor and that could cost him his life. A week following the meeting, Woo and his wife set out to furnish a new summer home near Pongiabu. The house had been a gift for his dedicated service, on the same day twenty six Christians set out on a pilgrimage to safety being led by a nun. They were overtaken by a group of Boxers and slaughtered. Woo and his wife was traveling that very same road.

Woo's coach was loaded with furnishings, window shades chairs, a small desk cooking and eating utensils. They traveled in silence and Woo heard horses approaching. Suddenly the coach jolted to a halt and his door was jerked open. A man dressed in a red turban and blue pantaloons and clutching a long quiang balefully regarded him. A second man leaped from his horse and threw Woo's driver to the ground and wrestled him to his knees.

"Esteemed leader this man is a Christian!" He foisted a string of rosary beads.

Woo was angry. "What is the meaning of this?"

"Settle down, rich man. Your driver is a Christian, a first level devil, and he must be destroyed."

Woo realized that the coach had been surrounded by men in peasant garb. They were well armed with ancient weapons: jians, fues and quians. One carried a tall banner of red cloth. The quian spears loomed above the swords and axes. Woo was frightened as the mob pressed him closer to the coach.

"Before you threaten me again, I am Woo - counselor to the Empress. That man is my driver! You will be punished for any harm that befalls me or him."

"I do not fear your punishment. He turned to the men restraining the driver, "kill him!"

They tied the driver hand and foot and stripped off his shirt and wrestled him to his knees. A large man stepped forward and with the point of his sword scored the driver's back as he arched against the pain the Boxer struck his neck nearly severing the head, a quick second blow sent it skittering to the road's edge.

Woo heard his wife's muffled cry from within, and lunged at the turbaned figure. He was promptly spun about and thrown against the coach.

"Counselor to the Empress, no you are a representative of the foreigners! You are a third level devil. You have done business with them."

Two men seized Woo's arms and spread them. The force of the leader's thrust sunk the quian deep between Woo's shoulder blades and emerged through his solar plexus. As he fell, the spear was jerked back. They pulled Woo's wife from the coach and delivered one swift blow with a fues. After ransacking the coach for valuables, one of the men noticed the coin suspended around Woo's neck and cut it loose.

"I found this esteemed leader."

"What is it?"

The man rubbed away the blood." It is an old coin made of copper, I think. There is a tree stamped on it. I do not see a value." He proffered it to the leader who carefully examined it.

"You are correct, copper. It can not be worth much." He gripped the coin on its edge and scaled it into the trees. "Let us make haste."

The group dragged the bodies into the forest stripped them and heaped them with the others. The coach was driven off around a bend in the road. This trail had proved to be an ideal ambush site.

In June 1900, the Boxers laid siege to the Western living areas and many fled to the embassy compound. The Allies made a determined stand. Attack followed attack and the Boxers suffered significant loses but steadily wore down the defenders. With water food and ammunition nearly expended and exhaustion wearing down confidence and resolve, the siege was lifted by an allied force in August. The Boxers and the Chinese army that supported them were never again were a threat to Western influences that continued to plunder the resources of China. Allied patrols spread into the area around Beijing walking the roads and byways to draw out the remaining Boxers. A patrol came upon the place where Woo and his wife were killed but the bodies were so entangled and in advanced decay that no one tried to identify them.

Chapter 40

Mindanao
Philippine Islands
1903

The war with Spain resulted in the partial destruction of their empire. The United States took only a small chunk of Cuba in the form of a permanent lease near Guantanamo Bay. However, as part of the reparations the Philippine Islands came as a possession. The islands already had a healthy revolution in progress with Spain, and when they realized they were not going to get much freedom under US domination the revolution was extended. Most was controlled; however the area around Lake Lanudo remained a hotbed of contention, the homelands of Moros. The Moros were Muslims and had been in the area for hundreds of years. They did not recognize any form of government beyond their own tribe and its alliances. They viewed the arrival of Americans as invaders from the West and commenced a jihad upon the troops. They were fierce contenders who believed that to die killing Americans would assure them a place in paradise. Pershing studied their culture and religion and extended America's friendship. The Moros regarded him highly and he was able to deflect many situations where lives would have been lost. Working through chiefs that he had won confidence, he brought many others to peaceful terms. He still had some fights on hand around Lake Lanudo. Pershing became ill and was recalled to the states and other responsibility. He later returned.

Billy had just settled down to his favorite meal, fresh fish fried in rice flour and a large bowl of fruit. He sought a querida and had bargained with her father to acquire her as a mistress, house keeper and cook. She was an excellent cook and he was happy with the bargain. He looked up from his meal to a sound at his door step.

"Ah, Corporal Brighton, to what do I owe this visit? As you can see, I am having my lunch."

"Sorry Sergeant Major, there is a Lieutenant down at HQ and he wants to talk to you."

"Very well, as soon as I am finished, sit down a minute."

"Sir, he insisted he wants to see you right away."

"No one told me any lieutenant was coming. What the hell does he want to see me for?"

"He came in this morning with a guide."

"One guide, did he talk to Drews? Another damn tourist and he can not a very bright one to come with only one guide."

"He already talked to Drews, what will I tell him? I have to report back."

"You won't have to tell him anything, I'll go back, tell him it took a while to find me, that's all." He mumbled around a piece of breadfruit, "did you get his name?"

"MacArthur, --he's a young guy."

"When they arrived at HQ, he dismissed Brighton and entered into Macarthur's presence.

"Sergeant Major Kavanaugh reporting as ordered, sir."

"At ease, Kavanaugh," he closed the folder on his desk and stood up. "Have a seat sergeant major, I'd like to discuss an event that occurred recently." Mac Arthur fired up a cigarette, balanced it on the edge of an ashtray and paced to the window.

Billy reviewed the officer before him. He was not as tall as he but with piercing eyes, a jutting square jaw and slick black hair. He returned to his cigarette gave it a puff and carefully replaced it on the ash tray then stretched to his full height.

"You have a distinguished record, Kavanaugh."

Billy did not respond and shifted uncomfortably in his chair. He thought, 'what the hell is up now?'

"I understand there was an incident lately when you accounted for three Moros?"

"Yes, sir, that was a couple weeks ago."

"I'd like the details of that encounter."

"Not much to tell, sir. Mulrooney, that is, Sergeant Mulrooney and I were going fishing, it was a Sunday. We stated down the trail to our spot and about twenty yards ahead this big Moro jumped out on the trail, sticks out his tongue, flourished his Kris and started at us. I shot him then two more even closer rushed us. Mulrooney did not have his sidearm so I shot them too." Billy ceased talking.

MacArthur carefully regarded him, "just like that?"

"Just like that, sir. We both were a little rattled. We never expected them to be that close. "We were only a couple hundred yards into the jungle." He saw MacArthur was intently listening. "And sir it played hell with our fishing trip." He laughed nervously." I reported it to Lieutenant Drews. We got some locals to drag them in and dug their graves. Lieutenant Drews smeared some bacon grease on them to deny them paradise and let the locals know what trying to kill Americans can do." Billy pointed out the window. "They're over there."

MacArthur returned from the window, puffed his cigarette and rubbed it out and began to pace again.

"I'm thinking about how we might defend these outposts. Obviously, those three were in very close."

"They often are I think, we just don't see them."

"You have been here for awhile?"

"Yes, sir, I came over with Captain Pershing."

"How would you defend this and other outposts like it?"

"We could just leave the Moros alone - withdraw from these outposts in the nowhere. Just let them alone like we could have done with our own native peoples"

"That is not a defense, we just can't withdraw. Our orders are to pacify. They would cause havoc like maverick braves from a reservation. We must continue to campaign against them, not let them alone. Hit them where they ain't an old baseball slogan goes. It will be difficult for them to take the offensive when they are forced to defend. You are an old Indian fighter, you must know this."

"Yes, sir, but it is different - disease is on their side this time. Half this post has turned over this year due to malaria. We can keep the skeeters down on post, but the jungle is another story. Every time we go in you can expect men to go down soon after."

The Lieutenant continued to pace his jaw jutting out both hands in his thigh pockets. The faster he walked the faster he talked.

"We can not just abandon the campaign; we must keep up the pressure. We are not quitters- we must win this. We must eliminate them when we can and eliminate all we can." He ceased striding between desk and window and looked at Billy. "Do you grasp this, Kavanaugh?"

Billy was taken aback by the passion of the man, straightened in his chair. "Beg your pardon, sir, I do not believe in just wiping them out like we did our native Sioux and Cheyenne. This land was theirs long before we arrived."

"Quite, quite, but this land was also Spain's. It is difficult to argue to the contrary. We paid for this with American blood that soaked the sands of Cuba. That is why we are here and to maintain it, we must control the Moros." He stared down on Billy with an intensity that was uncomfortable.

Billy stared back with an intensity of his own. "Yes, sir, some of that blood was mine."

MacArthur in turn was temporarily taken aback then continued his lecture less forcibly.

"Well, Sergeant Major we have these islands now and we will have them for many years to come. These islands will one day become our fortress of the Pacific." MacArthur returned to his desk sat down and glanced through the folder. "You were regimental rifle champion almost every year since your arrival."

"Yes, sir," Billy smiled. "I arrived too late to enter the first one."

MacArthur laughed aloud, "I must say you are competitive. I noticed that the enlisted under your command appear as genuine soldiers. I commend you on that, to maintain discipline at such a distant outpost is not easy."

"Thank you, sir I will pass your comments to the men. I was with Captain Pershing a few years. He set very high standards, we are not up to them yet, but we do fairly well. I have lost track of him but he was a fine officer."

"Yes Pershing, he is back in Washington convalescing. I do not think he will be there long; there is talk of him going to Japan. By the way Sergeant Kavanaugh, you are an excellent marksman what do you think of the Krag-Jorgenson rifle?"

"They asked me that a few years ago. It is an improvement over the old pumpkin slingers of the past, although we sure could use more stopping power against these Moros, they can take a couple slugs and keep on coming. The Krag is difficult to load especially when under threat therefore prone to jams, occasionally a round will go off early, especially under quick fire. But it shoots well, that is,-- accurately."

"Well you will be pleased to know that the Army will be issuing a new rifle. It will be thirty caliber, well designed, similar to the 1898 Mauser, no accidental firings and very accurate."

"Those Spanish Mausers they had on Cuba were the best I ever fired. I could have shot flies off a forehead with those rifled."

MacArthur laughed. "Would that be shooting from the front or the side, Sergeant?"

Billy also chortled, "that would have depended on whether they were Spaniards or Americans."

"I have enjoyed this conversation Sergeant Major. Perhaps we will meet again."

"You know what they say sir, the Army is one big family." He rose to leave. "May I ask you a question, sir?"

"Of course, what is it?" MacArthur withdrew another cigarette from his case.

"General Arthur MacArthur, are you related to him?"

"Yes he is my father. Why do you ask?"

"When I was in Cuba, I heard of him and men I respected and believed said he was the best, a real soldier's soldier. Captain Pershing thought a lot of him and how he managed these islands."

MacArthur exhaled a halo of smoke. "Yes and it is nice of you to remember, Kavanaugh."

Back at his cottage Billy was eating the remaining fruit from his lunch when he heard a familiar voice.

"Sarge?"

"What now, Brighton? Don't you have anything to do except interrupt my lunch?"

"I'm sorry, Sarge."

"Well what is it?"

"Are you going to play in the big game tonight?"

"I'm thinking about it – so what?"

"Well if you are going to play, I'm not."

"Come on Brighton! You play a fine hand of poker. Why stay away? I think you still have a red ass from the twenty bucks I won two days ago."

"Twenty? It was more like thirty! "

"There are lots of suckers you can scale, so don't feel too bad. Now I will play for sure."

"You are a hard man, Kavanaugh." He nodded despairingly and stepped back.

"So what other discoveries have you made lately?"

Chapter 41

San Francisco, California
April 1906

Billy joined the others at the rail and peered toward the shore. A dense pall of smoke hung where the city should have been. In the fading light large leaps of orange rose from fires yet to be extinguished. They had received word on board that a devastating earthquake had struck the city a week ago.

"Have a look Sergeant Major." An Army Captain named Grayson proffered his binoculars. "The place looks like it has been shelled for a month."

Billy studied the shoreline. "Holy shit sir, I have never seen anything like this! All this happened in less than a minute?"

"That's right. It is a scene no one else has seen not in our time or on this continent, in our country. It is a huge disaster!"

"I heard that they will land us tomorrow to pitch in with fire control or whatever."

"That's the word, tomorrow early. Are your men ready?"

"I 'm in transfer, I really don't have any men. They assigned me a detail- that's it. But we are ready for whatever"

"We will be sent to the city proper but the damage is spread for three hundred miles down the coast."

At precisely six am Billy and his men assembled behind Grayson. Among the men there was an undercurrent of curiosity, eagerness and wonder. None had ever seen such widespread destruction as they gawked about and felt the sense of the tragedy that pervaded. From the edge of the surf stretching toward the highlands there was a tangle of rubble streets disappeared into a jumble of junk. Looming behind the flattened area roofless, floorless structures and single wood and cement spikes reached to no where. Apartment buildings still striated by gaping walls had entire fronts missing, and bowed and buckled into precarious angles - the habitat for ghosts. Offshore winds had shifted smoke and choking smells of old wood burning and faint odors of charred pork. Billy recalled the smell of the burning settler wagon buried in the cottonwoods of Nebraska. It seemed so long ago but in the smells was recalled as yesterday.

The Captain called, "Kavanaugh, "I want you to take your three squads toward that church steeple there." He pointed at a broken steeple intact above the rubble. "Then work your way back to here. There is fire control, you are to look, listen for survivors. If you think you have located one, start digging. Your squad will draw picks and shovels and entrenching tools. If you can believe this, there is not a pick or shovel to be had around here. Take along a couple litters just in case. As I speak, the equipment will begin arriving."

"Yes sir."

"For if I am not mistaken, that launch yonder is bringing it. Can you believe it there is not a pick or shovel available in the HQ of the gold strikes?"

Billy turned and spotted the launch. "Yes Captain, kind of funny, isn't it all those miners and no picks and shovels."

"Nothing funny about it, god damn sad state of affairs this city is destroyed! All those picks and shovels are buried somewhere in it."

"Ironic is a better term. That church down there, how the hell are we supposed to get there- climb over all that shit?"

"Follow that street as best you can."

"Sir, there isn't any street."

"Climb over go around clear one as best you can. Keep your side arm, if you see any looters, shoot them"

"What if we find if we find somebody alive?"

"Pack them to where there is passage and send a runner here. If I don't miss my guess there won't be any; but take a couple of litters, anyway. Do you have rations?"

"Two days, sir. What do you want us to do if we find dead, pack them out too?"

"Stack and cover them, they will send along a wagon to pick them up, but it might not be any time soon. You will have tarps but there is no local water; extra canteens from ship's stores are with the gear. Assemble your squads, get your gear and get started. I'll try to get down there some time today."

After toiling through, clawing, dodging about obstacles and clearing when they could They reached the ruined chapel. An area near the chapel was not too cluttered and quickly cleared. All around their little clearing was broken masonry, charred beams, parts of roofs, pillars, twisted tin and tiles that rose above their heads. Most of the wooden structures had burned out and still smoldered.

"What now sergeant, have you ever seen such a mess?"

"No, first Arnie, take your squad to the buildings you can make out. There is a possibility there are people alive in those basements or collapsed apartments. Find a place you can holler into them, and then listen for a reply also any regular clicking, pounding or scratching sounds. If you think you have something, we will concentrate on finding them."

"I am going to take three men and start clearing the street to make way, so spread out and start yelling."

Billy and his three men cleared a narrow winding passage where the street once was. The work was exhausting the morning cool had dissipated in the hot sun and the heat and closeness sucked the strength out of them. They were resting propped among the ruins when Billy spotted Sergeant Arnold sprinting toward them.

"Kavy, we think we found a live one buried in that basement over there."
Kavanaugh could see the squad digging furiously at a collapsed basement.

"Private Hart heard this tick ticking and shouted into that mess over there. He thought he heard something in reply and banged away sure enough he heard second sounds and started rolling rocks away."

Kavanaugh looked into the hole and saw the top of Hart's head. He had braced his way down and was sending up the debris as he loosened it. He cleared to a small landing when they broke through. Trapped in scarce space was a man a woman. She was unconscious but the burst of fresh air revived them both. Both her legs were broken and he was battered badly. Carefully but quickly they extricated them and loaded on to litters the four bearers headed for the dock.

"I'd have never believed it if I didn't experience it. They been in that hole for over a week and lived."

"Me either, Kavy, it's a miracle. We did find a couple of dead ones they were not half as deep as the two survivors, just followed the rats and this big gray dog sniffing around."

"Gray dog, where the hell have you been Arnie? That was a coyote. Let's keep going here. Can Hart get through that wall down there? There may be people on the other side."

"Hart has been worth his weight in gold this day. Coal miner's kid, lost his dad and uncle in a cave in. In getting to those folks, he dug and braced his way in. He saved both their ass and our's too, we could have lost somebody with everything ready to fall in. I tell you he impressed us all. If it can be done, Hart will know how."

Kavanaugh again peered into the hole, he could hear the men working below street level and was about to leave, when two of the men climbed out greenish and gagging. He leaned over the hole and was assaulted by the stench of death, Hart presently appeared.

"Not good, Sarge, it's too late for the rest of them down there."

Billy descended into the hole and crawled through the opening to the other room. He sickened on the spot. He saw a woman and child dead just inside the light. "Drop down a rope." He secured the woman and guided her assent to the light and edged deeper into the rooms, struck a match recoiled at the sight and staggered back. When they had finished their task, six other children of various ages and size were hauled above. Kavy tried to climb out after the bodies were removed but the ordeal had so weakened him he required assistance. He ordered the men to take a break and sought shade in the rubble.

"You alright, Kavy?"

"No, I'm not alright I am puked out yet I think I am going to puke some more. I've seen a few dead children back awhile ago, but nothing like this. I've been a lot of places and done a lot of things but this is the worst job I have ever had. I keep imagining what it must have been like down in that hole, they all didn't all die at the same time. The panic, the fear they must have felt." He shook his head, "terrible!"

"I feel the same way." Arnold glanced to the road. "The Captain is coming with a cart and some men, we better get the men up."

"Bull shit, let them rest. If he says anything, I'll tell him to go down in that hole."

The Captain regarded Kavanaugh his hands on hips. "Well, well, you are to be commended. So far you are the only detail that has found anyone alive."

"Don't commend me for anything. Arnold and Private Hart did the lion's share - credit where credit is due, sir. I didn't do anything except help haul up the bodies." He shuddered, "Kids at that. Private Hart, sir is a coal miner and with out his know-how; we would never have found nor hauled them out."

"Noted, Sergeant Arnold, I will mention him in reports along with you two." Grayson looked toward Kavanaugh.

Kavanaugh waved off the mention of himself. "How are they doing, sir?

The woman is still in bad shape, the man talked a bit. It seems they thought at first it was just seasonal tremors as usual. They have these tremors often; no one paid much then wham!

The whole damn city crashed."

"You got them to help?"

"Yes, there was no place to send them, so we put them to the ship's infirmary. I brought some more water it is in the cart."

"We can use the water."

"It's not the only reason I am here. You are relieved of duty and are to report for transport. You can stay here if you want but your ride leaves at six am."

"Sir, I don't understand."

"Neither do I, but you Sergeants Arnold, Anderson and Lasko are to report aboard the Texas Star sailing to Galveston. She is in now. The only reason that makes any sense is you all have been cavalry scouts during Indian uprisings- that true?"

"Yes, sir Cheyenne, Arapahoe, Comanche and Apaches. Even chased a bunch of renegade Crows that jumped and raised hell and they were normally friendly folks."

"If I don't miss my guess, you were sent to get back into that fight. I will see you at six tomorrow morning." He prepared to leave. "Things are going from bad to worse on the Mexican border. They raid us we chase them for awhile, then we come back and it starts all over again. Each raid they make they become a little bolder they run off some horses and cattle and we go back after them. The Mexican Army isn't much help and as likely to shoot at us as the raiders. If I don't miss my guess the lid is going to blow off hell within the year. There is no love lost on Mexico, specially the Texas ranchers."

"One last thing, sir, altogether we found sixteen bodies." He nodded toward the mounded stack covered by tarps."

"They are gathering them up. We have found over a hundred today."

"Jesus wept!"

"There are thousands dead."

"I tell you one thing, sir; this is not my favorite line of work."

"That is true for most of us. Remember be at the dock at six am. After they have rested a bit get them going again."

The two Sergeants watched the captain around the corner of the narrow passage. The sun flared hotter and the two Sergeants moved deeper into the shadows.

I've wanted to say this Kavy. It's not very likely we will cross tracks again and I am getting out next month but I am damned proud to have served with you, damn proud."

"Thank you Arnie, but what brings this on?"

"A lot of reasons today for one you stayed down in that stinking hole and sent up those bodies yourself, you never expect credit for what some one else has done. I was on that Jolo raid and the medal is another reason. They asked me about it, you know."

"No, I didn't know, but what the hell is a medal? I know a lot of other people who deserved it more who couldn't or wouldn't get even a consideration like some of those black troops on Cuba."

"Don't try to bullshit me, Kavy – I was there and I saw Estevez and Bobby Rohaz get dragged into the cover by those four Moros and then you racing across the clearing right behind them with bullets kicking up shit all around and you disappeared into the cover. It was a goddamn miracle you made it across and I heard your .45 revolver banging away and Estevez coming back across like his ass was on fire then you stumbling out carrying Bobby, those two Moros right behind and drop Bobby down behind you reload that Colt and dropped them both.

394

I swear I thought the second one must have fallen near on top of you. So don't try to bullshit me. I have been in this army for 14 going on 15 years and I never saw anything like it."

"Come on Arnie, they were my men and I didn't want to find them staked out somewhere and skinned. You would have done the same thing."

"Like hell, Kavy all I did was try to put down some fire to keep any more of them from coming out. You all were in my line of fire to do much more."

"So you helped as best you could that is what it is all about. There is nothing particularly valorous about me. Now Vern Vilet, there was a man who wasn't afraid of anything. He should have five medals."

"Save it, Bill, I knew Vern Vilet and he was as crazy as a shit house rat. It is not the same thing."

"Well, maybe I am crazy too."

"Save it Kavanaugh, I was there. Another thing I don't want to rain on Grayson' parade, but I have never seen an Indian. I was mustered in at Fort Dix and they kept me on there for seven years teaching compass and map reading. Then to Fort Gordon doing the same thing then to Florida to Cuba, every officer and enlisted of any rank got sick and I ended up with a platoon in the midst of it leading patrols by compass mainly because you couldn't see shit. I was there two years. Then to the Philippines and I was there ever since. So I ain't ever seen a coyote and no god damn Indians neither."

Billy smiled at the consternation on Arnolds face. "Well, you will see coyotes in Texas." Billy stretched and rubbed the back of his neck. "Suppose we should get them up?"

"What ever you say, Sergeant Major."

For a moment Billy studied his hands. "Arnie, did you see the hands of that dead woman with all the kids? The bones were sticking out the ends of her fingers.

Chapter 42

Minsi, New York
Autumn 1907

The hills were bright fall colors the red and gold tones of the Catskills flowed for miles into the distance. Liam and a group of his friends had formed a hunting club called Pat's Club although the namesake had never shot a deer in his life. They stayed at the big house drank copious quantities enjoyed the best of Evelyn's cooking one of the few occasions she prepared food instead of supervising. They had finished dinner and Liam led them to the library. Most of the hunters had returned home only five had stayed for the meal and two left immediately after.

They gathered at a small table and settled into the stuffed chairs around it. Their wind burned faces reflected the day's activity and they were satisfied weary ready to review the day. Liam set a tray of glasses on the table. He snapped open his humidor and selected a dark Maduro cigar with out asking Mick selected one.

"Don't mind if I do." He smiled.

Liam laughed aloud. "No Mick you don't mind if I don't."

He was joined in laughter by the others and if Mick had been taken aback it never showed. The humidor made its rounds among the others and the room began to fill with smoke as they each huffed at getting an even light. Liam leaned back in his chair.

"Every one saw deer today?" He sent a smoke ring toward the ceiling.

"I saw a lot of doe but didn't get a shot at a buck until that last drive. I still don't know how I missed him."

"There is a lot of room around them, Henry and a lot more of them out there."

"You are right about that, Jack. I'll bet I saw thirty deer today."

"That is a nice fork horn you nailed."

"Yeah, Li but that eight point you got was a dandy. Banker John got a nice one too. It sure feels good to those three hanging."

"I noticed too, makes you feel good but I think your fork horn weighs more than either John's or mine. You can't eat the horns anyway. There were supposed to be three more guys show up this morning, but it's a week day and they couldn't get away. The gang is all going to be here this week end."

"With everyone here it should make for a good hunt. I do believe that Jack would make horn soup. That is why his nose is out of joint about that rack." Mick leaned back for the expected retribution.

"He makes a lot of noise for someone who didn't even shoot today."

A quiet mirth and contentment pervaded the men as they watched the fire.

"We had a family friend, a Chinese man we called Uncle Woo who treasured deer horns like gold. He believed horns were an aphrodisiac so Billy and Sara and I would gather a box full as a present for him. We really cared for him. Every Christmas he brought us a sleigh full of presents and went on about how strong and courageous Pat was."

"From what I have heard about your father that was all true." Henry enjoined.

Liam nodded and slid deeper into the chair. "Are any of you going to stay past Sunday?"

"I have to go home sometime tomorrow but I will be back on Saturday and stay over."

"What about you Jack, and you Henry?"

"I'm going to hunt through Monday. I don't get to escape very often."

"The same for me, this time of the year I would rather be in these woods than anywhere else."

"So only you are going home tomorrow, Jack."

"Yeah, but I'll be back Friday afternoon. There won't be any deer left in the woods by Monday knowing you guys. By the way, I want to donate that fork horn as camp meat. Maybe we can get Evelyn to roast a half outside for Saturday night?"

"I will see what I can do. Evelyn has recruited a couple fine cooks, a German lady and a French Canadian. Boy, you should hear that clatter when they are discussing something!"

"This is the only place I have ever been where the staff is better than the circus."

"That is the way Mary likes it. She is spending more time talking to the staff and hospital patients than ever before. She used to avoid the hospital, now she is down there almost as long as Sara is."

"It is funny how we change as life around us changes. There really nothing steady about it."

"You are right about that, Jack. Speaking about big changes how is your family?"

"Well, the boys are getting taller; my daughter Anne is in Albany working with the politicians and my wife is steadily slipping into a sausage."

A great guffaw followed the comment, Liam choked on his smoke which further added to the laughter.

"By God, Jack you should give some kind of a warning before you say something like that." Mick said wiping the laughter from his eyes." When next I see your wife I am going to tell her what you said." He added in jest, "slipping into a sausage, huh wait until she gets wind of that compliment."

"You tell her and I will disappear into the midst of her canning. She will probably put me up in jelly jars."

Another peal of laughter rocked the library.

"I swear, Jack, Henry managed holding his side, "I think sometimes you will be the death of me."

A moment of silence gripped the gathering that welled of friendship and good humor. Each of the men satisfied they belonged among the prevailing sentiment. Liam rose touched a match under the kindling in the fireplace and they watched the flame reach through the wood. He adjusted the damper and sat down and lighted his failing cigar.

"How are Elaine and your girl, Henrietta?"

"Talk abut big changes, she went off to Hunter College in September where your Sara went. We miss her. Elaine cried for a week and still can get teary about it. I damn near had to fetch her home because of Elaine. I knew in my heart I shouldn't do it so things are resolved some. She will be home in a couple weeks Elaine is elated now. I must admit it I am looking forward to the break."

"She is a very bright girl."

"There is a special bond between mothers and their daughters, like they share some secret vendetta."

"Yes, it is against men."

Another chuckle passed through them. The fire quickened and threw bright patches on the walls.

"Elaine worried about her living in the city. She wants the best for all of us. We have too big a house, an automobile - also too big and enough stuff to stock a year long fire sale and now she wants the right to vote."

"These damn women in bloomers and placards! To hell with them, what the hell do they know about politics?"

"Don't say that too loud. Mary thinks she is the grand dame of suffragettes in this county. If she hears us we all may well end up in jelly jars."

"Where is Mary she usually stops for a couple toasts a drink or two or threatens to play poker?"

Henry smiled. "The last time we were here she sat in."

"I remember she won two pots and left."

"She is in New Rochelle this week. Sara took her down yesterday and she is coming back tonight but Mary may be awhile. She opened a new store there selling Irish merchandise. This is her second one after her visit there with Pat she has all the relatives and whoever they can recruit a lot of different things. She can barely keep the shelves full. I'm afraid it may not last with war around the corner, even if the Irish manage to stay out of it."

"What is she selling? I might be interested in stocking some in the store."

"I really don't know. Sweaters shawls, woolen goods, lace beads and souvenirs. It is all authentic and expensive."

"Sounds good, but probably it's too rich for customers here in Minsi or Forestport."

"They are trying to meet the Christmas buyers and a large shipment arrived. Of course Mary wants to wants to see for herself what they sent."

"Nothing is inexpensive these days."

"I am", piped up Mick, "for the right woman I would be free."

Jack waggled his finger. "No doubt your wife will have to get rid of the chutney some where."

Liam laughed set a log on the stretching flames. "I have a special surprise. I got a case of this Monday, just in time for this hunt." He lifted the bottle so they all could see the label. "It is an especially good sherry, Harvey's Shooting Sherry rather appropriate don't you think?"

They all filled their glasses. Liam raised his glass. "Here's to the ladies."

"Yes, you can't get along with them and you can't get along without them."

They settled back in their chairs and watched the fire as it filled the silence with crackles and pops.

"I think you guys; the women will get the vote."

"They will, I know it too. The English already granted it. It's guaranteed, just a matter of time."

"Jack it can not be guaranteed until some one enforces it. Remember the South? They found ways to shut down the freed man votes."

"If it is the law, someone will enforce it. This will be an amendment to the Constitution and will be enforced nationally and once the women have it the men better pay attention for they won't get away with denial – too many eyes upon them."

"You are right, Li. I just wish we were more like the Indians. The men hunt and bring home the bacon and the women take care of the children, the house and cook."

"Tradition is in the toilet." Mick replied.

"By the way, Li I meant no offense about the Indians."

"None taken, now let's break out the cards. I'll take some of your money."

There was a general rejection of his claim for they all knew he was not a card shark and played less than average but did enjoy an occasional winning streak. They had played a few hands when Liam noticed Jack had not picked up his cards and was absorbed in a drawing on Liam's easel.

"Do you have any new drawings, Li? I don't remember that one. My God, Liam you really are talented."

"I've been busy lately. That's Lenin. I also have done Trotsky Marx and Stolypin."

"I know that its Lenin, there is no doubt about the identity. I like the cap and smile gives him cocky but kind of sinister look."

The others also looked at the drawing.

"It is an interesting drawing and makes you wonder what he is really up to."

"He is in command of a revolution really since '05 – Bloody Sunday. It has been building among the workers, riots work stoppage the Potemkin mutiny should have been the greatest clue. It provided a look into the military support the czar really had." Jack replied.

The Czar did back off and conceded some but now this Stolypin and his 'neckties' just hanging people right and left, a revolution is bound to result."

"The Czar dissolved two Dumas. That won't give the people much confidence either."

"The third one is still holding."

"You are right but one might wonder if it represents the people. How many reforms have been enacted?"

"Shit, we could ask the same thing about our own government."

"I get so confused", Mick said. Bolshevism, Mensheviks, communism, socialism this entire utopia stuff. What do Lenin and Trotsky really want?"

"It is confusing, you answer him, Jack. You are the politician. I couldn't get through Das Kapital. Marx was so layered and confusing, I gave up on it."

"It is deep alright. It is like the people who do the work share the swart as the fishermen called it. The people should get more back than they do and the government needs to insure that, so it acts like a supervisor to share the wealth. Another utopia and none of those groups do very well as witnessed by our own experiments here in America. The problem is power and those in government like all of us, take care of themselves first."

"This kind of crap starts in the city because farmers do not have time for it. I thought that Russia was primarily farmers supposedly the best butter in the world comes from there."

"Problem is they don't own their own farms, wealthy nobles do. It is similar in Ireland and there has been trouble aplenty over there."

"That is true. Russia wants to develop it's industry, develop cities with industry herd the people into town that way they will all have work, all will contribute and all will benefit more equally ; voila the ideal society. And by the way it's easier to manage and manipulate them all when they are in the cities."

"It seems like a good idea to me" Henry interjected. "What's wrong with that idea?"

"For one thing, you can organize the labor in the cities alright, but you must organize the farmers as well for they feed us all. Where will the wheat for flour for the bread, meat for the table and milk and eggs? If the people are gathered who can't feed themselves they will starve. There already appear to be problems people may have money but there may not be any food to buy."

"There must be land reform along with labor reform or it is not going to work and they will have to enlarge the government to control the citizens."

"And another utopian society goes down the creek."

"I tell you what I worry about and that is what may happen to our own country as a result of the labor unions - The International Workers of the World, Eugene Debs and all the others. I call them, the 'I won't work crowd.' What if they turn on us?"

"Don't worry Mick it won't happen here we are well educated with a representative government, sort of anyway, and no royal or privileged class based on heredity, a real working country. Organized labor is more likely to help in the long run."

"Great, ain't it? Russia is wracked with all kinds of troubles yet she and the rest of Europe are gathering up for a big war."

Henry stretched and stood up and set some wood on the fire. "That is what really concerns me."

"Germany and Austria against Great Britain, France and Russia, it will be a real shoot 'em up. We may end up in that squabble."

"That is a fight we can stay out of. We have enough troubles at home."

"We have more than enough with Mexico and things aren't going so well."

"To hell with all this politics, pick up your cards and let's play poker."

They resumed the game and exchanged bets that finally devolved to Li and Mick.

"I call all this talk about royalty and the working man, read 'em and weep, three queens."

"You have three queens, despite all this talk about the women? I have two red aces."

"The ladies love me."

"And that, Mick said is the story of another utopian society."

Chapter 43

The struggle for power to rule Mexico is an intrigue that involves foreign powers and domestic betrayals. Much of the trouble had to do with the 'latifunda system' where a very few wealthy people controlled huge grants of land and the lives of many peasants.

Following the Mexican War (1846 – 1848) the treaty with America ceded more than half of Mexico's territory to the United States. Following this travesty, in 1864 as the War between the States was in its final full year, the French Army, with the assistance of Mexican royalists, invaded under the command of Maxmillian von Hapsburg who became Emperor of Mexico.

Three years later, in 1867, a liberation army commanded by Juarez defeated Maxmillian and reestablished the Republic of Mexico with him as the President. After the death of Juarez in 1872, Sebastian Tajada became President. Four years later Tajada was over thrown by Porfirio Diaz who became President, re-electing himself seven times. His rule of 34 years became known as "The Porfiriato." The dictator was not popular with either the aristocracy or the peasantry.

In 1911 a visionary, reform-minded liberal from wealthy means, named Madero, over-threw the Diaz regime. Madero promised land reform and justice. Promising so much, he changed his life style to one closer to that of the peasants. He was a well meaning man with truly democratic principles; he listened to imaginary characters who gave directions for the management of Mexico. One of Madero's most trusted generals --- Victoriano Huerta betrayed him. He later murdered Madero and was set to assume power when he himself was over-thrown by an alliance of revolutionaries ---Venustiano Carranza and Pancho Villa. Before a year was up, the revolutionaries feuded among themselves. Carranzo defeated the forces led by Emiliano Zapata and Pancho Villa.

Near Guadalupe Bravos
Mexican Border
November 1911

Billy heaved his saddle into his tent and led his horse toward the rope line. He noticed two corporals standing near the end of the tent row - Nester and Layton who were joking on his approach. 'Here it comes he thought. ' He scanned them speculatively.

"You had a hard time his afternoon Sergeant Major?"

"What the hell are you talking about, Nester?"

"We both saw you skin out over the hill top with those steers hot on your behind."

"I was just getting out of their way."

"That wasn't quite what you ordered us to do get out of their way. We didn't expect to see you again 'till maybe tomorrow."

"We thought maybe you were headed for California."

"If I didn't know better I'd think you were flat skedaddled by those six mavericks. That what you thought, Nes?"

"Look you two; I don't want anything to do with steers, bulls, cows or what ever. Those goddamn animals flat surrounded me throwin' horns and tried to gore my horse. I'm no goddamn cow poke like you."

Billy's comment was met with a great guffaw. Layton was out of breath with laughing.

"I believe we got his goat, Layton!"

"I can't believe those long horns would spook you so."

"I'll admit I did not welcome the occasion."

"Not welcome the occasion?"

There s another great peal of laughter despite himself, Billy joined in.

"I swear, Kavanaugh you are a mystery. On one day jumpin' a renegade out of his saddle in a rolling knife fight and today ridin' from some steers like they was death itself."

"I thought you was goin' to pull your pistol and shoot 'em all." Nester chirped.

"I thought about it, and then I just left them for you two to round up."

The two Corporals smiled. Layton fished out a plug of tobacco, sliced of a chunk and popped it in his mouth.

"Those cows really did put the run on you."

"Like I said, I am not a drover or a rodeo rider. If I wanted to be, I could have been." Layton spit a trail into the dust. "Why do they make you so uneasy, outside the fact their horns were like hat racks was wild and big as box cars?"

"I can see you're not going to let go of this so I will tell you the story. About 30 years ago I was hunting buff with a bunch of my Indian friends. We stalked up close then rode right into them - my first real try at buffalo."

Billy paused and exhaled like he was blowing an unpleasant memory." I was just a kid and one of my pals was a young brave called Bright Feather. I was riding not fifty yards from him; we were right in the middle of the herd flying across the flats. The buff turned and Bright Feather went down. The buff just drove me along and I couldn't get back. I had to ride them out. I finally got turned around and found him."

Billy shuddered a bit as the memory worked through. "I never forgot it nor ever will. You could hardly tell what was left from the dirt. He was smashed to splatter. We tried to pick him up every bone in him was crushed. When we picked him up he ran like an egg. I was just a kid, but I never forgot Bright Feather."

The two corporals turned toward sympathy.

"That is a hell of a story, Kavanaugh." Nester observed and Layton nodded in affirmation.

"I have been a little anxious around herds ever since. I know that the trampling could well have been me. Know what beats hell? A couple years later I might have met Bright Feather in battle on those Dakota plains."

For a moment all three men looked north as if a distant memory was generated for them all.

"That's some story, Bill things have a funny way of turning out."

"Yeah, well I have lots of stories."

"No sense in lookin back, Kavy, something might be gaining on ya." Nester observed.

"I can understand why you scaled out. I been drivin' cattle since I was 15 or so and never saw anybody lost to a stampede."

"Don't misunderstand, Layton, I am not afraid of cows. I pulled my share of tits on Guernsey and Holsteins."

"I pulled my share of tits but they weren't Guernsey." He laughed, "I grew up in Saint Louis. I got to droving when I was eighteen or so. I still like pullin' tits better."

"Trust you to turn this discussion to sex. What the hell else do you know?"

"I know this; you get born – no choice and you get dead also no choice, what is betwixt - food, work and women."

"Cow poke's logic?"

"Maybe, but you can't eat that much and a lot of it is bad. You work but it ain't always that good, like ridin' drag all by your lonesome and that leaves the ladies."

Billy shook his head. "Speaking about work, don't you two have anything to do, because if you don't, I can find something?"

"No Sergeant, I want to write a letter, will you help me with it later?"

"I'll help you later, and how about you, Layton?"

"Oh, Sergeant, I have heaps to do. I have to go over and get a shirt starched; he was referring to the camp followers who did laundry and other favors for the troops. By the way, top sergeant, those whores are the most stinking bunch of women I have ever met and I have met a lot of them. Why don't you check for yourself?"

"Well, Layton why don't you do then go and get your shirt starched. You know, Layton, you should have been a sheep herder. I hear there might be some advantages for a man like you.'

This time the joke was on him and the look of consternation on his face.

"You would have food and work and a warm place to put it, even if it did have four legs attached."

Nester laughed and soon all three joined together.

Billy tied off his horse and again looked north and thought, 'I hate this damn duty, trailing cow herds taking them back just to have them stolen all over again. I get shot at by rustlers one day and another being chased by the Federales and another day by ranchers and some days I don't know who the hell is shooting at me. Maybe it really is time for me to wrap this tour up and go home.'

He trudged to his tent as the nostalgia bit deeply. Billy lay on his cot and closed his eyes and on the edge, Liam appeared dressed in a coat and bright tie his father voice echoed from behind him, then Sara appeared beside him dressed in a white coat. Evelyn's image of her in the kitchen providing counsel to a young man and woman he did not recognize. Then a bright image of Mary flowed like a spirit and washed it all away. He sat up with a start and became aware of a tapping at the tent flap. He jarred awake

"Sergeant Kavanaugh, Sergeant Kavanaugh, are you awake?"

"Yes, I am now." He rubbed at his eyes. "Come in Jorgensen, that's you isn't it?"

The tent flap separated and a pair of bright blue eyes surrounded by a sun burned face looked tentatively at him. "Yes sir. I am sorry to disturb you, Sarge."

"Private," he replied with a trace of admonishment and regret for the lost sleep and dream. "What is it?"

"Lieutenant Whiten wants to see you."

"Have any idea why he wants to see me?"

"He has new orders, I think; something about Presido."

Billy pulled on his boots and grabbed his hat. 'This could be a godsend he thought and followed Jorgensen down the tent row.

Whiten was a big man with watery eyes, a tight lip demeanor and prematurely bald giving him an intellectual, pertinacious look. He was arrogant but a bit in awe of Kavanaugh's record. He minimized this service and determined it would make little difference; after all he was still an enlisted man. He relished having Billy wait as he busied himself writing a letter.

"At ease, Kavanaugh," he looked up from his writing, "oh, I see that you already are."

Not with you, you son of a bitch' Billy thought but politely responded, "you sent for me, sir?"

"Yes, it appears the anticipated events with Mexico have transpired."

"What events might that be, sir, did Mexico collapse into the sea?"

Lieutenant Whiten looked carefully at Kavanaugh to discern if he was mocking him or whether it was just a frivolous comment. Finally he smiled. "No, Sergeant," he sat back in his chair and ruefully replied, "no, the revolution has turned to Madero."

"So, Diaz is out, who is the new one?"

"Madero? We don't much about him. A hacienda type who promises all kinds of reform he has not nor can not deliver. The usual promises: less suppression of the peasants, land reform. He is another idealist who probably doesn't know what is going on. The peasants know that he likely won't reform much because of his family's holdings despite his talk. He beats Diaz on the field then calls for an election instead of just taking over. That is a sign of a weak leader and the peasants know it."

'Like you', Billy thought but said nothing then asked, "what has this got to do with us, sir?"

"The locals in the north realize nothing will likely be done so they awe arming up for their own revolution. There are more reports that guns are being run into Mexico from U.S. sources and some of them are coming right through here or nearby. But before we get into what our new role will be, your last report leaves much to be desired. What exactly happened?"

Here we go again, Billy thought. "Sir, plainly spoken, we chased those god damn cows nearly to Lake Guzman and we got most of them back."

"Was there any action beyond that?"

"Well, they shot at us and we shot back and neither side hit anybody and I am not sure who they were."

"You got most of the cattle back?"

"Yes, sir they belonged to the El Paso Cattle Company. A few of their hands were with us, and they have already started the herd back. They left us three head figuring they owed us something. Layton and Nester drove them over to the mess tent, so I imagine we will be having some stringy steaks for dinner tonight."

"Is there anything else to tell?"

"Not about that, sir, but..."

"But what?"

"It is about the whores, sir."

"The whores, what about them?" He aired tiredly.

"Sir, they are filthy, they stink, and I can smell them a hundred yards away. They are wearing filthy frocks and some of the men have complained about it. Who ever rounded them up scraped the bottom of the barrel."

Whiten rubbed his eyes and wearily nodded. "I hadn't noticed, Sergeant." He set aside the letter he was composing.

"Sir, the shirt starchers are better off – hot water you know."

Whiten again fiddled with his letter then folded it aside. "What do you suggest Sergeant Major? I have enough on my plate already."

"Herd the whores down to the river and force them to wash up. We haven't let them near the river for almost three months, and it is not that far. I think most of them will be glad to clean up."

"No wonder they stink, hygiene is not one of their qualities. If it were up to me, they wouldn't be here. Why didn't we do this before?"

"Your orders, sir, you wanted to closely control them so they would not lure the men off post to meet them while they might be pulling duty. They need a chance to clean up. I suggest we borrow a couple of those big kettles and set them to boiling so they can clean up their clothes as well as themselves."

"Ha, perhaps I will have the Mess Sergeant prepare a picnic and you can make a day of it." He laughed quietly to himself.

"Sir, I don't see much humor in it."

Whiten sobered and squinted at Billy. "I assume they will all agree?"

"If not, sir, I will personally throw their asses into the river."

"Yes I bet you would." The Lieutenant mused. "Very well do what you have to; I do not want to be involved. Before you set to that task, I have some other news."

"New orders, sir?"

"Yes, Madero is presiding over mayhem. He has support now but the lid may blow off hell shortly. The people are impatient and the peasants are in revolt about the confiscation of ancestral lands and that frustration is just across the river, not Mexico City."

"What do they want us to do about it? I've already asked."

"It is complicated. We may have been helping things along. The Mexicans will find out sooner or later."

"You mean sir that we have been meddling in their affairs and will continue until someone we favor gets in."

"I would not put it so bluntly but essentially yes. Americans own a hell of a lot of Mexico more than a quarter of the land I'd guess. Also Americans have invested millions into the development of Mexican industry probably own at lest half of it. We will protect these interests."

Both men turned to strident voices outside the tent.

"I will take care of that when we are finished here. What are the orders?"

"See that you do." Whiten turned to a map suspended behind his desk. "There is a potential hot spot here. It is Presidio. We are here that is Guadalupe Bravos. Gun runners are coming down from the north. We thought we had them blocked instead they are going around us." He traced his finger along the map. They arrive at Van Horn on the map here and split. We expect some to come this way but others are going overland to Alpine, then to Presidio across the river into Ojinaga and south." He turned from the map.

"Begging your pardon, sir, we have not had any runners through here. That area north and east is the edge of Apache country and that is dangerous territory, especially sending patrols up in there. You never know what to expect from them hostility is about all."

"Then, Sergeant Major --expect that. The arms game has charged the peasants to up rise. They do not believe that Madero will deliver. We can not afford that. They want and need guns an arsenal was robbed in San Antonio last week and we expect that those arms are headed south of the border and it could be here or Presidio."

Billy anxiously studied the map. "We had better make our play along the river. I sure don't want to lead the men up into those hills. The runners take a great risk themselves. I'd rather catch up to them after their gauntlet than chase them all over that Apache country."

"You will do what you have to do. I want you to take twenty men to Presidio identify and guard river crossing points and vigorously patrol the region Apaches or not. Take ten day's rations and we will send more supplies in about five days."

"Yes sir, we had better pack more ammunition. I am not eager to put men at risk in that Apache country."

"I heard what you said, Kavanaugh! Let me clear, I want these runners brought to justice, but I also want them interrogated and find who is at the bottom of running this show. Who is ultimately responsible, especially the robbery of the arsenal. If that means going into Apache country then that is where you will go. I trust you know what an order is and I have just given you one."

"When do you want us to leave? I will ask for volunteers if I don't get enough I will pick some." He was miffed at the lieutenant's tirade but responded very evenly.

"You do that sergeant, and I expect you to leave no later than the day after tomorrow. I may send some more men later but we must remain on guard here."

"Is there anything else, sir?"

"No, go take care of the whores that should be an interesting task. Tell them to get the crud out of their crotch. You are dismissed; and find out who disturbed our conversation earlier."

True to his word, most of the women willingly went to the river and the men lined the banks to leer at them

The women stripped and acknowledged the gawkers with a variety of postures and gesticulations. Billy towered above the naked bathers. He had many volunteers of the fires underneath the kettles who were more interested in a closer look than in boiling water. A large, shapeless woman refused the request to bathe, so Billy wrestled her toward the water. She resisted, violently exclaiming "if they want to see me they will pay, god damn it!" There ensued an all out free for all where Billy ended on his backside acclaimed by cheers and jeers by the on- lookers, finally dumped her in the river but with a last kick she knocked Billy down and he promptly disappeared under the water. The current caught his hat and it started down stream where Nester fished it out and returned it. Billy wallowed toward shore and glared at the onlookers all around, stepped on to the beach, flourished his sodden hat and bowed. The banks and the river exploded in shouts, cheers and laughter.

They camped on the bank of the river identified crossing points twenty miles in both directions and began a regular patrolling. On one patrol they glimpsed some far off flashing in the hills Billy dismounted and scanned for other signs of Indian activity. As he remounted he turned to Jorgensen.

"I tell you Jorgensen, anyone who runs guns through here must be greedy or crazy or both."

Later Billy split the patrol and followed the river in opposite directions. One of the men reported he heard gunshots from the other patrol Layton was leading. Kavanaugh became more concerned when the patrol was late for the rendezvous. He was about to send out riders when he spied the late patrol was approaching. One look and Billy knew something was amiss.

'No sense in borrowing trouble, I'll wait until they get here,' he thought. A second glance alarmed him, but he sat down at his desk and waited.

A beleaguered trooper appeared at the tent.

"Private Clark, where is corporal Layton?" The question hung like a suspended spider.

"Bad news Sergeant Major, we lost Layton."

"What the hell do you mean 'lost him'? Anger flickered in his eyes. "Did he wander off – what?"

"No, sir they killed him." Clark looked down. "They shot him down."

"God damn it!" Billy brought his fist down the force collapsed his desk. "Who killed him?" Clark hesitated.

"God damn it –speak up! Who killed him? "

"Sir, we saw a wagon crossing the shallows. Layton shouted at them to stop and they opened up on us. We were right in the open, Dunn's horse went down and Layton got hit in the chest. I hauled him out of the river, but he was dead."

"Jesus wept!" Billy burst upright and stamped to the tent flap and Clark flinched as he passed close to him. In a moment Billy gained control and replied. "At ease, Clark, tell me where, when and what happened."

"It was down river about eight miles, by that big stand of cottonwoods, early this morning about eight. We rode up on them and they just started shootin' it took us by surprise. We returned fire and got one of them; they dumped him across the river and took off."

"God damn it! Clark you go out there and tell every one to saddle up, NOW!"

"Sergeant Kavanaugh, they are already well into Mexico."

"I don't give a shit if they are in Brazil. Saddle them up! No one and I mean no one, kills one of my men and gets away with it so long as I can do something about it. Tell them to saddle up – light. We are going after those bastards, and kill every one of them."

"Yes, sir," Clark looked down at his feet and was about to comment.

"Well, get going, don't just stand there!"

Clark disappeared and Billy gathered his gear and some extra cartridges. He left two men as guards and struck out. When they reached the crossing the dead renegade's body had already collected birds. Billy led the men over the river and sent Jorgensen at full gallop to scout ahead. Billy continued to lead following the wagon ruts. At one trail juncture there was evidence of a meeting a large group of horsemen and wagon tracks dispersed east while the tracks they had been following continued south.

They had proceeded just a few miles when Jorgensen returned having spotted the gun runners surrounded by locals. Billy slowed and split the men for an encircling movement. It appeared like there were goods being sold from the wagon and the runners were oblivious to their pursuers. Billy pressed the men forward the Mexicans fled to a safe distance to watch. The squadron pressed the wagon and was met with a bristling hostility.

"Which one of you bastards killed my friend?"

"What are you doing here blue belly? This is Mexico and you have no jurisdiction to do anything, we are just doing business." The man spoke with a cockney accent.

"Yeah, the gun business and you have already done all the business you will ever do. Now I am asking which one of you killed my friend."

"Fook you Sergeant," he snarled. "I am American citizen. I served two bleedin' years in the Army. So fook you and let us alone."

"Fook me, huh? Have it your way, your years of service should have taught you better. Nester put a rope on this son-of-a-bitch. Maybe a Mexican sleigh ride will improve his memory."

Before the man could move Nester had a rope around him and jerked him to the ground. Billy peered into the wagon that was nearly empty.

"This wasn't your first stop was it, you twit? You have already unloaded most of it."

"None of your business, saddle tramp. And get this rope off me."

"You are in a bad position to ask anything. If anybody is going to get fooked, it's you. One last try, which of you killed my friend?"

"You can't do this you son-of-a-bitch!"

"I can't? Take him for a ride, Nester."

Nester turned his horse galloped for a half mile raising dust and throwing panic into the Mexican spectators. He wheeled about and returned at a faster clip and reined up beside Billy. His cargo was unconscious and looked like a bundle of rags bleeding profusely from his bone scraped face with great swaths of peeled, raw skin leaking through what clothes were left.

"Now who killed my friend?" There was no reply from any of the three men. "Very well, Clark, get ropes on these people and search the wagon."

After a few minutes Clark called out. "There are a couple cases of rifles alright, not Army issue. Jesus, Sarge they have some dynamite in here - leaky dynamite. It could have blown at any time and it is a wonder it didn't. Not much else, general supplies: rope, hoes, buckets, and bags of beans, jerked beef and a couple jugs of rot gut."
"Check out those rifles."

In a moment Clark replied 1895 Marlins 32-40. Here is a note, the ammo is 44-40, and there ain't any fuse or caps for the dynamite."

"Jorgensen ride over there and bring back a couple of those locals." Billy swung down from the saddle and withdrew his Springfield. "Where did you get this stuff? I am talking to you." The man did not respond and with a swift stroke of his rifle Billy sent him spiraling into the dust. He approached the next man and asked again, "where did you get this?" The man cringed as Billy began to raise his rifle.

"We bought it all in San Antonio. We didn't steal it; I have a bill of sale. I don't remember his name. If you untie me I show it to you?"

"You assholes, why did you fire on my men? Billy snatched the slip of paper and glanced through it quickly. "You had other stuff you already peddled that is why we caught up to you."

I'm sorry Sergeant, very sorry. We were scared. We had so much trouble we were almost there and we didn't want to get stopped at the river. We just panicked, and we didn't want to kill anybody. It was an accident."

Billy turned to a new commotion behind him. Jorgensen had gathered up three of the Mexicans and the men had hemmed them in. "Do any of them speak English?" Jorgensen signaled no. Billy mounted and stood in his stirrups. Do any of you men speak Spanish? Ride forward."

Presently a rider appeared and reined up beside Billy. "Private Hurt, I would not have guessed."

"It is actually Huerta, Sarge and I can handle the lingo."

"Tell these men," he gestured at the peasants, "that these men were trying to cheat them. Tell them that the bullets do not fit the rifles and the dynamite would be more dangerous for them than whatever they would use it for." He waited as Hurt translated and motioned to Jorgensen. "Get out one of those rifles and some of that 44 ammo and show them."

Hurt finished and Jorgensen demonstrated the misfit cartridges. The Mexicans fully understood the situation and exchanged remarks and glares at the gun-runners.

"Clark, bring out a piece of that dynamite. Hurt tell them how dangerous this shit is and that it requires a fuse and there is none."

"Sarge, that dynamite is very, very unstable and if the sun even hits it, it may go off."

"Just be careful, Clark. Get one of them to carry it out there a hundred yards or so. That little rise in the ground out there." He pulled a red handkerchief from his pocket. "Wrap this around it and set it on end where I can see it."

Hurt completed his translation and Clark returned from his walk sweating not from the sun alone. "Tell the men to get a good hold on their horses." Billy steadied his Springfield over the wagon carefully sighted and squeezed off a shot. The dynamite exploded in a huge cloud of dust a few stones pummeled the men and sent some horses to bucking.

"Now Hurt, tell them that unless they can shoot as well as that or have a fuse, the dynamite is more of a danger to them than anyone else. Also tell them that these men put their lives at stake and should be treated like the murderers that they are. Tell them they can have the horses and the guns and wha ever else they want from the wagon."

The victim of the sleigh ride protested, "you can't do this."

"Weren't you the one who said fook you? I have already done it. You are the ones who have been fooked."

He waited until Hurt had finished translating and the Mexicans had plundered the wagon. He thought to himself about the Lieutenant's orders and smiled 'I captured them alive, I interrogated them and found they did not rob the arsenal and now I am delivering them to justice not exactly to the letter of the law but this is Mexico.'

"Jorgensen, tie these bastards to the wagon and fetch me one of those Marlins. It is time to go." He signaled the men to form a column and started back to the river.

They rode to a rise in the ground and he and when Jorgensen looked back, the wagon was afire and the Mexicans were headed away with the loot spread on the canvas from the wagon. The two turned to catch up with the others when a huge explosion raised a great dust cloud. They could see a body lifted high in the air then drop out of site.

"Justice ain't it grand?"

Sarge do you think we should have confiscated all the rifles?"

"Have you ever thought how helpless and powerless these people must feel? By the time they figure out what ammunition they need and where to get it the revolution will be over. Until they do something more than steal cattle and horses, revolts in Mexico should not be our problem."

Chapter 44

Minsi, New York
September 1912

The sky was a gray overcast and threatening rain. Mary and Sara were primping before the large mirror in Mary's sitting room. Liam announced his impending presence by nosily climbing the stairs.

"Come on in, Liam, we are both decent. I am dressed and you have already seen Sara in her underwear even better - without it."

"Mother," Sara began. "I don't think you should go."

"Cluck, cluck, cluck, I know what you are going to say' I have health limitations that might be aggravated by the strain of it all. The answer to your concern is why shouldn't I? I am not disabled!"

Li leaned on the large overstuffed chair without regard to the exchange between the two women.

"Are you sure you are up to all this? The parade may be long, the ceremony, the signing at the park plus the party tonight?"

"Liam, stop worrying! Just last week Billy, Mary C and me walked down to the fishing hole, that is two miles each way and you are worrying that I can't walk a mile in a parade? I think I can do that."

"Well, it is going to be a long day. The party begins at six and will end who knows when and there will be a lot of people here."

"Then I will sleep in tomorrow."

"I am going to have dinner, spend an hour at the party then go out to the hospital so I can get some sleep. I think I will have at least one delivery and It may be tonight." Sara slipped into a deep orange colored dress, turned and appraised her appearance. "Are the children ready?"

"They have clothes on."

"I expect they are clean?"

"I have Billy set and Mary C is dressing herself. I thought she was up here. Any way, we have a half hour before we must leave."

"Brian Shoemaker will be there?"

"Yes, Mary he is going to give the dedication speech and promised to include comments on suffrage."

"Did you read it?"

"Of course not; I don't think he had it written when last I spoke with him."

"I hope that blonde headed twit doesn't decide to give a speech about reelection."

"I think it will be about the monument and a few words about suffrage."

"We will see."

A huge crowd was milling around the park, talking, visiting the concession stands and listening to the band. One hawker estimated the crowd at two thousand. The crude speaker system growled for attention.

And the large assembly pressed toward the center bleacher bedecked with bunting. Mayor

Blum said a few words and summoned United States Senator Brian Shoemaker who stepped to center stage.

He was a man of medium height tending to portly with a heavy shock of blonde hair streaked with gray. The crowd hushed to hear him.

"Ladies, gentlemen, youngsters and veterans of the great civil conflict and the late war with Spain."

I thank you for the opportunity to join in the dedication of this monument to those that served and died in the Civil War now 50 years past. This long and bloody conflict pitted friend against friend brother against brother and fathers against sons. Time has diminished the urgency and it is now a glorious recollection or a sad recollection of the ultimate loss of a loved one. We have veterans with us today who served in that conflict."

He swept his arm toward a group of grizzled old men looking quite spiffy and enjoying the attention. A great cheer and clapping resounded and when they rose up together a second wave of resounding applause carried down the river and echoed from the hills. After a polite interval they sat down.

"Most of you know me. My father's shoe and boot repair shop is just down the street. Some of you may recall my campaign slogan, 'Brian Shoe maker, a shoe maker's son, give him support and see how he runs.'

Restrained laughter spread over the audience.

"Bear with me perhaps you will recall this tune." He nodded to the band that promptly belted out 'Marching through Georgia.' He raised his hands like a choirmaster. The band muted and he shouted above it. "Come on now join me. You know the words, they are in every child's song book. Hurrah, hurrah, we bring the jubilee. Hurrah, hurrah the flag that sets you free so we sang the chorus from Atlanta to the sea, while we were marching through Georgia." There was a faint compliance. "Come on now if you don't know all the words, sing the chorus. One more time, sing out for these veterans, sing out for the new monument and sing out for freedom." He stomped, jumped and waved his arms to lead the singers. This time there was a tremendous accord followed by loud acclaim cheers and laughter. The band went silent and the spectators gathered closer to the podium to hear Shoemaker more clearly. "Whew!" He swiped his brow with his handkerchief. "We folks from Minsi can really sing if we have a mind to." He waited for the crowd to quiet.

"That is a great line, 'the flag that sets you free and free' we did - NO MORE SLAVES." There was more applause. "And you know that black men were allowed the right to vote."

How do we maintain our freedom and our liberties?" He pointed to an adolescent in front of him. "Do you know, girl?"

"By voting for the right people."

"You're right. Speak up." By voting she shouted.

"Yes, by voting. I am afraid that we need another marching tune, one to bring the right to vote to the women of this country." There was a loud support from the suffragettes and their friends.

"The time has come. I want to tell you a story of another great American, familiar with war living on front at Washington DC during most of it. I wager many have heard but few have met Mary Cleary Kavanaugh, this county's most famous suffragette and quiet benefactor." He glanced at the suffragette's seating. "Mary Cleary Kavanaugh, will you please rise?"

Initially she refused then with Matilda assisting her she stood. The applause that greeted

411

her struck like a thunder. Everyone in the bleachers was standing, a crescendo of cheering, clapping and whistling. Mary had not expected the response and was visibly shaken. She leaned on Matilda who eased her into her chair.

"I didn't expect this, Mat."

"Hush Mary, sit down and enjoy it."

"You do know Mary Kavanaugh. She helped me get elected to Senator." He chuckled, "and I still get lots of advice from her. She is known through out the state for support of the women's vote."

Three years ago I visited Ireland. Mary told me to visit Listowel and the Raven's Prey pub. I was greeted and had a wonderful time. Pat Kavanaugh, who served in the war this celebration commemorates, hailed from that area. Mary's generosity reaches even there. It seems that Mary has her own private charity there assisting the ill, the widowed, and the destitute.

That should not surprise you, for down on Perch street there is a mission, a clean cot, a hot meal, for those locals down on their luck or transients in need also supported by Mary."

Brian observed the crowd was clinging to his speech. He took a gulp of water and continued." When I was in Listowel a farmer told me a British dealer bought up all of his stock at a price he decided to pay, left promising payment he never received. Mary loaned him enough money to restock his farm at a zero interest rate. You farmers out there, does Mary's assistance surprise you? Many of you had farms in foreclosure and the big city banks squeezed you for money and threatened to take your land. You went to Mary who bought those mortgages and held payment until you were back on your feet. Some of you were so broke you couldn't buy seed."

When work was hard to find how, many of us here worked on the D&H canal restoration where our kids swim and fish and skate in the winter? I worked for Mary too, repairing the road to Goshen, I knapped stone. It was hard work but I met people who have become my friends for life." He stopped and noticed that people were till attentive.

A few last stanzas and I will quit. Notice this park, the grass and benches and the picnic areas more than three acres right in the heart of Minsi. How many recall the run down tenements that used to be here? I do, they used to call them the Irish Pimple. Caffertys, Morans, O'Haras, O'Connels and O'Reilys lived here. I knew them all. Mary had the tenements razed and resettled those that still lived there and built this park.

Pat Kavanaugh helped with all the stonework. Any of you remember Pat? My mother used to say that he was like a match, scratch him and see where you light." The comment drew laughter and knowing nods from many of the assembled.

"There are so many more things Mary has done. I would be remiss if I did not mention the lying in hospital, 'The Cloister' as it is locally known. It is more than just for babies now. It started to assist women of the street and other women in need. The town might have resisted it had they known the original clientele. Mary persisted and now it is a renowned clinic, people from all over come to study it. Sara and Liam Kavanaugh operate the hospital together. Sara does the doctoring and Liam pays the bills and such. Please stand Sara and Li and be recognized." They were met with polite applause and quickly sat down."

I wish to share one final thought as we see the shadow of the monument reach away from the day before we become too nostalgic about the war it was to a large extent fought for equality. Both sides sacrificed equally and our southern states suffered untold loss in lives and property and to this day acutely feel the aftermath of the great tragedy. Many in Washington still want to punish them. I do not, but the struggle for equality goes on. And here is a secret that some of you may know. Mary Cleary Kavanaugh the great benefactor of this community was born on this very day in the state of Virginia.

Mary has done so much for all of us and now she needs your help. We are in the middle of a nation wide campaign for equality, the women's right to vote. Mary is asking for you make your mark or sign a petition that I personally with many other senators will deliver to the president. Please sign, Mary and her friends will have a table toward Perch street, I will be right here at my table with my wife and in-laws, Sara and Liam will be at the Trout avenue entrance and mayor Blum and city hall volunteers will have a table on the city hall walk. Please sign for equality and to honor our great benefactor Mary Kavanaugh. Thank you."

Applause for Shoemaker's speech resounded; he waved and pointed to the band that struck up 'The Stars and Stripes Forever' as hundreds began to line up before the benches. Mary bore up well initially to the crush of well wishers and signers but tired after the first hour. She got word to Liam who spirited her off in their auto.

"Liam I'm bushed and I need a cup of tea and some quiet before the party tonight."

"Maybe you should take it easy tonight just say hello and go to bed."

"Nonsense, I like birthday parties and I am sure not going to miss my own."

"What ever you say, you will do as you damn well please, so do it."

The evening meal began with many inquiries as to Mary's presence. Liam was about to seek her out when she appeared in the hall way. He rose to assist her. She was very pale and weak and made her way to her chair with deliberate steps and smiling all the way. Liam adjusted her chair and whispered, "Mary you don't look so good."

"I heard the same thing from your sister earlier. I am alright, if you really want to help fetch me a glass of port."

"Very well, I have some good news for you."

"Yes, "she looked up at him, "I can use some."

"Harriet Blum finished the petition count, eight hundred seventy."

"My God, Liam that is fantastic!"

"That is what I thought, happy birthday, Mary."

She grasped his hand, "is Brian Shoemaker here?"

"Not yet but we expect him any time now."

"Tell him I want to talk to him. That speech was long but he did a fantastic job."

"No, Mary you did."

Chapter 45

Kavanaugh Home
Minsi, New York
Summer 1913

Nearly a year had passed since the monument ceremony and over that time Mary did little other than answer the growing number of inquiries about the suffrage movement, local developments in particular and the national movement in general. She had help set up and fund a growing number of chapters in nearby counties. She had become quite frail but her mind was still active and her wit still sharp. Mary was propped up among her pillows looking out on the sun splashed meadows. She turned to the sound of his entrance. She wanly smiled and extended her hand toward him. Liam took her hand and sat in the chair beside the bed.

"How are you feeling, Mary? Sara said you are down today."

"Fine, better already since you're here." She released his hand. "Liam, how long have you been working for me?"

"If you start with the first book keeping, I worked for you about 20 years."

"I would like to start to put things in order. I'm not going to last forever and I want to start. What's the date today?"

"It is the thirteenth of August. And September is right around the corner, Mary," he replied impatiently. "You're going to get better, Sara said so."

"If we sold out all the holdings, how much would be the cash value?" She broke in.

"I don't know, Mary. I'd have to figure it out, but it would be a lot of money."

"What's your best guess?"

"One and a half maybe two million it could even be more. It would not be a good idea to cash out. Some must surely be invested. The Hacienda's gone, but there're still the boats, cash, real estate, I don't know. You know we have eight farms, still some Maryland property that Randolph recently sold to you and a couple pieces in downtown D.C. they could be worth a lot of money."

"If that were all sold, how much, then?"

"Maybe three million but that's just a guess. I don't really know, Mary, but I can figure it out, if you want me to."

She glanced out the window, and then turned her clear blue eyes to him. "What if we closed out? What if we offered the farms to those who are running them?"

"I don't know if they could afford them. Sell your gambling interests, then the clothing stores, all of it? It would amount to a lot of money."

"Cash it all out," Mary firmly said. "It wouldn't be that difficult, would it? Suppose we had buyers for the gambling? What about Guido?"

"He may buy you out, probably – at some sacrifice on our part. Mary, I don't know. You should invest at least a third and there are good investments out there."

"Guido would be fair."

"I doubt that, but I know he'd be surprised," Liam smiled, "and probably relieved."

"I want you to call on him; I'd like you to ask him to come here. I want to meet with him face to face."

"If you asked, he might come. Last time I saw him, he spoke about how savvy you were and how much he admires you. Giuseppe always speaks highly of pa."

"The pair of them," she smiled and looked out the window. "You see that pond out there?"

"I know the story, and the beautiful stonework and the hunting trips. Billy went out with him once or twice, he told him to give up his rifle and go with dynamite." Liam chuckled as he remembered.

It became quiet. Mary continued to contemplate the pond. "Oh, that Billy, where do you suppose he is? Why didn't he come home after he talked with you? Why doesn't he write or something? Why doesn't he come home?"

"Last time I heard of him was in that newspaper article, he was still in the Philippines I don't know where he is now."

"Yes, the medal. Did you know that...?"

"That my namesake, Liam O'Connell also won it? I've heard that story too."

"Yes, Kevin O'Connell, his second cousin, is one of our tenants. I was there when President Lincoln gave the medal to Liam. Your father once told me that he was one of a kind, a very special man"

"I know, Mary. Time seems to twist. Who would have thought that Billy would join the Army and also get the same medal?"

A heavy silence descended, each unwilling to speak. Suddenly Mary sat up, a bright flicker in her eyes and resolve engraved on her face.

"Let's do it, Liam. Let's cash out invest what you think is necessary to keep things going here. And I want to take care of everybody."

"Everybody, who do you mean everybody?"

"You, Sara, the kids, the family, I want to be sure that the money is spread evenly among you all.

Take care of the family first."

"We are already well taken care of."

"I want to put half at least if it's appropriate, into a foundation. I want to support the suffrage movement, some for girls to go to college, especially medical school. Maybe Sara will have some suggestions."

"I know she will." A deep seated excitement began to fill him.

"And money for her research," she paused. "What do you think? Can it be done?"

"Of course it can be done, if you're sure that's what you want to do."

"I want you to write something up like a will."

"A will, that is a good idea, you should write a will."

"You can do it?"

"Yes."

"Then do it."

"Very well," he resigned. "I'll do it."

"Soon, Liam," With a kindly look she regarded his face and lightly grasped his arm. "Li, I want to be buried beside your father. Will you add that to the will, and will you see that's it's done?"

"Yes Mary."

"I know you used to go to the woods where your mother is," she smiled. "Do you still go there?"

"Once in a while, I get lonely sometimes. I could have done better by her. As it was, Billy spent more time with her than I did."

"Have you taken the children there? They should know that I'm not their real grandma."

"Yes, we've taken them there, and we've told them about my mother and Sara's mother; but don't you think about bowing out on us. Those kids love you just as Sara and I do! You are the grandmother that they know. Someday, we'll tell them the whole story."

Once again she gazed out the window, separated to her own thoughts.

"Do you believe in heaven, Liam?"

"I believe there's someplace the spirits go."

"You're your mother's son." She sighed through her smile.

Liam shifted uneasily in the chair. Once more she reached out and took his hand.

"God, I miss him, Liam"

"Pat?"

"Yes, Pat. I do want to be with him again. I hope that I will be with him again."

"What do you believe, Mary?" His eyes met hers.

"That I will be with him."

"Then you will." He reassured and grinned in affirmation.

She squeezed his hand once more, looking out the window. "How long will it take to write this up? I want to put things in order."

"To write a will and to sell off all your holdings?"

"Yes."

"Not long to write a will, but selling out all of your holdings may take considerable time. It will be at least a year I think."

"I don't worry about the stores; the gambling interests are what I want done first. I know the stores are doing well and the current operators are both well off enough to buy me out. They've asked me about that in the past. "

"I think you're right. The Fifth Avenue store is doing particularly well."

"Oh, Liam, I'm so tired." She said quietly.

Liam did not reply but his eyes regarded her sympathetically.

"When can you have the will done?"

"I can do a draft pretty quickly, knowing what you want."

"Next week?"

Liam laughed. "Yes, Mary, I'll try to write it by next week. I'm glad you didn't ask for it today."

"So contact Guido – 'Geep the Bomb'." She matched Liam's smile. "Contact the tenants, if they need help, well, make it easy for them. You have a handle on all the property, right?"

"Yes, we could probably market the real estate in six months or so." He paused and carefully regarded her. "This is a big step, Mary."

"I'm not running from anything and I've been thinking it over for several months now."

"Mary, I don't think you have ever run away from anything."

She laughed aloud. "Once I made a beeline from Harrisburg, PA to Washington DC. I thought the Rebs were going to get it all; so I packed up and made a run for it."

Liam smiled, and in a slow reply said, "That was a long time ago."

"So you will contact Guido, the store managers, the tenants, the realtors and...," she resigned, "the bankers?"

"Yes, Mary."

"And draw up the will, half for the family, and half for the Foundation."

"Very well, I'll go to see Guido and ask him to come here and I'll call a meeting of the tenants, speak to the bankers, set our own local one on course and talk to shop keepers; there are already a couple of anxious realtors around the DC property."

"Next week."

"I'll start next week. It may be a year or so before it's all done. Could be even longer - Guido was in Sicily last I heard, but the bankers are around."

"Alright, let's get on with it." She released his hand and once again looked out the window. "Send the children up when you go downstairs."

"They've been at it today - Evelyn's got them under control now. I used to think that when kids got to be teen age they would be more responsible. Not so now it's what is mine and what is yours and leave mine alone. The other day they were fighting over books I will admit that Mary C is helping her mother and Billy is a fair farm hand. He sure can fix things better than I can. They don't seem to pay attention to Evelyn like we did."

Mary motioned with her hand, "And, Liam, take care of Evelyn. I don't wish her to ever want for anything so deal with her as a family member. The little house shall be hers as long as she wants it."

"Of course, I will do that."

"And Billy – don't forget Billy."

"Even though he's forgotten us," he replied with a trace of resentment.

"That's not true. It's just the way he is. I've resigned myself to it, but I don't like it any better than you do – not hearing, not knowing. True to his name he is like the lame wolf out of the pack - always wary and into himself. He is his namesake, Lame Wolf, just like your mother once said of him. If or when he comes home, I do not want him to come home to nothing."

"Yes, and you're right. That was unfair of me to say that. He sure did show up when I needed him."

She reached out and took Liam's hand again. "And you, dear Liam. I don't know what I would have done had you not been here to help me all these years."

"You would have done well, Mary, but I appreciated, always have appreciated, your confidence in me."

Mary released, and patted his hand. "I guess you have lots to do."

"I was getting bored, everything's been so quiet." He stood to leave.

"I love you, Liam. You have always been my favorite, you know."

"Mary, come on – you've treated us all equal, and you know it."

She smiled slightly and pushed a stray lock from her temple. "You'll send up the kids? Hand me that mirror, please. I can't have them finding me unprepared."

"Yes." He proffered the mirror, studied her face.

"And send up Evelyn with them. I want to talk with her."

"Yes, Mary I will tell her."

After talking with Evelyn, Liam made his way to his office and sat down heavily behind the desk. "Things are sure eerie sometimes. I wonder if she has some kind of telepathy or something. Sara and I talked about this very scenario. He leaned back in the chair, contemplated his law books, and then fished a cigar from the humidor beside him. He shook his head. "Just cash out -- next week, what the hell does she think, --I have some kind of a magic wand?" He lit the cigar, leaned back and smiled. "But it sure is Mary." The potential of the action began to work its way through his mind. He turned to the stack of ledgers on the bookshelf and selected the most recent notations. I must get started sometime; it might as well be now." He opened the large green book, picked up a legal pad and studied the first page.

Minsi
Kavanaugh Home
October 1913

Sara and Liam were both in the city and the house had a hollow feeling. August had passed on to October and the frosts and fading light had changed the landscape. Evelyn, balancing a tea tray in one hand, quietly opened the door and looked toward the bed across the room. Mary was dozing among the linens propped up by two oversized pillows. Light spilled across her lap to a colorful square on the dark floral rug. Evelyn softly closed the door behind her with the barest of clicks. Slowly she made her way to the night stand and set the tray down. Mary was settled like some bright small bird among the sheets and green comforter. She opened her eyes and smiled

"Miz Mary - I brought your tea. I made shortbread this morning, brought some of dat too."

"I knew you were baking something, I could smell it from here. I thought maybe it was shortbread."

"You need anything else, Miz Mary?"

"Oh, no but don't go, Evelyn." She sighed and adjusted her reach to the night stand. "I want to talk with you." There was sadness in her voice without a trace of her usually feisty demeanor.

"What do you want to talk about?" Evelyn smiled in an attempt to lift the gloom.

Mary lifted the cozy from the teapot. "Would you like some tea, Evelyn? There's a clean cup in the cabinet there." She paused. "Please, Evelyn, have a cup of tea with me."

"You sure about this, I have lots of work to do?" Evelyn smiled as she retrieved a delicate blue cup. "This is one of those fancy cups Mr. Woo bring."

"Nonsense - a cup's a cup. They're made to drink out of, you know."

"Yes, I knows that." She placed the cup on the tray and was about to reach for the pot when Mary plucked it up and filled both their cups.

"I was thinking just the other day. Do you remember those days in Washington?" She acknowledged Evelyn's nod of assent and continued. "We had tea together lots of times in those days in that big kitchen, especially after Donal." Her voice trailed. "We were like sisters and I still feel we are."

"I remember, Miz Mary, but only when I'se asked about it. No sense in thinkin' back. Ain't nuthin' you can do 'bout it and somethin' always raise up. Maybe you thinkin' back too much these days, Miz Mary."

Mary sipped her tea, stared out the window for a moment, and caught Evelyn's dark eyes in her own.

"Maybe," She sipped her tea. "I still miss him you know. I really loved him and I know he loved me."

"We all knows dat. Other people in this house who loves you too."

"Pat was so special." She sighed and looked out the window.

"I know dat too Miz Mary. No sense in wastin your sorrow on a wonder."

"How long have you been with me, Evelyn - how many years?"

"I don't rightly know. It's been awhile," she smiled at the lady in the bed.

"Fifty? Has it been fifty years?"

Evelyn looked out the window behind Mary and slowly passed her fingers across her lips. "Yes, I think fifty, maybe a few more, but sure fifty."

"All those years, you could have left at any time. I surely would have missed you though."

"I knows I could leave anytime. But why would I turn my back on you? You pay me well, you took me to your life and you cared 'bout me. Why would I want to leave?"

Mary smiled. "You know, Evelyn, since I've been sick I have been thinking about my will." She wiggled herself more upright against the headboard and again caught Evelyn's eyes. "I have Liam working on it and he has been given special instructions."

"Miz Mary, I don't want to hear it. I don't want to hear nuthin 'bout you dyin'. Not a word."

"But Evelyn, don't you want to know?"

"I don't wants to know nuthin 'bout it, Liam he come to me to talk, tolt him the same thing."

"Well, fifty years, you might have learned something about love and life, but I sure didn't teach you much business sense," she replied with a shade of impatience.

"I ain't expectin' any rewards on dis earth, that way I don't ever get disappointed. You been kind to me and..."

"You have been kind in turn. The whole family loves you."

"Miz Mary, you is my family. You give me more riches than I worth."

"That's not true. You never got enough so far as I was concerned. Your rewards were far short."

"You is my family like you said my sister. Your family is my family. I love Sara and those boys and the little ones like they was my own. There ain't no body else."

Mary's eyes began to blur on the large black lady with the white streaked hair. "Oh, Evelyn – you never – you could have left anytime." She snuffed her nose and drew a handkerchief from the sleeve of her flannel nightgown.

"Don't you be wastin' any tears on me, Miz Mary."

"I know, Evelyn. I know this, too, that those kids love you. Liam was so pleased when he heard my wishes; and Sara – she loves you like you were her favorite aunt. And now the grand children love you the way the Sara, Billy and Liam do. Hell, Evelyn, you are their favorite grandaunt, because you're like a sister to me."

Evelyn set her tea cup down. The tears were making streaks down her face to match those of Mary.

"Oh, Mary, I love them like they was my own. I pray for big Billy every night. I so miss him still. Rascal or not, and I'll tell you somethin' you already know – that grandchild Billy is just like him."

Mary nodded and smiled. "You remember the day father Flanagan came out to see us in

419

the church buggy?"

"And Master Billy rode out to greet him standin' on his hands on old Gray."

"And the priest's horse took a shy and ended up with a wheel in the pond."

"He didn't stay for dinner. Thought we were crazy, I guess." Mary mused with a smile.

"Oh, that Billy, He used to squeeze me so hard sometimes, I'd I lose my breath."

Both women looked out the window to the great turning clouds layered in a heavy pallet of gray. Across to the horizon there was only one light spot of sunlight, but it glowed like a coal.

Mary sighed loudly and placed her cup on the tray.
"Oh, Evelyn, I wish he would come home or write or something if he is still alive."

"Mary, I think he alive because I know if he was gone. Meantime Mr. Liam and the chillum, they is what is now."
"Sometimes I think that I did something wrong or Pat wasn't... or..."

"Bout Billy, hush, Miz Mary – Billy's Billy. He was a different kind of boy, always traipsing through the woods, shooting dis and dat; he was jest dat way."

"He surely didn't hesitate to tell you how he felt; he was too honest to live long in this life."

"He is alive, Miz Mary. I remember one day he come to the kitchen, not long before he left and he squeeze me and said, 'I love you, Evelyn,' I never felt so good." The tears welled in her eyes and she roughly wiped them away and smiled. "'Course I'd just baked some cookies and I watch while he fill his pockets, but I know he say the truth."

"That's a wonderful story, Evelyn. It sounds like Billy." She paused and looked at the flaming maples and yellow beech trees. "Another autumn, 1913 is nearly gone, hell, it's almost winter!"

Evelyn pushed up from the chair and began to gather up the tea set. "I'm gonna leave that shortbread, and you eat it. You're gettin' skinny, Miz Mary. You don't eat hardly nuthin' and I know you like shortbread, so..."
Mary smiled. "Thank you, Evelyn."

After the door shut behind Evelyn, Mary once again stared thoughtfully out the window. 'Oh, how fortunate I have been to have had so much love in my life. I had Pat and the children and Evelyn, and yes, Donal. I have had so much love, and that's what makes the difference – if I hadn't stayed open to it, I'd just be a rich whore in the Kingdom of Loneliness. I probably still would have made the money but it wouldn't have kept me from sorrow, sickness and melancholy. Oh, Pat, I sure hope you have worked things out with Donal, if I ever get to be with you." She smiled to herself, "loving two men in this life what more could I want?" She settled back beneath the covers and closed her eyes and said aloud "I should get up and get outside today, but what the hell, I really don't want to!"

A shout echoed up the stairwell, followed by the outside door banging closed. Mary rolled to her side, looked out the window spied Billy walking toward the barn with a large piece of shortbread in hand. A voice from the kitchen echoed after him.

"Damn you Billy, you didn't have to take that from my plate."

Mary smiled and resettled beneath the covers. "I wish they were all at home, who knows where the hell Billy is – if he's alive. Liam and Sara both in the city, Sara giving her report to the Medical Society convention, Liam selling off and here I am. It's funny how things change, yet are also the same. I should not have sent Liam down, but they will be home on the weekend and they needed some time together. If I hadn't insisted that he go, he would have been up here complaining about something. She adjusted to the pain between her shoulders and set them back against the pillow. "Oh, my damn rheumatism, arthritis, whatever the hell it is. It's getting cold and damp, and surely many must have it..."

She reached for the shortbread, took a bite, brushing crumbs from her bodice. She had no reason to suspect that Evelyn would be dead by winter.

Chapter 46

Minsi, New York
October 1914

The party was originally scheduled a month earlier, but Mary was not well, so the party celebrating her seventy third birthday had been rescheduled for October seventh. The big house was full with well wishers from all walks of life and the parking area outside was jammed with automobiles, parked beside horse buggies.

Inside the air was warmed by talk of war, women's rights and future alternatives for the United States. Mary, perched like a diva on one end of the long living room, was surrounded by a clutch of ladies nursing tea or brandy. The other end of the great house was filled with the overflow of dancers and men from the back parlor where Liam was holding court. A large blue cigar haze drifted from there over the dancers who were keeping pace to a lively band.

"The parade this year really made a point, don't you think, Mary?"

"Well, Anne, it surely was a lot different than what I remember in 'eighty-two'. Hell, Pat had to clear the bleachers of the men jeering us. And there were a lot of women doing the same thing. This year it was cheers instead of jeers – now that was something! I'd have given a tooth to have been able to walk in it!"

"We have so much support now! Forty men marched with us this year."

"I tell you, when Brian Shoemaker passed by wearing that big yellow bonnet. I just broke with laughter. He truly is a good natured man."

"It surely was a sight for sore eyes. We suffragettes have a lot of support and I feel it is growing. Brian Shoemaker is one of them."

"Helen, you are right." Anne Reynolds replied.

"I had hoped we would get the vote in my lifetime," Mary mused, "but I am not so sure it's possible. The lids have been lifted off hell in Europe. The fields of France are soaked in blood. I think we will have a war before the vote."

"Maybe not, mother. There are a lot of people who remember Cuba and the Philippine business. That's enough war, I think. What do you think about it, Martha?"

"Those men in Washington could do anything. We have so many more needs than another war – social ones, the women's vote, the poor, the emigrants. Let Germany and the rest of Europe solve their own problems."

"Marty, there will always be poor, and hope to God the door will stay open for emigrants; but think what a world war would bring." Mary sipped at her brandy and pointed toward the parlor. "So long as there are men running the country, there will always be shit in the wind. We not only need the vote, we need a woman in charge!"

"Mother, don't get started."

The women began to laugh, looking from Sara to Mary.

"You will have to forgive my daughter; she's having difficulty entering the arena. "She thinks I'm outrageous – which I probably am." A second round of laughter rose above the quiet waltz. Mary finished her brandy and signaled the waiter for another. "What the hell, I'm getting old, no sense in changing now," she bounced a glance off Sara's eyes.

"Well, Mary, how are we going to deal with all those men in Washington – since we can't vote yet?"

"I don't know, Helen. The secret I think is getting more sympathy from their wives. They can put the pressure on – women for women. You know, catch them by their needs."

"What might they be, or perhaps we don't want to hear," Marty chuckled.

"It's pretty simple really. Once you get beyond their ambition, it they're not all stiffed up and panting, give them a sandwich; if they are, give them what's obvious. Hell, once you catch their night-crawler you can put a hook in them."

There was a general convulsion of laughter as the small group caught up in the ribaldry was ogled by the swinging dancers.

"Mother..." Sara feigned disgust but smiled at the comment as the group's laughter became louder; even those under the blue haze looked toward the ladies.

"The trouble is, Mary, we don't even know the names of the senators' wives, so we can't get a message to them."

"Those wives should have figured out the message on their own, if they're not damn fools; women must have the right vote. They are politicians' wives and it should be obvious to them what needs to be done, if they care about voting themselves, they will find a way to enter the movement!"

"Maybe we could help organize them."

"Perhaps you're right, Anne, I've been in correspondence with a few of them but most of their men are already on our side. We need other men's support, I know it; and that's what really counts now. We need more women to write to these wives, stress how important an issue suffrage really is, and encourage them to use their influence on their husbands. That is one way. We must continue to write, not just me or the group representatives - individual letters are very important. They must know they have an active following. And we must keep the issue of women's rights before the public."

The women quieted, listening to the fading waltz becoming plaintive and then pale away. A great guffaw rolled from the parlor.

Anne spoke up. "Do you suppose they are talking about the same thing in there, only from the male point of view?" The women chuckled and looked toward the parlor.

"I don't know, Liam has drawn up a bunch of funny faces – caricatures, of mostly politicians. I bet that is what they are laughing about. You all should see them; they are really cute." Mary interjected.

"That Liam has a poison pen when he wants it to be. Once when we were in school, he drew a rather eccentric portrait of Miss Dowling and she caught him." Sara chuckled, "He went to the corner for that!"

The women laughed and after a moment Anne asked, "Do you suppose he would show them to us?"

"I think so, if we get him away from being the center of attention."

"Any of you ladies like a cigar? Liam has some nice small ones, cigarillos, he calls them. How about you, Marty? Helen? Is there anyone else? What about you, Anne?"

Anne laughed. "Only when I'm alone with you, Mary, Harvey would kill me."

"To hell with Harvey, it's my birthday. Let's all have one. Sara, go fetch some cigars and tell the boys we want to see those drawings."

The ladies joined in the spirit, nodding their assent.

"I don't think for me, Mary, I never have smoked."

"Always a first time Marty; try it, you might like it. Sara, go fetch some cigars for us, will you please?"

"You're going to cause trouble, mother," she gently scolded.

"So, what's new about that? While you're up, send Charley over with another tray of brandy."

Sara rose to leave and gave Mary a disparaging glance. "If you'll excuse me, I'll go and check in to hear what the men are saying about us." She grinned and disappeared among the dancers.

The women watched her out of sight.

"My, my, Sara is so lovely, Mary."

"Yes, she reminds me of her mother, except for her hair. When Hope - her mother - entered the room, men fell silent on seeing her. Her mother was striking and she gets more beautiful each day. Of course I am biased."

"What happened to her mother?"

"Oh, she died many years ago, Helen. Sara was just a toddler." Mary looked away over the dance floor as though suddenly pierced by thoughts of the past.

An awkward silence fell over the group, sensing that Mary did not wish to speak further on the topic. Anne spoke out after a minute had passed and knowing that the topic would bring some levity.

"You have any other suggestions about politicians?"

"My usual – they all are liars, they all can be bought, they forget their obligations to their constituents and their main goal after being elected is to be re-elected."

"I guess that about says it," a woman named Signe offered.

"And so far as I am concerned, they are just below child molesters on my scale of social desirables." Mary's comment brought another round of giggles, although a little suppressed at the imagery.

"So what do we do to get the vote, Mary?"

"Well, Sig, get enough of a crowd together so you can walk right over their shoulders and talk to the powers that be, eye to eye." Mary paused, spotting Sara approaching from across the dance floor. "It's all power, Sig. That's what they want. In a way, they are afraid of us; they want to keep us down, for we have the real power – home control."

Anne began to laugh. "And if they're all stiff?"

The comment was cut short by a crescendo of laughter at the moment Sara returned with a handful of cigars. She stepped up to Mary, and stepped back.

"Mother, are you still...?"

"Yes, dear, I am still talking suffrage, did you bring some matches?"

"I have some matches, but no drawings. I think I can get a couple when things thin out in there."

Liam was holding his audience at bay, flashing through his collection of caricatures and making comments on each.

"Here's little Nicky – the Tsar." The drawing showed Tsar Nicholas heaped with marching gear, holding a rifle drawn well oversize and appearing too much for him to carry.

"George, Willie and Nicky are all one unhappy family."

"That's right, Hal, by marriage or blood."

"The blood is flowing now all along the Marne," a guest intoned. The levity in the room faded to the war's dismal progress.

"It's a wonder the French have held. Paris was so close to going down."

"Well, General French also had something to do with that, and Petain is a tough general."

"I do believe Von Kluck would have carried the battle if it hadn't been for the British – few as they were."

"Von Kluck left his right flank open. He had to retreat or be encircled."

"Be that what it may, they're digging trenches from Switzerland to the English Channel and God know how long a siege it's going to be."

"Another good reason we shouldn't be there."

"Yes the artillery and machine guns will make it a slaughter house."

"It is a slaughter house, but maybe we should get into it now instead of later."

"Submarines – I'm hearing a lot about submarines."

"There's going to be hell to pay – even among the neutrals. Hell, none of those countries can feed themselves. They are trading with us for their very lives. It won't be long before they start sinking our ships, but business is very good especially commodities."

"Yes, you ought to get back into it, Liam. A lot of money can be made."

"No thanks, I'm cutting back. I rarely speculated with stocks and just a little with bonds and never commodities. That is a very volatile market. "

"But there're millions to be made."

"I agree those countries now at war are going to be need everything."

"Especially guns, 'munitions and food."

"Hell, a fortune can be made on wheat and corn. England will pay dearly for it, so will Germany."

"Well, gentlemen, it doesn't take a wizard to figure out how to make money on all that grief. Do you want to see some more of my drawings or are we done with that?"

"No, Liam, I want to see them all."

There was a general consensus that he continue to show the drawings.

"There are way too many; you would be bored to death." Liam smiled. "I would have done Taft, except I couldn't fit him on a single page."

Laughter greeted his acknowledgment.

"But Wilson did." He displayed a sketch of a skinny bespectacled Wilson holding a huge volume of War and Peace; below it the caption asked "Which?"

"What's going to happen with our cerebral Mister Wilson?"

"Well, he's been in for a year and we are not into the war yet."

"He talks so much about peace I don't trust him."

"It depends on what happens. If the Germans really start all out war on the shipping, we will have to do something."

"Wilson is fond of both Washington's farewell address and bulging prosperity."

"I think both are doomed to hell. It is just a matter of time before we enter the war, and there is no prosperity worth thousands of men's lives."

"We are going to end up in the middle of the greatest war in Europe, mark my words."

"Damn it! It's their problem. Who the hell in America does or should care about the archduke of Austria?"

"Li, it will be a war that will pale all others before it; the whole world is getting into it."

"We're surely not ready for that yet."

"You know the story. The press is already siding up with England. Do you recall, 'Remember the Maine – Kick out Spain' – yellow journalism? Get the press behind a cause, just or not, and they will influence the public and the world in any direction they choose."

"They're fanning sentiment for the Allies to be sure. France maybe, I could support that, but what the hell do we owe England outside of our language?"

"Too much press favoring France and England. There're a hell of a lot of Germans in America, good men and hard workers. I talked with one man recently, already naturalized, and he was fearful of what might happen if we go to war with Germany."

"They have good reason, remember the Haymarket fiasco?"

"You're right, Li. What do you think, Hal? Does the press favor the Germans or the Allies?"

"The allies I think, but in America there are more Germans than French, that's for sure, and the newspapers must recognize this."

"You should have heard my father about England." Liam interjected. "He didn't like the British at all; he was an Irish Republican to his underwear. He certainly would have condemned this press so in favor of England."

"They just want to preserve an empire without a stitch of democracy in it."

"Well, the Kaiser wants his living space – they have an empire, too."

"My father was dead against England. He told me that once, when he was a boy in Ireland, they hung a man for stealing a duck."

"I remember your father, Li. It seems he and my father once tried to break up a brawl on Perch street among some railroad strikers who were getting nasty with everyone. They were all milling around Caulfield's bar and blocked his entrance. I guess it was quite a fight. My father always laughed about it. He said he never was quite sure about what happened, but your father was the last one standing."

Liam laughed. "I heard that story, too. I think the workers had made some ethnic slur." Liam smiled." He was a little thin skinned about being Irish. He sure didn't like the British. I'm not sure I do either."

"Better than the Huns, although I am not sure if Willie the Kaiser has it all together."

"I don't know, Frank. Better than what? Kaiser, King, Tsar, none of those titles sound good to me." He rifled through the sketches he was holding. "I have one other drawing I want to show you."

"Let's see it."

"I'll be, Black Jack Pershing!"

"I drew him, because my brother knows him, he served with him a several years." Liam prepared to set aside his stack of drawings. "And if we go to war, Pershing will likely lead us."

"Wait, wait, Liam, I see one more there. Show us that one."

"It's not a caricature; it's a remembrance – just a portrait."

"Come on, let's see it."

He held up a handsome heroic-looking figure drawn in sharp, sure lines. It displayed a man with keen eyes and bold Sergeant Major stripes with a Medal of Honor on his chest.

The men were taken with the image and marveled at the strong stroked lines.

"Who is that, Liam?"

"That is my brother Billy – wherever he is."

O'Carroll Hotel
Minsi, New York
December, 1914

Three women were speaking quietly over tea in the hotel dining room.

"It's such a shame that she died so near Christmas, I'm glad there wasn't any snow for the funeral service yesterday. Did you ever see so many people? How old a woman was she?"

"She was seventy four or five, I think. I went to her birthday party in October. She sat in her chair, bright-eyed, talking away, had us all laughing – she was so outspoken refreshing some would say shocking."

"I've never been to that house before! I've never seen anything like it."

"I understand what you mean, it's pretty awesome. I've been there many times; she used to hold meetings there. Mary started the Suffragettes movement here, did you know that?"

"You're new to town, Mae, but I can assure you that had Mary known about your feelings for the vote, she would have invited you out too. She was a very kind and wise woman."

"I can't get over that room, --buried in flowers. Talk about rich – those carved walnut passageways; the bust of the lady with a veil – exquisite! Of course, the funeral and all was quite somber." She paused. "I loved the oil paintings, such beautiful English pastoral scenes."

"Oh, no, Mae, they were paintings of Ireland."

"Is that right? I thought sure that they were English Anne, are you sure?"

"Yes, I was interested in them myself; I asked Liam once – he said his parents bought them in Ireland."

"I should have known, I remember hearing that her husband was Irish. Did you ever meet him?"

"Not really to talk to, just to say hello, I saw him several times at O'Carroll's Hotel, and occasionally at Mass. He was friendly enough, but reserved."

"Yes, he and his mates used to play cards there and at Caulfield's. A giant of a man, very kind and good natured, very religious, but a hard man to shave, my Lester used to say. I remember one Fourth of July parade. He sure settled down the hooters when the suffragettes marched."

"I remember that too. What about the boys; I've heard that they aren't hers, is that true?" Mae asked.

"They were his." The woman lowered her voice. "By a Cheyenne woman, Sada I think was her name, Mary never had children. Billy, Liam's twin is kind of a wild one – lots of talk you know."

"Did you ever meet her?"

"Sada? No, nor do I know anyone who ever did." She thought a moment. "Oh, that's not true; Kevin O'Connell met her once when he was hunting. She didn't live in the house, you know, she had a Wickiup down by the river, refused to live in the house, I heard. He said she was pretty, for an Indian, and tall."

"That's strange, isn't it? That is such a beautiful big house with all those rooms. Someone said there were six bedrooms on the upper floor."

"It is peculiar, but there's no explaining Indians."

"Did you see that sitting room? Blue tile wainscot, I never saw that before. And the table setting in the reception room, two huge crystal punch-bowls —I bet they cost a dime or two. Beautiful chandeliers, leather chairs, bird's eye maple table with lace cloths."

"She was well off."

"I guess, and that library, --floor to ceiling books in those beautiful burled walnut cases."

"She added that later, I think when Liam came and began to manager her affairs. They are probably his books. But, Mary was very well read. She had a book group for awhile, but it didn't last long. The time, you know; reading takes so much time and there is so much to do."

"Isn't that the truth? I can't get over the house, that kitchen was beautiful. Cherry cabinets, I think well laid out. I'd like to have a kitchen like that. Those pots and pans so handy, lined out so orderly."

"Who wouldn't want a kitchen like that? I'll tell you a little story. She had a colored woman who ran that kitchen like it was her personal room. Evelyn her name was. It was at a suffragette meeting, I carried a plate out to the kitchen and I sure didn't feel welcome in there. Evelyn fixed me with a stare that would have turned me to stone had I not been so excited about the meeting." She paused and adjusted her purse to her other hand. "I never went back to that kitchen. She's dead now, died last November as I recall. Mary never got over her loss. She was like one of the family, I guess —Mary grieved her death to her own."

"I liked those wing backed chairs, and all the leather, --lovely lace doilies, and those window dressings, --just perfect for each room. I think they were silk."

"She had good taste."

"There were a couple rooms closed off. I saw a few of the men go in to smoke. I was very curious, but didn't venture in --the one door never was opened."

"Oh, they are the boys' rooms. The one never opened was Billy's room --Liam's brother. The one is a parlor now where the men went in; it looks out on to the porch. Liam does business there sometimes, so Lester says, at least. It is also like a studio. He draws and paints there."

"The frieze around the room —the one she was laid out in, just gorgeous, --harps, ivy, and angels. The carpet, no doubt, is Persian."

"Yes, all the carpets are Persian, --very expensive."

"And the tapestry's lovely, --just lovely. Although I don't think I would have that hunting scene over the fireplace —that fireplace, my gracious, --marble mantle and the flowers in every nook and cranny! Of course, you would expect that at a wake."

"She had such a lovely garden —beautiful flowers. Once I came by and she was out there working like a field hand, and she could well have afforded a gardener. Just about all the ladies I know have a slip or two of her plants. She liked birds, too and had a lot of very nice Audubon prints."

"Yes, a beautiful collection; did you see that tea set? All exotic birds; and such unusual silverware it must be expensive."

"The family had a Chinese friend for years. Quite a man, --I met him once at a Christmas party. He was all dressed up in robes, and fine jewelry."

"That explains the candle seats, ginger jars, and all that beautiful crockery, --I sneaked a peek into the kitchen and the breakfront is full of Chinese vessels.

"Mary had good taste and the money to display it."

"I think everyone in the county was there when we went in. The house was bulging, and the layout of the food! There were a lot of people there I didn't know."

"She had friends all over the state. Her business interests, you know."

"I must admit there were some people there who looked like overdressed criminals. A lot of the women, I would say looked – well, oddly overdressed, but there were some real fashion plates. I heard some of the men speaking Italian, but I couldn't make out much of it.

"Those Italians I've seen before. They came up every so often to meet with Liam, --the lawyer son."

"She can never be replaced, she was very generous."

"Do you have any idea how many patients have been cared for in the clinic, and how many of those don't have two coins to rub together? Many were farm families."

"She was a very kind and generous woman and from what Lester has said, drove a hard bargain."

"I guess she will be difficult to replace."

"No, Mae. She can never be replaced." But we should focus more on who she was rather than what she had. You will come to know more about her after you have been here a while."

Kavanaugh Home
Minsi, New York
December 1914

"I guess it's useless to ask you to go with me." He said with finality.

"Liam, I have so much to do; I just can't up and leave my patients."

"You mean you won't. You could but you won't. I can though right? I'm not working so; I can take the time to accompany her casket to Ireland. You could come with me."
Sara studied her hands in her lap and glanced to her husband. "No, I won't."

"But why, it would only be a couple months? You've never been to Ireland. You said you would like to visit Pa's grave."

"Li, we have gone over and over this. I'd like to go, but not now. Doc Wayland is getting old; he cannot handle it all. He just gets around now."

"Mary was more your mother than mine. Isn't there any doctor who can help? Couldn't you bring someone in? What about the advertisement for an associate? Don't you have any possibilities that you could expedite?"

"Li, there have been no women applicants. Some of the men – no, all of the men – that have applied are undesirables. The score so far is two alcoholics, one man older than Dr. Wayland, two with very questionable practices, two who were straight out and out pretenders, never even studied medicine; they were snake oil salesmen or something worse. The last one was barred from practice in the State of Pennsylvania. I just can't go to Ireland now. Do you have any idea how enormous a transgression I would be committing if I just up and left now? It would be unethical to say the least, and possibly malpractice, I could end up losing my license!"

"I imagine you'd have to kill somebody or something for that to happen; but I hear what you are saying, good help is hard to find."

"Dr. Wayland did interview another man who had some potential, but he had some very unkind words to say about women who practice medicine. Do I want to work with him? Not on your life!"

"All right, Sara, before I also say some unkind words about women who practice medicine, I'll go myself. I have to take the casket and the vault to New York, book passage to Liverpool and then to Cork. I don't know exactly what's going to happen after I get to Cork. I guess I'll get a wagon and haul it all to Listowel."

Sara did not acknowledge the comment about women in medicine – it simply strengthened her resolve. "Did you contact Pat's brother, sister, and family?"

"I sent a letter off the day after Mary died." He smoothed his forehead with his hand and fixed Sara with his eyes. "You know I'm not looking forward to this. Remember what happened the last time I visited a trouble spot? Remember Cuba and the Hacienda sale?"

"Of course I remember. Did you think I'd forgotten? And that is another reason we should stay behind. It's very risky for the whole family to travel over there together right now. Why don't you just forget about it or ship the casket and have Pat's family take care of it?"
"Because I promised Mary that I would do it, and I intend to keep my promise."
"I think, she would understand, Li."

"Well, I'm not sure about that, and I promised her." The emotions vented silenced the room and Sara leaned on the table, hand to cheek.
"I sure miss her, Li."

"So do I. I really don't like going by myself, but I don't mind going. It was one of her last wishes that I take her to Listowel."

"The children still are troubled by her death; God knows I would not want to lose you too. The seas are so unsafe; you never know when one of those U-boats will start to attack."

"I'm not going to dwell on that and I think the sooner I get started, the better." He looked at her then out the window. "You're right about the travel, kids and all."

She followed his gaze out the window, and quietly questioned, "Will you wait until after Christmas? The vault is safe in the mausoleum."

"Yes, but passage is booked for December twenty-ninth to Liverpool, so I'll have to celebrate New Year's on board ship. I've booked a state room with the White Star Line. It has plenty of room for the two of us .I don't need the space I hoped that you would join me."
"Have you booked return passage?"

"No, Sara. Shipping of all kinds is really difficult right now, so I really don't know when I'll be coming back home. It will probably take two months – at least that. I must get everything straightened out with the will and pa's family. Mary left them some money and business information. She made a couple of contracts I must straighten out; I can go on and on."

"Oh." The ticking of the grandfather clock became very apparent. Sara stared quietly at her hands and Liam studied the shadows from the clouds dappling the porch. "Li, you're not feeling much better after settling the estate. You seem so distant sometimes. Is it me, Li?"
He did not answer and continued to study the clouds passing shadows over the porch.

"You don't have a woman somewhere, do you?"

"Come on, Sara – no, and I don't want one. What the hell is the matter with you? You have said this before and you know I am tired of it. Do you have a man somewhere?"

"What do you want? There must be something."

"I want to spend more time with you and the kids."

"What's stopping you?"

"You, do you have a man somewhere, Sara?" He mocked and turned to face her.

"Of course not, I'm too busy for anything like that."

"And you're too busy for me. I can see that not too long from now I will have lots of time available. Will you?"

She did not reply and tears began to well up in her eyes. "I'm damned tired of this discussion. I have told you how important it is for me to work, my patients put great demands on me. My research is very significant and I must continue with it. I'm tired, too, Li!"

"Then why don't you just quit? Take it easy and come with me? Forget about the Clinic for awhile. It will be here when we get back."

"I can't do that! It's my patients – I have hundreds of them now. It's non-stop when I open the door to when I close it behind me."

"Ah, what the hell," Liam replied curtly and threw up his arms in exasperation. "Far be it for me to cause any additional demands." He slumped in his chair.

An uneasy silence surrounded them. From beyond the porch little Billy could be heard cajoling his horse and Mary C urging him on.
"Sara."

"Li, what? Get it out say what you want to say."

"Maybe it would be a good idea to be separated for awhile. This trip may be good for both of us."

"Maybe so, Li; your restlessness has been very evident, more so since you sold out Mary's businesses and now, Mary's death. She kept you busy, Li; I don't think you know what to do with yourself anymore. It's true. I think it is a good idea we separate for awhile and I think you need a holiday. Get away from here for a while."

"I've been away, Sara. So far as a holiday goes, I want you to be with me."

"And if that is not possible?"

"Maybe we could find another solution."

"A divorce, are you suggesting a divorce?"

"I didn't say that, nor do I want one."

"What do you say, then?"

"A separation, it would be a time for us both to think things over."

"What logic! A separation when we are already separated in our own home? Very well, suit yourself. You can book return passage earlier or later. Leave tomorrow if you like. Come back when you want to, if you want to. I am done talking about it."

Liam stared at the empty doorway and hastened to the disappearing sound of her footsteps in the hall. "Maybe I will," he intoned, although she was not close enough to hear him.

Christmas, 1914, had been barren and empty without Mary and Evelyn. Sara was sleeping in their bedroom and Liam in the downstairs guest room. Although the routines were familiar ones, the strained relationship was not easy to overcome. To avoid confrontation, each spoke little to the other and conversations were superficial exchanges of words.

On Christmas Day, Decker along with his wife and two boys, came for a dinner Sara cooked; but the day was heavy with unsaid thoughts, and its spirit limped by the absence of Pat, Mary, Evelyn and Billy who had not been heard from in several years. Woo had returned to China years before to try to piece his family back together, as the Boxers rose and fell and Western allies plundered the country. He too, had not been heard from for years. Liam guessed he had died during the purge of Western sympathizers or was killed in the uprising or shortly there after. Li and Decker separated from the others and retreated to his studio to share a smoke.

"You know Deck, life changes, --it's so difficult to hold on to what is worth it, and let go what is not."

Part IV

**Holding on and Letting Go
1915-1917**

Chapter 47

New York City and Ireland
January 1915

Liam departed New York City on December twenty ninth on a White Star liner and celebrated New Year's Day 1915, on the uneasy Atlantic. Despite heavy seas he remained well. Getting the casket and vault on board and clearing the port had been trying, but once at sea his thoughts returned to home and Sara's cold goodbye kiss. He felt tinged with sadness and guilt for what his mind projected to the future. He missed her and he was not even half way to Liverpool.

By the time he landed in Ireland, he had resolved three things. First, he would meet Mary's wishes; second, search his soul regarding the future; and third, look for a business opportunity in Ireland. He was bored despite the initial relief he felt being free of managing Mary's empire.

The graveside ceremony at Listowel was brief. Dozens of mourners attended and Mary's good works were remembered. Liam felt accepted, like a beloved cousin, his loneliness was abated and soon he settled easily into the life in Listowel and the Raven's Prey Pub. He enjoyed seeing his father's friends brighten as they spoke of Pat and the good ole days. He also met Gavin McBride and an interesting young man named Michael Collins. Two topics dominated pub conversation: the war in France and the creation of an Irish republic. Universal agreement was rare. The adage best applied was "put two Irishmen together and you have three arguments."

The casualty lists of Irish men dying for England's cause were posted in the window of the newspaper office. Many Irish saw Germany as an ally to the creation of a republic 'the enemy of my enemy is my friend.' Others hated the Huns. Home rule, through representation in the English Parliament, versus a completely autonomous republic were still hotly debated issues. Most of the men at Raven's Prey favored a true, Irish Republic.

Liam and his Uncle Tom had gone out to inspect a small property that was up for sale. They decided against the purchase, and the raw wind had licked their faces purple by the time they arrived back at the pub. Liam went to the loo, and Thomas joined the table surrounded by his regulars.

"Jesus wept! What were you doing mucking about in this weather? Have you lost your senses?" Michael Collins declared.

"I'll tell you, Michael. It was cold." Tom laughed. "That Liam's somethin' else, I was hurrying about tryin to check a boundary marker and he's just standin' there. Then he waves me over, 'give me a bump,' he says, 'I'm froze fast!'"

The table exploded in laughter, and when Liam joined them, he received a warm welcome at the table.

"Did you hear, Gavin" began to Liam, "we're in a war zone now."

"What," Liam said in surprise, "In a war zone?"

"So the Germans have decided," a man named Sean enjoined. "They have gone to war with every ship that ventures near here."

"Are you pullin' my leg?"

"He's not; the Germans have warned that after February 18th they will have immunity from any 'accidents' that might happen. I don't think you should be starting for home anytime soon. Even the sea lanes coming from America are unsafe but they have left the American vessels alone."

"There's been a lot of trouble with the U-boats, mines and such; and there's big trouble for America, they've been trading with both sides. That makes them fair game for the submarines. Did you know that English ships fly the American flag when it's convenient?"

"Sure we know that," Collins observed. "It's likely to result in a lot of American ships going down because the Germans can't tell who is what. The damned English! Our boys are going over to France, getting killed by the hundreds, for what? They'd be better off here at home, fighting against England!"

There was a general consensus about the table.

"Now is the time for Ireland to rise up and get rid of these English bastards who are so eager to tell us what to do."

"Rise up with what, Sean? Shovels and pitchforks?" Liam asked.

"I agree that it will be difficult, probably bloody but it's a time to de-anglicize Ireland."

"Pearce said, we need arms in Irish hands – the thought of arms, the sight of arms and the use of arms."

"Home rule is still a possibility and it's not so bad; a compromise that gives us some voice is better than blood in the streets." Gavin enjoined. "Pearce is a determined leader but what is the price for a republic?"

"I think the crack of a rifle speaks louder than words, and its message will be clear." Collins retorted.

Liam sensed that the conversation was beginning to take on hostile airs. "Do you know how much of this talk I've heard – my father, Tom, and all of you? I heard it for thirty years! Why don't you do something about it or stop talking about it? The Irish Republic – I've heard that theme all my life. Now there is a great war with thousands dying every day, isn't that enough blood shed for all of us?"

It became quiet around the table. The strident tones diminished to an uncomfortable silence. Liam felt all their eyes upon him. Then he stood up and smiled broadly. "Let's have a drink – it's on me." He added in a more hushed tone to his table mates, "I'll stand a round for the Republic!"

For the first time in many years, Liam felt that he was at the center of something important; that his opinion counted and was valued. He read any newspaper available, whether it was Irish, English, or American. The war seemed so close yet far away. It raged just a short way across the channel, at times the war news was equaled by republic rumors. He spoke to those returning from the front whenever he could and visited Cork, a hot bed of information on the war abroad and the rebellion within.

Kinsale Ireland
April 1915

Ireland was an exciting place to be but Listowel did not present any business interests for Liam, so on April seventeenth, the day the second battle of Ypres got underway; Liam made his way to Kinsale where Gavin McBride's cousin Mick had placed his fishing and refueling business up for sale. After two days of negotiating, Liam purchased the business and offered Mick a salary to stay on. Li developed seamanship skills with Mick as his tutor and tested them at every opportunity.

Liam enjoyed working the small netter; setting and hauling the nets tested his strength and resolve. He soon began to master stiff winds and tides and occasionally, on a quiet sea, they would offload the nets and go out with rod and reel, wandering close to the great sea lanes plied with ships and enjoying a day of sport fishing. On one occasion they were able to approach an American freighter and purchase some barrels of diesel fuel. Liam felt rather like a pirate, even though he had paid for it, and discovered that smuggling not only paid off but was exciting to boot.

May 7, 1915 began like many other days, with strands of fog that were dissipated by a light breeze. This weather was much different than the blustery week before, and the calm sea, smooth as a mirror, was a welcome sight. Liam and Mick were planning to go sport fishing and they had checked their gear the night before, had dinner together and vowed to get started by dawn. They were making their way toward Seven Heads, a fishing spot that was know for plentiful Pollock and cod, when they found themselves drifted over a ball of mackerel. They were so busy pulling in fish that they didn't see the great liner with the black smokestacks when it first heaved into view.

"Hey, look there Liam, that's a liner for you!" Mick nodded toward the distant vessel.

"Wow that is a big ship; can you make out her name?"

"I think it's the Cunard Lusitania; no red funnels, all darkened up for war. But, it's a Cunard alright and it most certainly is the Lusitania. She's a beautiful thing."

"What do you say we head back in? We have enough fish for everybody we know."

Mick laughed, "And for a few we don't."

Mick busied himself with the engine and struck a parallel course with the great liner following a few miles behind her. The ship had nearly faded from sight after rounding the Old Head of Kinsale as Mick reset the course for their approach to Kinsale harbor. Both men were looking ahead when they were startled by the sound of an explosion, followed by a second larger boom; it from the direction of the Kinsale lighthouse which they had just passed a short time before.

"Holy Christ" Mick exclaimed. "What the hell was that? Look at all that smoke!"

Liam grabbed up the binoculars and looked toward the lighthouse.

"My God, Mick they've struck the Lusitania! She's going down they're trying to launch boats! Let's get the hell out there! Full speed ahead, Mick --at full speed!"

Mick jerked the boat about as Liam looked into the binoculars, giving a running account of his vision.

"They're trying to launch boats! They're goin' over – my god, my god – they're hanging on the davits. Boats are capsizing. There're people in the water. They're swarming – the water's full of people. The rail of the upper deck is level with the sea – she's goin' down, she's going down! Hurry, Mick, hurry!"

"We're goin' as fast as we're gonna go!"

"She's sinking' by the bow – she's up on end."

"Saints preserve us!"

The great ship's bow went under as the stern rose and she struck bottom, the giant brass propellers could be seen glinting in the sunlight, then she started her final slide. There were hundreds of bobbing heads in the water and in the debris field spreading around the stricken ship. The floating mass contained remains of boats, crates, rafts, desk furniture, clothing and plants. The Lusitania's lifeboats were swinging like baleful toys on their davits as the ship slipped under. The water was boiling with frantic swimmers, twisting and grasping, their screams for help drifted over the sound of the waves. Many were trying desperately to avoid being sucked into the huge maw of the funnels or snared in ropes, funnel stays, and aerial wires. Both Liam and Mick could feel, as well as see, the terror driven scene.

"There are a lugger and a tug out there closing in," Mick observed. "They're picking up some swimmers. Bear starboard. I see people in the water."

The first humans they spotted were drowned, bobbing like buoys, and Mick maneuvered the boat toward a naked woman still weakly swimming. He extended the long handled net to her and the two hauled her into the boat. Liam immediately wrapped her in a blanket and propped her inside the cabin. Mick netted another young man covered him with their remaining blanket and set him in the cabin beside the woman. They rescued two more women and wrapped them in their jackets.

By now, there were several more boats picking up the swimmers. Mick had grabbed the hand of another man and tried to pull him aboard, but lost his grip and the man slowly sank from sight.

Liam took out his flask of whiskey and guided it to the lips of the first woman they had rescued. She sipped at it and gagged, vomiting up sea water. He made his way among the other three; the faces of the women were stark with shock. The man was sitting with his eyes closed trying to control the shivers that wracked him.

When he returned to the rail he drew back in shock. Mick was hoisting a dead child aboard. With in minutes, they collected seven bodies and placed them on the deck.

"We have to get these people back; I don't see any more swimmers. We'll come back later. Those people in the cabin are going to go into shock. They'll be dead before we get them back. How far out are we, Mick?"

"Twelve, fifteen miles, I think."

"We've got to get goin. There's nobody out there alive that I can see."

"You're right, Li. Those other boats will get any that are left."

"I've never seen anything like this." Li shook his head in despair.

"Torpedoed, who would have expected it within sight of Old Head?" Mick swung the boat toward Kinsale. "God, she sunk so fast, I can't believe it! I can't believe it! The war is too goddamned close!"

"We've got to hurry, Mick. These people are in a bad way." Liam quickly took stock of the passengers.

The small fishing boat began to pick up speed and lunged ahead. Liam hurried to the passengers cuddled together in the small cabin. The one woman implored him to hasten without a word and settled back trying to contain warmth.
"We're going in as fast as we can. We will soon be ashore, try to stay warm."

"My husband..." one of the women began. "My husband was right beside me." Tears welled up and she lowered her head to her hands.

"We only picked up this gentleman," he nodded toward the man buried in the blanket, "but there were other boats out there, one with a string of life boats full of people. You must not give up hope. He's probably in one of those boats. What's your name?"
"Helen."

"Helen we will get you in as fast as we can." Li glanced up and saw other boats arriving. He felt a surge of relief and turned again to his shivering passengers.

"I am so cold." She was blue and shaking.

"I'm sorry –I can't do much," he whispered helplessly. "We weren't prepared for this." He looked at the first woman they had wrapped in the blanket, her eyes were glazed and she was slumped against the cabin wall. Liam studied her closely – she was dead. He removed the blanket from her and placed it on the other women. "Cover yourself as best you can."

"Oh, she has no clothes", the woman observed.

"She's past caring, miss. I'll take her out of here."

"Suddenly a second woman blurted, "Oh my God! Oh my God there were people all around me going under the water. They were trying to hold on to me I pushed them away and they went under. I couldn't help them, I couldn't help them."

"I know it was terrible, but you had to save yourself or they would have dragged you under too. What is your name?"

"Joan," she whispered, Joan Connors."

"You're an American?"

"Yes."

439

"So am I." He began to adjust the blanket. "Joan, you and Helen share this blanket as best you can. What is your name?" --he asked the man whose teeth were chattering, and barely in control of his emotions.

"Harold Unsert, I was bringing my son to England. His mother's waiting in Liverpool. What will I say? He's not with me I had to throw him into a lifeboat that was being lowered. Someone caught him, but I think the boat went over." He began to sob.

"Harold, there're more boats out there besides than this one. They have already picked up swimmers. Don't lose hope; your boy may be on one of those." The visage of little Billy, Mary C, and Sara crashed into his awareness. He looked back at the sea swarming with boats and a large debris field. There was a great empty space where the Lusitania had slipped from sight. He shook his head in disbelief as a great loneliness, tinged with anger, rose within him. "This tragedy cannot be comprehended because it's beyond it," he explained to himself; "beyond belief!"

He once more moved to assist his cowed, trembling companions and a surge of remorse rushed through him. He took a draught from his flask and passed it on to Mick. Gently he dragged the body of the naked woman to where the dead lay. The bodies had slipped across the deck, lying akimbo at all angles. Liam pulled the bodies to the outside cabin wall. He looked about the boat; no tarps were on board. In gesture more than effect, he laid two large coils of rope on them, all the cover that was available. He silently recited a prayer taught to him by his mother. 'Great spirit that invests all life, take these souls to your keeping' he added 'when you return them be gentle, for they have had great despair in this life.' He stepped inside the cabin. "Mick, how are we doing?"

"Fifteen more minutes, but there is a tug over-taking us".

"Maybe they'll have some spare blankets. We are damn near out of fuel. We'll be lucky to make it in at this speed."

Liam reviewed the survivors, blue from the cold, one with her eyes rolling backward. "Jesus, Mick, they're not gonna make it. We've got to get them in; we can't slow down.

Liam focused on the approaching tug and began to wave his arms to attract their attention. Its deck was jammed with huddled figures in blankets and a ominous pile of bodies stacked along the rails. The tug drew within hailing distance and Liam directed Mick to guide their boat to the starboard side.

The tug, named Flying Fish, slowed and the skipper's voice boomed over the water. "You there on the Mary C, have you been to the Lusitania?"

"Yes, sir, we have three alive, eight bodies; we need more blankets. I'm afraid we will lose the rest. Can you take them?"

"Stand by, Mary C. We can't take them, but we have blankets. The tug Captain skillfully maneuvered the boat. The steady sea allowed them to toss three blankets to Liam. "We can spare the blankets but have no room. Head into Queenstown, they're waiting." The tug pulled away and Mick revved the engine and headed the boat toward the still invisible dock.

Liam made sure each passenger had a blanket, then took the vomit stained one and placed it over the bodies beneath the coil of rope. For a moment he studied the naked woman in bluish repose. Again he thought of Sara and wondered how she was and he felt a great sense of loss. He realized he was trembling like an ash tree. He ducked back inside the cabin and settled behind Mick. The passengers were huddled beneath their blankets with vacuous looks. Harold was sobbing and Joan moaned in pain; the other woman was silent.

The enormity of the tragedy descended like darkness. When they reached the Queenstown

440

pier, stretcher bearers removed the dead and the three survivors melded into the grim procession of others who had recently arrived half clad, soaked, shivering and disheveled by their bout with the sea. Local citizens were taking many into their homes; women wept, and others ran rosaries through their fingers. Men were bearing stretchers into a makeshift hospital.

Liam and Mick took in the scene, the Town Hall was serving as a morgue and its hallways and rooms were fast filling with the dead.

"This is bad, Liam, this is so very bad. We were lucky to make it in. We have to fuel up if you want to go back out."

They turned to a heartbroken shriek. A mother had just been presented the body of her daughter.

Liam swallowed back his tears as Mick, transfixed by the scene, began to sob openly. Liam put his hand on his shoulder.

"Let's get the hell out of here, Mick; enough is enough! We can't do anymore out there, let's fuel up and head for home. I sure hope that Harold finds his boy alive."

"I have no words for this. I can't believe my own eyes!"

They made their way through the havoc and back to their boat. Mick sat solemnly in the cabin as Liam backed and loaded some fuel. He steered to the southwest and headed away, following the coastline. I've had enough of this day." They made slow, steady progress toward the lights of Kinsale.

"This goddamn war is getting too close, Mick. Too goddamn close!"

There was no reply from behind him. He set his jaw and steered their way to port.

Kinsale Ireland
May 1915

On May eighth, the whole world new about the Lusitania. Wires were alive with the stories as the morgue in Queenstown grew with the lines of the dead. The grim total was not yet known, but ultimately it would reach 1,198 lives lost: 127 Americans, 79 children, 39 of which were infants. About 200 corpses were recovered from the sea; the rest were interred there forever.

Liam and Mick were out with many other locals who still searched for bodies in the miles-wide debris field and on the beaches. Salvage of the passenger baggage and valuable cargo also was going at a rapid rate.

"There're a couple suitcases floating to starboard, Mick. Do you see them?"

"Yes," the reply was matter-of-fact.

"Well, let's pick them up."

They hooked the luggage aboard and continued their slow crisscross of the edge of the mass of floating wreckage.

"You don't want to open any of these, do you, Li?"

"Nope, we will gather up what we can and take it to Queenstown. God knows the people that belong to this stuff have suffered enough." He paused, but Mick did not acknowledge his remark. "Can you believe what happened? I still can't."

"I don't know. It's such a tragedy, think of all the families and how this must affect them."

"It's a goddamn waste is what it is! It is like the war. Did you hear young Lowry was killed last week?" He guided the ship at a slight angle. "What the hell is that?" He pointed to a huge and layered bobbing bundle.

They drew up beside it and Liam hooked it to the side of the boat.

"What the hell is it?"

"I know what it is; it's beaver pelts."

"There must be more than a hundred of them."

"Beaver pelts? I've never seen one before."

"I've never seen so many, but my brother caught a few when we were kids."

"What do you want to do with these pelts?" Mick slowed the boat and let the engine idle, and his place beside Liam.

"I don't think the water has ruined them."

"I say we take them aboard. It's not like they belong to anybody, like the luggage, and now these are salvage, someone in Dublin will surely buy them."

"They belong to somebody, but on the other hand, its salvage – right?"

Mick smiled. "I don't know technically yes, but those hides sure don't belong to anybody I know."

Liam laughed. Then they both began to cackle like a roost of hens. Their laughter drifted over the water and carried its way toward the shore. "It's some catch," Liam burbled. "It would have taken my brother ten years to get this many. Beaver pelts in the middle of the Atlantic—I can't believe it."

The solemnity was broken, the sadness dissipated. It was time to let go of the tragedy and move life along.

Minsi, New York
May 1915

Sara sat alone in the small office near the entrance to the Cloister Clinic, as it was locally known. She was waiting to interview a new doctor; Henry Fowler who had replied to her ad in the Union Bugle newspaper. It was the third response she'd had in a week, although the other two should not have bothered to call. She was slowly turning through a pile of patient records when there was a sharp knock on the door.

"Come in," she responded. The door swung slowly open, and standing before her was a man about six feet tall with dark hair and dressed impeccably in a blue pinstriped suit with a high collared white shirt and a navy tie with dark red stripes. His black brogans were shined mirror bright.

"Dr. Kavanaugh, I am Doctor Henry Fowler. I called you yesterday." He fixed her in his deep green eyes partially shaded by long dark lashes.

Sara was taken aback. "Oh my! I guess I must have lost track of the time, I didn't expect you for another hour." She felt slight embarrassment due in part to her thoughts about his handsome appeal.

"I was in town and we did say morning? Another hour would be near midday," he smiled.

Sara recovered her composure, stood up, and extended her hand. "I am pleased to meet you."

Fowler took her hand and kissed it lightly, looking into her eyes as she smiled in response. "He is too charming and handsome to be real," she mused silently to herself.

"I have heard a great deal about you, Doctor Kavanaugh. You are quite a celebrity in some circles."

"Well, thank you, doctor. I don't know to which circles you refer, but I do hope they are commendable ones."

"Indeed they are," he smiled in reply.

For the first time Sara noted a bruise by his eye, and a small nick on his chin she guessed was a shaving accident. She returned to her chair and motioned for him to sit in the chair beside her desk.

"Well, Doctor Fowler, please tell me about yourself and why you might be interested in coming here to practice." Sara adjusted the edges of her lab coat closer together.

"Your advertisement indicated you were seeking someone with obstetrical experience – which I have had, and also I am interested in research. I read your paper on black Cohosh it was very well written. A neat controlled study, arguably the best research, certainly the best written report, in the New England Journal for some time. Equally surprising you are a woman and a very attractive one."

Sara felt a blush spreading from her ears and into her cheeks. She glanced at her watch.

"Thank you, doctor; I think women are better qualified to resolve women's problems. I trust that you do not harbor any resentment of women practitioners?"

"I assure you that I do not. Your research speaks for itself; male or female, it was well done."

Sara felt pleased by the compliment, but tried to appear casual, as she looked down and folded the patient records; she turned back to Fowler, his dark green eyes locked on her with an uncomfortable power. "Would you like to look around? I've already done rounds this morning except for a few patients in what we refer to as the second ward – mixed complaints and problems. They're all women and it's a good place to start. There's an extra lab coat on the door there. I'll explain things as we go along."

Fowler donned the lab coat and the pair made their way down the quiet hallway.

"How did the Cloister Clinic get started?"

"My stepmother created it more than thirty years ago; it was more like a private retreat then. When I finished med school I came back here to help out for a while and ended up staying; the place has grown steadily ever since. We have adjusted to the growth of the community although still primarily a maternity hospital; we do see a few male patients. We now have 80 beds, and plans in the works to expand to100. You, no doubt, saw the construction on the way in."

He nodded in assent and they proceeded down the hall. "Is your stepmother...?"

"She died last December and bequeathed a very generous endowment to the clinic. We'll finish the addition, actually a new building, later this year."

"Sounds like a remarkable and altruistic woman."

"She was all of that and much more too."

"If I may be so bold as to ask, are you married, Doctor Kavanaugh?"

"Yes, and we have two children, a boy and a girl. My husband is away in Ireland right now." Sara knew the moment she had uttered the comment that she had made a mistake. "He took mother's body there for internment," she added.

"I see," Fowler replied, looking a bit puzzled.

"Well, we're here. This is the second ward. Come in."

Fowler opened the door for her and touched her gently on the back as she passed through. Sara approached the first bed that contained a teenager, beautiful but wane, with dark circles beneath her eyes, a trace of jaundice.

"Your patient, doctor," she smiled, gesturing toward the bed.

Fowler picked up the chart from the foot of her bed and reviewed it carefully before addressing the patient. "Well, young lady, what seems to be the difficulty here?"

"I'm real sick, doctor. Some bad pains here." She placed her fingers on the right side of her abdomen, beneath her lower ribs." I was awful sick to my stomach and I had bad." She appeared embarrassed to continue.

"Diarrhea," Fowler finished her statement and draped her with the blanket as he carefully lifted her gown to expose her abdomen. Palpating gently from side to side, he noted her flinch as he pressed in the upper right quadrant. "When did this pain begin?" He quickly scanned the chart – "Annie?"

"A couple days ago; I bin so tired lately and didn't want to eat nothin', then I got sick to my stomach and threw up. I felt real hot so my ma brought me here." She added in dismay, "my pee is dark brown and I'm yellow!"

"Well, young lady, I think you're going to get a bit more yellow than you are now. It will be just about that time when you start feeling better."

"It will go away, won't it?"

"Oh yes, it will go away." He adjusted her gown and blanket. "Did you eat anything away from home the last couple weeks?

"No," she hesitated, "we went to the church picnic though, a couple weeks ago. I remember we had a lot of fun. I didn't feel sick or nothin and I ate a lot."

"Anybody else get sick at your house?"

"My brother Carl got a little sick, but he's better now. I want to go home."

"Annie, I think you ought to stay here and rest for a few days until you're feeling better. You are going to need to take it easy for several weeks, just think, you'll get out of chores for awhile." Fowler passed the chart back to Sara and they stepped away from the bed to confer.

"She has hepatitis, and if I guess you're about to receive some more patients with the same malady."

"My thoughts exactly, doctor. As a matter of fact, we had one more admitted this morning."

"Probably the source was at the church picnic. Depends on how many were there and who ate what."

Sara smiled. "You did very well with that girl, Doctor Fowler; very nice bedside manner."

"Thank you. I consider that a great compliment coming from you."

"What would you suggest for treatment?"

"In this case, ammonium chloride and some calomel might help."

"Well, doctor, ammonium chloride is appropriate, but she will likely recover without it. We have an herbal tonic that we have used made from milk thistle that grows in abundance around here. The Indians used it for jaundice. It's been used in Europe as well but we make up our own concoction. They completed the rounds of the second ward and made their way back to the office.

"You said you had practiced in Buffalo?"

"Yes, I have a letter here."

"Where did you go to medical school?"

"I attended Jefferson in Philadelphia."

"My." Sara glanced at the letter and returned it. "It appears you were well regarded. Why did you leave?"

"Oh," he replied absently, rubbing the small mar on his chin. "It was time to leave. I was actually on my way to New York City when I read your ad; --it was entirely by accident. The newspaper headlines caught my eye and then I found your ad. I prefer the city, but I freely admit I would like to work with you. I recognized your name because I read your paper on cohosh and I was impressed."

"So you said," Sara responded thoughtfully. She was tempted to ask about the bruise, but dismissed the idea.

"I have a partner –an older gentleman, Dr. Weyland. He comes in the afternoon, I'd like him to meet you, I'm sure he will approve of your credentials, and I'll offer my comments."

Fowler regarded her curiously. "Should you offer me the position and I choose to practice here, what are the details?"

"Oh, yes – salary and such. We will pay $20.00 per day for a six day week, 7 am to 4 pm –on call, of course, in emergency. It is rather isolated here, so we include some amenities. We will provide you with quarters, breakfast and lunch –the patient's fare, and an automobile that you may use." She paused, gathering her thoughts. "We have tennis courts, the local tennis club meets here on Fridays; and there is some fine fishing and hunting if you're interested. We have some riding horses, and also a number of walking trails. I think you would find this clinic an excellent place to work, and the surroundings relaxing."

"May I see the quarters, please?"

"Yes, of course, they're in the house just over there," she pointed through the window. We currently have a couple of nurses staying there, but that will change very soon. I neglected to ask, are you married, Doctor Fowler?"

"Please call me Hank, and the answer is no; never have been, but maybe some day. I've practiced in a number of places, moved a lot and never seemed to find time to get married. I prefer the city but, as I said, this opportunity is a very appealing one. I am especially interested in the research that you are doing here."

"Well, there is certainly plenty of research opportunity for us both here, I've merely cracked the jar," she smiled. "There's so much more. I plan to study some other Indian remedies for their efficacy."

"An interesting opportunity, I agree. I am curious about native medicine but never studied it."

"Shall we look at the quarters, then? I think that you will find them satisfactory. However, if you would prefer to live in town, there are a number of rooming houses with excellent accommodations. There is one room still unoccupied. The nurses will be here for a week or two more, before they can move into their new quarters in the new wing. Then you will have the whole house to yourself."

He slipped out of the lab coat, returning it to its peg and assisted Sara with her coat. Dr. Wayland reviewed Fowler's credentials though a concerned by the missing information about past practice gave into the exigency of need for another provider. He was not as impressed as Sara and suggested that they should inquire into his past activity and suggested probationary employment. Fowler accepted.

Kinsale, Ireland
August 1915

"Do you have any idea why Gavin wants to see me?"

"No, not exactly, I think I do, but I don't know. I really don't."

"All right, Mick, we will take the truck. It's about time I went to see Tom and the kids anyway." Liam smiled. "I sure do like those boys."

"It's done, then and we will go?"

"It's done. When do you want to leave?"

"You know there's to be a big 'ceilidh,' there always is on Friday night. Sure, you will hear the best music Ireland has to offer."

"That may well be, but we need to get things in order before we go. Any boats due for fueling today?"

"Only ours," Mick picked at his nose, examined the gray flake and flicked it aside. "If anyone comes the Finnegan lad will take care of them. I will talk to him before we leave." The idea of going to Listowel appealed to him and there was a slight tint of impatience in his reply.

"I suppose we can go today then, we can stop at Cork on the way back. We need some refitting supplies. I have a list at the office and I have to finish a letter to Sara, I'm not sure she has received any I've sent."

"You haven't heard from her?"

"No." A look of concern creased Liam's forehead and knotted between his eyes.

"Ah, she's busy and probably has other interests. She works all the time. Our disagreement over time is one of the reasons I decided to stay here, and I'm sure not planning to go home until I hear from her."

"Aye, Liam, best not to rush off anyway, there's so much trouble right now, and there may be trouble crossing; the U boats are busy!"

"Yeah, there was a Zeppelin raid on the coast again, the Russians are in full retreat from Poland and the lid is off hell at Gallipoli; lots of trouble."

"So when do we start for Listowel?"

Liam fished his watch from his pocket. "We might as well have lunch. I'll finish my note; in about an hour or so."

"I will get word to Joe Finnegan." He smiled, "can I drive?" Mick asked hopefully.

"You know, Mick," Liam petulantly rejoined, "sometimes you are a pain in the ass."

"I take that as a yes."

"The first twenty miles, then we will see if you can keep us on the road. Remember the last

446

time?" Liam smiled inwardly for there was only one thing more that Mick enjoyed doing more than driving a boat, and that was recklessly driving the Model T Ford truck Liam had purchased for the business. "You know Mick, it doesn't do any good to talk to the truck, you still have to steer it. Learn the pedal for reverse and you will not need to talk to it or push it around."

They drove to the Raven's Prey, without incident, just as the long soft evening was slipping toward dark. The streets were crowded with donkey carts and people thronging the square. Motor vehicles were still a bit of an oddity, and several children gathered around the Model T, eagerly exploring it. Inside the pub, lively music greeted them and they spotted Gavin drinking with his friend, Jim O'Hara, and two other men at a corner table. Liam did not recognize them at first; Gavin waved them over.

"Liam you know Jim. Do you know Michael Collins and Tom Barry? They're' both hard line Republicans."

"I know the Mr. Collins was in a discussion with him when I first arrived. Tom introduced me." Liam extended his hand.

Collins shook hands, and abruptly turned to Gavin. "Can he be trusted?"

"Trusted? Trusted I guess, --he's Kek Kavanaugh's grandson, --Pat's boy. They've had more time in Republican causes than you, young Collins."

The big man lapsed into silence and fingered a pack of cigarettes, on the table.

Liam laughed. "What the hell are we doing, planning a revolution or something?"

"Since 1911," Barry enjoined.

"So what happened in 1911?" He asked, a bit surprised at the answer.

"That's when 'Home Rule' was last turned down in Parliament and the Republic was traded for greed."

"That was 1911; you look as nervous a fresh fucked fox in a forest fire!"

Laughter ensued, and the tension broken. A round of Guinness was delivered. Liam leaned back in his chair smiling benignly; acutely aware he was in a situation with grave overtones. Suddenly it dawned on him; he queried, "so you ARE planning a revolution?" He reviewed the grave faces. "What does it have to do with me? Why the hell did you invite me here?"

"Since nineteen thirteen the 'Oglaigh Na L Eireann' has been active."

"Excuse me, Mr. Collins, but what does that mean? I don't speak nor understand Irish."

"In English – the Irish Volunteers were established."

"And?" Liam inquired.

"It is a nationalist organization devoted to the integration of Ireland, the preservation of Irish culture and the defense of Ireland's territory."

"And harmony and peace, I suppose? He scoffed. "You still haven't answered my question. --what am I doing here?"

The men about the table did not speak and the tension returned. Liam shifted uncomfortably in his seat.

"Liam, your father, 'may he rest in peace,' left here many years ago because he struck a blow for those who suffered at the hands of the English."

"I know the story, Mr. Barry, and I also know how adamant he was about an Irish Republic. But isn't there enough trouble to go around these days?"

"It is precisely the time to reassert the Republican ideal," Gavin interjected.

"Because the allies are gettin' their ass kicked, take advantage of the moment, --that's it, huh?"

"Yes," Collins brought his hand down hard on the table. "You can't help but see the conditions here. For Christ sakes, man, you're an American! Can't you see, feel and identify with what's going on here the heavy hand of Great Britain, the poverty of the people, and the persecution?"

Liam scratched his head, took a long drink from his glass. "I didn't think there was anybody being persecuted."

"There's no freedom here, you are so used to it, and you don't even see it missing?" Barry added with a twinge of disgust.

Collins did not reply immediately, then spoke adamantly. "There are hundreds of Irishmen in jail at this very moment; many of them don't even know why they are there. They are incarcerated while their brothers, uncles and cousins are bleeding and dying for the empire that put them there." Collins turned in his chair and pointed toward two men talking together across the crowded room. "Those two men are British spies –they are everywhere. Those two are shadowing me. Of course we have our own informers, --traitors too."

Liam's eyes followed the gesture.

"If that's the case, I'm probably going to be on somebody's list."

Collins smiled. "You already are, and were from the day you arrived."

A man who had not spoken leaned forward. "I've seen a list of people of interest to the crown, Mr. Kavanaugh, and you are on it."

"Gavin spoke. "What do you mean, Liam is on a list?"

"My cousin James is a very reliable source Gavin, I'm sure they flagged his name when he entered the country." Barry replied.

"Just great, I haven't done anything so to hell with their list!" Liam drained his glass, caught his nephew's attention and signaled another round.

"I have a proposition for you, Mr. Kavanaugh. It is offered in supreme confidence. Do you wish to hear it?" Collins asked.

The ardor of the men and their strict attention caught Liam's attention. An uneasy feeling was spreading inside him. He fought the impulse to stand up and walk away.

"Will it put me in harm's way?"

"Possibly."

"Is it illegal?"

"Exceedingly so."

Liam edged back in his chair as the second round of Guinness appeared. He slowly turned the glass on the table, lifted it and looked at Collins." Will it involve murder?"

"No." Collins fingered his cigarette package and flicked it aside.

"If I say no?" Liam replied.

"Then it is no, and nothing further will be said. All we ask is that you keep the conversation in confidence."

"It won't get you off the list Liam," Mick explained.

Liam glanced toward the two men across from him and back to the other faces. Gavin alone appeared anxious; the others were expressionless.

"You're sure about this list?" Barry nodded assent. "Well, that being the case, might as well be hung for a wolf as a sheep;" he thought for a moment. "All right, let's hear it."

"We are planning a rising, probably early next year and we are very short of weapons. Do you remember our first conversation when the question of arms came up and we talked about Pearce?"

"Vaguely, already this conversation doesn't sound too good," Liam observed.

"We have managed to purchase a number of rifles from Germany. The first consignment, relatively few, is already underway. A large consignment will follow."

Liam observed Collins carefully and glanced around the table; the looks had changed more to interest. He felt a small chill of excitement rising within him.

"You have studied navigation?"

"I know the rudiments; Mick and I can usually figure things out."

"If you were to have precise coordinates, could you find them at sea?"

"Probably, if not exactly, very close; I'd need to study the charts, but I don't foresee any problems there."

"Yes or no, are you familiar with navigation?"

"Yes, I could find them." Liam straightened in his chair, his curiosity now on full throttle.

"The rifles – and ammunition – are aboard a U boat and will enter these coordinates on August 15." Collins passed him a scrap of paper. "She will surface at exactly ten p.m."

"Wait a minute; you want me to make a rendezvous with a German submarine?"

"Yes, at ten p.m. on August 15."

"You know, Michael, I do not have much regard for U boats or the Germans."

Collins smiled. "Politics makes strange bedfellows."

"Why me, I'm no politician? One of these days I'm going to go back home."

"We thought you might be sympathetic to our cause." Collins looked across the table at Gavin, who adjusted uncomfortably before his gaze. "You have some experience and you're an American."

"Where the hell did I get all this experience? I understand the American part, alright. If I am caught they will deport me or throw me into jail. I've been in jail and I didn't like it much either." They would hang you. "

Collins smiled. "True, we also know you have dabbled a bit in smuggling diesel fuel and gasoline."

"You mean the American freighter Mick and I bought fuel from? The ship was dead in the water with a steerage problem; they offloaded thirty drums. That's not exactly smuggling."

"Nor was it quite legal."

"I'm a lawyer, for Christ sake, I didn't do anything illegal. Although I'm not sure if it belonged to somebody else, I didn't ask; I paid for it and that was that."

"Then there were two hundred or so beaver hides," Jim added.

"That was salvage. I've got this strange feeling it's not just those two men over there I have to worry about." His irritation was obvious as he canted his head toward the table by the wall.

"We have our ways, Mr. Kavanaugh." Barry rejoined. "You now know a lot about our activities."

The table silenced to a lively Irish reel that seemed about to burst the building. Some young dancers were stamping their way through it.

"You have yet to answer my question. Yes or no? We will pay you for the use of your boat."

"I don't want any pay," he wagged his finger in vigorous negation; "here are my conditions: I will do it this one time and that's it! ONCE, and call me Liam."

The tension at the table dissipated into the lively reel. And for a moment the attention turned to the musicians.

"Excellent then it is agreed. "Tom, Jim, Gavin, let's get along. We have other business this night."

"Wait a minute; what the hell do you want me to do with them? He lowered his voice, —the rifles, --when I get them from the submarine. I don't want to keep them very long."

"Gavin will provide details for you tomorrow." Collins stretched tall. "Don't worry, Liam, you won't have them long."

Liam watched them disappear into the crowd. When he looked across the dance floor, the table was empty of the men Collins had identified as spies. He looked at the coordinates in his hand; they were in waters he was familiar with.

"Collins and company appear to have attracted a pair of bloodhounds all right. They probably were British spies." He grimaced and looked at Mick.

"Ah, sure they were, Collins also has watchers everywhere and he means business."

"It looks like we have been drafted into the business too. These coordinates are not a mile offshore, near Seven Heads I think. By the way, Mick, you don't have to come, I cast the bargain. "Ah, Liam, I wouldn't miss it for the world."

The band suddenly went into remission and there was a scramble of people toward the bar.

"Want a drop of the hard stuff?"

Gentle swells lapped at the hull of the Mary C as they churned quietly through the fading evening light.

"What do you think, Mick?"

"I think we are there or damn close."

"It's getting dark. I hope they're not too far away. They might not even show up, that wouldn't break my heart."

"They will be up by dark, I'd guess. They have light to see us and if they used a signal light some body on shore would surely spot them."

"I don't..." Mick started as he felt a surge in the ship. "Wait, he's right there!" He pointed. "Jesus wept - he's coming' up damn near underneath us!"

In a rush of grey water, the U boat rose beside them like a surreal dolphin, tipping the Mary C with a wash of water. The coning tower rose above them, and before the rest of the ship had surfaced, the hatch was open and four sailors ran quickly down its deck. They quickly un-limbered the deck gear and the cargo hatch. The U boat was about thirty yards away. The tower hatch fell back and a man in a dark shouted across the water.

"Identifitzier!" It was a strident voice

"It's the Mary C, prepared to take cargo." Liam called out.

Mick maneuvered the boat, a bit unnerved when the deck gun was pointed at them.

"Mary C will take cargo," Liam shouted. Mick maneuvered the Mary C along side the submarine.

A work crew quickly assembled on the deck and ten long crates began to train up. Two

450

of the sailors hooked the Mary C as others began to pass the crates. There were ten cases, ten rifles each, and they were heavy for Liam and Mick to handle, but they managed to stow them in their fish hatch. The ammunition came across in cans, ten in all.

"Glück haben, Irishman are good!"

"I'm not Irish," Liam called. The men across from him were more attuned to enemy than to friends. "I'm an American."

"American good," he called some orders to his crew,

"Well, Fritz, tell that to the families of those you killed on the Lusitania."

"They had warning, sorry for the dead Americans. We apologized. Sorry. Good luck." The Captain disappeared below.

The sailors unhooked then pushed off the bow. There was a quick scramble as the men secured the deck gun, and as Mick worked to throttle the engine; the U boat sank like a shark. Barely fifteen minutes had passed.

"That was quick. Let's get the hell out of here, Mick! I sure hope Collins has arranged the pick up; I don't want to be sitting on these things."

"Don't worry, Liam, they will be picked up quickly. Collins wants the rifles right away."

Back in port, they were still making the Mary C fast, when a touring car appeared at the base of the dock.

"I hope that's not who I think it is."

"Ah, I told you not to worry, that's Danny O'Rourke from Cork. He's Irish Volunteers; I know his car."

The man was short and stout with a broad face, and he was puffing on a cigar when he reached the boat. Mick was in the cargo hold adjusting the cases.

"You have Mr. Collins' cargo?" At the sound of the voice Mick popped up his head. The man paused and smiled in recognition. "Hello, Mick."

"Hello, Dan."

"I'll take five and as many ammunition cans as we have room for." He motioned toward the car and two men approached at a fast walk. They lifted a crate and hurried toward the auto; "I'll move a little closer." Dan said as he disappeared into the growing dark. Soon the car was backing toward them and within minutes it was packed and gone.

Liam looked nervously at the remaining five crates, and then from the empty dock came the sound of a donkey cart. An old donkey, with an older man driving her, drew slowly near in the gathering gloom. Liam recognized him as the farmer from whom he had purchased potatoes.

"You're out late, aren't you, Herb O'Toumey?"

"Oh no, Mr. Kavanaugh, I'm out early. I'll be changing Mr. Collin's package for me milk can."

Liam laughed. "How many of these crates do you want?"

"All what's left."

"Herb, we can load them on for you, but how are you going to get them off?"

He smiled. "Well, me grandsons, they are strapping boys, they can do it."

A kind of grudging admiration entered Liam's mind. He wished he had a cause so dear that three generations of a single family would risk so much. It took less than half an hour to load the cart and cover the crates and cans with the straw and O'Toumey disappeared down the road.

They checked the boat's mooring and hurried down the dock toward town. The dockside pub, with its narrow windows glowing cheerily against the dark, called out an invitation. "Would you like a drop, Liam?" They stopped outside the door where the faint sound of laughter crept about its lighted edge.

"No, Mick, I'm feeling very tired." Liam took a deep breath and looked back at the dock and Mary C's mooring. "Things went off real well, but I'm glad to be done with it."

The last strand of the light had washed into the west and a brisk breeze worked its way toward distant trees. Mick made his way into the pub as Liam labored on up the hill to his house.

Nothing seemed changed, yet everything was changing.

Mick and Liam were seated at the kitchen table two days after their 'fete accompli' with the contraband. Liam began to pour a cup of coffee in the mug Mick was offering. At first he was not sure, then the sounds came again; the jangle of equipment and the distinct squeak of leather.

"Someone's coming!" Mick rose from the table to look out the window.

Liam set down the coffee pot and at the same moment the door exploded inward and four British regulars crashed into the kitchen. A sergeant pointed to them.

"Stand against the wall, both of you."

Liam, soon over the surprise, turned an angry look on the man and gestured toward the others.

"What the hell do you mean by breaking into my house?"

"I'll break your bones if you don't shut up. Now get up against the wall." He shoved the rifle butt into Liam's stomach then, with his rifle across his chest, slammed him back into the wall.

Mick made a move to help, and a second soldier crashed his rifle stock into Mick's ribs. He fell on to the floor with a great wheeze and the soldier kicked him over to his back. As Liam was forced to back up, he looked to the door. A tall, spare man stepped through wearing the rank captain.

"Greetings, Mr. Kavanaugh." He glanced at Mick on the floor, smiled slightly, "and Mr. McBride," he addressed the Sergeant. "Search this place top to bottom, not a cup unturned!"

The men responded quickly to the order. Cupboards were emptied; shelves, tables, dishes and cans were sent crashing; spices, salt and flour all mixed together on the floor as the containers and drawers were pulled and dumped.

"What the hell are you doing? You can't do this, this is my house! Who the hell do you think you are breaking into my house?"

"I am quite sure who I am, old man. I am Captain Anthony Pilkington of His Majesty's Home Guard. It is you who appears to have an identity problem."

Liam made a move to help Mick as he was struggling to gain his feet, bleeding profusely from his eyebrow.

"Stand where you are, Kavanaugh!" Pilkington watched as Mick stood. "Ah, Mr. McBride, both you and your cousin are courting the hangman, if someone doesn't shoot you sooner."

"Captain, I am a citizen of the United States of America."
"That means nothing here, Mr. Kavanaugh."

"Well, that's not what my passport says and that is not what my consulate in Dublin will say."

"I don't give a wit about your passport, Mr. Kavanaugh; we are at war and these Irish

Republicans mean to open a second front in this conflict. We believe that you are a smuggler and your uncle and cousin is also involved."

"Whatever your trouble, America is a neutral."

"Spare me the details, Mr. Kavanaugh. Rhodes, Richards, start looking upstairs."

"Well, here's a detail you might like to know. My late mother contributed ten thousand dollars to the British Relief Fund. I know, because I am the one who probated her will."

"Balderdash," Pilkington turned to the third soldier. "Currier, check the front rooms – thoroughly." He turned and pointed to the room. "I don't care a wit about that either. Where would a contemptible red nigger like you get such money? You would need to sell a great many blankets."

"You son-of-a-bitch, you're country would be starving at this moment if it were not for the American relief!"

Pilkington whirled and smashed the back of his hand across Liam's face, splitting his lip.

"Be more cautious with your words, Mr. Kavanaugh. I am quite out of patience with you. You will address me as captain or sir, or by all that is holy I will clap you into Irons and send you to jail."

Liam wiped his chin and observed the red streak on his hand. "You're out of patience? So am I, and if I could, I would cancel that bequest and give the money to the Turks. If I am a smuggler, then prove it!"

"I do not like to repeat myself. This is Ireland, itching to drive a blade into the back of the Kingdom. I could have you arrested simply because you are associated with Republicans. We know about your family, your father and grandfather, and the Raven's Prey pub – a mere gathering place for rebels and miscreants, which category are you? Both, I believe. We know of your meeting with Mr. Collins, Mr. Kavanaugh."

"I belong to neither category, although the second category may well fit you. You break into my home without a search permit rough up my employee and me on questionable authorization. You are the miscreant in a fancy red suit."

"Warrants are not required in a time of war, you twit."

"Well, Mr. Pilkington, whatever you say. I'm gonna have your ass, your commission and a letter of apology."

"I'll make an appointment for you at 10 Downing Street, or perhaps a soapbox in Hyde Park."

Liam could hear the bumps, crashes and thumps as the soldiers vented their orders with vengeance. Furniture, dresser drawers, vessels of any kind were being dumped in great abandon. After an hour of trashing the rooms of Liam's home, the four soldiers returned to the kitchen.

"What did you find worth reviewing?" Pilkington questioned.

"Nothing at all, sir, we could not find any rifles or firearms of any kind."

"Very well, then. Sergeant, prepare and search the shop and the boat."

"Are you satisfied that I am not at war with you, or England, or the Kingdom?" Liam noted with an air of disgust.

"Frankly, no, I do not trust you, Mr. Kavanaugh. There was a submarine sighting the day before yesterday and there has been word from Cork that you may have been involved in a transfer which we assume was weapons. My only regret is that we did not have the news sooner so that we could have caught you red-handed and gladly killed you. We will see what your boat and shop yield. Perhaps we will find something to hang you for yet."

"It will yield nothing, and I will protest this." Liam glared at the Major.

"Protest, yes, by all means protest! Like you protest about our ships being torpedoed, protest the activity of the Huns and protest the indignities of war. By all means, protest from your hiding place behind your borders. Yes, and by all means, give money; we give our blood! To hell with you, Mr. Kavanaugh, you have turned your back on the nation who peopled your country. America may be a great giant with greenbacks in its hands, but its liver is white as a lily. So, go protest, you little brown pip – protest!"

"I will be sure to mention your high regard for Americans when I file my letter protesting this travesty. It would behoove you to remember that without America you would be starving and your war machines stalled. You wouldn't have paper to wipe your ass on and the Huns would be having picnics in Trafalgar Square." His voice was still edged in anger. "You are God damn right I am going to protest! Now, why don't you get the hell out of here?"

"Quite, it's getting rather tedious." As an afterthought, Pilkington opened the oven door and peered inside, then popped it shut. "Mr. Kavanaugh your business is shut down and a guard posted until further notice."

"Did you find any contraband, you tumid popping jay?" Liam snapped." I am not going to tell you anything except I am going to build a fire under your ass."

Anger traced a faint line over Pilkington's face. "I would be most careful, Mr. Kavanaugh, with whom you associate. I must complete the rest of the search of your premises and shop, and we will talk."

"You won't find anything, and I'm done talking with you."

"Perhaps, Mr. Kavanaugh, perhaps a mistake has been made." He made a slight nod toward Liam and gathered his men. He paused in the doorway as his men started toward the dock. "Then, perhaps not, we will see what happens, good day, Mr. Kavanaugh."

"You made a mistake all right," Liam spoke aloud as they threaded out of sight, a big one." He wiped the taste of blood from his mouth and, selecting a dishtowel from the pile on the floor, he held it briefly under the faucet then folded it onto the gash in Mick's eyebrows. "You all right, Mick?"

"I'm mad and mean, those bloody English bastards." He flinched in pain at his movement.

"They don't realize it yet, but they made an error. A God damn big one, now they have made an enemy of me." Liam tenderly touched his lip and rubbed off the blood that stained his finger. "It is a good thing I didn't keep one of those rifles; I would have killed that son of a bitch! I'm thinking of old Herb O'Toumey and his grandchildren, three generations. I'm beginning to understand why three generations can have such firm resolve to remove British rule."

"Ah, Liam, it goes further back than that. You are three generations: Kek, Pat and you."

"I never really did get the story on my grandfather." He went to the window and looked out on the harbor.

"They hanged him." Mick followed his gaze over the moored boats.

"I know that much, but why?"

"He was accused of murdering' a man in prison. They first accused him of stealing a sheep and clapped him in jail, no proof mind you. There was a riot and some prisoners were killed, and the jailer said that Kek had been in on it. Ci Burke's father was in at the same time and swore Kek was with him in a cell when the murder happened. We didn't hear about the details until after the hanging."

Liam did not reply but thought, "It could or could not have been true."

"They brought the charges, everybody knew Kek had a temper so I've been told, but more believe he was innocent for it takes more than a temper for murder."

"Not always." Liam looked angrily across the wrecked kitchen toward the boat deck. "Are you still bleeding, Mick?"

"A little trickle, I'll be fine." He gently touched his eye brow.

It became quiet in the kitchen and anger passed in waves as Liam viewed the mess. "They have made a big mistake. I'm going to get even with those bastards! "

They listened carefully as sounds from within their shop carried up to them. Liam set his mouth and gritted his teeth, working the muscles of his jaw.

"There's a lot of gettin' even among the Republicans."

"You know, when Ci's dad, Aaron found out they had hanged Kek, he swore to get even. About three weeks after he was furloughed from Macroom, the sergeant of the guards at Kek's hanging just disappeared; they never did find him."

"The hanging caused quite a stir, did it?"

"From what I hear, my mother was there with all three of my uncles, she was just a young girl, but she always had the fondest regards for your father."

"Oh," Liam replied with interest, "Because of the hanging?"

"Yes. She said she remembered your dad at the hanging; he had found a long stick and tied a bit of cloth to it. Trying to keep off the birds, you know? He was just a little kid but he ran right up on to the gallows and when one of the soldiers chased him away, there was damn near a riot. It was as though everybody was just waiting for a reason to explode their anger on them."

"Jesus Christ!" Liam's eyes began to fill. "No wonder Pa hated these British bastards so much."

"The Ribbon boys came back the second night and cut him down." He paused and looked out the window. "Are you up to going down to the warehouse? I think they're gone now." Mick rose slowly from the table and double winced in pain. "I think he broke me ribs."

"We'll get somebody to bandage them. I've got a cane here, if that will help."

"Ah, I'll be all right, we would have to go to Cork to get bandaged. You can never find Doc Cronin when you need him."

"This place sure could use a hospital or a clinic or something."

"Indeed it could."

"I know just the person to do it," Liam smiled.

"Who would that be?"

"My wife, Sara she's one hell of a doctor."

"It would be fine if it was possible, but she is further away than Doc Cronin."

They made their way slowly down the hill. The warehouse had been sacked including a few pounds and dollars Liam had kept in a cigar box. They studied the damage and once again the anger rose in Liam.

"You know, Mick, I'm not going to write my protest today. I'm going to wait until tomorrow, then really give them hell."
"Make it a good one and sign it in blood."

Liam smiled, and then bent to pick some tools from the floor. He arose as the newest Irish Republican.

Minsi, New York
Fall 1915

Sara had yet to hear from Liam, and as August passed to September she fluctuated between anger and concern.

Dr. Fowler was competent and popular among the female patients and appeared to have excellent relations with the nurses and staff. After moving into Evelyn's former house, he had joined the tennis club and hosted several meetings. Sara also liked to play tennis and the two made a formidable team in the mixed doubles. She had resisted temptation to probe his life, and his courtly and considerate manners flattered and reminded her of Peter Mitchell and his attentions. Fowler often conferred with her or Wayland when he was perplexed about a patient. He appeared interested in research and proved to be a talented lab assistant. She was not at all reluctant to accept a dinner invitation following a Friday tennis match.

Sara did not knock and walked into the house that was filled with the most pleasant cooking smells.

"Where are you, Hank?"

"Hi, Sara, I'm in the kitchen."

"You're cooking?" She placed her shawl on the back of the chair; the table was laid out with a beautiful place setting for two. The blue lace table cloth was reflected in the water and wine glasses. "My, the table looks lovely!"

Hank appeared in the kitchen doorway, vigorously drying his hands on his apron.

"You approve?" he jested.

"Oh, yes, the wild flowers are so pretty."

"Well, I hope you approve of dinner, I am not much of a cook."

"It smells delicious."

"It's my mother's recipe – chicken breasts sautéed with pearl onions and carrots. Put the whole mess in a frying pan, dump in some sherry, garlic and basil, and cook it all down very simple, How about a glass of wine?" He cast the apron aside. "We have time before it's all done. I just finished mashing the potatoes, and put them in the oven, to brown a bit. I have this wonderful French Cabernet, a nice white wine."

"Hank, you know so much about so many things; you can talk about almost anything. Didn't I hear you speaking Italian to that fellow with the broken thumb yesterday?"

"Yes, that young man had one very mashed up finger!" He grinned, handing her a glass of wine just short of brimming over. "Salute." He touched her glass and watched as she took a deep swallow.

"Didn't want the glass to run over," she laughed. "It is good! Do you know any other languages?"

"I am pleased you enjoy it. And yes, I speak Italian, French, and a little bit of German."

"You learned all these languages in school?"

"Oh, no," He reached out his glass to her and they both drank deeply, nearly emptying their glasses. "I never spent a day in a language class. My parents were Swiss, my mother on the

456

French side, my father on the Italian. Mother spoke French to my grandmother, my father spoke Italian to his mother, and they all spoke a bit of German. I had to learn the languages to survive."

Hank poured a second glass of wine, and they settled back into the leather couch.

"You truly are a remarkable man, gourmet cook, connoisseur of wine, and a linguist. That is quite a list."

"And you, Sara, are a remarkable woman, expert clinician, researcher, and mother."

"Not so that anybody would know."

They drank their wine, looking at the fireplace and the large stag's head that returned a glassy stare.

"All those 'anybodies' may not know, but Jim and Margaret, our rivals from today's match, sure will remember you. You are one hell of a tennis player. Those three backhands you hit today - I sincerely believe if they had volleyed them, the ball would have popped their racquets. You look so soft, but you are so strong and so aggressive. I can't believe the shots you make!"

"Grew up with two brothers, I had to be strong and aggressive."

"You had two brothers? Liam is your husband's name."

"One and the same, we are not blood related. Billy and Liam were fraternal twins from my father's first wife, Sada, the Cheyenne woman who taught me so much."

"Your husband is in Ireland, right?"

"Yes, we don't have any idea where Billy is, in the Army somewhere. Last we heard of him, he was in the Philippines, won a big medal. Neither one of them are very reliable correspondents. I haven't heard from Liam in months." She drained the last of her wine from her glass, briefly regretting her admission.

"It sounds quite complicated. Would you like another glass of wine?"

"No. I've gone quite beyond my usual limits."

"Oh, don't worry about limits. There's just a little left in the bottle, we might as well finish it and celebrate our hard earned win in the match today. I'll split it with you."

"Very well, Hank, but I didn't have much of a lunch and I'm already feeling a little tipsy."

"What possessed me? I need to pay attention to dinner. I'll be back in a bit – enjoy the wine." He grasped his apron and fled toward the kitchen, calling over his shoulder, "I've brought some wood in. Do you know how to lay a fire?"

"Yes, I know how," she called to the voice from the kitchen. She paused for a moment, smiling to herself at the rattle of pans.

"I had a little bad news today." She said raising her voice above the din.

"Oh?" the reply sounded far away.

"Beatrice quit."

"What?" Hank suddenly appeared in the kitchen doorway, with a look of concern. "She's the best nurse we have. Why?"

"I don't know, she didn't say. I got back from the tennis court, hurried to the clinic after my shower and she was waiting to do rounds."

"How long has she worked for you? She is an excellent nurse."

"I agree; she's been with us two years. She was good with the lie-ins and outstanding with children. She had a way of calming them, even cranky infants."

"Yes, she did."

"She was one of your original housemates, wasn't she?" Sara laughed. "I must admit that your arrival was not expected."

"Yes, she was," he disappeared into the kitchen. "I'm just as happy that I moved into here, it's larger and more quiet now without the women. When did she tell you she was leaving?"

"We were just doing rounds, talking girl talk, you know. I told her I was coming here for dinner tonight. She was rather quiet after that. I got back to the office, was reviewing charts and she dropped off her letter. She insisted on being paid, said it was personal, and she was not coming back; then she asked me for a reference letter. Of course, I agreed."

He reappeared with a look of concern. "Just like that; nothing else, she didn't say anything else?"

"No, I paid her and told her I would send her the letter within a week." He ducked back inside the kitchen.

Sara began to lay the fire, first the tinder, then a lattice of progressively larger sticks, and tented three larger logs over it.

"I think the fire's ready and I opened the draft – do you want me to light it?"

"No, dinner's ready also. If you want to wash up, you'd better hurry."

They passed small talk over dinner then sat together on the sofa after. Hank lit the fire and he presented her with a glass of dark red wine.

"This is a delicious port. It is my very favorite spirit."

"French?" she asked with a smile.

"No," he laughed. "As a matter of fact, it's English"

"Mmm, it is good!" she purred, looking over the rim of her glass into his eyes.

The fire licked up through the lattice, collapsing the large pieces of wood on top of it, and burned with a low hiss, dancing the walls with light and shadow. They sat without speaking, watching the pattern of flames among the logs.

"Ever get lonely, Sara?" he asked quietly.

"Sometimes, but the kids and work keep me very busy. I don't have time to get lonely. I fear Mary C will miss Beatrice; often she spent time with her when I was making calls. Perhaps I can still convince her to stay, I will write the letter she asked for, but try to get her back."

"I wouldn't bother, she's gone. He quickly replied. "There's lots of potential help around here and hiring back help who quit is usually not a good idea." He paused, watching the fire's yellow and blue flames spreading among the wood. "I don't see your kids very often."

"I don't see them often enough. Billy is working and helping manage one of our farms. Mary C is working in town at the bank and stays in an apartment over it."

"I was never close to my family after I left for residency; my loneliness is in my heart."

"Loneliness is understandable, we are quite isolated here. I'm used to it, have been here all my life, if you did get to town, there's not much there just a few stores, a couple banks, saloons and one halfway decent restaurant at the hotel; that's it. But it has grown a lot since I was a little girl - the railroaders and all."

"A town is not what I need. I've been in a town." He spread his arm across her shoulder. She did not resist, instead she settled against him.

"Sara, I do admire you. You're not only a fine physician, but also very beautiful."

"Not so anyone would notice." The compliment lingered in the satisfied shroud that hung over her mind.

"Oh, don't be so naïve! All the men I know in the tennis club, town, wherever I meet them often comment on your beauty. You know what else? We look good together. Don't you feel the men's eyes on you, on us, when we're together? I don't know what it is with your husband, I would not want to be away from you long, perhaps he has other interests."

"I don't know either," she quietly slurred. He leaned forward and kissed her lightly on the neck. She turned her face toward him. "Kiss me, Hank, I like the way I feel with you, loved and appreciated." She turned up her mouth as he leaned toward her. Circling a breast with his hand, slowly he caressed her nipple until it erected. She slipped her hand and began to stroke him to arousal.

He pulled her up. "Sara, you are so beautiful! I want to be in you." Slowly he undid the buttons of her blouse, stripped it aside and buried his face in her breasts.

"Wait a minute, Hank let's make this easier." She unhooked her brassiere, letting her full dark-tipped nipples fall into the light. Eagerly he began to suck one breast and manipulate the other. She abruptly stood for a moment and dropped her skirt and panties. Hank undressed quickly and pulled a blanket from a chair and spread it the large bear rug.

Sara slipped under him and moved slightly as he passed his hand over her mons and his searching finger found her clitoris.

"Oh, yes," she arched her back.

"Fold your legs up, Sara, I have something for you." He pressed into her introitus, lifted her buttocks and drove into her.

She responded with a moan and he began slow thrusts into her. She lifted to his efforts and he began deep thrusts and drove to orgasm. She gasped and shattered into her own. He collapsed heavily on her; slid off with his back to her. She curled into the hollow of his back.

"You were magnificent," she whispered.

"You liked that?" He relaxed and quietly went to sleep.

For more than an hour she lay by him, hundreds of thoughts floating through her mind. At first there was a persistent image of Liam and a feeling of betrayal. She rationalized to herself. 'If he really cared, he would have written. He doesn't value me as much as money and his freedom. He was never satisfied with his work, the family or me. He's tired of me and never really approved my work. To hell with him - he's the one that mentioned divorce. If he really cared, he would have written.' Hank showed some signs of revival; she went to the fireplace and fed in another log.

"How are you, Sara?" he murmured.

"I feel real good."

"No regrets?"

"No regrets."

The sound of the fire crackling filled the room. Hank sat up and pulled on his underpants. "Another glass of port, Sara?"

"Oh, why not, I'm not in a hurry to go anywhere and I don't have far to go."

She draped the blanket around her shoulders and opened her legs to the fire and absently brushed at her sticky pubic hair. Hank presented her with a glass and sat down beside her. She leaned her head against him.

"I feel so good, Hank. What an evening!"

"It's not over yet." He smiled and cupped her breast beneath the blanket. "I do care for you, Sara. I really do."

"I care for you too, Hank," she laughed. "You're good at what you do."

"You know, Sara, we could have quite a future together, between the care, the research and the tennis. We could travel Europe, hell travel the world. You could press your remedy. We would not have to work."

Sara grinned. "I never thought of it quite that way. I don't think I could do that. I enjoy work and feel very good helping people."

"We could quit, you know. The foundation is financially quite secure. You could help people through it."

"Oh?" she asked curiously." How do you know that?"

"Well, that's what Doc Wayland indicated. He just mentioned it one day."

"It's true; my mother was very generous and had a considerable sum to be generous with."

"Millions, true?" He looked into her eyes. "You don't really have to work."

"That's true; we are very well off - the foundation, me, the children and my husband also. She separated it all in her will. She was an extraordinary business person, a suffragette, just a generous and remarkable woman."

The room quieted to the fire sounds. Sara set down her glass and settled once more into Hank's chest.

"Sara, were you left a lot of money?" The question was quite matter of fact as he ran his hand along the inside of her leg.

"Yes, a lot." She closed her legs against his hand.

"Sara," he took her hand and placed it on his erection.

"Oh," she demurred. "Are you ready again?"

He eased her up and she wriggled over his erect penis. "Just take me by the shoulders and hold on." She righted over him, a new sweat streaking her forehead. When they finished they both entered a deep and dreamless sleep.

Saturday morning seemed especially bright as Sara made her way to the clinic. She rehearsed briefly what she intended to say to Hank and quickened her pace. A satisfied and assured smile creased her lips. There was a mountain of mail for the end of the week, and she searched quickly through it and stopped short when she saw an envelope rowed with British stamps. She recognized Liam's hand writing and began to tremble as she opened the letter.

June 01, 1915
Dear Sara,
My darling, darling, I miss you so much. This is my fifth try to reach you. It is so very difficult to get any mail in or out. I have so much to say to you but above all I want you to know how much I love you.

The letter blurred as she read on to the account of the Lusitanian. An anxious guilt began to grow; slowly she walked to and locked the door. "My god," she murmured, "what have I done?" There was a loud tap at the door.

"Sara, are you in there?"

She did not respond and sank deep into the chair. Hank tried the lock, she heard him

walk down the hall, mumbling, "isn't that it? Give a woman what she needs and wants and they disappear on you. She is probably is counting up the accounts."
She folded her arms on the desk and nestled her head into them.

"Damn, damn, damn you, Liam Kavanaugh, Damn you!" Anguish and anger argued adamantly through the range of her emotions. The objective and emotional raged at one another. She began to tremble with the force.

"What have I really done?" she argued aloud, "If there was advantage taken, I took my share from him and he took his of me. Shall I tell Hank to move on, that it's an impossible situation?" She sat up in the chair and slipped her hand to her crotch and quickly withdrew it. "If I send him along, who will take his place? It was so damn difficult to find someone to begin with."

The sound of the construction workers echoed from the site of the new building. She listened to them and the sounds were somehow reassuring. She studied the letter and cast it to the floor. Maybe I should tell Liam, let him decide to go his own way if he wants."

She fumed to herself, "You still don't say when you're coming home. It probably is a woman." But she knew it was unlikely and couldn't get the thought to stick. "It's just as well you are not walking in the door today," she reasoned aloud. She slowly rubbed her forehead.
"What am I going to do with Hank? How am I going to work with him? Damn you, Liam! Why" Exasperation collided with reason. "Why didn't you write? Why, why can't you make me feel like Hank did? You take me for granted, you always have and it serves you right" She knew in her heart it was a lie and her rationalization was an empty one. She sighed and continued to herself.

"What's done is done. All I have to decide is what I am going to do now. First, I must put some distance between Hank and me until I figure something out, no more dinners with port and firelight. Second, I will stay away from Hank; let him find a new doubles partner. Sally Harrington would be good. I'll talk to Sal. Things were all right before last night, it can be the same again." In her heart she knew nothing would be the same. She listened to the men working, one of them laughing loudly, another with a string of oaths in reply.

"No more private dinners. No more OB consults together. I'll take the lying-ins and he can do the clinic. If he doesn't like it, he can quit. I'll do my own research, I really don't need him in my way anyhow."

She looked down at the floor and retrieved Liam's letter, and read it carefully. When she finished there was a heavy feeling in her chest. She looked toward the sounds of the men at work and tears welled in her eyes. She sniffed them back. "And what will I tell you, dear kind Liam, and most innocent of all?"

There were approaching footsteps, light and fast. She guessed it was one of the nurses. The door rattled, after a few seconds, the footfalls disappeared away. "Nothing, I will tell you nothing Liam, but I will tell you the truth if you ask me." She whispered to herself as she rose from behind the desk, patted her cheeks dry with the sleeve of her coat. "Well. It's time to join the world, time to go to work."

Sara adjusted her lab coat and sat down behind her desk. She had just finished a meeting with the building contractor who assured her the wing would open in two weeks. She anticipated his report, but she was not so sure about the meeting about to transpire. She was anxious but resolved, and a tap at the door set her on edge and when the door opened she consciously braced her mind.

"Hello, Sara." He paused in the doorway, taken aback by the steely set to her face.
"Come in, Hank."

461

He eased the door shut, and started toward her smiling.

"Please leave the door open."

Hank responded by opening it to a narrow crack. He circled the desk and tried to pull Sara's face to his.

"Don't, Hank, don't."

He kissed her cheek and smiled and slipped his hand under her breast giving it a gentle lift upward.

"Stop it; I didn't call you here for a kiss and a mauling." She pushed his hand away.

He withdrew with a tight lipped smile. "A pity it's not." He sat down across from her and her. "Is there something wrong?"

"Hank, I've been thinking things over. I want you to leave." Her command lay heavy in the air. Surprised he leaned toward her.

"I can't believe you just said that. What on earth for?"

"I think you know what for. We made a big mistake."

"You mean our evening together last week?"

"Yes." Sara stirred uncomfortably. "It was a terrible mistake. I can't work with you under these conditions."

"What conditions?" He asked with earnestly. "We had an intimate evening together, so what? It was delightful; I was looking forward to another. I've been wondering why you've been avoiding me."

"There will be no more evenings." Her reply was emphatic. "It is over! It was a mistake. I'm as much to blame as you, but I do not want the remotest possibly of an opportunity for it to happen again."

"I see you're upset with yourself, more with yourself than with me. You enjoyed it and now you don't want another. I would consider it carefully before you let me go."

"I've considered nothing since the night it happened and I believe it best for all parties that you leave the employ of this hospital. I am ashamed of what I did and I know there's no future with you. I have my family to consider."

"And your money --I remind you, I have a contract."

"I am offering you one year's pay as severance." She passed her hand along the edge of her desk, "I'd prefer if you moved away from the area."

"Generous, but who will take care of the patients? You can't do it alone and Wayland's so old he can barely totter around."

"I hired a couple yesterday, both well recommended physicians, Reginald and Sharon Merver. I expect them here for the opening of the new building."

"All bases covered, eh, Sara? Just like that, pack me up and send me on. You feel guilty and it is easier to send me on than to accept your part in it and by all means, get rid of the temptation you feel and the intimacy you hunger for. You have crossed over and it was sweet, there will be another man within the year." He glanced out the window beside her desk, "when would you like for me to leave?"

"I prefer that you leave before the end of the month." She fidgeted with the desk blotter and did not look at him. Some of what he said, she knew to be true. The room filled with an uneasy silence. Hank did not move to leave.

"Did I not provide excellent patient care?"

"Your patient care is excellent and will be difficult to replace, but I am confident in the

462

couple I have hired."

"What about my lab work, who will help you with that?"

"Yes, you assisted well. I appreciate that."

"So this departure is all over our caring for one another?" Hostility trimmed his tone. "What's the matter, Sara," he asked with a tinge of bitterness, "too much or not enough?"

"I do not want to work with you anymore, Hank. We made the mistake of twisting our private lives into our work." She adjusted her lab coat. "I also now have a good idea of why Beatrice left the Cloister and why you left Buffalo. Does an altercation with a certain Cecil Bonnard ring up any memories? The reason for the altercation was your seduction of Bonnard's wife. You still showed the marks of the fight at our interview."

He was taken aback, and countered, "so now you want me gone because of that? What did you do have a detective check my past? And what does Bonnard or Bea has to do with us?"

"Doctor Wayland received the information from Buffalo yesterday and he did do a check through channels. You took advantage of Bea like you took advantage of me. You gave her wine, dinner and promises and then seduced her. She told me. Yes, I want you to leave."

"You're not upset with me, you're upset with yourself. What does my relationship with Bea have to do with our relationship? We are a damn good team and Bea is gone, so what?"

"Were Hank, we 'were' a team. I don't like your attitude now and your attitude toward women in general. Bea was my friend before you ever came here; we were very close and worked hand in hand developing the service."

"Then there's no alternative?"

"No. I want you to go." She insisted.

"Very well, let me think. You said a years' pay for severance. That would be one hundred twenty dollars a week for fifty-two weeks. Let's see. He thought for a moment. That's six thousand two hundred and forty dollars. Make it seven for my inconvenience and I will be gone the day after tomorrow."

"I don't have to pay you anything you are a probationary appointment." Sara fought the anger rising in her.

"That's right, but I know the foundation can well afford it. There were some extraordinary benefits to the job, so make it seven thousand and call us even." He brushed a lock from his forehead. "After all, you received some additional benefits from me," he smirked, focusing his eyes on her breasts.

Aware of his stare, she responded. "You're disgusting, Hank. I don't know how I could have misjudged you so —disgusting!"

"You protest too much! Let me tell you what you are, Doctor Kavanaugh. You are a whore about to happen. You won't admit it, but you are greedy for sex and attention and when you feel you don't get enough you will get it whenever and where ever you can. That little taste you got from me was just a start. After I am gone, even if your husband comes home, you will spread your legs again, and the next man might not be as talented as I am and you will look for another one. You won't even be aware of what you are doing, but believe me you will be doing it, --you will be sending out signals. Few people know me here and I will say nothing to sully your reputation, the locals will get the picture soon enough."

"Get out of my office, Hank! You'll get your seven thousand. Now, get out of my sight." Her voice was calm in its resolve.

"I'll get out of your sight, but I won't be out of your mind. You will have me over and over and over again because you liked it. As for me, you will be the source of many an erection and I will have you over and over again. Trust me; I know women and you, Sara, are a whore in the making."

Hank raised quickly from the chair and swung through the door, leaving it open. His parting words hovered like a dreary bird of prey over her thoughts. She fought the dim memory of her mother and Mary's frank accounts of her life. She rested her head on her hand and pushed at a stray lock of hair that had fallen forward. The angry undertones faded toward guilt, and split to fear.

"I will not let it happen again," she whispered aloud. "It's what you would have done, Mary." Then for a moment her mind flashed back to the lusty image on the floor before the fireplace.

She dismissed the thought. Suddenly a bright and fuzzy image of the family came to her -- Mary, Evelyn, Pat, Billy, Liam --all were there, arms locked in a circle around her. It grew large in her consciousness, brightened and passed. A kind of clarity followed it. She thought of Liam's last letter. It had read hopeful as though he had found new and exciting interests. He loved her, missed her, and told her of how much the Irish needed health care and the challenge of it was also mentioned.

"To hell with all of it, all this here, the clinic will go on even if I'm not here. I can find a manager and it is well funded. It's not worth my family. I will gather up the children, and by damn, we will go to Ireland." A great relief surged through her and when she looked up, the contractor was standing in the doorway.

"I hate to bother you, Doctor Kavanaugh, but there's a load, a big load of furniture out here, and we don't know exactly where to put it."
"I'm coming!" With a light step, she fell in behind him.

On November 10, 1915, when the North Atlantic supposedly was covered in squalls and storms, Sara and the children set out from New York. Dire predictions about weather and submarines failed to materialize. After arriving in Liverpool, she had some difficulty booking a voyage to Bantry, but little getting on to Kinsale. The packet boat hugged the pier and Sara, glanced down the dock, and saw a familiar figure about to board a boat. Billy and Mary C also saw the man and went hurdling toward him. The figure glanced up at first perplexed and then recognized them.
"Daddy" Mary C shrieked.

Liam leapt from the boat and opening his arms nearly went down with the double impact. He could not contain his tears as he looked toward the woman beyond. Sara hurried toward him and he crushed her to him.

"Oh, Sara, how much I have missed you and wanted to hold you! What a surprise! I did not get any word and had no idea you were coming! I was on my way out of Kinsale another five minutes I would have missed you." He kissed her over and over as the tears streamed down her face.

"Liam, how much I have missed you. We knew we had to get to Kinsale and we made it." She clung to him tightly.

"I'm so glad you're here. I love you Sara."

"And I love you." She wiped at her tears. "I took a page from Mary's book; act on your hunches. Those two," she gestured toward Billy and Mary C, "they came along for the adventure of it."

"Come on, Mom we wanted to be sure you got here safely." Billy said as he looked over the town spread from the long dock.

Chapter 48

Kinsale, Ireland
March 1916

The Ford truck heaved and pitched down the muddy Post Road toward Listowel. Mick McBride, wrestled the steering wheel, wove from one side of the road to the other as he tried to avoid the deep rutted puddles. A steady rain pelted the vehicle. A donkey cart approached and Mick swerved into a deep rut with a bone crunching bang and subsequent pitch of the passenger to the roof.

"Jesus wept, Mick will you slow down? You will have us both killed."

"Ah, 'tis the weather, have you ever seen it so bad?"

"Beware the ides of March."

"Beware; all right I can barely see the road, more or less drive it."

"Want me to drive?" Liam smiled.

He smiled back, reluctant to give up the wheel. "No, not necessary, I'll slow a bit."
They continued to shatter from one side to the other, but Mick slowed and so too the impacts.

"Do you know what this meeting is all about, Mick?"

"No, but it's important."

"I trust it will not be another submarine event."
"I think not, there will just be you and me and Gavin so far as I know."

"Who the hell is this Collins? I like the man and I told him I'd help out. We have helped out, but I'll not do murders for him."

"Don't know much more than you. His father has ninety acres over in West Cork. He has seven brothers and sisters, a bad temper, and he's been in the Brotherhood quite a while, ten years I expect."
"How old is he?"

"That I wouldn't know, maybe twenty five or six - he's a Republican, though." Mick cranked the wheel away from a puddle.
"There must be something up."

The Raven's Prey was nearly empty when the two of them walked in and spotted Collins in an animated conference with Gavin McBride and Tom Barry. They had stopped their confab only long enough to welcome Liam and Mick.
"Sit down, boys. I don't have much time but a lot to say." Collins greeted.

"Well, it better be good," laughed Liam. "I'm lucky to get here alive; I think I'll hire a chauffeur." The men chuckled at Mick's silent protest.

"First things first, Liam, I want to thank you for looking after young McCrey."

"I didn't do anything – my wife did."

"Was she curious about the wound?"

"Very likely, but she didn't ask me and I did not venture any explanation."

"Good, women talk." Collins leaned back in his chair.

"Not this one, she considers patient care information as very privileged and she has had a lot of practice." Liam took a deep swallow from his glass. "I have a feeling we're not here to receive your thanks, Mike."

"True." He glanced about the room, and leaned forward in a confidential manner. "Next month will be the rising."

The comment came like the jolt of a fist.

"Next month?" Liam queried incredulously.

"On or about the twenty fourth," Collins acknowledged.

"Can you share some details? I didn't think we were ready for this."

"I can share what I know at the moment, and you're right, it's a damn fool plan."

The men at the table did not respond to Collins' sentiment, but curiosity surged around the table.

"Connolly and Pearce have decided to seize the government buildings in Dublin, the castle, the post office, houses and rooftops that command the canals."

Liam looked at him carefully. "And that's it?"

"They expect a general rising in Dublin and the provinces."

"That is expecting a lot," He looked directly at Collins. "There is a fine line between expecting and speculating. Battles must be based on known factors not expectations."

"Too much expectation is exactly what I told them. I don't think more than a thousand in all Ireland will join in. We do not have enough arms and if we did have them, we would have difficulty getting them where needed."

"I hope you have more than what I helped to bring it."

"Yes, and there are some that have been purchased and should be here."

"Jesus, Mike that sounds like more speculation. Going to get more guns from the Germans? Is this a sure thing?"

Collins frowned. "Who else but the Germans and they have been reliable." He paused. "But to be fair, there is a lot of money from America involved." Collins lit a cigarette and continued. "What puzzles me is you Americans know these British bastards and freedom and democracy and all that, yet your government persists in supporting them and their stranglehold here. It is a bit puzzling."

"If it doesn't make sense it is politics. I don't know about Wilson and his cronies, I didn't vote for any of them. But this much support I can pledge, and that's myself. I want to be in Dublin."

Collins puffed impatiently at his cigarette and exhaled a blue cloud over the table.

"Are you daft, man? We need you outside this. It is going to fail! It has about as much chance for success as for a stone to speak. What we need are flying columns, hit and run the bastards ragged until they give up. Hit one place, then another, scatter the attacks, ambush the pursuit."

"Still I'd like to be there. In Dublin, I mean."

"No. It will be over and there will be a great more yet to do. What we need now and in the future is information. You can be a vital part of that plan if you stay outside the rebels, get lost in the Kinsale community, listen to what is being said by them, by the Brits, the Yanks, help us fill in their plans, who is who, who is doing what. Even the possible ways a person might think and suspected to act. We will need this; without it we are doomed to a future failure, can and will you do that? Can we count on your wife's support? There may be wounded with no care available and if they go to treatment they will also go to jail."

Liam took a sip from his glass and looked directly at Collins. "Yes, you can count on us."

"Then it's done. I must get on to Cork." He stubbed out the cigarette and lifted his glass. "Here's to a free Ireland."

After Collins and Barry left, Liam sat with Mick and Gavin into the early morning, long after the shutters were closed. The men had quietly discussed the pending event, an air of anticipation mixed well with their patriotism. They were also sobered by what Collins had said. They would have to wait and see, and they did not have long to wait. The rising began on April twenty fourth.

Liam slipped quietly into the infirmary. Sara and her nurse assistant were bent over the operating table. Sara suddenly straightened and threw down the clamp she had been holding. She was not aware of his presence.

"He's gone, May," she said to the nurse beside her.

She shook her head in despair and saw Liam looking toward her. Sara's frock was stained in broad bands of red, the sleeve of the coat soaked in blood. Even her shoes were dark and wet. As she walked toward Liam, she wiped the sweat from her brow, leaving a red smear on her temple. She was agitated and exhausted and collapsed into a chair. Liam sat down beside her; the steady rain drowned the sounds of the nurse as she put the operating instruments into a metal pan.

"Are you all right, Sis?"

"No, I am no all right, and don't call me Sis! Goddamn it, Liam! I am NOT a surgeon. That boy over there, he's not much older than our Billy, this is madness!"

She slumped back into her chair, and Liam took the handkerchief from his pocket and dabbed the blood from her temple.

"You look so tired. I think you need some rest."

"Sixteen gunshot wounds, very serious ones, I have treated in two days. The boy is, was, the seventh abdominal wound. I couldn't find the bullet, went through his intestine. I probed, couldn't find it. It was all the way back to his spine. I was starting to close when he died. I am not a surgeon! I don't have the equipment and I can't keep up this pace!" Anger, frustration and sadness welled in her eyes. "Damn it, I deliver babies to life, not sons to death." She began to sob and abruptly stopped. Liam put his arm around her shoulders and held her tight. "That boy over there, what's his mother going to think?" Her voice began to break up. "I don't even know his name."

Liam took in a breath and shuddered. "I don't know it either. They have no other place to go. Sara, they are getting better care here than anywhere else. Some are in barns, hay racks, and back rooms with no care whatsoever. This I do know, I'll get some more equipment. I'll get some more surgery stuff. What do you need?"

"I don't need so much equipment as I need some more help. Did you know, your son was down here until three o'clock this morning? Your son, God bless him, he was a lot of help. Mary came too, but she got sick. I could have used your help, but I knew you were on the boat."

"I know, I talked with her but Billy was asleep. I will inquire about some help for you. We must be careful in recruiting help they could be informers. The worst may well be over. It's been five days and according to the Irish Times the rebels are cordoned off. There will not be many more coming out, if any at all. I'm sorry I wasn't here when you needed more help."

"Where are you taking them? Both those men in there," she nodded toward the small row of beds in the adjoining room, "They will probably be dead by morning, they lost so much blood. Where will you take them? If it's still going on they may be coming here for days."

"Of the six that were badly wounded that came in yesterday, three are at Coleman's and three at Desmond's."

"In the barn, I suppose?"

"I don't know. The Desmond place is a big house. I don't know."

"I don't know either but I wish this Irish Republic that you so fondly speak of would not be washing in on a sea of blood."

"They have tried negotiations for many years."

"I know the stories, Liam." She pointed to the bed and the blood stained sheet pulled over the face. "But that's the reality."

He stood, rubbed her shoulder and kissed her on the cheek.

"I'm going to head down to the pub, I think Gavin is there. Maybe he will have more news from Dublin. Maybe he has a place to bury the boy. It's best we move the body along in case someone uninvited stops by."

Sara watched the door close behind him. She sat and braced her shoulders back.

"Yes, by all means, go down to the pub it is a good place to share pipedreams."

Liam was surprised when he saw Jim, not Gavin, in conversation with Mick McBride. He had not expected to see Jim in Kinsale for he had gone to Dublin but there he was, sipping whiskey and speaking quietly. "I didn't expect to see you here, Jim."

"Liam, he's just come from Dublin."

"Aye, it's true."

"What's happening?"

"'Tis a lost cause, I'm afraid. I just got out in the nick of time. Sure, they have brought in the big guns and hammering us down."

"What's going on?"

"Well, it was a surprise, they were not ready, and things went fast. The guards at the Castle were taken first, no British officers anywhere. There were only three men there."

"There were not any British officers?"

"Oh, maybe a few were in town, somebody said they all were at the races."

Liam smiled. "Then what happened?"

"Well, at first I was near the town center - that was Monday the first day. Ah, we waltzed right in. The countess took her position in the park."

"That's countess who?"

"Why, Countess Markievicz, of course. She set up on Saint Stevens Green. We took the biscuit factory, the post office and the houses by the canal bridges. I was at the telephone exchange. A very indignant lady turned us away at the door, 'there was no one there to operate', she said and we didn't go in."

"That was a mistake, why didn't you check? You should have shut down the exchange, indignant lady or not. You should have made sure it was not operating. They must have been able to call where ever they wanted to."

"Ah, Mick, everything was movin' so fast. We thought she was telling the truth. The biggest mistake was not to take Trinity College. They barricaded up and just played hell with us from there." Jim paused and threw down his whiskey, his deeply lined face reflected fatigue.

"Then what happened, Jim?"

"Michael sent me down to Haddington Road. We had a fierce fight there, that's when I got this." He touched his leg.

For the first time Liam noticed the bump on the side of Jim's leg that spread across his thigh.

"Went clear through," Jim acknowledged.

"How many of our men were there?"

"I think, thousands, Liam, thousands."

"You shut Dublin down, that's for sure. But thousands, they still were not enough, were they?"

"We could have used more. Those bastard Irish Volunteers, may they burn in hell. They took up against us marchin' down the roads. May the flail consume them in this life and the fire in the next! I heard the Dubliners were giving the Brits water on the streets. They that did are traitors, traitors!"

Liam waited for Jim's anger to dissolve and watched while he slowly poured another glass of whiskey.

"If there were thousands..."

"Liam, they just couldn't get it going. They were here, there, everywhere, the numbers were great but their organization poor. They didn't get together, a piece here, a piece there. The downtown streets belonged to us. We killed hundreds of them in the streets, hand to hand, eye to eye, and we gave as good as we got and then some." He tossed off the whiskey and offered the bottle. "Have a drink."

Liam was dubious about the report and extended his glass. "When did you get out?"

"It started to go sour on Wednesday. I had three bullets left and my revolver, none for my rifle. The house I was in was gettin riddled with bullets. We held 'til dark. I hid my rifle and we made a run for it. We got about a block and ran right into a patrol. Both the Carrick boys went down, I emptied my revolver, dived into a house, climbed out the other side. I was almost away when the bullet struck me. It knocked me down but I got up quick and got away. An old lady bandaged my leg, I was pretty bloody, so she handed me her husband's trousers and I started for here."

"Jesus, Jim, you're lucky to be alive." Liam downed his whiskey.

"I am indeed," he rubbed his neck and rested back against the chair.

"What happened to Mike Collins?"

"I don't know, Mick. Last I saw him; he was at the post office. When I left, the center of Dublin was on fire, you could see the flames, they lit the night. The post office was in the middle of it. The flames were shootin' high in the sky. The big fire started Thursday."

"From what I have heard so far, not much happened outside of Dublin. But the news is slow. I heard of no risings outside of Dublin. Few if any at all I'll wager."

"I didn't see much else. I got picked up just outside Dublin when it was just getting light. A man named O'Geary brought me clear to Waterford. Then I came here."

"Things don't look good, Jim. I fear Michael was right, too little, too soon."

"Well," McBride offered. "The people know we mean business. The world will know that too."

"The world is awash with blood in France, in Belgium, and Turkey. I'm afraid more blood lost in Ireland will not be noticed very much."

"You may be right, Liam, but the Irish won't forget."

"True, but we won't be able to do much further with the leaders at Richmond Barracks. There will be reprisals, Pearse, Connolly, O'Rossa, all of them will probably be executed, even the countess."

"I don't think they will execute a woman - that would be a bad precedent indeed."

"I hope you're right, Mick." Liam looked over to Jim. "You'd better get on down to the clinic and have my wife take a look at that leg."

Jim nodded affirmatively.

Liam turned to Mick. "See if you can find old man O'Toumey. He should be in here today sometime. Tell him we have a package at the clinic that needs to be delivered and if he has a place for it, tell him it's addressed to God. Come on, Jim, I'll walk with you. We will have Sara take a look at that wound."

The two men slowly made their way down the narrow streets. Shortly after delivering Jim to Sara's care he returned to the pub. Mick was still at the bar and Li motioned him to a table.

"We lost, Li. From what I heard it was a disaster, just as you predicted."

"True Mick, we lost but we also learned. Indeed we lost this battle, now all Ireland and the whole world knows we are serious about independence. We lost this battle, but not the cause and I for one am not going to quit."

Chihuahua, Mexico
1916

Pancho Villa was born c1878 as Doroteo Arango. He was the oldest of five children when his father died at an early age Doroteo surrendered his schooling to help support his family by working on a nearby hacienda.

Doroteo's first run in with the law occurred when he murdered an attempted rapist of his sister. He fled into the harsh hills of Nueva Viscaya. About 1891 he assumed the name Francisco Villa and began in earnest a career of looting and murder. In peaceful interludes he was a butcher by trade. He became a legend in his time by the duality of his nature – a ruthless murderer and a defender of women and the poor, --- a kind of desert Robin Hood. Many of his deeds were to bring attention to his greater glory. Between 1900 and 1911 he looted and murdered across Chihuahua. Villa was moved by the idealism of Madero and when Victoriano Hurtas overthrew and murdered Madero, he and Venustiano Caranza defeated Huertas. Within a year, a falling out occurred among the revolutionaries and they began warring amongst themselves. Caranza ultimately won the war, but Villa had stunning victories against Huertas while leading his infamous Northern Division with reckless abandon. These victories came at great cost in the lives of thousands of his followers. Villa was a paradox --- a complex man who believed in justice without juries, and that ends were to be gained whatever the cost of the means; he murdered, without remorse, thousands of federales prisoners, yet released the peasants who had served in the same cause. He never forgave a slight, yet sought forgiveness; he murdered masses, yet loved children. On March 9, 1916 Villa attacked Columbus, New Mexico ---a small border town. The motivation for the raid was as complex as the man:

His star was falling, ---the United States had recently recognized Caranza, ---even though it had highly touted Villa in the past and he had remained steadfastly loyal. Caranza may also have had a hand in it; his ties to Germanic funding had already been disclosed and it is thought that the Germans may have helped sponsor the raid to keep America busy at home and out of the war in Europe. Villa was concerned that the US would swallow-up Mexico, so it would not have been hard for him to justify the attack, plus he needed supplies.

About 600 raiders looted, murdered, and raped their way through the small town leaving 18 Americans and at least 90 raiders dead, in exchange for a small cache of weapons, military supplies, and food. After gathering some horses the raiders fled into Chihuahua and were never caught. Villa's raid was the last successful attack on US soil until World War II.

President Wilson's response was immediate and 10,000 troops, under General John Pershing, were sent to capture and punish Villa. Attack they did, ---with over 100 types of motor vehicles, planes, and an active Cavalry force. For eleven months Pershing combed Chihuahua but never caught Villa who spent a large amount of this time holed-up in a carefully camouflaged cave.

"You wanted to see me, sir?" Pershing looked up, carefully reviewing the man before him.

"Button your collar button, sergeant. I think this is the third or fourth time I have told you to do so."

"Yes, sir well noted."

"Billy, damn it, you're a sergeant major and you have to set an example." He picked up a cigar from the ashtray, puffed a cloud of blue smoke and sat back. "At the very least button it when you come in my presence."

"Yes, sir, I will try to remember next time." Billy snapped the clasp, uncomfortable under the gaze. Pershing softened his voice. "Want a cigar?"

"I'll take one for later, thank you, sir."

Pershing jumbled through a box on his desk and handed Billy a large dark cigar. "They're made in Cuba." He smiled. "You remember Cuba."

"Yes sir." He took the cigar, "Thank you, sir. You did want to see me."

"Sit down, Billy." Billy looked beside him and sat down, carefully holding the cigar. Pershing continued, "Yes, Billy. Tomorrow I want you to go out with Lieutenant Patton. He wants to take the motor cars down to Salsito Village. You were there the first time, remember?"

"Yes, sir, we weren't' very successful in getting information last time."

"Yes, I remember." Pershing stood and walked to open flaps of the tent. "How are the men?"

"You see them everyday, sir."

"I know that," he replied with an edge to his voice. "I'm asking you. I know you will tell me how it is, not what I want to hear."

"It's been hot and they're tired and we really need to get some fresh meat again. The kitchen had to throw away half that last batch - It spoiled. The water is been scanty and muddy; and the horses aren't' much better. But they're soldiers, sir; I think I'd worry more if they didn't complain. Most of the cars are running' for once."

"What have you heard them saying about the leadership?"

"Well, sir they don't say much, the usual complaining, not much about you personally. Leaders lead, sir."

Pershing puffed on his cigar and blew a stream of smoke toward the tent flap.

"They call you "Black Jack, but it's nothing disrespectful."

"Like everyone else." Thoughtfully he puffed again. "Did I ever tell you what they called me back at the Point?"

"No, sir I haven't heard."

"They called me Nigger Jack. They sure didn't like me back there." He smiled and shook his head, reviewing the company street outside the tent.

"Well, sir, according to Marcus Aurelius, warriors should consider the source of complaints about them."

Pershing turned and burst into a laugh. "Where in the hell did you hear about Marcus Aurelius?"

"Lieutenant Patton, sir. He's been teaching me a lot of things; he's smart as hell, sir, and doesn't waste many words."

Pershing chuckled and drew on his cigar, then leaned back in his chair. "How long has it been since we first met? It was 1890, right?"

Billy nodded his head "Yes, sir at Wounded Knee."

"Yes, that was a tragedy that should have been prevented. You look after the Lieutenant tomorrow. I'll have to tell George he has an avid student. George has been talking to me about his sister, Nita they call her."

Pershing stood up abruptly and motioned with his hand for Billy to stay seated.

"I know he has one. He mentioned her once or twice. He is quite fond of her, she sends him stuff."

"He suggested that I meet with her, perhaps get together. She's not married."

"Yes, sir," Billy shifted uncomfortably he had not anticipated the turn in the conversation. He adjusted his posture to better view the spare officer before him.

"I don't know, I think it's too soon." He slowly exhaled and turned back toward his desk and absently fingered some papers on it. "Too soon since the Presido, you know what I mean?"

"Yes, sir, I know."

473

"I miss them so." He slowly exhaled a puff of smoke. "Still, I don't know if I want to get involved."

"How's your boy doing, sir?"

"Warren? Oh, he is just fine, writes notes to me often."

It became very quiet in the tent. Billy again adjusted his chair. He was well aware of Pershing's loss, his wife and two daughters in a fire at the Presido military base in San Francisco.

"Too soon," Pershing said.

"Yes, sir, I've never really wanted another woman since Calling Jays died. I mean a full time, night-time woman, sir."

Once again it became quiet in the tent. Pershing suddenly straightened and slapped his desk. "Goddamn it! I wish we could just catch this son of a bitch Villa or kill him so we could get out of here and get on with our lives!"

"I know, sir, it is pretty damn discouraging sometimes. What are the latest rumors?"

"He's nearby; he's in Tampico, up in the Sierra Madres, down on the coast, back up on the Rio Grande. I wish I knew where the hell he is." He gesticulated angrily, the frustration clearly showed in his voice. "We will check out the haciendas again. Maybe we can get more information. Damn him, he's just disappeared. One of those press men, he was here the other day; he said he thought Villa was down in Santa Rosalia." Pershing shook his head and smiled. "Hell, I told him his guess was as good as mine."

"His guess was as good as mine?" Despite trying to stifle a laugh, Billy guffawed and fumbled with the cigar.

Pershing still smiling said, "All right, Sergeant Kavanaugh, take a ride in the car tomorrow." He laughed again. "Rest your horse. You're dismissed."

Billy stood, snapped a salute and stepped out into the sunshine. He felt better for the encounter. Across the camp he saw Patton resting outside his tent, puffing on his large curved stem pipe.

"What a wild goose chase," he thought. "With a wilder goose tomorrow, what a shitteree this chase turned out to be." Smiling to himself, he ambled toward Patton.

The tent flaps burst inward as the lieutenant, coated in alkali dust, burst through into the lantern light. He resembled a raccoon; his dust goggles had left a white band around his eyes.

"George, I wondered where you were. Any luck?"

"I think we can be assured we nailed one of them, Jack."

"Oh?" The spare man with the brigadier star leaned back in his chair.

"We followed up on that rumor and damned if we didn't luck out." He began to beat the alkali dust from his uniform.

Pershing watched him for a moment and delivered a sharp rebuke. "You could have done that before you came in, you know."

"I know, Jack, but it's late. Sorry, I didn't want to wait until morning to report." Patton let Pershing's rebuke slide by. Pershing did not pursue his initial comment.

"Well then, let's hear it, cigar?"

"No, I've brought my pipe; Nina sent me some good English tobacco back at Fort Sam. It is about the only goddamn thing even remotely civilized in this goddamn, godforsaken place." He raised his hand as if to forestall a comment. "But I love the work." A broad grin creased his dust encrusted face.

"You were saying?" The general smiled at the explosive bluster.

"We got down there, checked out the town and the two cantinas and pulled out some of the harder looking bandits - nothing. Didn't have the trucks, you know that, just the two cars, and didn't want to wait too long the Goddamn things may quit and it could be a long walk."
"Yes, from what I gather, they are not holding up too well."

"True, but they're Dodges and until two days ago I hadn't found any mechanics worth a fiddler's fart. A couple men, infantry, I might add, came forward. They had a couple up and going and the touring car will be ready in the morning. Anyway, Jack, they're holding up pretty well when you consider this place." He began to pack his pipe.

The general smiled. "It's not exactly Michigan. The aero-planes are all down. That dust storm the other day did them in, but I hope they will be back. You know they're calling the Jennies suicide buses." Nevertheless, when they are up they reconnoiter a lot of ground." He puffed on his cigar. "So what happened today?"

"One of the men we pulled was scared damn near to death when we put a rope around his neck. And then he said there were a couple Villistas just outside of town holed up in an old shepherd's shack. So I took six men, left the others in town to finish questioning and rode out. Shaw, Sergeant Kavanaugh and some others went with me." He paused, struck a match and puffed the pipe alive, a cloud of smoke enveloping him.
"And then what happened?" General Pershing inquired.

"They were there. They had spotted the cars because of the dust we were raising. There were three and one threw a couple shots at us, and took off. They went over this little hill, showed up on the other side, riding like the devil was on them. We sent a couple shots after them, and then Kavanaugh climbed out of the auto and Jack, I swear, the sons of bitches were four hundred yards away riding like hell, and I'll be goddamned if Kavanaugh didn't clean one out of the saddle. Don't know for sure he killed him because we couldn't get over there. It was some shot! I don't think even I could have made it."

Pershing leaned back in his chair and smiled, "Well, George, that's quite an admission." He laughed. "It must have been quite a shot, but it hardly surprises me."
"Oh? Who the hell is this Kavanaugh?"

"A man I swore into this Army myself." Pershing replied with some satisfaction in his voice.
"Is that right?" He puffed his pipe and pushed back his chair.

"It's quite a story; I picked him up back at Wounded Knee. Found him naked as a jaybird, unconscious and damn near frozen to death. He recovered after a couple days and joined up."

"So you go back a long way."

"Yes, he was with me in Cuba, then to the Philippines."

"Is that where he got the medal?"

"Yes, but it was after I left the first time. He was with me on the march around Lake Lanao - at Bacolad he accounted for a few Moros who were foolish enough to put their heads above the parapet, but he received the medal for action at Mount Bud Dajo on Jolo Island. That

475

was sometime in '06, there was a hot fight and two of his Philippine scouts were down, dragged away by the Moros and he waded right into them. Carried one lad back and took out four Moros face to face, or so I read."

"I believe that, I sure would not want him set up against me. He has a warrior's soul and the skills to go with it."

"He was with me at Nebraska, taught marksmanship, and went to Fort Assiniboine in Montana. I lost track of him but he showed up with the Tenth in Tampa when we were saddling up for Cuba. He did a hell of a job in the jungle before we broke on to the heights. He was wounded three times in the same day, shot some of his ear off, plus arm and shoulder wounds. He is a natural leader – generates enormous respect among his men. Before I left Zamboanga, I recommended he be promoted to second lieutenant and I recommended him again while we were at Fort Bliss. When he showed up with that squadron from the Tenth, I transferred him over for this goose hunt."

"He would be an excellent officer. No doubt in my mind, he rode along with me in Namquipa in the auto last week you know that's when we hit the smallpox scare. He sure was relieved when we sent that Mexican packing off to his home, and so was I."

"Kavanaugh has the drive; he seems to call up his Cheyenne ancestors when the occasion merits careful when he has to be. He is observant; he misses nothing with those sharp eyes." Pershing adjusted in his chair. "Want a drink, George? I've a flask of good brandy."

"Hell, yes. The boys brought me some cactus juice from the cantina and let me tell you, we will be lucky if they' don't go blind drinking that piss."

Pershing rose, went to a pack and produced a bottle and two cups. "This will cut the dust."

They both leaned back and sipped at the brandy. From outside the voices of the men carried to them and then faded into the wind.

Patton listened for a moment, sipped his brandy and spoke, "I'd like to see Kavanaugh get a commission. With all the trouble in Europe, we're going to need some good men. The sinking of the Lusitania, I thought that was going to do it."

"Ah, Wilson, I don't think he'd be much of a war president, George. But I never would have guessed that he would send us be here either. And secretary of state Bryan, even less inclined to war."
Patton laughed. "What was it Senator Ashurst said?"
"We need less grape juice and more grape shot."

"Here, here!" Pershing replied and lifted his cup. "What are you up to tomorrow, George? We need to get a better assessment of the horses. I understand we lost four in a lightning strike. We need to check on that mess and the war correspondents have been clamoring for another press conference. There's a lot to do, so if you have no other plans, I need help with the press. So...."

"General," Patton broke in, "You remember that tip we got about Cardenas being at the Rubio Ranch?"

"The tip you strangled out of his uncle at San Miguelito about two weeks ago? That was a raw point with the correspondents and was a little rash, don't you think?"
"Yes, sir, but this isn't a goddamn Sunday school picnic and I thought..."

"I know where we are, Lieutenant." Firmness had crept into Pershing's voice. "We do not really need any negative publicity and how reliable is a tip like that? It sounded to me that you recently threatened it again. There are many who think we shouldn't be here - that we have invaded Mexico. Some of the press represent their interests and could encourage problems for the Army."

"Yes, sir, but the tip, General, I think it would be worthwhile to check it out. I know that son of a bitch is around there somewhere. Cardenas's wife and kid were at that house, or the other place, Saltillo. I'd like to check it out, sir."

"I want you to take some men and see if you can purchase some corn from the farmers over by Coyote or Salsito. We are getting short and who knows where the hell we will be next."

"Yes, sir, I can check for horse feed." Patton still sensed the impact his remark had made. He took a long draw from his pipe.

Pershing looked steadily at the lieutenant before him.

"If the situation merits, use your best judgment to find out what you can about Villaistas. Take some men and a couple cars, see what you can find out, but be sure you arrange for the delivery of corn. Might take Kavanaugh along as scout, he thinks like an Indian. Hell, he is one." Pershing finished his brandy. "And, George – there will be no more hanging."

Patton quaffed the last in his glass. "Yes, sir," he stood to leave and smartly saluted.

Pershing returned the salute. "You're dismissed, George. Look after yourself, get the corn."

"Yes, sir," Patton turned on his heel and left.

Pershing looked at the flaps through which Patton had disappeared and smiled to himself. "You will do well and you have a lovely sister."

He turned over the piece of stationery that was lying on the small desk and reviewed the message.

Dear Nita,

There is not a day that goes by that I do not think of you and the gracious kindness that...

He picked up his pen and began to write.

Kavanaugh and the second scout were riding with Patton in the first car as they set out on the corn buying excursion. Behind them were two other automobiles crammed with eight soldiers and four civilians. The road was rough and rutted and the drivers displayed extraordinary skills in skirting boulders and shifting according to grade. They had successfully negotiated the purchase and delivery of the corn at Coyote and its nearby neighboring town of Salsito. The task being accomplished, Lieutenant Patton had decided to push on to Rubio, a larger town.

Kavanaugh stood beside Patton outside the cantina and looked the men seated about.

"Some rough looking men in town today."

"Yes, sir, there are quite a few here today."

"What do you think, Kavanaugh?"

"I think there probably are Villaistas among them. They have been doing some hard riding from the looks of those horses. Might be more of that bunch we ran into the other day."

"Could be right, Sergeant." He reviewed the horses more carefully. "Damn fools, don't take care of their animals. Skinniest things I ever saw."

"Not just old men and pregnant women today, sir. I'd say there was something up and they sure as hell don't like our presence here a lot of hard looks. There's three to the right and one on that balcony to the left that have been watching us very carefully."

"I've got a feeling Cardenas is around." He turned to the men standing about the automobiles and motioned, "Get back in the autos, men."

The men crowded themselves into the vehicles and once outside the view of town, Patton gathered them around him.

"I think this son of a bitch Cardenas is up at his place in Saltillo, the Rubio Ranch. Now it's about six miles from here and I've been there before. If the son-of-a-bitch is there, I don't want him to get away. Matter of fact, I want to kill the bastard, any questions?"

"He's probably not alone."

"You're right, Sergeant Kavanaugh, and if he isn't alone I want to kill them, too."

Patton reviewed the men's faces around him. "Any questions," None of the men responded; some looked down, others carefully observed him. "Now this is what we're going to do. First it's a big square house and it's off the road. He traced the outline with his boot. "It has a courtyard."

"There could be men in there, a lot of 'em."

"That's true, so we have to surprise them. So when we see the house I'm going to roar right by it fast as we can go. Then I'll stop past it. I and the two scouts," he pointed to Billy and his companion, "are going to run across to the north end of the house. The other two vehicles will stop short of the house and three men from each will converge on the main gate. The rest of you will watch the road. When we get in, we're going to search the place top to bottom. Clear?"

"The three men from each..." one soldier began.

"Work that out. We will have to be fast. So load and lock and be careful, goddamn it. I don't want you to shoot one another."

As they approached the house and Patton sped by, they noticed three older men and a boy skinning a cow. One of the men ran into the house, and returned. He paid no heed to the Americans sprinting toward the house lead by the young Lieutenant. Armed Mexicans appeared riding at full speed and were bearing down on Patton. Kavanaugh was fast closing the distance and drew up to shoot. Patton was in his line of fire and blazing away at the riders. He dropped the first horse and the rider fled. Patton chased him around the corner of the building then ducked back, almost being buried by oncoming riders. Patton fired and the second horse went down but the rider leapt up, pistol in hand. Patton and the others sent a fusillade of shots that killed him. Billy did not fire but picked out a third rider, now a hundred yards distant. Other men who saw him began firing at him, including Patton. Billy also fired; the man went down. The first man, obviously wounded, was dashing along the patio wall when shots from the soldiers brought him down. Patton started toward him and Billy also ran toward the crippled rider. As they approached he raised a pistol. Billy shot him dead. The brief mayhem was over and Patton walked up to where Billy was standing.

"Dead?" he asked, and briefly reviewed the body.

"Yes, sir, he is dead - one who didn't get away."

"Come on." He looked to where the four men had returned to skinning the cow. "You come over here." None of them responded. "Come here, goddamn it, or I'll kill you all." Immediately the men moved toward them. Patton turned to Billy. "We will use them as shields and check the rest of this place out." Patton pushed the Mexicans ahead and motioned to two other soldiers to follow. Only a few old men and women were inside. Patton looked at those gathered. "Any of you speak English?" An old man nodded and stepped forward. "Who were those men? That man with the silver studded saddle. Do you know him?" Patton's voice was sharp and threatening. He was still holding his pistol and reviled the faces before him.

"That is my cousin, Julio Cardenas, senor." There was not a sign of emotion in the deep black eyes.

Patton smiled, turned and walked back toward his men, holstering his revolver. "Load them up, boys. We'll take them back to General Jack, one on each car. Throw them over the hoods. You, Corporal, I want that saddle and saber."

"Yes, sir," He moved off toward the dead horse.

Patton turned back to Kavanaugh and smiled. "Goddamn good day, Bill! We bagged three." With Kavanaugh at his side, they walked back toward the automobile. "You're good luck to me, Sergeant Major, and you did a damn fine job. I will be sure to tell the General."

"Thank you, Lieutenant. You did damn well yourself. I thought that rider had you. I couldn't get off a shot."

"You got one off at that other rider?"

"Yes Lieutenant, a couple. I thought I hit him but I don't know. There was a lot of lead headed in his direction."

Patton smiled. "There might be some question about that one. I got off three shots off myself." Suddenly he clapped Kavanaugh on the back. "You did a fine job here today. Let's load up the trophies and go home. See to it."

"Yes, sir," Billy smiled as he walked to where they were loading the three bodies. "Man, if the lieutenant lives past this campaign, he's going to be heard from."

It was October third, 1916, and a trace of winter had already whitened the hills west of Namiquipa. The sparse grass was encrusted with frost and the sky a turquoise blue bereft of clouds. Billy had returned the night before after a week of scouting out another rumor. The campaign had drawn near to a halt but he and the Apache scouts, Pershing's Pets according to the enlisted lingo, had been busy. Neither nor the scouts tolerated inactivity. He stopped and glanced toward the building that housed the camp whores that had been provided with full knowledge and encouragement of the commander. The ladies were more or less confined, and occasionally inspected for sexually transmitted disease. They were much better off than the ones at the river. They were provided hot water and the opportunity to clean up; the 'Remount Station' was a welcome comfort to the troops.

There was no sentry on duty as he approached Pershing's CO tent. He slapped the flaps and was greeted by a terse "enter."

Billy pushed through the flap, saluted and snapped to attention. "Sir, Sergeant Kavanaugh reporting."

Pershing returned his salute, a sly smile picked at the corner of his lips. "At ease," he said, his smile growing wider. "You're back – that's good, so what did you find?"

"Nothing, sir, there was nothing there --no signs, no nothing. We did spot some Carrangjistas miles from where Pancho was supposed to be."

"Goddamn!" Pershing's countenance darkened as he fixed Billy's eyes in his own. "I'd like to catch him one of these days."

"General, the natives don't even know who's who, and you know what, sir? I don't think there are many left. Villa himself maybe, he can't have many with him. He can't be creating men out of the thin air. I don't think he is such a hero anymore to attract recruits, he may not even be in Chihuahua."

"I think a successful outlaw like Villa will always appeal to the Mexican people. That's why we need to catch him – if we can." Pershing stood up from his desk, stretched his back and turned his chair more toward Billy and sat down again.

"I've a second star, Billy, did you hear?"

"No, sir, but congratulations, you sure as hell deserve it."

Pershing leaned back in his chair and spoke very quietly. "Not all the promotions in the world are worth much these days."

Billy sensed an impending sadness did not reply but shifted uncomfortably in his chair.

"Since I lost Frankie and the girls, you remember them, Billy?"

"Yes, sir, I do. She was a nice lady, sir. Whenever I saw her on post she always said hello to me."

"Yes, she was very kind, my love and sunshine."

"Yes, sir, I really felt bad when I heard about what happened."

"Damn! If I had not had those floors varnished the fire never would have happened. The Army and all this Mexican business, I might have been there otherwise. If Frances had not opened the door upstairs the fire might not have spread." Pershing settled into a fierce lipped silence. The room filled with the quiet.

"Did I ever tell you, sir, how I lost my wife and little boy," Billy asked, the silence resonating to his hushed voice.

Pershing pulled from his own remorse and studied Billy carefully. "You mentioned that you were married but I never did know the details."

"Well I was not married in the usual way, no priest or pastor joined us, but I was married in the Cheyenne way, to 'Woman Who Calls to Jays.' I called her Calling Jays. It was a long time ago, sir."

"What happened, if you don't mind telling me?"

"I was in Dakota country, I was trapping. I left her alone to do a run over the sets. When I got back I found her," he grimaced at the pressing memory. "A bear had taken her, she was all pulled apart." He paused, and solemnly intoned, "I never found my little boy."

"You found her like that?"

Billy nodded.

Pershing did not reply but a deep understanding seemed to loom, filling some unknown gap between them. "And that is some of the long version." Pershing enjoined with a somber smile.

"Yes, sir, I didn't realize you remembered the long version comment. Well, I'd best be going, some horses to look after."

"Stay a while. We're not yet finished here." Pershing leaned forward in his chair. "I met Villa once in August, 1914. He impressed me as being a strong man, and a true patriot that would help his country. Hell, he even sent me a note after the Presidio fire. I never thought I'd be chasing him across Mexico. What a state, us chasing Villa, the Carranqistas fighting Zapata.

No one knows for sure what's going on. You need a damned scorecard."

"Well, sir, I think this game of hare and hounds is about up. Every time we've met them, we've smashed them and they were surprised, and they're the ones that are supposed to be surprising us."

"There was the unfortunate event at Carrizal."

"Well, sir, that was Boyd's fault, not every lieutenant in this man's army has sense enough to pour piss out of a boot, even if it was marked on the heel."

Pershing laughed. "I agree, which brings me to the next order of business. You do remember that I requested you be awarded a commission?"

"I gave up on that, sir." He smiled.

"Well, you shouldn't have. When my second star came through, so did your commission. My sincere congratulations, there is not another man in this man's Army who deserves it more."

Billy was stunned. He tried to speak, but nothing emerged. He swallowed, exhaled and managed, "I don't know what to say. I'd given up on it."

"I made another request while we were at Fort Bliss. It does not surprise me; I believe we will shortly be in great need of competent officers. We will need officers who also have experience and wisdom. A young man graduating from West Point today will take years to reach the maturity, competence and valor you so often have projected." Pershing stood and went back to his desk. "I happen to have a pair of Second Lieutenant bars courtesy of my bandit, George. He said he would like to be here for this occasion, but I had to send him off to find out where half the expedition is. So I will present them to you." He extended his hand and Billy gingerly picked them from his grasp.

"So, Mr. Kavanaugh, you can strip those stripes from your sleeve and pin these bars on your collar."

Pershing stepped back and reviewed Billy briefly. "And as soon as we get back, get over to supply and see what they can do for a new uniform. I welcome you to the commissioned ranks of the United States Army." Pershing extended his hand.

Billy stood, awkwardly holding the bars in his hand. "Thank you, sir. I'll try to be worthy of your trust." He reached for Pershing's hand and gripped it.

"You are already worthy of that, but there is a time coming I fear will test us all."

"What do you mean, sir?"

"Germany, I was there a few years ago. They had the most complete and organized military I have ever observed. Of course, you know what's going on now. I fear France and England will not outlast them. We will be drawn into the conflict despite what Wilson has said in the past." Pershing released his hand but remained standing looking into Billy's face.

"When do you think we will be in it?"

"Soon - next year, I expect. It's going badly for the Allies, the U boats are beginning to strangle off all supplies to England. England is also besieged within –the Irish business."

"So I have heard. Wasn't it a U boat sank three British gun ships on the same day? I know that a lot of ships have gone down. I thought we would be in it after the Lusitanian went down."

"Yes, so did many others. What's going on in Europe is a hard but distinct lesson for us. We must be prepared. There will be war with Germany. I don't see how we can avoid it. This expedition proved for all time we cannot be so self assured and must be ready for a military response. And if we do not foster a military spirit in our young men, our nation will not long endure with so many potential enemies."

"Well, sir, there's the militia. They can be mustered up."

"Militia will never be enough, Billy, and it would be absurd to depend on them. We need regular Army. Well trained and led by good men."

"Yes, sir," Billy looked down at the bars in his hand, then back to Pershing.

"I think we might have a little private celebration. I know the other officers are planning a little something later when George gets back." Pershing turned back to his desk and produced two cups and filled them halfway with brandy. He smiled with such force, his whole face lighted to the creases round his eyes.

"Here's to Lieutenant William Patrick Kavanaugh." He extended his cup to the toast and chuckled. You can pour piss out of a boot I trust."

"I think so, sir," He laughed "It's the first time I've been called William since I sent a parish priest buggy and all into a lake. I think he wanted to call me more than William that day. And here's to Major General John Pershing."

"Here, here!" Pershing laughed. "That sounds like another story I will have to hear sometime."

"It was a long time ago, but it gets better every time I tell it."

They both laughed and settled into chairs, sipping at the brandy.

"On a more serious note, Billy, I think this expedition will finish up by December – January at the latest. You may also be right about Villa; with all his losses, I do not believe he has the stature he once had, and I think things in Europe may force our withdrawal."

"Yes, I think so too, sir."

"When we got stateside I'm going to keep you close, lieutenant, Patton also. It will take a while to stand down; I think our commitment to Europe is just around the corner."

"Do you think you will be ordered over, sir?"

"I believe so. I am the general officer with the most experience abroad. They will most surely call upon me. I'll need some good men around me to help organize and train the troops. I am convinced that you can make a significant contribution in the training of reconnaissance personnel and scouts."

"Of course, sir, I'd be honored, sir. You have made a good choice in Lieutenant Patton. He's an excellent officer and not afraid to mix it up."

"You will stay on with me, attached to headquarters until the expedition is dissolved, then depending on circumstances, I'll decide your future assignment."

"Yes, sir, that will be fine, sir."

Pershing took a swallow from the brandy cup. "Do you speak French, Billy?"

"No, sir, I can speak a few words." He smiled inwardly as the specter of Micheline passed through his mind. "You know, directions, food and such and a few romantic ones."

Both Billy and Pershing broke into grins.

"Why do you ask, sir?"

"Because, Billy, if we go over, France will be the place we go." Pershing finished his brandy and set down his cup. Billy took a deep swallow and quaffed his own cup.

"By the way, sir, we did bag a couple deer and brought them back to the mess."

"Excellent, Billy, it's time to get on with the day. That venison will make a good addition to what the other officers have planned for you tonight."

Billy stood to leave. "Thank you, sir and thank you in recommending the commission."

Pershing smiled and returned to his desk.

482

"Get on with it, Lieutenant."

The full impact of the promotion did not register on him at first. He walked back to his tent and was removing his stripes when Riker, one of his friends, popped in. He observed the sewing scene, and stammered, "Jesus, Bill, what the hell did you do to lose your stripes?"

"I didn't lose them, thank you. I am trading them."

"What the hell?"

"I've been promoted to Lieutenant."

"Lieutenant, well, I'll be goddamned."

"Exactly what I thought, Riker, and as the General would say, 'don't that beat hell?'"

Chapter 49

France
August, 1917

"Billy, I am sending you on a special reconnaissance, a mission that is very important."

"Yes, sir, what do you want me to do?" He watched with interest as the general began to unroll a map.

"I'd like you to look at this map." Pershing rolled out the map on his desk, anchoring both sides with books. "This is the city of Verdun and not three miles distant are the trenches."

"They're damn near in town."

"Yes and the Germans have been trying to get into that town since the outset of the war. The front lines drawn here are those as of now and have been so since December of last year."

"They were accurate then, what about now?"

"They are as accurate as they possibly can be. General Petain is planning an offensive to begin next month. We will be there when they start out, but I'd like to have information before then." Pershing looked into Billy's eyes. "It's an important offensive."

"Yes, sir, we have been expecting an offensive."

"Billy, this ten or so square miles before Verdun is probably the bloodiest piece of real estate the world has ever known. It is estimated that more than 250,000 Germans have already died there and more than 300,000 French." His tone was dead serious like a recitation of a mathematical theorem.

"Jesus Christ, general! That is one hell of a lot of casualties!" Billy was awed and his voice reflected it.

"And thousands upon thousands more wounded on both sides, probably four times more than those killed. We are talking more than a million casualties here when wounded are accounted for."

"But why the slaughter for this piece of ground, sir?"

"Prussian pride in general, Van Fallkenhayn's in particular, French endurance and the threat to Germany's source of steel, the Briey basin. Do you know what the phrase 'ne passerant' means?"

"Something like 'they shall not pass'."

"That's the French phrase for valor at Verdun."

They straightened from the map and Pershing gestured toward a chair.

"Sit down, Billy."

"The casualty rates are beyond my ability to imagine – millions of casualties in a year, what a waste!"

"Precisely, Petain is preparing for a new offensive. He has concentrated artillery in a great mass at Verdun. Two thousand five hundred guns, that's about forty thousand artillery men alone. Plus eight divisions of infantry, all aimed at the German salient within these bloody acres. The French want to dislodge them so they never again will have to worry about their passage."

"And the Germans no doubt are expecting them?"

"During some weeks, they exchange more than a thousand artillery rounds every day.

484

Petain intends to concentrate his fire in zones, racking the area from the front lines back as far as there is movement to the front. You can count on it; the German defenders will be well prepared, well entrenched, and well armed. We are about to witness one of the largest battles in history."

"If will be a lot different from chasing Pancho around Chihuahua," Billy smiled.

"Yes," Pershing laughed and leaned back in his chair.

"What do you want me to do, sir?"

"Billy, I want you to go over there and work closely with the French. I want some idea of their morale and their preparations. I mean the everyday soldier. I want you to be my eyes and ears among the men and conscripted non-commission officers." He fixed Billy's eyes with his own.

"Yes, sir."

"I want to know how well trained they are, their complaints, their morale, their weapons, and I want to know what the ordinary soldier thinks of their officers and what they think about us. You can do this?"

"I'll try my best, sir, but why me?"

"You fooled me." He shook his head. "I didn't know you spoke French as well as you do. I thought I was beyond being surprised by you, Kavanaugh."

"I don't speak it very well. Captain Patton really speaks it."

"Well enough to shame the rest of us."

"I had a girl friend once," Billy smiled. "I always had a knack for languages. A few words are all I know."

"You didn't know your success with the language while we were coming over on the Baltic would pay such rich dividends." Pershing chuckled. "A girl friend, huh she must have been quite a teacher as well."

"Yes, general, she was quite a teacher."

"I want a report back in a week, report to Captain Quekemeyer at G-3. He will arrange transport."

"Yes, sir, you want me to go today?"

"Yes, and Billy, when you get back, I want you to set up a sniper group. Canvass the companies for outstanding marksmen. We will need them. I don't care how you do it, but you will report to me personally when you get back. In the meantime, you might think about their recruitment and training." Pershing tented his fingers and settled Billy with a stare. "Don't take any unnecessary risks." He saluted. "Get cracking."

"Yes, sir," he saluted smartly and smiled, "but taking risks is part of it."

Billy made his way trough the bustle in the fine house on Rue de Varenne that Pershing had been granted as headquarters. A brief meeting at G-3 yielded up a car with a French driver and they made their way over the crowded roads toward the bilateral annihilation acres referred to as Verdun.

The road nearer the front reminded Billy of a swamp after a fierce rainstorm. Ruined buildings, houses, offices and farm sites lined the ruts to whole villages devastated into rubble.

A grave and haunting desolation inundated the road and Billy and the driver said little. At one village not a single building had a roof. It was surrounded by truncated trees that once were verdant in foliage, now without a single limb. A few white geese waddled over the moonscape of shell craters, making a solemn parade towards a small pond. They were the only living things visible to the eye. The town pump had miraculously survived the shelling, so they stopped and drew some water.

Billy looked about while leaning on a wall that was once a home. Across from him, one wall of the church still stood, but the interior had been entirely burned out. A few blackened timbers remained, wet down by an earlier rain. He looked into the ruins of another small house and saw a colorful rocking horse amidst the remains of broken furniture, shards of glass, wood and broken crockery. He wondered vaguely what had happened to the family that once lived there. The fields were tossed and cratered as though some giant astride a pernicious pogo stick had cratered them, after tearing up the town and twisting the foliage from the trees.

Most of the buildings were mere skeletons, the empty windows–mournful maws through which the wind hissed and sighed of sadness. On the edge of the village was a cemetery, Billy counted thirty-six new graves, many marked merely by a stake. There was not the sound of a voice, the call of a bird or the squeak of summer frogs. It was as though something bright had been, but was now gone and the somber silence was homage to its passing.

Billy turned and started walking back to the car. "What madness is this?" he thought. "And I am madder to be a part of it?"

The desolate landscape did not prepare him for his initial visit to Verdun. The large city was also in ruins. Although there was ample evidence of activity, few of the thousands of troops were visible; most were massed in trenches among the buildings and camped in alleys. There was some wounded being transported on wheel-less sledges towed by horses. The town ruins had been pushed to the sides of the thoroughfares, abject palisades raised to the fierce artillery. He walked carefully down the empty street, casting his eyes over the destruction. Outside a sandbagged redoubt he spotted a French captain sucking on a pipe. He appeared to have a casual air about him and smiled at Billy when he recognized the American uniform.

"Captain, I wonder if you could help me." He spoke in French and extended his hand. "Lieutenant Billy Kavanaugh."

The officer shook his hand vigorously. "Captain Chevert at your service," the officer replied in English.

Billy took off his cap and scratched his head. "I've been sent down to take a look at things. You know the preparations for the offensive?"
"Ah, but of course. How can I help?"

"Well, I'd like to take a tour of the trenches. See what it's like, I'm an old Indian fighter, I haven't a grasp of this trench stuff."

"You would like a tour of the trenches?" He tapped out his pipe. "Mon ami! It can be very dangerous. You first need a helmet before you venture there."

"I have one in the car."

"Well, get it then and I can show you, are you armed?"

"Naw." Billy replied and wondered at the perplexed look from his host.

"Naw – that is negative?"

"Yes. I mean, no." Billy laughed. "I have a side arm in the car."

"If you would like to go forward you had best take it also."

486

"Yes, I'll get it before we start."

"Verdun is quiet now except the morning and night greetings the Bosche artillery sends."

"I feel that quiet, a little creepy with all the ruins. I guess I did not think how dangerous it would be." Billy returned to the car, put on his equipment and directed the driver to hide the vehicle. Chevert looked curiously at the Colt automatic Billy wore.

"Would you like to see it, Captain? It is very different from the revolver I used to carry." He unsnapped the holster and offered the pistol. "It's a bit complicated, has a double safety, one grip, one trigger. It's streamlined and a good pointing weapon. It's forty-five caliber and packs a wallop."

"A bit heavy, I think." He offered his revolver to Billy. "This is a Chemlot - Del Vigne revolver. A double action eleven millimeter, model eighteen seventy and is accurate once you learn how to use it."

"That's a mouthful. We call this a Colt Forty-five, model nineteen eleven. I used to carry a forty five revolver."

"The Chemlot revolver is not so advanced as your automatic, but quite effective up close. The Bosche have automatics called Lugers. They are a prize many soldiers try to get one."

"I've heard they are very good."

"Quite so." They exchanged weapons. "Are you ready, lieutenant?"

"Yes." Billy snapped his holster shut. "Lead the way, Captain."

"The entrance is just there, eight feet below the surface of the ground." He gestured to some sandbags beside the street. The entrance opened into a long winding trench, the sides of which were reinforced with beams and boards. The ruined landscape and blasted buildings were no preparation for the subterranean town planning that had been provided by high explosives. Wherever the trench had been struck, the cavities had been developed into redoubts. The supply trench they had entered was actually a series of trenches spread like a network of blood vessels reaching from the road, branching east, west and center. Along the deep ditches were a series of revetments and bomb-proofing, composed of complex wooden supports and sand bagged walls.

"Here is our secondary aid station, Lieutenant Billy. Let's drop in," Chevert laughed.

Billy realized to his amusement Chevert was literally speaking for the first step was like plummeting into a deep pit. They made their way into the interior, descending a steep path downward into darkness. It was illuminated by periodic placement of lanterns. The deeper they descended, the closer the air became and the sickening smell of unwashed bodies, decay and ether increased in proportion. The tunnel opened into a large room packed with cots filled with soldiers in various degrees of stress, the smell was overpowering, and Billy experienced some difficulty in breathing. The floor was muddy despite its depth.

One of the surgeons focused on Billy. "An American, eh?" He spoke French in an accent Billy had trouble following. "Come to review the misery?"

"There seems to be much," he replied. Carefully he reviewed the reinforced walls above and around and the wounded men. Some of them were studying Billy, who continued in French.   "When were these men wounded?"

"Yesterday and the day before, we cannot do much for them here. We stop the blood, treat the shock, and give them some tea and biscuit. The more serious wounds have already been sent back. Unfortunately," he gestured to a pile of bodies against one wall, "some were more serious than we expected. It would have been more merciful to let them die outside." The surgeon sat wearily down. "The harvest of the guns, the ground has a dear price around Verdun."

As they returned through the tunnel, they stepped aside as men hurried toward them bearing a great pot of soup suspended on a long pole. Others were bearing bags of bread. They regained the fresh air and Billy inhaled deeply, exhaling through his nose to clear the smell.

"Captain, I felt like I was in a coal mine. How deep are they?"

"Let me think – fifteen meters, about forty English feet."

"How far ahead is the front, then?"

"Three, maybe four kilometers."

"That's a lot of digging. It must have taken awhile to prepare all this."

"True, it has taken us more than two years, done by men with shovels and picks, sweat, and blood. As you may know, the front is nearly – let me think – two hundred miles long but really from Switzerland to Belgium, however far that is."

"How do you keep your left hand aware of what your right hand is doing through all these trenches?" They kept advancing at a brisk pace. "These trenches are vast and complicated."

"Telephones and miles of wires, there you see," he pointed to the wall, "hundreds of miles of wires from front to back, from left to right. They lead to command posts --like where I was standing, from the front to the big guns – artillery. One can call up death."

"How long have you been here?" Billy was disconcerted by the remark of calling death.

"I am in my third year. Last year I was on Hill 304. The Bosche came hard at us there, forty thousand of them in a dense and deep formation. Our artillery concentrated on them, 'mon dieu,' what a butcher's market. It was an efficient example of defense, the gun, the trench. At Dead Man's Hill, the other end of the attack, a hundred thousand Germans died, to win five hundred yards."

Billy shook his head in disbelief, transfixed by the revelation. "I can't even imagine that. I don't believe I have ever seen that many people at one time."

"They did not pass," Chevert smiled. "We must be careful now, for this supply trench will open out. We are under observation every hour of daylight and listened to every hour of the night. They know where we are and we know where they are. Their artillery is registered on our entire line."

"You mean if they spot just the two of us moving, they will put artillery on us?"

"One never knows about the Bosche, maybe yes, maybe no. More than one man moving could bring on the cannon."

"Seems like a great waste to me, getting artillery to fire on a couple of men - using a broom to kill a gnat."

Chevert laughed. "They hold off mostly because our return shells may do worse."

They had arrived at a crossing in the maze of trenches. On either side there was no one obvious to view. A series of revetments hid most of the troops. The sand bagged entrances were present the length of the trench until it curved out of sight. A few men could be seen backed into spider holes, their knees folded before them, but no officers were visible.

"Where is everyone?"

"They are sleeping, for it is at night that this becomes a very busy place. All our new building of obstacles, our supplies come in, and our patrols go out, --leaving the trenches for their bloody hunts. Even then we must be careful how many men we gather to work or send out.

In the daytime it would be foolish to assemble that many together. Do you wish to continue forward?"

"Yes. Captain, how are the men doing?" They began to move ahead.

"The trench is a difficulty, they complain. Most are here for months, crowded, exhausted from the work; the food is not good, and danger is their constant companion. The men would get lazy and lose their spirit if we did not work them hard. Complaining is good because there still is something there, when they become quiet, well, that is not a good sign."

"I've observed that, too. So you keep them busy on improving the trenches and enforce discipline to detail."

"Yes, but you must know the limit - too much will not help, but too little is worse. Mostly we keep them busy."

"That's a seventy-five emplacement," Billy remarked as he spotted an artillery piece carefully camouflaged and sand bagged. He slowed his stride for a better look.

"We cannot tarry here, Billy. An observer may take too close a look."

"I expected to see more artillery."

"It is located beyond the city, but there are many guns here. Sometimes we shell the Bosche to remind the men to believe in the war. When the Germans return fire it draws them together against those who would take their lives. It encourages their reliance on one another and the officers."

"What breaks them down – mostly?"

"Ah, the boredom spiced with terror and the snipers that strike and hide. The longer exposed, the more likely the break."

They had passed the third "T" to the supply trench and paused at the juncture.

"Are we getting close? How much farther is it to the line?"

"We will not go to the fire trench; it becomes very dangerous to be observed. They are men with less protection --shallow trenches and more heavily armed, mostly with machine guns. Even now as we near the reserve trenches, our danger increases." Concern clearly edged his voice.

"What about the snipers, Captain? Are they a big factor in morale?"

"Yes, yes, they must be mastered or they will master morale. It is the fire trenches that they watch – one careless moment in view is death. I know." He tapped a long crease in his helmet.

"I'm supposed to help train some of our men to become snipers."

"It is a thankless task not even your own men will like them. They are needed but reviled. We are now in a very dangerous area. Somewhere up there sits a German, deep in a hole, observing this very trench through a periscope. He may have already seen us. The second trench line is about two hundred meters ahead, and the fire trench just beyond. Have you seen enough?"

"I'd like to talk to some of the men up this far."

"But of course." He gestured toward a large revetment with a small portico where a few men were clustered.

Suddenly there came a sound like a great locomotive approaching through the air. Immediately following was the flash-crash of a shell. The concussion knocked both Billy and Chevert to the ground, half covering them with dirt and debris. Billy was stunned and could hear nothing except a great roar in his ears, but he could see Chevert motioning him toward the revetment. He struggled to his feet as the next locomotive approached, he started to run.

Pershing's office suite occupied most of the first floor of the fire house on Rue de Varenne. The surroundings reflected nineteenth century opulence, rococo, flamboyant paintings, tapestries, broad marble steps and a garden large enough to gallop a horse. The communications center dominated the activity with telephone lines reaching in every direction and the installation was constantly undergoing change. Pershing's office was quite austere, a large desk and chair with maps on the wall. There was also a table with chairs and a coat rack with a single hat impaled upon it. Pershing straightened at the tap on the door and folded the sheaf of papers to the side, turning the last page to its reverse.

"Come in. Entré," he added.

The door swung inward, outlining the figure of James Harford.

"Come in, Jim a bit of surprise to see you. What brings you here? I thought you would be up to your ears in officer's billets. Have you a report on that already?"

"I completed most of them for the First Division, but..." Harford paused. Pershing looked at him in a quizzical way.

"What is it, Jim?"

"Some bad news, I'm afraid, General."

490

"Okay – out with it."

"Lieutenant Bill Kavanaugh was killed yesterday."

"Oh, no," Pershing stood from his chair and with his back to Harford. "What happened?" His voice was barely audible.

"From what I gather, he and a French Captain were touring the trenches and artillery, probably just harassing fire, killed them both. I'm sorry, Jack. I know how much you liked him. Hell, I don't know anyone who had a bad word about Billy."

"I sent him just two days ago. I told him not to take any unnecessary risks."

"I don't know that he was, Jack. I don't know."

"Where is the body?"

"The round was a direct hit or very close. The Captain and Bill were in bits and pieces and gathered up. They couldn't tell – anyway, they put the pieces in bags."

Pershing raised hand, his back still to Harford. "That's enough, Jim." He turned from the window and exhaled deeply, and with sorrow in his voice. "Send his effects home but not the body or whatever."

"Very well, where do you want to send them? He listed his home as Belle Forche, Nebraska, but from what I gathered he was from upstate New York somewhere."

"I believe so ...some Indian name – Minsi, I think. I do not believe he ever told me." Pershing retraced his steps toward his desk. "You know, Jim, you serve with a man for more then twenty five years, on and off, and you think you know him, but you really don't."

"I know, Jack. I really liked him. There was a perpetual air of youth about him, not a gray hair on his head, clear-eyes and such great enthusiasm about him."

"Yes. Life was always an adventure for him. I will dearly miss him, Jim." Pershing's voice grew thick with emotion, and once again he turned and walked to the window. "Jim, give a call over to Captain Patton." He lapsed into silence.

"Yes, sir do you just want me to inform him, or do you want me to ask him something?"

"Billy and George were friendly in Mexico; he may know where Billy's home is. Did you know he had a twin brother?"

"No, I didn't."

"I don't know much of his life before the Army. I used to chide him about telling the rest of his story, and he always put me off. He could have had something shady back there." Again he looked to the window, "it doesn't make any difference now. He was one hell of a good soldier!"

"Well, he would not have been the first to rediscover life in the cavalry."

"True enough." He once more turned from the window. "Contact Captain Patton and tell me what you find out. You're dismissed, Jim."

"There are a couple of French officers waiting, and a Moroccan. There's also an artist – a lady."

"An artist? Tell them I'll see them in a few minutes."

Harford left the office, paused for a minute to speak with the waiting officers, and disappeared into the bustle of the office. Pershing once more looked to the window "Damn, damn, I am going to miss him."

Outside, thunderclouds were gathering with the promise of more rain in their shadows. Down the roads that networked toward Verdun, a more ominous thunder was looming.

Kinsale Ireland
Winter 1917

December 1, 1917

Dear Bea,

Congratulations! I was so happy to hear of your engagement. Thank you for the photograph. You now know what can happen when we opened the clinic to admissions from doctors other than our own. Not only do you get more patients, you also get a crop of doctors to review. It sounds like you found a good candidate for a husband among the crop. I'm so glad the Mercers are doing well and you find them easy to work with. I thought they might be just right for the clinic

From what you have written about Doctor Kenyon, it appears he is a brilliant young man. Isn't it wonderful to have a doctor in Minsi so interested in children and so interested in you? Handsome at that, I am looking forward to meeting him, but I don't know when we will be home - after this nasty war is over. You must not worry about being two years older than he is — I am older than Liam. I think he will be a wonderful husband.

Liam has some interesting friends and some with quite interesting injuries. I do so much like Ireland. These people are so devoted to their faith, to the land and to each other. It is a wonderful thing. We have come to know many, not just clinic patients or Liam's business associates, but people from all walks of life. Liam is highly regarded and inspires family confidence; he is more curious about things than ever before. Where ever he goes he asks lots of questions and people respond to his interests and his concerns for them.

The other day a mysterious man came in and asked to see Gray Wolf. What a shock! I didn't think a dozen people in the world knew Liam's given name. Somehow his Cheyenne name got out. Sada named him Gray Wolf, you know. I laugh at him sometimes and ask if it will be used as a pen name or a code word. He has become more interested in his Cheyenne roots, much more so than when Sada was alive. Billy was much closer to her when she was alive.

For the first time Liam is actively writing a diary, it is quite amusing for he sometimes is so secretive about it. He says he will write a book some day. He writes lots of notes and keeps very busy in his business---very successful as you might imagine and he is able to get most anything we or the clinic needs. He has said that the Volstead Act — prohibition as it is known – may provide him with business opportunities. I told him I didn't want to hear anything about it. He has also again taken to sketching some – he is so good at it.

The Kinsale Clinic is also doing a land office business – not so profitable – but lots of patients. I have trained some local girls as nurses (wish you were here) and we deliver some services in the countryside. I am also working with the local midwives and occasionally they will tend their patients in our small cottage hospital. Keeps the patient load lighter in the clinic and gets service to the people who would not ordinarily get in. We do encourage the primiparas and older women to come in, but home delivery is the way of most. Prenatal care is so important; unfortunately even though what we know will improve outcomes, it can't always be carried out (diet, etc.), because the people are too poor.

I have been considering how we might train nurses for the clinic when I return. Please ask Mr. Murray to contract an architect to prepare plans for a nurse's dorm and training center. Make it to accommodate twenty student (two per room), three class rooms, a small library and an office reception area. Tell him also to go ahead with the extra storage space at the clinic. Thank him for his fine report and keeping it so straight forward and short.

By all means, you must use the house for your wedding reception and Bea; I do insist that you and Dr. Kenyon move into it. Such a large grand house and no one in it except a few household staff. After all, you are patient care director while I am away. I trust that you are getting along with Mr. Murray; his administrative reports appear to support that. We will work out new arrangements when I return.

Thank you for sending on my brother Billy's things. It was a sad day here. Liam took it particularly hard. I had not seen Billy in so many years. Among his things we found a picture of the opening of the new building (the photo the New York World published). The family and staff were all in the picture, except Liam of course --he was here. Billy must have somehow cared. General Pershing's letter seemed so warm in concern, as though he really knew Billy. Perhaps he did know him even better than we did. Poor man, he must be writing many such letters in these troubled times.

Ireland is awash in sorrow. The war in France has killed and maimed many young men there and the troubles continue here. Also, in Billy's things there was a photo of Mary's twelfth wedding anniversary. I remember it well. We were all there, Mary and I all dolled up – even Pat with a derby looking so serious. And there were the two of them, they'd been hunting and looked bedraggled, just out of the bush. They pulled the same thing the following year. There was another photo with Liam and Uncle Woo, and the pictures brought the tears.

We are blessed with a full social life. Young Billy has learned so much Irish. He speaks it like a native and he and Mary C talk it all the time. Drives me mad for I do not know what they are saying. The people are not supposed to speak it, but many do anyway.

We all go riding at least once a week, weather permitting often on a Sunday afternoon, --one of our English friends has quite a stable. We have very interesting conversations; -- there was an English officer joined us one day-- genteel, polite and my, quite handsome as well very charming. Liam, of course, doesn't care for anything British, but he's polite to them.

Sometimes the family goes fishing on Sunday afternoons there is a French family living on the estate of one of our neighbors and the kids come over, or more likely, we send Billy and Mary C there; their ages are well matched. We have had them out fishing. The wife spoke little English and my French is terrible, but we managed to enjoy the day. Liam speaks the language better than I and he has never studied it a day in his life.

We go to Listowel whenever the chance presents. My, when the races are on it's an exciting spot! Liam's Uncle Tom is an avid fan of the races he knows each horse, how they run in the mud, their win records all in great detail. He is quite aged and is not well – congestive failure I fear. He is a living link to the past. We frequently stop at the cemetery, look after Mary and Pat's graves and say a prayer or two.

Whenever I go there I always recall how so much in love they were. I do believe in love, Liam is so devoted to me and the family, and we love him so. It's like it is the only real thing in the world, yet you can't measure it. I believe Billy loved us all; he just loved adventure more. You know, Bea, that it's been more than two years since she is gone. I miss her so much even now. How much we owe her for our good life and how many other lives she touched. Many she helped did not even know her name. I don't think there will ever be the likes of her again.

Do use the house, Bea, to the fullest extent. Until we see each other again -
Love, Sara